READER'S DIGEST
SELECT EDITIONS

READER'S DIGEST
SELECT EDITIONS

The condensations in this volume
are published with the consent of the authors
and the publishers © 2007 Reader's Digest.

www.readersdigest.co.uk

The Reader's Digest Association Limited
11 Westferry Circus Canary Wharf London E14 4HE

For information as to ownership of
copyright in the material of this book,
and acknowledgments, see last page.

Printed in Germany
ISBN 978 0 276 44283 4

**SELECTED AND CONDENSED
BY READER'S DIGEST**

THE READER'S DIGEST ASSOCIATION LIMITED, LONDON

CONTENTS

Jeffery Deaver displays his world-class talent as a master of the roller-coaster thriller ride in this, his latest book. When a killer escapes prison, Kathryn Dance, a brilliant interrogator and body-language specialist, is in hot pursuit. But Daniel Pell is no ordinary criminal. Controlled and brilliant, he skilfully mesmerises and exploits people—especially his devoted followers—for his own ends. To outwit him, Dance must get right inside his mind—a terrifying place to be.

THE SLEEPING DOLL

JEFFERY DEAVER

9

In this delightful new collection of fictional memoirs based on his time as a schools inspector in the Yorkshire Dales, Gervase Phinn proves once again that he is 'the James Herriot of the classroom'. His humorous observations get to the heart of what makes the people of 'God's own county' tick, while he affectionately mocks his eccentric, officious, and linguistically challenged colleagues. Best of all, though, are the disarmingly down-to-earth children of the Dales with their delightfully cheeky wit.

HEART OF THE DALES

GERVASE PHINN

169

THE SACRED BONES
MICHAEL BYRNES

285

A long-hidden vault beneath Jerusalem's Temple Mount is raided and a unique artefact disappears, causing political and religious uproar. At the same time, across the Mediterranean Sea, American scientist Charlotte Hennesey has been hired by the Vatican to examine some ancient bones. When she discusses her strange findings with her colleague, Italian anthropologist Giovanni Bersei, she realises that the implications are staggering and could change history, science, and her own life, for ever.

When she travels to Crete to unravel the mystery of her mother's childhood, Alexis Fielding finds herself irresistibly drawn to Spinalonga, a tiny island off the mainland, once Greece's main leper colony. Sophia Fielding has steadfastly refused to discuss her Greek past, but by reawakening long-dormant memories in those familiar with local history, Alexis uncovers a powerful story of four proud generations linked by tragedy. This fine debut novel was a recent winner at the Galaxy British Book Awards.

THE ISLAND
VICTORIA HISLOP

427

JEFFERY DEAVER

the sleeping doll

Eight years ago, the murders of William Croyton, his wife and two of their three children shocked a nation. Daniel Pell, dubbed the 'Son of Manson' for his sinister and charismatic leadership of a secretive cult, was convicted of the crime. Now Pell has escaped from prison and is on the run and, like a creature of the night, impossible for the forces of justice to catch. . .

'SON OF MANSON' FOUND GUILTY
IN CROYTON FAMILY MURDERS

Salinas, California—Daniel Raymond Pell, 35, was convicted today on four counts of first-degree murder and one count of manslaughter by a Monterey County jury after only five hours of deliberations.

'Justice has been done,' lead prosecutor James J. Reynolds told reporters after the verdict was announced. 'This is an extremely dangerous man who committed horrendous crimes.'

Pell became known as the Son of Manson because of the parallels between his life and that of convicted murderer Charles Manson, who in 1969 was responsible for the ritualistic slayings of the actress Sharon Tate and several others in Southern California. Police found books and articles about Manson in Pell's house following his arrest.

The murder convictions were for the May 7 deaths of William Croyton, 56, a wealthy computer innovator, and of his wife and two of their three children in Carmel, California. The manslaughter charge arose from the death of James Newberg, 24, who accompanied Pell to the Croyton house on the night of the murders. The prosecutor asserted that Newberg initially intended to assist in the murders but was killed by Pell after he changed his mind.

One child survived the attack—a daughter, Theresa, 9. Pell overlooked the girl, who was in her bed asleep and hidden by her toys. Because of this, she became known as the Sleeping Doll.

Because of Pell's interest in Manson, there was speculation that the killings had ideological overtones, but robbery was the most likely reason for the break-in, Reynolds said. Pell has dozens of prior convictions for shoplifting, burglary and robbery. Like Manson, Pell exuded a dark charisma and attracted a group of fanatical followers, whom he called his Family—a term borrowed from the Manson clan—and over whom he exercised absolute control. At the time of the Croyton murders, this group included Newberg and three women: Rebecca Sheffield, 26; Linda Whitfield, 20; and Samantha McCoy, 19. They all lived together in a shabby house in Seaside, north of Monterey.

The women were not charged in the deaths of the Croytons or Newberg but were convicted of multiple counts of larceny, trespass, fraud and receiving stolen property. Whitfield was also convicted of hampering an investigation, perjury and destroying evidence. As part of a plea bargain, Sheffield and McCoy were sentenced to three years in prison, Whitfield to four and a half.

Pell's behaviour at trial also echoed Charles Manson's. He would sit motionless at the defence table and stare at jurors and witnesses in apparent attempts to intimidate them. There were reports that he believed he had psychic powers.

The jury begins sentencing deliberations tomorrow. Pell could get the death penalty.

Monday
Chapter 1

The interrogation began like any other.

Kathryn Dance entered the interview room and found the forty-three-year-old man sitting at a metal table, shackled, looking up at her closely. Subjects always did this, of course, though never with such astonishing blue eyes.

'Good morning,' she said, sitting down across from him.

'And to you,' replied Daniel Pell, the man who eight years ago had knifed to death four members of a family for reasons he'd never shared. His voice was soft. A slight smile on his bearded face, the small, sinewy man sat back, relaxed and perfectly still. His head, covered with long grey-black hair, was cocked to the side.

To Dance, a specialist in interrogation and kinesics—body language—Pell's demeanour and posture suggested caution, but also confidence and, curiously, amusement. He wore an orange jumpsuit stencilled with CAPITOLA

CORRECTIONAL FACILITY on the chest. At the moment, though, Pell and Dance were not in Capitola but, rather, a secure interview room at the county courthouse in Salinas, forty miles away.

Pell continued his examination. First, he took in Dance's eyes—a green complementary to his blue—and framed by square, black-rimmed glasses. He then regarded her French-braided dark blonde hair, the black jacket and unrevealing white blouse. He noted too the empty holster on her hip. He was meticulous and in no hurry. (Interviewers and interviewees share mutual curiosity. She told the students in her interrogation seminars, 'They're studying you as hard as you're studying them—usually even harder, since they have more to lose.')

Dance fished in her blue leather bag for her ID card, not reacting as she saw a tiny toy bat, from last year's Halloween, that either twelve-year-old Wes or his younger sister, Maggie, had slipped into her bag as a practical joke. She thought: How's this for a contrasting life? An hour ago she was having breakfast with her children in the kitchen of their comfortable Victorian house in Pacific Grove, their two dogs begging for bacon, and now here she sat across a very different table from a convicted murderer.

She found the ID and displayed it. Pell stared for a long moment, easing forward. 'Dance. Interesting name. Wonder where it comes from. And the California Bureau . . . What is that?'

'Bureau of Investigation. Like an FBI for the state. Now, Mr Pell, you understand this conversation is being recorded.'

He glanced at the mirror, behind which a video camera was humming.

'You can withdraw from this interview any time, and you have a right to an attorney.'

'I know more criminal procedure than the entire graduating class of Hastings Law rolled up together.'

More articulate than Dance expected. Cleverer too.

The previous week, Daniel Raymond Pell, serving a life sentence for the 1999 murders of William Croyton, his wife and two of their children, had approached a fellow prisoner due to be released from Capitola and tried to bribe him to run an errand after he was free. Pell told him about some evidence he'd disposed of in a Salinas well years ago and explained that he was worried the items would implicate him in the unsolved murder of a wealthy farm owner. Pell had read recently that Salinas was revamping its water system, and he'd grown concerned that the evidence would be discovered. He'd wanted the prisoner to find and dispose of it.

Pell picked the wrong man to enlist, though. The short-timer spilled to the warden, who called the Monterey County Sheriff's Office. Investigators wondered if Pell was talking about farm owner Robert Herron, beaten to death a decade ago. The murder weapon, probably a claw hammer, was never found. The Sheriff's Office sent a team to search the wells and, sure enough, they found a tattered T-shirt, a claw hammer and an empty wallet with the initials R.H. stamped on it. Two fingerprints on the hammer were Pell's. The Monterey County prosecutor asked CBI agent Kathryn Dance to interview Pell in hopes of a confession.

Dance asked, 'How long did you live in the Monterey area?'

'A few years.'

'Where?'

'Seaside.' A town of about 30,000 north of Monterey on Highway 1. 'You got more for your money there,' he explained. 'More than in your fancy Carmel.' His eyes alighted on her face.

Ignoring his fishing expedition for information about her residence, Dance continued to ask about his life in Seaside and in prison, observing how he behaved when she asked questions and how he behaved when he answered. She'd done her homework and knew the answers, but she was establishing his behavioural baseline.

In spotting lies, interrogators consider three factors: nonverbal behaviour (body language, or kinesics), verbal quality (pitch of voice or pauses), and verbal content. The first two are far more reliable indications of deception, since it's easier to control *what* we say than *how* we say it and our body's natural reaction when we do.

The baseline is a catalogue of those behaviours exhibited when the subject is telling the truth. This is the standard the interrogator will compare later to the subject's behaviour when he might have a reason to lie. Any differences between the two suggest deception.

Finally Dance had a good profile of the truthful Daniel Pell and moved to the crux of her mission this foggy morning in June. 'I'd like to ask you a few questions about Robert Herron.'

Eyes sweeping hers, now refining their examination: the abalone shell necklace, which her mother had made, at her throat. Then Dance's short pink-polished nails. The grey pearl ring on the wedding-band finger got two glances.

'Where were you living in January of 1996?'

'Monterey.'

'What street?'

He pursed his lips. 'Beats me. North part of town, I think.'

Interesting. Deceptive subjects often avoid specifics, which can be checked. And it was rare not to remember where you lived. Still, his kinesic responses weren't suggesting deception.

'How did you meet Robert Herron?'

'You're assuming I did. Never met him in my life. I swear.'

The last sentence was a deception flag, though his body language wasn't giving off signals that suggested he was lying.

'But you told the prisoner in Capitola that you wanted him to go to the well and find the hammer and wallet.'

'No, that's what *he* told the warden.' Pell offered an amused smile. 'Why don't you talk to him about it? You've got sharp eyes, Officer Dance. I've seen them looking me over, deciding if I'm being straight with you. I'll bet you could tell in a flash that boy was lying.'

She gave no reaction, but reflected that it was very rare for a suspect to realise he was being analysed kinesically. 'But then how did he know about the evidence in the well?'

'Oh, I've got that figured out. Somebody stole a hammer of mine, killed Herron with it and planted it to blame me. They wore gloves. Those rubber ones everybody wears on *CSI.*'

Still relaxed. Pell's body language wasn't any different from his baseline. He was showing only emblems—common gestures that tended to substitute for words, like shrugs and finger pointing. There were no adaptors, which signal tension, or affect displays—signs that he was experiencing emotion.

'But if he wanted to do that,' Dance pointed out, 'wouldn't the killer just call the police *then*? Why wait more than ten years?'

'Being smart, I'd guess. Better to bide his time. Then spring the trap.'

'But why call the prisoner in Capitola? Why not just call the police?'

A hesitation. Then a laugh. His blue eyes shone with excitement. 'Because the police are involved too. The case is unsolved, and they want to blame someone. Why not *me*? I'll bet the cops planted the hammer themselves.'

'Let's work with this a little. There are two different things you're saying. First, somebody stole your hammer *before* Herron was killed, murdered him with it, and now, all this time later, dimes you out. But your second version is that the police got your hammer *after* Herron was killed by someone else altogether and planted it in the well to blame you. Those are contradictory. It's one or the other. Which do you think?'

'Hmm.' Pell thought for a few seconds. 'OK, I'll go with number two. The police. It's a set-up. I'm sure that's what happened.'

She nodded agreeably. 'Let's consider that. First, where would the police have gotten the hammer?'

He thought. 'When they arrested me for that Carmel thing.'

'The Croyton murders in '99?'

'Right. All the evidence they took from my house in Seaside.'

Dance's brows furrowed. 'I doubt that. Evidence is accounted for too closely. No, I'd go for a more credible scenario: that the hammer was stolen recently. Where else could somebody find a hammer of yours? Do you have any property in the state?'

'No.'

'Any relatives or friends who could've had tools of yours?'

'Not really.'

Which was even slipperier than 'I don't recall'. Dance noticed too that Pell had put his hands on the table at the word 'relatives'. This was a deviation from baseline behaviour. It didn't mean lying, but he *was* feeling stress. The questions were upsetting him.

'Daniel, do you have any relations living in California?'

He hesitated, must have assessed that she was the sort to check out every comment—which she was—and said, 'The only one left's my aunt. Down in Bakersfield.'

'Is her name Pell?'

'Yep. . . . That's good thinking, Officer Dance. I'll bet the deputies who dropped the ball on the Herron case stole that hammer from her house and planted it. Why don't you talk to them?'

'All right. Now let's think about the wallet. Where could that've come from? . . . Here's a thought. What if it's not Robert Herron's wallet at all? What if this rogue cop just bought a wallet, had R.H. stamped in the leather, then hid that and the hammer in the well?'

Pell lowered his head and said nothing.

It was unfolding just as she'd planned. Dance had forced him to pick the more credible of two explanations for his innocence—and proceeded to prove it wasn't credible at all. No jury would believe that the police had fabricated evidence and stolen tools hundreds of miles from the crime scene. Pell was now realising the mistake he'd made.

Checkmate. Her heart thumped a bit, and she was thinking that the next words out of his mouth might be about a plea bargain.

She was wrong.

His eyes bored into hers with pure malevolence. He lunged forward as far as he could. Only the chains hooked to the chair and bolted to the floor stopped him from sinking his teeth into her.

She jerked back, gasping.

'You goddamn bitch! Oh, I get it now. Sure, you're part of it too! Yeah, yeah, blame Daniel. It's always my fault! I'm the easy target.'

Her heart was pounding furiously now, and she was afraid. But the restraints were secure, and he couldn't reach her.

Suddenly Pell's fury was replaced with a cold calm. He sat back, caught his breath and looked her over again. 'You're in your thirties, Officer Dance. You're somewhat pretty. I guarantee there's a man in your life. Or has been.' Another glance at the pearl ring. 'And you've got children, right? Close in age and not too old, I'll bet.'

This unnerved her, but she struggled not to react. He *doesn't* know I have children. He can't. But he acts as if he's certain. Was there something about *my* behaviour he noted? Something that suggested to him that I'm a mother?

'Daniel,' she said smoothly, 'an outburst isn't going to help.'

'I've got friends on the outside, you know. They owe me. They'd love to hang with your husband and children. Yeah, it's a tough life being a cop. The little ones spend a lot of time alone, don't they? They'd probably love friends to play with.'

Dance returned his gaze, never flinching. She asked, 'Could you tell me about your relationship with that prisoner in Capitola?'

'Yes, I could. But I won't.' His emotionless words mocked her, suggesting that for a professional interrogator, she'd phrased her question carelessly. In a soft voice he added, 'I think it's time to go back to my cell.'

ALONZO 'SANDY' SANDOVAL, the Monterey County prosecutor, was a handsome round man with black hair and an ample moustache. He sat in his office, two flights above the lockup, behind a desk littered with files. 'Hi, Kathryn. So, our boy, did he beat his breast and cry, "*Mea culpa*"?'

'Not exactly.' Dance sat down and peered into the coffee cup she'd left on the desk forty-five minutes ago. 'I rate it as, oh, one of the least successful interrogations of all time.'

'You look shook, Boss,' said a short, wiry young man with curly red hair, wearing jeans and a plaid sports jacket. TJ's outfit was unconventional for an investigative agent with the CBI—the most conservative law-enforcement agency in the state, but so was pretty much everything about him. Thirty and single, TJ Scanlon tended to work solo, surveillance and undercover, rather than pairing up with another CBI agent, which was the bureau's standard procedure. But Dance's regular partner was in Mexico on an extradition and TJ had jumped at the chance to see the Son of Manson.

'Not shook. Just *curious*.' She explained that the interview had been going fine when suddenly Pell turned on her. Under TJ's sceptical gaze, she conceded, 'OK, I'm a *little* shook. I've been threatened before. But his were *calm* threats.'

The little ones spend a lot of time alone . . .

'What happened?' Sandoval asked.

'When he denied knowing Herron, there was no stress reaction at all. It was only when I had him talking about police conspiracy that he started to exhibit aversion and negation.'

Kathryn Dance was often called a human lie detector, but that wasn't accurate; in reality, she, like all successful kinesic analysts and interrogators, was a *stress* detector. This was the key to deception; once she spotted stress, she'd probe the topic that gave rise to it and dig until the subject broke.

Kinesics experts identify several different types of stress. Some types arise primarily when someone isn't telling the whole truth. Dance called this 'deception stress'. But people also experience general stress, which has nothing to do with lying. She'd found that different kinesic behaviours signal the two different kinds of stress.

She explained this, and added, 'My sense was that he'd lost control of the interview, so he went ballistic.' Then her mind made one of its curious jumps. A to B to X. She couldn't explain how they happened. But she always paid attention. 'Where was Robert Herron murdered?' She walked to a map of Monterey County on Sandoval's wall.

'Here.' The prosecutor touched an area in the yellow trapezoid.

'And the well where they found the hammer and wallet?'

'About here, make it.' It was a quarter mile from the crime scene, in a residential area.

Dance stared at the map. 'You have a picture of the well?'

Sandoval dug in the file. 'Forensics shot a lot of pics.' He riffled through a stack of photographs until he found the ones he sought.

Gazing at them, Dance asked TJ, 'We ran a case there six, eight months ago, remember?'

'The arson, sure. In that new housing development.'

Tapping the spot on the map where the well was located, Dance continued. 'The development is still under construction. And that'—she nodded at a photograph—'is a hard-rock well.'

Everybody in the area knew that water was at such a premium in this part of California that hard-rock wells, with their low output, were never used for agriculture, only for private homes.

'Hell,' Sandoval said. 'Ten years ago, when Herron was killed, that was all farmland. The well wouldn't have been there then.'

'It wasn't there *one* year ago,' Dance muttered. *'That's* why Pell was so stressed. I was getting close to the truth—somebody *did* get the hammer from his aunt's in Bakersfield and had a fake wallet made up, then planted them there recently. Only it wasn't to frame him.'

'Oh, no,' TJ whispered.

Dance nodded. 'Pell set the whole thing up himself.'

'Why?' Sandoval asked.

'Because he couldn't escape from Capitola,' she said. That facility was a high-tech superprison, reserved for the most dangerous prisoners. 'But he could from here.'

Kathryn Dance lunged for the phone.

IN A SPECIAL holding cell, segregated from the other prisoners, Daniel Pell studied his cage and the corridor beyond, leading to the courthouse. To all appearances he was calm, but his heart was in turmoil. The woman cop had spooked him badly. He hadn't expected somebody to get inside his mind so deeply or so fast. It was like she could read his thoughts.

Kathryn Dance . . .

Pell turned back to Baxter, the guard who was outside the cage. He was a decent hack, not like Pell's escort from Capitola, a burly black man now sitting silently at the far door, watching everything.

'What I was saying . . .' Pell continued his conversation with Baxter. 'Jesus helped me. I was up to three packs a day. And He took time outta His schedule to help me. I quit pretty much cold.'

'Could use some of that help,' the hack confided. 'I tried the patch you put on your arm. Wasn't so good. Maybe I'll pray for help tomorrow.'

Pell had seen Baxter's lapel pin in the shape of a fish. 'Good for you.'

Baxter's phone rang. An instant later an alarm brayed.

The Capitola escort leaped to his feet just as a huge ball of fire filled the parking lot. The cell's barred window was open, and flames shot through it.

Pell dropped to the floor as black, greasy smoke streamed into the room. 'My dear Lord.'

Baxter stared at the flames engulfing the lot behind the courthouse. He grabbed the phone but apparently the line was dead. He pulled his walkie-talkie off his belt and reported the fire.

Daniel Pell lowered his head and began to mutter the Lord's Prayer.

'Yo, Pell!'

The con looked up.

The massive Capitola escort was holding a Taser. He tossed leg shackles to Pell. 'Put 'em on. We're going down that corridor, out the front door and into the van.' More flames streamed in. A car's gas tank had exploded. 'You're going to stay right beside me. You understand?'

'Yeah, sure.' Pell ratcheted on the shackles. 'Let's go! Please!'

Sweating, Baxter said, 'Whaddaya think it is? Terrorists?'

Ignoring the panicked hack, the Capitola escort pointed the Taser at Pell. 'If you don't do 'xactly what I say, you'll get fifty thousand volts.'

'Yessir. Let's go. Please,' said Pell. 'I'll do whatever you want.'

'Open it,' the escort barked to Baxter, who hit a button.

With a buzz, the door eased outwards. The three men started down the corridor, which was filling with smoke. The alarm was braying.

But wait, Pell thought. It was a second alarm—the first had sounded *before* the explosions. Had someone figured out what he was going to do?

Kathryn Dance . . .

Just as they passed a fire door, Pell glanced back. Thick smoke was filling the corridor around them. He cried to Baxter, 'No, it's too late. The whole building's going to go! Let's get out of here.'

'He's right.' Baxter reached to the alarm bar of the exit door.

'No,' the Capitola escort said calmly. 'Out the front to the prison van.'

'You're crazy!' Pell snapped. 'For the love of God. We'll die.'

As he shoved the fire door open, the men were hit with a blast of fierce heat, smoke and sparks. Outside, a wall of fire consumed cars and shrubbery.

Pell dropped to his knees, covering his face. 'My eyes!' he screamed.

'Goddamn it, Pell—' The escort stepped forward, lifting the Taser.

'Put that down. He's not going anywhere,' Baxter said angrily. 'He's hurt.'

'I can't see,' Pell moaned. 'Somebody, help me!'

Baxter turned towards him, bent down.

'Don't!' the escort shouted.

Then Baxter staggered back, a bewildered expression on his face, as Pell repeatedly shoved a knife into his belly. Bleeding in cascades, the county hack fell to his knees. As Pell shoved him aside, the huge escort fired the Taser. It discharged, but the probes went wide. Pell moved towards him.

The big man froze, staring at the knife. The useless Taser dropped from his hand and his massive fists balled up. 'Don't do it, Daniel.'

Pell charged forward, dodging the man's blows, and struck him hard a dozen times, the knife edge facing out and down from his clenched hand. Punching was the most effective way to use a knife against a strong opponent.

His face contorting, the escort fell, gripping his throat. A moment later he stopped moving. Pell grabbed the shackle keys and undid the irons. He stepped to the door again, covered his eyes, and grabbed the metallic fire-proof bag, where he'd got the knife, just outside the door.

At that moment, the gas tank of the car nearest the door exploded; a flare of orange flame shot through the doorway.

Flames licked his cheek, but he stood his ground. *Hold fast . . .*

KATHRYN DANCE put down the phone just as the courthouse security chief, a grizzled, crew-cut retired cop, stuck his head into the office.

'Who's running the search?' he asked. 'Who's in charge?'

Sandoval glanced at Dance. 'You're senior.'

Dance had never encountered a situation like this—a fire bomb and an escape by a killer like Daniel Pell—but then, she didn't know of *anybody* on the Peninsula who had. It was vital to move fast and decisively.

'OK,' she said. And instructed the security chief to get other guards downstairs immediately and to the doors where people were exiting.

Screams outside. People running in the corridor.

'Look,' TJ said, nodding towards the window, where black smoke obscured the view completely. 'Oh, man.'

Despite the fire, which might be raging inside now, Dance decided to remain in Alonzo Sandoval's office. She wouldn't waste time by relocating or evacuating. If the building was engulfed they could jump out of the windows to the roofs of cars parked in the front lot, ten feet below.

She turned back to the security chief. 'We need a room-by-room search of the building.'

'Yes, ma'am,' he said, and trotted off.

'And in case he gets out, I want roadblocks,' Dance said to TJ. 'Here, here, here.' Her short nails tapped loudly on the laminated map of Salinas.

Noting the places she had indicated, TJ made calls to the Highway Patrol—

California's state police—and the Monterey County Sheriff's Office.

Sandoval, the prosecutor—grim and dazed—stared at the smoky parking lot. Flashing lights reflected in the window. He said nothing. Reports came in. No sign of Pell in the building or outside.

The courthouse security chief returned a few minutes later, coughing hard. 'Fire's under control,' he said shakily. 'But Jim Baxter's dead; so's the Capitola guard. Stabbed. Pell got a knife somehow.'

'No,' Sandoval whispered. 'Oh, no.'

'We can't figure out where he went,' the chief went on. 'Somebody opened the fire door, but there were flames everywhere that way.'

Looking up from his phone, TJ called, 'Monterey and CHP should have the main highways sealed in fifteen minutes.'

It worked to their advantage that Salinas wasn't a huge town, and agricultural fields covered most of the surrounding area, with limited highways and roads. On foot, Pell would be very visible in the fields of low crops.

Dance ordered TJ to have Pell's mug shots sent to the sheriff's office and the highway patrol officers manning the roadblocks. She nodded to the security chief. 'What about Baxter's weapon?'

'No weapon.'

Damn. 'TJ, tell everybody Pell's armed.'

'Roger that.'

Dance looked up to see Sandoval staring numbly at the map. 'Who helped him?' he muttered. 'And where the hell is he?'

These two questions were also spinning through Kathryn Dance's mind. Along with another: What could I have done to read him better? What could I have done to avoid this tragedy altogether?

Chapter 2

D ance was outside in the parking lot, surveying the scene, when she got a call from her boss. Charles Overby was the agent in charge of the west-central regional office of the CBI.

'I'm on my way to the courthouse. What've we got, Kathryn?'

She updated him, including the deaths of the guard and the escort.

'Sorry to hear that. Any leads, anything we can tell the press?'

'I don't know, Charles. Pell could be anywhere. I've ordered roadblocks, and we're doing a room-by-room search.'

Overby sighed. 'OK. By the way, you're in charge of the manhunt.'

'Me?' She was surprised. CBI certainly had jurisdiction; it was the state's highest-ranking law-enforcement agency, and she was a senior agent. Still, the CBI was investigative and didn't have a large staff. The California Highway Patrol and the sheriff's office would have to provide manpower. 'Why not somebody from CHP or the Mercer County Sheriff's Office?'

'I think we need central coordination on this one. Besides, it's a done deal. I've cleared it with everybody.'

'OK, but I want Michael on board.' Michael O'Neil was the Monterey County Sheriff's Office detective Dance worked with most often. She and the soft-spoken officer had worked together for years; in fact, he'd been a mentor when she'd joined the CBI.

'That's fine with me. I'll be there soon. I want another briefing before the press conference.' Overby disconnected.

Dance was heading towards the back of the courthouse when flashing lights caught her eye. She recognised one of the CBI's Tauruses, the grille pulsing red and blue.

Rey Carraneo, the most recent addition to the office, pulled up nearby and joined her. The slim man, with black eyes sunk beneath thick brows, had only two months on the job. But he had been a cop near Reno for three years—a tough venue before moving to the Peninsula. He was a tireless, reliable law enforcer. And that counted for a lot.

Carraneo was only six years younger than Dance, but he couldn't bring himself to call her Kathryn, as she frequently offered. His usual greeting was a nod. He gave her a respectful one now.

'Come with me,' Dance said. 'He's probably got an accomplice, and we know he's got a weapon. So eyes open.' They continued to the back of the courthouse, where arson investigators and crime-scene officers were looking over the carnage. Four cars had burned to the frames, and the back of the building was black with soot.

Her eyes slipped to the open fire door.

'No way he got out *there*,' Carraneo said, echoing Dance's thought.

From the destroyed cars and the scorch marks on the pavement, it was clear that the fire had surrounded the door; the flames were meant to be a diversion. But where *had* he gone?

'These cars all accounted for?' she asked a fireman.

'Yeah. They're all employees'.'

'Hey, Kathryn, we have the device,' a man in a uniform said to her. He was the county's chief fire marshal.

She nodded a greeting. 'What was it?'

'Wheelie suitcase, big one, filled with plastic milk containers of gasoline. The doer planted it under that Saab there. Slow-burning fuse.'

'A pro?'

'Probably not. We found the fuse residue. You can make 'em out of clothes line and chemicals. Got instructions from the Internet, I'd say. The sort of things kids make to blow stuff up with.'

'Can you trace anything?'

'Maybe. We'll have it sent to the MCSO lab and then we'll see.'

'You know when it was left?'

He nodded at the Saab. 'The driver got here about nine fifteen, so it'd be after that.'

'Any hope for prints?'

'Doubt it.'

Dance stood with her hands on her hips surveying the battleground. Something felt wrong.

The dim corridor, visible through the open door. Blood on the concrete. The open door.

Turning slowly, studying the area, Dance noticed behind the building something in a nearby pine and cypress grove, a tree from which dangled an orange ribbon—the sort used to mark shrubs and trees scheduled for cutting. Walking closer, she noticed that the mound of pine needles at its base was larger than those beneath the others. Dance dropped to her knees and dug into it. She unearthed a large scorched bag made of metallic cloth.

'Rey, need some gloves.' She coughed from the smoke.

The young agent got a pair from an MCSO crime-scene deputy and brought them to her. Inside the bag were Pell's orange prison uniform and a set of grey hooded overalls, which turned out to be some kind of fire suit.

Her shoulders slumped in disgust. *What are we up against here?*

'I don't get it,' Rey Carraneo said.

Dance explained that Pell's partner had probably set the bomb and left the fireproof bag outside the door; it had contained the fire suit and a knife. Pell had donned the garment and run through the flames to the tree marked with the orange tag, where the partner had hidden some civilian clothes. He'd changed and sprinted off.

She called on her Motorola and reported what she'd found, then gave the evidence to one of the crime-scene officers.

Carraneo called her to a patch of earth not far away. 'Footprints.'

Several impressions left by someone running. The two CBI agents started jogging in the direction they led.

Pell's footsteps ended at a nearby street, San Benito Way, along which were vacant lots, a liquor store, a dingy taqueria, a quick-copy and shipping franchise, a pawnshop and a bar.

'So here's where the partner picked him up,' Carraneo said.

'Could be.' Dance scanned the area, coughing again. Finally her eyes focused across the street. 'Come on, let's move!'

THE MAN—in his late twenties, wearing shorts and a Worldwide Express uniform shirt—drove his green panel truck through the streets of Salinas. He was intensely aware of the gun barrel resting on his shoulder, and he was crying. 'Look, mister, really, we don't carry cash. I've got about fifty on me, personal money—'

'Give me your wallet.' The hijacker wore shorts, a windcheater and an Oakland A's cap. His face was streaked with soot and his beard was burnt. His eyes were a weird light blue.

'Whatever you want, mister. Just don't hurt me. I've got a family.'

'Wal-let?'

The stocky young man prised the billfold out of his tight shorts. 'Here!'

The hijacker flipped through it. 'Now, William Gilmore, of 3435 Rio Grande Avenue, Marina, California, father of these two fine children, if the photo gallery's up to date. And husband of this lovely wife. Look at those curls. Natural, I'll bet any money.'

Dread unravelled inside Billy Gilmore.

'Keep going where I told you and hand me your cellphone.'

Billy gave him the phone and heard the man punch in a number.

''Lo. It's me. Write this down.' He repeated Billy's address. 'He's got a wife and two kids. Wife's real pretty.'

Billy whispered, 'Who's that you're calling? Please, mister . . . Please. Take the truck, take anything. I'll give you as much time as you want to get away. An hour. Two hours. Just don't—'

'Shhhh.' The man continued his phone conversation. 'If I don't show up, that'll mean I didn't make it through the roadblocks because William here wasn't convincing enough. You go visit his family. They're all yours.'

KATHRYN DANCE and Rey Carraneo were in the You Mail It franchise on San Benito Way, where they'd just learned that a package delivery company, Worldwide Express, had made its morning drop-off moments after the escape.

A to B to X . . .

Dance realised that Pell could hijack a truck to get by the roadblocks. She called the Worldwide Express Salinas operations director, who confirmed that the driver on that route had missed all remaining deliveries. Dance got the tag number of his truck and relayed it to the MCSO.

They returned to Sandy Sandoval's office to coordinate efforts to find the truck. There were twenty-five Worldwide trucks in the area, so Dance told the director to order the drivers to pull over immediately at the nearest gas station. The truck that kept moving would contain Daniel Pell.

This was taking some time, though. The director had to call them on their cellphones, since a radio broadcast would alert Pell that they knew about his means of escape.

A figure walked slowly through the doorway. Dance turned to see Michael O'Neil, the Sheriff's Office chief deputy, walk in. She nodded at him with a smile, greatly relieved he was here.

O'Neil had been with the MCSO for years. A solid investigator with a stunning conviction record, he was now a chief deputy and detective with the investigations division. He'd resisted offers to join bigger law-enforcement ops that required extensive travel. O'Neil's lifelong home was the Monterey Peninsula, and he had no desire to be anywhere else. With his love of the bay, fishing and his boat, Michael O'Neil could be the unwavering, unobtrusive hero in a John Steinbeck novel.

The MCSO uniform was typical khaki, but O'Neil often dressed soft, and today he was in a navy suit with a tieless charcoal-grey shirt, matching about half the hair on his head. His brown eyes moved slowly as they examined the map of the area. His physique was columnar and his arms thick, from genes and from playing tug-of-war with muscular seafood in Monterey Bay when time and the weather allowed him to get his boat out.

He nodded a greeting to TJ and Sandoval, then answered a phone call and walked to the map. He tucked the phone between ear and shoulder, picked up a pack of self-adhesive notes and began sticking them up.

Roadblocks, Dance realised.

He hung up. 'They're on 68, 183, the 101. We've got the back roads to Hollister covered, and Soledad and Greenfield.'

Sandoval said, 'If Pell's partner didn't drive getaway, where is *he*?'

TJ offered, 'Rendezvous point somewhere?'

'Or staying around,' Dance said, 'to find out what we know.'

O'Neil suggested, 'Or maybe he wants to slow us up.'

But as it turned out, they had no time to speculate about whether the partner was nearby. The plan about the Worldwide Express trucks had paid off. A call to O'Neil from MCSO's central radio dispatch unit reported that two policemen had found Pell and were presently in pursuit.

THE DARK GREEN delivery truck was kicking up a rooster tail of dust.

One uniformed officer gripped the wheel of the squad car. His partner gripped the microphone. 'Salinas Police Mobile Seven. We're still with him. On a dirt road off Natividad.'

'Roger. Central to Seven, all available units are en route.'

'Roger that.'

The driver muttered, 'Where's he going? There's nothing here.'

The road was used mostly for farm equipment. It led to no major highways. But Pell would not know that it ended abruptly in the middle of an artichoke field. Ahead of them, Pell braked in panic and the truck began to skid. Its front wheels dropped into an irrigation ditch, and the rear end lifted off the ground, then slammed back with a crash.

The squad car braked. 'This is Seven. Pell's off the road.'

'Roger, is he—?'

The officers leapt out of the car with their pistols drawn. 'He's going to bail, he's going to bail!' But nobody exited the truck.

They approached it. The back door had flown open in the crash, and they could see dozens of packages and envelopes littering the floor.

'There he is, look.'

Pell lay stunned, face down, on the floor of the vehicle. The men cuffed and dragged him out of the space where he was wedged.

'Nice try, buddy, but—'

'Fuck. It's not him.'

'What?'

'Does *that* look like a forty-three-year-old white guy?'

The officer bent down to the groggy teenager, a gang teardrop tat on his cheek, and snapped, 'Who are you?' in Spanish, a language that every law enforcer in and around Salinas could speak.

The kid avoided their eyes. 'I no saying nothing.'

'Oh, man.' The cop glanced into the cab, where the keys dangled from the dash. He understood: Pell had left the truck on a city street with the engine on, knowing it would be stolen—in about sixty seconds—so the police would follow it, giving Pell a chance to escape.

Another thought. Not a good one. He turned to his partner. 'You don't think, when they called all availables for back-up, they pulled 'em off the roadblocks, do you?'

The men looked at each other.

'Christ.' The partner raced to the squad car and grabbed the microphone.

'A HONDA CIVIC,' TJ reported, hanging up from a call with the Department of Motor Vehicles. 'Five years old. Red. I've got the tags.' They knew Pell was now in the Worldwide Express driver's personal car, which was missing from the company lot. 'I'll let the roadblocks know.'

'*When* they get back on site,' Dance muttered.

To the dismay of the agents, some local dispatcher had ordered the nearby roadblocks abandoned for the pursuit of the Worldwide Express truck. His placid face registering disgust, O'Neil had sent the cars back on site immediately.

They were in a meeting room up the hall from Sandoval's office. A figure strode confidently through the door. Charles Overby, a fifty-five-year-old career law enforcer, greeted his agents. Brown-haired and sunburnt, Overby was the newly appointed head of the CBI's west-central office.

'He wasn't in the truck?' Overby asked Dance.

'No. Local gangbanger. Pell left the truck running. He knew somebody'd snatch it. He took off in the delivery driver's own car. No sign of the driver.'

'Ouch.'

They updated Overby, adding the details of Pell's new wheels.

'Nobody's spotted the Civic,' said O'Neil, 'but he could've gotten through on the 101.' The 101, wide as an interstate, would take Pell to every major expressway in the state. 'They're setting up new checkpoints in Gilroy. And about thirty miles south,' O'Neil added.

'And you've got the bus terminals and airport secure?'

'That's right,' Dance said.

'And San Jose and Oakland PD are in the loop?'

'Yep. And the other nearby counties.'

Overby jotted a few notes. 'Good. Oh, I just talked to Amy Grabe.'

Amy Grabe was the SAC—the special agent in charge of the FBI's San Francisco field office. Dance knew the sharp, focused law enforcer well, and she'd had a number of opportunities to work with her. Dance's late husband, an agent with the FBI's local resident agency, had too.

Overby continued, 'If we don't get Pell soon, they've got a specialist I want on board. A cult expert. Deals with people like Pell.'

Dance shrugged. 'Well, I'm not sure how useful that'd be.'

But Overby had clearly made up his mind already. 'He's a brilliant profiler, can really get into their minds. The cult mentality is a lot different from your typical perp's.' Overby handed Dance a slip of paper with a name and phone number on it. 'He'll be here tomorrow morning.'

'You sure about this, Charles?'

'With Pell we can use all the help we can get. Absolutely. And a big gun from Washington? More expertise, more person power.'

More places to stash the blame, Dance thought cynically. But she kept the smile on her face. 'All right, then.'

'OK, I've got that press conference. If you hear anything else, let me know. I'll be on in about ten minutes.' The man left.

O'Neil stifled a smile.

'Don't get me started,' Dance muttered.

She looked out the window at the people milling in front of the building. 'I'm worried about that partner. Where is he?'

'Who'd bust somebody like Pell outta the joint?' asked TJ.

Dance recalled Pell's kinesic reactions in the interrogation when the subject of his aunt in Bakersfield arose. 'I think whoever's helping him got the hammer from his aunt. Pell's her last name. Find her.' She had another thought. 'Oh, and check this guy out, discreetly.' She gave TJ the slip of paper with the FBI profiler's name on it.

O'Neil took a call and had a brief conversation. He hung up and explained, 'That was the warden at Capitola. I thought we should talk to the supervising guard on Pell's cell block, see if he can tell us anything. Also, a fellow prisoner claims to have information.'

'Good,' Dance said. Her cellphone rang, a croaking frog.

O'Neil lifted an eyebrow. 'Wes or Maggie've been busy.'

It was a family joke. The kids would reprogramme the ringer of her phone when Dance wasn't looking. She hit the RECEIVE button. 'Hello?'

'It's me, Agent Dance.'

She recognised the voice of Rey Carraneo. 'What's up, Rey?'

'No sign of his partner or any other devices. Security wants to know if they can let everybody back inside the courthouse.'

Dance debated the matter with O'Neil. They decided to wait.

'TJ, go outside and help them search. I don't like it that the accomplice is unaccounted for.'

She recalled what her father had told her after he'd nearly had a run-in with a great white in the waters off northern Australia. 'The shark you don't see is always more dangerous than the one you do.'

THE STOCKY, bearded, balding man in his hard-worn fifties stood near the courthouse looking over the chaos, his sharp eyes checking out everyone—the police, the guards, the civilians.

'Hey, Officer, how you doing? You got a minute? Just like to ask you a few questions . . . You mind saying a few words into the tape recorder? . . . Oh, sure, I understand. I'll catch you later. Sure. Good luck.'

Morton Nagle had watched the men and women conducting the search, their strategy—and faces—making clear that they'd never run an escape. He'd also watched the uneasy crowds, thinking accidental fire, then thinking terrorists, then hearing the truth and looking even more scared. As well they should, Nagle reflected.

'Excuse me, do you have a minute to talk? . . . Oh, sure. Not a problem. Sorry to bother you, Officer.'

Nagle milled through the crowds. Smoothing his wispy hair, tugging up saggy tan slacks, he studied the fire trucks, the squad cars, the smoky courthouse. He snapped some pictures through the foggy haze.

A middle-aged woman looked over his battered camera bag. She snapped, 'You people, you *journalists*, you're like vultures. Why don't you let the police do their job?'

He gave a chuckle. 'I didn't know I wasn't.'

'You're all the same.' The woman turned away angrily.

Nagle hitched up his slacks and scanned the crowd. Off to the side he spotted a tall, young Latino in a suit, clearly a plain-clothes detective. The man was speaking to an elderly woman who wore a juror badge. Nagle sized up the officer. Good. Just what he wanted—young, gullible, trusting. Nagle began slowly moving towards him. Closing the distance.

The man moved on, oblivious, looking for more people to interview.

When he was ten feet away, Nagle slipped the camera strap round his neck, unzipped the bag, reached inside. He stepped closer yet.

And felt a strong hand close round his arm. Nagle gasped and felt his heart give a jolt.

'Just keep those hands where I can see them.' The man was a short, fidgety officer with the CBI. Nagle read the ID dangling from his neck.

'Hey, what—?'

'Shhhhh.' The officer had curly red hair. 'Hey, Rey.'

The Latino detective joined them. He too had a CBI ID card. Together they led Nagle to the side of the courthouse.

'Look, I don't know—'

'Shhhhh,' the red-haired officer hissed again.

The Latino frisked him carefully and nodded. Then he lifted Nagle's press pass off his chest. 'This is four years out of date.'

'I must've picked up the wrong one. I've been a reporter for—'

'So if we called this paper, they'd say you're an employee?'

If they called the paper, they'd get a nonworking number. 'I can explain.'

The short officer frowned. 'I sure *would* like an explanation. See, one of the groundskeepers told me a man fitting your description was here at eight thirty this morning. *Before* the escape. So before you do any explaining, turn around and put your hands behind your back.'

IN THE CONFERENCE ROOM on the second floor of the courthouse, TJ handed Dance what he'd found on Morton Nagle.

No weapons, no incendiary fuse, just a wallet, camera, tape recorder and notebook. Along with three true-crime books, his name on the cover and his picture on the back, where he was described as 'a former police reporter'.

'This doesn't let you off the hook,' Dance snapped. 'Why were you at the courthouse before the fire?'

'I got here early to get some interviews.'

O'Neil said, 'With Pell? He doesn't give them.'

'No, no, not Pell. With the family of Robert Herron. I heard they were coming to testify to the grand jury.'

'What about the fake press pass?'

'OK, it's been four years since I've been credentialled with a newspaper. I've been writing books full-time. But without a press pass, you can't get anywhere. Nobody ever looks at the date.'

TJ looked up from his laptop. 'He's clean, Boss. At least no priors. DMV pic checks out too.'

'I'm writing a book. It's all legit. You can check.' He gave them the name of his editor in Manhattan.

Dance called and spoke to the woman, whose attitude was, Oh, hell, what's Morton got himself into now? But she confirmed that he'd signed a contract for a new book about Pell.

Dance then said to TJ, 'Uncuff him.'

O'Neil turned to the author. 'What's the book about?'

'It isn't like any true crime you've read before. It's not about the murders. That's been done. My book's about the *victims* of Daniel Pell—what their lives were like before the murders and, the ones who survived, what they're like now. It's about Theresa Croyton—the girl who survived—and the family's relatives and friends. The title's going to be *The Sleeping Doll*. That's what they called Theresa. I'm also going to include the women who were in Pell's "Family", the ones he brainwashed. Pell has hundreds of victims when you think about it. I see violent crime like dropping a stone into a pond. The ripples of consequence can spread almost for ever.'

'Mr Nagle, do you have any information that could help us?' Dance asked. 'What Pell might be up to? Who's helping him?'

Nagle shook his head. 'No idea. I'm sorry. I really just got started on the project a month or so ago. I've been doing the background research.'

'The women in Pell's Family, have you contacted them?'

'Two of them. I asked if they'd let me interview them.'

O'Neil asked, 'They're out of jail?'

'Oh, yes. They weren't involved in the Croyton murders. They got short terms, mostly for larceny-related offences.'

'Could one of them—or both, I guess—be his accomplice?'

Nagle considered this. 'I can't see it. They think Pell's the worst thing that ever happened to them.'

'Who are they?' O'Neil asked.

'Rebecca Sheffield and Linda Whitfield.'

'Have they kept out of trouble?'

'Think so. No police records I could find. Linda Whitfield lives with her brother in Portland. She works for a church. Rebecca Sheffield runs a consulting service in San Diego.'

'You have their numbers?'

The writer flipped through a notebook of fat pages. His handwriting was sloppy and large, the notes voluminous.

'There was a third woman in the Family,' Dance recalled.

'Samantha McCoy. She disappeared years ago. Rebecca said she changed her name and moved away. I've done a little searching, but I haven't been able to find her yet.'

'Find her, TJ,' Dance said.

The agent bounded off to the corner of the room. Nagle gave her the numbers for the other two women, and she placed a call to Rebecca Sheffield.

'Women's Initiatives,' a receptionist said. 'May I help you?'

A moment later Dance found herself speaking to the head of the company, a no-nonsense woman with a low, raspy voice. The agent explained about Pell's escape.

Rebecca Sheffield was shocked. Dance asked if she had any thoughts on where Pell might go or who his accomplice could be.

Rebecca didn't, though. She said that she'd met Pell just a few months before the Croyton murders. And she could offer nothing about Samantha McCoy's whereabouts. Then, uneasy, she said, 'Back then I didn't turn him in, but I did cooperate with the police. Do you think I'm in danger?'

'I couldn't say. But you might want to contact San Diego police.' Dance gave the woman her numbers at CBI and her mobile, and Rebecca told her she'd try to think of anyone who might help Pell or know where he'd go.

The agent pushed down the button on the phone cradle and dialled the second number, which turned out to be the Church of the Holy Brethren in Portland. She was connected to Linda Whitfield, whose reaction was completely different: silence, broken by nearly inaudible muttering. All Dance caught was 'dear Jesus'. Praying, it seemed, not an exclamation. The voice faded, or she was cut off.

'Hello?' Dance asked.

'Yes, I'm here,' Linda said.

Dance asked the same questions she'd put to Rebecca Sheffield and received the same answers. Linda hadn't heard from Pell in years and could offer no leads as to where Pell would go or who his accomplice might be. Nor did she have any information about Samantha McCoy's whereabouts.

'We don't know what Pell has in mind,' Dance told her. 'We have no reason to believe you're in danger, but—'

'Oh, Daniel wouldn't hurt me,' she said quickly.

'Still, you might want to tell your local police. And if you can think of anything else, please call.' Dance gave her the phone numbers and hung up.

A few moments later, CBI chief Charles Overby strode into the room. 'Press conference went well, I think. They asked some prickly questions, but I fielded them OK. You see it?' He nodded at the TV in the corner. No one had bothered to turn up the volume to hear his performance.

'Missed it, Charles. Been on the phone.'

Overby stared at Nagle. 'Who's he?'

Dance introduced them; then the writer instantly disappeared from the agent in charge's radar screen. 'Any progress at all?' A glance at the maps.

'No reports,' Dance said. She told him she'd contacted two of the women who'd been in Pell's Family. 'One's in San Diego, one's in Portland. So at least we know they aren't the accomplice.'

Overby nodded and announced he was headed back to the CBI office. He left the conference room.

Dance turned to Morton Nagle. 'Do you have any research about Pell I could look at?'

'Well, I suppose,' the writer said. 'But copies, not the originals.'

'That's fine,' Dance told him. 'One of us'll come by later and pick them up. Where's your office?'

Nagle gave Dance the address and phone number of the house he was renting in Monterey, then began packing up his camera bag.

Dance glanced down at it. 'Hold on. Your camera. Did you take any pictures this morning before the fire?'

'Yes, I did.'

'Can we see them?'

Nagle picked up the Canon and began to push buttons. Dance and O'Neil hunched over the tiny screen as the writer scrolled through the photos. Most were of people walking into the courthouse, a few artistic shots of the front of the building in the fog.

Then the detective and the agent simultaneously said, 'Wait.' The image they were looking at depicted the driveway that led to where the fire had occurred. They could make out someone behind a car wearing a blue jacket, a baseball cap and sunglasses.

'Look at the arm.'

Dance nodded. It seemed the person's arm trailed behind, as if wheeling a suitcase. 'Is that time stamped?'

Nagle called up the read-out. 'Nine twenty-two.'

'That'd work out,' Dance said, recalling the fire marshal's estimate of the time the gas bomb had been planted. 'Can you blow up the image?'

'Not in the camera.'

TJ said he could on his computer, though, no problem. Nagle gave the memory card to him, and Dance sent TJ back to CBI headquarters, reminding him, 'And Samantha McCoy. Track her down. The aunt too. Bakersfield.'

'You bet, Boss.'

Chapter 3

At lunch hour a woman in her mid-twenties was sitting on a patio outside the Whole Foods grocery store in Monterey's Del Monte Center. A pale disk of sun was slowly emerging as the blanket of fog melted away. The scent of pine filled the cool air. A typical California day on the coast, but everything about it was intensified. Which is what happens when you're in love and about to meet your boyfriend.

Blonde, *authentic* California blonde, Jennie Marston sipped her coffee. It was expensive but good. This wasn't her kind of store (the part-time caterer was a Safeway girl), but it was a good meeting place.

She was wearing close-fitting jeans, a light pink blouse and, underneath, a red Victoria's Secret bra and panties. Like the coffee, the lingerie was a luxury she couldn't afford. But some things you had to splurge on, Jennie reflected, rubbing the bump on her nose.

Stop it, she told herself. But she didn't.

Why couldn't she have met him a year later? She'd've had the cosmetic work done by then and be beautiful. At least she could do *something* about the nose and boobs. She only wished she could fix the toothpick shoulders and the boyish hips.

Jennie watched the unsmiling women wheeling their grocery carts to their mommy vans, thinking they couldn't possibly be as much in love with their husbands as she was with her boyfriend. She felt sorry for them.

She finished her coffee and returned to the store, wondering if the intensity she felt for her boyfriend was simply because it was new. But this wasn't teenage passion. They were mature people. And most important was their souls' connection. Each knew exactly how the other felt.

'Your favourite colour's green,' he'd shared with her the first time they'd spoken, 'I'll bet you sleep under a green comforter. It soothes you at night.'

Oh, he was *so* right. It was a blanket, not a comforter. But it was green as grass. What kind of man had *that* intuition?

Suddenly she paused, aware of a conversation between two women nearby.

'Somebody's dead. Stabbed. In Salinas. It just happened.'

Salinas? Jennie thought.

'Oh, the prison escape? Yeah, I just heard about it.'

'David Pell, no, Daniel. I heard some guards got killed.'

Her palms damp, heart uneasy, Jennie walked away. She checked her phone. Her boyfriend had called a while ago but nothing since then. She tried the number. He didn't answer.

Jennie returned to the turquoise Thunderbird, put on the radio news, then twisted the rearview mirror towards her. She pulled her make-up from her purse. *Some guards got killed . . .*

Don't worry about it, she told herself. Working on her face, concentrating the way her mother had taught her. It was one of the nice things the woman had done for her. *Smooth it in, blend it. Good.*

Though her mother often took away the nice. *It looked fine until you messed it up. Honestly, what's wrong with you?*

DANIEL PELL was strolling down the sidewalk from the small garage connected to an office building in Monterey. He'd abandoned Billy's Honda Civic earlier than planned. He'd heard on the news that the police had found the Worldwide Express truck, which meant they would probably assume he was in the Civic. He'd apparently evaded the roadblocks just in time.

How 'bout *that*, Kathryn?

He wasn't concerned about being out in public, not yet. Nobody would expect him here. Besides, he looked different. After dumping Billy's car, he'd slipped into the back parking lot of a motel, where he'd found a discarded razor and a tiny bottle of the motel's giveaway body lotion in the trash. He'd used them to shave off his beard.

A squad car went past. *Hold fast . . .* Pell was careful to maintain his pace, not looking around, not deviating from his route. Changing your behaviour draws attention. Smart people can figure out *why* you changed, then use it against you.

That's what had happened at the courthouse. *Kathryn . . .* To his astonishment, she'd learned exactly what he was doing. If she'd anticipated him just five minutes earlier, he would have been back in the Capitola prison van. The escape plan would have turned to dust.

Another squad car drove quickly past.

Still no glances his way. But Pell knew it was time to get out of Monterey. He slipped into the open-air shopping centre, which was packed. It was June; many schools were out of session.

One girl, college age, came out of a store, a bag over her shoulder. Beneath her jacket was a tight red tank top. One glance at it, and the swelling began inside him. The bubble, expanding. He stared at her, following only a few feet behind, enjoying the sight of the hair and her tight jeans, trying to smell her, trying to get close enough to brush against her as he walked past. Ah, but then she turned into another store and vanished.

In the parking lot, Pell saw a turquoise Ford Thunderbird. Inside he could just make out a woman brushing her long blonde hair.

Ah . . .

Walking closer. Her nose was bumpy and she was a skinny little thing, not much in the chest department. But that didn't stop the balloon within him growing, ten times, a hundred. It was going to burst soon.

Daniel Pell looked around. Nobody else nearby.

He walked forward through the rows of cars, closing the distance.

JENNIE MARSTON finished with her hair. She reached for the door handle and gave a gasp. It was opening on its own. She froze, staring at the wiry man who was leaning down. For three or four seconds, neither of them moved. Then he pulled the door open.

'You're prettier than I imagined, Jennie Marston,' he said.

'Oh, Daniel.' Overwhelmed with emotion, Jennie slipped out of the car and flew into her boyfriend's arms.

She pressed her head against his neck as Daniel carefully surveyed the parking lot. When they got back into the car, Jennie thought about how difficult the past month had been, forging a relationship through email, rare phone calls and fantasy. Then she felt the tears start. No, no, stop it. Men get mad when you cry.

But he asked gently, 'What's the matter, lovely?'

'I'm just so happy.'

'Come on, tell me.'

Well, he didn't sound mad. She debated, then said, 'I was wondering. I heard two guards were killed. Stabbed.' Daniel had said he just wanted the knife to threaten the guards. He wasn't going to hurt anybody.

'What?' he snapped. His blue eyes grew hard.

No, no, what are you doing? Jennie asked herself. You made him mad! Now you've messed everything up! Her heart fluttered.

'When I left, nobody was hurt. I was so careful! I got out the fire door just like we'd planned.' Then he nodded. 'There were other prisoners in a cell near mine. They wanted me to let them out too. I'll bet they started to riot, and when the guards went to stop them, that's when those two got killed. Some of them had shivs. But the police are blaming me, like they always do.' His lean face was red. 'I'm the easy target.'

'Just like that family eight years ago,' she said timidly.

Daniel had told her how he and his friend had gone to the Croytons' to pitch an idea to the computer genius. But his friend decided to rob the couple, knocked Daniel out, and started killing the family. Daniel had come to and tried to stop him. Finally he'd had to kill his friend in self-defence.

'They need somebody to blame. It's human nature.'

He was right, Jennie reflected. She was relieved, but also terrified that she'd upset him. 'I'm sorry. I shouldn't've mentioned it.'

He smiled and stroked her hair. 'You can ask me anything.'

She hugged him again. Felt more tears on her cheek. 'I've been worried you wouldn't like me.'

'Baby, I love you. What I emailed you, remember?'

Jennie remembered every word he'd written. She looked into his eyes. 'Oh, you're such a beautiful person.' She pressed her lips against his. She slipped her hand along his bare, muscular leg.

He gave a laugh. 'Tell you what, lovely, maybe we'd better get out of here. You have the phone I called you on?' Daniel had told her to buy three prepaid cellphones with cash.

She handed him the phone she'd answered when he'd called just after he'd escaped. He pulled the battery and SIM card out, threw them into a trash can and returned to the car. She produced the other two phones, and he put one in his pocket.

A siren sounded nearby. They froze. Then the sirens faded.

'Let's go, lovely.'

She nodded after the sirens. 'They might come back.'

Daniel smiled. 'I'm not worried about that. I just want to be alone with you.'

Jennie felt a shiver of happiness down her spine. It almost hurt.

THE WEST-CENTRAL regional headquarters of the California Bureau of Investigation was a two-storey modern structure, a functional rectangle of glass and stone, near Highway 68. Kathryn Dance and Michael O'Neil were standing in the ground-floor conference room, directly beneath her office, staring at a large map on which the roadblocks were indicated—this time with push-pins. There had been no sightings of the Worldwide Express driver's Honda.

Dance glanced at O'Neil's face and read in it determination and concern. She knew him well. They'd met years ago when she was a jury consultant, and when she'd joined the CBI she found herself working frequently with him. O'Neil taught her more about the art of investigation in six months than she'd learned during her entire formal training. Though their talents differed, their instincts were identical. She was amused to see that while he'd been staring at the map, he'd been sensing signals from her too.

'What is it?' he asked. 'Something's bothering you.'

'Yep.' She thought for a minute. 'Bad feeling about Pell. I got this idea it doesn't matter to him if people live or die, as long as he gets what he wants. I think that Worldwide Express driver's dead. But let's hope I'm wrong.'

'You're never wrong, Boss.' TJ appeared and set up a laptop on the battered conference table. 'Check this out.'

They hovered round the computer screen, on which was a high-resolution enlarged image of Morton Nagle's photo. It revealed a figure in a denim jacket on the driveway. A shadow had morphed into a large black suitcase.

'Woman?' O'Neil asked.

They judged the person's height against the automobile nearby. About Dance's height, five six. Slimmer too, she noted. The cap and sunglasses obscured the head and face, but through the vehicle's window you could see hips slightly broader than a man's would be for that height.

'A blonde woman, about five six or so,' O'Neil summarised.

Dance said, 'Weight one ten, give or take.' She had a thought. She called Rey Carranco in his office upstairs, asked him to join them.

He appeared a moment later. 'Agent Dance.'

'Go back to the You Mail It store on San Benito. See if anyone there remembers a woman fitting her general description. If so, get a picture on EFIS.' The Electronic Facial Identification System is a computer program used by investigators to re-create suspects' likenesses.

'Sure, Agent Dance,' said Carraneo.

TJ hit some buttons, and the image zipped wirelessly to a colour printer in his office, where Carraneo would pick it up. Then his phone rang.

After a brief conversation, TJ hung up. 'Vital statistics clerk in Sacramento. Five years ago Samantha McCoy changed her name to Sarah Monroe. Three years ago she married Ronald Starkey. They live in San Jose.'

'San Jose,' O'Neil said. 'That's close enough.' Samantha could have planted the gas bomb that morning and been home in an hour and a half.

'Does she work?' Dance asked.

'I'll check that out.' TJ's call to the tax department revealed that Sarah Starkey was employed by a small educational publisher in San Jose.

Dance got the number. 'Let's see if she was in this morning.'

She called the publisher from a caller ID–blocked line. When a woman answered, she said, 'Hi. This is the El Camino Boutique. We have an order for Sarah Starkey, but the driver said she wasn't there this morning. Do you know when she'll be getting in? . . . Really? Well, I'll talk to him again. Might be better to deliver it to her house. If you could not mention anything to Mrs Starkey, I'd appreciate it. It's a surprise.'

Dance hung up. 'She's been there all morning, since eight thirty.'

The conference-room phone trilled. She listened for a moment and said, 'Have somebody bring him to my office right away.'

THE LARGE MAN, in a California prison guard's uniform, sat in front of Dance's desk, on which lay a dozen files, random pens and various photos: of the two children, of Dance with a handsome silver-haired man, of her mother and father, and of two dogs, each paired with one of the youngsters.

'This is terrible,' said Tony Waters, a senior guard from Capitola, in a distraught voice. 'I can't tell you.'

'You were in charge of Pell's wing?' Dance asked.

'That's right.' Bulky and with stooped shoulders, Waters sat forward in the chair. He was in his mid-fifties, she estimated.

'Did Pell say anything to you about where he's headed?'

'No, ma'am. Daniel didn't talk a lot. Not to us hacks.'

'Did he have any visitors?'

'Nobody in the last year.'

'And telephone calls? Are they logged?'

'Yes, ma'am. But not recorded. He didn't have many. I think he talked to his aunt once or twice.'

'What about computers, email?'

'Not for the prisoners. We do for ourselves, of course. They're in a special area—a control zone. We're very strict about that.'

'Did you get our request for the contents of his cell?'

The guard looked down. 'Yes, ma'am. But it was empty. Had been empty for a couple of days, actually.' He looked up, his lips tight. 'I didn't catch it.'

'Catch what?'

'We learn to look for certain things. If something big's going down, the con's cell changes, because he knows we'll look over the cell with a microscope after. But we never had an escape from Capitola. And they're watched so close.' The man's face was flushed. 'I should've thought better.'

'That'd be a tough leap to make,' Dance reassured him.

He shrugged and examined his nails.

'Sounds like you've been in this business for a while.'

'Long time. Been there ever since I left the army.' He brushed his crew cut, grinning. 'Two years till I retire. In a funny way, I'll miss it.'

She asked about where he lived, his family. He was married and had two children, both bound for college, he said proudly. But while they chatted, a silent alarm was pulsing within Dance. She had a situation on her hands.

Tony Waters was lying.

Dance had asked him here only to get information. If Waters had been a suspect or a hostile witness, she'd have been looking for stress signs, then kept probing those topics until he admitted lying. But this process only works if you determine the subject's nondeceptive baseline behaviour *before* you ask sensitive questions. Even without a baseline comparison, though, a perceptive kinesic interrogator can sometimes spot deception. One clue is a very slight increase in the pitch of the voice, because lying triggers an emotional response within most people and vocal cords tighten. Another clue is pausing, since lying is mentally challenging.

In her conversation with the guard, Dance had become aware that at several points his voice had risen and he'd paused with no reason. She looked back to other behaviours that suggested deception: offering more information than necessary, digressing, and aversion, turning away from her.

It was at that point in their conversation that Dance had begun talking about topics that Waters would have no reason to lie about. At the same time she performed her standard four-part analysis of the subject himself.

First, she asked, what was his role in the incident? She concluded that Waters was, at worst, an accomplice of Pell's.

Second, did he have a motive to lie? Of course. Waters didn't want to be arrested or lose his job because intentionally, or through negligence, he'd helped Pell escape.

Third, what was his personality type? Some officers simply determine if the subject is an introvert or extrovert. Dance preferred the Myers-Briggs personality type indicator, which includes three additional attributes: thinking or feeling, sensing or intuitive, judging or perceiving. She concluded that Waters was a thinking-sensing-judging-extrovert. This meant she could use reward-punishment techniques.

Finally, she asked, what kind of 'liar's personality' does Waters have? There are several types. For instance, manipulators lie with impunity, seeing nothing wrong with it, using deceit to achieve goals in love, business, politics—or crime. Other types include social liars, who lie to entertain, and adaptors, insecure people who lie to make positive impressions.

Waters, Dance decided, was in yet another category. He was an 'actor', someone for whom control was important. They lie only when necessary and are less skilled than manipulators.

Dance rose, walked round the desk, and sat beside him. 'Now, Tony, I'd like to go over things one more time.'

'Sure.' He lifted his ankle to his knee—a defence manoeuvre.

She returned to a topic that she now knew raised significant stress indicators. 'Tell me again about the computers at Capitola.'

'Computers?'

Responding with a question was a classic indicator of deception.

'Yes, what kind do you have?'

'Oh, I'm not a tech guy.' His foot tapped. 'Dells, I think.'

'Now tell me about *access* to computers again.'

'Like I said, cons aren't allowed to use them. The computers are in an area of limited access. Only the nonviolent cons who help out in the office are allowed there. But they can't use the computers.'

'And Pell couldn't get in there?'

'He's classified as One A.' A scratch of his eyelid—a blocking gesture.

'Whether authorised or not, have Daniel Pell and a computer ever been in the same room at the same time at Capitola?'

'I've never seen him on a computer, I swear. Honestly.'

The stress that people experience when lying pushes them into one of four emotional states: they're angry, they're depressed, they're in denial, or they want to bargain their way out of trouble. The words 'I swear' and 'honestly' told Dance that Waters was in the denial stage; he couldn't accept the truth of whatever he'd done and was dodging responsibility.

In the case of denial, you attack with the facts. 'You have access to the office where the computers are kept, right?'

'Yeah, but so what? All the hacks do.'

'And has Pell ever been in there?'

'Nonviolent felons are the only ones allowed in—'

'Has Pell ever been in there?'

'I swear to God I never saw him.'

Dance noted adaptors—gestures meant to relieve tension: finger-flexing, foot-tapping. 'That's the fourth time you haven't answered my question, Tony,' she said. 'Now, was Pell ever in any room in Capitola with a computer?'

The guard grimaced. 'I'm sorry. I never saw him on a computer, really. You can imagine I've been pretty upset by this whole thing.'

'Sure I can, Tony.'

'Maybe Daniel could've been.'

Her attack had made Waters realise that it was more painful to endure the interrogation than to own up to what he was lying about. Waters was now in the bargaining phase of deception, and Dance knew she had to offer him a way to save face. In an interrogation, the enemy isn't the liar, but the lie.

'So,' she said in a friendly voice, 'it's possible that, at some point, Pell could've gotten access to a computer?'

'I guess it could've happened. But I don't know for sure he was on one.' His head drooped, his voice was soft. 'It's just . . . people don't understand. Being a hack. What it's like.'

'I'm sure they don't,' Dance agreed.

'We have to be teachers, cops, everything. Admin's always looking over our shoulders, telling us do this, do that.'

'Obviously, you care about doing a good job.'

'It was nothing, really, what happened.'

'Go ahead,' Dance said.

'OK, see, Daniel was different. He's got this . . . power or something over people. People do things for him, people tell him things.'

'And so he gave you information. Is that it?'

'*Good* information. Stuff nobody could've got otherwise. Like, there was a guard selling meth. And Pell let me know.'

'Saved lives, I'll bet. So you cut him some slack.'

'Yeah. The TV in the office had cable, and sometimes he wanted to watch games nobody else was interested in. I went on rounds, and he watched games. It happened three or four times.'

'So he could've been online. When, most recently?'

'Maybe yesterday.'

'OK, Tony. Now tell me about the telephones.' Dance recalled seeing a stress reaction when he'd told her Pell had made no calls. Waters had touched his lips, a blocking gesture.

Waters said, 'The other thing about Pell, he was into sex, way into sex. He wanted to make some phone-sex calls, and I let him.'

But Dance immediately noticed deviation from baseline. 'Did he, now?' she asked bluntly. 'And how did he pay for it? Credit card?'

A pause. Waters had forgotten you had to pay for phone sex. 'I don't mean like you'd call up one of those numbers in the backs of newspapers. Daniel called some woman who'd written him.'

'But when you listened, there wasn't any sex, was there?'

'No, I — No. They were just talking.'

'You heard both of them?'

'Yeah. I was on a third line.'

'When was it?'

'A month ago, the first time. And yesterday. In the office.'

'If it was long distance, it would be logged.'

Waters looked at the floor. 'I got him a phone card. You call an eight hundred number and punch in a code, then the number you want.'

Dance knew them. Untraceable. 'What were they talking about?' she asked in a friendly voice.

'Just stuff. Money, I remember. Pell asked how much she'd put together, and she said ninety-two hundred bucks.'

'Any idea of where she was?'

'He mentioned Bakersfield. He said, "To Bakersfield".'

Telling her to go to his aunt's place and get the hammer to plant in the well.

'Did her voice have an ethnic or regional accent?'

'Not that I could tell.'

'Was it low or high, her voice?'

'Low, I guess. Kind of sexy.'

'Is there anything else that's helpful? Come on, Tony.'

'Not that I can think of. I'm sorry.' He sounded exhausted.

She looked him over. 'OK. That'll do it for the time being.'

Chapter 4

She'd done well, his little lovely. Followed the instructions perfectly. Getting the hammer from his aunt's garage in Bakersfield, embossing the wallet, then planting them in the well in Salinas. Making the fuse for the gas bomb. Planting the bag containing the fire suit and knife.

Pell, though, hadn't been sure of her ability to look people in the eye and lie to them. So he hadn't used her as a getaway driver. He didn't want her stopped at a roadblock and giving everything away because she stammered and flushed with guilt.

Now, shoes off as she drove, a happy smile on her face, Jennie Marston was chattering away. Pell had wondered if she'd believed the story about his innocence in the deaths at the courthouse. But one thing that never ceased to astonish him was how often people flung logic and self-preservation to the wind and believed what he wanted them to believe.

They drove through a complicated route of surface streets, avoiding the highways with their potential roadblocks.

'I'm glad you're here,' she said, voice tentative as she rested a hand on his knee with ambivalent desperation. He knew what she was feeling: torn between pouring out her love for him and not wanting to scare him off. The gushing would win out. Always did with women like her.

Daniel Pell knew all about the Jennie Marstons of the world, the women breathlessly seduced by bad boys. Pell got a lot of mail from them. Plenty of romantic overtures too. But it was her passionate letters and extraordinary gullibility that had made Pell decide on her for the escape.

He now asked, 'You were careful about everything, weren't you? Nobody can trace the T-bird?'

'No. I stole it from a restaurant. There was this guy I went out with, he worked there, and I saw that nobody paid any attention to the valet-parking key box. So Friday, when the valets were busy, I got the keys. I was on the One-oh-one in, like, ten minutes.'

'And you burned all the emails, right? Before you left?'

'Uh-huh. And I have the maps.' She patted her purse.

He looked over her body. The small swell of her chest, the long blonde hair. Women let you know right up front the kind of licence you have, and Pell knew he could touch her whenever he wanted. He put his hand on the nape of her neck. She made a sound that was actually purring. The swelling within him continued to grow.

'Pull over there, baby.' He pointed towards an abandoned farmhouse.

She turned down the driveway, and he looked around.

'This's good.' His hand slid from her neck down the front of her pink blouse. It looked new. She'd bought it just for him.

He lifted her face and pressed his lips against hers softly, then backed away. She grew more and more frantic the more he teased.

'I want you,' she whispered.

'We don't have much time, baby. They're looking for us.'

She got the message. Minutes later he was finished.

'You're wonderful, lovely. That was special.' He reassembled his clothes.

Jennie buttoned her blouse. Pell looked at the pink cloth, the embroidery, the metal tips on the collar.

She noticed him. 'You like?'

'It's nice.' He glanced out of the window and studied the fields.

Hesitantly Jennie said, 'It's awfully pink. Maybe too much.'

'No, it's fine. It's interesting.'

'I'll change later if you want.'

'No. If you like it, that's fine,' he said. 'We should get going.'

'Sure.' She wanted him to tell her more about the blouse. What was wrong with it? But, of course, he said nothing.

Jennie smiled when he touched her leg, and she put the car in gear. She returned to the road, glancing down one last time at the blouse, which, Pell knew, she would never wear again.

And the irony was that it looked really good on her.

But he had a nice picture of how controllable she was, how loyal. A good teacher always knew the exact state of his student's progress.

MICHAEL O'NEIL sat in a chair in Kathryn Dance's office, feet on her coffee table. He, TJ Scanlon and Dance were gazing at her phone.

A computer tech from Capitola was explaining through the speaker-phone, 'Pell *did* get online yesterday, but he didn't send any emails. He only browsed the Web. He erased the sites he visited, but he forgot about erasing search requests. He did a Google search for "Alison" and "Nimue" together. Then he did another. "Helter Skelter".'

O'Neil and Dance shared a troubled glance. The phrase was the title of the award-winning book about cult leader Charles Manson.

'Then he went to Visual Earth dot com. Like Google Earth. You can see satellite pictures of practically everywhere on the planet. But there's no way to narrow down what he'd looked for.'

'And what's "Nimue"?' asked Dance.

'No idea.'

'Any employees at Capitola named Alison?'

The techie said, 'Nope. But I might be able to find out what sites he logged on to. It depends on whether he just erased them or shredded them.'

'Anything you can do would be appreciated,' Dance said. She thanked him and disconnected. 'TJ, check out "Nimue".'

TJ's fingers flew over his keyboard. The results came up, and he scrolled through them. 'Hundreds of thousands of hits,' he said. 'Looks like people use it as a screen name.' He scrolled again. 'Most references are to King Arthur. Nimue was the Lady of the Lake. Merlin fell in love with her.'

'I like the idea it's someone he was trying to find,' said Dance. 'Cross-check Nimue with "Alison" and "Croyton". Anything else?'

O'Neil suggested, 'The women: Sheffield, McCoy and Whitfield.'

'Good,' said Dance.

After minutes of typing, TJ looked at her. 'Sorry, Boss. Zip.'

'Check the search terms out with the main criminal data bases.'

'Will do.'

'What about the forensics?' Dance asked O'Neil.

The detective consulted his notes. 'No red flags. Almost everything was burnt or melted. The gas was in plastic milk jugs inside a cheap roller suit-case, sold in a dozen places. The fireproof bag and fire suit were made by Protection Equipment, Inc., New Jersey. Most are sold in Southern California for stuntmen. No serial numbers. They couldn't lift any prints. The fuse was homemade: rope soaked in slow-burning chemicals, none of them traceable.'

'TJ, what's the word on the aunt?'

'Zip, so far. I'm expecting a breakthrough any moment.'

Her phone rang. It was a call from Capitola. The warden was with a pris-oner up for parole in six months who claimed he had information about Pell. Did Dance want to talk to him now?

'Sure.' She hit the speakerphone button. 'This is Agent Dance. I'm here with Detective O'Neil.'

'Hey. I'm Eddie Chang.'

'Eddie, how well did you know Daniel Pell?' Dance asked.

'Not really good. Nobody did. But I was somebody who wasn't no threat to him. So he kind of opened up to me.'

O'Neil asked, 'Did Pell talk about girlfriends on the outside?'

'He bragged about the women he'd had.'

'You remember any names? Someone named Alison?'

'He never mentioned any.'

'So what do you want to tell us?' Dance asked.

'I have this idea where he might be headed. A couple times he mentioned Utah. He liked that you could have a lot of wives.'

The Family . . .

'He said the police there don't give you any shit, because it's the

Mormons who run the place and they don't like the FBI or the state police snooping around. You can do whatever you want in Utah.'

'When did he tell you that?'

'I don't know. Last year. Then maybe a month ago.'

Dance glanced at O'Neil. 'Eddie, thanks. Anything else about Pell you can remember? Things he said, things he did.'

Chang talked for a few more minutes. As soon as the call ended, the frog croaked again. The caller was Rey Carraneo, reporting that the manager of the You Mail It franchise *did* remember a woman about a week ago.

'Only, she didn't mail anything, Agent Dance. She just asked about when the different delivery services stopped there. Worldwide Express was the most regular, he told her. Like clockwork. He wouldn't've thought anything about it, except that he saw her outside a few days later, sitting on a park bench across the street. I'd guess she was checking the times herself.'

Unfortunately, she'd worn the baseball cap and dark sunglasses then, too. And the manager hadn't seen her car.

They disconnected, and Dance wondered again when the Worldwide Express driver's body would be found. *The ripples of consequence can spread almost for ever.* Morton Nagle's words were passing through her mind when Michael O'Neil got a call. Coincidentally, the message was about the fate of that very driver.

DANCE WAS in her Taurus. A song by the original Fairfield Four gospel singers was on the CD player. Music was Dance's salvation. Police work for her was people, and her job required her to blend her mind and heart with theirs so that she could discern the truth. The interrogations were sometimes wrenching and never left her memory completely. If music was in her ears and thoughts, she tended not to hear the shocking replays of rapists, murderers and terrorists.

Dance now lost herself in the tones of the music from sixty years ago.

Five minutes later she pulled into an office park in downtown Monterey and climbed out. She walked into the garage, where the Worldwide driver's red Civic sat, trunk open, blood smeared on the metal. O'Neil and a town cop were standing beside it.

Someone else was with them.

Billy Gilmore, the driver Dance had been sure was Pell's next victim. To her shock, he'd been found very much alive.

The heavyset man had some bruises and a large sticking plaster on his forehead but, it turned out, the injuries weren't from being beaten by Pell; he'd cut himself shifting around in the trunk to get comfortable.

'I wasn't trying to get out. I was afraid to. But somebody heard me, I guess, and called the police. I was supposed to stay in there for three hours, Pell told me. If I didn't he said he'd kill my wife and kids.'

'They're OK,' O'Neil explained to Dance. 'We've got them in protection.' He related Billy's story about Pell and the hijacking.

'What was Pell wearing?'

'Shorts, a dark windcheater, baseball cap, I think,' said Billy.

O'Neil called in the new description to the roadblocks.

'Do you remember anything else?' Dance asked.

Just after the trunk lid slammed, Billy heard the man's voice again. 'I think he was making a call. He had my phone.'

Dance glanced at O'Neil, who immediately called the MCSO technical-support people and had them get in touch with the driver's cellphone service provider to set up a trace. A few minutes later his mobile rang.

He listened for a while, then said to Dance, 'Nope. It's either destroyed or the battery's out. They can't find a signal.'

Dance looked around. 'He's dumped it somewhere. Let's hope nearby. We should have somebody check.'

O'Neil sent two of his deputies off on the task.

TJ joined them, shaking his head. 'Call me crazy, Boss, but this isn't on the route I *myself* would take to Utah.'

Pell's coming to downtown Monterey was surprising. There were fewer escape routes than if he'd gone east, north or south. A risky place to meet his accomplice, but a brilliant move. This was the last place they'd expect him.

'Why don't you go be with your family?' Dance suggested to Billy, and a medical tech led him back to the ambulance.

'Detective, I found a phone,' an MCSO deputy called as he joined them. 'Up the street in a trash can. The battery was in another can, across the street.'

'Good catch,' O'Neil told the man.

Dance pulled on a pair of latex gloves, then took the phone and replaced the battery. She turned it on and scrolled through recent calls, reading them out to O'Neil, who was on the phone with his tech people again.

The first wasn't a working number—the call to the accomplice about Billy's family had been faked. The second and third calls were to a prepaid mobile phone, but there was no signal now. The last two numbers were directory assistance for Utah and an RV campsite outside Salt Lake City.

'Bingo,' TJ said.

Dance called the number and identified herself. She asked if they'd received a call forty minutes ago. The clerk said that she had, a man driving west, curious how much it cost to park a small Winnebago by the week.

'Did the man say when he'd be arriving?'

'No. That was all.'

Dance told the woman to call immediately if he contacted them again. She then phoned the Utah State Police and told them the situation. They said they would send a surveillance team to the campsite straight away.

'Should I tell Overby about Utah?' TJ asked. 'He'll want to get word out.'

'Hold on,' Dance told him, and answered a phone call. The computer specialist from Capitola had managed to find one site that Pell had visited. It had to do with the Helter Skelter search.

'It was pretty smart,' the man said. 'He used the term to find a bulletin board where people post messages about crime and murder. Helter Skelter is devoted to cult murders. I found a message that had been posted on Saturday, and I think it was meant for him.'

'Clever,' Dance said. 'Can you find out who posted it?'

'It was anonymous. No way to trace it.' He read her the few lines. There was no doubt it was for Pell; it gave the last-minute details of the escape. The message added something else at the end, but it made no sense to Dance.

'OK,' she said. 'Appreciate it. Forward me a copy of that.' She gave her email address and disconnected.

Dance silently came to a decision. She called Charles Overby and told him about the camper park in Utah. Her boss was delighted at the news.

Then, thinking about her conversation with Eddie Chang, she called Rey Carraneo and sent him on another assignment.

'Pull out all the stops,' she said. 'Move fast.'

'WE'RE GETTING sand dabs.'

'OK,' Jennie agreed. 'What's that?'

'These little fish. Like anchovies, but they're not salty. We'll get sandwiches. I'm having two. You want two?'

'Just one, honey.'

Jennie and Pell were in Moss Landing, north of Monterey. Across the highway from the massive Duke Power plant was a small spit of land accessible only by bridge. On this strip of sandy soil were marine service companies, docks and the structure where they now sat: Jack's Seafood.

Jack's was a commercial fishery, seafood market and restaurant that had been in business for three quarters of a century. Pell remembered it from the days when the Family lived in Seaside. He had some business to take care of on the Peninsula, but there'd be a little delay. Besides, he was starving and figured the police wouldn't be looking for a happy tourist couple here, since according to the radio he was halfway to Utah by now.

Jack's had an outdoor patio with a view of the fishing boats and the bay, but Pell had wanted to stay inside. Jennie sat beside him at the table, pressing her knee against his. He sipped his iced tea and glanced at her.

'Let's look over the maps,' he said.

She opened her bag and took them out. Pell unfolded one, then paused, aware of a curious feeling he couldn't quite figure out.

Then he realised: he was free. He could now start his life over again. After finishing up his missions here, he'd leave for good and start another Family. Pell glanced around him, at the other patrons in the restaurant, noting in particular the teenage girl, two tables away, her silent parents hunched over their food. The girl, a bit plump, could be easily seduced away from home when she was alone in an arcade or Starbucks.

And at the counter, the young man of about twenty, inked with tattoos. He wore shabby clothes, which, along with his meal of soup, suggested money problems. His eyes zipped around the restaurant, settling on every female older than sixteen. Pell knew exactly what it would take to sign the boy up in a matter of hours.

He was lulled from his daydreams by the waitress bringing their food.

'Looks scrumptious, sweetie,' Jennie said, staring at her plate.

Pell handed her a bottle. 'Here's the malt vinegar. You put that on them. Just sprinkle it on.'

'OK.'

He took one more look around the restaurant: the sullen girl, the edgy boy . . . He was ecstatic to see that so many opportunities beckoned. After life was settled, he'd begin hunting again.

THE CARS SPED NORTH on Highway 1.

Michael O'Neil was behind the wheel of his unmarked MCSO Ford, Dance beside him. TJ was in a CBI pool Taurus right behind them, and two Monterey police cruisers were tailing them. The highway patrol was sending several cars to the party too.

O'Neil was doing close to eighty. Traffic was heavy, and they used only lights, no sirens. They were en route to where they believed Daniel Pell and his blonde accomplice were, against all odds, eating a leisurely lunch.

Dance had had her doubts about Pell's destination of Utah. Her intuition told her that it probably was a false lead, especially after the mobile phone had been conveniently found. And most important, Pell had left the driver alive to report about his making a call.

And then she'd heard from the computer tech at Capitola, who'd read her the message on the 'Helter Skelter' bulletin board: 'Package will be there about 9.20. WWE delivery truck at San Benito at 9.50. Orange ribbon on pine tree. Will meet in front of store we mentioned.'

This was the first part of the message, a confirmation of the escape plan. What had surprised Dance was the final sentence: 'Room all set and checking on those locations around Monterey you wanted.—Your lovely.'

Which suggested that Pell might be staying nearby.

Dance and O'Neil could deduce no reason for this. It was madness. But if he *was* staying, Dance decided to make him feel confident enough to show himself. She knew that once she told Charles Overby about Utah, he'd run to the press and announce that the search was now focused on the routes east. This would, she hoped, give Pell a false sense of security and make him more likely to appear in public. But where?

She'd hoped the answer to that question might be found in her conversation with Eddie Chang, when she'd got a sense of what appealed to Pell, his interests and urges. Sex figured prominently. So did food.

Daniel Pell, it seemed, had a particular love of seafood, especially a tiny fish known as the sand dab. He had mentioned on several occasions that there were only four or five restaurants in the Central Coast area that knew how to cook them right. Three had closed since Pell had gone into prison, but one at Fisherman's Wharf and one in Moss Landing were still open.

Dance had Rey Carraneo call those two restaurants—and any others on the Central Coast with similar menus. It was a long shot, but Carraneo had just heard back from the manager of Jack's Seafood, at Moss Landing. A couple was in there at the moment, the man clean-shaven and wearing sunglasses and a cap, the woman apparently blonde, though she too wore a cap and shades. Dance spoke to the manager and asked if someone could find out which car the couple had arrived in. One of the busboys gave Dance the tag numbers of all the cars parked in the lot. A fast DMV check revealed that one, a turquoise Thunderbird, had been stolen last Friday in Los Angeles.

Dance decided to move on the place; if nothing else, they'd collar a car thief. She'd alerted O'Neil, then told the manager, 'We'll be there as soon as we can. Just ignore him and act normally.'

'Act normal,' the manager said, voice shaking. 'Yeah, right.'

Cruising through Sand City, traffic grew lighter, and O'Neil punched the accelerator hard. They'd be at the restaurant in ten minutes.

'ARE THOSE THE BEST thing you ever tasted?'

'Oh, honey, they're good. Sandy dabs.'

'Sand dabs,' Pell corrected. He was thinking of having a third sandwich.

'So, that was my ex,' Jennie continued. 'I never see him or hear from him. Thank God.' She'd just given him the details of the husband—an accountant and wimpy little guy—who'd put her in the hospital twice with internal injuries, once with a broken arm.

Then he heard the further instalments of the soap opera: the boyfriends after the divorce. They seemed like him, but Pell Lite, he thought. One worked low-stakes scams. One sold drugs. One was just a shit.

Pell could have told her: By the way, lovely, we never, ever change. Write that down and keep it close to your heart.

She stopped eating. 'Honey? Can I ask you a question?'

'Sure, lovely.'

'You never said anything about those, you know, girls you were living with. The Family. What were their names?'

'Samantha, Rebecca and Linda,' he recited.

'Did they turn you in?'

'Not exactly. They didn't even know we were going to the Croytons', Jimmy and me. But they didn't back me up after I got arrested.' A sour laugh.

'Are you upset? I don't want to upset you.'

'No.' Pell smiled. 'It's OK, lovely.'

'Do you think about them much?'

Ah, so that's it. Pell realised that Jennie was jealous.

'Nope. I haven't heard from them for years. I was mad at first, but then I understood that I made a mistake with them. I picked wrong. Not like you.'

She lifted his hand and kissed his knuckles one at a time.

Pell was studying the map again. Now Jennie pointed out some locations, and he took in the information. But, as always, he was also listening to everything around him. To bits of people's conversations.

'He's a good puppy. Just needs more training.'

'It's a long drive, but if we take our time, it'll be a blast. You know?'

'I ordered ten minutes ago. What's taking so long?'

At this last comment, Pell glanced towards the counter.

'Sorry,' explained a man at the cash register to a customer. 'Short-staffed today.' The man looked everywhere except at Pell and Jennie.

When Pell had ordered their food, there were three or four waitresses. Now this man was the only one working.

He'd sent all his employees into hiding.

Pell leapt up. Jennie dropped her fork and jumped to her feet. The manager stared at them in alarm.

'You son of a bitch.' Pell pulled his pistol from his waistband.

Jennie screamed.

'No, no . . . I—' The manager fled to the kitchen, abandoning his customers, who spilled onto the floor for cover.

'Let's go. The car.' Pell grabbed the map, and they fled.

Outside, in the distance, south, he could see flashing lights.

Jennie froze, panicked.

'Come on!'

They leapt in. He gunned the engine and sped over the narrow bridge. On Highway 1 he turned north, got a hundred yards, then skidded to a stop. Coming the other way was another police car.

Pell glanced to his right and floored the accelerator, heading directly for the front gate of the massive power plant.

DANCE AND O'NEIL were five minutes from Moss Landing. The Ford squealed round a corner, and O'Neil muttered, 'Oh, hell . . .'

He jammed the brake pedal. The car skidded to a stop. The highway was completely blocked all the way to Moss Landing. Miles ahead Dance could see flashing lights and realised that officers were turning back the traffic.

A roadblock?

O'Neil called MCSO central dispatch. 'It's O'Neil. We're on One, northbound, just short of Moss Landing. Traffic's stopped. What's the story?'

'Be advised, sir. They're evacuating Duke Power. Fire or something. They've got multiple injuries. Two fatalities.'

Oh, no, Dance thought, not more deaths. She could see a column of black smoke. Security at the power facility would have frozen Highway 1 and started to evacuate anyone nearby.

O'Neil snapped, 'Tell Monterey Fire or whoever's running the scene to clear a path. We're in pursuit of that escapee. Over.'

'Roger, Detective . . . Hold on . . .' Silence for a minute. 'OK, the plant's *not* burning. The fire's just a car in front of the main gate. I don't know who called in the eleven-forty-one. No injuries. That was a false report. We've got some calls from Jack's. The suspect pulled a gun and fled.'

'Hell, he made us,' O'Neil muttered. He hit the siren and started along the shoulder, which was rocky and barely passable.

It took twenty minutes to drive a distance that should have taken three. And when they arrived at Moss Landing, Pell and his girlfriend were nowhere to be seen.

Dance and O'Neil parked. A moment later TJ pulled up too, beside the burnt-out Thunderbird, still smouldering.

'Pell's car,' she pointed out. 'The one stolen from LA on Friday.'

O'Neil and the other officers spread out to search for witnesses. Several people reported that a wiry man and a blonde, driving the Thunderbird, had sped over the bridge from Jack's Seafood and stopped abruptly in front of the plant. They'd got out, and the car had erupted in flames. The couple had run across the road, but nobody saw what became of them after that.

Dance looked around her. They'd need another car; you couldn't escape from here on foot. She noticed a store across the highway, a shack selling souvenirs. There was a CLOSED sign on the door, but inside Dance believed she could see a woman's face looking out.

Was Pell inside with her?

Dance gestured to a deputy, and together they stepped to the door. She rapped on it.

Slowly the door opened. A round woman with short hair glanced in alarm at their hands, which were resting on their guns. 'Yes?'

Eyes on the dim interior behind her, Dance asked, 'Is anyone else in there?'

'No. What—?'

The deputy pushed past her and flicked the lights on. Dance joined him. A fast search revealed that the tiny place was unoccupied.

Dance returned to the woman. 'Sorry for the disturbance.'

'That's OK. This is scary. Did you get them?'

'We're still searching. Did you see what happened?'

'No. I was inside. When I looked out, there was the car burning.'

'Why did you say "them"?'

A pause. 'I . . . I think I talked to somebody about it. Outside.'

I think . . . A denial flag expression.

'Where's your car?' Dance asked.

'My—?'

Eyes can be revealing in kinesic analysis. Dance had noticed the woman looking at a particular place in the parking lot, displaying general stress indicators. Dance understood: Pell had stolen her car and said that he would kill her family if she said anything. Just like the Worldwide Express driver.

'I—' The woman started to cry.

'We'll make sure you're safe. What kind of car?'

'A dark blue Ford Focus. Three years old. There's a dent—'

'Where did they go?'

'North.'

Dance got the tag number and called O'Neil. She stared at the lingering cloud of smoke around the Thunderbird. She was angry. She'd made a sharp deduction from Eddie Chang's information, but it had been a waste.

TJ joined her with the manager of Jack's Seafood. He gave his story of the events and put the woman's age at mid-twenties. He added that they'd pored over a Monterey County map for a good portion of the meal.

O'Neil came over, flipping closed his phone. 'No reports of the Focus,' he said. 'Hell, he could've driven right past us.'

Dance called Carraneo over. 'Start calling motels from Watsonville down to Big Sur. See if any blonde women checked in Friday, Saturday or Sunday and listed a Thunderbird as their car.'

'Sure, Agent Dance.'

She and O'Neil both stared west, over the calm water. The sun was low, a wide, flat disk; the bay looked like a hazy blue desert. O'Neil said, 'Pell's taking a huge risk staying around. He's got something important in mind.'

It was just then that she got a call from someone who, she realised, might have some thoughts about that very subject.

Chapter 5

James Reynolds, the retired prosecutor who'd won Daniel Pell's conviction eight years earlier, had a Carmel zip code, though his street wasn't in the cute part of town that got flooded with tourists at weekends. Reynolds was in working Carmel, but it was not exactly the wrong side of the tracks. He had a precious three-quarters of an acre of secluded property.

Dance pulled into the long driveway. The tanned, balding man in his mid-sixties met her at the door, ushered her inside.

'I'm cooking dinner,' he said. 'Come on into the kitchen.'

As she followed him along the hallway, Dance could read the man's history in the frames on the wall. The East Coast schools, Stanford Law, his wedding, raising two sons and a daughter, their graduations.

The most recent photos had yet to be framed: a stack of pictures, the top one of which was of a young woman, blonde and beautiful in her elaborate white dress, surrounded by her maids of honour. She also noticed a number of framed newspaper pages: big convictions he'd won. And trials he'd lost.

He noticed her looking at one and chuckled. 'I'd take the high ground and say I learned something from the not-guilties. But the fact is, sometimes juries are just out to lunch. Like with our boy Pell. They should've recommended the death penalty.'

'But they didn't have a problem convicting him.'

'Oh, no. The case was solid. I ran the prosecution hard. I picked up on the Son of Manson theme; I pointed out all the parallels. Pell actually helped get himself convicted by playing the part. He'd sit in court and stare at the jurors, trying to scare them. He tried it with me too. I laughed at him and said I didn't think psychic powers had any effect on lawyers. The jury laughed too. It broke the spell.'

'You also prosecuted the three women in the Family?'

'I pled them out. It was pretty much minor stuff. They didn't have anything to do with the Croyton thing . . . Jimmy Newberg was different. He had some aggravateds and felony drug charges.'

Reynolds had called Dance after he'd been in touch with Sandoval and learned the latest details of the manhunt. Now, in the spacious yellow kitchen, he put on an apron. A large skillet was filled with cooking seafood.

'I'll do whatever I can to help you nail this bastard.' Reynolds meticulously sliced a tomato. 'Just name it. The county storage company's bringing me all my notes from the case. There could be a nugget or two, and I'll go through every page if I have to.'

'That'd be very helpful, James. Appreciate it. I didn't even know you were in the area. I'd heard you retired to Santa Barbara.'

'We have a place there. But we're here most of the year.'

'Well, I told Michael O'Neil I'd like a deputy stationed outside.'

Reynolds dismissed the idea. 'I've got a good alarm system. I'm virtually untraceable. When I became lead prosecutor I started getting threats. I had my phone unlisted and transferred title to the house to a trust. There's no way he could find me.'

Dance wasn't going to take no for an answer. 'Pell's already killed several times today.'

A shrug. 'Sure, what the hell, I'll take a baby sitter. My younger son's here visiting. Why take chances?'

Dance scooted onto a stool, resting her maroon Aldo wedges on the supports. The straps were inlaid with bright daisies; shoes were one of her passions. 'For now, you could you tell me something about the Croyton murders. It might give me an idea of what he's up to.'

Reynolds ran through the facts of the case: how Pell and Jimmy Newberg had broken into the house of William Croyton in Carmel, stabbed to death the businessman, his wife and two of their three children.

'Newberg too. My theory was that he baulked at killing the kids and got into a fight with Pell, who killed *him*.'

'Any history between Pell and Croyton?'

'Not that we could establish. But Silicon Valley was at its peak then, and Croyton was one of the big boys. He designed most of his company's computer programs and was chief of sales too. Larger-than-life kind of guy. Big, loud, tanned. Work hard, play hard. Ruthless businessman, rumours of affairs, disgruntled employees.'

'What happened to his estate after he died?'

'Most of it went in trust to his daughter, and to the aunt who took custody of the girl. Croyton had been in computers ever since he was a kid. He left probably ten, twenty million dollars' worth of old hardware and programs to Cal State, Monterey Bay—the computer museum there. He was way ahead of his time, it seems.'

'And rich. Was that the actual motive for the killings?'

'Well, on the facts, it was a plain-vanilla burglary. But Pell's take was pretty skimpy. Would've been a small case, except for five dead bodies— almost six. Good thing that little girl was upstairs.'

'Where is the girl now?'

'No idea. The aunt and uncle moved away.'

'What was Pell's defence?'

'They'd gone there with some business idea. Newberg snapped and killed everybody. Pell tried to stop him, they fought and Pell, quote, "had" to kill him. But the forensics were clear: Jimmy probably stabbed Croyton's wife, but Pell killed everyone else.'

'In prison, he got unsupervised access to a computer. We found some things he searched for. Does "Alison" mean anything to you?'

'I don't remember anybody connected to him with that name.'

'Another word he searched was "Nimue".'

'Sorry, nothing.'

'Any other ideas about what he might have in mind?'

Reynolds shook his head. 'Sorry. It was a big case for me. But the fact is, it wasn't remarkable. He was caught red-handed; the forensics were waterproof. I'd have had to screw up pretty bad to lose.'

'All right, James. I should get going,' she said. 'Appreciate the help. If you find something in the files, let me know.'

He gave her a solemn nod.

SEVERAL HUNDRED YARDS apart, they made their way on foot to a motel in quaint Pacific Grove, right in the heart of the Peninsula.

Pell's pace was leisurely and he walked wide-eyed, like a dumbfounded tourist who'd never seen surf outside *Baywatch*. They'd bought a change of clothing at a Goodwill store in Seaside. Pell was now in a grey windcheater, cords and running shoes, a baseball cap on backwards.

He and Jennie had driven east from Moss Landing in the stolen Ford Focus, taking none of the major roads. Eventually they headed back towards Pacific Grove, but when the area became more populous, Pell hid the Focus in tall grass in a large field. He decided they should separate on the hike to the motel, staying in touch via their prepaid mobiles. Jennie called every five minutes until he told her the police might be listening in.

Which they weren't, of course, but he was tired of the honey-bunny chatter and wanted to think. Daniel Pell was worried.

How had the police tracked them to Jack's? Maybe the cap, sunglasses, and shaved face hadn't fooled the restaurant manager. Finding the stolen T-bird was another possibility. But the cops were supposed to believe he was headed to Salt Lake City.

Kathryn?

He had a feeling she hadn't bought into the Utah idea, even wondered if she'd put out the announcement to the press to flush him into the open. Which had, in fact, worked, he reflected angrily.

Pell wondered where she lived. He thought again about his assessment of her in the interview—her children, her husband—and recalled when she'd given her subtle reactions, when she hadn't.

Kids, yes, husband, probably not. A divorce didn't seem likely.

Kathryn as a widow. Interesting idea.

He bought a few things at a little bodega, which he picked because he knew his picture wouldn't be on the news every five minutes. He met up with Jennie in Asilomar, the beautiful shoreline park.

'Everything all right?' she asked cautiously.

'Fine, lovely. We're doing fine.'

She led him through the quiet streets of Pacific Grove, filled with colourful Victorian and Tudor-style bungalows. In five minutes, she announced, 'Here we are.' The Sea View Motel was brown, with small leaded windows, a wooden shingle roof. 'It's cute, isn't it?'

What mattered to Pell was that the room faced away from the road and there were driveways off the parking lot. 'It's perfect, lovely. Just like you. Which one's ours?'

She pointed. 'Come on, honey. I have a surprise for you.'

Hmm. Pell didn't like surprises.

She unlocked the door. He followed her inside and looked around. The place was ritzy. Expensive furniture, paintings, drapes, towels, bathrobes. And candles. Everywhere. That was the surprise.

'Hey, lovely.' He kissed her head. 'You were real steady today at Jack's.'

'I got kind of freaked.' She rubbed her nose.

'No, no, you held fast. We're a team, lovely.' Which got her to stop rubbing her nose. Pell noted that.

He went into the bathroom and washed up. When he stepped out, Jennie was wearing only a bra and panties, holding a cigarette lighter, working on the candles.

He grinned, walked to her. Ran his hand down her bony spine.

'Oh, I want you, baby,' she whispered.

He took the lighter. 'We'll do atmosphere later.' He kissed her.

She smiled. 'I think you want me too.'

THE EXPANSE OF GREY, pressure-treated wood, extending from the kitchen of Dance's house and filled with mismatched lawn chairs, loungers and tables, was known as the Deck. Tiny electric Christmas lights, a sink and a large refrigerator were the main decorations. A narrow stairway led down to the back yard, which was filled with scrub oak, lupine and renegade grass.

A stockade fence provided separation from the neighbours. The classic Victorian house—dark green with grey, weathered shutters and trim—was in northwest Pacific Grove; if you were willing to risk a precarious lean, you could catch a glimpse of ocean.

Dance spent plenty of time on the Deck. It was often too cold for an early breakfast, but on lazy weekends, after sun had melted the fog, she and the children might come here after a walk on the beach with the dogs and have bagels, coffee and hot chocolate. Hundreds of parties, large and small, had been hosted on the uneven planks.

The Deck was where her late husband, Bill, had told his parents firmly that, yes, he was marrying Kathryn Dance and, by corollary, not the Napa socialite his mother had championed—an act braver than much of what he'd done with the FBI.

The Deck was where they'd had his memorial service.

It was also a gathering place for friends both inside and outside the law-enforcement community. There was beer and soda in the outdoor fridge and usually a bottle or two of chardonnay or pinot grigio and cabernet. A rusty but functional barbecue grill sat here as well. It wasn't unusual for Dance to come home and find her mother or father, friends or colleagues, enjoying a beer or coffee.

Dance now climbed the steep stairs onto the Deck carrying a box of Morton Nagle's photocopies and tapes, on top of which was perched a prepared chicken dinner from Albertsons. The dogs greeted her: Patsy, a black flat-coated retriever, and Dylan, a black and tan German shepherd. She rubbed ears and flung a few mangy stuffed toys, then continued on to two men sitting in plastic chairs.

'Hi, honey.' Stuart Dance looked younger than his seventy years. He was tall, with broad shoulders and a full head of unruly white hair. A retired marine biologist, he still worked at the aquarium several days a week.

He and his daughter brushed cheeks.

'Hnnn.' From Albert Stemple, another major crimes agent with the CBI. The massive man had a shaved head and wore boots, jeans, a black T-shirt. The CBI was not known for its cowboys, but Stemple was your basic make-my-own-rules Wild Bill Hickok. He had more collars than any other agent.

'Thanks for keeping an eye on things, Al. Sorry it's later than I'd planned.' Thinking of Pell's threats during the interrogation, Dance had asked Stemple to baby-sit (and O'Neil had arranged for local officers to keep an eye on her house).

Stemple grunted. 'Not a problem. Overby'll buy me dinner.'

'Charles said that?'

'Naw. But he'll buy me dinner. Quiet here. Nothin' strange.'

'You want a soda for the road?'

'Sure.' The big man helped himself to two Anchor Steams from the fridge. 'Don't worry. I'll finish 'em 'fore I get in the car. So long, Stu.' He clomped along the Deck and disappeared, and she heard the Crown Victoria peel away fifteen seconds later.

'Thanks again, Dad.'

'No worries.' He turned away, rapped on the window. 'Bye!'

'Grandpa, wait!' Maggie ran outside, clutching a book. 'Hi, Mom,' she said enthusiastically. 'When'd you get home?'

'Just now. Where's your brother?'

'I don't know. His room.' Maggie held the book up to her grandfather and pointed out a seashell. 'Look, Grandpa. You were right.'

'A Columbian Amphissa,' he said. 'A tide-drift shell, very rare here. But Maggie found one.'

'It was just *there*,' the girl said.

'OK, I'm headed home. Night, all.'

Her father climbed down the stairs, and Dance thanked fate for a good, dependable male figure in the life of a widow with children.

On her way to the kitchen, Dance's phone rang. Rey Carraneo reported the Thunderbird had been stolen from the valet parking lot of a restaurant in LA. There were no suspects. Also, he'd had no luck finding the motel the woman might have checked into. 'There are a lot of them,' he said.

Welcome to the Monterey Peninsula. 'We've got to stash the tourists somewhere, Rey. Keep at it.'

Dance unpacked dinner. A lean boy with sandy hair wandered into the kitchen. He was on the phone. Though only twelve, Wes was nearly as tall as his mother. She kissed him on the forehead, and he didn't cringe. Which was the same as 'I love you very much, Mother dear.'

'Off the phone,' she said. 'Dinnertime.'

'Like, gotta go.' The boy hung up. 'What are we having?'

'Chicken.'

'Oh, mashed potatoes too. You rock, Mom.'

Maggie and Wes set the table. Wes asked, 'Mom, aren't you going to change?' He was looking at her black suit.

'I'm starving. I can't wait.' Not sharing that the real reason she'd kept the outfit on was as an excuse to wear her weapon. *Yeah, it's a tough life being a cop. The little ones spend a lot of time alone . . .*

They turned to the food, talking about their day—the children's, at least. Wes was in a tennis camp in Monterey, Maggie at a music camp in Carmel, each enjoying the experience.

When dinner was over, the trio did the dishes. Then Wes and Maggie headed into the living room, and Dance logged onto her computer and checked email. Her phone rang again. She looked at the caller ID number.

'Well, hello.'

'Hey there,' Michael O'Neil said. 'How'd it go with Judge Reynolds?'

'Nothing particularly helpful. But he's checking his old files from the Croyton case. She added that she'd picked up Morton Nagle's material too, but hadn't had a chance to look through it yet.

O'Neil told her that the stolen Focus hadn't been located, but the techs had lifted fingerprints from the T-bird and the utensils at Jack's Seafood—Pell's and presumably the woman's. A search through state and federal data bases revealed she had no record.

Dance relayed Carraneo's information about the T-bird.

'Not racing forward at the speed of light, are we? I'm headed your way right now. Want help looking through Nagle's papers?'

'You're on.'

'Hi, Michael,' Wes said, slapping him a high five.

'Hey there.'

They talked about the boy's tennis camp—O'Neil played too. Dance's son was skillful at most sports he tried, though she deflected him from karate and aikido, as sometimes the boy boiled over with anger—he'd been shaken hard by his father's death.

O'Neil had undertaken a mission to keep Wes occupied with healthy diversions. Now and then he would take the boy out on his boat in Monterey Bay, fishing or whale watching. They talked now about a fishing trip in a few weeks, then Wes said good night and wandered off to his room.

Dance poured some wine, then spread Nagle's sheets out in front of them. The quantity was daunting.

O'Neil flipped through a stack of notes. 'Nagle have any thoughts yet about what Pell's up to?'

'Not really. He's writing us a bio.'

For the next hour, they sifted through the photocopies, looking for references to any place or person in the area that Pell might have had an interest in. There was no reference to Alison or Nimue. Nothing.

Most of the videotapes were feature TV magazine reports about Pell, the Croyton murders, or about Croyton himself. 'Sensationalist crap,' O'Neil announced. But there were two police interview tapes, one for a burglary bust thirteen years earlier.

'Who are your next of kin, Daniel?'
    'I don't have any family. I'm an orphan, you could say.'
    'When did your parents die?'
    'When I was seventeen. But my dad left before that. My father . . . that's a hard story.'

Pell gave the officer an account of his abusive father, who had forced young Daniel to pay rent from the age of thirteen. He would beat the boy if he didn't come up with the money—and beat the mother if she defended him. This, he explained, was why he'd taken to stealing. Finally the father had abandoned them. Coincidentally, his separated parents had died the same year—his mother of cancer, his father in a drunk-driving accident.

'And no siblings, hmm?'
    'No, sir. . . . And I don't have any children myself, either. That's a regret, I must say. But I'm young. I've got time, right?'
    'Oh, if you get your act together, Daniel, there's no reason you couldn't have a family of your own.'
    'Thank you for saying that, Officer. Thank you.'

The second police tape was from a town in the Central Valley twelve years ago, where he'd been arrested for petty larceny.

'Daniel, listen here, I'm gonna be askin' you a few questions. Don't go and lie to us, OK? That'll go bad for you.'
    'No, sir, Sheriff. I'm here to be honest. Tell God's truth.'
    'You do that. Now, how come you was found with Jake Peabody's TV set and VCR in the back of your car?'
    'I bought 'em, Sheriff. I swear to you. On the street. This Mexican fellow? We was talking, and he said he needed some money. Him and his wife had a sick kid, he told me.'

'See what he's doing?' Dance asked.
O'Neil shook his head.
'The first interviewer speaks well. Pell responds the same way. The second officer makes grammatical mistakes. Pell echoes him. 'We was talking',

'Him and his wife'. It's a trick manipulators use. He's in total control.'

They looked through the material for another half hour, but nothing else was useful.

O'Neil looked at his watch. 'Got to go.' Wearily he rose, and she walked him outside. He scratched the dogs' heads.

'Hope you can make it to Dad's party tomorrow,' Dance said.

'Let's hope it's all over with by then.' He climbed into his Volvo and headed down the misty street.

Her phone croaked. ''Lo?'

'Hey, Boss. Pell's aunt? Her name's Barbara Pell. But she's brain-fried. Bakersfield PD say she's got Alzheimer's. But there's a work shed behind the house with some things of Pell's in it. Anybody could've strolled in and walked out with the hammer.'

'Bakersfield's going to keep an eye on the woman's house?'

'Affirmative. Now, Boss, I got the skinny for you on Winston.'

'Who?'

'Winston Kellogg, the FBI guy that Overby's bringing in to baby-sit you.'

Baby-sit . . . 'Could you pick a different word?'

'To oversee you. To ride herd. Subjugate.'

'TJ.'

'OK, here's the scoop. He's forty-four. Lives in Washington now. Former military, army. Detective with Seattle PD, then joined the bureau. He's with a division that tracks down cult leaders and hooks up cult members with deprogrammers. It was formed after the Waco siege. He's got a good rep in the bureau. He's a bit of a straight arrow, but he's not afraid to get his hands dirty. That's a direct quote, and I have no clue what it means.'

'OK. Thanks, TJ.'

Dance ended the call and let Dylan and Patsy out for their bedtime business, then checked that no unrecognised cars were parked nearby. She got the animals back inside. Normally they slept in the kitchen, but tonight she gave them the run of the house. She also armed the window and door alarms.

Dance went into Maggie's room, kissed her good night and turned out the light. She then sat for a few minutes with Wes while he told her about a new kid at camp. They'd enjoyed playing practice matches today.

'Want to ask him to Grandpa's birthday tomorrow?' she asked.

'Naw, I don't think so.' After his father's death Wes had also grown shyer and more reclusive. 'Maybe later. I don't know . . . Mom? How come you've still got your gun?'

Children—nothing whatsoever gets by them. 'I forgot all about it. It's going in the safe right now.'

'Can I read for a while?'

'Sure. Fifteen minutes.'

'Night, Mom.'

Dance slipped the Glock into her gun safe. She reset the lock, then showered, donned sweats and slipped under the thick comforter.

Where are you? she asked Daniel Pell. Who's your partner? Are you planning to kill again?

As she drifted off to sleep, she heard in her mind lines from the tape she and Michael O'Neil had just listened to.

Dance's eyes opened. Pulling on slippers, she made her way to the living room. 'Go back to sleep,' she said to the dogs, but they watched her attentively for the next hour as she prowled once again through Morton Nagle's box.

Tuesday
Chapter 6

Kathryn Dance, TJ beside her, was in Overby's office, early morning rain pelting the windows. 'I need something, Charles.'

'What's that?'

'An OK for some expenses.'

'For what?'

'We're not making any headway. There are no leads from Capitola, the forensics aren't giving us answers, no sightings of him . . . And most important, I don't know why he's staying in the area.'

'What do you mean, expenses?'

'I want to interview the three women who were in the Family. They lived with him; they've got to know him pretty well.'

Oh, if you get your act together, Daniel, there's no reason you couldn't have a family of your own . . .

It was this line from the tape that had inspired the idea. *A to B to X . . .*

'But they'd be sympathetic to him, wouldn't they?'

'No. I've talked to two of them, and they have no sympathy for Pell. The third changed her identity to put that life behind her.'

'Why here? Why not interview them where they live?'

'I want them together. It's a Gestalt interviewing approach. Their memories would trigger each other's. I was up till two reading about them. Rebecca wasn't with the Family very long—just a few months—but Linda lived with Pell for over a year, and Samantha for two.'

Overby shook his head. 'Air fare, guards, transportation . . . It's too out of the box.' He noticed a frayed thread on his cuff and plucked it out. 'I'm afraid I have to say no. Utah. I'm sure that's where he's headed now. After the scare at Moss Landing, it'd be crazy for him to stay around.'

'Charles, Utah's a false lead. He's not going to point us there and—'

'Unless,' her boss said triumphantly, 'it's a double twist.'

'It's not Pell's profile. I really want to go with my idea.'

A voice came from behind her. 'Can I ask what that idea is?'

Dance turned to see a man in a dark suit, powder-blue shirt, and striped blue and black tie. Not classically handsome—he had a bit of a belly, and if he were to look down, a double chin would blossom. But he had amused brown eyes and a flop of brown hair over his forehead that suggested an easy-going nature. He had a faint smile on his lips.

Overby asked, 'Can I help you?'

Stepping closer, the man offered an FBI identification card. Special Agent Winston Kellogg.

'The baby sitter is in the building,' TJ said, *sotto voce.*

'Charles Overby. Thanks for coming, Agent Kellogg.'

'Please, call me Win. I'm with the bureau's Multiple Victims Coercive Crimes Division.'

'That's the new term for cults?' Dance asked.

'We used to call it cult unit. But that wasn't politically correct.'

She laughed. 'I'm Kathryn Dance.'

'TJ Scanlon.'

'Thomas Jefferson?'

TJ gave a cryptic smile. Even Dance didn't know his full name.

Addressing all the agents, Kellogg offered, 'I want to say something up front. Yeah, I'm the Fed. But I don't want to ruffle feathers. I'm here to give whatever insights I can about how Pell thinks. I'm happy to take a back seat.'

Even if he didn't mean it, Dance gave him credit for the reassurance. It was unusual in the world of law-enforcement egos.

'Appreciate that,' Overby said.

Kellogg turned to Dance. 'What idea were you just suggesting?'

Dance reiterated it.

The FBI agent nodded. 'Getting the Family back together. Very good. I think we should pursue it.'

There was silence for a moment. Overby finally said, 'The only problem is budget. See, recently we—'

'We'll pay,' Kellogg said. 'I'll get a Bureau jet to fly them here if we need one. Sound OK to you?'

DANCE, KELLOGG and TJ were in her office when Michael O'Neil stepped inside. He shook the FBI agent's hand, and they introduced themselves.

'It might be helpful to give you all some insights into the cult mentality,' Kellogg said. 'At MVCC we've put together a general profile, and I'm sure some or all of it applies to Pell.'

'Good,' O'Neil said. 'I don't think we've ever seen anyone like this guy.'

Kellogg leaned against Dance's desk. 'First, like the name of my unit suggests, we consider the members of a cult "victims". But we have to remember that they can be just as dangerous as the leader. Charles Manson wasn't even present at the Tate–La Bianca killings. It was the members who committed the murders.

'So here's the basic profile. A cult leader is always in charge one hundred per cent. He dictates how the subjects spend every minute of their time. He'll make the subjects believe it's morally right to do what he tells them— or what he suggests. Subjects are expected to give everything to him—their time, their money, their bodies. He'll pick vulnerable people and play on their insecurities. They come to see him as a source of support and nurture. He'll threaten to withhold himself—and that's his most powerful weapon.'

Kellogg lifted his hands. 'What does this all mean for us? For one thing, it says something about his vulnerabilities. It's tiring to be a cult leader. You have to monitor constantly, so when external influences exist—like out on the street—they're particularly wary. In their own environments, they're more relaxed. At that restaurant, he was constantly monitoring. If he'd been in his own house, you probably would've gotten him.

'The other implication is this: the accomplice, that woman, will believe that Pell is justified in killing. So we won't get help from her, and she's as dangerous as he is. Yes, she's a victim, but that doesn't mean she won't kill you . . . Well, those are some general thoughts.'

Dance thanked Kellogg, and the meeting broke up. Dance pulled out her mobile and found Linda Whitfield's and Rebecca Sheffield's numbers in the call log. Now all she had to do was convince them to come to Monterey.

IN THE SEA VIEW Motel, Daniel Pell looked up from Jennie's computer and saw the woman easing towards him seductively.

'Come on back to bed, baby,' Jennie whispered.

Pell switched screens so she wouldn't see what he was searching for. He grinned, and looked at her body as if he were sorely tempted. 'I wish I could, lovely, but you tired me out. Anyway, I need you to run an errand for me.'

'Me?'

'Yep. Now that they know I'm here, I need you to do it by yourself.' The news stories were reporting he was probably still in the vicinity, so he had to be much more careful.

'Oh, all right.' A little pout.

He said, 'Now, go cut your hair.'

'My hair.'

'Yeah. And dye it. The people at the restaurant saw you. I bought some brown dye at the Mexican store.' He pulled a box out of the bag.

'Oh, I thought that was for you.' She smiled awkwardly.

Daniel Pell had no agenda with the haircut other than making it more difficult to recognise her. He understood, though, that there was another issue. He remembered her proudly brushing away in the T-bird. He supposed she'd let it grow long as protection from her vicious self-image.

After a moment, Jennie said, 'Sweetheart, I'll cut it. Whatever you want.' Another pause. 'I was thinking. Wouldn't it be better if we left? After what happened at the restaurant? Let's get a car and go to Anaheim! We'll have a nice life. I'll support us. You can stay home until they forget about you.'

'That sounds wonderful, lovely. But we can't leave yet.'

'Oh.'

She wanted an explanation. Pell said only, 'Now go cut it.' He added in a whisper, 'Cut it short. Real short.'

DANCE WAS HEADING north on Highway 1, getting a beautiful view of the bay. She hadn't needed to ask Rebecca Sheffield to come to Monterey; the woman had suggested it herself. Linda Whitfield had been reluctant, however, and had told Dance that she would have to ask Jesus.

Dance had just pulled into a gas station when she got a call from FBI Agent Winston Kellogg in his new temporary CBI quarters.

'Kathryn, I've got the jet tanked up in Oakland, if Linda Whitfield gets the OK from on high,' he said. 'Have you called the third woman?'

'Samantha McCoy? No. I'm driving up to San Jose now. If she's gone to this much trouble to keep her identity quiet, it'll take more than a phone call to convince her to help us out.'

Dance disconnected, then flipped through her notebook and found the number of Samantha McCoy's employer. She called, and asked to be connected, ready to hang up if she answered. But the receptionist said McCoy was working at home that day. Dance then had TJ text-message her Mapquest directions to the woman's house.

A few minutes later, when she was back on the highway, the phone rang. It was Linda Whitfield, calling from her church office.

'Agent Dance—'

'Call me Kathryn. Please.'

'I just wanted you to know I'll be there in the morning, if you still want me.'

'Yes, I'd love for you to come. Somebody from my office will call about the arrangements. Thank you so much.'

A hesitation. Then she said in a formal voice, 'You're welcome.'

Two out of three. Dance wondered if the reunion might work after all.

SITTING IN FRONT of the open window of the Sea View Motel, Daniel Pell typed awkwardly on the computer keyboard. He'd managed some access to computers at Capitola, but hadn't had time to get to know how they worked. He'd been pounding away on Jennie's all morning. Ads, news, porn . . . It was astonishing. He searched for some people from his past, but he didn't have much luck. He tried tax records, deeds offices, vital statistics. But you needed a credit card for most things. And credit cards left trails.

Then he had a brainstorm and searched through the archives of the local newspapers and TV stations. That proved much more helpful.

Among the names on his list was Kathryn Dance.

Always aware of his surroundings, he noticed a black Toyota Camry pull into the lot and pause outside the window. He gripped the gun. Then he smiled as the car parked exactly seven spaces away. She climbed out.

That's my girl. *Holding fast* . . .

Jennie walked inside.

'You did it, lovely.' Pell glanced at the Camry. 'Looks nice.'

She kissed him fast. Her hands were shaking. And she couldn't control her excitement. 'It went great! It really did, sweetie. At first he was freaked about the plates, but I did what you said and he agreed.'

'Good for you, lovely.'

Jennie had used some of her cash to buy a car from a man who lived in

Marina. It would be too risky to register it in her real name, so she'd told him that her car had broken down in Modesto, she'd have the licence plates in a day or two and she'd mail his back. This was illegal and stupid. No man would ever do that for another guy, even one paying cash. But Pell had sent Jennie in tight jeans, a half-buttoned blouse, and red bra on fine display.

'Nice. Oh, can I have the car keys?'

She handed them over. 'Here's what else you wanted.' Jennie set two shopping bags on the bed.

Pell nodded approvingly. Then he looked down at the map. Jennie clearly wanted to ask what he had in mind, but couldn't bring herself to.

'I've got a few things to take care of, baby. I'll need a ride.'

'Sure. Just say when.'

THE DOOR OPENED, and Kathryn Dance found herself looking at a slim woman with a narrow, pretty face, blue-framed glasses and curly brown hair.

'Mrs Starkey?'

'That's right.' The face was very different from the one in the pictures of eight years ago; Samantha McCoy had had extensive cosmetic surgery. But Dance knew from her eyes that there was no doubt of her identity. Not from their appearance, but from their flash of horror, then dismay.

The agent said, 'I'm Kathryn Dance. California Bureau of Investigation.'

The woman glanced at the ID. From inside, a man's voice called, 'Who is it, honey?'

Samantha's eyes remained fixed on Dance's. 'That woman from up the street. The one I met at Safeway I told you about.'

Which answered the question about how secret her past was. Dance also thought: smooth. Good liars are always prepared with credible answers, and they know the person they're lying to. Samantha's response told Dance that her husband had a bad memory of casual conversation and that Samantha had thought out every likely situation in which she'd need to lie.

Samantha stepped outside, closed the door, and they walked halfway to the street. The woman looked haggard. Her eyes were red, and the crescents beneath were dark. It seemed she hadn't slept.

A glance back at the house. Then she turned to Dance and, with imploring eyes, whispered, 'I had nothing to do with it, I swear. I heard he had somebody helping him, a woman, I saw that on the news, but –'

'No, no, that's not what I'm here about.'

The woman rubbed her face, then crossed her arms.

'That was your husband?' Dance asked.

She nodded.

'He doesn't know?'

'He doesn't even suspect.'

Amazing, Dance reflected. 'Does *anyone* know?'

'My parole officer.'

'What about friends and family?'

'My mother's dead. My father couldn't care less about me. After the Croyton murders, they stopped returning my phone calls. And my old friends found excuses to disappear from my life as fast as they could. Everybody I know now I met after I became Sarah.' A whisper. 'What do you want?'

'Pell's staying in the Monterey area, and we don't know why. Rebecca and Linda are coming to help us. I'd like you to come.'

Her jaw trembled. 'No, no, I couldn't. I don't know anything. Really. Daniel Pell's a monster. I couldn't begin to tell you what was going on in his mind. You have to believe me. I swear.'

Classic denial flags signalling stress from a past she couldn't confront. 'You'll be completely protected, if that's what—'

'No. I'm sorry. You have to understand, I've created a whole new life for myself. But it's so fragile. I'm sorry. I just can't do it.'

'I understand,' Dance said.

Samantha turned and walked to the house. At the door, she looked back and gave a big smile.

Has she changed her mind? Dance was momentarily hopeful.

Then the woman waved. 'Bye!' she called. 'Good seeing you again.'

Samantha McCoy and her lie stepped back into the house.

'DID YOU HEAR about that?' Susan Pemberton asked César Gutierrez, sitting across from her in the hotel bar as she poured sugar into her latte. She was gesturing towards a TV from which a picture of Daniel Pell was staring out above a local phone number. The caption was: ESCAPEE HOT LINE.

'Wouldn't it be Escap*er?*' Gutierrez asked.

Susan blinked. 'I don't know.'

The businessman continued: 'I didn't mean to be light about it. It's terrible. He killed two people, I heard.' The handsome Latino sprinkled cinnamon into his cappuccino, then sipped, spilling a bit of spice on his slacks. 'Oh, look at that. I'm such a klutz.'

This was a business meeting. Susan, who worked for an event-planning company, was going to put together an anniversary party for his parents—but, being single, the thirty-nine-year-old woman automatically noted that this soft-spoken man wore no wedding ring.

They'd disposed of the details of the party—cash bar, chicken and fish, open wine, dancing to a DJ—and were now chatting over coffee before she went back to the office to work up an estimate.

'You'd think they'd have got him by now,' Gutierrez said, then glanced outside, frowning.

'Something wrong?' Susan asked.

'It sounds funny, I know, but just as I was getting here, I saw this car pull up. And somebody who looked a little like him got out.'

'Who? The killer?'

He nodded at the TV. 'And there was a woman driving.'

'Where did he go?'

'I wasn't paying attention. I think by the bank.'

She looked towards the place.

Then the businessman smiled. 'But that's crazy. He wouldn't be here.' He nodded past where they were looking. 'What's that banner? I saw it before.'

'Oh, the concert on Friday. Part of a John Steinbeck celebration.'

'What kind of music?' Gutierrez asked.

'Jazz—because of the Monterey Jazz Festival. It's my favourite.'

'I love jazz,' he said. 'I go to the festival whenever I can.'

'Really?' Susan resisted an urge to touch his arm.

'Maybe we'll run into each other at the next one.'

Susan said, 'I worry . . . Well, I just wish more people would listen to music like that. Real music.'

'Here's to that.' Gutierrez tapped his cup to hers. 'My ex . . . She lets our son listen to rap. Some of those lyrics? Disgusting. And he's only twelve.'

'It's not music,' Susan announced. Thinking: So, he has an ex.

Gutierrez hesitated and asked, 'You think you might be there?'

'Yeah, I will.'

'Well, if you go, you want to hook up there?'

'Oh, César, that'd be fun.'

Gutierrez stretched. He said he wanted to get on the road. Then he added he'd enjoyed meeting her and, without hesitating, gave her the holy trinity of phone numbers: work, home and mobile. He picked up his briefcase, and they started for the door together. She noticed, though, that he was pausing, his eyes examining the lobby.

'Something wrong?'

'I think it's that guy,' he whispered. 'The one I saw before. There, you see him? He was looking our way.'

The lobby was filled with tropical plants. She had a vague image of someone walking out of the door. 'Daniel Pell?'

'It couldn't be.' Gutierrez looked out through the door. 'He's gone.'

'Think we should tell somebody at the desk?'

'I'll give the police a call. I'm probably wrong, but what can it hurt?' He pulled out his cellphone, dialled 911 and spoke for a few minutes. 'They'll check it out. Of course, they're probably getting a hundred calls an hour. I can walk you to your car if you want.'

'Wouldn't mind that.'

They walked along Alvarado, their conversation subdued, and Susan realised the streets were unusually deserted. She began to feel uneasy.

Her car was next to a construction site a block from Alvarado. If Pell had come this way, she reflected, he could easily be hiding behind the piles of materials. She slowed.

'Something wrong?' Gutierrez asked.

Susan gave an embarrassed laugh and told him her fears.

He smiled. 'He wouldn't attack two of us together. Come on.'

'César, wait,' she said, reaching into her bag. She handed him a small red cylinder. 'Here. Pepper spray. Just in case.'

'I think we'll be OK,' he said, but took the spray.

They continued to the car, and by the time they got there Susan was feeling foolish. No crazed killers were lurking behind the piles of bricks. She unlocked the doors.

'I better give this back to you,' he said, holding out the spray.

Susan reached for it. But Gutierrez lunged fast and jerked her head back. He shoved the nozzle into her mouth, open in a stifled scream.

AGONY IS PERHAPS the fastest way to control somebody, reflected Daniel Pell as he drove Susan Pemberton's car to a deserted location near the ocean south of Carmel.

Agony . . . Hurt them bad, give them a little time to recover, then threaten to hurt them again. Experts say torture isn't efficient. That's wrong. It isn't *elegant*. It isn't *tidy*. But it works real well.

Oh, it had been nice! Playing Susan like a fish was a luxurious high. Practising his art in the real world once again.

Pell found the turnoff. It led through a dense grove of trees to the ocean. Jennie had spent the Saturday before the escape doing reconnaissance and had discovered this deserted place. He continued along the sand-swept road, beached Susan's car in sand at the end and climbed out. Surf crashed over an old pier. The sun was low and spectacular.

He didn't have to wait long. Jennie was early. She parked, climbed out and walked to him. She hungrily closed her mouth around his, gripping his face in both her hands. Desperate.

Pell came up for air.

She laughed. 'It's hard to get used to you like this. I mean, I knew it was you, but still, I did a double take. But it's like me and my short hair—it'll grow back, and you'll be white again.'

'Come here.' He took her hand and sat on a low sand dune, pulled her down next to him.

'Aren't we leaving?' she asked.

'Not quite yet.'

A nod at the Lexus. 'Whose car is that? I thought your friend was going to drop you off.'

He said nothing. They looked west at the Pacific Ocean. She'd be thinking: What's going on? Uncertainty—Pell let it run. She'd notice that he wasn't smiling. Concern flowed in like high tide, tension in her hand.

Finally he asked, 'How much do you love me?'

She didn't hesitate. 'As big as the universe.'

Pell was quiet.

'What's the matter, Daniel?'

'I have a problem, and I don't know what to do about it.'

'A problem, sweetheart?'

So it's 'sweetie' when she's happy, 'sweetheart' when she's troubled. 'That meeting I had? The business thing?'

'Uh-huh.'

'Something went wrong. This woman was going to pay me back a lot of money I'd loaned her, but she lied to me. She had her own plans. She was going to use me. You too.'

'Me? She knows me?'

'Not your name. But from the news, she knows we're together. She wanted me to leave you so she could be with me.'

'This was somebody you used to know?'

'That's right.'

'Oh.' Jennie fell silent. *Jealousy* . . .

'I told her no. Susan got mad. She said she would turn us both in.' Pell's face contorted with pain. 'I tried to talk her out of it.'

'What happened?'

He glanced at the car. 'I brought her here. I didn't have any choice. She was trying to call the police.'

Alarmed, Jennie looked up. 'In the trunk? Oh, God. Is she—?'

'She's tied up. I don't know what to do,' he said breathlessly. 'She's not right in the head. Like your husband, remember? She can't control herself.' He sighed angrily. 'I was going to pay you. For everything you've done.'

'You don't have to worry about the money, sweetheart.'

'No, I'm going to pay you back.' He kissed her in a preoccupied way. 'But what are we going to do?'

Jennie avoided his gaze. 'I . . . I don't know, sweetheart. I'm not . . .' Her voice ran out of steam.

'I can't let anything hurt us. I love you so much.'

Faintly: 'And I love you, Daniel.'

He took the knife from his pocket. Stared at it. 'I don't want to. I really don't. People've been hurt yesterday because of us. But that was accidental. This . . .' He turned the knife over and over in his hand.

She pressed against him, staring at the blade, shivering hard.

'Will you help me, lovely? I can't do it by myself.'

Jennie started to cry. 'I don't know, sweetheart. I don't think I can.'

Pell kissed her head. 'We can't let anything hurt us. I couldn't live without you.'

'Me too.' She sucked in breath.

'Help me, please.' A whisper. He helped her to her feet, and they continued to the Lexus. He gave her the knife, closed his hand round hers. 'I'm not strong enough alone,' he confessed. 'But together . . .' He looked at her, eyes bright. 'It'll be like a pact.'

He reached into the car and hit the trunk-release button. Jennie barked a faint scream at the sound.

'Help me, lovely. Please.' He led her towards the trunk.

Then she stopped. She handed him the knife, sobbing. 'Please, I'm so sorry. Don't be mad. I can't do it. I just can't.'

Pell just nodded. Her miserable eyes, her tears reflecting red from the melting sun. It was an intoxicating sight.

'Don't be mad at me, Daniel. I couldn't stand it if you were mad.'

Pell hesitated three heartbeats, the perfect length of time to foment uncertainty. 'I'm not mad.'

'Am I still your lovely?'

Another pause. 'Of course you are. Go wait for me. It's OK.'

Jennie walked back to the Toyota. He continued to the trunk and looked down—at Susan Pemberton's lifeless body.

He'd known Jennie would baulk. In fact, he'd planned on it.

But she'd moved a step closer to where he wanted her. Death and violence were on the table now. For at least ten seconds she'd considered slipping the knife into a human body, watching a life vanish.

Next week she'd consider it for a longer period.

Chapter 7

He was a curious man, Kathryn Dance was thinking.

Morton Nagle tugged at his sagging trousers and sat down at the coffee table in her office, opening a battered briefcase.

He was a bit of a slob, his thinning hair dishevelled, shirt cuffs frayed, body spongy. But he seemed comfortable with his physique, his mannerisms stress-free. His eyes, with their elfin twinkle, deciding instantly what was important. He'd ignored her decor, noted the exhaustion on her face, glanced at Rey Carraneo and fixed immediately on Winston Kellogg.

Kellogg was dressed quite unfederal compared with this morning—checked sports jacket, dark slacks, blue shirt. Still, his noncommittal behaviour was right out of the Bureau. He told Nagle only that he was an observer. The writer offered one of his chuckles.

'Rebecca and Linda have agreed to help,' Dance told him.

He lifted an eyebrow. 'Really? And the other one—Samantha?'

'No, not her.'

Nagle set three sheets of paper on the table. 'My mini-opus, if that's not an oxymoron. A brief history of Daniel Pell. The *real* story. It's interesting—Pell changes his autobiography depending on whom he's talking to. But here's the truth. Daniel didn't have a bad life as a kid. Joseph Pell, his father, was a salesman; his mother, Elizabeth, was a receptionist. Middle-class family. Mom drank a lot, died of cirrhosis when Daniel was in his midteens. Father did what he could to raise the boy, but Daniel couldn't take anyone else being in charge. Didn't do well with authority figures—teachers, bosses and especially his old man.'

Dance mentioned the tape that she and Michael O'Neil had watched, the comments about his father charging rent, beating him, abandoning the family, his parents dying.

Nagle said, 'All a lie. But his father was undoubtedly a hard character for Pell to deal with. He was very religious, very strict. An ordained minister—some conservative Presbyterian sect—but he never got a church of his own, so he ended up selling religious books and icons. When he retired, he moved to Phoenix and remarried. His second wife died two years ago, and Joseph died last year, heart attack. Pell apparently had never stayed in touch. No uncles on either side, and his only aunt is the woman in Bakersfield.'

'The one with Alzheimer's?'

'Yes. But he does have an older brother. Moved to London years ago, runs the sales operation of a US importer/exporter. Doesn't give interviews. All I have is a name. Richard Pell.'

Dance said to Kellogg, 'I'll have somebody track him down.'

'Cousins?' the FBI agent asked.

'The aunt never married. Now, in Pell's later teens, he was constantly in and out of juvenile detention—mostly for larceny, shoplifting, car theft. But there's no early evidence of violent assault. One officer suggested that it seemed Pell would hurt somebody only if it was tactically useful and that he didn't enjoy—or hate—violence. It was a tool.' The writer looked up. 'Which, if you ask me, is scarier.'

'What about education?' Dance asked.

'Now that's interesting. He's brilliant. In high school he got A's in independent study classes but never showed up when attendance was required. In prison, he taught himself law and handled his own appeal in the Croyton case. Took it all the way to the California Supreme Court.'

'Well, he may be smart but he's not smart enough to stay out of jail.' Kellogg tapped a paragraph of the bio that described maybe seventy-five arrests. *'That's* a rap sheet.'

'It's the tip of the iceberg; Pell usually got *other* people to commit the crimes. Robbery, burglary, shoplifting. Anyway, he left Bakersfield and went to San Francisco. Hung out with people there, was picked up for a few things, nothing serious. No word for a while—until he's picked up in northern California in a homicide investigation.'

'Homicide?'

'Yep. The murder of Charles Pickering, a county worker, near Redding. He was stabbed to death in the hills outside of town about an hour after he was seen talking to somebody who looked like Pell. Vicious killing. He was slashed dozens of times. But Pell's girlfriend at the time swore he was with her at the time of the killing. And there was no physical evidence. The case was never solved.

'Then he gets the Family together in Seaside. A few more years of theft, shoplifting. Some assaults. An arson or two. Suspected beating of a biker. After that came the Croyton murders.'

'What does the girl have to say?'

'Girl?'

'The Sleeping Doll. Theresa Croyton.'

'What could she tell you? She was asleep at the time of the murders. That was established, I assume.'

'She'd be, let's see, seventeen now,' Dance calculated. 'I'd like to talk to her. She's living with her aunt and uncle, right?'

'Yes. They adopted her.'

'Could I have their number?'

Nagle hesitated. 'I promised the aunt I wouldn't say anything about the girl. She's very protective of her niece. Even *I* haven't met her yet. The woman was dead set against my talking to her. I think she might agree eventually, but not if I gave you her number.'

'Just tell us where she lives. We'll get the name from directory assistance. I won't mention you.'

'They changed their last name, moved out of the area.'

'*You* found them,' Dance said.

'Through some confidential sources. But I'll tell you what I'll do. I'll go see the aunt in person. If she says no, that's it.'

Kellogg nodded. 'That's all we're asking. Thanks.'

'I HAVE TO GET HOME,' Dance said after Nagle left. Her mother and children were awaiting her arrival for her father's party.

Kellogg tossed the comma of hair off his forehead. She glanced at the gesture and noticed something she hadn't seen before—a bandage protruding above the collar of his shirt.

'You hurt?' she asked.

A shrug. 'Got winged. A takedown in Chicago the other day.'

His body language told her he didn't want to talk about it. But then he said, 'The perp didn't make it.' With a glance and in a certain tone. It was how she told people she was a widow.

'I'm sorry. You handling it OK?'

'Fine.' Then he added, 'OK, not fine. But I'm handling it.'

On impulse, she asked, 'Hey, you have plans tonight?'

'Brief the SAC, then a bath at the hotel, a Scotch, a burger and sleep. Well, OK, two Scotches.'

'You like birthday cake?'

He lifted an eyebrow. 'It's one of my favourite food groups.'

'MOM, LOOK. We deck-orated it! *D-E-C-K*.'

Dance kissed her daughter. 'Mags, that's funny.' She knew the girl had been bursting, waiting to share the pun.

The Deck did look nice. The kids had been busy all afternoon. Banners, Chinese lanterns, candles everywhere.

'When can Grandpa open his presents?' Wes and Maggie had saved up allowance money and bought Stuart Dance outdoor gear—waders and a net.

'Presents after the cake,' Edie Dance announced. She was a stocky woman with grey hair and an ageless face.

'Hi, Mom.' Dance and her mother hugged.

Maggie asked, 'Mom, can we let Dylan and Patsy out?'

'We'll see.' The dogs could be a little boisterous at parties. And tended to get too much food for their own good. 'Where's your brother?'

'In his room, doing stuff.'

Dance locked her weapon away—an MCSO deputy on security detail was parked outside. She showered fast and changed.

She found Wes in the hallway. 'No T-shirt. It's your grandpa's birthday.'

'Mom. It's clean.'

'Go change.'

Ten minutes later she was setting out mounds of luscious appetisers, offering a silent prayer of thanks to Trader Joe's. In a dress shirt, cuffs buttoned and tails tucked, Wes strafed past and grabbed a handful of nuts.

She pitched him a bag of pretzels, which he caught with his spare hand. 'Set those out for the guests.'

Carting beer outside onto the Deck, she found her father with Maggie. 'Happy birthday, Dad.' She hugged him.

'Thank you, dear.'

Dance dumped the beer in the cooler, then walked into the kitchen and pulled out her mobile. She checked in with TJ and Carraneo. They'd had no luck with the physical search for Pell, nor come across any leads to the missing Ford Focus, the names Nimue or Alison, or hotels or motels.

She was tempted to call Winston Kellogg, thinking he might be shying, but she decided not to. He'd either show or not.

Dance helped her mother with more food and, returning to the Deck, greeted the neighbours, Tom and Sarah Barber, who brought with them wine, a birthday present and their gangly dog, Fawlty.

'Mom, please!' Maggie called, her meaning clear.

'OK, OK, let 'em out of doggy jail.'

Maggie freed Patsy and Dylan from the bedroom, and the three canines galloped into the back yard.

A few minutes later another couple appeared on the Deck. Fortyish Steven Cahill, with salt-and-pepper ponytail. His wife, Martine, sultry, dark and voluptuous, part Ohlone Indian.

Some years ago Dance had met Martine at a concert in Monterey. The women had hit it off instantly, and had soon become best friends. It was Martine who'd kept Dance from sinking into the seductive world of reclusive widowhood following Bill's death. Embarking on a campaign that could be called ignoring sorrow, Martine cajoled, joked and plotted, and was perhaps the biggest influence in getting Dance's life back on track.

Steve and Martine's children, twin boys a year younger than Maggie, followed behind. After greetings, Maggie herded the boys into the back yard. The adults gravitated to a rickety candlelit table. Dance saw that Wes was happier than he'd been in a long time. He was a natural social director and was now organising a game for the children.

'The escape. Are you . . . ?' Martine's melodious voice faded once she saw that Dance knew what she was talking about.

'Yep. I'm running it. If I have to run off before the cake and candles, that's why.'

Sarah Barber added, 'People are staying home. All over the Peninsula. They're afraid.'

'Only reason I'm here,' Steve said, 'is I knew there'd be folks packing heat.' Dance laughed.

Michael O'Neil arrived with his wife, Anne, and their two children. Anne, a tall and attractive blonde, ran a photography gallery in Carmel and was also a stringer for several big daily newspapers.

Dance pointed out wine and beer, then headed into the kitchen to help, but her mother said, 'You've got another guest.' She indicated the front door, where Dance found Winston Kellogg.

'I'm empty-handed,' he confessed.

'I've got more than we'll ever eat. You'll have to take a doggy bag home.'

Kellogg had changed again, into a polo shirt and jeans. She directed him through the kitchen and introduced him to Edie, then continued onto the Deck. There he was inundated with more introductions, and said merely that he was 'working with Kathryn on a few projects'.

Then she took him down to the back yard and introduced him to the children. Dance caught Wes looking at him closely for armament. When O'Neil joined the two agents, Wes waved enthusiastically to him and returned to the game he was playing with the kids.

'Did you tell Michael about Morton Nagle?' Kellogg asked.

She told the detective what they'd learned about Pell's history, and added that the writer was going to see if Theresa Croyton would talk to them.

'So you think Pell's here because of the murders?' O'Neil asked.

'I don't know,' she said. 'But I need all the information I can get.'

O'Neil gave a smile and said to Kellogg, 'No stone left unturned. That's how I describe her policing style.'

'Which I learned from him,' Dance said, laughing.

Kellogg sipped his wine and smiled. O'Neil looked past Dance's shoulder. 'Hey, happy birthday, young man.'

Stuart Dance, wearing a badge that said BIRTHDAY BOY, handmade by Wes and Maggie, shook hands, refilled O'Neil's and Dance's wineglasses, and said to Kellogg, 'You're talking shop. Not allowed. I'm stealing you away.'

Kellogg gave a shy laugh and followed the man to the candlelit table. Dance and O'Neil stood alone.

'He seems good,' O'Neil said, tilting his head towards Kellogg.

'Winston? Yes.'

'He take a hit recently?' O'Neil tapped his neck.

'How'd you know?' The bandage wasn't visible tonight.

'He was touching it the way you touch a wound.'

She laughed. 'Good kinesic analysis. Yeah, happened in Chicago. The perp got a round off first, I guess, and Win took him out.'

They fell silent, looking over the back yard, the children, the dogs, the bright lights. 'We'll get him,' said O'Neil.

'Will we?' she asked.

'Yeah. He'll make a mistake. They always do.'

'I don't know. He's something different. Don't you feel that?'

'No, he's not different. He's just *more*.' O'Neil had surprisingly simple philosophies of life. He didn't believe in evil or good. Just destructive forces that had to be stopped.

Dance turned to see how her mother was coming with dinner. She saw O'Neil's wife looking at them. Anne smiled.

Dance smiled back. 'So, let's go join the others.'

After a half-hour of music, gossip and laughter, Edie Dance set out Worcestershire-marinated flank steak, salad, asparagus and potatoes au gratin. Dance sat beside Winston Kellogg, who was holding his own very well among strangers. He even told a few jokes, with a deadpan delivery that reminded her of her late husband.

The conversation ambled from music to Anne O'Neil's critique of San Francisco arts, to politics in Sacramento and Washington, to the sea otter pup born at the aquarium two days ago. It was a comfortable gathering.

Of course, complete comfort eluded Dance. Pervading the otherwise fine evening was the thought that Daniel Pell was still at large.

Wednesday
Chapter 8

Kathryn Dance was sitting in a cabin at the Point Lobos Inn, an expensive lodge on a quiet road off Highway 1, south of Carmel, abutting the ruggedly beautiful state park after which the inn was named. A long driveway separated it from the road, and the deputy in the MCSO car stationed in front had a perfect view of all approaches.

Dance checked in with Carranco, who said he was still having no luck finding a cheap motel or hotel where Pell might be staying. 'I've tried all the way up to Gilroy and—'

'*Cheap* hotels?'

A pause. 'I didn't think an escapee'd have much money to spend.'

Dance recalled Pell's secret phone conversation in Capitola, the reference to $9,200. 'Pell's probably thinking that's exactly what *you're* thinking. Which means . . .'

'Hmm. OK. I'll get on it, Agent Dance.'

She hung up and looked at her watch.

Five minutes later there was a knock on the door. Dance opened it to see massive CBI agent Albert Stemple overshadowing a woman in her late twenties. Stocky Linda Whitfield had a pretty face, untouched by make-up, and short red hair. Her red sweater's V-neck framed a pewter cross.

The women shook hands. Dance thanked the big agent, and he set down Linda's suitcase and ambled off. Dance locked the door.

Linda walked into the living room of the two-bedroom cabin. She looked around at the elegant place. 'My,' she said.

'I've got coffee going.' A gesture towards the small kitchen.

'Tea, if there's any. Any more on Daniel?'

Dance made a cup. 'Nothing new.'

Linda looked at the bedrooms, picked one, and took her suitcase inside. She returned a moment later and accepted the cup of tea.

'I haven't been on an airplane in years,' she said. 'That FBI jet was amazing.' They sat on comfortable couches, a coffee table between them. Linda looked around again. 'My, this is nice.'

It sure was. What would the FBI accountants say when they saw the bill? The cabin was nearly $600 a night.

'Rebecca's on her way. But maybe you and I could get started.'

'And Samantha?' asked Linda.

'She wouldn't come. I went to see her.'

'Where is she? . . . No, wait, you can't tell me that. I heard she had plastic surgery and changed her name.'

'That's true, yes.' Dance smiled.

'I bought a newspaper at the airport. It said there's no doubt he killed those guards.' Linda set down the tea. 'I was surprised by that. Daniel wasn't violent. He'd only hurt someone in self-defence.'

Dance asked about the killing of the man in Redding.

'Charles Pickering? I never heard Daniel mention him. But if the police let him go, I guess that means he didn't do it.'

Interesting logic. 'How did you meet Pell?' Dance asked.

'It was about ten years ago. In Golden Gate Park. San Francisco. I'd run away from home and was sleeping there. Daniel, Samantha and Jimmy were living in Seaside, along with a few other people. They'd travel up and down the coast like Gypsies, selling things they'd bought or made. Sam and Jimmy were pretty talented; they'd make picture frames, CD holders, tie racks. Things like that. Anyway, Daniel saw me near the Japanese Garden.

He sat down, and we started talking. Daniel has this gift. He listens to you like you're the centre of the universe. It's really seductive.'

'And you never went back home?'

'No, I did. I always wanted to run away and just keep going, but I wasn't brave enough. My parents, they were real strict. Like drill instructors. My father was head of Santa Clara Bank and Trust, and—'

'Wait, *that* Whitfield?'

'Yep. The multimillionaire Whitfield. The one who financed a good portion of Silicon Valley. The one who was going into politics—until a certain daughter of his made the press.' A wry smile. 'Ever met anybody who's been disowned by her parents? You have now . . . Anyway, when I was growing up, they were very authoritarian. I got spanked until I was fourteen.

'So I went back home, but all the time I was there, I couldn't get Daniel out of my head. He told me that I was smart and pretty.' A grimace. 'Oh, I wasn't really, but when he said it, I believed him.

'One morning my mother told me we were going to visit my aunt and I was supposed to wear a skirt. I wanted to wear jeans. She screamed at me. Well, I grabbed my backpack and just left. I remembered Daniel had told me he'd be in Santa Cruz at a flea market on the boardwalk.'

The boardwalk was a famous amusement park on the beach. A lot of young people hung out there. Dance reflected that it would make a good hunting ground if Daniel Pell was on the prowl for victims.

'So I hitched a ride down Highway One, and there he was. He looked happy to see me. I asked if he knew a place I could stay, hinting. He said, "You bet I do. With us."'

'In Seaside?'

'Uh-huh. We had a little bungalow there. It was nice.'

'You, Samantha, Jimmy and Pell?'

'Right.'

Her body language told Dance she was enjoying the memory: the easy position of the shoulders, the crinkles beside the eyes, the illustrator hand gestures suggesting the intensity of her reaction to what she was saying.

Linda sipped her tea. 'Whatever the papers said—cult, drug orgies—that was wrong. No drugs at all. Wine at dinner sometimes. It was nice. I loved being around people who saw you for who you were. I ran the house. It was so nice to be in charge for a change, not getting yelled at for having my own opinion.'

'What about the crimes?'

Linda grew tense. 'There was *that*. Some. Not as much as people say. A little shoplifting, things like that. And I never liked it. Never.'

A few negation gestures here, but Dance sensed she wasn't being deceptive; the kinesic stress was due to her minimising the severity of the crimes. The Family had done much worse than just shoplifting. There were burglary counts and grand larceny, purse snatching and pickpocketing.

'But we didn't have any choice. To be in the Family, you had to participate. You had to do what Daniel wanted.'

'And if you didn't?'

'He never hurt us physically. Mostly he'd withdraw. And you'd get scared. You never knew if you'd get thrown out.'

Responding to Dance's questions, Linda mentioned more about her recent life. In jail, she'd become devoutly religious, and after her release she'd got a job in Portland working for a local Protestant church, where her brother was a deacon. She was seeing a man in Portland, but the church was her whole life. She wanted to become a foster parent, but that was hard with the prison conviction.

A knock on the door intruded. 'It's TJ, Boss.'

Dance opened the door, and the young agent entered with another woman. Slim and tall, in her mid-thirties, Rebecca Sheffield was gorgeous, though the short crop of prematurely grey hair, the brash jewellery, and the absence of make-up made her look austere. She wore jeans and a white silk T-shirt under a brown suede jacket, and carried a leather backpack.

Rebecca shook Dance's hand firmly, but she immediately turned her attention to Linda, who was rising and gazing at her with a steady smile.

'Well, look who it is.' Rebecca stepped forward and hugged her.

'After all these years.' Linda's voice choked. 'My, I think I'm going to cry.' And she did.

Rebecca held her hand. 'It's good to see you, Linda.'

'Oh, Rebecca . . . I've prayed for you a lot.'

'You're into that now? You didn't used to know a cross from a Star of David. Well, thanks for the prayers. Not sure they took.'

'No, no. You're doing such good things. Really! The church office has a computer. I saw your website. It's wonderful.'

Rebecca seemed surprised that Linda had kept up with her.

Linda picked up her teacup, fiddled with it, not taking a sip. How people love their props in stressful situations, Dance reflected. She poured Rebecca coffee and set out milk and sugar.

Sipping the coffee, Rebecca said, 'You're looking good, Linda.'

A blush. 'Oh, I don't know. I'm not in the shape I'd like. You're glamorous. And thin! I *love* your hair.'

Rebecca laughed. 'Hey, nothing like a couple years in prison to turn you grey, hmm? Hey, no ring. You're not married?'

'Nope.'

'Me neither.'

'You're kidding. I thought for sure you'd be hooked up.'

'Not easy to find Mr Right when they hear your boyfriend was Daniel Pell.' Linda shook her head. 'You still paint?'

'Not professionally. Just sketch some for fun,' said Rebecca.

They spent a few minutes catching up, then Dance got down to work, asking Rebecca the same basic questions she'd asked Linda.

'I was the last one to get suckered in by Mr Pell,' the thin woman said. 'It was only . . . When?' A glance at Linda.

'January. Just four months before the Croyton situation.'

Situation. Not *murders*.

'How did you meet Pell?' Dance asked.

'Back then I was bumming around the West Coast, making money doing sketches of people at street fairs and on the beach. I had my easel set up, and Pell stopped by. He wanted his portrait done.'

Linda gave a coy smile. 'I seem to remember you didn't do much sketching. You two ended up in the back of the van.'

Rebecca's smile was of embarrassment. 'Well, Daniel has *that* side to him, sure . . . In any case, we *did* talk. And he asked me if I wanted to hang out with them in Seaside. I just said to myself, Hell, I'm a bohemian; I'm a rebel and artist. Screw my lily-white suburban upbringing . . . And it worked out well. There were good people around me, I didn't have to work nine to five and I could paint as much as I wanted. Who could ask for anything more in life? Of course, it turned out I'd also joined a band of thieves.'

Dance noticed Linda's placid face darken at the comment.

After release from jail, Rebecca became involved in the women's movement and started a consulting service to help women finance small businesses. She'd been at it ever since.

Another knock on the door. Winston Kellogg arrived. Dance was happy to see him—professionally and personally. She'd enjoyed getting to know him on the Deck last night. He'd been surprisingly social for a hard-travelling Fed, and, along with her parents, had been the last to leave the party.

He now greeted the two women and, in keeping with protocol, showed them his ID. He poured himself some coffee. It was time to get to the crux of the interview.

'All right, here's the situation,' Dance said. 'Pell is probably still in the area. We can't figure out where or why. Most escapees get as far away as they can.' She told them the developments to date. 'First, let me ask you about his accomplice.'

'That woman I read about?' Linda asked. 'Who is she?'

'We don't know. Apparently, blonde, age roughly mid-twenties.'

'He's got a new girlfriend,' Rebecca said. 'That's our Daniel.'

'There's a chance,' Dance said, 'that she isn't a stranger. She'd have been very young at the time the Family was together, but I was wondering if she could be somebody you know.'

Linda frowned. 'Mid-twenties now . . . She'd have been a teenager then. I don't remember anyone like that.'

Rebecca added, 'When I was in the Family, it was only the five of us.'

'Were there any friends in Seaside he had a connection with?'

'We didn't have friends,' Rebecca said.

'But people he'd met would come by, stay for a while.' Linda said, 'Daniel gave them food, money sometimes.'

The conversation didn't trigger any recollections of who the houseguests might have been. Dance moved on.

'There are some things he searched for online recently. I was wondering if they mean anything to you. One was "Nimue", a computer nickname, maybe. And any recollection of an Alison?'

Neither woman could suggest any reason why Pell had searched for those words. The discussion meandered and revealed nothing helpful.

In interviewing and interrogation, it's a well-known rule that abstractions obscure memories. Dance now said, 'Pick a particular holiday: Thanksgiving, Christmas. Tell me about it.'

Linda shrugged. 'How about that Easter?'

Rebecca nodded. 'My *only* holiday there. Sure.'

Linda described making an elaborate dinner with food that Sam, Jimmy and Rebecca had 'come up with'.

Prodding, Dance asked, 'Jimmy Newberg. Tell us about him.'

Rebecca said, 'He was a funny little puppy. He'd been a stoner.'

'But he was a genius with his hands,' said Linda. 'Carpentry, electronics, everything. He was totally into computers, even wrote his own programs.'

Dance steered them back to the Easter holiday.

'It was a pretty day,' Linda continued. 'The sun was out. We played some games in the yard. Frisbee, badminton. Then I put dinner out.'

Rebecca said, 'I'd boosted some good cabernet, and we girls and Jimmy had wine—Pell didn't drink. Oh, I got pretty wasted.'

Linda added, 'After dinner, we just hung out and talked.'

'You remember what you talked about?'

'Oh, just stuff, you know . . .' Linda fell silent. Then she said, 'Wait. That reminds me of one thing.' She tilted her head slightly. 'It was another dinner, not Easter. Daniel and I were in the kitchen. He was watching me cook. And there was a big crash next door. The neighbours were fighting. He said he couldn't wait to get out of Seaside. To his mountaintop.'

'*His* mountaintop? Did he own some property?'

'He never mentioned anything specific. Maybe he meant "his" in the sense that it was something he *wanted* to have someday.'

Rebecca knew nothing about it.

Linda said, 'I remember it clearly. He wanted to get away from everybody. Just us, just the Family. Nobody else around. I don't think he'd said anything about it before or after that.'

'He ever mention Utah?'

'No.' Rebecca agreed. 'But wait . . . Along those same lines, we were in bed one night, and he said, "I need to get enough money just to get away from everybody." I remember that.'

Mountaintop . . . Could that have been what he'd been looking for in Capitola on the Visual Earth website?

Dance's phone rang. 'Excuse me.' She answered it.

'Kathryn. It's me.'

She pressed the phone closer to her head. 'TJ, what's up?'

And steeled herself. The fact that he hadn't called her 'Boss' meant he was about to deliver bad news.

KATHRYN DANCE and Winston Kellogg walked along a road covered with a thin coat of damp sand towards TJ and Michael O'Neil, who stood at the open trunk of a late-model Lexus.

Another man was there too, one of the officers from the coroner's division, part of the Monterey County Sheriff's Office. The balding round deputy greeted her. 'Kathryn.'

Dance introduced him to Kellogg, then peered into the trunk. The victim, a woman, lay on her side. Her hands and mouth were duct-taped. Her nose and face were bright red.

O'Neil said, 'Susan Pemberton. Lived in Monterey.'

'Probable COD is suffocation?'

The coroner's officer added, 'We've got capillary dilation and membrane inflammation and distension. That residue there? It's capsicum oleoresin.'

'He hit her with pepper spray and then duct-taped her.'

'Terrible,' O'Neil muttered.

A burst of anger swept through Dance. 'We're sure it's Pell?'

'It's him. Prints match,' the coroner's officer said.

O'Neil added, 'She worked for an event-planning company. He apparently used her to get in and tell him where all the files were. Crime scene's been through the office. Nothing conclusive, except his prints. He stole everything.'

'Any clue why?' Kellogg asked.

'Nope.'

'How'd he find her?'

'Her boss said she left the office about five last night to meet a prospective client for drinks. Her boss didn't know who. Maybe Pell followed them.'

'Time of death?'

'Last night, maybe seven to nine,' the coroner's officer said.

Pell had left little evidence except a few footsteps in the sand that seemed to lead towards the beach, then were lost in the dunes.

What was in the files he'd stolen? What didn't he want them to know? Dance looked around. 'Why'd he abandon the car here? He could've gone into the woods. It's a lot more visible here.'

O'Neil pointed at a narrow pier extending into the ocean. 'He's ditched the Ford Focus by now. Maybe he got away by boat.'

Kellogg said, 'It's a little rough to dock a boat there. My thinking is that he started that way maybe to lead us off.' He looked around. 'But I think he was drawn here not because of the pier but because it's deserted and it's a beach. Most cult leaders have a mystical bent, and water often figures in that. Something happened here, almost ceremonial, I'd say. It might have involved the woman with him. Maybe she met him here.'

'But,' O'Neil pointed out, 'there's no evidence of another car, no prints indicating that he turned around and walked back to the road.'

'He could've covered his tracks.' Kellogg pointed to the sand-covered road. 'Those marks don't look natural. He could've swept them over with brush or leaves. I'd excavate that whole area.'

O'Neil. 'I'm thinking it can't hurt to check on stolen vessels. And I'd rather crime scene ran the pier now.'

The tennis volley continued, the FBI agent offering, 'With this wind and rain, I really think the road should be first.'

'You know, Win,' Dance said, 'I think we'll go with the pier.'

Kellogg tipped his head, meaning: It's your team; I'm backing down. 'Fine with me. I'll search it myself, if you don't mind.'

'Sure. Go right ahead.'

Without a look at Dance—he had no desire to test loyalties—Kellogg returned to the area with the dubious markings.

Dance turned and walked along a clean zone back to her car, glad to leave the crime scene behind. Forensic evidence wasn't her expertise. Neither were strong-willed rams butting horns.

THE VISAGE OF GRIEF.

Kathryn Dance knew it well. From life as a cop. And as a widow: looking in the mirror, staring at a very different Kathryn Dance.

Now Dance was seeing the same look as she sat in Susan Pemberton's office across from the woman's boss, Eve Brock.

'It's not real to me.'

The crying was over but only temporarily, Dance sensed. The middle-aged woman held herself in tight rein. Sitting forward, legs tucked under the chair, shoulders rigid, jaw set. The kinesics of grief matched the face.

'I don't understand why he took the computer and the files.'

'Maybe he was at an event years ago, and he didn't want anybody to know about it.' Dance asked about the client Susan was going to meet, but the woman knew nothing. The crying began again.

'Would you excuse me for a moment?' Eve Brock grabbed a key from her desk and headed for the ladies' room.

Dance looked at Susan Pemberton's walls, filled with photos of weddings, bar and bat mitzvahs, anniversary parties, outings for local corporations. She called TJ, gave him the address, and told him to meet her on the street in ten minutes. She also asked him to check with the phone company about calls to Susan's phone. She read out the number from a card on the desk.

Eve Brock returned, her face red, eyes puffy. 'I'm sorry.'

'Not a problem at all. What would be in the files that were stolen?'

'Oh, everything. Clients, hotels, suppliers, caterers, restaurants, liquor stores, florists, photographers . . .' The recitation seemed to exhaust her.

'Did you ever work for William Croyton or his company?'

'I suppose we could have. We do corporate functions.'

'Do you have back-ups of the material?'

'Copies of the invoices would be at my accountant's.'

'Could you get as many of them as possible? Up to May of '99.' It was then that Dance's mind did another of its clicks. 'All your upcoming jobs too.'

'I'll do what I can.'

The woman seemed crushed by the tragedy, paralysed with grief. Dance thought of Morton Nagle's words: *I see violent crime like dropping a stone into a pond. The ripples of consequence can spread almost for ever.*

She got a picture of Susan to give to TJ and walked downstairs to the street to meet him.

IN HER OFFICE at CBI headquarters, Kathryn Dance dropped her jacket onto a chair and sat down. She looked through her email. Pell's brother, Richard, had replied from London that yes, he had heard of his brother's escape from prison but that he had not had any contact with Daniel for twelve years. So much for that lead.

Her mobile rang. The caller was Morton Nagle. In an alarmed voice, he asked, 'He killed someone else? I just saw the news.'

'I'm afraid so.' She gave him the details.

'I'm so sorry. Are there other developments?'

'No.' Dance told him that she'd spoken with Rebecca and Linda.

Nagle had come across nothing in his research about a mountaintop. Nor had his other efforts been successful. He'd talked to Theresa Croyton's aunt, but she was refusing to let him or the police see the girl.

'She threatened me,' he said, his voice troubled.

'Where are you?'

He didn't say anything.

Dance filled in: 'You're not going to tell me, are you?' She glanced at the caller ID, but he was on his mobile. 'Is she going to change her mind?'

'I really doubt it. You should've seen her. When she saw me, she abandoned a hundred dollars' worth of groceries and just ran.'

Dance was disappointed. 'I appreciate your help.'

'I did try. Really.'

After hanging up, Dance talked to Rey Carraneo. Still no luck on the motels and no reports of boats stolen from marinas. A few moments later her phone rang again.

'Hey. It's me.' It was Michael O'Neil, his voice laden with exhaustion. 'I just talked to Rey. He tells me there are no reports of any stolen boat so far. Maybe I was off base. And negative on sources for the duct tape, and the pepper spray's sold in ten thousand stores and mail-order outlets.'

She told him that Nagle's attempt to contact Theresa had failed.

'I liked the idea,' he said. 'She's the only nexus to Pell and that night.'

'We'll have to try harder without her.'

A few minutes after they disconnected, Winston Kellogg arrived.

Dance asked, 'Any luck at the Pemberton crime scene, the road?'

'Nope. We searched for an hour. No treadmarks, no discarded evidence. Maybe Michael was right, and Pell did get away by boat from that pier.'

Dance laughed to herself. She updated Kellogg, then glanced at her watch. 'Got an important meeting. Want to come?'

'Is it about Pell?'

'Nope. It's about snack time.'

AS THEY WALKED down the halls of CBI's headquarters, Dance asked Kellogg where he lived.

'Washington, DC. Grew up in the Northwest—Seattle—but didn't really mind the move east. I'm not a rainy-day kind of guy.'

The talk meandered to personal lives, and he volunteered that he and his ex had no children, though he himself had four brothers.

'I was the youngest. I think my parents ran out of names and started on consumer products. So I'm Winston, like cigarettes. Which is a really bad idea when your last name is cornflakes.'

Dance laughed. 'I'm convinced I didn't get invited to the junior prom because nobody wanted to take a Dance to the dance.'

Kellogg had received a degree in psychology from the University of Washington, then gone into the army.

'CID?' She was thinking about her late husband's stint in the army, where he'd been a Criminal Investigations Division officer.

'No. Tactical planning. Which meant paper, paper, paper. Well, computer, computer, computer. So I left and joined the Seattle police. Did profiling and negotiations, but I found the cult mentality interesting, so I thought I'd specialise. I know it sounds lame, but I just didn't like the idea of bullies preying on vulnerable people.'

She didn't think it was lame at all.

'How'd *you* get into this line?' he asked her.

Dance gave him a brief version of the story. After she grew tired of being a crime reporter, she got degrees in psychology and communications, improving her natural gift of observation. She became a jury consultant. But a sense that her talents would be more worthwhile in law enforcement led her to the CBI.

'And your husband was like me, a feebie?'

'Been doing your homework?' Her late husband, William Swenson, had been a dependable career special agent for the FBI, but there was no reason for Kellogg to have heard of him.

A bashful grin. 'I like to know who I'm going to meet on assignments. Hope you're not offended.'

'Not at all. When I interview a subject, I like to know everything about his "terrarium".' Not sharing with Kellogg that she'd had TJ scope him out.

A moment passed, and he asked, 'Can I ask what happened to your husband? Line of duty?'

The thud in her belly generated by that question had become less pronounced over the years. 'It was a traffic accident.'

'I'm sorry.'

'Thank you . . . Now, welcome to Chez CBI.'

Dance waved him into the lunchroom. They poured coffee and sat at one of the cheap tables. Her cell chirped.

It was TJ. 'I found out where the Pemberton woman was before she was killed—in the bar at the Doubletree with some Latino guy. A business meeting, the waiter thinks. They left about six thirty.'

'You get a credit-card receipt?'

'Yep, but she paid. Business expense.'

'What about Susan's phone log?'

'About forty calls yesterday. I'll check them out when I'm back in the office. Oh, and statewide real-estate tax records? Nope, Pell don't own any mountaintops or anything else. I checked Utah too. Nothing.'

'Good. I forgot about that.'

They hung up, and she relayed the information to Kellogg. A moment later her mother and children walked into the lunchroom. The kids were going to spend the night at her parents' house, so she'd arranged for them to stop by. Dance made sure to see her children whenever she could.

'Hi, honey,' Dance said to Maggie, then hugged her son. There'd be a day when public hugs would be verboten, and she was storing up for the drought.

Edie Dance and Kellogg greeted each other.

'Mom, Carly moved Mr Bledsoe's wastebasket!' Maggie told Dance breathlessly. 'Every time he threw something out, it went on the floor.'

'Did you keep from giggling?'

'For a while. But then Brendon did and we couldn't stop.'

'Say hello to Agent Kellogg.'

Maggie did, but Wes only nodded. His eyes shifted away.

'You guys want hot chocolate?' Dance asked.

'Yay!' Maggie cried. Wes said he would too.

Dance patted her jacket pockets. Coffee was gratis, but anything fancier took cash, and she'd left her purse in her office. Edie had no change.

'I'll treat,' Kellogg said, digging into his pocket.

Wes said quickly, 'Mom, I want coffee instead.' The boy had sipped coffee once or twice in his life and hated it.

'No coffee. It's hot chocolate or soda.' What was going on here? Then Dance remembered Wes's eyes scanning Kellogg on the Deck the other night. She thought he'd been looking for his weapon. Was he sizing up the man Mom had brought to his grandfather's party?

Wes muttered, 'That's OK. I don't want anything.'

'Come on, I'll loan it to your Mom,' Kellogg said, dispensing the coins.

'Thanks,' Wes said reluctantly.

Edie poured coffee, and they sat at the table. Kellogg thanked Dance's mother again for the dinner the previous night. Then turned to the children and wondered aloud if they liked to fish.

Maggie said sort of. She didn't.

Wes loved to but responded, 'Not really. You know, it's boring.'

Dance knew the agent had no motive but breaking the ice. She noted some stress reactions—he was trying too hard to make a good impression, she guessed.

Wes fell silent and sipped his chocolate while Maggie inundated the adults with the morning's events at music camp. But Dance knew the tricks of parenting and soon had Wes talking enthusiastically about a tennis match. Kellogg's posture changed once or twice, and the body language told Dance that he too was a tennis player and wanted to contribute. But he'd caught on that Wes was ambivalent about him and smiled as he listened, but didn't add anything.

Finally Dance told them she needed to get back to work, she'd walk them outside. Kellogg said goodbye and wandered up the hallway to his temporary office.

Dance led her mother and children through the parking lot to Edie's Prius hybrid. After she said goodbye to them, she headed back towards the front door of the CBI building. She was nearing the stairs when she heard a scrape of footstep on the asphalt and turned quickly to see a young woman wearing sunglasses and a cap come up behind her. Dance stopped fast.

The woman did too. She shifted her weight.

'Agent Dance . . . I . . .'

Neither woman spoke for a moment.

Then Samantha McCoy said, 'I've changed my mind. When I heard he'd killed somebody else, I knew I *had* to come.'

Chapter 9

The Toyota smelt of cigarette smoke, which Daniel Pell hated. It reminded him of his father, of growing up. He himself never smoked, though he'd bartered cigarettes like a floor broker on a stock exchange inside Capitola.

He and Jennie were now driving with the windows down. She was doing that rubby-nose thing, but she was back on track. His distance last night had worked just fine. They'd returned to the Sea View, and she'd done the only thing she knew would win back his love—for two strenuous hours.

Later he'd stepped outside and pretended to make a phone call. Just to keep her on edge. When he returned, he'd carried on flipping through Susan Pemberton's material, and went online once more.

This morning he'd told her he had to see someone. Let that sit, watched her insecurities roll up. Then finally he'd said, 'I'd like it if you came along.'

'Really?' A thirsty dog lapping up water.

'Yep. But I don't know . . . It might be too hard for you.'

'No, I want to. Please.'

'We'll see.'

Now, as they drove, he was firmly in control.

'You understand about yesterday at the beach? I was in a funny mood. I get that way when something precious to me is endangered.' This was a bit of an apology—who can resist that?—along with the reminder that it might happen again.

'That's one thing I love about you, sweetie.'

Not 'sweetheart' now. Good. 'We have another problem now, lovely.'

'Oh.' Rub-a-dub on the nose. It was a wonderful barometer. 'I told you, honey, I don't care about the money.'

'This doesn't have anything to do with that. It's much more important. I'm not asking you to hurt anybody. But I need some help.'

STANDING IN THE open doorway of the cabin at Point Lobos Inn, Rebecca Sheffield said to Dance, 'Welcome back. We've been gossiping and spending your money on room service.' She nodded towards a bottle of Jordan cabernet, which only she was drinking.

Rebecca glanced at Samantha and, not recognising her, said, 'Hello.' Probably thinking she was an officer involved in the case.

The women walked inside. Dance shut and double-locked the door.

Samantha looked as if she'd lost her voice.

Rebecca did a double take. 'Wait. Oh my God.'

Linda didn't get it, her brows furrowed.

Rebecca said, 'Don't you recognise her?'

'What do you—? Wait. It's you, Sam?'

'Hello.' The slim woman was racked with uneasiness.

'Your face,' Linda said. 'You're so different. My.'

'Uh-huh, prettier.' Rebecca walked forward and hugged Samantha firmly. 'Great job. What'd they do?'

'Implants on my jaw and cheeks. Lips and eyes, mostly.'

Linda, crying: 'I can't believe it.' Another hug. 'What's your new name?'

Not looking at either of them, Samantha said, 'I'd rather not say. And please, you can't tell anybody about me.'

'Your husband doesn't know?' Linda asked, glancing at Samantha's engagement and wedding rings.

Samantha shook her head and swallowed. 'I lied. I didn't have any choice.' Dance recognised the kinesic attributes of defensiveness, body parts folding, stature shrinking, aversions. She was a volcano of stress.

Rebecca said, 'But he has to know you did time?'

'Yes. I told him it was a white-collar thing. I helped my boss embezzle some stocks because his wife needed an operation. He'd walk out the door if he knew the truth, that I was in a cult—'

'It wasn't a cult,' Linda said quickly.

'Do your parents know anything?' Rebecca asked.

'My mother's dead, and my father's as involved in my life as he always was. Which is not at all. But you remember that.'

'Sure, Sam,' Rebecca said.

Dance now returned to the case. First, she gave them the details of the Pemberton killing, the theft of the company's files. None of them could recall any catered events Pell might have gone to.

'Wasn't a black-tie kind of life back then,' Rebecca said.

Dance asked Samantha about Pell's accomplice, but like the others, she had no idea who the woman might be. Nor did she recall any references to Charles Pickering in Redding.

'Linda mentioned that Pell wanted to move to the country somewhere, a mountaintop,' Dance continued. 'Do you have any idea what that was about?'

'Well, Daniel told me a bunch of times he wanted to get out to the country,' said Samantha. 'He didn't like neighbours, didn't like the government. He wanted space for more people. He wanted the Family to grow.'

'Did he ever mention Utah?'

'No. He didn't say where he had in mind.'

'Now, about his motives for staying here,' Dance said. 'I was thinking he hid money or something valuable here. Maybe from a big heist. Or has unfinished business. Something to do with the Croyton murders.'

'Money?' Samantha shook her head. 'I don't think that's it. And not a big heist. He didn't like crimes that'd be too visible. We broke into houses—'

'Well, hardly any,' Linda corrected.

Rebecca sighed. 'Well . . . we pretty much *did*, Linda.'

Samantha shrugged. 'Anyway, the stealing was never about money. Daniel liked getting people to do things they didn't want to.'

'I think he was definitely into making money,' Rebecca said.

Samantha smiled uncertainly. 'Well, I just had this sense it was more about manipulating people. But I could be wrong.'

Dance sensed this was a key to understanding Pell, so she asked them about their criminal activities, hoping it might spark specific memories.

Samantha said, 'He was good, Daniel was. He'd know the best places to go for pickpocketing or breaking into houses. How security worked in department stores, which labels had security tags.'

Linda said, 'But we'd have disguises, remember? Wigs, different clothes, fake glasses . . . It was really just a *game* to him.'

'What about the Charles Manson connection?' Dance asked.

'Oh,' Samantha said. 'There *was* no Manson connection.'

Dance was surprised. 'But all the press said so.'

'Well, you know the press. Daniel thought Manson was an example of what *not* to do.'

But Linda shook her head. 'No, no, he had all those books and articles about him.'

'The only parallels were that he lived with several women and had us doing crimes for him,' Samantha said. 'But Manson wasn't in control of *himself*. He claimed he was Jesus; he tattooed a swastika on his forehead; he thought he had psychic powers.'

Glancing at her notebook, Dance asked the newcomer about the key words Pell had searched in prison.

'"Nimue"?' Samantha repeated. 'No. But he had a girlfriend named Alison once. When he was in San Francisco, before the Family. She was in this group, sort of like the Family. He was fascinated with it, but they got suspicious of him—he wouldn't really commit. So he and Alison left. They hitchhiked around the state; then he got arrested or something and she went back to San Francisco. He tried to find her, but he never could.'

'What was her last name?'

'I don't know.'

Dance wondered if Pell was looking for this Alison—or Nimue—for revenge. 'After all, he'd need a pretty good reason to risk going online in Capitola to find somebody.'

'Oh,' Samantha said, 'Daniel didn't believe in revenge.'

Rebecca said, 'I don't know, Sam. What about that biker? That punk up the street? Daniel beat the crap out of him. Nearly killed him.'

'But the police let him go,' Linda said.

'Only because the guy didn't press charges,' Rebecca said.

Samantha shrugged. 'But that wasn't about revenge. See, the biker thought he was some kind of neighbourhood godfather. He tried to blackmail Daniel about something that never even happened. Daniel started playing mind games with him. But the biker just laughed at him. Next thing, the biker's wrists and ankles were broken. But that wasn't revenge. It was because he was immune to Daniel. If you're immune, then Daniel can't control you, and that makes you a threat. And he said all the time, "Threats have to be eliminated."'

'Control,' Dance said. 'That sums up Daniel Pell, doesn't it?'

This, it seemed, was one premise of their past that all three members of the Family could agree on.

FROM THE PATROL CAR, the MCSO deputy kept his vigilant eye on his turf: the grounds, the trees, the road. Guard duty—it had to be the most boring part of being a cop. Especially baby-sitting good guys when the bad guys don't even know where they are. And now he needed a bathroom break. He'd have to ask to use one inside.

He climbed out of the car and walked down the road, looking around. Nothing odd. Typical of what you'd see, considering the posh place where he was: a limo driving past, a housewife having her gardener arrange flowers beneath her mailbox before he planted them.

The woman looked up and nodded his way. Then she waved to him and approached. 'Are you here about that car?' she asked.

'Car?'

She gestured. 'Up there. About ten minutes ago the driver sort of pulled up in between some trees. I thought it was a little funny, parking that way. You know, we've had a few break-ins around here lately.'

Alarmed, the deputy stepped closer to where she was indicating. Through the bushes, he saw a glint of chrome or glass. The only reason to drive a car that far off the road was to hide it. Pell, he thought, reaching for his gun.

Wsssssh.

He glanced back just as the shovel slammed into his shoulder and neck.

DANIEL PELL DRAGGED the cop into the bushes, where he couldn't be seen. The man wasn't dead, just groggy and hurting.

Quickly he stripped off his dirt-stained gardener outfit and put on the deputy's uniform. He duct-taped the officer's mouth, cuffed him with his own bracelets and slipped the cop's gun into his pocket.

Glancing behind him, he saw Jennie retrieving the flowers from the soil around the neighbour's mailbox and dumping them into a shopping bag.

'Get the car, lovely.' He handed her the clothes.

A smile blossoming, full. 'I'll have it ready.' She hurried up the street with the clothes, bag and shovel. She glanced back, mouthing, 'I love you.'

Pell turned and walked up the drive to the house. He peered through a crack in the curtain of a front window. He could see James Reynolds on a cordless phone, holding a bottle of wine in his other hand. A woman—his wife, Pell guessed—walked into the kitchen.

Pell had thought it would be easy to find almost anybody nowadays—computers, the Internet, Google. But James Reynolds had been invisible. No phone listing, no tax records, no addresses.

But then he'd had his brainstorm and found a listing in the *Peninsula Times* archives about the prosecutor's daughter's wedding. He'd called the venue where the event was held and found the name of the wedding planner. And now here he was.

More motion inside. A man in his late twenties, it seemed, was also in the house. Maybe a son. He'd have to kill them all, of course, to have time to get away. With some luck, the bodies wouldn't be found until after he finished his other mission here on the Peninsula and was long gone.

Seeing the prosecutor hang up his phone, Pell ducked back, checked his pistol, and pressed the doorbell. There was the rustle of noise from inside, a shadow in the peephole. Pell stood where he could be seen in his uniform, though he was looking down casually.

'Yes? Who is it?'

'Mr Reynolds, it's Officer Ramos. The relief deputy. I'd like to talk to you.'

'Just a second. I've got something on the stove.'

Gripping his pistol, Pell stepped back into the shadows of a large, tangled tree beside the door, enjoying the feel of the heavy gun. A minute passed. Then another. He knocked again. 'Mr Reynolds?'

'Pell, don't move!' a voice shouted behind him. 'Drop the weapon.' The voice was Reynolds's. 'I'm armed.'

No! What had happened? Pell shivered with anger.

'Listen to me, Pell. If you move one inch, I'll shoot you.'

'What? Sir, what are you talking about?'

No, no! He'd planned this so perfectly! He was breathless with rage. Pell gave a brief glance behind him. There was Reynolds, holding a large revolver in both hands.

'Wait, wait, my name's Hector Ramos, sir. I'm the relief—'

He heard the click as the hammer on Reynolds's gun cocked.

'OK! I don't know what this is about. But OK.' Pell took the barrel in his left hand and lowered it to the deck.

With a screech, the black Toyota skidded into the driveway and braked to a stop, the horn blaring.

Pell dropped flat to his belly, swept up the gun and began firing. The prosecutor crouched and fired several shots himself, but, panicked, he missed. Pell then heard the distant keening of sirens. Torn between self-preservation and his raw need to kill the man, he hesitated. But survival won out. He sprinted down the driveway towards Jennie, who had opened the passenger door. He tumbled inside the car, and they sped away.

KATHRYN DANCE and James Reynolds stood in his dewy front lawn, amid pristine landscaping, lit by the pulse of coloured lights.

The prosecutor's first concern, he explained, was that no one had been injured by a stray shot. He'd run to the street to look at the car's tags, but the vehicle was gone. The deputy in the bushes would have some bad bruises and a concussion.

When 'Officer Ramos' rang the doorbell, Reynolds had actually been on the phone with Dance, who was telling him urgently that Pell knew where he lived and was planning to kill him. The prosecutor had sent his wife and son into the basement to call 911, slipped out through a side door and come up behind the man.

Reynolds now said, 'Pell took all this risk just for revenge?'

'No, James, it wasn't revenge.' Dance told him about the incident that Samantha McCoy had described, where the biker had laughed at Pell. 'You did the same thing in court. When he tried to control you, remember? That meant you were immune to him. And even worse, you controlled him—you turned him into Manson, into somebody else. He was your puppet. Pell couldn't allow that. You were too much of a danger to him.'

'That's not revenge?'

'No. It was about his future plans,' Dance said. 'He knew you wouldn't be afraid to help us catch him. And like he said, threats have to be eliminated.'

'But how did you manage to call minutes before he showed up?'

'The woman killed yesterday worked for Eve Brock.'

His eyes flashed in recognition. 'The event planner who handled Julia's wedding. He found me through her? Brilliant.'

'I kept thinking about why he'd kill Susan Pemberton . . . and I kept picturing her office, all the photos on the walls. Some were of local politicians, some were of weddings. Then I remembered seeing the pictures of your daughter's wedding in your house. The connection clicked. I called Eve Brock and she told me that, yes, you'd been a client.'

'How'd you know about the Latino disguise?'

She explained that Susan had been seen with a slim Latino man not long before she'd been killed. And Linda had told them about Pell's use of disguises. 'Becoming Latino seemed a bit far-fetched, but apparently it wasn't.'

Finished with their canvassing, TJ and Rey Carraneo arrived to report that there'd been no sightings of the killer's new wheels.

Michael O'Neil joined them too, and nodded politely towards Kellogg. He'd been with the crime-scene officers as they'd worked the street and the front yard. They hadn't discovered much, he reported. Shell casings, some worn tyre prints 'that'll lead us nowhere'. Frustrated, he added that the guard gave only a groggy description of his attacker and the girl with him.

Reynolds called his daughter and told her to leave town until the killer was recaptured. His wife and other son would join them, but Reynolds was going to stay at a hotel under police guard until he'd reviewed the files from county court archives. He was more determined than ever to help them get Pell.

THEY SAT AROUND the TV, leaning forward, watching the news like three reunited sisters. Which in a way they were, thought Samantha McCoy.

'Can you believe that?' Rebecca asked in a low, angry voice.

Linda shook her head in dismay.

James Reynolds, the prosecutor, had been the target of Daniel Pell.

Sam was very disturbed by the assault. She remembered Reynolds well. A stern but reasonable man, he'd negotiated what her lawyer had said were fair plea bargains.

A picture came on the TV: an artist's rendering of Pell with darker skin and black hair, glasses and a vague Latino look. His disguise.

'That's way bizarre,' Rebecca offered.

The knock on the door startled them. Kathryn Dance's voice announced her arrival. Linda rose to let her in.

The woman entered with Winston Kellogg. Glancing at the TV screen, Dance asked, 'You heard?'

Linda said, 'I'm so happy Reynolds is all right. His family too.'

'They mentioned a deputy was hurt?' Rebecca asked.

Kellogg said, 'He'll be all right.' He went on to explain how Pell and his partner had planned the prosecutor's murder, killing Susan Pemberton yesterday to find out where Reynolds lived.

Sam thought of what had struck her years ago: the obsessed, unstoppable mind of Daniel Pell.

Dance said, 'I wanted to thank you. The information you gave us saved his life.' She explained how observations they'd offered earlier—particularly about Pell's reaction to being laughed at and about disguises—had let her deduce what the killer might be up to.

'But he did get away from you, I noticed,' Rebecca said, her lips tight.

'He did,' Dance said, looking the taller woman in the eyes. 'We didn't get there in time. Now, there's another deputy outside. There's no reason to believe that Pell has any clue you're here, but I thought it couldn't hurt.'

'Won't say no to that,' Rebecca said.

The agent glanced at the clock. It was ten fifteen. 'I propose we call it quits for tonight. You've got to be exhausted.'

Samantha said, 'Reunions have a way of doing that.'

PARKING IN THE BACK of the Sea View, Jennie shut off the Toyota's engine. Daniel Pell didn't get out. He felt numb.

'Are you all right, sweetie?'

He said nothing. He was shivering in rage.

'You look upset. Can you tell me?'

Pell told Jennie the story about prosecutor James Reynolds laughing at him in court and the danger he represented—a story no one knew.

'That's terrible. My mother would do that—laugh at me in front of people. And hit me. I think the laughing was worse. A lot worse.'

He was actually moved by her sympathy. 'Hey, lovely? You held fast tonight. I'm proud of you. Let's go inside.'

But Jennie didn't move. 'I was thinking. How did Reynolds figure it out?'

'Saw me, I suppose. Recognised me.'

'No, I don't think so. It sounded like the sirens were coming, you know, *before* you knocked on the door.'

'They were?'

Kathryn . . . Eyes as green as mine are blue, red rubber band round her braid, pearl on her finger. He could picture her perfectly.

'Well, there's this policewoman. She's a problem.'

'Tell me about her.'

Pell kissed her and slipped his hand into the waistband of her slacks, felt the lace. 'Not here. Let's go inside. I'll tell you about her inside.'

'I'VE HAD ENOUGH of that,' Linda said, nodding towards the TV, where news stories about Pell kept looping over and over.

Samantha agreed. Linda walked to the kitchen and made decaf coffee and tea, brought out cups and milk and sugar, along with some cookies. Rebecca took the coffee but continued to sip her wine.

During their room-service dinner, the conversation had been superficial: the weather, what they thought of Kathryn Dance. Now Rebecca, who'd had plenty of wine, tried to draw Linda out, find out what made her so religious, but the woman deflected the questions. Linda did talk about running the church's neighbourhood centre and added that she was dating a man from her church. 'Nice' was how she described him. 'He works at Macy's.'

Rebecca was more forthcoming about Women's Initiatives, her condo overlooking the water and her latest boyfriend, a landscape designer fifteen years older. She mentioned other boyfriends too.

Both Linda and Rebecca tried to get Sam to talk about herself. She demurred. She didn't want anyone, least of all these women, to have any possible clues as to her life as Sarah Starkey. If word got out, Ron would leave her—and take their son with him.

Linda ate half a cookie. 'Oh, Sam, before you got here, we were telling Kathryn about that last Easter dinner. Remember?'

'Remember it? It was fantastic.' It had been a wonderful day, Sam recalled. Great music from Jimmy's stereo, piles of food. 'That turkey,' she said, shaking her head at the memory. 'You smoked it, right?'

Linda nodded. 'About eight hours. In that smoker Daniel made for me.'

'The what?' Rebecca asked.

'That smoker out back. The one he made.'

'I remember. But he didn't make it.' Rebecca looked perplexed. 'He got it from what's-her-name up the street.'

'Up the street?' Linda frowned. 'You're wrong. He made it out of an old oil drum. He surprised me with it.'

'Wait, it was . . . Rachel. Yeah, remember her? Bright red hair.'

'I remember Rachel.' Linda's response was stiff.

Rachel had caused serious disharmony within the Family before Rebecca arrived because Pell had spent a lot of time at her house doing what he loved to do most. Sam hadn't cared—anything to avoid Pell's unpleasantries in the bedroom was fine with her. But Linda had been jealous.

'He got the smoker from her,' said Rebecca.

'No, he didn't. He made it for my birthday.'

Rebecca sipped the wine. 'Linda, he gave it to you on your birthday because he was with her that morning and she gave it to him. Some surfer dude made it for her, but she didn't cook.'

'He was with her?' Linda whispered. 'On my birthday?'

'Yeah. And, like, three times a week. You didn't know?'

'It doesn't matter,' Sam said. 'It was a long—'

'Shut up,' Linda snapped. She turned to Rebecca. 'You're wrong.'

'What? You're surprised Daniel lied to you?' Rebecca laughed.

'Why would he lie to me? You're the one who's lying, because Daniel never made anything for you.'

'Oh, please. Are we back in high school?' Rebecca looked Linda over. 'Oh, I get it. You were jealous of *me*! That's why you were so pissed off.'

'I was with him for more than a year. You? A few months.'

'Daniel asked me, Linda. I didn't force my way in.'

'We were going along fine, and then *you* show up.'

'"Going along fine"?' Rebecca set down her wineglass and sat forward. 'Are you hearing what you're saying?'

'Please, Rebecca,' Sam said. Her heart was pounding. 'Don't.'

Rebecca ignored her. 'Linda, I've been listening to you since I got here. Saying we didn't steal all that much, maybe Daniel didn't kill so-and-so. Well, that's crap. The Family was sick, totally sick.'

'Don't say that! It's not true.'

'Goddamn it, it *is* true. And Daniel Pell's a monster. Think what he did to you.' Rebecca's eyes were glowing. 'He saw somebody whose parents never gave her an inch of freedom. So what does he do? He puts you in charge of the house. He gives you power. He hooks you in with that. Then the Family breaks up, we go to jail, and where do you end up? With a domineering male again—only this time, Daddy is God.'

'Don't say that,' Sam began. 'She's—'

Rebecca turned on her. 'And *you*. Just like the old days. Little Miss United Nations, don't want anybody upset. Is it because you *care* about us? Or because you're terrified we'll self-destruct and you'll be even *more* alone? Back then it was your parents who didn't know you existed. Now you don't exist to *anyone*. Because you're not Samantha. You became somebody else.'

'Stop it!' Sam was crying now. The harsh words stung deeply.

'And what gives you the right to talk?' Linda's voice shook with anger. 'You were just some tramp pretending to be this bohemian artist. You weren't any better!'

Rebecca's face grew still. She said in a soft voice, 'You're right, Linda. You're absolutely right. I fell for it too.'

'You?' Linda snapped. 'You were just there for sex.'

'Exactly,' Rebecca said with a sad smile. 'How do you think he got me hooked? He taught me that sex was good. It wasn't just something dirty that happened when my father got home from work.'

'Oh,' Sam whispered. 'I'm so sorry. You never said anything.'

'And now look at me—I'm thirty-three and I've dated four different men this year and, you know, I can't remember the name of the second one. No, I'm not any better than you guys.'

Linda's face was unmoved. After a moment she said, 'I'm sorry for your misfortune. I'll pray for you. Now please excuse me, I'm going to bed.' Clutching her Bible, she went off to the bedroom.

'That didn't go over very well,' Rebecca said. She leaned back, eyes closed, sighing. 'Funny about trying to escape the past. It's like a dog on a tether. No matter how much he runs, he just can't get away.'

DANCE AND KELLOGG were in her office at CBI headquarters, where they'd briefed Overby, working late for a change, on the events at Reynolds's house. The time was just after 11 p.m.

She put her computer on standby. 'OK, I'm calling it a night.'

'I'm with you there.' As they walked down the dim hallway, Kellogg said, 'I was thinking, they really are a family.'

'Back there? At the lodge?'

'Right. The three of them. They're not related. They don't even like each other particularly. But they *are* a family.'

His tone suggesting that he defined the word from the perspective of its absence. The interaction of the three women had touched him in some way. She noted his shoulders lift slightly, evidence of general stress.

'You going to pick up the children?' he asked.

'No. They'll stay at their grandparents tonight.'

'They're great; they really are.'

'You never thought about having kids?'

'Not really.' His voice faded. 'We were both working. I was on the road a lot. You know—professional couples.'

In kinesic analysis, the content of speech is usually secondary to the tone with which the words are delivered. Dance had heard many people tell her they'd never had children, and the resonance of the words explained whether that fact was inconsequential, a comfortable choice, a lingering sorrow.

She'd sensed something significant in Kellogg's statement. Maybe a physical problem on his part or his wife's. Maybe it had been a big issue between them, the source of their breakup.

'Wes has his doubts about me.'

'Ah, he's just sensitive about Mom meeting other men.'

'Got it,' Kellogg said. 'Though he seemed to be comfortable when you're with Michael.'

'Oh, that's different. Michael's a friend. And he's married. He's no threat.'

There was a faint hesitation. 'Sure, I can see that.'

They walked outside. The air was so crisp, Dance's fingers were quivering from the chill. But she liked the sensation.

'I'll drive you to yours,' she said. His car was parked behind the building.

They both got in, and she drove to Kellogg's rental. Neither of them moved for a minute. She put the transmission in park. She closed her eyes, stretched and pressed her head back again the rest. It felt good.

She opened her eyes and saw him turning towards her. Leaving one hand on the dash, he touched the shoulder closest to him. He was waiting for some signal. She gave him none, but looked into his eyes and remained silent. Both of which, of course, were signals in themselves.

In any case, he leaned forward and kissed her, then backed off slightly, giving Dance a moment to decide how she was going to handle it.

When he eased in again she met him halfway, and kissed back fervently. She slipped her arms up to his shoulders, which were as muscular as she'd thought they'd be. His beard stubble troubled her cheek.

His hand slipped behind her neck, pulling her harder into him. She felt that uncurling within her, heart stepping up its pace. She pressed her nose and lips against the bone beneath his ear.

Then Kellogg's hand found her chin, easing her face to him again. Their whole mouths participated now. She felt his fingers moving tentatively to her shoulder, locating the satin strap and, using it as a road map, slowly moving down, outside her blouse.

Her response was to kiss him harder. Images of her husband came to mind, but she observed them from a distance. She was completely with Winston Kellogg at this moment.

His hand reached the tiny metal hoop where the strap transitioned to the white Victoria's Secret cup. And he stopped.

The hand retreated. The kisses became less frequent.

But this seemed to her exactly right, under the circumstances—which included the manhunt for a killer, the short time they'd known each other, and the terrible deaths that had occurred.

'I think—' he whispered.

'It's OK.' She smiled and lightly kissed away any more words.

He sat back and squeezed her hand. She curled against him, feeling the perfect stasis of reluctance and relief.

'But one thing?' he said. 'The case won't go on for ever. If you'd be interested in going out afterwards. How does that sound?'

'"Afterwards" has a nice ring to it. Real nice.'

A HALF HOUR LATER Dance was parking in front of her house.

She went through the standard routine: a check of security, a glass of pinot grigio, two pieces of cold leftover flank steak enjoyed to the sound track of phone messages. Then came canine feeding and their back-yard tasks and stowing her Glock. Alarms on.

Shower, a clean T-shirt and shorts. She opened the window to the guards, about six inches, and dropped into bed. Thinking: Golly damn, girl, making out in a car with the man of the hour. She recalled his hands, the flop of hair.

She thought too of his tentativeness about children, the stress he exhibited. She wondered if it was because he was uneasy around youngsters and was now forming a connection with a woman who came with a pair of them. How would he deal with that?

But, hold on here, let's not get ahead of ourselves. You were making out. You enjoyed it. Don't call the wedding caterer yet.

For a long time, she lay in bed listening to the sounds of nature—throaty sea mammals, temperamental birds, the surf. It was at moments like this that she was most vulnerable to loneliness. How nice it was to hear the adagio of shallow breath next to you, to awake at dawn to the rustling of rising: sounds that were the comforting heartbeats of a life together.

Kathryn Dance supposed that longing for these things revealed a sign of dependency. But what was wrong with that?

Ah, Bill . . . She thought to her late husband. Bill . . .

Distant memories tugged. But so did fresh ones.

. . . afterwards. How does that sound?

Thursday
Chapter 10

In her back yard again.

Her Shire, her Narnia, her Hogwarts, her Secret Garden.

Seventeen-year-old Theresa Croyton Bolling sat in the grey teak Smith & Hawken glider and read the slim volume in her hand, turning pages slowly. It was a magnificent day. The air was sweet, and the nearby Napa hills were covered with verdant grapevines and pine and gnarly cypress.

Theresa was thinking lyrically because of what she was reading—beautiful, heartfelt . . . and totally *boring* poetry.

She sighed loudly. The paperback drooped in her hand, and she gazed over the place where she seemed to spend half her life. The green prison, she sometimes called it.

She was here at the moment, not in school at Vallejo Springs High, because of an unplanned trip to New York that she and her aunt and uncle were taking. Which was why her aunt had taken her out of school at 10 a.m. on Monday. Only—*hello*—they hadn't left yet, which was odd. Her aunt explained there were some 'logistical difficulties'.

Of course, it was all bull. There *was* no trip. It was just an excuse to keep her in the green prison. Why the lies? Because the man who'd killed her parents, brother and sister had escaped from prison. Which her aunt actually seemed to believe she could keep secret.

Like, please. The news was the first thing you saw on Yahoo's home page. And everybody in California was talking about it on MySpace and Facebook. (Her aunt had disabled the family's wireless router somehow, but Theresa had simply piggybacked through a neighbour's unsecured system.)

Theresa was certainly grateful for what her aunt had done for her. After those terrible days in Carmel, Theresa found herself adopted, relocated, renamed and plopped down on the chairs of therapists while time worked its patient magic and Theresa became someone other than the Sleeping Doll. She was a student, friend, occasional girlfriend, veterinary assistant, and not bad sprinter in the fifty- and hundred-yard dash.

Now, though, eight years later, all the gains were erased. Her aunt was edgy and paranoid. The Sleeping Doll was in lockdown.

Hey, that's sweet, Theresa thought bitterly: Daniel Pell is out of prison, and I'm stuck inside one.

Thinking of her English test, she read two more lines of poetry.

Borrrring.

Theresa then noticed, through the chain-link fence at the end of the property, a car ease past, braking quickly as the driver looked her way.

Theresa planted her feet. The car could belong to anyone. Still, she stood and headed for the house, looking behind her at the gap through the bushes. No car. Nothing.

Turning back to the house, she stopped fast.

A man had scaled the tall fence twenty feet away, between her and the house. He'd landed on his knees beside two azaleas, and now he looked up, breathing hard from the effort. It was him. It was Daniel Pell!

She gasped. A smile on his face, he walked towards her.

'No, it's all right,' the man said in a whisper as he approached. 'Shhhh. I'm not going to hurt you.'

Theresa told herself to run, but fear paralysed her. Besides, there was nowhere to go. Tasting the fear, she looked for a weapon. Nothing: only *The Collected Poems of Emily Dickinson*.

She looked back at Pell. 'You killed my parents. Don't hurt me!'

A frown. 'No, my God,' the man said, eyes wide. 'Oh, no, I just want to talk to you. I'm not Daniel Pell. I swear. Look.' He tossed something in her direction. 'Look at the back. Turn it over.'

She stepped forward and glanced down. It was a book. *A Stranger in the Night*, by Morton Nagle. With her foot, she eased it over. On the back cover was a picture of a younger version of the man in front of her.

Theresa wiped her face. Anger exploded inside her, a popped balloon. 'What are you doing here? You scared me!'

The man pulled his sagging trousers up. 'There was no other way to talk to you. I wanted your aunt to ask you something.'

Theresa glanced at the chain link.

'I know, I saw the alarm on the fence. The police'll be here in three, four minutes, and they'll arrest me. That's fine. But I have to tell you that the man who killed your parents escaped from prison.'

'I know. Just leave me alone!'

'There's a policewoman who's trying to catch him, but she needs to talk to you. Your aunt wouldn't tell you. But you're old enough to make up your own mind. Please, just call her. She's in Monterey. You can— Oh, God.'

The gunshot from behind Theresa was astonishingly loud. She cringed and dropped to her knees, watching Morton Nagle tumble back onto the wet grass, his arms flailing in the air.

Eyes wide in horror, the girl looked at the deck behind the house.

Weird, she hadn't even known that her aunt owned a gun, much less knew how to shoot it.

TJ Scanlon's canvassing of James Reynolds's neighbourhood had yielded no helpful witnesses or evidence. 'No vee-hicles. No nothin'.' He was calling from a street near the prosecutor's house.

Dance, in her office, badly wanted an ID of Pell's new car, if not a tag number; Reynolds had reported only that it was a dark sedan.

She thanked TJ and disconnected, then joined O'Neil and Kellogg in the conference room. Overby was about to arrive to ask for fodder for the next press conference—and his daily update to Amy Grabe and the head of the CBI in Sacramento, both extremely troubled that Pell was still free.

Her eyes caught Kellogg's, and they both looked away.

. . . afterwards. How does that sound?

Young Rey Carraneo stuck his head into the room and said breathlessly, 'Agent Dance, I'm sorry to interrupt.'

'What, Rey? What is it?'

'I think . . . Agent Dance, I think I've found him.'

The young agent explained that a woman had checked into the upscale Sea View Motel in Pacific Grove—only a few miles from where Dance lived—on Saturday. She was mid-twenties, blonde, slightly built. On Tuesday night, the desk clerk had seen her and a Latino man go into her room.

'The clincher's the car, though,' Carraneo said. 'On the registration, she put down Mazda. With a fake tag number—I just ran it. But the manager saw a turquoise T-bird for a day or two. It's not there any more.'

'They're at the motel now?'

'He thinks so. The curtain's drawn, but he saw motion and lights inside.'

'What's her name?'

'Carrie Madison. But she paid cash and showed a military ID in a scratched plastic sleeve. Might've been faked.'

Dance stared at the map. 'Occupancy of the motel?'

'No vacancies.'

She grimaced. Plenty of innocents in the place.

Kellogg said, 'Let's plan the takedown.' To Michael O'Neil: 'You have MCSO tactical on alert?'

O'Neil was looking at Dance's troubled face. 'We can get teams there in twenty minutes.' He sounded reluctant.

Dance was reluctant as well. 'I'm not sure,' she said. 'We know he's armed and he'll target civilians. I know the motel. The rooms look out on a parking lot. Hardly any cover. If we empty the nearby rooms, he'd spot us. If we don't, people are going to get hurt.'

'What are you thinking?' Kellogg asked.

'Surveillance. When he leaves, take him on the street.'

O'Neil nodded. 'I'd vote for that too.'

'Vote for what?' Charles Overby asked, joining them.

Dance explained the situation.

'We've found him? All *right*!' Overby turned to Kellogg. 'What about *your* tactical teams?'

'They can't get here in time. We'll have to go with county SWAT'

'Michael, you've called them?'

'Not yet. Kathryn and I have some problems with a takedown.'

'What?' Overby asked testily.

She explained the risk. 'If he gets any hint we're moving in, he'll go barricade. If there's a door to the adjoining room—'

'There is,' Carraneo said. 'I asked.'

She gave him a nod. 'Then he could take hostages. I say we get a team on the roof across the way and watch. When he leaves, we'll tail him, and when he hits a deserted intersection, we block him in.'

'He's too slippery for that,' Kellogg countered. 'We surprise him in the motel; we move fast; he'll give up.'

'And go back to Capitola? I don't think so. Everything the women have told me makes me believe he'll fight tooth and nail.'

Dance was in an odd situation. She had a strong gut feel that moving too fast was a mistake. But with Pell, she was wary of trusting her instinct.

Overby said, 'If we *do* end up with a barricade, would the three women talk him out? They're the closest thing to family Pell's got.' He stepped towards her phone. 'I'll give them a call.'

The last thing Dance wanted was Overby scaring them off. 'No, I'll do it.'

She called and spoke to Samantha, who begged Dance not to involve her. Rebecca and Linda, though, said they were willing to do what they could.

Overby said, 'Well, there's your back-up plan. Good.'

Dance wasn't convinced. 'I still say surveillance.'

O'Neil said firmly, 'I agree.'

Kellogg looked at Dance. 'Remember what I was saying about the cult profile. When he goes out on the street, he'll be alert. In the motel, he'll be complacent. He won't have a clue we're coming.'

That was true, Dance reflected.

'It *is* Winston's expertise, Kathryn,' Overby said. 'That's why he's here. I really think we should move.'

She glanced at Kellogg's confident eyes. 'OK. We go in.'

LYING IN BED, Daniel Pell was thinking that they'd now have to be particularly careful. The police would know what he looked like in the Latino disguise. Still, he couldn't leave yet. He had one more mission on the Peninsula, the whole reason for his remaining here.

Pell made coffee, and when he returned to the bed carrying the two cups, he found Jennie looking at him. Like last night, her expression seemed more mature than when they'd first met.

'What, lovely?'

'Can I ask you something?'

'Sure.'

'You're not coming to my house in Anaheim, are you?'

He hesitated. 'Why do you think that?'

'I just feel it.'

Pell set the coffee on the table. He started to lie. But instead he said, 'I have other plans for us, lovely. I haven't told you yet.'

'I know. I had a feeling all along.'

'After we take care of things here, we're going somewhere. A place I have. We won't be bothered there. Do you like mountains?'

'Sure, I guess.'

That was good. Because Daniel Pell owned one.

Pell's aunt, in Bakersfield, was the only decent person in the family, as far as he was concerned. Aunt Barbara spent money on Daniel as a boy, took him places. She also shared her views with him. One was that there'd be a wildfire of a race war in the country, so she bought 200 acres of forest in northern California, a mountaintop near Shasta. Daniel Pell had never been racist, but neither was he stupid, and when the aunt ranted about the forthcoming Great War of Black and White, he was with her one hundred per cent. She deeded over the land to him so that he and other 'decent, good, right-thinking people' could escape to it when the shooting started.

Pell hadn't thought much about the place at the time, being young. But then he'd hitchhiked up there and knew instantly it was the place for him. He loved the view and the air, mostly loved the idea that it was so unreachable by the government and unwelcome neighbours. He did some clearing and built a shack by hand. He bought books about hiding ownership of property, which was surprisingly easy.

Pell's mountaintop.

Only one glitch had interfered with his plan. After he and a girl he'd met in San Francisco, Alison, had hitched up there, he ran into a guy who worked for the county assessor's office, a guy named Charles Pickering. He'd heard rumours of building supplies being delivered there. Did that mean improvements? And by the worst of all coincidences, Pickering had family in Marin County and recognised Pell from a story in the paper about his arrest for a break-in.

'Hey, I know you,' Pickering had said.

Which turned out to be his last words. Out came the knife, and Pickering was dead in thirty seconds.

He'd escaped that one, though the police had held him for a time—long enough for Alison to decide it was over and head back south. (He'd been searching for her ever since; she'd have to die, of course, since she knew where his property was.)

The mountaintop was what sustained Pell in Capitola. He dreamed of it constantly, of living there with a new Family. Lying now in the Sea View Motel, he told Jennie about the place—in general terms, of course.

But Jennie was excited about the few facts he shared. 'I'll go wherever you are, sweetie.' She set his coffee cup aside and lay back. 'Make love to me, Daniel. Please?'

He smoothed a strand of dyed hair off her forehead and kissed her. His hands began that familiar, yet always new, exploration. Which was interrupted by a jarring ring.

He picked up the phone, listened, then held his hand over the mouthpiece. 'Housekeeping saw the DO NOT DISTURB sign. They want to know when they can make up the room.'

Jennie gave a coy smile. 'Tell them we need at least an hour.'

'I'll tell her two. Just to be sure.'

THE STAGING AREA for the assault was an intersection round the corner from the Sea View Motel. Albert Stemple and TJ represented the CBI on the takedown teams, made up mostly of Monterey County SWAT deputies and highway patrol officers. The eight men and two women were gathered beside a nondescript truck, which held enough weapons to put down a modest riot.

Pell was still inside the room that the woman had rented; the lights were off, but a surveillance officer clapped a microphone on the back wall and reported that it sounded like they were having sex.

Good news, thought Dance. A naked suspect is a vulnerable suspect.

The room to Pell's left was empty; the guests had just left with fishing tackle, which meant they wouldn't be back until much later. Unfortunately, though, a family appeared to still be in the room on the other side. Dance's initial reaction was to call them and tell them to get down on the floor in the back. But they'd flee, of course. And Pell had the instincts of a cat.

Kellogg arrived, in black jeans, a black shirt and a bulletproof vest. He walked up to the tactical officers and introduced himself.

In this garb, with his attentive eyes, he reminded her even more of her late husband. She watched Kellogg load and chamber a round in a large silver automatic pistol.

'Now that's some weapon of mass destruction,' TJ said. 'The new SIG-Sauer P two-twenty. Forty-five calibre.'

Kellogg pulled on an FBI windcheater and joined her and O'Neil, who was today in his khaki chief deputy uniform—body armour too.

Rey Carraneo radioed in; the lot was empty of people, and the housekeepers were going about their business, as instructed, until the last minute.

Kellogg spoke to the officers. 'I want a rolling entry—one team through the door, the second, back-up, right behind.' He held up a sketch the manager had drawn. 'First team, to the bed. Second, closets and bathroom. I need some flash-bangs.' He was referring to the loud, blinding hand grenades used to disorient suspects without causing serious injury. One of the officers handed him several. 'I'll take the first team in. I'm on point.'

Dance wished he wouldn't; there were far younger officers with military combat experience.

The FBI agent continued: 'Now, we'll circle round the side and move in fast along the front. Those going past his window, stay on your bellies. And don't assume there are only two perps in there.' He turned to Dance. 'That sound OK to you?' He was giving her one last chance to pull the plug.

She debated only a moment. 'It's fine. Do it.'

O'Neil didn't look at her, just drew his Glock and, along with TJ and Stemple, moved out with a back-up team.

Dance joined Carraneo on surveillance and plugged in her headset. Her radio crackled. Kellogg, saying, 'On my five, we move.'

Affirmative responses came in from the leaders of the various teams.

'Let's do it. One . . . two . . .'

Dance wiped her palm on her slacks and closed it round the grip of her weapon. Please, she thought. No more deaths.

'. . . three . . . four . . . five, go!'

Kellogg got to the door first, giving a nod to an MCSO officer whose weighty battering ram crashed it open. Kellogg pitched in a grenade. It detonated with a stunning explosion, and his and O'Neil's teams raced inside.

Then: silence. No gunshots, no screams. Finally Dance heard Kellogg's voice lost in a staticky transmission.

'Say again,' she transmitted. 'Win, do you have him?'

A crackle. 'Negative. He's gone.'

As THEY DROVE AWAY from the motel, Jennie Marston looked back. No squad cars yet, no lights, no sirens.

Her Daniel was brilliant. Her Daniel was a genius.

Twenty minutes ago, he'd frozen, sitting up in bed.

'What, honey?' she'd asked, alarmed.

'Housekeeping. Have they ever called about making up the room?'

'I don't think so.'

'Why would they today? And it's early. Somebody wanted to see if we were in. The police! Get dressed. Now!'

She leapt from bed.

'Grab what you can. Get your computer, and don't leave anything personal.' He tossed things into a bag. Holding the gun up, he kicked in the adjoining door, startling two young men inside.

At first she thought he'd kill them, but he just told them to turn around, tied their hands with fishing line and taped washcloths in their mouths. He pulled out their wallets. 'You stay here and be quiet. If you say anything to anybody, your families are dead. OK?'

They nodded, and Daniel dumped out the contents of the fishermen's cooler and tackle boxes and put their own bags inside. They dressed in the men's yellow slickers and, wearing baseball caps, they carried the gear and the fishing rods outside.

'Don't look round. Walk right to our car. But slow,' Pell told her.

They headed across the parking lot. He spent some minutes loading the car. Jennie wanted to cry, she was so nervous. But she had to admit that driving away was a total high.

They passed four police cars speeding towards the motel. Now they were miles away from the inn and no one was after them.

Finally he laughed. 'How 'bout that, lovely?'

'We did it, sweetie!' She whooped wildly.

Soon they were pulling into the parking lot of the Butterfly Inn, a small dump of a motel on the commercial strip in Monterey. Daniel told her, 'Go get a room. Get it for a week; it'll be less suspicious.'

Jennie registered and returned to the car. He carried the cooler and boxes inside, then lay on the bed, arms behind his neck. She curled up next to him.

'We're going to have to hide out here,' Pell said. 'There's a grocery store up the street. Go get some food, would you, lovely?'

'And more hair dye? Can I be a redhead?'

'You can be green if you want. I'd love you anyway.'

God, he was perfect . . .

She heard the crackle of the TV coming on as she stepped out the door, slipping the cap on. A few days ago she'd never have thought she'd be OK with Daniel hurting people, and leaving her house in Anaheim for ever. Now it seemed perfectly natural.

Anything for you, Daniel. Anything.

'AND HOW DID HE KNOW you were there?' Overby asked, standing in Dance's office. The man was jumpy. Now he was on record as supporting a bad tactical decision.

'Must've sensed something,' Kellogg replied. 'Like in the restaurant at Moss Landing. He's got the instincts of a cat.'

'And I thought your people heard him inside, Michael.'

'He had porn on pay-per-view,' the detective explained.

Kellogg was upset but not apologetic. He'd made a judgment call. His plan could have worked, but fate had intervened. Now he was focused on the next steps.

Overby's assistant joined them. She told her boss he had a call from Sacramento, and SAC Amy Grabe, from the FBI, was holding on two.

With an angry grunt, Overby followed her back to his office.

An MCSO deputy arrived with a large packet. O'Neil set out photos and a list of physical evidence. The fingerprints were of Pell and his accomplice. Clothes, food wrappers, personal hygiene items, some cosmetics, condoms.

O'Neil's phone rang, and he took the call. 'Good. Send it to Agent Dance's computer . . . Thanks.' He looked at Dance. 'Crime scene found an email in the woman's jeans.'

Minutes later Dance called up the message on the screen.

From: CentralAdmin2235@Capitolacorrectional.com
To: JMSUNGIRL@Euroserve.co.uk

Jennie, my lovely—

Bargained my way into the office to write this. I had to. I woke up thinking about you—our plans to go out to the beach, and the desert, and watching the fireworks every night in your back yard. I was thinking, you're smart and beautiful—who could ask for anything more in a girl? We've danced around it a lot and haven't said it but I want to now. I love you. There's no doubt in my mind. You're unlike anybody I've ever met.

Soon, Daniel

So Pell *had* sent emails from Capitola, Dance noted.

O'Neil said, 'Our tech department's contacting her ISP. Foreign servers aren't very cooperative, but we'll keep our fingers crossed.'

Dance was staring at the email. 'Beach, desert and fireworks every night. All near her house. That ought to give us some ideas.'

Kellogg said, 'Beach and desert, that's Southern California. But fireworks every night?'

'Anaheim,' Dance said. 'Disneyland.'

O'Neil said, 'How about we contact banks there and see if any women customers have made withdrawals of nine thousand two hundred dollars in the past month or two? Now we know her first name, possibly an initial— M. Can your people handle this, Win?'

'That'd be manageable,' Kellogg said, and called the LA field office.

Dance phoned the women at the Point Lobos Inn. She explained what had happened at the motel and gave the details of the email, but no one could recall anybody with that name.

It was only a few minutes later that Kellogg received a call. His eyes flashed in surprise. 'A woman named Jennie Marston withdrew nine thousand two hundred dollars from Pacific Trust in Anaheim last week. Cash. We're getting a warrant to raid her house.'

Sometimes you *do* get a break.

O'Neil grabbed his phone, and in five minutes a JPEG of a driver's licence photo was on Dance's computer. She called TJ in and nodded at the screen. 'Do an EFIS image. Make her a brunette, redhead, long hair, short. Get it to the Sea View. I want to make sure it's her.'

'You bet, Boss.' He typed on her keyboard, then hurried out.

Overby stepped into the doorway. Dance briefed him on the latest news.

'Well, a lead. At last. Anyway, we've got another issue. Napa County Sheriff's Office has someone named Morton Nagle in jail.'

Dance nodded slowly. She hadn't told Overby about enlisting the writer's aid to find the Sleeping Doll.

'What did Nagle do?' Kellogg asked, lifting an eyebrow.

'The Croyton girl lives up there somewhere with her aunt and uncle. Nagle wanted to talk her into being interviewed by you.'

'That's right,' said Dance.

'Oh. I didn't hear about it.' Overby let that linger. 'The aunt told him no. But this morning he sneaked onto their property to try to convince the girl in person. The aunt took a shot at him.'

'*What?*'

'She missed, but if the deputies hadn't shown up, the sheriff thinks she would've taken him out on the second try.'

'I'll handle it,' Dance told him.

Overby gave her the sheriff's number and headed back to his office. Dance called the sheriff and told him the situation.

The man grunted. 'Well, Agent Dance, I appreciate the problem, Pell and all. But the magistrate set bail at a hundred thousand.'

'Can I talk to the prosecutor?'

'He's on trial. Will be all day.'

Nagle would have to spend a little time in jail. She felt bad for him, but there was nothing she could do. 'I'd like to talk to the girl's aunt or uncle.'

A pause. 'Well now, I really don't think they'd be inclined. In fact, I can pretty much guarantee it. Goodbye, Agent Dance.'

DANCE AND O'NEIL were alone in her office.

She'd learned from the Orange County Sheriff's Department that Jennie Marston's father was dead and her mother had a history of petty crime, drug abuse and emotional disabilities. Jennie had gone to community college for a year, before dropping out. She'd worked for Hair Cuttery for a year, then went into food service, employed by a number of caterers and bakeries. No friends were found, and her ex-husband hadn't talked to her in years. Deputies had been summoned by hospital workers at least a half-dozen times on suspicion of domestic abuse involving the ex and four other partners.

Just the sort to fall prey to someone like Daniel Pell.

Dance mentioned this to O'Neil. The detective nodded. He was looking out of Dance's window at two pine trees that had grafted themselves to each other over the years, producing a knucklelike knot that Dance would often stare at when the facts of a case refused to coalesce into helpful insights.

'So what's on your mind?' she asked.

'You want to know?'

'I asked, didn't I?' In a tone of good humour.

It wasn't reciprocated. He said testily, 'You were right. He was wrong.'

'Kellogg? At the motel?'

'We should've set up a surveillance perimeter, not spent a half-hour assembling tactical. Somebody gave something away.'

'A takedown made sense at the time; a lot was happening.'

'No, it didn't make sense. His plan was a prescription for a shoot-out.'

O'Neil crossed his arms—a protective gesture, which was ironic because he still had on the bulletproof vest. 'You're giving up control of the operation. *Your* operation. He's a consultant.'

'He's the specialist, Michael. I'm not. You're not.'

'He is? I'm sorry, but I don't see *him* closing in on Pell. You're the one who's been doing that. Look, we've handled pressure before, the two of us. We could've backed him down.'

'Are you saying I'm deferring to him for some other reason?'

O'Neil looked away. 'I'm saying you're giving him too much control over the operation. And frankly, over yourself.'

She snapped, 'Because he reminds me of my husband? Is that what you're saying?'

'I don't know. You tell me. *Does* he remind you of Bill?'

'This is ridiculous.'

'You brought it up,' O'Neil said tersely.

'Well, anything other than professional judgment's none of your business.'

'Fine. I'll stick to professional judgment. Winston was off base. And you acquiesced to him, knowing he was wrong.'

She and O'Neil had fought before; you can't have friendship and a working relationship without wrinkles. But never with an edge this sharp. And why was he slipping over the bounds into her personal life? This was a first.

The kinesics read almost as jealousy.

They fell silent. The detective lifted his hands and shrugged. This was an emblem gesture, which translated: I've said my piece. The tension in the room was as tight as that entwined pine knot.

They resumed their discussion of the next steps: checking for more details about Jennie Marston, sending out the woman's picture, following up on the crime scene. But the climate in the office had dropped significantly, and when Winston Kellogg came into the room, O'Neil retreated, saying a perfunctory goodbye that was aimed at neither of them.

MORTON NAGLE gazed at the big Latino guard outside the holding cell of Napa County Men's Detention.

'Stand up.' The door opened. 'Hold out your hands.'

Nagle watched the cuffs clatter round his wrists.

'This way.' The man's strong fingers closed round his arm. They walked like this down a dim corridor to an interview room. The guard opened the door and gestured Nagle inside.

Theresa Croyton, the Sleeping Doll, sat at a table.

The guard pushed him forward and he sat down across from her.

'Hello again,' he said.

The girl nodded. She was only seventeen, but there was nothing young about her except the white delicacy of her skin. She hadn't died in Daniel Pell's attack, Nagle thought. But her childhood had.

The guard stepped back, but he remained close; Nagle could hear his large body absorbing sounds.

Theresa focused on the writer. 'Tell me what you were going to say in my back yard. About Daniel Pell.'

'He's staying in the Monterey area. The police can't figure out why.'

'And he tried to kill the prosecutor who sent him to jail?'

'James Reynolds, that's right. The policewoman I was telling you about saved him.'

'I want to go see her.'

Nagle wasn't sure he'd heard correctly. 'You want what?'

'I want to go down to Monterey. Meet her in person. I'll have my aunt drive me there. You can come with us.'

'There's one problem.' Nagle chuckled. 'I'm in jail.'

She looked towards the guard, surprise in her eyes. 'Didn't you tell him?' The guard shook his head.

Theresa said, 'I bailed you out.'

'You?'

'My father was worth a lot of money.' Now she gave a laugh—a small one, but genuine and from her heart. 'I'm a rich girl.'

Chapter 11

Footsteps approaching.

The gun was in Daniel Pell's hand instantly.

In the cheap hotel, with its aroma of air freshener and insecticide, he glanced outside and slipped the pistol back into his waistband, seeing that it was Jennie. He shut off the TV and opened the door. She stepped inside, carrying a heavy shopping bag. He set it on the bedside table.

'How'd it go, lovely? See any police?'

'None.' She pulled her cap off. Pell kissed her head.

Another glance out of the window. After a long moment, he came to a decision. 'Let's get out of here for a bit, lovely.'

'Outside? I thought you didn't think it was a good idea.'

'Oh, I know a place. It'll be safe.'

She kissed him. 'Like we're going on a date.'

'Like a date.'

They put their caps on and walked to the door. Her smile gone, Jennie looked him over. 'You OK, sweetheart?'

Sweetheart. 'Sure am, lovely. Just that scare back at the motel. But everything's fine now. Fine as could be.'

They drove south along a complicated route of surface streets to a beach on the way to Big Sur. Wooden walkways wound past rocks and dunes. Sea otters and seals hovered in the raging surf. It was one of the most beautiful beaches on the Central Coast. Normally it would be crowded, but now, with the day's sweeping fog, wind and mist, the area was deserted. Daniel Pell and his lovely walked down to the water.

'Oh, it's beautiful. But it's cold. Put your arm round me.'

Pell did. Felt her shivering.

'This is amazing. Near my house, the beaches there? They're all flat. Just sand and surf. Nothing like this. It's very spiritual here. Where we're going—your mountain? Is it as pretty as this?'

'Prettier. And a lot more deserted. We don't want tourists, do we?'

'Nope.' Her hand went to her nose. Was she sensing that something was wrong? He leaned back and looked at her face.

The same face that had been on the motel TV screen a half hour earlier while she'd been out shopping.

Apparently, Jennie left something in the Sea View after all.

He turned her to face the raging ocean, stood behind her. Pell held her tight, gazing at the beach. 'Look at that rock there, in the sand.' He bent down and unearthed a smooth grey stone, which weighed maybe five pounds. 'What do you think it looks like?'

'Oh, when you hold it that way, it's like a cat, don't you think? A cat sleeping all curled up. Like my Jasmine.'

'That was your cat?' Pell hefted it in his hand.

'When I was a little girl. My mother loved it. She'd hurt me; she'd hurt a lot of people. But never Jasmine. Isn't that funny?'

'That's what I was thinking, lovely. It looks just like a cat.'

DANCE CALLED O'NEIL first with the news.

He didn't pick up, so she left a message. It wasn't like him not to answer, but she knew he wasn't screening. Even his outburst—well, not outburst, OK—even his *criticism* earlier had been grounded in a law enforcer's desire to run a case most efficiently.

Dance found Kellogg in the conference room. She said, 'We've got Theresa Croyton. Nagle just called from Napa. Get this. She bailed him out.'

'How 'bout that. Are you going up there to talk to her?'

'No. She's coming here. With her aunt.'

'*Here?* With Pell still loose?'

'She wanted to come. Insisted, in fact. It was the only way she'd agree.'

'Gutsy.'

'I'll say.'

Dance called massive Albert Stemple and arranged for him to take over Theresa's guard detail when they arrived.

She looked up and found Kellogg studying the pictures on her desk, the ones of her children. His face was still. She wondered again if there was something about the fact that she was a mother that touched, or troubled, him.

She said, 'Theresa won't be here for a while. I'd like to go back to the inn, see our guests again.'

'I'll leave that up to you. I think a male figure's a distraction.'

Dance agreed, and said she appreciated his understanding.

She started to rise, but he surprised her by saying, 'Wait, please.'

Dance sat back. He gave a faint laugh and looked into her eyes.

'I haven't been completely honest with you, Kathryn. And it wouldn't mean anything . . . except for last night.'

What was this? she wondered.

'About children.'

Dance sat forward, giving him her full attention.

'The fact is, my wife and I did have a child. She died in a car accident when she was sixteen.

'Oh, Win . . .'

'I couldn't handle it. I tried to be there for Jill, but I wasn't, not the way I should've been. We got divorced, and it was bad for a few years. We patched it up and we're friends now, sort of. And she's remarried. But I have to say, it's hard for me to be natural with kids. So if I act stiff, it's not Wes or Maggie.'

'I'm so sorry, Win.' She took his hand, pressed it. 'I'm glad you told me. I did see something. I wasn't sure what, though.'

'Eagle eye.'

She laughed. 'I've got my own issues because of Bill.'

'We'll take things slow.'

'Slow is good,' she said.

She walked him to his temporary office, then drove back to the Point Lobos Inn.

As soon as she got there, though, she knew the atmosphere had changed. The kinesics were wholly different from yesterday. The women were restless and edgy. She noted postures and facial expressions that suggest tension, defensiveness and outright hostility. Dance was discouraged, and assessed that it might take long hours, if not days, to get them in a place mentally where they could once again provide helpful information.

Still, she gave it a shot. She ran through what she'd learned about Jennie Marston and asked if the women knew anything about her. They didn't. Dance then tried to resume the conversation of yesterday, but today the comments and recollections were superficial.

Linda seemed to be speaking for all of them when she said, 'I just don't know how much more I can add. I'd like to go home.'

Dance wanted them to stay until she'd interviewed Theresa Croyton. They agreed, reluctantly, to wait a few more hours.

As Dance left, Rebecca accompanied her outside. They stood under an awning; a light drizzle was falling.

'Maybe it's obvious,' Rebecca said. 'But I thought I should mention something. Sam doesn't appreciate how dangerous Pell is, and Linda thinks he's a misunderstood product of his childhood.'

'Go on.'

'What we were telling you yesterday about him—all that psychological stuff—well, it's true. You've managed to stop him and nearly caught him a couple of times. Does he know your name?'

A nod. 'Do you think he'd waste time coming after me?'

'Are you immune to him?' Rebecca asked, cocking an eyebrow.

And that answered the question right there. Yes, she was immune to his control. And therefore she was a risk.

Threats have to be eliminated . . .

'I have a feeling he's worried. You're a danger to him, and he gets to people through their family. You have family in the area?'

'My parents and children,' said Dance.

'Are the children with your husband?'

'I'm a widow. But they're not at home right now. And I've got a deputy guarding them.'

'Good, but watch *your* back.'

'Thank you.' Dance nodded back into the cabin. 'Did something happen last night? Between all of you?'

She laughed. 'I think we've had a little more past than we can handle. We aired some laundry. It should've been aired years ago. But I'm not sure everybody felt that way.'

Rebecca walked back inside and closed and locked the door.

KATHRYN DANCE had been gone half an hour when one of the deputies called the cabin to check up on the women.

'Everything's fine,' Samantha replied—apart from the broiling tensions inside the suite.

He had her make sure the doors and windows were locked. Sealed in, nice and tight. She felt a burst of anger that Daniel Pell had them trapped once again, stuck in this little box.

'I'm going stir crazy,' Rebecca announced. 'I've got to get outside.'

Linda looked up from her Bible. 'Oh, I don't think you should.'

Rebecca shrugged. 'I'll just go out a little ways.' She gestured towards Point Lobos State Park. 'I'll be careful. I'll wear my galoshes and look both ways.'

'It's stupid, but do what you want,' Linda said, and went back to her Bible. Sam said, 'You'll get wet.'

'I'll go to one of the shelters. I want to do some drawing.' Rebecca picked up her pad and pencils, put on her leather jacket and pulled the hood up. She unlatched the back door and stepped outside. 'Lock it after me.'

Sam double locked the door and put the chain on.

DANIEL PELL PARKED the Camry in a deserted lot off Highway 1 near Carmel River State Beach. He was alone in the car.

He caught a whiff of Jennie's perfume.

Climbing out of the car, he noticed Jennie's blood in the crescent of his nails. He spat on his fingers and wiped it off.

Pell looked around at the cypress and pine and oak woods and the rugged outcroppings of granite and Carmelo formation rock. Head down, Pell moved south through the thick trees. There was a path nearby, but he didn't dare take it, though the park seemed deserted.

The rain had stopped. After ten minutes, Pell came to the dozen cabins of the Point Lobos Inn. Crouching, he circled to the rear of the place. He froze, gripping his gun, when a deputy appeared, surveyed the grounds, then returned to the front of the cabin.

Easy, he told himself. Take your time.

About a hundred yards away, invisible to the cabins, was a small shelter. Someone sat at a picnic bench underneath it.

Pell's heart gave an uncharacteristic thud.

The woman was looking out over the ocean, a pad in her hand. Whatever she was drawing, he knew it would be good. Rebecca Sheffield was talented.

He looked around once more, then made his way towards her until he was right behind her. 'Hello,' he whispered.

She gasped and turned. 'Jesus.' A moment of silence.

Then her face lurched into a smile. 'Damn, I missed you.'

'Come here, lovely,' he said, and pulled her towards him.

THEY'D MOVED INTO the grove of trees so there was no chance of being spotted by anyone at the inn.

'They know about Jennie,' Rebecca said.

'I know. I saw it on the TV.' He grimaced. 'She left something in the room. They tracked her down. But she won't be a problem.' Glanced down at the blood in his nails. 'Lovely, if you hadn't called, I don't know what would've happened.'

After they'd checked in to the Sea View, Pell had left a message on Rebecca's home voicemail, giving her the name of the motel he and Jennie were in. The call he'd received supposedly from housekeeping was Rebecca, telling him in a frantic whisper that the police were on their way.

'That was lucky,' Rebecca said, wiping mist from her face.

She looked good, Pell thought. He got a twist inside him and kissed her again. 'You're the best, baby. I'm here only 'cause of you.'

Jennie Marston had been just a pawn in the escape; it was Rebecca who'd planned everything. Pell had managed some unsupervised phone time in Capitola and spoken to Rebecca. For some time she'd been considering how to break Pell out. She came up with an idea when she read about the unsolved Robert Herron killing—which Pell had nothing to do with. She decided to make him the prime suspect so he'd be transferred to a lower-security facility for the trial. Rebecca had found some of his tools, which she'd had from the days of the Family, and slipped them into his aunt's garage in Bakersfield.

Pell had sifted through his fan letters to look for a candidate who'd help.

He settled on Jennie Marston, a woman who seemed wonderfully desperate and vulnerable. Pell had limited access to computers, so Rebecca had set up an untraceable email address and masqueraded as Pell to win Jennie's heart, convince her that he was innocent of the Croyton killings and get her to help him escape. Rebecca had sent the woman instructions: stealing the hammer, making up the fake wallet, planting them in Salinas. And how to construct the gas bomb and where to buy the fire suit and bag.

Pell now asked, 'That was Sam when I phoned, wasn't it?'

The call—thirty minutes ago—purporting to be the guard checking up on them was Pell. His arrangement with Rebecca was that he'd ask whoever answered—if she didn't—to check the window locks. That meant he'd be there soon and Rebecca was supposed to go to the shelter and wait for him.

'She didn't catch on. The poor thing just doesn't get it.'

'I want to get out of here soon, lovely. I've got Dance's address.'

'Oh, one thing you'll want to know. Her kids aren't at home. I found a Stuart Dance—probably her father—in the phone book. I'd guess they're there. Oh, and there's a cop guarding them. There's no husband.'

'A widow, right? I just knew.'

Rebecca eased back and studied him. 'For an undocumented alien, you look pretty damn good. You really do.'

MICHAEL O'NEIL finally called. Dance was glad to hear his voice, though the tone was purely professional. He was, she sensed, still angry. Which was odd for him. It bothered her, but there was no time to consider their grievances, given his news.

'Got a call from CHP,' he said. 'Some hikers halfway to Big Sur found a handbag on the beach. Jennie Marston's. Blood on the sand, and blood and scalp tissue on a rock that crime scene found. Pell's prints are on the rock. No body, but the coastguard is out looking.'

He killed her . . . Dance closed her eyes. Pell had seen her picture on TV, and she'd become a liability. 'How long ago?' she asked.

'Crime scene's estimating an hour. We're checking along One and the cross roads, but no witnesses.'

'Thanks, Michael.' She waited for him to say something else, something about their earlier discussion.

'Bye.' *Click.*

Just then the CBI's front desk called on the intercom to tell her that Theresa Croyton, the Sleeping Doll, had arrived.

THE GIRL wasn't what Kathryn Dance had expected.

In baggy sweats, Theresa Croyton Bolling was tall and slim and wore her light brown hair long, to the middle of her back. Four metallic dots were in her left ear, and the majority of her fingers were encircled by silver rings. Her face, free of make-up, was narrow and pretty and pale.

Morton Nagle ushered the girl and her aunt into Dance's office. Mary Bolling was stiff and cautious as hands were shaken and greetings exchanged. The girl was casual and friendly but nervous.

Nagle said he'd be at home if anybody needed him.

Dance gave him a sincere 'Thank you.'

He nodded a farewell, tugged up his saggy trousers, and left.

'Thank you for coming. You go by "Theresa"?'

'Mostly "Tare".'

'Do you mind if I talk to your niece alone?' Dance asked the aunt.

'It's OK.' This was from the girl. The aunt hesitated. 'It's OK,' the girl repeated more firmly. A hint of exasperation.

TJ escorted the aunt to the office of Albert Stemple.

Dance came out from around the desk and closed her door. She didn't know if the girl could help lead them to Pell. Despite her gutsy foray here, Theresa would be raising subconscious barriers to the pain of recollection.

Dance directed her to the couch. 'You comfortable?'

'Sure.' She smiled at Dance with her lips taut. 'Mr Nagle said you wanted to ask about the night my parents and brother and sister were killed.'

'That's right. I know you were asleep at the time, but—'

'What? Who told you that?'

'Well, all the news stories. The police.'

'No, no, I was awake.'

Dance blinked in surprise. 'You were?'

'Like, yeah. I thought *that's* why you wanted to see me.'

Dance felt her heart tapping fast. The girl tugged at her studded ear lobe, and the top of her shoe rose, indicating curling toes. *Stress*.

'Go ahead, Tare.'

'I was asleep earlier, for a while. I wasn't feeling good. I had a dream I don't remember, but I think it was scary. I woke myself up with a kind of moaning. Only . . .' Her voice faded.

'You're not sure it was *you* making the noise?'

The girl swallowed. 'Right.'

'Did you hear anything after that?'

'Yeah. Voices. Men's voices. But not my father or brother.'

'Tare, did you tell anybody this back then?'

'Yeah.' She nodded. 'But nobody was interested.'

How on earth had Reynolds missed it? 'What did you hear?'

'A couple of things. First I heard somebody mention four hundred dollars.'

Pell had more than that when he was arrested. Maybe he and Newberg were going through Croyton's wallet. 'What else?'

'OK, then a different man said something about Canada. And somebody else asked about Quebec.'

'And what was the question?'

'He just wanted to know what Quebec was.'

So, a Canadian connection. Is that where Pell wanted to escape to? A lot of mountaintops. Dance sat forward. 'Go on, Tare. You're doing great.'

'Then,' Theresa continued, 'somebody was talking about used cars. He had a really low voice. He talked fast.'

Used-car dealerships were popular for money laundering. Or escape. And it hadn't been just Pell and Newberg. A third person had been there.

'Did your father do business in Canada?'

'He travelled a lot. But I don't think he ever mentioned Canada.'

'Anything else?' Dance asked.

'No. I guess I fell back asleep. The next thing I knew'—she swallowed again—'there was this policewoman there.'

Dance reflected: $400, a car dealership, a French Canadian province. And a third man.

Was Pell intent on heading north now? Homeland Security and Immigration could keep an eye on the northern border crossings.

Dance tried again, walking the girl through the events of that terrible night. But Theresa knew nothing more.

And then Dance had an idea. 'Tare,' she asked reluctantly, 'you think this was around seven p.m. or so?'

'Yeah, maybe.'

'Where did your family eat?'

'The den most of the time.'

'Did you watch TV while you were having dinner?'

'Yeah. A lot. Me and my brother and sister, at least.'

'Did you ever watch *Jeopardy*?'

She frowned. 'Yeah.'

'Tare, I'm wondering if maybe the voices you heard were from the show.

Maybe somebody picking the category of geography for four hundred dollars. And if the answer was "The French-speaking province of Canada", the question would be "What is Quebec?"'

The girl fell silent. 'No, that wasn't it. I'm sure.'

'And the car dealership—could it have been a commercial?'

The girl's face flushed with dismay. Then anger. 'No!'

'But maybe?' Dance asked gently.

Theresa's eyes closed. 'No.' A whisper. Then, 'Maybe. I don't know.'

That was why Reynolds hadn't pursued the child's testimony. The mysterious third man was the TV host, or an advertising actor.

Theresa's shoulders slumped forward, the clear kinesic signal of defeat and sorrow. The girl realised that her efforts to remember something helpful had been pointless. Tears pooled in her eyes.

Dance smiled. 'Tare, don't worry. It's nothing.' She gave the girl a Kleenex.

'Nothing? It's terrible. I wanted to help so bad . . .'

Another smile. 'Oh, Tare, believe me, we're just getting warmed up.'

The art of interviewing isn't only about analysing answers and body language and demeanour; it's also about asking the right questions.

The Croytons' murders and every moment afterwards had been documented by police and reporters. So Kathryn Dance decided to enquire about the one period of time that no one had ever asked about.

'Tare, I want to hear about what happened earlier that day.'

Theresa frowned. 'Oh, I don't remember much about it.'

'Give it a try. Think back. It was May. What day of the week?'

'Um, it was Friday.'

'You remembered that pretty fast.'

'Oh, because on a lot of Fridays, Dad would take us kids places. That day, we were going to the carnival rides in Santa Cruz. Only everything got messed up.' Theresa rubbed her eyes. 'We were, like, on our way, but'—she looked down—'I got sick. In the car. So we turned around and went home.'

'What did you have? A cold?'

Theresa winced. 'Stomach flu.'

'Oh, I just hate that. And you got back about when?'

'Five thirty, maybe.'

'And you went straight to bed.'

'Yeah, that's right.' She looked out of the window at the gnarled tree.

'And then you woke up hearing the TV show.'

The girl twined a strand of hair round a finger. 'Quebec.' A grimace.

At this point, Kathryn Dance paused. She had a decision to make.

When Theresa had been talking about what she'd overheard from the TV room, her kinesic behaviour was relaxed and open, though she obviously was experiencing general stress. But as soon as she started talking about the trip to Santa Cruz, she displayed hesitations of speech, she covered parts of her face—negation gestures—and looked out of the window—aversion. Dance sensed that there were things the girl wasn't sharing.

'Tare, something troubling happened on the drive, didn't it?'

'Troubling? No. Really. I swear.'

A triple play there: two denial flag expressions, along with answering a question with a question.

'Go on, tell me. It's all right. There's nothing to worry about.'

'Like, you know. My parents, my brother and sister—they were *killed*. Who wouldn't be upset?' A bit of anger now.

Dance nodded sympathetically. 'I mean before that. You're driving to Santa Cruz. You're not feeling well. You go home. What was there about that drive that bothered you?'

'I don't know. I can't remember. It was a long time ago.'

That phrase, from a person in a denial state, means: I remember perfectly well, but I don't want to think about it. The memory's too painful.

'You're driving along and—

'I—' Theresa began, then she fell silent. She lowered head to hands, breaking into breathless sobbing.

'Tare.' Dance rose and handed her a wad of tissues as the girl cried. 'It's OK,' the agent said compassionately. 'Don't worry.'

'I . . .' The girl was paralysed; Dance could see she was trying to make a decision. She'd either spill everything or stonewall.

Finally Theresa said, 'Oh, I've wanted to tell somebody. I just couldn't. Not the counsellors or friends, my aunt.' More sobbing. Collapsed chest, hands in her lap when not mopping her face. The textbook kinesic signs that Theresa Croyton had moved into the acceptance stage of emotional response. The terrible burden of what she'd been living with was lifting at last.

'It's all my fault they're dead!' She pressed back against the couch. 'Brenda and Steve and Mom and Dad, all because of me!'

'Because you got sick?'

'No! Because I *pretended* to be sick! I didn't want to go to the board-walk. I couldn't stand going. I hated it! All I could think of was to pretend to be sick. I remembered about these models who put their fingers down their throats so they throw up and don't get fat. I did that when no one was looking. I threw up in the back seat, and said I had the flu. It was all gross, and everybody was mad, and Dad drove back home.'

'Tell me, Tare. Why didn't you want to go to the pier?'

'I just didn't. It wasn't fun.'

'Why not? You can tell me. Go on.'

'Well, Dad was always busy, so he'd give us money and go off and make phone calls and things. It was boring.'

Her feet tapped again. The stress was eating her up.

Yet it wasn't only the kinesics that were sending deception signals. What Theresa was telling Dance didn't make sense—from Dance's knowledge of children and the place in question. Wes and Maggie, for instance, loved Santa Cruz and would have leaped at the chance to spend hours there unsupervised with a pocketful of money. There were carnival rides, food, music, games.

And why hadn't Theresa simply said she wanted to stay home? It was as if she didn't want anyone to go to Santa Cruz.

Dance considered this for a moment. *A to B* . . .

'Tare, you said your father worked and made phone calls when you and your brother and sister went on the rides. Where did he go to make the calls?'

She looked down. 'I don't know. He had a cellphone. Not a lot of people had them then. But he did.'

'Did he ever meet anybody there?'

'I don't know. Maybe.'

'Tare, these other people he'd be with? Were they other women?'

Theresa was silent, looking everywhere but at Dance. Finally she said, 'Maybe. Some, yeah.'

'And you think they might've been girlfriends of his?'

A nod. Through clenched teeth, she said, 'And he said that when we got home, if Mom asked, we were supposed to say he was with us. Because she'd be mad he was working and not having fun.'

Dance recalled Reynolds hinting that Croyton was a womaniser.

A bitter laugh escaped the girl's trembling lips. 'I saw him. Brenda and me. We were supposed to stay on the boardwalk, but we went to an ice cream place and I saw him. There was this woman getting into his car, and he was kissing her. And I saw him later with somebody else, going into her house by the beach. *That's* why I didn't want him to go there. I wanted him to go back home and be with Mommy and us.' She wiped her face.

So he'd meet his mistresses in Santa Cruz—and take his own children to allay his wife's suspicion, abandoning them till he and his lover were finished.

'And my family got killed. And it was my fault.'

Dance leaned forward and said, 'No, Tare. It's not your fault at all. Daniel Pell *intended* to kill your father. It wasn't random.'

She grew quiet. 'Yeah?'

Dance wasn't sure about this at all. But she absolutely couldn't let the girl live with the terrible burden of her guilt. 'Yeah.'

Theresa calmed at this tentative comfort. 'It's all so stupid. I wanted to help you catch him. And I haven't done anything except act like a baby.'

'Oh, we're doing fine,' Dance said. 'In fact, I hope you're up for some more questions.' Her stomach gave a peculiar, and opportune, growl just at that moment. They both laughed, and Dance added, 'Provided there are Frappuccinos and cookies in the near future.'

Theresa wiped her eyes. 'I could go for that, yeah.'

PARKED UP THE ROAD from the Point Lobos Inn, out of sight of the guards, Daniel Pell stared at the space between the cypress trees.

'Come on,' he muttered.

And just a few seconds later, there she was, with her backpack. Rebecca climbed into the car and kissed him firmly.

'Lousy weather,' she said, then grinned and kissed him again.

'Nobody saw you?'

'Climbed out the window. They think I went to bed early.'

He put the car in gear, and they started up the highway.

This was Daniel Pell's last night in the Monterey Peninsula. Later they'd steal another car and head north, winding along the increasingly narrow and rugged roads until they came to Pell's mountain property. He'd be king of the mountain, king of the Family, not answering to anybody. A dozen young people, two dozen, seduced by the Pied Piper. *Heaven . . .*

But first his mission here. He had to guarantee his future.

Pell handed her the map of Monterey County. She opened a slip of paper and read the street and number as she studied the map.

'It's not far. Shouldn't take us more than fifteen minutes.'

EDIE DANCE glanced out of the window of the front of her house and observed the police car. It certainly made her feel comfortable, with an escaped killer somewhere in the area.

Stuart would be back with the children soon. She was happy that Wes and Mags were staying here, but she'd be a lot happier when that terrible man was arrested again and thrown back in jail—

The woman cocked her head. A noise from the back yard. She glanced up to see if Stu had arrived. No, the carport was empty except for her Prius.

Then she heard the sound again. The clatter of rocks.

Edie and Stu lived off Ocean, on the long hill descending from downtown to Carmel Beach. Their back yard was a stepped series of gardens, bordered by rock walls. Walking to or from the neighbour's back yard sometimes set loose a tiny spill of gravel down the face of those walls. That's what the noise sounded like.

She opened the back door. She couldn't see anyone and heard nothing else. Probably just a cat or a dog.

Hearing Stu's car pull into the driveway, she closed the door, then walked to the refrigerator to find a snack for the children.

THE INTERVIEW with the Sleeping Doll had come to an intriguing conclusion.

Back in her office, Dance checked up on the girl and her aunt, both safely ensconced in the hotel and protected by a 250-pound monolith of a CBI agent, who carried two large weapons. They were fine, Albert Stemple reported, then added, 'The girl's nice. I like her. The aunt you can keep.'

Dance read over the notes she'd taken in the interview and then called TJ. 'Bring me what we've got so far on Pell.'

'The whole ball of wax, Boss? Whatever that means.'

'All the wax we've got.'

TJ arrived three or four minutes later. She took the files he carted and spread them out until they covered her desk.

'The girl, was she helpful?'

'Yep,' the agent replied absently, riffling through reports.

TJ made another comment, but she was flipping through more pages. Finally she said, 'I've got a computer question. Go check this out. It's fishy.' She circled some words on a sheet.

He glanced down. 'I'm on the case.'

'WE'VE GOT A SITUATION.'

Dance was addressing Charles Overby, Winston Kellogg and TJ. They were in Overby's office, and he was playing with a bronze golf ball mounted on a wooden stand. Wishing O'Neil were here, Dance dropped the bomb.

'Rebecca Sheffield's working with Pell.'

'What?' Overby blurted.

'I think she was behind the whole escape.'

Her boss shook his head, the theory clearly troubling him.

But Winston Kellogg encouraged her. 'Interesting. Go on.'

'I looked back over the evidence. Remember that email we found in the Sea View? Supposedly, Pell sent it, but look.' She showed the print-out. 'His address says Capitola Correctional. But it has a dot-com extension. If it was really a Department of Corrections address it would've had dot gov.'

Kellogg grimaced. 'Hell, yes. Missed that completely.'

'I just had TJ check out the address.'

The young agent explained, 'The company's a service provider in Seattle. You can create your own domain. It's an anonymous account, but we're getting a warrant to look at the archives.'

'Anonymous? Then why do you think it was Rebecca?' Overby asked.

'Look at the email. That phrase. 'Who could ask for anything more in a girl?' It stuck with me because it echoes a line in an old Gershwin song. One Rebecca used the first time I met her.'

Overby said, 'Still—'

She pushed forward. 'Now, let's look at the facts. Jennie stole the Thunderbird in LA on Friday and checked into the Sea View on Saturday. Her phone and credit-card records show she was in Orange County all last week. But the woman who checked out the You Mail It office was there on Wednesday. We faxed a warrant to Rebecca's credit-card companies. She flew from San Diego to Monterey on Tuesday, flew back on Thursday.'

'OK, good,' Overby allowed.

'Now, I'm guessing that in Capitola it wasn't Jennie that Pell was talking to; it was Rebecca.'

Kellogg added, 'So she knows what Pell's doing here.'

'Has to.'

Overby said, 'Let's pick her up. You can work your magic, Kathryn.'

'I want her in custody, but I need some more information before I interrogate her. I want to talk to Nagle.'

'The writer?'

She nodded, then said to Kellogg, 'Can you bring Rebecca in?'

'Sure, if you can get some back-up for me.'

Overby said he'd call the MCSO and have another officer meet Kellogg outside the Point Lobos Inn.

Dance nodded at TJ. 'Let's go see Nagle.'

DANCE AND TJ were en route to their destination when her phone rang.

'Hello?'

Winston Kellogg said in an uncharacteristically urgent voice, 'Kathryn, Rebecca's gone. Linda said Rebecca wasn't feeling well and went to lie down. We found her bedroom window open but her car's still at CBI.'

'So Pell picked her up. How long ago?'

'She went to bed an hour ago. They don't know when she slipped out.'

'Where are you now?'

'Going back to CBI. I'll talk to Michael about setting up roadblocks again.'

When they hung up, she called Morton Nagle. 'It's Kathryn. Listen, Rebecca's with Pell.'

'What? He kidnapped her?'

'They're working together. She was behind the escape.'

'No!'

'There's a chance you're in danger.'

'Me?'

'Lock your doors. Don't let anybody in. We'll be there in five minutes.'

It took them closer to ten. They skidded to a stop in front of the house and walked to the front door. Dance knocked. The writer answered a moment later, then scanned the street. The agents stepped inside.

Nagle closed the door. 'I'm sorry.' His voice broke. 'He told me if I gave anything away on the phone, he'd kill my family. I'm so sorry.'

Daniel Pell, standing behind the door, touched the back of her head with a pistol.

Chapter 12

'It's my friend. The cat to my mouse. With the funny name. Kathryn *Dance*.' Nagle continued. 'When you phoned, your number came up on caller ID. He made me tell him who it was. My children. I—'

'It's all right—' she began.

'Shhhhh, Mr Writer and Ms Interrogator. Shush.'

In a bedroom to the left, Dance could see Nagle's wife and son and daughter lying belly-down on the floor, their hands on their heads. Rebecca sat on the bed, holding a knife. She gazed at Dance without a flicker of emotion.

'Come on out here, baby, lend a hand.'

Rebecca slid off the bed and joined them.

'Get their guns and phones.' Pell held the gun to Dance's ear while Rebecca took her weapon. Then he told Dance to cuff herself.

She did.

'Not tight enough.' He squeezed the bracelets. Dance winced.

They did the same with TJ and pushed them down on the couch.

'Is anybody else coming?' Pell said to Dance.

'I didn't call anyone.'

'That's not what I asked.' The essence of calm.

'As far as I know, no. I was coming here to ask Morton some questions.'

Pell set their phones on a coffee table. 'Anybody calls you, tell them everything's fine. We clear on that? Or I pick one of the kiddies in there and—'

'Clear,' she said.

'Now, no more words from anybody until later. We've—'

'This is not smart,' TJ said.

No! Dance thought. Let him control you! With Pell, you can't be defiant.

Pell touched his gun almost casually to the man's throat. 'What did I tell you? Why would you say something? What a stupid, stupid thing to do.'

He's going to kill him, Dance thought. 'Pell, listen to me—'

'You're talking too.' The killer swung the gun towards her.

'I'm sorry,' TJ whispered.

'That's more words.' Pell turned to Nagle. 'Keep going.'

Nagle returned to the task that Dance and TJ had apparently interrupted: burning his notes and research material.

Pell watched the bonfire and added absently, 'If you miss something, I will cut your wife's fingers off. And quit crying. It's not dignified.'

Ten agonising minutes passed as Nagle tossed his notes into the fire. Dance knew that as soon as he'd finished and Pell had learned from her and TJ whatever he needed to know, they'd be dead.

Nagle moaned as the last note went up in flames.

'Hush there.' Pell rose and stirred the fire with a poker to keep the pages burning. 'OK, then.' He turned to Dance. 'Now, I understand from your call earlier you figured out about Rebecca. What do you know about us? And who else knows it? And understand this, Agent Dance, Rebecca found another address for me. The home of one Stuart Dance.'

Dance felt this news like a slap in the face. She struggled to keep from being sick. A wash of heat enveloped her face and chest.

'You son of a bitch,' TJ raged.

'I was right about your brood, wasn't I? At our first get-together. And no husband. You, a poor widow. Anyway, if you tell me the truth, your mom and pop and kiddies'll be fine.'

At that moment, Kathryn Dance came to a decision. It was a gamble, and under other circumstances a difficult choice. Now there was no option. She had no weapons except words and intuition. *A to B to X* . . .

'Aren't you curious why we're here?' she asked Pell.

'That's a question. I didn't want a question. I wanted an answer.'

Make sure he remains in charge—Daniel Pell's trademark. 'Please, think about it. Why would we come here in such a hurry?'

Rebecca scowled. 'She's stalling, baby. Let's go.'

Dance said, 'Because I had to warn Morton—'

Rebecca whispered, 'Let's finish up and get going. Jesus, we're wasting—'

'Quiet, lovely.' Pell turned his bright blue eyes back to Dance. 'Yeah, you wanted to warn him about me. So?'

'No. I wanted to warn him about Rebecca.'

'What are you talking about?'

Dance held Pell's eyes as she said, 'I wanted to warn him that she was going to use you to kill him. Just like she used you at William Croyton's house eight years ago.'

Dance saw the flicker in Pell's otherworldly eyes.

'This is such bullshit,' Rebecca snapped.

The agent eased forward. 'She set you up, Daniel. And you want to know why? To kill William Croyton's wife.'

He was shaking his head, but he was listening to every word.

'Rebecca was Croyton's lover. And when his wife wouldn't give him a divorce, she decided to use you and Jimmy Newberg to kill her. Remember the Sleeping Doll? Theresa Croyton? I just talked to her.'

Rebecca was shocked. 'You what?'

'We had a long conversation. It was quite revealing.'

'Daniel, she's bluffing to save her ass.'

But Dance asked, 'Was *Jeopardy* on the TV in the den the night you broke in? She told me it was. Who else would have known that?'

The killer blinked. Dance saw she had his complete attention. 'Theresa told me that her father was having affairs. He'd drop the children off at the Santa Cruz boardwalk and meet his lovers there. One night he spotted Rebecca doing sketches and picked her up. They started an affair. She wanted him to get a divorce but he wouldn't, or couldn't, because of his wife. So Rebecca decided to kill her.'

'Oh, this is ridiculous. She doesn't *know* any of this,' Rebecca raged.

'The boardwalk . . . Rebecca would've heard about you there, wouldn't she, Daniel? That's where the Family went to sell things at flea markets and to steal and shoplift. Gypsies, they called you. It made the news. Rebecca needed a fall guy, a killer. You thought you seduced her? No, it was the other way around.'

Rebecca's voice remained calm. 'Shut up! She's lying, Dan—'

'Quiet!' Pell snapped.

'She joined your clan when? Not long before the Croyton murders. A few months?' Dance pressed forward relentlessly. 'Didn't you wonder why? Linda and Samantha and Jimmy, they were children. But Rebecca was different. Independent, aggressive. Once she was in the Family, she used Jimmy Newberg too. She told him that Croyton had something valuable in his house, and he suggested that the two of you break in and steal it. Right?'

Dance saw that she was. 'But Rebecca had made *other* plans with Jimmy. Once you were in the Croytons' house, he was supposed to kill Croyton's wife, then kill *you*. With you gone, he and Rebecca could be in charge. After a suitable period of mourning, William Croyton would marry her.'

'Honey, no. This is—'

Pell lunged forward and grabbed Rebecca's hair. 'Let her talk!'

Moaning in pain, cringing, Rebecca slipped to the floor.

Dance caught TJ's eye, then continued. 'Rebecca thought only Croyton's wife would be home. But the whole family was there because Theresa said she was sick, and everybody ended up dead. And when you called the Family to tell them what happened, Rebecca made the call that got you arrested. *She* turned you in.'

'That's bullshit,' Rebecca said. 'I just got him out of jail!'

Dance laughed coldly. She said to Pell, 'She needed to use you again, Daniel. To kill Morton. A few months ago she got a call from him about his book, *The Sleeping Doll*. She knew he'd learn about the affairs Croyton had. It was just a matter of time before somebody put the pieces together.'

'So Rebecca came up with the plan to break you out of Capitola.' Dance frowned. 'One thing I don't know is what she said to you, Daniel, to convince you to murder him.' She glanced angrily at Rebecca, as if she were offended by what the woman had done to her good friend Daniel Pell. 'So what lies *did* you tell him?'

Pell shouted at Rebecca, 'What you told me Is it true or not?' But before she could speak, Pell grabbed Nagle, who cringed. 'That book you're writing! What were you going to say about me?'

'It wasn't about *you*. It was about Theresa and the Croytons and the girls in the Family. It was about your *victims*, not you.'

Pell grabbed Nagle, pushed the man to the floor. 'No, no! You were going to write about my land!'

'Land? What are you talking about?'

'My land, my mountaintop. You found out where it was!'

Ah, Dance finally understood. Pell's precious mountaintop. Rebecca had convinced him that the only way to keep it secret was to kill Morton Nagle and destroy the notes.

'I don't know anything about that. I swear.'

Pell looked him over closely. He believed the writer, Dance could see.

'Daniel, you know what was coming next, don't you? Rebecca was going to murder *you*. Claim you kidnapped her from the inn.' Dance gave a sad laugh. 'And you thought you were in charge.'

Pell rose and charged towards Rebecca as he lifted the gun.

The woman cringed but suddenly swung the knife madly, slicing into Pell's arm, grabbing at his gun. The weapon went off, the bullet digging a chunk of rosy brick out of the fireplace.

Instantly, Dance and TJ were on their feet. The young agent kicked Rebecca hard in the ribs and grabbed Pell's gun hand. They wrestled for control of the weapon, sliding to the floor.

'Call nine-one-one,' Dance shouted to Nagle, who scrabbled for a phone. She started for the guns on the table.

'Kathryn,' TJ shouted.

She saw Pell twist the gun towards her. It fired. Dance dropped to the ground. The bullet streaked past.

TJ was young and strong, but his wrists were cuffed, and Pell had desperation and adrenaline coursing through him. With his free hand, he pounded at TJ's neck and head. Finally the killer broke away, holding the gun, as the young agent rolled desperately for cover under a table.

A huge explosion. Another.

Dance looked behind her.

Morton Nagle had picked up one of their guns and was firing the weapon towards Pell. The bullets were wide, but he stood his ground and kept firing. 'You son of a bitch!'

Crouching, Pell fired one round into Rebecca's belly, then flung the door open and ran outside.

Dance took the gun from Nagle, grabbed TJ's as well, and shoved it into his cuffed hands.

The agents got to the half-open door just as a round slammed into the jamb, peppering them with splinters. They jumped back, crouching. Dance fished the cuff keys from her jacket and undid the bracelets. TJ did the same.

Cautiously they glanced outside at the empty street. A moment later they heard the screech of an accelerating car.

WHILE TJ CALLED IN the escape, Kathryn Dance phoned the deputy guarding her parents and children and had him take them to CBI headquarters. She doubted Pell would waste time at this point carrying out his threats, but she wasn't taking any chances.

Rebecca was badly wounded and unconscious. O'Neil had sent a deputy with her in the ambulance. The moment she was able to talk, he would call the detective.

Dance now joined Kellogg and O'Neil, who stood nearby, heads bowed, as they discussed the case. They were quickly coordinating roadblocks and planning a search strategy.

O'Neil took a phone call. He hung up and announced, 'Got a lead. Man fitting Pell's description—and bleeding—snatched a black Infiniti in Marina. Had a gun. He must be headed north.' He climbed into his car. 'I'll set up a command post in Gilroy. And Watsonville.'

She watched him drive off.

'Let's get up there too,' Kellogg said, turning to his car.

Following him, Dance heard her phone ring. The call was from James Reynolds. She briefed him on what had just happened, and then the former prosecutor said he'd been through the files from the Croyton murders. He'd found something that might be helpful. Did Dance have a minute now?

'You bet.'

SAM AND LINDA huddled together, watching the news reports about yet another attempted murder. Pell had once again escaped.

'Oh, my,' Linda whispered.

'Rebecca was with him all along.' Sam stared at the TV screen, her face a mask of shock. 'But who shot her? The police?'

The newscaster described the woman who'd been shot, Rebecca Sheffield, as founder of Women's Initiatives in San Diego, and one of the women in the Family eight years ago. She mentioned that Sheffield had been born in Southern California. Her father had died when she was six and she'd been raised by her mother, who had never remarried.

'Six years old,' Linda muttered.

Sam blinked. 'She lied. That stuff with her father never happened.'

She jumped when the phone rang. It was Kathryn Dance.

'Oh, we just heard—' Sam began.

But the agent said, 'Listen to me, Sam. I don't think he's headed north. I think he's coming for you.'

'What?'

'James Reynolds just told me that after the Croyton deaths he was questioning Pell about the Charles Pickering murder, and he went crazy and tried to attack him—because he was getting close to something important. James was thinking he killed Pickering because the man knew about his mountain.'

'But why hurt us?'

'Because he told *you* about Alison, his girlfriend, who knew about the mountain too. Maybe you wouldn't make the connection, but that place is so important to him he's willing to murder anybody who's a risk. The officers outside, they'll take you and Linda to CBI. Agent Kellogg and I are on our way. We're going to wait in the cabin and see if Pell shows up.'

Sam hung up. 'Linda!' she said breathlessly, 'Kathryn thinks he might be coming this way.'

'No!' The curtains were drawn, but the women instinctively looked towards the windows. There was a knock on the door.

'Ladies, it's Deputy Larkin.' They froze; then Linda slowly walked to the peephole, looked out and opened the door. The MCSO deputy stepped inside. 'Just leave everything and come with me.' The other deputy was outside, looking around the parking lot.

Samantha grabbed her bag. 'Let's go.' Her voice was shaking.

The deputy, hand near his pistol, nodded them forward.

At that moment, a bullet struck him in the side of his head. He dropped fast. Another shot, and the second deputy slumped to the ground.

Linda gasped. 'No, no!'

Footsteps were running on the pavement. Daniel Pell was sprinting towards the cabin. Sam was paralysed.

Then she leapt forward and slammed the door, managed to get the chain on and lunged for the phone.

Pell gave two solid kicks. The second one cracked the lock, though the chain held. The door opened only a few inches.

'Rebecca's room!' Sam cried. She ran to Linda and grabbed her arm, but the woman stood rooted in the doorway.

'What are you doing?' Sam screamed. 'Come on!'

Pell kicked the door again, but the chain continued to hold.

'Daniel,' Linda called. 'Please, listen to me. It's not too late. You can give yourself up. We'll get you a lawyer. I'll make sure you're—'

Pell shot her in the abdomen. He aimed the gun through the gap in the door, as casually as if he were swatting a fly. He tried to shoot again, but Sam dragged her into the bedroom. Pell kicked the door once more. This time it crashed open.

Sam locked Rebecca's door. Pell kicked the panel, but the door held firmly against his blows.

Sam helped Linda to the windowsill, pushed her out, then tumbled after her onto the damp earth. Linda was whimpering in pain and clutching her side. Sam helped her up and, holding her arm in a bruising grip, guided her, jogging towards Point Lobos State Park.

'No,' KATHRYN Dance gasped. 'No . . .'

Win Kellogg skidded the car to a stop beside the two deputies sprawled on the sidewalk. 'See how they are,' he told her, and pulled out his cellphone to call for back-up.

Gun in her sweating hand, Dance knelt beside the deputy, saw he was dead. The other officer as well. 'They're gone.'

Kellogg joined her. Though they'd had no tactical training together, they approached the cabin like seasoned partners.

'I'm going in,' Kellogg said. 'Just back me up. Keep an eye on the doorways inside. Constantly scan them. He'll lead with the gun.'

Dance nodded. 'Got it.'

'Ready?'

No, not the least bit. But she nodded. He touched her arm, then took several deep breaths and pushed through the doorway fast, weapon up, swinging it back and forth.

Dance was right behind him, remembering to target the doors—and raise her muzzle when he passed in front of her. Scan, scan, scan . . . Glance behind, check the open door.

Kellogg called, 'Clear.'

And inside, thank God, no bodies. Bloodstains, though. Fresh ones on the sill of an open window, footprints in the dirt beneath it.

She told Kellogg, 'I think we have to assume he's after them.'

The FBI agent said, 'I'll go. Why don't you wait for back-up?'

'No,' she said automatically. 'The reunion was *my* idea. And I'm not letting them die. I owe them that.'

LINDA WANTED TO LIE DOWN. She whispered this to Sam, but Samantha said nothing. She kept her jogging, in agony, along the twisty paths of the park.

The pain in Linda's heart was nearly as bad as the pain in her side. She had forgiven Daniel for the past. She was ready to forgive him for the present. Yet he'd *shot* her.

'Keep going,' was Sam's whisper. 'Kathryn will be here any minute.'

'Daniel shot me.' Linda's vision crinkled. She was going to faint.

Through the sound of the waves, the wind hissing through the slippery pines and cypress, Linda heard Pell behind them. The snap of a branch, a rustle of leaves. They hurried on. Until a root caught her foot and she went down hard, screaming with pain.

'Shhhh.' Sam's voice was shaking with fear. 'Get up, Linda!'

'I can't.'

More footfalls. 'Please!'

Linda turned to look. Daniel Pell was fifty feet away.

She turned to Sam, but the woman was no longer there.

'MY LOVELY, my Linda.'

He approached slowly.

She winced at the pain. 'Daniel, listen to me. It's not too late. God will forgive you. Turn yourself in.'

He laughed. 'Rebecca told me you'd gone religious. Where's Sam?'

'Please! You don't need to do this. You can change.'

'Change? Oh, Linda, people don't change. Never, never, never. Why, you're still the same person you were when I found you, all red-eyed and lumpy, under that tree in Golden Gate Park.'

Linda felt her vision turning to black sand and yellow lights. The pain ebbed as she nearly fainted. When she floated back to the surface, he was leaning forward with his knife.

'I'm sorry, baby. I've got to do it this way.' An absurd but genuine apology. 'But I'll be fast. You won't feel much.'

And then a tree fell.

Daniel Pell grunted and slammed into the rocky ground.

Samantha McCoy leapt off the killer, climbed to her feet and swung the solid tree branch onto his head and arms. Daniel slashed at her with the knife but she was too fast for him. He grabbed for the gun, which had fallen to the trail. But the rough branch connected hard again and again. Lashing out with his fist, he caught her in the knee and she dropped hard. Daniel dived for the gun, grabbed it. He scrabbled upright and swung the pistol muzzle her way. But Samantha rolled to her feet and struck with the branch again, two-handed. It connected with his shoulder. He stepped back, flinching. Samantha swung the branch again, but now Daniel managed to catch it with his left hand. For a moment, they stared at each other, the wood connecting them like a live wire. Daniel gave a sad smile and lifted the gun.

'No,' Linda croaked.

Samantha gave a smile too. And she pushed towards him, hard, and let go of the branch. Daniel stepped back—into the air. He'd been standing on the edge of a cliff, twenty feet above another trail.

He cried out and tumbled backwards down the rough rock face.

Samantha glanced down with a grimace, then helped Linda to her feet. 'We've got to go. Now. We have to hide.'

Exhausted, she struggled to keep Linda upright. The woman was pale, but the bleeding wasn't bad.

They continued for another fifty feet, then Linda started to falter. 'No, no. . . . I can't go on. I'm sorry.'

Sam found some reserve of strength and managed to get Linda another twenty feet. But then she collapsed—at the worst possible place, a clearing visible for a hundred yards all around.

A shallow trough in the rocks was nearby; it would hide them well enough. 'Come on, we've got to go.'

'You go. Please.' Linda began to whisper a prayer.

'You are not going to die here! Stand up!'

She struggled to her feet, and together they staggered off the path to the shallow ravine. They were on a promontory about fifty feet above the ocean. The low sunlight hit them full on in an orange wash. They'd lie down in the ravine, pull leaves over themselves.

Suddenly, with the sound of crackling underbrush, a figure pushed out of the woods, coming right at them.

'No,' Sam cried. Then, gasping, she barked a hysterical laugh.

Kathryn Dance, crouching, whispered, 'Where is he?'

Her heart slamming, Sam mouthed, 'I don't know.'

Dance scanned the area around them, squinting into the sun. She then assessed Linda's condition. 'Get her down there.' Nodding at the ravine. 'Press something on the wound.'

Together they eased the woman into the depression.

'Please, stay with us,' Sam whispered.

'Don't worry,' Dance said. 'I'm not going anywhere.'

DANCE CALLED WINSTON KELLOGG from her mobile phone. 'Win, I've got Sam and Linda. We're about a hundred yards west from where we split up.'

'Do they know where Pell is?'

'He was near here. Below us and to our left about fifty yards.' Then she tensed, looking down. 'Win, where are you? Are you on the beach?'

'No, I'm on a path. The beach is below me, a hundred yards away.'

'OK, he's there! You see that small island about fifty feet into the water, gulls all over it? The beach in front of that.'

'I can't see it from here, but I'm moving that way.'

'No, Win. There's no cover. We need tactical. Wait.'

'We don't have time. I'm not letting him get away again.'

The gunslinger attitude . . . It bothered her a lot. Suddenly she really didn't want anything to happen to Winston Kellogg. 'Just be careful. I lost sight of him. He was on the beach, but he's in the rocks now.' Dance stood up, scanning the beach. Where was he?

She found out a second later. A bullet slammed into the rocks not far from her. Samantha screamed, and Dance dropped to cover, furious that she'd presented a target.

'Kathryn,' Kellogg called on the radio, 'are you firing?'

'No, that was Pell. We're fine.'

'Where did it come from?'

'I couldn't see. Win, you could walk right into a trap.'

'Hold on. I think I see something. I'll call you back.'

'Wait . . . Win, are you there?'

Moving some distance away, she looked out between two rocks. Couldn't see a thing. Then she noticed Winston Kellogg making his way towards the beach. Against the massive rocks, the expanse of ocean, he seemed so fragile.

Please . . . Dance sent him a silent message to stop, to wait.

But, of course, he kept on moving.

DANIEL PELL KNEW more cops were on their way. But he was confident that there were just two or three immediate pursuers. They must have stopped at the cabin, seen the dead deputies, then pursued him. And it seemed that only one was actually nearby.

He closed his eyes momentarily against the pain. He pressed the stab wound, which had opened in the fall down the rocks.

He wondered if one of the pursuers was Kathryn Dance. Well, one way or the other, she wasn't going to be a threat too much longer.

The cop pursuing him was getting close. There were only two approaches to where he now was, a rocky inlet near the beach. Whoever came after him would either have to climb down a twenty-foot-high exposed rock face or— taking the path—would turn a sharp corner and be a perfect target.

Pell hunkered down and waited, resting the gun on a boulder.

He wouldn't shoot to kill. He'd wound. And then, when he was down, blind him with the knife. He'd leave the radio nearby so the cop would scream for help and distract the other officers. Pell could escape into a deserted area of the park.

He heard someone approaching, trying to be quiet. But Pell had hearing like a wild animal. He curled his hand round his gun.

The emotion was gone. Rebecca and Jennie and Kathryn Dance were far from his thoughts. He was in perfect control.

DANCE, in yet another spot on the ridge, looked out fast.

Winston Kellogg was on the beach now, close to where Pell must have been when he'd fired at her. The agent was moving slowly, gun in both hands. Seeming to notice marks in the sand, he crouched and moved closer to them, pausing at an outcropping.

'What's going on?' Samantha asked.

Dance shook her head. She looked down at Linda, who had lost a lot of blood, and called MCSO and asked for the status of the troops.

'First tac responders in five minutes.'

Dance sighed. Why was it taking the cavalry so damn long? She glanced out again and saw Winston Kellogg ease round the rock, which was glistening burgundy in the low sun.

A long minute passed. Two. Where was he? What—?

The boom of an explosion.

What the hell was that?

A series of gunshots, a pause, then more pistol cracks.

'What happened?' Samantha called.

'I don't know.' Dance got her radio out. 'Win! Are you there?'

But the only sounds she heard were the rush of the waves and the edgy cries of the frightened, fleeing gulls.

KATHRYN DANCE HURRIED ALONG the beach, her Aldo shoes ruined by the salt water. She didn't care.

Behind her, back on the ridge, medical technicians were trundling Linda to an ambulance, Samantha with her. Dance nodded to two MCSO officers, ringing yellow tape from rock to rock, though the only intruder to trouble the crime scene would be the rising tide. Dance ducked under it and turned the corner, continuing to the scene of the death.

She paused. Then walked straight up to Winston Kellogg and hugged him. He seemed shaken and kept staring at what lay in front of them.

Daniel Pell was on his back, his sand-stained knees in the air, arms out to the sides. His pistol lay where it had flown from his hand. His eyes were partly open, intensely blue no longer but hazy in death.

Dance realised that her hand remained on Kellogg's back. She dropped it and stepped aside. 'What happened?' she asked.

'He was hiding there.' He pointed out a stand of rocks. 'I saw him just in time. I pitched a flash-bang his way, and he started shooting. I was lucky. The sun blinded him, I guess. I returned fire.'

'You're OK?'

'Oh, sure.' He shrugged. 'Little scraped up from the rocks.'

One of the CS officers said to Kellogg, 'Hey, congrats.'

The FBI agent smiled noncommittally.

A smile, kinesics experts know, is the most elusive signal that the human face generates. A frown, a perplexed gaze or an amorous glance means only one thing. A smile, though, can telegraph hate, indifference, humour or love.

Dance wasn't sure exactly what this smile meant. But she noticed that an instant later, as he stared at the man he'd just killed, the expression vanished, as if it had never existed.

DANCE STOPPED BY Monterey Bay Hospital to see Linda, who was conscious and doing well. Then the agent drove Samantha to the Point Lobos Inn. Sam's husband was on his way to pick her up, and, whatever the outcome, she was determined to tell him everything.

Dance returned to CBI, where Theresa Croyton Bolling and her aunt stood by their car, apparently awaiting her return to say goodbye. The girl's face brightened when she saw Dance. They greeted each other warmly.

'We heard,' the aunt said, unsmiling. 'He's dead?'

'That's right.' Dance gave them the details of the incident at Point Lobos. Theresa nodded and took the news unemotionally.

'We can't thank you enough. What you did saved lives,' the agent said. 'You're driving back tonight?'

'Yeah,' the girl said. 'And Mr Nagle's going to come to Napa and interview me. For that book. *The Sleeping Doll*. That's the title. Isn't it weird having a book written about you?'

Dance hugged Theresa, shook her aunt's hand and wished them a safe trip. Five minutes later she was back in her office.

She kicked off the damaged Aldos and dug in her closet for sandals. Then she stretched and sat, searching through her desk for a pack of M&Ms she'd stashed there. She ate them quickly, looking at the pictures of her children.

Her phone chirped. She glanced at the screen, and her stomach did a small jump, relieved. 'Hi,' she said to Michael O'Neil.

'Hey. Just got the news. You OK? Heard there were rounds exchanged.'

'Pell parked one near me. That's all.'

Dance gave him the details. She was glad to hear his voice, but something was off. He wasn't overly pleased to be speaking to her. She wished that the rough seas between them would calm.

She asked, 'You all right?'

'Fine,' he said.

She suggested he come by the Deck that night.

'Can't, sorry. Anne and I have plans. Anyway, better go.'

'Sure, take care.'

Ten minutes later, Winston Kellogg appeared in the door. She gestured towards the chair, and he dropped down into it, his clothes still muddy and sandy. He saw her salt-stained shoes and laughed. 'Probably nothing in your closet there that'd work for me.'

'Sorry,' she answered, deadpan. 'They're all a size six.'

They discussed the reports that needed to be completed. She realised that, whether or not he asked her out, he'd stay for four or five days; a shooting review board could take that long to hear testimony.

. . . afterwards. How does that sound?

Like Dance herself a few minutes ago, Kellogg stretched. His face gave a very faint signal—he was troubled. It would be the shoot-out, of course.

Dance had never even fired her weapon at a suspect, and here Kellogg had killed twice in a relatively short period of time.

'So what's next for you?' she asked.

'I'm giving a seminar in Washington, then some time off. If the real world cooperates, of course.' He slouched and closed his eyes.

In his smudged slacks, and with floppy hair and a bit of five-o'clock shadow, he was really an appealing man.

'Sorry,' he said, opening his eyes and laughing. 'Bad form to fall asleep in colleagues' offices.' He paused. 'Oh, one thing. I've got paperwork tonight, but tomorrow can I hold you to that dinner date? It *is* afterwards, remember?'

She said, 'You know, tomorrow'd be great.'

AT HOME, after pancakes with Wes and Maggie, Dance spent the next few hours fielding phone calls, including one from Morton Nagle, thanking her again for what she'd done for his family.

Michael O'Neil did not call.

Rebecca Sheffield was in stable condition after surgery. She'd be in the hospital, under guard, for six or seven days.

Dance found a Wallace and Gromit Claymation tape, cued it up, and was pouring popcorn into a bowl when her phone rang yet again.

'Boss, who's getting all the stuff? Evidence, reports, everything, the ball of wax?' TJ meant for the final disposition report. It would be massive in this case, with the multiple felonies and the interagency paperwork.

'Me. Well, I should say *us*.'

'I liked the first answer better, Boss. Oh, by the way, remember "Nimue"? I just found another reference to it. I'll follow up, OK?'

Friday
Chapter 13

Kathryn Dance, in a black suit and burgundy cotton sweater—not the warmest of outfits—was sitting outside at the Bay View Restaurant near Fisherman's Wharf in Monterey.

The place lived up to its name, offering a postcard image of the coast all the way up to Santa Cruz, which was, however, invisible at the moment. The morning was a perfect example of June Gloom on the Peninsula. Fog like smoke from a damp fire surrounded the wharf. The temperature was fifty-five degrees.

Last night she'd been in an elated mood. Daniel Pell had been stopped; Linda would be all right; Nagle and his family had survived. She and Winston Kellogg had made plans.

Today, though, things were different. A darkness hung over her, and it had nothing to do with the weather. There were many things contributing to it, not the least of which was planning the memorial services and funerals for the deputies killed at the Point Lobos Inn.

'Hello.' Winston Kellogg came up behind her, slipped his arm round her shoulders and kissed her on the cheek. She smiled and hugged him.

He sat down. Dance waved to the waitress, who refilled her coffee cup and poured one for Kellogg.

'So I was doing some research,' he said. 'I thought we could go down to Big Sur tonight. Someplace called Ventana.'

'I haven't been for years. It's wonderful. Bit of a drive.'

'I'm game. Highway One, right?'

Which would take them right past Point Lobos. She flashed back to the gunshots, the blood, Daniel Pell lying on his back.

'Thanks for getting up so early,' Dance said.

'Breakfast *and* dinner with you. The pleasure's mine.'

She gave him another smile. 'Here's the situation. We finally found the answer to Nimue, I think. But we need your help. TJ found a file on Jennie Marston's computer. The name was'—Dance found a slip of paper and read—'"Nimue—cult suicide in LA".'

'What was inside?'

'That's the problem. He tried to open it, but it's password-protected. We'll send it to CBI headquarters in Sacramento to crack, but frankly that'll take weeks. It might not be important, but I was hoping you'd have somebody in the Bureau who could decrypt it faster.'

Kellogg knew of a computer wiz in the San Jose field office. 'If anybody can break it, they can. I'll get it to him today.'

She thanked him and handed over the Dell, in a plastic bag and with a chain-of-custody tag attached. He signed the card.

Dance waved for the waitress. Toast was about all she could manage this morning, but Kellogg ordered a full breakfast.

He said, 'Now, Big Sur. It's supposed to be pretty.'

'Breathtaking,' she said. 'One of the most romantic places you'll ever see.'

DANCE WAS IN HER OFFICE when Kellogg came to collect her at five thirty for their date. He was in formal casual. He and Dance came close to matching—brown jackets, light shirts and jeans. Ventana was an upscale restaurant, but this was, after all, California.

'First, let's get work out of the way.' He opened his attaché case and handed her the plastic evidence bag containing the computer.

'Oh, you've got it already,' she said. 'The mystery of Nimue is about to be solved.'

He grimaced. 'Afraid not, sorry.'

'Nothing?' she asked.

'The file had a wipe bomb on it.'

'Wipe bomb?'

'Like a digital booby trap. When TJ tried to open it, it turned to mush, my guys said. Just random characters.'

'No way to reconstruct it?'

'Nope. And, believe me, they're the best in the business.'

Dance shrugged. 'Not that it matters that much, I suppose.'

He smiled. 'So are you ready to go?'

'Just a second or two.' She walked to the door and nodded.

Massive Albert Stemple stepped into the office, with TJ right behind him. Both men drew their weapons, and in a few seconds Winston Kellogg was disarmed, cuffs on his hands.

'What the hell's going on?' he raged.

Dance provided the answer. 'Winston Kellogg, you're under arrest for the murder of Daniel Pell.'

THEY WERE IN interrogation room 3, and it was Dance's favourite. It had a small window, and if the curtains were open you could see a tree outside. Today the curtain was closed.

Dance and Kellogg were alone. Behind the mirror, the video camera was set up and running. TJ was there, along with Charles Overby, both unseen, though the mirror, of course, implied observers.

Winston Kellogg had declined an attorney and was willing to talk. Which he did in an eerily calm voice. 'Kathryn, let's just step back here, can we? Is that all right? I don't know what you think is going on, but this isn't the way to handle it. Believe me.'

The subtext of these words was arrogance—and the corollary, betrayal. She tried to push the pain away as she replied simply, 'Let's get started.'

'Maybe you've got bad information. Why don't you tell me what you *think* the problem is, and we'll see what's really going on?'

As if he were talking to a child.

She looked Winston Kellogg over closely. It's an interrogation just like any other, Dance told herself. Though it wasn't, of course. Here was a man who'd lied to her personally. Someone she'd felt romantic towards. Someone who'd used her.

Then she forced aside her own emotion, hard though that was, and concentrated on the task in front of her. She was going to break him. Nothing would stop her.

As she knew him well by now, the analysis unfolded quickly in her mind.

First, how should he be categorised in the context of the crime? A suspect in a homicide.

Second, does he have a motive to lie? Yes.

Third, what's his personality type? Extroverted, thinking, sensing, judging. She could be as tough with him as she needed to be.

Fourth, what is his liar's personality? A manipulator. He's intelligent, has a good memory, is adept at the techniques of deception, and will use all those skills to create lies that work to his advantage. He'll give up lying if he's caught, and use other weapons to shift the blame, threaten or attack. He'll demean and patronise, trying to unnerve her and exploit her own emotional responses, a dark mirror image of her own mission as an interrogator. He'll try to get information to use against me later.

You had to be very careful with manipulators.

The next step in her kinesic analysis would be to determine what response state he fell into when lying—anger, denial, depression or bargaining—and to probe his story when she recognised one.

But here was the problem. She was one of the best kinesics analysts in the country, yet she hadn't spotted Kellogg's lies. He was, she decided, in that rare class of individuals virtually immune to kinesic analysts, including subjects like the mentally ill and serial killers. And zealots. Which was what she now believed he was. Not the leader of a cult, but someone just as fanatical and just as dangerous, a man convinced of his own righteousness.

She needed to break him. So she attacked. Hard. Fast.

'Winston, Pell didn't write anything about Nimue or suicides. I created that file last night.'

He could only stare at her.

She said, 'Nimue was a red herring. TJ did find a reference, but it was just an interview with an Alison Sharpe in a Montana paper—"My Month with Daniel Pell", something like that. They met in San Francisco when she was living in a group like the Family and going by the name Nimue. The leader named everyone after Arthurian characters. She and Pell hitchhiked around the state but she left him after he was picked up in Redding on that murder charge. He probably didn't know her surname and searched the only names he knew—Alison and Nimue—to find her. And probably kill her because she knew where his mountaintop was.'

'So you faked this file and asked me to help you crack it. Why the masquerade, Kathryn?'

'I'll tell you why. Body language isn't limited to the living, you know You can read a lot into a *corpse*'s posture too. Last night I was looking over the crime-scene pictures from Point Lobos. Pell wasn't hiding behind the rocks. He was out in the open, on his back, and there were water and sand stains on both his knees. People *crouch* when they're fighting. Why would he leave cover, get down on both knees, and shoot at you?'

'I don't know what you're talking about.'

'And the coroner's report said that from the downward angle of the bullets, you were standing full height, not crouching. And I remembered the sequence of sounds: the flash-bang went off, and then, after a delay, I heard the shots. I think that you saw where he was, tossed the flash-bang and moved in fast, disarmed him. Then had him kneel and tossed your cuffs on the ground. When he was reaching for them, you shot him.'

'Ridiculous.'

'And the flash-bang? After the assault at Sea View you were supposed to check all the ordnance back in. That's standard procedure. Why keep it? Because you were waiting for a chance to move in and kill him.' She held up a hand. 'I got your file from a friend of my husband's on Ninth Street. You'd been involved in the shooting deaths of suspected cult leaders during attempts to apprehend. And two cult leaders died of suicides under suspicious circumstances when you were consulting in their investigations.

'So I had to test you, Winston. I wrote the document in that file. It was a fake email that suggested a girl with the name of Nimue was in the LA suicide victim's cult and had information that the death was suspicious. I put a simple Windows password on the file and handed over the computer. If you'd told me you'd read the file, that would've been the end of the matter. You and I'd be on our way to Big Sur right now.

'But no, you read the file and destroyed it yourself. You were afraid we'd catch on to the fact that for six years you've been travelling around the country and murdering people like Daniel Pell.'

Kellogg gave a laugh. Now faint kinesic deviation; the tone was different. 'Please, Kathryn. Why on earth would I do that?'

'Because of your daughter,' she said, not without sympathy.

The fact that he gave no response, merely held her eye as if in pain, was a tiny indication that she was narrowing in on the truth.

'Your daughter did die in a car accident, yes, but you apparently destroyed the Seattle police report. TJ and I pieced together the story.

'When she was sixteen, your daughter ran away from home because you and your wife were getting divorced. She ended up with a group in Seattle—very much like the Family. She and three other members died in a suicide pact because the leader told them to leave; they hadn't been loyal enough. They drove their car into Puget Sound.

'Then you joined the MVCC and made it your life's work to stop people like that. Only sometimes the law didn't cooperate. You had to take it into your own hands. I wondered why you wanted to be first through the door at the Sea View. The answer is so that you'd have a clear shot at Pell. And yesterday, at Point Lobos, you got him on his knees. And you killed him.'

'That's your evidence that I murdered him? His posture? Really, Kathryn.'

'And MCSO crime scene found the bullet of the slug you fired at me on the ridge. You wanted to keep me there so I wouldn't interfere.'

'It was an accidental discharge,' Kellogg said matter-of-factly. 'Careless of me. I should've owned up, but it was embarrassing.'

Lie . . .

Under her gaze, his shoulders dipped slightly. His lips tightened. Dance knew there'd be no confession, but he did shift into a different stress state. He wasn't a completely emotionless machine, it seemed.

'I don't talk about my past and what happened with my daughter. I should've shared more with you, maybe, but you don't talk about your husband much either, I notice.' He fell silent for a moment. 'Look, Kathryn, these people have to be stopped. I'm aggressive about it; I get results. But I don't cross the line.'

'You don't cross *your* line, Winston. But it's not your own standards you have to apply. Daniel Pell never thought he was doing anything wrong either.'

He gave her a smile and a shrug, the emblem gesture, which she took to mean, You see it your way, I see it mine. But to Dance it was as clear as saying, 'I'm guilty.'

Then the smile faded, 'One thing,' he said. 'Us? That was real. Whatever else you think about me, that was real.'

As a kinesic analyst, she could see his comment was absolutely honest. But it was also not worth the breath to respond to.

Dance knew it was the end of the interrogation. But she had her answers, she had the truth—or at least an approximation of it. Which, according to the elusive science of kinesic analysis and interrogation, is usually enough.

DANCE AND TJ were in Charles Overby's office. The CBI chief sat behind his desk looking at his desk clock. It was 8.30 p.m. Two straight nights the agent in charge had been working late. A record.

'I saw the interview. You got some good stuff. But he was pretty slick. Didn't really admit anything. Hardly a confession.'

'He's a manipulator with an antisocial personality, Charles. He's not the sort to confess. I was just probing to see how he'd structure the denials. He destroyed computer files when he thought they implicated him in a suspicious suicide? He used unauthorised ordnance? His gun went off accidentally in my direction? A jury'd laugh all the way to a guilty verdict. He'll be a good defendant—*if* he takes the stand. But tactically his case is hopeless.'

'He was arresting an armed killer. And you're claiming that his motive is that his daughter died because of some cult thing? That's not compelling.'

'I never worry too much about motive. Murder's murder. It'll become a lot less soap opera when we link Kellogg to the others who've been killed.'

Dance told him about other deaths. The takedown in Chicago last week had been suspicious, and there were others, in Fort Worth and New York. The two suicides. One troubling case in Florida.

'What about forensics from the beach?' her boss asked.

'The slug fired at Kathryn conclusively matches his SIG,' TJ said.

Overby grunted. 'Accidental discharge . . . Relax, Kathryn. Somebody's got to be the devil's advocate here.'

'The shell casings from Pell's gun were found closer to Kellogg's position than Pell's. Kellogg probably fired Pell's weapon himself to make it look like self-defence. Look, Charles, I'm not saying it'll be a shoe-in, but Sandoval can win it. The pose of the body's clear.'

'Our motive for bringing the case? It'll come up, you know.'

'Winston Kellogg murdered someone within our jurisdiction.'

Overby's phone rang. He answered. When he hung up, he straightened his tie. 'We've got visitors. The FBI's here.'

'CHARLES, KATHRYN . . .'

Amy Grabe took the coffee cup offered by Overby's assistant and sat. She gave a nod to TJ.

Dance chose an upright chair near the attractive but no-nonsense special agent in charge of the San Francisco field office, and proceeded to tell her the details about Kellogg.

Grabe knew some, but not all, of the tale. She frowned as she listened, motionless. Her right arm rested on the opposite sleeve of her stylish suit.

Dance made her case. 'He's an active duty agent killing these people, Amy. He lied to us. He staged a dynamic entry when there was no need to. Some people could've been killed.'

Overby's pen bounced like a drumstick, and TJ's kinesics read: OK now, *this* is an awkward moment.

Grabe's eyes, beneath perfect brows, scanned the room. 'It's all very complicated and difficult. I understand that. But whatever happened, they'd like him released.'

'They—Ninth Street?'

She nodded. 'And higher. Kellogg's a star. Great collar record. Saved hundreds of people from these cults. Now I talked to them, and they'll have an inquiry. Look into the takedowns, to see if he used excessive force.'

'Look into them?' Dance asked, her voice incredulous. 'We're talking questionable deaths, Amy. Oh, please. It's a vendetta. And who knows what else he's done.'

'Kathryn,' her boss warned.

The FBI agent said, 'He's a federal agent investigating crimes in which the perps are particularly dangerous. In some instances, they've been killed resisting. Happens all the time.'

'Pell *wasn't* resisting. He was murdered. My concern is presenting a single homicide case to Sandy Sandoval, whether Washington likes it or not.'

Tap, tap . . . The pen bounced, and Overby cleared his throat.

'It's not even a great case,' Grabe pointed out. She'd apparently read all the details on her flight to the Peninsula. She levelled hard eyes at Overby. 'Charles, they've asked that you don't pursue it.'

Overby looked down at his desk. 'It's a tough situation.'

Grabe said in a soft tone, 'Kathryn, Daniel Pell was a dangerous man. He killed law enforcers, and he killed innocents. You've done a great job in an impossible situation. You stopped an evil-doer. And Kellogg contributed to that. It's a gold star for everybody.'

'Absolutely,' Overby said. He set down the bouncing pen. 'You know what this reminds me of, Amy? Jack Ruby killing Kennedy's assassin. I don't think anybody had a problem with Ruby gunning Oswald down.'

Dance's jaw closed, her teeth pressing together firmly.

'Exactly,' Grabe said. 'So—'

Overby held up a hand. 'But a funny thing about that case.'

'What case?' the FBI agent asked.

'The Ruby case. Texas *arrested* him for murder. And guess what? Jack Ruby got convicted and sent to jail.' A shrug. 'Amy, I'm submitting the Kellogg case to the Monterey County Prosecutor. I'm going to recommend indictment for murder. Oh, and aggravated assault on a CBI agent. Kellogg did take a shot at Kathryn, after all.'

Dance felt her heart thud. TJ glanced at her with a raised eyebrow.

Overby was looking at Dance. 'And we should go for misuse of legal process and lying to an investigative agent. Kathryn, what do you think?'

Those hadn't occurred to her. 'Excellent.'

Grabe rubbed her cheek. 'Do you really think this is a good idea, Charles?'

'Oh, I do. Absolutely.'

Saturday
Chapter 14

Tears pooling in her eyes, a woman lay on the bed of the cheap transient hotel off Del Monte, near Highway 1. Listening to the hiss of traffic, she was staring at the ceiling.

She wished she could stop crying. But she couldn't.

Because he was dead. Her Daniel was gone.

Jennie Marston touched her head, which stung furiously under the sticking plaster. She kept replaying the last few hours of their time together, Thursday. Standing on the beach south of Carmel, as he held the rock in the shape of Jasmine, her mother's cat, the one thing her mother would never hurt.

She recalled Daniel gripping the rock, turning it over and over.

'That's exactly what I was thinking, lovely. It looks just like a cat.' Then he'd held her tighter and whispered, 'I was watching the news.'

'Oh, back at the motel?'

'That's right. Lovely, the police found out about you.'

'About—?' She'd started shaking.

'Your name. They know who you are.'

'They do? Oh, no. Daniel, sweetheart, I'm sorry.' She'd started shaking.

'You left something in the room, right?'

Then she remembered. The email. It was in her jeans. In a weak voice, she said, 'It was the first one where you said you loved me. I couldn't throw it out. I'm so sorry. I—'

'It's OK, lovely. But now we have to talk.'

'Sure, sweetheart,' she'd said, resigned to the worst. He was going to leave her. Make her go away.

But it seemed that one of the women in the Family was working with him to get another Family together and go to his mountaintop.

'You weren't supposed to be part of it, lovely, but when I got to know you, I knew I couldn't live without you. I'll talk to Rebecca. She's . . . difficult. But eventually she'll do what I say. You'll become friends.'

'I don't know.'

'You and me, lovely, we'll be the team. But now we have to be careful. The police know you. So you've got to disappear.'

'Disappear?'

'For a month or two. Oh, I don't like it either. I'll miss you.'

And she could see that he would.

'Everything'll work out. We're going to pretend that I killed you. I'm going to have to cut you a little. They'll think I hit you with the rock and threw you into the ocean. It'll hurt.'

'If it means we can be together, it's OK.'

'Sit down here. Hold my leg tight. It'll hurt less that way.'

The pain was terrible, but she bit down on her sleeve and squeezed his leg hard and managed not to scream as the knife cut and the blood flowed.

He gave her the address of a place to stay in San Francisco, a transient hotel on Sutter. He'd call her when it was safe.

They'd driven to where he'd hidden the blue Ford Focus stolen at Moss Landing, and he gave her the keys and said goodbye. She'd got a room in this cheap hotel, and just as she'd turned on the TV, she'd seen on the news that he'd been shot dead at Point Lobos.

She'd screamed into the pillow, beaten the mattress with her bony hands. Finally she'd sobbed herself into a tortured sleep. Then she'd woken and lain in bed, staring at the ceiling, her eyes flicking from one corner to the other. Endlessly. The compulsive gazing.

Jennie knew she had to get up, get moving. The police were looking for her—she'd seen her driver's licence picture on TV. Yet for the past few hours, as she lay on the bed, she'd felt something curious within her. A sudden change, like the first frost of autumn. She wondered what the feeling was. Then she understood.

Anger. She was angry. Her hands shook, and her breath came fast. And then, though the fury remained, she found herself calm.

Cold, hard anger, that's what Jennie felt within her heart.

Teeth set, heart pounding, she walked into the bathroom and took a shower. She sat at the cheap desk in front of a mirror and put on her makeup. She looked at herself. And she liked what she saw.

She was thinking back to Thursday, as they'd stood beside the Focus, Jennie crying, hugging Daniel hard.

'I'll miss you *so* much, sweetie,' she said.

Then his voice had lowered. 'Now, lovely, I've got to go make sure our mountaintop is safe. But there's one thing you need to do. Remember when I needed you to help me with that woman in the trunk?'

She nodded. 'You . . . you want me to help you do something like that?'

His blue eyes staring into hers. 'I don't want you to *help*. I need you to do it yourself. If you don't, we'll never have peace; we'll never be together.'

She slowly nodded. He handed her the pistol he'd taken from the deputy guarding James Reynolds's house, and showed her how to use it. Jennie was surprised at how easy it was.

Now, feeling the splintery anger within her, Jennie shook out the contents of a small shopping bag. There was the gun, her remaining money, some personal effects, and the other thing Daniel had given her: a slip of paper. Jennie opened the note and stared at the names and addresses.

He'd smiled as he'd slipped the gun into the bag and handed it to her. 'Be patient, lovely. Take your time.'

LEAVING HEADQUARTERS, Dance headed down to the Point Lobos Inn to see about transferring the bill from Kellogg's credit card to the CBI's own account.

Overby had whined mightily about the expenditure, of course, but there was a conflict of interest in having a criminal defendant pay for expenses to help out the very institution that had arrested him.

As she was driving, Dance listened to some Celtic music. The melody was haunting, which seemed appropriate en route to the location where people had died.

The bad weather had returned. Dance saw only one car behind her on the road, a blue sedan trailing behind her half a mile.

Dance turned off and headed to the Point Lobos Inn. She glanced at her phone. Still no message from O'Neil. Dance could call him on the pretence of a case, but it was probably better to keep some distance.

She parked, went into the office and took care of the paperwork.

As she was returning to the car, she was aware of a woman nearby, looking out into the mists towards the ocean, her jacket fluttering in the breeze. As Dance walked on, the woman fell into pace not far behind.

A blue car was parked nearby. It was familiar. Was this the driver who'd been behind her? It was a blue Ford Focus, and Dance recalled that the vehicle stolen at Moss Landing had never been recovered. Were there any other loose ends that—?

At that moment, the woman walked up to her quickly and called, a harsh voice over the wind, 'Are you Kathryn Dance?'

Surprised, the agent turned. 'That's right. Do I know you?'

The woman continued until she was a few feet away. She took off her sunglasses, revealing a familiar face, though Dance couldn't place it.

'We've never met. But we kind of know each other. I'm Daniel Pell's girlfriend.'

'You're—' Dance gasped.

'Jennie Marston.'

Dance's hand dropped to her pistol.

But before she touched the weapon's grip, Jennie said, 'I want to turn myself in.' She held her wrists out, apparently for the handcuffs. A considerate gesture Dance had never seen in all her years as a law-enforcement agent.

'I WAS SUPPOSED to kill you.'

This news didn't alarm her as much as it might, considering that Jennie's hands were cuffed, and Dance had found no weapons on her or in the car.

'He gave me a gun, but it's back at the motel. Really, I'd never hurt you.'

She didn't seem capable of it, true.

'He said no policeman had ever gotten into his mind like you had. He was afraid of you.'

'So he faked your death?'

'He cut me.' Jennie displayed a sticking plaster on the back of her head. 'Your head bleeds a *lot*. Then he gave me your address and your parents'. I was supposed to kill you. He knew you'd never let him get away.'

'You agreed?'

'I didn't really say anything one way or the other. He just assumed I would. I'd always done what he wanted. He wanted me to kill you and come live with him and Rebecca somewhere. We'd start a new Family.'

'You knew about Rebecca?'

'He told me.' In a wisp of a voice: 'Did she write the emails to me? Pretending to be him?'

'Yes.'

Her lips pressed together tightly. 'They didn't sound like the way he talked. But I didn't want to ask.'

'How did you get here? Did you follow me?'

'That's right. I wanted to talk to you in person. I thought if I just turned myself in, they'd take me right to jail. But I had to ask. Were you there when he was shot? Did he say anything?'

'No, I'm sorry.'

'Oh. I was just wondering.' Her lips tightened, a kinesic clue to remorse. Then a glance at Dance. 'I didn't mean to scare you.'

'I've had worse scares lately,' Dance told her. 'Why didn't you run, though? You could've gotten to Mexico or Canada.'

'I guess I just got out from underneath his spell. I thought we'd developed this real connection. But then I figured that was all a lie. Just like my husband and boyfriends. All my life I've had this idea I was like a flashlight and men were the batteries. I couldn't shine without one. But then after Daniel was killed, I was in this motel room, and all of a sudden, I got mad. It was weird. And I knew I had to do something about it. But not moaning about Daniel, not going out and finding a new man. No, I wanted to do something for *me*. And what's the best thing I could do for me? Get arrested.' She gave a laugh. 'Sounds stupid, but it's my decision. Nobody else's.'

'I think that's a good one.'

Dance escorted Jennie back to her Taurus. As they drove to Salinas, she mentally tallied up the charges. Arson, felony, murder, conspiracy, harbouring a fugitive, several others.

Still, the woman had surrendered voluntarily and appeared as contrite as they came. Dance would interview her later, and if Jennie was as sincere as she seemed, she'd go to bat for her with Sandoval.

At the lockup in the courthouse, Dance processed her into the system. 'Is there anybody you want me to call?' she asked.

'No. I think it's best, you know, just to start over. I'm fine.'

'They'll get you a lawyer; then maybe you and I could spend some more time talking.'

'Sure.'

And she was led down the very hallway her lover had escaped down almost one week before.

THE EVENING SKY was clear, the fog busy elsewhere.

Kathryn was on the Deck alone, though the dogs were nearby, roaming the back yard. She was sipping a German beer while listening to 'A Prairie Home Companion'. When the variety show concluded, she shut off the radio and heard in its stead the distant sound track of Maggie playing scales and the faint bass of Coldplay on Wes's stereo.

Dance walked into her bedroom, pushed aside the sea of shoes and found her forty-year-old Martin 00-18 guitar. She carried it out to the Deck, sat down, and with fingers clumsy from lack of practice, tuned up and started to play. First, some scales and arpeggios, then the Bob Dylan song 'Tomorrow Is a Long Time'.

Her thoughts were meandering to the front seat of the CBI Taurus and Winston Kellogg.

As she played, she noticed motion inside the house. Dance saw her son beeline to the refrigerator and cart a cookie and glass of milk back into his room. The raid took all of thirty seconds.

She found herself thinking that she'd been treating Wes's attitude as a flaw to be fixed. Maybe she'd been taking him for granted. Here I am, she thought, a kinesic expert, establishing baselines and looking for deviations from them as signals that something's not right.

With Winston Kellogg, was I deviating from my own baseline?

Maybe the boy's reaction was a clue that she had.

She was halfway through a Paul Simon song, humming the melody, not sure of the lyrics, when she heard the creak of the gate leading up to the Deck.

The instrument went silent as she glanced over to see Michael O'Neil breach the stairs. He was wearing the grey and maroon sweater she'd bought for him when she'd been skiing in Colorado a year ago.

'Hey,' he said. 'Intruding?'

'Never.'

'Anne's got an opening in an hour. But I thought I'd stop by first, say hi.'

'Glad you did.'

He pulled a beer from the fridge and got another for her. He sat down next to her. The Beck's snapped open crisply.

She started playing an old Celtic tune. O'Neil said nothing, just drank the beer and nodded with the rhythm. His eyes, she noticed, were turned towards the ocean, though the view was obscured by lush pines. When she finished, they sat in silence for a moment.

Then O'Neil said, 'Heard about Winston Kellogg. Never would have called that one.'

Word travels fast.

'Yep.'

'TJ gave me all the gruesome details.' He shook his head and gestured for Dylan and Patsy. The dogs bounded over. He handed out Milk Bones from a cookie jar that sat beside a bottle of tequila. He said, 'Sounds like it'll be a tough case. Pressure from Washington to drop it, I'll bet.'

'Oh, yeah. Uphill all the way.'

'If you're interested, we might want to make some calls.'

'Chicago, Miami or LA?'

O'Neil blinked, then gave a laugh. 'You've been considering it too, hmm? What's the strongest?'

Dance replied, 'I'd go with LA. It's in state, so CBI's got jurisdiction?' She'd decided that if Kellogg got off the hook on the Pell killing, which was a possibility, she wouldn't let the matter rest there. She'd pursue the case against him in other venues.

And apparently, she wasn't going to do it alone.

'Good,' O'Neil said. 'Let's get together tomorrow, look over the evidence.'

She nodded.

The detective finished the beer and got another one. 'I don't suppose Overby would spring for a trip to LA.'

'Believe it or not, I think he would.'

'Really?'

'If we fly coach.'

'And standby,' O'Neil added. They laughed.

'Any requests?' She tapped the old Martin, which resounded like a crisp drum.

'Nope.' He leaned back and stretched his scuffed shoes out in front of him. 'Whatever you're in the mood for.'

Kathryn Dance thought for a moment and began to play.

JEFFERY DEAVER

Born: 1950, Chicago
Homes: California and North Carolina
Books in print: 20 million worldwide

RD: Did you always want to become a writer?
JD: Yes. I wrote my first 'book' at age eleven.
RD: How did your first writing get into print?
JD: I was a reporter for the school newspaper and editor of my high-school literary magazine.
RD: How do you find fresh story ideas?
JD: I'm often asked where the ideas for my books come from. To answer that I have to describe what I think is my responsibility as a thriller writer: to give my readers the most exciting roller-coaster ride of a suspense story I can possibly think of. This means that, rather than looking through newspapers or magazines for inspiration, I spend much of my time during the early stages sitting in a dark room and trying to think up a story line that features strong (though possibly flawed) heroes, sick and twisted bad guys, deadlines every few chapters, a short time frame for the entire story (eight to forty-eight hours or so), lots of surprising plot twists and turns and plenty of cliffhangers.

RD: Does writing come easily to you?
JD: I wouldn't say it comes easily to me but I thoroughly enjoy doing it so I'm lucky in that sense. I revise a great deal. My publisher doesn't even get a peek at my manuscript until I've revised it at least twenty or thirty times (and I mean major revisions).

RD: Where do you like to write?
JD: I write pretty much anywhere—on planes, in hotel rooms, anywhere in my house. (My office sometimes gets so cluttered I end up working in the kitchen. When the kitchen goes, it's up to my bedroom. And so on. I wish I had a bigger house.) I like the writing area to be silent, or with jazz or classical accompaniment occasionally, and either windowless or shaded. When it comes time to write the book itself I'll shut the lights out, picture the scene I'm about to write, then close my eyes and go at it.

RD: Are there any books about writing you would recommend? Did you take writing classes?
JD: I never took classes. There aren't any books that I would recommend. The best way to learn about writing is to study the work of writers you admire.

RD: Do you ever have 'writer's block'?

JD: I've often said that there's no such thing as writer's block; the problem is 'idea block'. If you have a craftsman's command of the language and basic writing techniques you'll be able to write—as long as you know what you want to say. This is not to belittle the affliction, of course, because figuring out what you want to communicate can be one hell of a daunting task. When I find myself frozen it's usually because I'm trying to shoehorn an idea into a passage or story where it has no place. I ask myself: What am I trying to say? If I can't answer that, or if the answer doesn't enhance the work, I back off and try another approach. Trying to write books in a genre or style you're not familiar with is the best way to find the Big Block looming.

RD: Why do you think forensics are so popular now in commercial fiction?

JD: The recent fascination, I think, reflects the shift in approach by law enforcement officials to embrace technology as wholeheartedly as the rest of the world. After all, a psychotic criminal can fool the best psychologists and lie detectors, but he can't beat a DNA match.

RD: How much of what you write comes from your real life experiences?

JD: In my case, none. I was an attorney but I practised corporate law. It means working harder to do the research but I don't really mind—I don't think I have what it takes to chase criminals through back alleys and wade through blood at crime scenes. Of course, all writers draw upon their personal experiences in describing day-to-day life and human relationships, but I tend to keep my own experiences largely separate from my stories.

RD: And how do you pick the settings for your books?

JD: Rule one: write about settings you're familiar with. If I'm setting a book outside of New York (where I lived for twenty years) or Northern Virginia or California (where I live now), I'll travel there and spend some weeks researching. I try to add some local colour and description, but also try not to go overboard—too much description can detract from the story.

RD: Why do you think so many lawyers and doctors become novelists?

JD: The easy answer is that writing novels is a lot more fun than practising law. But there is an analytical component—a left-brained component—to writing crime fiction that I think is an element of such professions as law, and medicine as well. For me a thriller is a very carefully structured story. I spend eight months outlining and researching the novel before I begin to write a single word. The skills I use to do that are the same I used when researching and structuring a legal document or case.

RD: What is the best advice about writing, and who gave it?

JD: Mickey Spillane: 'People don't read books to get to the middle. They read to get to the end.'

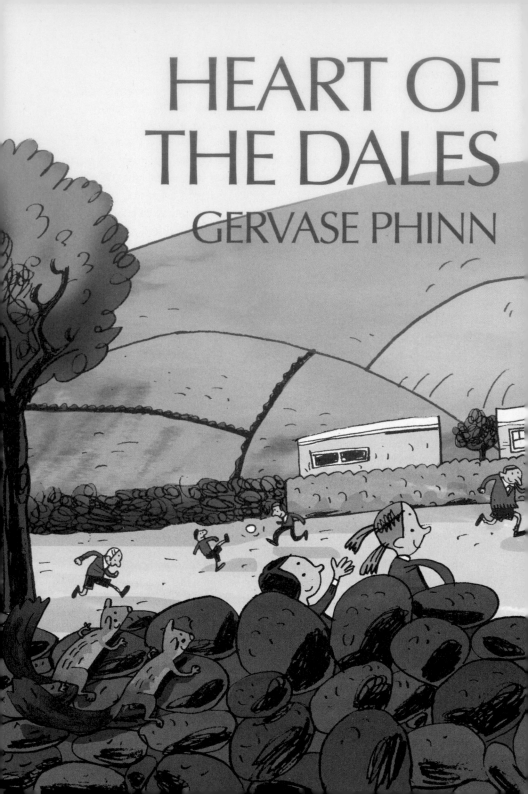

HEART OF
THE DALES

GERVASE PHINN

If there's one thing that Gervase Phinn has learned to expect during his years as a schools inspector, it's the unexpected. Whether he's dealing with inspiring, eccentric or incompetent teachers, or with lively young children, the job is always a challenge.

And never more so than when a child fixes him with a stare and asks, as they regularly do, 'What are you for?'

1

David Pritchard, the inspector for Mathematics, PE and Games, was in a rare good mood that Friday morning. It was during the schools' summer holidays and the two of us had been busily occupied for a good couple of hours packing up all our belongings in our old place of work, ready to take to the school inspectors' new office downstairs. We were having a break from our exertions and David, perched on the edge of a desk, was entertaining me with some amusing anecdotes related to his school visits the previous term.

'There was the occasion,' he said, smiling widely at the memory of the incident, 'when the teacher, in an effort to test the children in their numeracy skills, asked his class of nine-years-olds: "Now, children, if I laid eight eggs over here and nine eggs over there, what would I have?" "A bloody miracle," had come a muttered voice from the back of the room.'

David and I were both laughing uproariously—I just loved the things these young 'innocents' came out with—when a figure appeared at the door.

Mrs Brenda Savage, Personal Assistant to Dr Gore, the Chief Education Officer, stood framed in the doorway with the usual haughty expression on her carefully made-up face. She was dressed in a tailored grey tweed jacket, tight pencil skirt, cream silk blouse with a lace collar and black patent-leather shoes, and was garlanded in an assortment of expensive-looking jewellery.

'May I help you, Mrs Savage?' asked my colleague.

'Mr Pritchard,' she said, giving him a chilly look, 'I had assumed that by this time the school inspectors would have relocated themselves.'

'My dear Mrs Savage,' said David calmly, 'I have no desire to be impolite, much less disobliging, but we are in the very process of moving.'

'Well, as far as I can see, Mr Pritchard,' continued Mrs Savage, surveying the room, 'you haven't got very far. You have to vacate these premises by today so that the Social Services team can move in at the beginning of next week. It's on my schedule here.' She tapped a long scarlet-painted fingernail on the clipboard she held in front of her. 'I did send a memorandum.'

'Indeed you did, Mrs Savage,' replied David, 'I will vacate the office by the end of the day.' He returned to sorting through some papers on his desk.

She remained at the door, looking at David with a stern expression. Since starting my job as a school inspector some four years before, I had found Mrs Savage, as had my three colleagues, extremely prickly and sometimes downright objectionable. This dramatically good-looking widow of indeterminate age, always immaculately turned out, could be by turns rude and deferential, depending on the status of the person to whom she was talking. And it was clear she did not like talking to the school inspectors, whom she felt had far too much clout and influence.

Getting no further response from David, she now turned her frosty eye in my direction. 'Mr Phinn. May I have *your* assurance that this office will be cleared and available for the Social Services team by Monday morning?'

'You have my assurance, Mrs Savage,' I told her. 'The day is yet young.'

'It's just that there appears to be still so much to pack,' she said, glancing around the room. 'That corner area looks as if it hasn't been touched at all.'

'That's because it hasn't,' said David airily. 'That's Mr Clamp's domain. And he's away in Italy.'

'Away in Italy!' she exclaimed.

'Even school inspectors have holidays, Mrs Savage,' said David, looking up. 'As the inspector for Visual and Creative Arts, he is spending two *creative* weeks in Venice, Florence and Rome, where he is collecting material for next term's art courses. Then he is spending a third week in Sorrento.'

'But Mr Clamp should have kept this week free,' she said peevishly. 'And when will Mr Clamp be back, may I ask?'

'Mrs Savage,' sighed David, 'I am not my colleague's keeper. What he does is entirely his own concern.'

'But what about all his files and all these pictures and boxes?' Mrs Savage asked. 'They can't remain here.'

'Don't worry, Mrs Savage,' I said, 'we'll move his things for him.'

David gave a hollow laugh. '*We* most certainly will not!' he cried. 'I've got quite enough of my own stuff without lugging all Sidney's rubbish down two flights of stairs.'

'Well, this is most unsatisfactory,' said Mrs Savage. 'It is imperative that this room is cleared today.' She glanced at the only area of the room that was cleared. 'It's a pity that all the inspectors aren't as efficient and well organised as Dr Mullarkey. I notice that she has moved everything of hers.'

'We can't all be as efficient and well organised as the inspector for Science and Technology,' said David.

'More's the pity,' she muttered.

'Mrs Savage—' began David in a voice threatening to brim over with fury.

'Don't worry,' I interrupted, 'the room will be cleared by the end of the day.'

'I sincerely hope so,' she said. She gave a look like the sweep of a scythe and departed angrily in a whiff of Chanel No. 5.

'In all my years in education,' said David, removing his spectacles, 'I have never, never met such a pettifogging and infuriating person as Mrs Savage. Who does she think she is, swanning over here, speaking to us like an infants head teacher telling off some naughty children? Goodness knows how Dr Gore puts up with her.'

'She does have some abilities,' I said. 'She's quite efficient in her own way. It's just her manner.'

'I've a good mind—'

David was interrupted by the appearance at the door of Julie, the inspectors' secretary. 'Has she gone?' she asked in hushed voice.

'She has,' I told her.

'Thank goodness for that,' she sighed. 'I just couldn't face she of the joyless countenance and the viper's tongue this morning. What did she want?'

'To see if we'd cleared the office,' I told her.

'Well, what's it got to do with her?' asked Julie.

'As you know, Julie,' said David, 'everything in the Education Department has to do with the meddlesome Brenda. But I shall move out in my own good time. And there's no way I'm shifting all Sidney's stuff downstairs.'

'Don't worry about that,' said Julie. 'I'll sort it out later.'

'We'll do it together, Julie,' I said. 'When I've finished moving my things.'

'And, despite what I told the wicked witch of County Hall,' said David, 'I suppose I shall reluctantly have to help you move all Sidney's stuff or I'll never hear the last of it.'

'I'll put the kettle on,' said Julie, laughing, and headed for the door.

If the man in the street were to describe what he imagined a school inspectors' secretary might look like, I guess he would picture a small, inconspicuous woman, dressed soberly with sensible flat-heeled shoes. Well, Julie could not have been more different. She wore short skirts, tight-fitting jumpers and outrageously high heels, and had thick bubbly dyed-blonde hair. Heads turned whenever this young woman with the hourglass figure sashayed down the marbled corridors of County Hall.

Everyone in the inspectors' office loved Julie and relied heavily upon her. She had the qualities of many a Yorkshire lass: she was funny, talkative, outspoken and big-hearted but also possessed the sterling qualities of the really good secretary. Julie was industrious, highly organised and entirely loyal.

By the end of the afternoon, the small, cramped room was clear of everything. David, Julie and I had made journey after journey up and down the narrow stairs, struggling with boxes full of reports and guidelines, balancing armfuls of files and folders. The worst stuff to carry down was, of course, everything that belonged to Sidney. By five o'clock, all that remained in the office was the furniture.

David, Julie and I surveyed the room, hot, tired and ready for home.

'Well, that's a job well done,' I said.

At that very moment we heard heavy footsteps on the stairs, accompanied by a rendering of 'Come Back to Sorrento'.

'Tell me I am imagining things,' whispered David.

'No,' said Julie, 'it's Mr Clamp all right.'

The great bearded figure appeared at the door like a pantomime villain. Sidney stopped singing, removed a large fedora hat in a flourish and beamed at us. Then he stared beyond us and around the empty office.

'Sweet angels of mercy!' he cried. 'Where is everything?'

David raised his eyes heavenwards but said nothing.

'Hello, Sidney,' I said.

'Did you forget, Mr Clamp,' asked Julie, 'that we were moving into the new office this week?'

'Aaaaah,' groaned Sidney. 'The move, the move! I only popped in to collect my mail. Was it this week we were supposed to be moving?'

'We have to be out of here by the end of the day,' said Julie. 'The three of us have had to take all your stuff downstairs to the new office for you.'

'How awfully decent of you,' said Sidney. Then his face clouded over. 'I say, I do hope that you have taken great care with my things. Dear God,' he said, 'what have you done with Aphrodite?'

Sidney had a fairly ghastly white plaster model of the Goddess of Love, which he used in his drawing classes.

'Aphrodite is safe and well in the new office,' replied David who, amid loud complaining, had carried the scantily clad female downstairs.

The telephone on Sidney's desk suddenly rang, echoing round the almost empty room. Julie, standing nearest, picked it up. 'Inspectors' office,' she said. She listened for a moment, then replaced the receiver. 'That was Mr Reid of Social Services. He said that we shouldn't rush as they are somewhat behind schedule and won't be ready to move up here till Tuesday at the earliest.'

'Open the window, Gervase,' said David, slowly and quietly. 'I am about to jump out.'

THURSDAY MORNING of the first week of the new autumn term found me at Ugglemattersby County Junior School to undertake what I imagined to be a routine follow-up inspection. I had visited the school some two years earlier. On that occasion, I had not been impressed with the standard of education provided, and my largely critical report had led to the enforced early retirement of the head teacher. Mr Sharples, a dour man with the smile of a martyr about to be burnt at the stake, had rattled on about the pressures and problems he had to face day after day. He had bemoaned the awkward parents, interfering governors, disillusioned teachers and wilful children.

A new head teacher, Mr Harrison, was appointed. I had sat on the interview panel and had been impressed with the enthusiastic, bright-eyed deputy head teacher from a large school in inner-city London.

Sadly, on this September morning, what I thought would be a pleasant, uneventful routine visit turned out to be quite different.

'It's been difficult, Mr Phinn,' Mr Harrison told me, tugging nervously at his small moustache. 'I rather imagined that moving north to become the head teacher of a village school in rural Yorkshire would be idyllic and certainly less stressful than my last school. I little imagined the problems I would have to face.' He sounded unnervingly like his predecessor.

As I sat in his cramped office that morning, I was concerned at the change I saw in the head teacher after so short a time. Gone were the broad and winning smile, the bright eyes and the confident manner. He looked ashen and stared at me with the doleful eyes of a sick spaniel.

'Perhaps you would like to tell me about it,' I said.

Mr Harrison took a deep, audible breath. 'I came from a large multicultural inner-city school where the staff worked hard and pulled together. The children were challenging and we had our fair share of problems, but it was a very positive environment. Ugglemattersby is completely different. In terms of discipline, the children are biddable enough, though rather blunt, but your report on Mr Sharples' regime quite rightly mentioned the lack of rigour and creativity in the curriculum. I have attempted to change things but with little success. People in this part of the world seem very resistant to change.'

He rose from his chair and stood looking pensively out of the window. 'The two teachers I inherited are not exactly incompetent but, my goodness, they can be difficult. They do the very minimum, and spend most of the day complaining. Mrs Battersby, who teaches the top Juniors, has been here all her teaching career. Her husband owns a shop in the village. He's a parish councillor, churchwarden, a stalwart of the community. Mrs Battersby leaves school two seconds after the bell to help her husband in the shop.

'The other teacher, Mrs Sidebottom—which she prefers to be pro-nounced Siddybothome—has been here many years too, and is far, far pricklier. Of course, I followed your recommendations to send them both on courses but they came back saying what a waste of time it had been. Again, as you suggested, I insisted that they planned their lessons more carefully, which they now do—more or less—but I have got nowhere with my requests that they should contribute rather more to the life and work of the school. Mention out-of-school activities and they look fit to faint.'

'Perhaps you should have contacted the Education Office,' I said. 'The situation sounds serious.'

'I did think of doing just that, but a newly appointed head teacher running to the Education Office, complaining he was having problems, would not have gone down very well, would it?' He paused, then looked straight at me. 'Actually, Mr Phinn,' he continued, 'your report did say you would check on how things were progressing. I rather expected you to get in touch before now.'

He had been right, of course. I had promised to return to monitor progress but I had failed to do so. 'Yes,' I replied now, rather sheepishly. 'I did. I'm afraid I've been so very busy. It was remiss of me.'

'I'm not blaming you, Mr Phinn,' the head teacher told me. 'I am respon-sible for the effective running of the school and it is down to me to implement your recommendations and make the necessary changes.'

Nevertheless, I thought, I should have followed things up.

'I assumed,' he continued, 'that once I had gained the confidence of the governors, parents and my teaching colleagues, I could develop so many interesting initiatives and move the school forward. Sadly, I have not been very successful. Many parents of the children at the Infant School don't want their children educated at Ugglemattersby Juniors and opt for other schools when their offspring reach seven. There's been a steady haemorrhaging of children and I've not been able to stem the flow. It's all very depressing.'

'I assume the governors are aware of your concerns?'

'In some parts, yes, but there lies another difficulty. I get little support from the present governing body. The governors who appointed me at my interview unfortunately resigned—for perfectly valid reasons—before I took up my position. They were replaced by Councillor Sidebottom, who is now the chairman of the board, assisted by the parish council nominee Mr Battersby. The clerk is Mrs Battersby's sister-in-law. It's all terribly incestuous.'

'Then the Education Office must assist you to grasp this particular nettle,' I told him. 'I've not seen the two teachers since my last visit, when I was not impressed. But if things have not improved, then we have to go down the road of competency proceedings, which may lead to their dismissal.'

'You imagine that it might come to that?' Mr Harrison asked.

'Children only have the one chance at education,' I told him. 'They deserve enthusiastic, optimistic, committed teachers who have high expectations of the pupils in their care. From what you have told me, the children in this school are getting a poor deal.'

'It's not going to be easy,' the head teacher told me sadly. He looked completely defeated and weary. 'I sometimes wish I had never left London.'

I SPENT the next part of the morning observing the lower Juniors, a class of seven- to nine-year-olds and their prickly teacher.

Mrs Sidebottom, tall and thin with a pale, melancholy, beaked face, was like a heron in her prim white blouse buttoned up to the neck and tight grey skirt from which protruded skeletal legs. When I entered her classroom, she drew her lips together into a tight little line.

'Good morning,' I said heartily.

'Good morning,' Mrs Sidebottom replied, with cool, immutable gravity.

'Good morning, children,' I said.

'Good mo-or-ning, Hinspector Phinn,' they chorused.

'We were expecting you, Mr Phinn,' the teacher said in a coldly formal voice. Her eyes refused to meet mine. 'I assumed that you would be here at the very start of the lesson.' She glanced theatrically at her wristwatch.

'I have been with the head teacher since I arrived at eight thirty.'

'I see.' She gave me a little smile—but wouldn't look directly at me. 'Well, now you are here, I'll explain a little of what we are about.'

'Perhaps one of the children could tell me.'

'Very well,' the teacher said, bristling a little. 'Simone, could you explain to Mr Phinn what we do on Thursday mornings?'

'We're learnin' 'ow to speyk proper,' a large, healthy-looking girl informed me in her strong Yorkshire accent. 'All on us in t'class 'ave to—'

'I am endeavouring, Mr Phinn,' the teacher cut in sharply, 'to encourage the children to speak clearly, expressively and accurately so that they can be understood by those with whom they converse. Most of the children come from the immediate locality and their accents do tend to be—'

'An' on Thursday mornin', we 'ave to—' Simone started to say.

'One moment, Simone,' the teacher intervened irritably. 'It's rude to interrupt when someone else is speaking.' It had been, of course, exactly what she herself had done. 'Put down your hand and sit up properly.' She turned in my direction again. 'One hears such slovenly use of the English language these days, doesn't one, the dreadful jargon, colloquial vulgarisms and awful slang. So, once a week, we do a little work on our spoken English.'

'I see,' I said, my heart beginning to plummet.

'So, if you would like to take a chair, we shall continue. Page forty-seven,' she said, turning to face the class, 'exercise one. Off you go.'

The children then proceeded to chant various elocutionary exercises.

'Gertie Gordon from Glasgow grew a gross of gaudy gay gladioli.'

'Good!' the teacher snapped out. 'And the next.'

'They thought they had fought to defeat the fort but they found they had fought for naught.'

'Good! Next.'

Exercise three caused some problems for the children:

> 'Enery 'All 'ops on 'is 'eels.
> What an odd 'abit.
> 'Ow 'orrid hit feels.
> 'Oppin' on 'is 'eels
> Hisn't 'oppin' at all.
> So why not 'op properly, 'Enery 'All?

There was a long deep audible exhalation from Mrs Sidebottom. 'No, no, no!' she cried. 'How many *more* times do I have to tell you not to drop your aitches?' She then demonstrated how the poem should be recited, over-enunciating every syllable. 'Now, children, let us try again.'

Despite several more attempts the children continued to drop every aitch possible and add the letter where none was required.

'Let's try exercise number four,' Mrs Sidebottom said, sighing again.

And so the lesson dragged on for a further wearisome quarter of an hour until the teacher told the children to write out the exercises in their books and to learn them at home. This gave me a chance to examine the children's books.

The door suddenly flew open and a boy with long black hair tied back in a ponytail burst in. 'Sorry I'm late, missis,' he said in a pronounced Irish brogue, 'but the 'ossis got out again and I 'ad to 'elp mi da get 'em back.'

'Come in, Niall,' the teacher said. She stared at the boy as a rattlesnake might stare at a rat. 'Sit down quickly and get on with your work.'

'Yes, missis,' he said, heading for a desk near to where I was sitting.

'We are copying out the exercises on page forty-seven in your textbook.'

Mrs Sidebottom sidled over to me and informed me *sotto voce* that the boy was from a travellers' family, and missed more time at school than he attended. 'A gaggle of them always sets up camp near here for the summer, making a nuisance of themselves. My husband, County Councillor Sidebottom, is trying to stop them coming here. Have you met my husband, by the way?' she asked.

'No, I haven't,' I replied.

'He's recently been elected to the County Council,' Mrs Sidebottom informed me, 'and is a colleague of Councillor Peterson, who, as you are no doubt aware, is very influential on the Education Committee.'

I detected a veiled threat in her voice.

When Mrs Sidebottom returned to her desk at the front of the classroom, I approached the boy who had been the topic of the conversation.

'Hello,' I said, pulling up the hard wooden chair to sit beside him.

'How are ya?' he asked, with nonchalant confidence. He was a handsome lad with tanned skin and a ready smile.

'I'm fine. May I look at your book?' I asked.

'Now, who would ya be?'

'A school inspector. I visit schools to hear children read and look at their work.'

'Well, now, that sounds like a great number to be on. Now, how would ya be getting a job like that?'

'By working hard at school,' I told him, reaching for his exercise book.

'Now, don't yous be expecting much in there,' he said. 'I'm not one for the reading and the writing and the mental arithmetics. I just can't get my head around this fraction and percentages business.'

'You need to know about fractions and percentages, Niall, because if you don't, people might cheat you.'

'They won't be cheating *me*,' he said vehemently. 'Just let 'em try!'

'What do you want to do when you leave school?' I asked the boy.

'I want to do what my da does. He collects scrap metal and sells it.'

'And what sort of scrap gives you the greatest profit?'

'Oil drums,' he answered. 'There's a good market for used oil drums.'

'Now suppose someone told you he'd got a hundred oil drums and that he would sell you a quarter of them—that's twenty-five of them. Because you don't know about fractions you wouldn't know, would you, if he sold you the right amount? He could sell you ten or fifteen rather than the twenty-five because you wouldn't know what a quarter of a hundred is.'

Niall considered what I had said for a moment, rubbed his chin and then nodded. 'He wouldn't cheat me because if he said you can have a quarter of them there oil drums, I'd say to him, "I'll have the lot or none at all".'

There was little chance, I thought, of anyone cheating one so canny.

As I looked through the boy's book, Simone piped up, 'Miss, I can't find mi readin' book. I've gorran putten it down someweer an' I don't know where I've putten it.'

'I have put it down somewhere, Simone,' corrected Mrs Sidebottom, 'but I do not know where I have put it.'

'Have ya, miss?' the child asked innocently.

'No, *you* have put it down,' the teacher said, drawing an exasperated breath.

'I know, miss, that's wor I just said,' the girl answered.

'There is no such word, Simone, as "putten",' the teacher explained. 'The word is "put". "I have put down my book".'

'Miss!' another child piped. 'She's gone an' putten it on *my* desk, It's 'ere.'

'Put, William, put,' the teacher corrected sharply. Mrs Sidebottom sighed dramatically. 'You know, Mr Phinn,' she said, 'sometimes I really ask myself why I bother.' I asked myself the self-same question.

Just before morning break, the teacher wrote a sentence in large white letters on the blackboard: 'I have putten my book on the teacher's desk.'

'Now, children,' she said, facing the class. 'On the blackboard I have written a sentence. Who can tell me what is wrong with it?'

Young William waved his hand. 'I know, miss!' he shouted out.

'Come along then, William, what is wrong with the sentence?'

'Miss,' the boy replied, 'tha's gone and putten "putten" when tha should 'ave putten "put".'

I HAD LOOKED at a range of children's workbooks, most of which I judged to be unsatisfactory. I was dismayed to find that my various recommendations seemed to have been largely ignored. During the break, therefore, I found a secluded area in the small school library. I was just starting to jot down my observations when I was aware of a figure standing a few feet away.

He was a small wiry lad of about ten or eleven with an earnest face, wild, tufty ginger hair sprouting up from his head like a clump of dry grass, a scattering of freckles around his nose and bright, intelligent eyes.

He stuck out his chin and demanded, 'So, what are you for?'

I smiled. 'I'm a school inspector,' I told him.

'I knows that,' he sighed. 'Mester 'arrison told us that you'd be comin' in today—but what I wants to know is what are you *for*?'

A large girl with a pale moon face and two big bunches of thick straw-coloured hair tied with crimson ribbons, appeared from behind a shelf of books and stared at me impassively. I smiled at her but she stared back at me as if I were some strange and rather unpleasant exhibit displayed in a museum case. She then proceeded to explore her nose with her index finger.

'Well,' I said, 'I go into schools and see what children are doing.'

'Dunt you 'ave a proper job, like?' the child asked brusquely.

I laughed. 'I think it *is* a proper job,' I told him. This question had been put to me a good few times before by pupils, so I was well used to answering it.

The large girl was now examining the contents of her nose critically. Then she wiped her finger on her T-shirt, ran a small finger across the base of her nose and departed. The boy remained resolutely in front of me.

'Dooan't mind 'yacinth,' he informed me. He tapped the side of his nose knowingly. 'She's got what they calls especial needs, tha knaas. She's not much cop at yer writin' an' yer readin' but by the 'ell, she can't 'arf arm wrestle. Champion at conkers an' all, an' good at footie in t'goal.'

'Thank you for telling me,' I said.

'So what do you actually *do*, then?' said the ginger-headed boy.

'I hear children read,' I informed him patiently. 'I look at their books and examine the work, see how well they write, if they can spell, use punctuation, and then I talk to the teachers to see that everything is as it should be.'

'Well, if tha asks me,' he confided, 'I think tha's got a reight job on 'ere.'

'Really? So, if you had a magic wand and could change things in this school, what would you change?'

He puffed out his cheeks and exhaled noisily. ''Ow long 'as tha got?'

'All right,' I said. 'What is the best part of your day in this school?'

'Goin' 'ome,' he replied, without pause for thought.

'I see. Isn't it morning break?' I asked pleasantly. 'So shouldn't you be out in the playground getting some fresh air and exercise?'

'I'd like to be,' he told me, grimacing, 'but I've been kept in. Missis Battersby, she's my teacher, she said I 'ad to stop in 'cos I've been chatterin' too much this mornin' an' not gerrin on wi' mi work.'

I could see the teacher's point of view.

'I'm writin' about what I did on Sat'day,' he told me.

'Really?' I could see that I was in for another long conversation.

'Missis Battersby 'as gor us to write abaat summat interestin' we did over t'weekend.'

'So what did you—' I began.

The boy continued without seeming to draw breath. 'I know what Missis Battersby's been doin' over t'weekend,' he said with a knowing wink. 'She's gone an' putten that display up theer on t'yonder wall in t'corridor outside 'er classroom. She never puts owt much up out theer but she's gone to town wi' this 'un. It's all abaat t'Gret Fire o' London so tha berrer tek a look at it or she'll not be best pleased. It's been purrup special like. There's never much on t'walls usually 'cept what Mester 'arrison puts up.'

'It's very impressive,' I said. 'So what can you tell me about the Great Fire of London?' I asked.

'Nowt.'

'I thought you'd been studying it.'

'Nay, I din't say we'd been studyin' it. Last 'istory topic we did were on t'Vikings. I can tell thee owt abaat t'Vikings if tha wants but I know nowt about t'Gret Fire o' London.'

'Before you go,' I said, 'you might like to tell me your name.'

'Well, mi mam an' dad calls me Charlie but mi teacher calls me Charles.'

'Tell me, Charlie, what is your account about?'

'Tha what?'

'The piece of writing you are finishing. What is it about?'

'Oh, that. Me an' mi brother 'elped mi dad castrate three bullocks.' With a cheerful wave, the boy returned to his desk leaving the Inspector of Schools with open mouth.

FOLLOWING THE BREAK, I joined Mrs Battersby's class and met Charlie again.

'Hey up, Mester Phinn,' he said as I entered the classroom. 'It's Mester Phinn, miss,' Charlie informed her enthusiastically. 'I've met 'im.'

'I do have eyes, Charles,' said the teacher. 'It's nice to see you, Mr Phinn,' she said unconvincingly.

My report of her lesson on the last visit had been critical so I was prepared for the tightlipped and solemn countenance.

'Sit down, Charles,' instructed the teacher. 'You're jumping up and down like a jack-in-the-box with fleas.' There was a slight tremble in her voice.

'Good morning, children,' I said brightly.

'Mornin', Mester Phinn,' they replied in unison.

'So you've met Charles,' said the teacher, raising a hand to her throat where a small red nervous rash was appearing.

'Yes, we were having a little chatter at break time,' I said.

'When he should have been completing his work,' said the teacher. 'I hope that he behaved himself.'

'Oh, he was very polite,' I told her. 'We were talking about the Great Fire of London and I was admiring your display.'

Mrs Battersby's face coloured a little. 'I'm pleased to hear it,' she said.

Mrs Battersby was a dumpy, sharp-eyed woman wearing a bright pink turtleneck jumper and grey, shapeless skirt. To complete the ensemble she sported a large rope of amber beads and heavy brown brogues.

During the lesson the children worked quietly, copying up their accounts of their weekend activities. Mrs Battersby sat at her desk and a small queue of readers formed to read to her from their books. As I wandered round talking to the children and examining their work, the teacher constantly looked up and watched my progress with small black suspicious eyes.

The first child to whom I spoke, a stout girl called Ruby, was only too pleased to show me her book. It was neat and contained some interesting stories, poems and language exercises but the teacher had been very heavy-handed with the marking pen.

'We usually have the Leprosy Hour every Thursday after break,' Ruby told me, 'but we've got to finish our account of what we did over the weekend.'

'Whatever is the Leprosy Hour?' I asked mystified.

'It's really called the Literacy Hour,' the girl told me, 'but miss calls it the Leprosy Hour because she hates it. When Mr Harrison came, he said we all had to do an hour of English and maths every morning.'

'I see. So what is your account about?' I asked.

'Well,' replied the girl, swivelling round to face me, 'I'm writing about helping my Grandpa Morrison build a dry-stone wall.'

'Really? That sounds very interesting.'

Her account was clear and detailed. She described how at six thirty on the Saturday morning she had set off with her grandfather and two of his friends to repair a hundred-year-old wall on the estate of Lord Marrick. 'If my Grandpa Morrison can't get a stone just right,' she told me, 'he sometimes pushes it in really hard and says, "Get in, tha bugger!" and then says, "Pardon mi French".' She giggled. 'My Grandpa Morrison says dry-stone walls make cosy homes for all sorts of creatures—voles, wizzles, lizards, slow-worms, hedgepigs, spiders and bees—so they're very important. Did you know that?'

'I didn't,' I said. What a confident girl, I thought.

I found Hyacinth poring over a large picture book.

'Hello,' I said.

She wiped her nose with the back of a finger and eyed me apprehensively.

'Let's see what you are doing, shall we?' She didn't object as I slid her reading book across the desk and started to examine it.

'Would you like to read a little of your book to me?' I asked.

She shook her head. She wiped her nose on her finger again and then told me in a loud voice, 'I'm special needs.' Perhaps she thought that this revelation might convince me to leave her in peace. The girl reluctantly read to me, slowly and with fierce concentration on her face, her finger following each word on the page. There was no expression in her voice and not once did she pause for breath but read on, determined to get the ordeal over and done with.

'Hyacinth,' I said, when she snapped the book shut, 'that was very good, but what do you do when you come to a full stop?'

She eyed me like an expert in the presence of an ignoramus. 'You gerroff t'bus,' she replied.

I chuckled. 'Of course you do,' I said.

She sniffed noisily and then asked me, 'So, what are you for?'

BEFORE I LEFT the school at the end of the morning I spoke to both the teachers before seeing the head teacher. A wary resentful look crept across Mrs Battersby's face when I gave her the feedback on her lesson.

'Goodness knows, I try my best,' she told me. 'And let's be fair. I can't be expected to make silk purses out of pigs' ears. I mean, these children are not going to end up brain surgeons or nuclear scientists, are they now? All they want to do when they leave school is work on their parents' farms.'

'That is my point, Mrs Battersby,' I told her. 'I think your expectation of these children is too low and the work they do lacks challenge and variety.'

The reaction of Mrs Battersby's colleague to my comments was aggressively defiant. Mrs Sidebottom sat before me tightlipped, straight-backed and steely-eyed. As diplomatically as possible, I told her that, in my opinion, it was misguided to try and change the children's natural way of speaking with one lesson a week in which they chanted doggerel.

'Far from being a deviation of the standard form of the language, dialect is an earlier form of English and has its own vocabulary, syntax and grammar. Children do need to learn standard forms of English but trying to change their accents is undesirable.'

'Mr Phinn,' she said with slow deliberation in her voice, 'I am of the opinion that it is my job to eradicate the slovenly, lazy and inaccurate way the children speak. You may call it dialect if you wish. I call it bad English.'

I then told her straight that I was very disappointed that very few of my recommendations had been addressed, and I was not impressed with what I had seen that morning. The teacher's eyes bulged in indignation. I rather expected a spirited defence of her teaching, but Mrs Sidebottom glanced up at the clock on the wall and informed me that it was her lunch hour and it was in her contract that she should have a one-hour break in the middle of the day.

I promised Mr Harrison that I would return before half-term with my colleagues to undertake a more thorough inspection. In the interim, I told him, I would discuss with the Chief Inspector of Schools the possibility of starting competency proceedings. I advised him to keep a record of all incidents and refusals to carry out instructions on the part of the two teachers. I agreed with him that it would prove difficult to dismiss either of them, particularly since both teachers were so well connected locally. The teachers were not incompetent, it was just that their teaching was lacklustre and short of challenge and they both had an unfortunate manner with the children.

'I can assure you, Mr Harrison,' I told him as I made a move to leave, 'that I will follow things up this time.'

2

I arrived at Ugglemattersby Infant School, on the other side of the village, just as the bell was sounding for the end of lunchtime. I watched for a moment from the gate as the small children, who had been running and jumping, chattering and playing games, lined up obediently in the playground. Dressed identically in their bright red jumpers, white shirts and grey shorts or skirts, they resembled a miniature army as they marched smartly into school behind their teachers. This looked a happy and well-ordered school.

In contrast to the Junior School, Ugglemattersby Infant School was a modern, attractive building. It was set among open fields, enclosed by silvered limestone walls, with views stretching to the nearby moors. A coloured mural depicting rows of happy children had been painted on one exterior wall. It was a cheerful, welcoming environment.

The head teacher, Mrs Braddock-Smith, a young woman in a very stylish black suit and frilly white blouse, took me on a tour of the school, proudly telling me about the interesting work the children were undertaking and their achievements. She bubbled with enthusiasm as she tripped along a corridor resplendent with the pupils' paintings, poems and stories, all of which were carefully mounted. Each child we passed said, 'Hello, miss,' cheerfully, and in all the classrooms I could see busy little people hard at work.

I explained to Mrs Braddock-Smith that I wished to spend the first part of the afternoon with the top Infants. Then I would join the youngest children for the remainder of the day, meeting her after school to report back.

'Certainly,' trilled the head teacher. 'I think you will be very impressed with what you see and hear, Mr Phinn. Our standards are extremely high, even if I do say so myself, and this last couple of years have been so very successful that we have attracted a growing number of "G and T" children.'

'"G and T" children?' I repeated.

'Gifted and talented,' the head teacher explained. 'An increasing number of parents from the professional classes have moved into the village, and we have had an influx of very bright children with most supportive and ambitious parents. Indeed, there's a long waiting list for places for children who live outside the catchment area. Perhaps I shouldn't blow our own trumpet but we do very well here indeed.'

There were twenty bright-eyed six-year-old pupils in the top Infants, in the charge of a plump, red-faced teacher called Mrs Hartley. They listened attentively to her as she finished reading the fairy story of *The Princess and the Pea*. She then set them to write about the story, and to draw pictures to illustrate their work. I sat in the small reading corner and heard one child after another read to me. The head teacher's proud boasts were certainly not unfounded since all the infants read clearly and accurately.

When it came to a boy called Joshua's turn, he scurried over, clearly eager to demonstrate his ability.

'Mrs Hartley lets me choose my own books,' he informed me before I could open my mouth.

'Really?'

'I'm between books at the moment so I haven't brought one to read to you.'

'Don't worry,' I said, 'we'll pick one from the shelf.'

'I've just finished a novel. And I know all my times tables.'

'Good gracious!'

'Do you want me to do the eleven times table? I can if you want.'

Clearly here was one of the head teacher's 'G and T' pupils. 'Not at the moment,' I told him. 'I would like you to read to me. Now, let's see what we have on the shelf, shall we?'

The boy started busily rummaging through the bookcase. 'May I have this one with the snail on the front?' he asked. 'I like snails.'

He presented me with a brightly coloured pop-up picture book called *Little Snail's Big Surprise*.

'This looks interesting,' I said.

'Snails are called gastropods, you know,' he told me seriously. 'That's a sort of mollusc with a shell. I learnt that at the Natural History Museum in London. I went there with my father during the summer holidays.'

The boy began to read with gusto. 'Sandy Snail lived in a beautiful garden filled with delicious plants. One day Daddy Snail said, "Go to your Mother. She has a big surprise for you! Go straight there. And don't talk to strangers!" You're not supposed to start a sentence with "and", are you, Mr Phinn?' he asked, looking up at me with wide, inquisitive eyes.

'Some writers do,' I told him. 'Would you like to continue, Joshua?' I said, not wishing to engage in a debate about the technicalities of the English language with a six-year-old.

The boy read on: 'Sandy raced off. Let's follow his tracks.' He stopped again. 'Mr Phinn, snails can't race. They're very slow creatures.'

'It's supposed to be funny,' I told him. 'The writer knows snails move slowly and has used "raced" to make us smile.'

'Oh,' said Joshua, his small brow furrowing. He shrugged and continued until he came to the final page where Sandy Snail meets his mother. '"Here I am. Where's my BIG surprise? Can I have it now, please?"' Two little snails, one with a blue shell and the other with a pink shell, popped up from behind a leaf. '"We're your big surprise, your new brother and sister!"'

'You read that very well, Joshua,' I told the boy. 'You're an excellent reader. And wasn't it a delightful story?'

He scowled. 'I didn't think much of it.'

'Why is that?' I asked.

'Well, for a start, snails don't have blue or pink shells. They are more of a greeny-brown colour. And snails and those other creatures can't talk.'

'No, but then neither can Peter Rabbit. It's only a story.'

'And another thing,' said Joshua. 'You can't have boy and girl snails. Everyone knows that snails are hermaphrodites.'

AFTER MY VISIT to the Ugglemattersby schools I decided to return to the office and write up my report while things were fresh in my mind.

Little did I expect to find Sidney and David at their desks and I was even more surprised to find Geraldine Mullarkey there, too.

'Ah!' cried Sidney as I entered the room, 'a full complement! What a rarity. We must celebrate. We shall retire to the local hostelry for a little drinkie and catch up on what we did over the summer.'

'Not for me, Sidney,' said Geraldine hastily. 'I must be going in a minute. I have a little boy to get home to.'

'And I've a meeting at the golf club at seven,' said David.

'Well, that just leaves us, Gervase,' said Sidney. 'Fancy a pint, old boy?'

'No thanks, Sidney,' I told him. 'I have this report to write up.'

'Pish!' he exclaimed. 'It can wait until tomorrow.'

'Not this one,' I said.

'Oh dear,' said David, 'that sounds serious. Gerry was just telling us about her holiday to the Emerald Isle this summer.'

'Oh sure and beggora,' said Sidney, adopting a mock-Irish accent, 'don't I just feel one of my mawkish Irish melodies a-comin' on, to be sure.'

'Behave yourself, Sidney,' interrupted Geraldine, laughing.

'The Welsh have a great deal in common with the Irish, you know,' said David.

'Here we go,' mumbled Sidney.

'And, of course,' continued David blithely, 'the shared Celtic heritage explains why both races have such a love of and talent in music and poetry.'

'I will grant you that the Welsh and the Irish do have something in common when it comes to language,' said Sidney, 'and that is their inability to shut up. Get a group of you Celts together and nobody can get a word in.'

'When I hear you expounding thus, Sidney,' said David, 'three words come to mind: "kettle", "pot" and "black".'

'Speaking of pots,' said Sidney, 'have any of you seen my ceramic vase? I've searched high and low for it and it seems to have disappeared into thin air.'

David and I exchanged glances.

'Ceramic pot?' said David innocently.

'The one that was on the windowsill,' said Sidney. 'I made it on my pottery course last term.'

'I've not seen it,' said Geraldine. 'Have you asked Julie?'

'Yes, and she doesn't know where it's gone either,' replied Sidney. He looked at David and me. 'Do either of you know where it is?'

David and I did indeed know where it was. The remains of the vase were in the skip at the back of County Hall where I had deposited them. The item in question had slipped from my hands during the office move.

'I'm sure it will turn up, Sidney,' said David, knowing full well that it would not. 'Well, I shall have to be going.' He rose from his chair and stretched. 'Good night, Gervase. Don't stay too late. Come along, Sidney, let's leave the man to finish his report.'

'And I must be away, too,' said Geraldine, giving me a small wave.

'I'll see you all tomorrow,' I said.

The three of them departed and in the silence of the office I thought back to my previous visit to the Ugglemattersby Junior School, when I had presented such a critical report. I should have followed things up. Now I had to face Miss de la Mare, the Chief Inspector, and explain myself.

I ARRIVED HOME to my cottage in the pretty little Dales village of Hawksrill on that wet and windy evening with Ugglemattersby still on my mind. I parked the car on the narrow track that ran along the side of the cottage, turned off the engine and sat in the silent darkness, considering what I would say to the Chief Inspector.

Through the car window, the cottage looked cheerful and welcoming, and I knew the two people I loved most in the world would be waiting for me.

Christine and I had wanted Peewit Cottage in the village of Hawksrill as soon as we had set eyes upon it. Colleagues at work thought we had taken leave of our senses, cobbling together every penny we had to buy this rundown, dark stone barn of a building but, standing in the overgrown garden, surrounded by waist-high weeds and rampant rose bushes, we had gazed across a panorama of green undulating fields crisscrossed with silvered limestone walls that rose to the craggy fell-tops, and we had marvelled. We knew we could transform this old cottage into our dream home.

Our 'dream home', in fact, turned out to be something of a house of horrors. We soon discovered that we had an expanding family of woodworm in the quaint beams, persistent dry rot in the cosy little sitting room, a leaking roof and nearly every conceivable problem that could face the homeowner. But we had been optimistic and cheerful and now, after nearly two years, having spent most of our spare time renovating and refurbishing, Peewit Cottage was beginning to take shape.

There was a rap on the side of the car, which made me jump. Outside the car window was a wide-boned, weathered face. It was our nearest neighbour, Harry Cotton, a man whose long beak of a nose was invariably poking in everyone else's business. He was a man of strong opinions, most of which were usually complaints and pieces of unwanted advice.

I wound down the window. 'Hello, Harry,' I said wearily.

'I thowt it were thee,' he said, scratching his impressive shock of white hair. 'What's tha doin' out 'ere, sittin' in t'dark by thissen?'

'Just thinking,' I told him.

'I thowt tha were deead or summat, just sittin' theer. I was tekkin' Buster out for 'is constitutional an' I saw thee.' Buster was Harry's wire-haired Border terrier. ''As tha 'ad a bit of a barney wi' t'missis, then?' he asked.

'Harry,' I said, getting out of the car, 'Christine and I have not had any barney, as you put it. We are very very happy and everything is fine.'

I headed for the cottage, but Harry and his dog followed me up the path. 'By the way, I've had a word with thy missis about yon garden,' he called after me. 'It needs sooarting out. It's t'time o'year when it wants fettlin'.'

'I'll see to it,' I told him shortly.

'An' that allotment of yourn needs a bit o' work on it an' all. It's goin' dahn t'nick, by looks on it. Now, if it was up to me—'

'I'll see to it, Harry. Good night,' I said, going into the cottage.

Christine was in the kitchen preparing supper. The cottage was as cheerful and welcoming as I knew it would be, and I could see that a lazy fire burned in the sitting-room grate. It was good to be home.

'You're late,' said Christine as I wrapped my arms around her and gave her a kiss on the cheek.

'Yes,' I sighed, 'and I need a strong drink,' I said, bending over Richard's carry-cot. Our baby son looked washed and scrubbed and was gurgling away contentedly. As I sat at the kitchen table nursing a dark brown whisky, Christine had to endure a detailed account of my day. She was, as always, a sympathetic listener, and by the time supper was ready I felt better.

'Would you take Richard up, then we can eat,' she said.

When I came downstairs, having tucked the sleepy baby into his cot, supper was on the table.

'Harry's been round today,' Christine said, heaping beef stew onto my plate.

'So I hear. He was lying in wait for me outside,' I told her.

'He's not that bad,' said Christine, 'and it's good to have a neighbour who keeps an eye on things. He told me he's a bit down in the dumps at the moment because of the new landlord at the pub. Apparently, the man's causing a few waves, upsetting the regulars by changing things.'

'Harry doesn't like change and that's for sure,' I said.

'Well, in my opinion, the Royal Oak wants changing,' Christine said. 'It's very old-fashioned. People nowadays want a more cheerful place.'

'It's not that bad,' I said. 'It's got character, although I must admit it could do with a lick of paint and some new furniture.'

'Harry also mentioned the garden,' said Christine, 'and he wondered if we might be interested in his—er, brother's grandson, I think, tidying it up a bit. Richard takes so much of my time, and I know you're not up to it.'

'It's not that I'm not up to it,' I replied, a little annoyed by the comment. 'It's just that I'm up to my eyes at work.'

'Don't be so touchy,' said Christine, stretching out her hand to mine. 'What I meant was that you're far too busy. Anyway, Harry's brother's grandson, Andy, leaves school next summer and could do with some extra money. He's working up at Ted Poskitt's farm at the weekends but it's not a regular job and he's trying to save enough to put himself through Askham Bryan Agricultural College near York. From what Harry says, he seems a willing enough lad and would be a real help with the digging and weeding and doing a few repairs. What do you think?'

'So long as it doesn't cost too much,' I said, 'it sounds like a good idea.'

'I thought you'd say that,' said Christine, 'so I've asked Andy to come up and see you.'

THAT NIGHT my thoughts kept returning to the situation at Ugglemattersby Junior School and what I would say to Miss de la Mare the next morning. Finally I drifted off into a fretful sleep but was soon wide awake again, with Christine jabbing me in the back.

'Gervase! Wake up!' she whispered.

'What is it?' I mumbled.

'Can you hear that noise?' Christine asked in a hushed voice.

I rubbed my eyes and sat up. 'What noise? I can't hear anything.'

'It's a sort of scratching noise, coming from the loft. There's something up there, moving about.'

'Oh no,' I said, sitting up and gazing at the ceiling, 'I bet we've got mice.'

'Don't say that!' exclaimed Christine, clamping her arms around me. 'You know I hate mice—' She stopped. 'There it is again.'

There was certainly something moving about above us, a sort of scraping noise then a skittering sound. 'Yes, I can hear it,' I said.

'You don't think it's a rat, do you?' asked Christine shuddering.

'No, no, of course not,' I told her in a matter-of-fact tone of voice, as much to reassure myself as my wife. 'Rats wouldn't be up in a loft. They don't like heights.'

'It sounds huge. Go and look,' Christine told me, getting out of bed and putting on her slippers and dressing gown.

'Go and look?' I repeated. 'What, now? At this time of night?'

'I can't sleep with a rat in the house. I'm moving the baby in with us until you find it. The thought of a rat scuttling about makes me feel ill.'

I plodded downstairs to fetch a ladder and I poked my head up through the hatch but I saw nothing in the torch's beam except the black water tank and a few cardboard boxes. The rest of the loft was dark and dusty. The creature, whatever it was, was probably in some dark corner, watching me.

I found Christine sitting in the kitchen, feeding Richard.

'I can't see anything,' I told her, 'but I'll have another look in the morning.'

'What about giving Mr Hinderwell a call?' suggested Christine.

Maurice Hinderwell was the County Pest Control Officer. He was a strange little man, not unlike the rodents he caught and killed, with dark inquisitive eyes, small pointed nose, protuberant white teeth and glossy black hair bristling on his scalp. When rats appeared in the garden of Peewit Cottage, I had called on his services and since then not a rat had been seen.

'I'll call him in the morning,' I said.

As soon as it was light, I climbed the ladder to the loft, armed with a poker. I pushed my head charily through the hatch. Sitting on its haunches and staring at me with large black eyes was a grey squirrel. I could also see light coming through a hole in the corner where a slate had come loose.

'It's a squirrel,' I called down to Christine. 'A cute, little bushy-tailed squirrel. He's getting in through a hole under the eaves.'

I could hear the relief in Christine's voice. 'Well, I'm glad it's not a rat,' she said, 'but I still don't want a squirrel taking up residence.'

A moment later, I came down from the loft. 'Well, he'll not be back,' I said. 'I've blocked up his entrance and that should stop him getting in. That's the end of our little visitor.'

3

The following day was the day of the first autumn-term meeting of the team of inspectors. I wanted to get to the Staff Development Centre before my colleagues to discuss the situation at Ugglemattersby Junior School with Winifred de la Mare, the Chief Inspector.

Winifred de la Mare had only been in post for a term. Our new boss was extremely efficient, clear-sighted, frighteningly intelligent and, for anyone foolish enough to take her on, a formidable adversary. When the Education Committee on the County Council had proposed the closure of two small schools that were greatly valued by the small communities they served, Miss de la Mare had persuaded the councillors to scrap the idea. She was also supportive and someone for whom we inspectors had a great deal of respect.

The Staff Development Centre, where all the courses and conferences for teachers and most of the staff meetings took place, had once been a secondary-modern school. The biggest classrooms and the hall had been adapted for lectures and courses, and the smaller rooms had been converted into meeting rooms. There was a small staff room, reference library, kitchen, spacious lounge area and office. The SDC was as a good school should be—bright, cheerful and welcoming and, above all, spotlessly clean and orderly. This was as a result of the devotion of the caretaker, Connie.

Connie was a colourful and assertive character—a warm-hearted, down-to-earth Yorkshirewoman who had no understanding whatsoever of rank or status. She was known by Sidney Clamp as 'that virago with the feather duster', 'the tyrant with the teapot', 'the termagant in pink', and various other cognomens. Everyone who crossed the threshold of her domain was greeted with the same forthright manner, usually with the words, 'I hope you've parked your vehicle in the correct specificated areas.'

Connie had a delightfully eccentric command of the English language. For her, English was not a dull and dreary business, it was something to distort and reinterpret. She could mangle words like a mincer shredding meat.

She had a somewhat explosive relationship with Sidney who, being loud, expressive, untidy and larger than life, was guaranteed to cross swords with her. 'The mess that man leaves behind,' she frequently complained, 'with all his artificated courses. I'm sick and tired of clearing up after him.'

On this damp, dreary September morning, Connie was standing at the entrance in her familiar pose as I entered the Centre.

'Oh, it's you, is it?' she said. No 'Good morning, Mr Phinn.'

'Good morning, Connie,' I replied, trying to sound cheerful.

'You're early. The meeting doesn't start till eight thirty.'

'I was hoping to see Miss de la Mare before the start,' I told her. 'Has she arrived yet?'

'She's in Meeting Room One, rooting through a pile of papers,' Connie replied. 'I suppose you'll be wanting a cup of coffee?'

'That would be splendid,' I said.

'I've only got the ordinary kind,' she said, staring at me fiercely as if expecting some sort of confrontation. 'Not that decaffeinicated stuff.'

'That's fine,' I replied.

'I had a head teacher in here last term asking for "proper" coffee. "What's proper coffee when it's at home?" I asked her. "Proper ground coffee," she said, "that you get in one of those caf . . . er, cath . . . um, catheters."'

'Cafetières,' I murmured.

'Well, I'll go and put the kettle on,' she muttered as she strode off in the direction of the kitchen, flicking her feather duster along the walls as she went.

I found Miss de la Mare at a large table in the meeting room scribbling some notes on a vast pad of paper. Dressed in a rather loud red and green tweed suit, she looked more like the Madam Chairman of the Yorkshire Countrywomen's Association than the Chief Inspector of Schools.

'Good morning,' I said, feeling my stomach churning.

'Oh, good morning, Gervase,' she replied, looking over the top of her rimless half-moon spectacles. 'You're bright and early.'

'Yes,' I said. 'I was hoping to have a word with you before the meeting.'

'That's a coincidence,' she replied, putting her pen down, and removing her spectacles. 'I was hoping to have a word with you, too.'

'Really?'

'Yes, about something—how shall I put it—of a somewhat delicate nature.'

'That sounds ominous,' I said.

'Well, it might blow up into something serious if it's not handled carefully. Dr Gore has asked for it to be dealt with as a matter of some urgency.'

'And it concerns me?' I asked.

'Yes, it does,' she replied. 'Are you able to remain behind after the meeting?'

'Yes, of course,' I said. 'My first appointment this afternoon is at one thirty.'

'Now, if you'll excuse me,' she said. 'I really don't wish to appear rude but I have to finish the agenda for this morning's meeting.'

I joined Connie in the kitchen.

'There's no Garibaldis,' she said bluntly, pouring boiling water into a mug. 'It might be a pigment of my imagination but I could swear blind there was a full two packets of biscuits at the beginning of this week. I've an idea it's Mr Clamp who's the culprit. He's always got his hands in my biscuit barrel, nibbling away like a half-starved squirrel. Anyway, there are only custard creams, though I dare say it's a bit early for biscuits.'

'Your grandchildren are back at school this week.' I said. I knew from experience that once I moved the conversation on to the topic of her grandchildren, little Damien and Lucy, the thin line of her mouth would disappear and her eyes would sparkle.

'Keen as mustard to get back to school, they were. You should have seen the school report from their head teacher at the end of last term. At the confrontation meeting, Miss Pilkington told my daughter that they are a delight to teach and doing really well. As sharp as buttons and very good little readers.'

'I'm glad they like reading,' I said. 'You know, if every parent in the country read with their children every night for just half an hour it would make so much difference.'

'Oh, they get a story every night,' said Connie. Then her smile went. 'But, if you was to ask me, I think that my daughter—Tricia, that is—tends to spoil Lucy when it comes to food. Damien eats like there's no tomorrow, but Lucy's very fernickity. She wants all this fancy stuff, wholemeal bread and high-fibre cereals. Won't touch butter. Has to have this margarine with that monoglutinous sodomite. I told her that when I was a girl you ate what you were given. None of this decaffeinicated coffee and orgasmic vegetables. They were lean years in the nineteen-thirties and forties. I remember we went berserk at the sight of an orange, and I remember my first banana. You couldn't get them during the war.'

I glanced surreptitiously at my watch. 'I had better make a move,' I said.

'To be honest, it came as a bit of a surprise that first banana.' She said, smiling at the memory.

I was now intrigued. 'In what way?' I asked.

'Well, Ted and me were on our first date. My father was very strict. I had to be in by a certain time or there'd be fireworks. My mother was like my father and forever warning me about boys and what they would like to get up to. Anyway, Dad wanted to meet Ted to give him the once over and warn him to watch his step. He insisted Ted should see me back home after the film, ten thirty at the latest. In those days the Tivoli Cinema in the High Street had these double seats at the back for courting couples where it's all dark and secluded. There were no arm rests separating them so some of them were having a right old kiss and canoodle.'

'And the bananas?' I prompted.

'I'm about to tell you,' said Connie. 'We were halfway through *Brief Encounter* and Ted had his arm around me, and he says, "I've got a surprise for you." Oooh, I thought, a box of chocolates or a pair of silk stockings or something of that sort. Then Ted thrusts this banana into my hand. Course, it was pitch black so I couldn't see what it was. "Here you are," he whispers, "get hold of that." I screamed blue murder, the manager came running down the aisle and we were asked to leave the cinema.'

'Connie!' I said in a mock-outraged voice. 'I'm shocked!'

'Go on with you! Mind you, I'd been married for twenty-five years before I told Dad about it. How he laughed. And I always remembers that time if anyone mentions bananas.'

DAVID PRITCHARD and Sidney Clamp were arguing as usual as they arrived for the meeting.

'The Welsh are not stand-offish at all, Sidney,' David was saying angrily.

'As soon as you go into a shop in Wales they all stop talking English and break into that spluttery incomprehensible language of yours,' Sidney replied. 'I find it infuriating.'

They arrived at the hatch to the kitchen and I moved out of the kitchen to meet them. 'Good morning,' I said.

'Gervase,' said Sidney, not returning my greeting, 'is it not a fact that the Welsh are less than friendly, in particular when it comes to the English?'

'Not at all,' I replied. 'I have always found them a most agreeable race.'

Connie poked her head through the hatch and glowered. 'It's like a Punch and Judy show out there,' she said. 'Will you keep your voices down?'

'Ah, Connie,' said Sidney, 'what a delight to see your happy, smiling countenance on such a wet, windy and incredibly inhospitable morning.'

Connie grimaced and thrust two large mugs of coffee through the hatch.

Geraldine Mullarkey was chatting to Miss de la Mare when the three of us arrived in the meeting room. Gerry was a pretty young woman with short black hair, a pale, delicately boned face and great blue long-lashed Irish eyes. She was clever, personable and very efficient but was an exceptionally private person who, when she wasn't visiting schools, tended to work away from the office, preferring either the SDC or her own home.

We took our places around Miss de la Mare. 'Good morning,' she said cheerfully. 'All ready for a challenging term, I hope. Now, we have a lot to get through this morning—'

Miss de la Mare's introduction was cut short when Connie poked her head round the door. 'I'm sorry to disturb your deliberations, Miss de la Mare,' she said, 'but I have an urgent message for Mr Phinn. His wife's phoned and said to tell him that the squirrel has returned.'

'Thanks, Connie,' I said.

'How very intriguing,' said Sidney. 'You're not some secret agent are you, Gervase? This is not some sort of coded message: "The eagle has landed", "The lion is on the loose", "The squirrel has returned"?'

'We have a squirrel in the loft,' I told him.

'Colleagues,' interrupted the Chief Inspector, 'we really must proceed. Gervase will deal with his squirrel later.' She caught sight of Connie still standing by the door. 'Was there something else, Connie?' she asked.

'Will you remind them about the painters?'

'Painters!' exclaimed Sidney. 'And what painters pray are these?'

'Not your sort,' said Connie. 'Painters and decorators. They'll be in the Centre next week so some of the rooms will be unavailable.'

'But I am running a course next week!' exclaimed Sidney.

'Perhaps you might like to discuss the matter with Connie after the meeting, Sidney,' Miss de la Mare said firmly. 'We really must get on. Thank you once again, Connie.'

Connie departed, mumbling something under her breath.

'Now, as I was saying,' continued the Chief Inspector, 'the term ahead promises to be very challenging but I have every confidence that we will all rise to that challenge.' She picked up a large red folder and placed it before her. 'The main business of the morning concerns reorganisation.'

'Oh no,' sighed Sidney. 'Not more change.'

'I'm afraid so,' said Miss de la Mare. 'The numbers of children attending the county schools has declined considerably over the last few years, which will mean some closures. As you are all aware, I fought long and hard to stop the closures of some schools last year, but I'm afraid I've had to bow to the inevitable with those schools that are less successful.' She picked up a paper. 'Now, I have here a rather convoluted memorandum from Dr Gore.'

'Written by Mrs Savage, no doubt,' added David, 'in her usual incomprehensible style.'

'I have to say,' said the Chief Inspector, 'that the CEO's Personal Assistant does have an excessively wordy way of saying things.'

'I've another name for it,' said David. 'Twaddle!'

'Well, let me read it,' said Miss de la Mare. '"The Education Department, as part of the rigorous ongoing process of consolidating and in the light of the increasing pupil shortfall in the county and in concert with the Education Sub-Committee Staffing and Resources, will be instituting an initiative in which the school inspectorate will take a leading strategic part. The Chief Education Officer is looking for an ongoing 360-degree feedback before the necessary restructuring of the educational provision takes place."'

'Give me strength,' sighed David. 'What is that supposed to mean?'

'It means,' explained the Chief Inspector, 'that we will be responsible for consulting interested parties and seeing through the closures.'

'We will be about as popular with schools as King Herod at a playgroup,' said Sidney.

'If I may continue,' said Miss de la Mare, allowing herself a slight smile, 'an initial selection of the five schools has already been made by Mrs Savage.'

'She has been a busy bee over the summer,' said David.

'I have to say that you are rather hard on Mrs Savage,' said the Chief Inspector. 'I have always found her very professional. Let's move on. Each of us,' she continued, 'will take one of these schools, explain things to the head teacher and governing body, address the parents' meeting, attend the consultative discussions, and submit a report for Dr Gore to take to the Education Sub-Committee. Then final decisions will be made. I am sure I do not need to stress that this is likely to be an extremely sensitive issue, so it requires a great deal of diplomacy and discretion.'

'COUNTY COUNCILLOR PETERSON is on the warpath,' said Miss de la Mare. The other inspectors had gone about their business and I was alone, with dry mouth and beating heart, facing the Chief Inspector.

As I suspected, Councillor Sidebottom hadn't wasted any time in getting in touch with his pal on the Education Committee just as soon as his wife had got home that afternoon to complain about my visit.

County Councillor George Peterson was an insufferably self-opinionated man who always succeeded in irritating me with his sarcastic comments and vacuous views. If I saw his barrel-bodied figure striding down the top corridor at County Hall, or if I caught sight of the ponderous, fleshy face appearing around a corner in Fettlesham High Street, I did a fast disappearing act.

'Councillor Peterson?' I said. 'So he's involved, is he?'

'Yes, I'm afraid he has seen fit to take up the matter,' Miss de la Mare replied. 'Now,' she said, reaching for a substantial file, 'I have the school report here and need to check on a few things. What can you tell me about Mr Hornchurch at Tarncliffe Primary School?' she asked.

'Tarncliffe!' I exclaimed. 'Is this about Tarncliffe?'

'Yes, it is,' the Chief Inspector replied. 'There has been a serious complaint about a teacher called Mr Hornchurch. I believe you have seen this young man teach on a number of occasions.'

I had geared myself up to discuss Ugglemattersby and was so taken by surprise that I was lost for words. 'Well, let's see,' I said. 'Um—he's an unusual man but a real enthusiast. He's keen, hard-working, spends many hours outside school time, organises trips, coaches the football team, conducts the choir, runs an astronomy club. You'll find details of the outstanding results his class achieves in my report. He's just a bit unconventional. I did see Dr Yeats about him because he's, well, rather different from your run-of-the-mill teacher.'

'And what did Dr Yeats say?' asked Miss de la Mare.

'As I recall, he said Mr Hornchurch was a successful deviant—deviant in the sense of diverging from accepted standards of behaviour—and that education would be a dull business if teachers were all the same. He said there is a place in education for the teacher who is a bit out of kilter and that these were the teachers we tend to remember most from our own schooldays.'

'And how is Mr Hornchurch different?' enquired Miss de la Mare.

'He's idiosyncratic,' I said. 'He dresses like a down-at-heel student and his classroom looks as if a hurricane has hit it.' I recalled the man in question—tall, pale-faced, with an explosion of wild woolly hair. I decided not to tell the Chief Inspector how, on that visit, Mr Hornchurch had sat cross-legged on his desk, a cardboard box on his head, his face peering out of a large hole in the front. This was, he explained, to simulate a television set. He then proceeded to tell the children a story, and I have rarely seen a class of children so engrossed.

'I found his planning virtually non-existent and the record system was incomprehensible. But I must add that the quality of the pupils' work was of the very best, and the progress the children made under him was excellent.'

'The proof of the pudding,' murmured Miss de la Mare.

'So what's this all about?'

'A parent of a child in Mr Hornchurch's class has complained to Councillor Peterson that his daughter's teacher uses bad language in the classroom. The parent owns a building firm, NBG Construction, on which Councillor

Peterson is a non-executive director, and he mentioned it to him.'

'Bad language?' I repeated.

'Yes,' replied the Chief Inspector. 'But there is more to it than that. This parent was in a public house and was apparently telling all and sundry how he had made a formal complaint. A reporter from the *Fettlesham Gazette* overheard the conversation, and is writing an article based upon this over-heard discussion about the decline in standards in schools which will appear in next Friday's newspaper. The Editor of the *Gazette* contacted Dr Gore yesterday for a comment, hence the panic at County Hall. The Chief Education Officer, understandably, does not like negative publicity.'

'And what were these words Mr Hornchurch has supposedly used?' I asked.

'I don't know,' replied Miss de la Mare, 'but I am led to believe that they were extremely vulgar and offensive. Of course, Councillor Peterson hurried to County Hall to see Dr Gore, demanding action. Have you ever heard this teacher say anything inappropriate in front of his class?'

'No, I haven't,' I replied, 'and it seems to me it would be so out of charac-ter. He has a very gentle, positive and encouraging manner with the children.'

'Very well,' said Miss de la Mare. 'I would like you to go into the school this afternoon and report back to me first thing on Monday morning. Then we shall have to report back to Dr Gore.'

'Right,' I said, getting up from my chair, 'I had better cancel this after-noon's appointments and get straight on to it.'

'Before you go, wasn't there something you wished to discuss with me?' asked the Chief Inspector.

'Oh that,' I said. 'That can wait.'

4

As soon as I got back to the office, I telephoned Miss Drayton, the head teacher of Tarncliffe Primary School, to arrange the visit for the afternoon. I then called Maurice Hinderwell.

'A squirrel, eh? Oh dear. It'll be a grey squirrel, of course. Oh dear, oh dear,' he sighed, in a prophet-of-doom voice. 'It was in your loft, was it? Sure it wasn't a rat? They are far more active than squirrels at night.'

'No, no, it was definitely a squirrel.'

'You see, Mr Phinn, your grey squirrel is most lively at dawn and dusk, not in the middle of the night,' said Mr Hinderwell.

'Well, I want to get rid of it,' I said. 'It's disturbing our sleep, and my wife's getting into a bit of a state about it.'

He gave a hollow laugh. 'Disturbing your sleep is not all it'll be doing. It'll be chewing and gnawing with its incisors. Squirrels can cause untold damage, biting through your electric cables, nibbling your woodwork, defecating all over the place. They can be bloody pests, can grey squirrels.'

'So, can you help me?' I asked.

'That is what I do, Mr Phinn, help people with a pest problem. I'm the County Pest Control Officer, known affectionately as the Verminator. Now, your squirrel is a rodent like the rat but not quite as elusive and as clever as your average Samuel Whiskers. Have no fear, I'll tell you how to get him.'

'I should be very much obliged,' I said, greatly relieved.

'It's not a good idea to try and poison him. If you put poisoned nuts out, the birds will eat them. Do you know anyone who has a gun?'

'Mr Hinderwell, I really would rather not kill him.'

'Not kill him!' exclaimed Mr Hinderwell. 'It's no use being sentimental about squirrels, Mr Phinn.'

'All the same,' I said, 'is there some other way? I just want to catch him.'

'Well, you could use a trap, I suppose,' he said. 'I could drop one off at the Education Office next week.'

'I'm very grateful, Mr Hinderwell.'

I ARRIVED AT TARNCLIFFE at the very end of the lunch hour. The small primary school, which faced the village green, was a typical Dales stone building, with a porch and mullioned windows. On one side was the village shop, on the other the grey brick Primitive Methodist Chapel.

The head teacher, Miss Drayton, was an optimistic and cheerful person, but when I informed her of the reason for my impromptu visit her face fell.

'Bad language!' she exclaimed. 'Mr Hornchurch? There must be some mistake. As you know, the school comprises one large room divided by a partition. I can hear virtually everything that is said next door to me and I would know if he had used any offensive words. I'm certain Mr Hornchurch would never use inappropriate language with his class. He's very professional. Who made the complaint?'

'A Mr Gaskell,' I told her.

'Oh well, that explains a great deal! I hate to say it, but Mr Gaskell is a most disagreeable man. His daughter only started school last term and already he's been in complaining that we spend too much time on art, poetry and music, which he considers largely a waste of time. And he is always at great pains to tell me how one of the directors of his company is a councillor on the Education Committee and that he agrees with his views.'

'That would be Councillor Peterson. It was Councillor Peterson who brought the matter to the attention of the Chief Education Officer.'

'Was it indeed?' said Miss Drayton, bristling. 'Well, Mr Gaskell's daughter, when she started, hardly said a word—and stuttered when she did. Mr Hornchurch brought her out of her shell. He's mild-mannered and, as I have said before, highly professional. The very idea of him using bad language is inconceivable.' Miss Drayton sighed. 'Anyway, I suppose you had better have a word with Mr Hornchurch.'

'I would prefer it, Miss Drayton,' I said, 'if you were present. I really feel you need to be there when this interview takes place. Perhaps I could join you and the infants for the first part of the afternoon, observe Mr Hornchurch for the remainder and then speak to you both after school.'

'Very well,' she agreed. She looked extremely angry.

'I am certain it's a storm in a teacup,' I reassured her, 'but I am sure that you understand that I do have to investigate it.'

'Very well then,' she said, 'we will leave it until after school. I cannot for the life of me understand why Mr Gaskell never mentioned the matter to me, going to County Hall instead.'

WHEN I ENTERED the infants' class, Miss Drayton gave me a selection of the children's workbooks to look at while she marked the register.

'You might care to browse through these,' she said. 'As you will see, children do very well in this school.' I could tell she was making a point.

I sat in the corner of the classroom in the small carpeted reading area adjacent to the partition to examine them. I could hear Mr Hornchurch quite clearly behind the partition, telling the children about the effects of pollution on the environment in a clear and interesting manner.

I was so engrossed in his account that I didn't see the girl who had appeared at my side. She tugged at my sleeve.

'Hello,' she said.

'Hello,' I replied.

She was a small child with sparkling, intelligent eyes and corkscrew curls. She stared at me intently. 'Who are you?' she asked.

'Mr Phinn,' I answered.

'I'm Rhiannon. It's a Welsh name. My mummy and daddy can speak Welsh and I know some words.'

'Really.'

'Yes, big words. I know a lot of four-letter words.'

'Do you really?' I must have sounded very impressed.

'And some five-letter ones too. *Cwtch*—that means cuddle,' explained the child. 'I have a *cwtch* every night when I have my story. We'll be having a story this afternoon, after we've finished our poems.'

'And what are your poems about?' I asked.

'We're writing poems about excuses. We have to think of lots of reasons for coming late to school.'

'I see. And what excuses have you thought of so far?' I asked.

'The alarm clock didn't go off,' the child told me, 'I forgot my PE kit and had to go back home to get it.'

'Those are very good excuses,' I told her.

'I've got another one, too,' she said. 'A really good one because it really happened once,' the child informed me.

'And what's that?' I asked.

'Our electric gates wouldn't open,' she told me.

With that, she took off, sat at her table, and got on with her poem.

I have had so many conversations like this with young children and have so often been brought out of a black mood by their chatter. Small children are a delight. Everything in the world to them is new and exciting. They are fascinated by people, and are wonderfully forthcoming in their talk. With age, one tends to become far more self-conscious. One has only to travel in a lift with a group of adults: they stare at the ceiling, examine their shoes, look anywhere as long as their eyes don't meet yours. If a child is in the lift, it is a different matter. He or she will stare intently at you, taking everything in, and then very often make a comment such as: 'I have my Mickey Mouse knickers on', or '*I'm going to the pet department, where're you going?*'

I was brought out of my reverie by Miss Drayton. 'Mr Phinn? I was wondering if you might like to tell the children a story.'

'Of course,' I said.

'I was about to start *The Three Billy Goats Gruff*,' she said, handing me a book. 'While you are telling them the story, I'll take the opportunity of making a phone call.' She lowered her voice. 'I think it might be prudent for me to have a word with someone in my professional association. Mr

Hornchurch might need to have his union representative present.'

'I really don't think, Miss Drayton—' I began.

'I am sure you'll be all right with the class by yourself, won't you?' enquired the head teacher, giving me little chance of arguing with her. She clapped her hands to gain the children's attention. 'We are very lucky, children,' she announced, 'to have Mr Phinn, a very special visitor, with us this afternoon and he has asked if he might tell today's story. I know'—at this point she stared intently at a small boy with a shock of ginger hair and his two front teeth missing—'that we will all be on our very best behaviour, won't we?'

'Yes, Miss Drayton,' chanted the class obediently.

Without any bidding, the children gathered around me in the reading area, and sat with crossed legs and folded arms, their faces staring up at me expectantly. Miss Drayton quietly left the room. Anyone who thinks that handling a group of twenty infant children is an easy job should have a go. It demands a great deal of expertise, as I was soon to discover.

'Good afternoon, children,' I said cheerfully.

'Good afternoon, Mr Thin,' they all chorused.

'Is that your real name?' asked the ginger-haired boy. He had a small green candle of mucus appearing from his nose. He sniffed it away noisily but it re-emerged immediately. 'Because you're not very thin, are you?'

'It's Mr Phinn,' I said. 'Like on the back of a shark.'

'I like sharks,' said the boy.

'I don't,' said a tiny, elfin-faced child with long black plaits and impressive pink-framed glasses. 'I'm frightened of sharks.'

'I'm frightened of spiders,' said another.

'Well, this story isn't about sharks or spiders.' I told the class, smiling. 'It's about three goats, called the Billy Goats Gruff.'

'Goats have horns,' volunteered Rhiannon. 'And they butt,' she added.

The ginger-haired boy immediately began to butt the girl next to him.

'Don't do that,' I said. 'It's not very nice to butt other people, is it?' The boy pulled a face but stopped. 'So, children,' I said, continuing, 'this is a famous story called *The Three Billy Goats Gruff*.'

'I've heard it before,' announced the ginger-haired boy, sniffing loudly.

'And what's your name?' I asked.

'James Oliver Jonathan Ormerod,' he replied. 'My granddad calls me Jo-Jo but my dad calls me Jack.'

'Well, Jack,' I said pleasantly, 'you're going to hear the story again. Now, let us all sit up nice and straight, children, ready to listen.' I began. 'Once upon a time there were three Billy Goats Gruff. There was the father, Big Billy Goat Gruff; the mother, Medium-sized Billy Goat Gruff; and—'

'Little Billy Goat Gruff,' cut in Jack.

'And Little Billy Goat Gruff,' I repeated, fixing Jack with an eagle eye. 'They lived in a valley in the winter to keep warm, but when spring came they climbed up to the rich green meadow on the hillside to eat the fresh green grass that grew there. Each morning they would run across the fields and cross the rickety-rackety old wooden bridge that spanned the river.'

'I wouldn't like to go over a rickety-rackety old wooden bridge,' said the child who was afraid of sharks. 'It sounds dangerous.'

'Well, the Billy Goats Gruff were very careful,' I told her.

'And there's this troll under it,' said Jack, growling. 'Grrr! Grrr!'

'Yes, I know there is,' I said, 'and we haven't got to the troll yet. Now, be a good boy, Jack, and listen. You're spoiling it for everyone else.' I proceeded. 'Now under the bridge there lived a mean and ugly troll, with eyes as big as saucers, ears as sharp as knives and a nose as long as a poker. Now this troll was very bad-tempered and unfriendly.'

'Like my granny,' said the child frightened of spiders. 'She's very bad-tempered and unfriendly.'

I moved on hurriedly: 'and the troll was always hungry. He waited under the bridge for creatures to cross, and then he gobbled them up with great sharp teeth and claws.'

'I know what I'd do if an ugly troll jumped out on me,' said Jack.

'And what would you do, Jack?' I asked wearily.

'I'd shit myself!'

'Perhaps we ought to have another story,' I suggested, reaching over to the bookcase.

MR HORNCHURCH greeted me enthusiastically when I entered his classroom later that afternoon. I feared that this warm welcome was going to make my meeting with him later in the afternoon all the more difficult.

The teacher seemed to have followed the recommendations in my last report. On my first visit, the mass of clutter and colour would have been the perfect set for a film version of *The Old Curiosity Shop*. On two large tables there had been bleached skulls and old bird feathers, shards of pottery and clay models. Now it looked more like the conventional classroom, far better organised and neater but, I guessed for the children, a great deal less interesting.

Mr Hornchurch's appearance had undergone a change, too. He was now dressed more conservatively in a pair of baggy blue corduroy trousers, shapeless tweed jacket, white shirt, and a loud kipper tie. However, he still had the wild and woolly head of mousy hair surrounding his long, pale face.

Having wished me good afternoon, the junior class resumed their activities. One group of children was gathered round the teacher as he conducted an experiment involving a tank of water. They were predicting whether various objects would sink or float, and I listened for a while to a fascinating and impressive discussion. Another group was busy writing a play the class would perform at the end of term, while a third group was writing stories.

'May I look?' I asked a blond-haired boy with large ears.

'Sure,' he replied. I sat next to him and examined his exercise book. 'I'm writing a newspaper article about the effects of pollution on the marine environment. We went on a trip with Mr Hornchurch to an aquarium last Saturday and I've got lots of facts and figures.'

It was an excellent piece of work—clear, well structured and neat.

'You're a fine writer,' I told the boy.

'Thanks,' he said. 'I want to be a journalist when I leave school.'

'And you seem to be a very good speller,' I said. 'How old are you?'

The boy smiled broadly. 'Eleven,' he replied.

'Is everyone in the class as good as you?' I asked.

'Mostly,' he told me. 'You see, we do quite a bit on spellings with Mr Hornchurch. We do rules for a start.'

'Such as?'

'There's "i" before "e" except after "c". Of course, it doesn't always work. Mr Hornchurch says that where there's a rule, there's generally an exception. That rule works with me,' the boy continued, 'because I'm called Kieran but it doesn't work with my mum, she's called Sheila, and it doesn't work with my dad, he's call Keith. They're what's called "irregulars". We list any irregulars in our spelling book.' The boy produced a notebook. On each page was a different spelling rule neatly written out.

'Mr Hornchurch appears to have taught you very well indeed.' I told him.

'We don't just do rules,' the boy continued. 'We learn what Mr Hornchurch calls "little wrinkles".'

'Go on,' I said, intrigued.

'Say if you want to learn a word like "necessary". We learn "one coffee and two sugars", then you remember it has one letter "c" and two letter "s"s.'

'That's very good,' I said, laughing.

'Then we do mnemonics,' said the boy. 'We work out mnemonics for difficult words. Take "because"—"big elephants can always understand small elephants"; "rhythm"—"rejoice heartily, your teacher has measles". You can work out a mnemonic for any difficult spelling.'

I was reminded of the word that was almost consistently misspelt in letters I received from parents when I was a teacher: 'diarrhoea'. One very inventive parent wrote to me saying that, 'Debbie is off with dire rear', another that his son was absent with 'diahr, dihia, diahrh,' with all three attempts crossed out and then the phrase 'the shits' written after it.

'Do you know how to spell "diarrhoea"?'

The boy shook his blond head.

'Look the word up in the dictionary, and then see if you can think of a sentence to help you remember how to spell that.'

'I'll have a go,' he said and off he went to find a dictionary.

I turned my attention now to two girls working together on the next table.

'May I ask what you're doing?'

'Me and Miranda—I'm Rowena, by the way—' said the first girl, 'are writing a guide for the aquarium of the future. We all visited the aquarium last Saturday and—'

'I d-didn't,' interrupted her partner, a mousy little girl with large glasses. 'My f-father wouldn't l-let me g-go,' stuttered Miranda. 'He d-doesn't believe in s-school trips. He s-says they're a waste of t-time.'

Undoubtedly, this diffident girl with the stutter, sad eyes and small pinched face was the child who had innocently been the cause of all the upset.

'So what have you written so far?' I asked.

Rowena shuffled through the papers. 'This is our second draft. We've just got it back from Mr Hornchurch with ideas on how we can improve it.'

'It sounds very interesting,' I said, turning to the other girl. 'And how are you getting on at school then, Miranda?'

She nodded. 'I l-like it here. It's much b-better than my l-last school.'

'Good,' I said, but before I could question her further, Kieran was at my side.

'Diarrhoea!' he announced loudly and spelt out the word: 'D-I-A-R-R-H-O-E-A.' Then he recited his mnemonic: '"Died in a Rolls-Royce having over-eaten again".'

'Very good,' I said, clapping my hands.

'There's more,' he said. 'This is the best,' he told me with a cheeky grin on his face. '"Dash in a real rush, help or exploding arse!"'

'Excellent!' I said. Biting my bottom lip to stifle my laughter, I suggested that perhaps he might like to tweak the ending a little bit, so it became: 'Dash in a real rush, help or else accident.'

AFTER SCHOOL had broken up, I stood by the window in the head teacher's office listening as Miss Drayton explained to Mr Hornchurch the real reason for my visit. To my surprise, the man did not look at all concerned as he listened patiently until the head teacher asked for his comments.

He smiled and shook his head. 'I assure you,' he said, 'that I have never used any inappropriate language in front of the children.'

After questioning him in more detail, Miss Drayton seemed satisfied that her colleague had nothing for which to answer, and I agreed with her. Then she looked out of the window. 'Ah, here comes Mr Gaskell,' she said, rising from her chair. 'Now we will get to the bottom of this matter.' She shot out of the room, leaving the door open for us to see what was going on.

'May I have a word with you, Mr Gaskell?' she said as he headed for the classroom to collect his daughter.

'I'm in a hurry, Miss Drayton,' he replied, not stopping. 'I'm late for a meeting already.' He sounded an ill-mannered individual.

'It is important,' she said stiffly, 'very important. I should be grateful if you would step into my room for a moment.'

'Well, you'll have to be quick,' he said, looking at his watch.

Miss Drayton returned to the room, accompanied by the parent, a stout man with a florid face and precious little hair. Mr Hornchurch got to his feet, but while Mr Gaskell eyed me suspiciously, he did not acknowledge the teacher in any way. Miss Drayton sat down behind her desk. 'Do take a seat, Mr Gaskell,' she said, her tone of voice glacial. 'This will hopefully only take a moment.'

He flopped in the chair and breathed noisily. 'What is it, then?'

'This gentleman, Mr Gaskell,' said the head teacher, 'is Mr Phinn, the County Inspector for English and Drama.'

'Oh yes,' said the parent. 'So what's this all about?'

'Mr Phinn has been sent from the Education Department at County Hall regarding a complaint you have made; I believe you have had reason to contact County Councillor Peterson about Mr Hornchurch,' she said.

The parent coloured up. 'Yes, I—er—did mention something to Councillor Peterson,' he said. 'I was unhappy about Miranda coming out with some of the words Mr Hornchurch had used in his lesson.' The man puffed himself up like a huge turkey.

'And might I ask why you did not bring this complaint to me?' asked the head teacher.

'I've complained about things before, Miss Drayton, as you well know,' said the parent defensively, 'and nothing's been done.'

'Your other complaints were curricular matters, Mr Gaskell,' said the head teacher. 'As I explained to you, I do not seek to tell you how to build houses and asked you not to tell me how to run a school.'

'Yes, well as a parent—'

'And now,' continued Miss Drayton, ignoring his response, 'perhaps you would tell us what these words were.'

'I don't like repeating them,' he said, sticking out his chin. 'They're rude, vulgar words, swear words.'

'Maybe you could tell us then what letters these words begin with?'

'There was the "b" word,' he said.

'The "b" word,' mused Miss Drayton. 'There are quite a few of those.'

'Balls!' said the parent. 'That's the word he used. When my Miranda came out with it, I couldn't believe my ears.'

'Is it not possible that your daughter could have heard this word on your building site?' asked Miss Drayton.

'No!' exclaimed the parent. 'I asked her where she had heard it and she said in the classroom from Mr Hornchurch. "It's cold enough to freeze the balls of a brass monkey this morning," she said, and then later she asked me if there'd been a "cock-up" when I told her I was collecting her from school and not her mother. This is not the sort of thing you expect your child to learn at school.'

Miss Drayton turned to the accused. 'Mr Hornchurch?'

'I did indeed use these expressions,' he admitted.

I saw the head teacher close her eyes momentarily and take a short breath.

'But the expressions are in no way vulgar, Mr Gaskell,' explained Mr Hornchurch, who still appeared quite unruffled.

'They are in *my* book!' the parent snapped.

'Well, they are not vulgar in the *Oxford English Dictionary*,' said the teacher, 'where you will find the origins and the meanings of these old expressions. If I might elucidate? You see,' enthused Mr Hornchurch, 'we are doing a history topic on Admiral Lord Nelson and I was explaining to the children that some of the expressions in common parlance today date back centuries and often have nautical origins. For example, something done inefficiently is known as a "cock-up" and the expression has a long provenance. The "cock" is the firing lever of the pistol, which can be raised to release the trigger. If the cock is up too far, the gun will not fire, hence the expression a "cock-up". I imagine you were thinking of something else.' He gave a small smile.

'As to "freezing the balls of a brass monkey". I was describing the scene at Trafalgar and what could happen if the sailors were not prepared. The "monkey" was a brass rack on which the cannonballs were stored. In very cold weather this monkey contracted thus ejecting the balls. The expression actually is "cold enough to freeze the balls off"—and not "of"—"a brass monkey". You see, English is a rich and poetic language, full of interesting expressions, which I think children should know about, and always seem to enjoy. If you had listened to Miranda she might have explained things.'

'Well, I wasn't aware that's what these expressions meant,' said Mr Gaskell, beginning to rise from his chair.

'Do sit down, Mr Gaskell,' said the head teacher, 'I haven't quite finished with this matter yet. You have made a serious allegation against a member of my staff, a false accusation which might very well have damaged his reputation. Further to that, it appears that you have repeated these unfounded allegations in a public house and now a newspaper article is to appear, so I hope you know the meaning of the word "libel", too. It seems to me, Mr Gaskell, you are in very hot water indeed.'

'Well, I wasn't to know,' he whined. 'I thought—as most people do, I reckon—that these expressions were rude.' He squirmed in the chair.

The head teacher nodded at me. 'Have you anything to add, Mr Phinn?'

'I think Mr Gaskell should contact the *Fettlesham Gazette* and explain it was all a misunderstanding,' I said.

'That goes without question,' said Miss Drayton. 'The reputation of the school could very well have been tarnished by such accusations.' She turned to her colleague. 'Have you anything to add, Mr Hornchurch?'

'It's just a misunderstanding,' he said. 'Let's forget all about it. I'm taking the children on a trip to the Science Museum next Saturday. It would be very nice if your Miranda could come after all.'

'I don't know about that,' Mr Gaskell replied quietly.

'School trips are an important part of the curriculum,' said the head teacher.

The parent stood up. 'Well, I must be off.'

'Yes,' said Miss Drayton, rising from her chair and giving Mr Gaskell a tight little smile of dismissal. 'I suggest we conclude this very unfortunate meeting. But before you go, Mr Gaskell,' said Miss Drayton, 'I rather think you have something to say to Mr Hornchurch.'

'Something to say?'

'An apology?'

The man coughed nervously. 'Yes, well . . . er . . . I'm sorry for the . . . er . . . trouble, I'm sure,' he mumbled. 'And . . . er . . . I'll let you know about Miranda and the trip.' And with that, he lumbered from the room.

'One expression from this rich and poetic language of ours,' I observed, 'which comes to my mind is being "taken down a peg or two".'

'Ah yes,' said Mr Hornchurch. 'Now that's another very interesting nautical expression. At the time of Nelson—'

'I think we have had enough expressions for one day, thank you,' said Miss Drayton, laughing.

I WAS at the office early on the Monday morning, eager to report back to Miss de la Mare about Tarncliffe. Julie was already tapping away noisily at the keyboard in the adjoining office when I arrived.

'Morning, Mr Phinn,' she said. 'Miss de la Mare rang through and asked me to tell you she's running a bit late and she'll ring when she's ready for you.

'So I have an extra ten minutes, good,' I said.

'Well, there's plenty of work for you on your desk and there're some calls to make from Friday afternoon.'

'No peace for the wicked,' I said, looking through the papers on my desk.

'So, how's that little squirrel of yours, then?' she asked.

'Who told you about the squirrel?' I asked.

'Mr Clamp, who else?' She perched herself on the end of my desk and straightened her strip of emerald-green skirt. 'We were having a laugh about it on Friday.'

'Well, I can tell you that Christine and I aren't laughing at the moment. We keep being woken up in the dead of night by its scratching and scuttling about in the loft. It is driving us mad. I'm expecting Mr Hinderwell to deliver a squirrel trap this week. Keep an eye out for it, will you?'

'Certainly. I'll put it by your desk when it arrives.' And with that, she tottered off on her bright green high heels. A moment later, she popped her head round the door. 'I meant to say, will you *please* give that double-barrelled woman a call before your meeting? I've left a note with her number on your desk.' She then adopted a frightfully upper-class accent. 'I hev to speak to Mr Phinn abite something very himportant. It's abslewtly hessential he rings me.'

The urgent call was from the Honourable Margot Cleaver-Canning. I had met this formidable woman with purple-tinted bouffant hair a couple of years before when I had been inveigled by her into taking a minor part in an amateur production of *The Sound of Music*. As the curtain had fallen, I had been informed that Christine had been rushed into hospital to have our first child. There had been no time to change out of our costumes. Her long-suffering husband, Winco—Wing Commander Norman Cleaver-Canning (Rtd) DFC—resplendent in a German admiral's uniform, had driven me in his Mercedes at breakneck speed to Fettlesham Royal Infirmary, with the Mother Abbess (Mrs Cleaver-Canning) directing proceedings from the passenger seat. I had arrived just in time to see my son being born.

I made the call.

'Gervase, how are you?' came a high-pitched voice down the line.

'I'm fine, thank you, Mrs Cleaver-Canning,' I replied.

'I do wish you would call me Margot.'

'Well, I'm fine, thank you, Margot, and how are you?'

'Top notch. And how is that dear little child of yours?'

'He's thriving.'

'I am so glad to hear it,' she said. 'Now, I'll come straight to the point. I am desperate for a man again.'

'Oh, no, Mrs Cleaver-Canning—er, Margot. I really cannot. I'm afraid—'

'Now, before you turn me down,' she interrupted, 'please hear me out. It's not a big part and you would only make a short entrance at the very end, just as you did when you gave that barnstorming performance as the SS lieutenant in *The Sound of Music*. There would be minimal attendance at rehearsals. So please don't turn me down.'

'I'm up to my eyes at the moment and—' I began again.

'It's called *The Dame of Sark* by William Douglas-Home,' Mrs Cleaver-Canning continued. 'A poignant piece set in one of the Channel Islands at the time of the German Occupation. I will be playing the lead part of Sybil, the courageous Dame of Sark, who comes to respect and even like the Commander of the German forces. Winco will be playing him. You would take the part of Colonel Graham who liberates the island in the last scene. It's a little gem of a part, a mere eighteen lines, and you're just ideal for it. Winco will drop a copy of the play off and you can peruse it at your leisure.'

'That's just the point, Margot,' I said, trying to sound forceful. 'I don't seem to have any leisure at the moment.' There was a touch of desperation in my voice. 'I really am so very busy.'

'Oh *please*, Gervase,' she said. '*Please* don't disappoint me.' And then she played her trump card. 'And you do owe me a favour. I mean, if it hadn't been for Winco driving you to the hospital . . .'

'The least I can do is look at the play,' I said feebly.

'Thank you *so* much,' oozed Mrs Cleaver-Canning.

Of course I knew, and so did Mrs Cleaver-Canning, that in effect I had agreed to take the part. I couldn't very well look through the script and then refuse to do it. When I thought about it later, I was quite pleased I had agreed. I had enjoyed the badinage at the rehearsals and meeting people outside the world of education. And, as Mrs C-C had reminded me, I did owe her a favour. However, I decided to pick the right moment to tell Christine.

MISS DE LA MARE'S office was on the top corridor of County Hall, near Dr Gore's. I presented a full written report on Tarncliffe School and explained to the Chief Inspector how the confusion had arisen.

'Thank you for dealing with it, Gervase,' Miss de la Mare said. 'I shall explain matters to Dr Gore and Councillor Peterson when I meet with them later this morning. I will also ring the Editor of the *Gazette* to make sure that article doesn't go ahead.'

I took a deep breath. 'There was another matter I wanted to speak to you about,' I said. 'Ugglemattersby Junior School.'

The Chief Inspector gave a slight smile. 'Go on,' she said.

She listened patiently as I admitted that I had been at fault for not having returned to the school to check on progress. There was what I felt to be an interminable silence before the Chief Inspector spoke. 'You are right,' she said at last, 'you should have followed things up. It's all very well writing critical reports on schools but if nothing is done about them it is a pointless exercise.'

'I see that,' I said quietly. 'I know it's a case of closing the stable door after the horse has bolted,' I said, 'but I've suggested in my new report that the team undertakes a full inspection of the school and that competency proceedings be considered with regard to the two teachers.'

'That might not be necessary,' said the Chief Inspector. 'You see, Ugglemattersby Junior is on the list of schools we are thinking of closing.'

'Closing!' I exclaimed.

'We have it in mind to amalgamate the Junior and the Infant Schools,' she told me. 'Numbers in the Juniors are declining and the Infant School is on a spacious site which could be further developed to accommodate the older children. It seems the best course of action in the circumstances.'

'I see,' I murmured.

'Quite fortuitous really, isn't it, Gervase?' said the Chief Inspector, giving a small, enigmatic smile.

5

Andy was a large pink-faced bear of a boy, with coarse bristly brown hair and enormous ears. I had just come down to the kitchen on Saturday morning in my dressing gown, and was making an early-morning cup of tea, when his great beaming face appeared at the window.

'You must be Andy?' I said as I let him into the kitchen.

'That's reight, Mester Phinn,' he said. 'Up wi' t'lark and rarin' to go. Is that a pot o' tea tha brewin'?'

'It is. Would you like a cup?' I asked.

'Cup o' tea gus down a treat this time o' t'mornin',' he said, seating himself at the kitchen table. 'Mi Uncle 'arry 'appen told thee I'd be comin' up this mornin', did 'e?'

'Yes, he did,' I replied, 'but not quite this early. It's only eight o'clock.'

'Well, tha sees,' he said, 'after I've sooarted thy garden out, I'm down to owld Missis Poskitt's to paint 'er iron yats. Then I've got sheep to fettle and beasts to feed an' toneet I'm goin' to Young Farmers pea and pie supper.'

I passed the boy a mug from the dresser. 'Busy man,' I said.

'I'm tryin' to save a bit o' money, tha sees, to get me through college. When I leave school next year, I'm 'opin' to go to Askham Bryan Agricultural College, but there's fees an' such. I can't wait to leave school.'

'Which school do you go to?' I asked him.

'West Challerton 'igh. 'Eadmaster, Mester Pennington-Smith, is only bothered abaat bright kids an' them what are good at sports. Wunt know me from Adam.'

I decided not to probe any more. 'So,' I said, 'do you think you can sort out my garden?'

'Oh, I can fettle it all reight. I can see there's a fair bit o' work needs doin', mind. It's like a jungle out theer.'

'I've not had much time to do it lately,' I said. 'I meant to make a start after we got back from our holidays but I didn't and now autumn is here.'

'Nivver thee mind, Mester Phinn, I'll soon 'ave it fettle,' said the boy.

'We haven't discussed your—' I started.

'We can sooart that out later,' he told me, 'when tha's seen what I've done. I'll do a good job for thee, Mester Phinn. Tha'll not be disappointed.'

'Fair enough,' I said.

'Oh, and yer gutterin' needs replacin' round t'side otherwise tha'll get watter comin' in. I'll bring mi ladders next week.'

Andy drained the mug and banged it down onto the kitchen table just as Christine came into the kitchen with the baby.

'You must be Andy,' she said.

'I am, missis,' he replied, standing up and extending a hand as large as a spade. 'Pleased to meet you.' He then pushed his large pink face close to the child. 'And this must be t'little un. Hey up, he's a bobby dazzler, is't 'e?' Andy tickled little Richard gently under his chin.

'So,' said Christine, 'is everything arranged?'

'It appears so,' I said.

'So what's wi' t'squirrels, then?' Andy asked.

'Who told you about the squirrel? I said.

'Well, there's a brace on 'em round back in a cage,' replied the boy.

Maurice Hinderwell had delivered a squirrel cage and as he suggested I had positioned the wire cage with the trap door in a corner of the back garden, close to the squirrel's point of entry under the eaves. I stocked it with a handful of honey-coated peanuts. However, each morning, I would check the trap but it remained irritatingly empty.

'So we've caught *two* squirrels?' I asked Andy now.

'Big uns, an' all,' said the boy. 'Dust tha want to look at 'em?'

Christine gently covered Richard with a shawl, then the Phinn family went out into the garden with Andy to view our bushy-tailed captives.

'Ahh', said Christine, 'aren't they sweet with their little furry faces?'

'Tree rats,' said Andy bluntly. 'Does tha want me to get rid of 'em for you?'

'Not kill them!' exclaimed Christine, looking aghast.

'Best thing, missis,' replied the boy. 'They're vermin. I'll just drop t'cage in your watter butt an' drown t'little devils.'

'No, no,' said Christine firmly, 'I won't let you do that. My husband will take them somewhere and set them free.'

'Will I?' I asked.

'Yes, you will,' she said firmly.

'Suit thissen, missis,' said Andy, shrugging, 'but you mark my words. This is their territory an', sure as sixpence, they'll be back.'

'Not if I take them a good distance,' I said.

'Want to bet on it?' asked Andy. 'I'll wager thee a fiver they'll be back.'

'How will you know?' I asked. 'One squirrel looks much like another.'

'I'll show thee,' said Andy, 'hang on a mo,' and he walked across to the back door where he had left an old holdall. He rifled through the contents and returned holding a spray can. 'I'll put a touch of this rust-repellent undercoat on t'tails of these two critters and then we'll know whether or not it's t'same squirrels if we catch any more.' Before I could argue, he liberally sprayed the tails of the two terrified creatures with the dark red paint. 'Now, if a couple o' grey squirrels wi' red tails are in your trap next week, we'll know I was reight, won't we, an' you, Mester Phinn, will be 'andin' over a fiver.'

ANDY WORKED HARD in the garden for the next three hours, and when he left the place looked a whole lot better. The sun had come out, and it had turned into a glorious autumn day. I suggested to Christine that we should load the squirrels into the car and take them up to the moors to release them.

So, with the caged creatures safely in the boot of the car and baby Richard strapped in the back, we set off through Hawksrill village with its cluster of grey stone cottages, ancient Norman church and the little school.

As we passed the pub, the Royal Oak, Christine pointed. 'Look,' she said, 'it's been done up.' The window frames and door had been painted a bright green and there were two stone troughs on either side planted with dahlias.

We drove on for several miles, past pale green fields where flocks of black-faced sheep meandered between bleached limestone walls and sleepy-looking cattle, chewing the cud, stared impassively.

After about fifteen minutes, Christine said suddenly, 'What about there? You could release the squirrels in that little copse.'

Beyond a field was a clump of tall firs surrounded by thick bushes.

'It's right off the road,' I said. 'It would be easier if I put them out here.'

'It's not that far and, look, there's a track down the side of the field leading to it. We don't want them to get run over, do we?'

'All right,' I grumbled. I set off with the cage down the track to the little covert. It took some time to persuade the wretched creatures to leave the cage but finally they left their prison and scampered off into the grass.

I had just set off back down the track when a loud voice sounded behind me. 'Hey, you there! What do you think you're doing?'

I stopped and turned to see a small, sinister-looking man, with a face as wrinkled and brown as an old russet apple. He was wearing leather gaiters and a green padded waistcoat and carried a shotgun under his arm.

'Good morning,' I croaked somewhat nervously.

He glowered at me in return and raised the shotgun.

'This is Lord Marrick's estate,' he told me, eyeing the cage I was holding. 'What are you doing?'

'I'm sorry, I didn't realise,' I replied. 'I was releasing some squirrels.'

The man lowered the gun. 'Releasing some squirrels?' he repeated very slowly, as if I had said something highly offensive.

I attempted to explain. 'They decided to make their home in my cottage. I managed to catch them and was just setting them free. I wasn't aware that it was Lord Marrick's land.'

'Well, it is. I'm Lord Marrick's gamekeeper,' he told me, 'and I spend most of my time killing vermin that eat the eggs of His Lordship's game birds and seeing off poachers and trespassers. Are you aware of the damage they cause?' he asked. 'Young saplings, which we plant in this woodland at great expense, are destroyed by your squirrels. They gnaw through the bark to get at the sap. They leave a raw scar, which encourages a fungus, which can kill or deform trees. Did you know that?'

'I wasn't aware of that, but—' I started.

'And were you aware that it is illegal to either keep or release grey squirrels unless you have a special licence from the Ministry of Agriculture. Have you such a licence?'

'No. I'm sorry,' I said. 'I didn't realise.'

The gamekeeper sucked in his bottom lip. 'I'm minded to take you up to Manston Hall with me and get you to explain yourself to His Lordship.'

'I won't do it again.' I sounded like a naughty schoolboy caught in the act by an angry head teacher. The last thing I wanted was to be hauled up in front of Lord Marrick, who happened to sit on the Education Committee.

'Well, make sure you don't. Now, get off this land,' ordered the gamekeeper, 'and if I see you again, you'll get a backside full of buckshot.'

'YOU WERE A LONG TIME,' said Christine when I arrived, hot and flustered, back at the car. 'I was beginning to worry. Have you released them?'

'I have,' I said shortly. I was keen to be on our way.

'I think they'll be happy in that little wood, don't you?' she asked.

'Idyllically,' I replied, thinking of what awaited them if they so much as showed a glimpse of their red tails.

'COME ALONG,' said Christine the following day before lunch. 'Get your coat. I'm taking you for a drink.'

'I thought you wanted me to dig the allotment this afternoon—'

'I think it's about time we met the new landlord at the Royal Oak,' she told me. 'He's obviously been treading on a lot of toes in the village. I thought we'd pop in and have a look for ourselves.'

'Will your mother keep an eye on Richard?' I asked.

'Yes, and she's also offered to do the vegetables, so we've got an hour before lunch is ready.'

'But if I have a pint now, I'll be no good for digging the allotment after lunch.'

'Look,' said Christine, putting her hands on her hips, 'we have precious little time to go out together, so when my mother agrees to look after Richard for an hour, we're going out. No arguments. Now come along, chop, chop.'

'I love it when you play the head teacher,' I said, laughing. 'You're like a dominatrix.'

'If you don't hurry up,' she said, 'I'll get my whip out. I want to see what changes the new landlord's made. It's about time that old pub was brought into the twentieth century.'

'I like it like that,' I said. 'It's rather quaint.'

'Quaint!' exclaimed Christine. 'My understanding of the word "quaint" is "attractively old-fashioned". There is nothing attractive about the Royal Oak. It is—or, rather, was—smoky, dirty, noisy and uncomfortable. The place needed more than a lick of paint, and the changes may not be that bad.'

'Yes, well, I still wouldn't like to see the old place being altered too much,' I said, wrapping my arms around her waist. 'It's part of the history of the village. It's all about tradition.'

THE ROYAL OAK hadn't, until now, changed in years. Outside, a dilapidated wooden board depicting a bewigged Charles II, one hand holding high a sword, and standing regally beneath a huge oak tree, had hung at the front of the inn. The public bar had been dim and smoky, reeking of beer and tobacco. There had been four ancient and sticky-topped trestle-style tables, rickety wooden chairs, a dusty inglenook, and a flagged and heavily stained floor. There had been no attempt to provide any physical comfort for customers.

On Thursday and Friday nights, it was the custom for Harry Cotton and three other worthies of the village to arrive at the Royal Oak and take their places at the corner table to play dominoes. The foursome comprised Harry, George Hemmings, Thomas Umpleby and Hezekiah Longton. Harry, George and Thomas were peas out of the same pod: all three had full heads of silver hair, thick bristling eyebrows, wide, weather-beaten faces and small, shrewd eyes set amid nests of wrinkles.

Mr Longton was very different. He was a tall, lean individual who, despite his advancing age, walked with a straight back and without the aid of a stick. When this quietly spoken man did venture an opinion, which was rarely, it was clear that he had a lively, intelligent mind. He always made an effort to look smart and was never seen in the village without a clean white collar and tie, a waistcoat with a heavy silver fob dangling across his chest, a tweed jacket, green cord trousers and highly polished brown boots.

The 'gang of four' would ensconce themselves in their corner and discuss the day's events before settling down to their game. When the serious business of the dominoes was over and tankards were filled with frothing ale, Harry would light his old black briar pipe and sometimes Thomas Umpleby could be persuaded to recite a poem. His *pièce de résistance* was 'The Wensley Lass', a wonderfully expressive dialect poem, which he would declaim passionately, hand on heart, in his rough, rich, racy native idiom.

When we arrived at the pub that Sunday morning we were expecting change but, even so, were surprised by the extent of it.

'I see that the Merry Monarch has been given his marching orders,' I said, looking up. The old inn sign had gone and in its place hung a brightly painted board with the outline of an oak tree and the lettering 'THE OAK'.

We went into the public bar. Gone was the old stone-flagged floor; instead there were polished anaemic-looking floorboards. The ancient trestles and hard wooden chairs had been replaced by high round tubular-steel stools and matching tables. In the fireplace, where there used to be a blazing log fire, there was now a modern electric unit with flickering false coal. Perched on the stools like strange and shabby birds sat three of the regulars, looking far from happy.

'Hey up,' said Harry as we entered. 'It's t'schoil hinspector.'

'Hello,' I said cheerfully.

'Don't offen see thee in 'ere,' said George Hemmings and then, raising his hand in greeting, said, 'Mornin', Missis Phinn.'

'Good morning,' replied Christine, giving him a stunning smile.

'I was wantin' to speak to you, Mester Phinn,' said George Hemmings, 'about that allotment of yourn. It wants fettlin'.'

'Tha right there,' agreed Harry.

I began to wish that we had never set foot in the pub.

'Now you tek 'ezekiah 'ere,' observed Thomas Umpleby. Mr Longton smiled. 'Best gardener in Yorkshire. I'll tell thee what, Mester Phinn, tha wants to let 'im 'ave a look at thy hallotment and tell thee what to plant.'

'I'd be more than happy,' said Hezekiah. 'More than happy.'

'That's very kind of you, Mr Longton,' I said. 'I might very well take you up on that.' I was keen to move the conversation on, so, looking around me, commented, 'It certainly looks a great deal brighter in here.'

'Oh aye,' said Harry, 'it does that an' I'll tell thee summat else an' all, some of us dunt like it.'

'Nay,' agreed George, and shifted uncomfortably on the high stool. 'I gets vertigo up 'ere.'

'Is somebody serving?' asked Christine, looking towards the empty bar.

'You 'ave to tinkle that little brass bell on t'bar to get attention now,' Harry scoffed.

I rang the bell and a fresh-faced young man with a ready smile emerged from the back. His black brilliantined hair was slicked back from the forehead in one smooth wave, and he wore a brightly coloured open-necked shirt and sported a gold chain and a heavy gold ring.

'Good morning,' I said. 'A pint of your best bitter, please, and a glass of red wine.'

'We have a selection of fine wines,' he told me. 'There's a particularly good Rioja, a couple of nice French wines—a Fitou Reserve and a Rhône from a small vineyard—and, if you like Italian wine, a *gallo nero* Chianti.'

A selection of disapproving noises emanated from the stools.

'The house red will be fine,' said Christine.

'Just passing through, are you?' the landlord asked.

'That's what Winston Churchill asked this fancy American general during t'last war,' announced Harry in a loud voice. 'This Yank said to Winnie that in 'is opinion Britain was the asshole of Europe. "Just passing through?" asked Churchill.' This was followed by raucous laughter.

The landlord look extremely embarrassed. 'I'm sorry about that.'

'We're used to it,' I told him. 'We live here. We're locals.'

The young man stretched a hand across the bar, and smiled. 'I'm very pleased to meet you. I'm David Fidler, the new landlord.'

'You've certainly made a big difference,' Christine said.

He lowered his voice. 'Well, I have tried to brighten up the place. Modernise it. It was like going back hundreds of years when I first walked in. But as soon as I saw the place, I saw the potential. With professional people like yourselves coming to live here, it could be very good. I want eventually to offer high-quality food.' He leaned over the bar. 'Quite frankly, I want to attract a rather better clientele. I have big plans for the Oak.'

'Well, I wish you luck,' I said, thinking that he would certainly need it. I carried the drinks over to join the regulars, and the landlord returned to the lounge bar.

''As tha sooarted out them squirrels yet, then?' Harry asked me.

'Andy told you about the squirrels then?' I asked.

'Aye, he said you'd 'ad an infestation. Tha got rid on 'em, then?'

'Yes, I got rid of them.'

'That's what thy thinks,' chuckled Harry. 'They'll be back. Mark my words.' Ever the prophet of doom, I thought.

'YOU KNOW, I do feel sorry for Harry and his pals,' said Christine later when we were back at the cottage. She took a steaming casserole out of the oven and placed it on the table. 'They were so out of place sitting on those horrible modern stools,' she said. 'They looked like parrots on a perch.'

'You're the best cook in Yorkshire, Mrs Phinn, do you know that?' I said, lifting the lid of the large metal dish and sniffing the contents. 'Mmmmm.'

'It's such a pity,' she said. 'To lose that traditional eighteenth-century inn with its timber frames, oak beams and horse brasses.'

'You've changed your tune,' I said. 'You were all for change before we went out.'

'That was before I saw the changes,' she said. 'The place now looks so pseudo. It's lost all its character.'

THE STAFF DEVELOPMENT CENTRE looked particularly clean and bright when I arrived there to prepare for a course I was to direct the following day. Since I had last been in, everything—the walls, ceiling, window frames, shelving and cupboards—had been painted a startling white.

I found Connie, in her regulation pink overall, up her stepladder scraping paint off a window with a vicious-looking kitchen knife. 'If you want a cup of anything, you'll have to get it yourself,' she told me bluntly. 'I'm busy.'

'So I see,' I said.

'I spent all day Monday on my hands and knees and I'm still not finished. The mess those decorators have left behind!' she complained. 'They were worse than Mr Clamp on a bad day, and that's saying something.'

'Well, the Centre looks a lot cleaner and brighter,' I said.

Connie peered down at me. 'Mr Phinn, what are you incinerating? I'll have you know, this Centre is *always* clean and bright. I makes sure of that.'

'Of course,' I said quickly. 'I didn't mean it was dirty or anything like that. You always keep the Centre pristine. I meant it looks . . .' I struggled for the right word. 'It looks . . . whiter.'

'Whiter?' she repeated. 'Well, of course it does,' she said. 'It's white paint they've used. I must say for the inspector in charge of English you do say some funny things. Anyway, I can't tell you how glad I was to see the back of the decorators. You would never believe the carry-on we had here last week. Fire alarm going off, fire brigade, ambulance, paramedics, hospitalisation—you name it, we've had it.'

'Why? What happened?' I should never have asked.

'One of the decorators, a young lad with more silver rings through his ears than they have in a jeweller's, ended up in hospital with a broken leg.'

'Ladders can be dangerous,' I said.

'Oh, he didn't fall off a ladder,' said Connie. 'He was sitting on the toilet.'

'How on earth do you break a leg sitting on the toilet?' I asked, intrigued.

'I'll tell you, if you let me finish,' she said. 'His mate, Shane, legarthic individual with more hair than a sheepdog, had just finished painting the toilet doors in the Gents and before he sets off home he goes and puts his brushes in a jar of turpentine substitute to stop them getting hard. Anyway, next morning the silly lad pours the contents of the jar down the toilet bowl but doesn't flush the toilet. Fancy putting inflammatory material down the toilet. Then in goes this Kevin and he sits on the toilet and lights up a cigarette.'

'Oh, no,' I said. I could predict what was to follow.

'Well, when he'd finished his cigarette, what does he do? He puts the lighted tab-end down the toilet and he does it while he's still sitting there.'

'Oh no!'

'Oh yes. There was this great big flash and the next thing you know he's emerging from the gents, screaming and shouting, and jumping down the corridor like a kangaroo with rabies. I've been on a first-aid course and did what I could. I can tell you it was very embarrassing for yours truly, not to mention the lad himself, with me having to put all my clean tea-towels on that particular part of his anatomy.'

'But how did he break his leg?' I asked.

'I'm coming to that,' said Connie. 'I called the ambulance and the lad was carted off. "So how did it happen?" asks one of the ambulance men as they were carrying the injured party down the steps. Well, when I told him he began to laugh and this started the other ambulance man off laughing and they laughed so much that they dropped the stretcher and Kevin broke a leg.'

'You are joking,' I said.

'As God is my judge. The lad was tipped off the stretcher, rolled down the steps and he broke a leg.' Connie stood and brushed the creases out of her overall. 'Mind you,' she said, 'there was one good thing about it all.'

'What's that?' I asked.

'He'd finished painting the Centre before he had the accident.'

6

The first school visit of the following week was to the primary school at Foxton. I was due to observe the lessons of a young probationary teacher. It was one of the inspectors' responsibilities to assess the competency of those new to the profession by observing their lessons three or four times over the course of their first year, evaluating their teaching, assessing their planning materials and examining the children's exercise books. It was understandably a nerve-racking time for many a young teacher.

Foxton School was a sprawling, flat-roofed structure erected in the 1950s to cater for the children who lived on the large council estate surrounding it. Knowing the area that Foxton School served, with its reputation as one of the most socially deprived parts of the county, I guessed that Miss Bailey would need all the encouragement she could get.

On my last visit, Mrs Smart, the head teacher, had listed for me a whole catalogue of difficulties faced by those who lived on the estate: petty crime, drug-related problems, absentee fathers, poverty and unemployment, all of which had a real impact on the children's achievement. But she was by nature a steadfastly optimistic and enthusiastic woman, and she was fortunate to lead a team of committed, experienced teachers who had a genuine concern for the children, and the school was achieving pretty good results.

I arrived at Foxton just as the bell sounded for the start of school, and I joined the throng of chattering children as they made their way down the long corridor to their various classrooms. Mrs Smart, a small, tubby woman with a jolly pinkish face and large blue eyes, was at her classroom door and greeted me with a broad smile. Unlike many of her head-teacher colleagues, she insisted on doing some teaching.

'Good morning, Mr Phinn,' she said in a hearty, welcoming voice, 'and how are you this bright Monday morning?'

'All the better for seeing you, Mrs Smart,' I said.

'Here to see our new member of staff, are you? I think you will find Miss Bailey a real gem. She's settled in really well.'

'Yes, but I thought I'd pop in to see you first.'

'Always a pleasure,' she replied. 'Come into the classroom for a minute, while I mark the register. I'm sure the children would like to meet you.'

The class of eight- to nine-year-olds stared at me inquisitively as they filed into the room and took their seats.

'Sit up smartly, children,' the head teacher said. The children did as they were told. 'We have a very important visitor. This is Mr Phinn, children.'

'Good morning, Mr Phinn,' the children chanted.

'Good morning,' I replied.

'Some of you might remember Mr Phinn when he came into our school last time,' said Mrs Smart.

'I remember him, miss!' called out a boy with a thin-boned face, very short hair and large, low-set ears.

'Yes, I thought you might, Justin,' said the head teacher, giving me a knowing look. 'As I recall, you and Mr Phinn had a very interesting conversation at the school office when you were sent there to cool off.'

'I couldn't stop winking,' said the boy, a grin spreading across his face.

'I am glad to say, Mr Phinn,' said the head teacher, 'that Justin has now got out of the habit of winking at everybody.'

'I am very pleased to hear it,' I said in a mock-serious tone of voice.

'Now,' said Mrs Smart, addressing the class, 'before I collect in the dinner money, are there any absence notes?'

Three children came forward, two of whom passed the head teacher scraps of crumpled paper. The third child, a pale-faced girl with large glasses and untidy hair, leaned over the teacher's desk.

'Miss,' she said, 'mi mam says can mi name be changed in t'register? She said she dunt want me called Darlene Nixon any more. She wants me to be called Darlene Smith.'

'But why?' asked the head teacher, clearly as puzzled as I was.

'Because mi dad keeps goin' off wi' women an' my mam says she's not 'avin' 'im back this time. Mi mam's sick of 'im goin' off wi' women an' then comin' back an' causin' trouble. Mi mam's got a new boyfriend now an' 'e's moved in wi' us, an' she wants me to 'ave 'is name.'

'I think I had better have a word with your mother, Darlene,' Mrs Smart told her. 'I can't just change your name like that.'

'But mi mam says you've *got* to change mi name to Darlene Smith from now on cos she's got this new boyfriend called Ron Smith.'

Justin, who had been eavesdropping on the conversation, nodded wisely and remarked, 'We 'ad 'im—'e were rubbish!'

WHEN I OBSERVE young teachers, I find I can usually tell within just a few minutes how good he or she really is; it is the way they react to the children. The teacher must be first and foremost a performer, able to interest and entertain as well as having a sound knowledge of their subject; they must be always in command of the classroom, their stage. I was impressed immediately by Miss Bailey, who had that certain presence. She had a winning smile and a patient and even-tempered manner, it was clear that the six-year-olds in her care liked her enormously. They clustered round her desk, chattering excitedly about what they had been doing over the weekend, and several had brought her little presents of flowers and sweets.

'It's my birthday,' she explained.

'I suppose the last thing you were expecting on your birthday,' I told her, 'was a visit from the school inspector.'

'I could think of a pleasanter present,' she replied good-humouredly.

If she was nervous about my visit, Miss Bailey certainly didn't show it. I had an idea that the head teacher's assessment of her was spot on.

'We usually have a story on Monday mornings,' Miss Bailey told me. 'So if you would like to join us in the reading corner, Mr Phinn, we'll start.'

The children gathered round the teacher on the small square of carpet, with me sitting at the back. 'This morning's story,' she began, 'is *The Tale of Chicken Licken*. It's about a rather silly chicken that spreads a foolish rumour.'

As soon as the teacher began reading, in a loud, expressive voice, the children turned their attention to her and listened intently.

'"Once upon a time there was a little chicken called Chicken Licken One day an acorn fell from a tree and hit Chicken Licken on the head."'

'I bet that hurt,' observed a little boy. 'A conker fell on my head once, miss, and it really hurt.'

'Philip,' said the teacher in a patient voice, 'I would like you to listen. We can talk about your accident with the conker later. "Now, when the acorn fell on Chicken Licken's head, the silly bird thought that the sky was falling down so he ran off to tell the king."'

'Miss,' interrupted Philip, 'Chicken Licken wouldn't be a *he*.'

'And why's that, Philip?' asked the teacher.

'Because a chicken would be a *she*. If it was a *he*, it would be a cockerel.'

The teacher smiled. 'Do you know, you're right, Philip. I shall change it to a *she*.' The teacher continued with the age-old story of the foolish chicken that, on the way to tell the king that the sky was falling down, meets a series of equally silly fowl that agree to join her on her trek.

At last Miss Bailey finished the tale and closed the book. She paused and looked up at the children. 'I wonder,' she pondered, 'what the wise old king would have said to Chicken Licken when the silly bird told him that the sky was falling down. What do you think he would have said, Philip?'

The child thought for a moment and scratched his chin before replying. 'Bloody hell, a talking chicken!' he said.

At morning break, I discussed the lesson with Miss Bailey.

'I'm glad you saw the funny side,' the young woman said. 'I always imagined that school inspectors were rather serious-minded people. You just don't know what they will say, do you?'

'I think you will find, Miss Bailey,' I said, 'that children are a constant surprise. One of the best pieces of advice given to me when I started as a teacher was from the first head teacher I worked for. "With young people," he once told me, "always expect the unexpected." I suppose that is why teaching has got to be the most interesting job in the world—nothing is predictable, every day is different.'

I had smiled when I saw the children giving Miss Bailey her little birthday gifts. It reminded me of an occasion when I was observing another probationary teacher. It was just before Easter and an angelic-looking girl had presented the teacher with a small bag of sugar-coated chocolate eggs.

'These are for you, miss,' the child had whispered sweetly.

The teacher had blushed with embarrassment and obvious pleasure. 'Oh, what a kind thought,' she had said. 'Thank you so much, Amy. Do you think I might have one now?'

The little girl had nodded and watched as her teacher had popped one of the chocolate eggs in her mouth.

A small boy had then approached with a little egg in the palm of his hand. 'This is for you, miss,' he had told her.

'My goodness,' the teacher had said, 'another present. Thank you so much.' She had popped that egg in her mouth—just as the small boy announced proudly, 'Our budgie laid it this morning.'

THE CHIEF EDUCATION OFFICER for the county of Yorkshire sat at a huge desk set in the middle of the room, his fingers before him. Dr Gore was a tall man with deep-set, earnest eyes and the unabashed gaze of one who knows his position in the world. Next to him, straight-backed and severe, sat his Personal Assistant, the redoubtable Mrs Brenda Savage.

'Do sit down, will you, Gervase,' said Dr Gore, indicating a chair facing his desk. 'Thank you for coming to see me. Now, I have a little job for you.'

I might have guessed as much, I thought to myself. Over the four years I had been a school inspector in the county, I had been summoned to the CEO's office about nine or ten times and on every occasion I had left the room with one of Dr Gore's 'little jobs'—conduct a countywide reading survey, undertake an audit of the secondary school libraries, chair working parties, organise a poetry festival. And they were never ever 'little jobs'.

'Strictly speaking,' continued the CEO, unsteepling his fingers and smiling like a basking shark, 'it doesn't fall into your bailiwick, but you have had the experience of organising conferences and events and such—very successfully, too, I may add. I am sure that this little job will not take up too much of your time. Mrs Savage will, of course, be working closely with you to deal with all the administration.'

'So, it's a conference you wish me organise, is it, Dr Gore?' I asked.

'Not as such,' said the CEO. 'Much of the work was done early last term when I selected the speakers. I just want you to deal with one or two aspects. You may or may not be aware that I have been elected the President of NACADS for this academic year.'

'The National Association of Chief Administrators and Directors of Schools,' explained Mrs Savage.

'Thank you, Mrs Savage,' said the CEO, holding up a hand to stop her speaking, 'I am sure Mr Phinn has heard of NACADS.'

'In my capacity as the President of NACADS,' said Dr Gore, 'it falls upon me to host the annual weekend conference.'

'It is an opportunity for delegates to hear the very best national speakers and for chief administrators and directors of schools and colleges to network,' said Mrs Savage, adding that 'Sir Brian Holyoake, the Minister of Education and Science, has already intimated that he might be present.'

'Where is the conference to be held?' I asked.

'Ah,' Dr Gore beamed at me, with obvious satisfaction. 'We have been most fortunate with the venue. Lord Marrick, in his capacity as Chairman of the Education Committee, has very kindly offered his own country residence,

Manston Hall, as the venue for the conference. What I would like you to do, Gervase, is organise things from the school side. I was thinking that it would be appropriate to have a display of children's work, a performance from a school choir, perhaps an art exhibition, that sort of thing. I want the delegates to leave the county with a very good impression.'

'If I might be allowed to say something, Mr Gore,' said Mrs Savage.

'Yes, of course,' sighed the CEO.

'I just wish to impress on Mr Phinn that he needs to liaise closely with me and keep me fully up to speed on everything that he intends to do.' Her voice dripped with condescension.

'Be assured, Mrs Savage,' I told her smiling, 'I will fill you in.'

'That's settled, then,' said Dr Gore. 'I look forward to hearing about how things are progressing.'

'There is just one other thing, Dr Gore,' I said. 'What are the dates for this conference? Some time next term, I assume?'

'No, no,' replied the CEO, 'the end of next month.'

'SO WHAT WAS your little tête-à-tête with the good Dr Gore about?' asked Sidney when I arrived back at the inspectors' office at lunchtime. He was leaning back precariously in his chair, with his feet on the desk.

'He's given me another of his little jobs,' I grumbled.

'You shouldn't be so malleable,' said my colleague. 'You should have told him you were far too busy and stressed.'

'Well, I am busy,' I said, 'but I don't know about being stressed.'

'I have to say, my dear friend, that I have perceived that you have recently been without your usual *joie de vivre*. There is a *froideur* about you, a lassitude which is quite *outré*. You are positively neurasthenic.'

'Hark at Dr Freud,' said David, looking up from his papers. 'Sidney, you are the last person in the world to counsel anybody. You may recall that when you went on one of those stress-management courses, the tutor told you that you didn't suffer from stress, you were more of a carrier. And, anyway, what's with all this French? You spent your holidays in Italy.'

'I am a man of the world,' said Sidney, spreading his arms expansively.

'Give me strength,' said David. 'The man gets worse.'

'Things are a bit heavy-going at the moment,' I told them.

'Tell me about it,' said David. 'These school closures are highly contentious and I have had to brave two acrimonious meetings with governors. I am dreading speaking to the parents' association next week.'

'You should have told Dr Gore that you were suffering from mental, physical and emotional strain and couldn't possibly take on anything else at the moment,' said Sidney.

'What?' I exclaimed. 'Tell Dr Gore that? I'd have got the sack.'

'Of course,' continued his colleague unabashed, 'I put it down to post-natal depression.'

'Post-natal depression?' I repeated.

'Oh yes,' said Sidney. 'It doesn't just affect mothers, you know. Fathers are susceptible too. It happened to me when my daughter, Tanya, was born. After all the euphoria of the birth the despondency and dejection set in. I couldn't put paintbrush to canvas for a whole year. I had sleepless night after sleepless night. I would doze off and then be woken up in the early hours to feed this wrinkled little piggy-faced whelp. And then having to change her and get her off to sleep again. It was a waking nightmare.'

'My dear departed Welsh grandmother had thirteen children and brought them up in a terraced house with only one tin bath,' said David. 'You never heard her complain.'

'Sweet angels of mercy!' cried Sidney, 'Please, oh please, spare us from the dear departed Welsh grandmother.'

'Actually I don't mind changing the baby,' I told Sidney, 'and since Christine is breastfeeding, I don't have to get up in the middle of the night, so it's certainly nothing to do with that.'

However, there was no doubt that the problems at Ugglemattersby were still preying on my mind. I would shortly be attending a meeting of the parents of the children at both schools, something I was not looking forward to.

David asked, 'So what's this little job that Dr Gore has given you, Gervase?'

'He's asked me to help organise a NACADS conference,' I said. 'I've been given the job of organising various exhibitions and events,' I told them. 'Displays of children's work, the usual sort of thing.'

'And does it mean having to liaise with Mrs Savage?' asked David.

'Yes, it does,' I replied glumly.

'Well, I wish you luck working with that woman, I really do,' said David.

'In the long tradition of *esprit de corps* that exists in our little team, Gervase, you know that if we can be of any help we would be only too happy to oblige—*tous ensemble*,' said Sidney.

'Of course,' agreed David. 'I am more than happy to produce an exhibition of mathematics teaching and children's work.

'That sounds excellent,' I said.

'And I shall be only too pleased to mount *une exposition magnifique* of children's painting and sculpture,' said Sidney. 'I shall get onto it, *pronto*.'

'Give me strength!' cried David. 'He's gone into Italian now.'

'I'm feeling better already,' I said.

At that moment my telephone rang.

'Brenda Savage here,' came a sharp voice down the line.

'Oh, hello, Mrs Savage,' I said, emphasising her name to let my colleagues know to whom I was speaking. Sidney pulled a gruesome face.

'Following our discussions with Dr Gore this morning,' she said formally, 'I feel that we need to expedite matters ASAP. Are you available?'

'Now?' I asked. 'This very minute?' Better get the inevitable meeting with her over and done with, I thought. 'I am free until two o'clock, and then I have to join an appointments panel.'

'Then I shall come over and see you straight away,' she said.

'DO YOU THINK I'm malleable?' I was helping Christine wash the dishes that evening when I put the question to her.

'Think you're malleable?' she repeated. 'You mean like a lump of clay that's moulded into shape?'

'Well, not really like a lump of clay,' I said. 'What I mean is "easily persuaded". Sidney says I'm malleable, that I take too much on because I can't say No to people.'

'Well, for once I think Sidney's got it right,' said Christine, 'You do take on too much and do tend to say Yes to people far too often.'

When Winco Cleaver-Canning had shown his whiskered face at the door that morning, clutching the script of *The Dame of Sark*, Christine had discovered that I had virtually agreed to join the cast. When I arrived home, she had asked me crossly why I hadn't said I was too busy.

'It's a simple enough word,' she told me. 'Just say No.'

BY THE END of that week, I was feeling under less strain. On Saturday, Andy fixed the guttering and finished tidying up the garden, and on Sunday, a gloriously sunny day, we decided to give ourselves a day off, and went to Whitby. The tide was out, and Christine and I strolled along the vast sandy beach to Sandsend with little Richard strapped on my back. That evening I read *The Dame of Sark*, which I enjoyed hugely, and became quite excited about 'treading the boards' once again with the Fettlesham Literary Players.

I also felt happier about Dr Gore's latest little job. The discussions with

Mrs Savage had gone surprisingly well, and we had arranged to visit Manston Hall this coming week. Both David and Sidney had been busy planning their contributions for the exhibition, and Geraldine had immediately agreed to put on a science display. As well as telephoning the schools that I wanted to provide material for an exhibition of children's writing, I had contacted the County Music Adviser, Pierce Gordon, and enlisted the services of the Young People's Brass Band to entertain the delegates on the Sunday morning. All in all, things were progressing well.

I was in excellent spirits, therefore, when I walked into the entrance of Daleside Primary School on the Monday lunchtime. I was there to observe Miss Graham, a probationary teacher.

In the head teacher's room, with a cup of coffee in my hand, I explained to Mrs Blackett, a small, dark-haired, softly spoken woman, what I intended to do that morning before I went into the first class.

'You don't remember me, do you?' she enquired. A small smile played on the woman's lips.

I looked at her a little more closely. 'I'm afraid not,' I replied. I looked again at the smiling face but no recognition dawned. 'I'm sorry but you will have to remind me.'

'We were on interview together,' she replied, 'at County Hall for the post of inspector.'

'Of course!' I said. 'I remember now,' I said. 'Dorothy Blackett.'

'That's right,' she said, 'neither of us thought we were in with a chance.'

'It was a pretty daunting experience,' I said. 'I remember your saying, when you congratulated me, that you were rather relieved that you didn't get the job because you weren't sure whether you wanted the post or not.'

'I did,' she replied, 'and I guess that uncertainty came over at the interview. But my dream was to work in the Yorkshire Dales. I was brought up here and wanted to return to my roots.'

'And your dream came true,' I said. 'I'm so pleased, and if I can—'

A sharp rap on the door interrupted me.

'I'm sorry to disturb you, Mrs Blackett.' It was the school secretary. 'I thought you ought to know that Gavin is in a bit of a state. His, er . . .' she paused, struggling for the right word—'er . . . little problem seems to have flared up again. Shall I send for his mother to come and collect him?'

'Yes please, Vera,' said the head teacher, 'that would be a good idea and I would like a word with her when she arrives. I really don't think he should have been sent to school in this state.' The secretary nodded, and after she had closed the door behind her the head teacher shook her head. 'Little Gavin, all of seven,' she said, 'arrived at school this morning obviously in some discomfort. During assembly I had to tell him to sit still on a couple of occasions. At the end of assembly, I saw him heading out of the hall like a miniature cowboy who had just got off his horse after a hard day in the saddle. In the classroom, Gavin produced a note from his mother explaining that he was "a bit sore in the downstairs department" because he'd been castrated.'

'Castrated!' I exclaimed.

'Yes, castrated,' said the head teacher. 'Well, a very red-faced Miss Graham—she's of a rather delicate disposition—brought little Gavin and the note straight along to me. I discovered that he had not, in fact, been castrated—he'd been circumcised. I thought it more appropriate that the deputy head teacher, Mr Johnson, rather than myself, should have a look at it. Les was not at all keen, telling me that he could get thirty years for "looking at it". Eventually, he was prevailed upon to examine the little boy's problem but only in the presence of the caretaker as a witness that nothing untoward happened. Les reported back to me that Gavin's little problem didn't look that bad and that the child had been sent back to his class. Gavin seemed a lot better. Then just before morning break, Miss Graham noticed to her horror that little Gavin, sitting at his desk, had his trousers and pants round his ankles and had everything on display for the entire world to see. "Whatever are you doing?" she asked him and he replied, "Mr Johnson told me to stick it out for the rest of the day."'

I spluttered and spilt coffee all down the front of my suit.

A SHORT WHILE LATER, I joined Miss Graham in her classroom. Miss Graham was indeed of a rather delicate disposition. She was a tall, mousy-haired, pale-faced woman whose dark brown eyes were alarmingly magnified behind large, round glasses. She looked agitated when I joined her.

'I must tell you, Mr Phinn,' she said at once, 'that I've never had a school inspector watching me before so I am rather apprehensive.'

'I'm quite harmless, Miss Graham,' I said, wondering how she would cope in a career where she was likely to come across some very demanding children. I complimented her instead on the splendid classroom displays.

'Art was my specialist study at college,' she told me, allowing herself a small self-conscious smile.

'And where was that?' I asked.

'The College of Ripon and York St John,' she replied.

'Ah, a very fine college,' I said. 'One of the very best teacher-training institutions in the country. You can't go far wrong if you have studied there.' I was attempting to put her at ease. 'And how are you getting on?'

'Oh, it's not too bad,' she said, 'but I have to admit I do find the children very blunt and to the point.'

'That's Yorkshire children for you,' I told her.

'Yes, and it's a very mixed catchment area. A growing number of children come from the estate, some from the village and a large number live on the surrounding farms. The world of the estate children usually centres on what is on the television, and for the farming children it revolves around sheep, cows and pigs. The farming children will insist on bringing things to school,' she told me. 'Sheep's skulls, dead birds, hedgehogs in boxes, wasps' nests, newts in jam jars, frog spawn. It's all very interesting, I'm sure, but I have an aversion to anything like that. I don't mind cats and small dogs but snakes and spiders and creepy-crawlies just freak me out.'

Having listened to this rather anxious young woman, I had to admit that I was not expecting the most riveting of lessons that afternoon, but I was pleasantly surprised. Miss Graham seemed to come to life. The nervousness disappeared, and she became animated and encouraging. The children listened attentively and readily responded to her questions. After she had set the children the task of writing a story entitled 'A Day to Remember', Miss Graham moved from table to table, smiling and helping the children with their work. She clearly had forgotten about me.

After a while, I joined a small group of children to talk to them about their work and to look at their books. One boy, a large lad with a rather mournful expression, sat staring at the blank piece of paper before him.

'I don't know what to write about,' he told me, screwing up his nose and scratching his thatch of thick fair hair.

'There must have been a special day in your life which stays in your mind,' I said. 'What about your birthday?'

'I had mumps.'

'Christmas?'

'My granddad died.'

'Well,' I said giving up, 'you put on your thinking cap. I'm sure something will occur to you.'

It was towards the end of the lesson that things went wrong for Miss Graham. She went into the storeroom and emerged a moment later carrying a little toy bat, black with rubbery wings and a furry body.

She held the toy between her finger and thumb. 'Now, this is very silly,' she said. 'Firstly, you know I don't allow anyone in my storeroom. Secondly, you all know I don't like creepy-crawlies. I don't find it at all funny. Now,' she continued, 'who does this toy bat belong to?'

The question was greeted with complete silence. 'Come along, whose is it?' Still there was no response. 'Well, if the person who brought it to school doesn't own up, then I shall put it in the wastepaper basket.' Just as she was about to deposit the toy in the basket, the thing moved. It was a real bat. The little creature turned its head and squeaked. Miss Graham went rigid. The children stared dumbstruck. I could see by the teacher's expression that she was having some difficulty in maintaining a measure of perpendicularity so, grabbing the blackboard duster, I rushed to her assistance.

'You go to the staff room,' I whispered in the teacher's ear, taking the small trembling creature from her in the soft material. 'I'll deal with the visitor.' Miss Graham, ashen-faced, headed for the door without a word.

Having deposited the bat in a small box and quietened down the now very excited class, I told the children to get on with their stories.

The taciturn boy with the blank piece of paper suddenly came to life. He waved his hand madly in the air. 'Sir, please, sir!' he cried.

'Whatever is it?' I asked.

'I've got something to write about now, sir,' he said with a great beaming smile. '"The Day Our Teacher Went Batty!"'

I MADE MY WAY towards the main entrance of Castlesnelling High School for the rehearsal of *The Dame of Sark*. It was the last thing I wanted on a Friday evening but Raymond, the producer, had very nearly burst into tears when I had told him that it was going to be very difficult for me to attend.

'No, no!' he had moaned, when I explained that I had a meeting that evening. 'But, Gervase, you have only made one or two of the rehearsals so far, and tonight is when I go through the play's *dénouement*.'

'Very well,' I had told him resignedly. 'I'll be there.'

Raymond was a frenetic little man with cropped dyed blond hair and a round, pixie-like face; he invariably wore a pair of extremely tight jeans and a close-fitting T-shirt. He seemed to live constantly on his nerves. If someone fluffed a line or missed a cue, he would utter a sort of strangled cry before calling out in a piercing voice, 'No, no, no, no, no!' Then he would add, brushing his brow dramatically with the back of his hand, 'Why, oh why, do I have to work with amateurs?'

'That's because we are amateurs,' one brave member of the cast had once informed him.

In the hall, a knot of people, wrapped up in thick coats, was standing on stage with Raymond. The producer was encased in a bright red duffle coat, a woolly hat pulled down over his ears, barking out instructions.

'I know it's cold, my lovelies,' Raymond was telling them. 'Unfortunately the heating's off, but the sooner we get moving about, the sooner we will get warm. Now, from the beginning of the act, please, and Cecile, darling, your line is: "That young soldier's at the door, madam, with a message for you" and not "with a massage for you". There is a subtle difference.'

'But I'm tryin' to do mi French accent,' said the girl peevishly. She was a large young woman swathed in a vast khaki anorak with a fur-lined hood and wearing substantial brown boots. 'It sounds more sexy to 'ave a French accent,' she said. 'Anyway, my mam says that if I was called Cecile I would be French and I'd 'ave a French accent.'

'Tell me, Sharon,' asked Raymond, 'is your mother producing this play?'

'No,' replied the girl, defensively folding her arms across her chest.

'Well, I am,' he told her, raising his voice, 'and what I say, goes. This is not a Whitehall farce, it is a deeply poignant drama about the triumph of courage and perseverance over tyranny and oppression and there is no place in it for a sexy French maid. So—stick to the English accent, please, but try not to make it so Yorkshire.'

'It'd liven things up a bit,' observed one of the actors, 'a sexy French maid and a German soldier offering the Dame of Sark a massage.'

'I could do with a massage,' announced a tall man in a black overcoat. 'It's colder than a morgue in here—and I should know.'

The figure in black was George Furnival, proprietor of Furnival's Funeral Parlour. He was a tall, cadaverous and sinister-looking individual with short black hair parted down the middle. He played the sinister Dr Braun, covert Gestapo officer. He suddenly caught sight of me standing at the back.

''Eye up, Colonel Blimp's arrived,' he called up to the stage.

Raymond swivelled round. 'At last,' he sighed. 'We were going to send out a search party. I can't tell you how stressful it's been, Gervase. This is one of the last rehearsals and half the cast is missing. There's no sign of Margot and Winco.'

'I'm sorry,' I said, 'the meeting went on rather longer than I thought.'

'Well, shall we get on with it, then?' called George. 'The sooner we do, the sooner we'll be on our way.'

'Give me strength,' said Raymond. 'Why do I put myself through this? On stage, please, Gervase. I'll read in the lines of the Dame. Cecile, you enter stage right with Colonel Graham behind you. You stride into the room, Gervase, the conquering hero, having just taken the German surrender. You look pretty pleased with yourself. You smile, look round, nod knowingly. Then you salute and extend a hand to the Dame.'

The rehearsal continued until, ten minutes later, the redoubtable Mrs Cleaver-Canning made her grand entrance followed by her husband, Winco. He was an elderly, slightly stooping man with thin wisps of sandy-grey hair and a great handlebar moustache, and he was struggling with a large hamper. The Dame of Sark was attired in a substantial fur coat with matching hat, puce leather gloves and knee-length black boots.

'Margot!' exclaimed Raymond, throwing up his hands. 'You've arrived.'

'With some hot soup and little nibbles to keep us going,' she said.

Despite Raymond's protestations, the whole cast descended on Winco chattering like a bunch of excited schoolchildren.

'I give up,' Raymond moaned, flopping onto a chair. 'I give up.'

7

'It's the Black Widow on the phone for you,' said Julie, grimacing, and passing over the receiver as if it harboured some dire infection.

'Mrs Savage?'

'Right! And, as usual, she sounds as sharp as a bottle full of sulphuric acid. Shall I say you've already left?'

'No, no,' I said hurriedly. 'I had better speak to her.'

I took the receiver from Julie who waited, listening.

'Mr Phinn?' came the imperious voice. 'Brenda Savage here. There is a slight problem with regard to our visit to Manston Hall this afternoon. I'm afraid my car is . . . well, it won't start . . . so I shall have to travel with you.'

'Travel with me?' I repeated. 'The problem is that I have a couple of calls to make on my way to Manston Hall. I agreed to collect some things for Sister Brendan at St Bartholomew's.'

'Collect some things?' She sounded like an echo.

'Yes, Sister Brendan is organising a charity auction next week and is collecting contributions. Fettlesham Social Club has donated a television, Fine Wines of Fettlesham a couple of cases of wine, and there's a hamper from Roper's Salesroom. I have agreed to collect them on my way to Manston Hall, so I can drop them off when I visit St Bartholomew's on Friday. So you see, I have to set off quite a bit earlier—in fact, I am just leaving now. So I suggest you get a taxi.'

'That is out of the question!' she retorted. 'The County Treasurer would not be best pleased to receive a claim for a taxi fare right out to Manston Hall, particularly when another member of the Education Department will be going there. No, no, I shall have to travel with you. When will you be ready?'

I looked heavenwards and sighed. 'As I said, I'm just about to set off.'

'Very well, Mr Phinn,' she said. 'I shall be with you directly.'

'I'll meet you in the car park.' I put down the phone.

'Well done!' Julie said sarcastically. 'The trouble with you is that you're too easily persuaded. Dr Gore gives you all those "little jobs", Sister Brendan has you collecting things for her raffle, and now the Bride of Dracula has you chauffeuring her around. You ought to put your foot down.' Before I could respond, Julie was through the door. 'See you tomorrow,' she called over her shoulder, 'if you survive this afternoon, that is.'

Strolling down the path leading from County Hall to where I was parked, Mrs Savage looked like a model from a fashion magazine. She was wearing a grey tweed jacket with black velvet collar and cuffs, a blue pencil skirt and navy suede shoes. Around her shoulders was draped a pale brown woollen overcoat; tucked under one arm was an expensive-looking ruched velvet handbag, and she was carrying a slim leather document case. She would appear very much at home among the aristocrats at Manston Hall.

As she climbed into the car, she sniffed the air.

'Babies,' I said.

'I beg your pardon?'

'The smell of babies,' I said. 'It's my little boy. He tends to splash a bit when he has his milk. The smell lingers.'

'Yes, it does,' she agreed, winding down the window a fraction.

After I had collected the wine from Fine Wines of Fettlesham and the hamper from Roper's Salesroom, we headed for the rather insalubrious northern side of the town. I pulled up outside an ugly grey building. A sign above the entrance announced in large letters, 'FETTLESHAM WORKING MEN'S CLUB'. The building was protected by security cameras and alarms.

'I shan't be a moment,' I told Mrs Savage.

'I don't intend to remain in the car,' she told me curtly. 'This area does not look at all safe. I shall come in with you.'

Pasted on the wall outside the club, between the graffiti, was a series of posters advertising the 'star turns' that were due to appear. The first stated: *Featuring the ravishing and adorable Big Brenda of the Body Beautiful. She's pert, pleasing and tasty.*

'Are we going to be long in this establishment?' asked Mrs Savage, looking decidedly uncomfortable.

'Not long,' I replied jovially.

After repeated ringing and banging, I managed to gain the attention of someone who poked his tousled head out of an upstairs window.

'What?' he shouted.

'It's Mr Phinn,' I shouted back.

'You're early!' he snapped. 'I was told you'd be arriving at six.'

'I can't recall giving a time,' I replied. 'Shall I call back later?'

'No, hang on, I'll come down.'

After a great deal of noise from chains and bolts from the other side, the door finally opened. An overweight and under-shaved man, dressed in a threadbare cardigan and shapeless grey trousers, peered myopically at me.

'You'd better come in,' he said. 'I'm Reg, by the way. Watch them barrels. I'll have to shift them before tonight's show. You'll be pleased to hear that it's a full house. Very popular is Friday night.'

I had no idea why the man thought I would be interested in this information but I nodded politely and said, 'Really?', following the man, with Mrs Savage close behind.

Reg took us into the vast hall, which had a big stage at the far end, a long curved bar area, and an assortment of tables and chairs; the unmistakable smell of stale beer, old smoke and toilets permeated the air.

The caretaker stared at Mrs Savage as she walked into the room as one might study a strange decorative item on show in someone's house. She sat down at a small round plastic-topped table near the door, having first dusted down the plastic chair with her hand. She looked ill at ease.

'Would you like a drink?' Reg asked, his eyes still fixed on Mrs Savage.

'No, thank you,' I replied.

'What about . . . er . . .' he gestured in Mrs Savage's direction.

'I don't think so,' I said.

The man turned slightly so we were facing away from Mrs Savage and whispered. 'You'd never tell, would you?'

'Tell what?' I asked, recoiling from the man's foul breath.

'You know.' He came closer. 'That it was a man.'

'What?' I said. 'I honestly don't know what you're on about.'

'It's the hands that are the giveaway, that and the prominent Adam's apple. Yes, I've seen one or two in my time,' he continued in a hushed voice, 'but I have to say, he's the best. He's incredible. Spitting image of Danny La Rue.'

'What on earth are you talking about?' I asked.

He tilted his head in the direction of Mrs Savage. 'Him, the female impersonator.'

'Female impersonator!' I exclaimed.

'You're the agent for Veronica, the drag act who's appearing here tonight.' Then a shadow of doubt crossed his face. 'Aren't you?'

I nearly choked. 'No, no, I've come to collect the television for Sister Brendan's charity auction. That's . . . that's not a man—it's Mrs Savage!'

'Bloody Nora!' he exclaimed. 'I'm sorry, mate, I thought you were this evening's drag act. I've been expecting them for a sound and lighting check before the show.'

The man started to stifle a laugh and so did I. Thankfully, it appeared that Mrs Savage hadn't heard any of the previous exchange.

A few minutes later, the television set was safely stowed on the back seat, and we set off for Manston Hall.

YORKSHIRE IS BLESSED with many gracious stately homes. Manston Hall, although not a large house by the standards of Castle Howard or Harewood, is undoubtedly one of the most elegant. The visitor drives through great black ornate gates and along an avenue of beech trees, until he arrives at this perfectly proportioned early eighteenth-century mansion, built in warm red brick and standing among lawns, rose gardens and woodland.

I pulled up in front of the flight of steps that climbed up to the great black front door. As Mrs Savage and I got out of the car, the door opened and a tall man appeared and stood at the top of the steps, his hands in the pockets of his dark green corduroy trousers.

'Mr Phinn, is it?' he called down.

'That's right.'

'You were expected,' he said. 'Do come along up.'

The speaker was a striking-looking man with a broad brown face creased around the eyes, and with a crop of curly brown hair flecked with grey at the temples. His gaze settled on Mrs Savage as she came up the steps.

'This is Mrs Savage,' I told him.

'I say,' he murmured, clearly taken with the vision who, having got to the top of the steps, looked around imperiously.

'I'm Tadge, by the way,' he said giving, her a broad smile.

The spacious entrance hall, which was decorated in the palest of yellows and blues, was dominated by a magnificent ornately carved chimneypiece in white Italian marble. Hanging above was a large oil painting depicting a heavily bemedalled and moustachioed soldier in crimson uniform.

'One of the ancestors,' Tadge explained, seeing me look up at it.

Tadge led us from the hall and down a long corridor to the library. In this elegant room the walls were lined with bookcases, from floor to ceiling, and over the fireplace was a large portrait of a young woman with pale blue eyes. Dressed for the hunt, she was astride a dashing chestnut horse.

'What a handsome room,' observed Mrs Savage.

Our host indicated a large green leather armchair. 'Do have a seat, Mr Phinn,' he said to me. He waited until Mrs Savage was seated on the matching chesterfield sofa and then sat down beside her. The man stared at her like a hungry cat might watch a bowlful of goldfish. 'I've arranged for a cup of tea later,' he said. 'I thought we'd discuss your requirements first and then have a look round the house.'

Mrs Savage opened the leather document case, removed a wad of papers and put on a pair of stylish gold-rimmed spectacles.

'We have two halls,' said Tadge, 'North and South. Either would be suitable as the main conference hall. I suggest you have the lectures in one and the exhibition in the other. Delegates are very welcome to use the billiard room, this room and the dining room but the drawing room and the morning room will not be available. Of course, the grounds are—'

'Excuse me,' interrupted Mrs Savage, her carefully plucked eyebrows arching, 'do I take it that *you* will be liaising with us?'

'That's right,' Tadge replied good-humouredly.

'Oh,' she said, clearly sounding disappointed. 'My understanding was that Lord Marrick would be meeting with us.'

'He's with the gamekeeper at the moment, but he will be along later.'

'I take it then, Mr Tadge, that you are Lord Marrick's secretary or an administrator of some kind?'

'I suppose I am, in a way,' said Tadge, smiling widely.

'Well, you are or you are not,' said Mrs Savage, somewhat coldly. Her tone bordered on the brusque. 'I do like to know with whom I am liaising.'

'I clearly didn't introduce myself properly,' said our host amiably. 'I deal with most of the business now at Manston Hall, running the estate, managing the business interests.'

'Oh, I see,' she said. 'So you are the Estate Manager?'

'I'm Lord Marrick's son,' replied the man. 'Tadge Manson. Tadge comes from my names, Thomas, Arthur, D'Aubney, George, Edmund Courtnay-Cunninghame—Viscount Manston, if you want the full thing.'

Mrs Savage jumped as if touched by a cattle prod. 'Oh!' she exclaimed. Her demeanour changed completely. 'Oh,' she cooed, smiling so widely that it was a wonder she didn't leave traces of her red lipstick on the lobes of her ears. 'I'm so very sorry, Lord Manston. You must have thought me extremely rude. I had no idea you were Lord Marrick's son.'

'Please, please, Mrs Savage,' he said, patting her hand. 'Think nothing of it. I don't stand on my dignity.'

Tadge took us on a tour of the rooms that the conference delegates would be permitted to use. When we returned to the library, a tray with the promised pot of tea was waiting for us. As we finalised the arrangements for the conference, Mrs Savage never took her fluttering eyes off Tadge Manston. He, too, seemed equally struck with Mrs Savage.

'Well, Lord Manston,' said Mrs Savage finally, 'I think we have dealt with everything most satisfactorily, and may I say it has been a very great pleasure to have met you.'

'The pleasure was entirely mine, Mrs Savage,' he replied, patting her hand, 'and do please call me Tadge.'

'And I do hope you will call me Brenda,' she said with a small smile.

I was beginning to feel like a gooseberry, so to put an end to their little *conversazione*—as Sidney would have said—I coughed. 'Was it your son, Tadge, that I met when I visited Manston School?' I enquired.

'Young Tommy?' His Lordship asked. 'Yes, he's at prep school now, and doing very well. He's had a rough time of it over the last couple of years.' Tadge turned to Mrs Savage. 'His mother died when he was six,' he said sadly, looking up at the portrait above the fireplace.

'I am so sorry,' said Mrs Savage, following his gaze to the portrait. 'Was that your wife?'

'It was. She had a riding accident, broke her neck.'

'How tragic,' said Mrs Savage, with a rare show of sympathy. 'I too lost a spouse and know full well how it feels to be left alone.'

'Really?' Tadge said, leaning forward.

Much to my relief, the door burst open and Lord Marrick made his ebullient entrance. Valentine Courtnay-Cunninghame, the 9th Earl Marrick, MC, DL was a rotund, ruddy-cheeked individual with a great walrus moustache. I had met Lord Marrick on a number of previous occasions and always found him an extremely warm, good-humoured and plain-spoken man.

'My apologies for not being here to greet you,' he growled, slamming the door shut behind him. 'Bit of business with the gamekeeper. Good to see you, Mrs Savage, Mr Phinn. I hope my son has been taking care of you both? Everything's sorted out for this conference, is it?'

'Yes, indeed,' replied Mrs Savage.

Lord Marrick turned to his son. 'Still trying to catch the blighters,' he said. 'Jameson's set a couple more traps near the forty-acre.' Then he turned to me. 'Do you know anything about squirrels, Mr Phinn?'

'Squirrels?' I murmured. I could feel myself colouring up. The gamekeeper had told him about my releasing the squirrels on his land, I was sure of it. 'I can't say I know a great deal about squirrels,' I said.

'We have rather an odd problem with squirrels on the estate at the moment. The first we knew about it was when the local rag printed a report of a new breed of squirrels having been seen up in the woods. A party of ramblers claimed to have seen a cross between a red and a grey squirrel—had grey coats, white bellies and bright red tails, would you believe. Stuff and nonsense, of course, reds and greys don't interbreed. Any damn fool knows that.'

I gulped. 'Really? Squirrels with red tails. How unusual.'

'I've no idea what they are. Had the fellows from CAPOW sniffing around—that's the Countryside Association for the Protection of Wildlife,' he expanded. 'It won't be a case of "protection", I can tell you, when we catch up with the varmints. Wreck my trees, they do. Once we catch them,' said Lord Marrick, 'the wildlife people can do what they like with them—so long as it is a long way away from my woods.'

'You think you'll catch them, then?' I asked in the most innocent of voices.

'Oh, we'll catch them all right,' growled the peer, 'and then we'll get to the bottom of this daft bloody business.'

'Perhaps we should be making tracks, Mrs Savage,' I said, keen to put an end to the conversation.

CROMPTON PRIMARY SCHOOL was built in the latter part of the nineteenth century for the children of the workers employed in the mills, factories and steelworks. It looked more like a Victorian workhouse than a school, with its shiny red brick exterior, cold grey slate roof, mean little windows and enveloping black iron fencing, despite the efforts of the head teacher and staff to brighten up the interior with pictures and plants.

Mrs Gardiner, the head teacher, a big-boned woman with bobbed silver hair and thin lips, had the no-nonsense look of someone who is very confident of her own abilities. Despite the dismal environment and a relatively large proportion of children one might euphemistically describe as having 'challenging behaviour', she ran a well-ordered and successful school and was highly respected in the Education Department at County Hall. Mrs Gardiner was, by her own admission, not one to beat about the bush.

'Overslept?' she asked bluntly, as I hastened into the building.

'I'm really sorry, Mrs Gardiner,' I explained. 'I called in at St Bartholomew's and just couldn't get away.'

She gave a small smile. 'Sister Brendan. You have to be firm with our dear Sister Brendan. Anyway, now you are here, you are in time for assembly and you can do me a great service this morning.'

'Oh?' This sounded slightly ominous.

'I want you to sit at the front with me, and I want you to glower at the boys I have asked to remain behind.'

'Glower? Why?'

'All will be explained at the end of the assembly,' said Mrs Gardiner.

The children marched into the hall, heads up, arms swinging, accompanied by stirring martial music played on an old upright piano with great gusto by a small man who bobbed up and down on the piano stool in time with the beat. Mrs Gardiner took centre stage, legs slightly apart, her hands clasped before her. I was placed behind her on a large wooden chair with arms. The children lined up in rows, sang the hymn lustily, said the prayer with downcast eyes and then, at the signal from the head teacher, they sat cross-legged on the floor, looking at Mrs Gardiner expectantly.

'Good morning, children,' said the head teacher.

'Good morning, Mrs Gardiner,' chanted the children.

'I would like to introduce our visitor. This is Mr Phinn, a school inspector.'

'Good morning, Mr Phinn,' chorused the children loudly.

'Good morning, children,' I said seriously. I felt like a king, enthroned in my heavy wooden chair, set high on the stage.

There followed a small homily from Mrs Gardiner about good manners and then the children, with the exception of the upper junior boys, were dismissed.

Mrs Gardiner turned to face me and, in a hushed voice, said, 'Now, Mr Phinn, I want you to look really angry.' She turned to the pupils. 'Down to the front, you boys!' A nervous group of pupils lined up before her. 'You are a group of dirty, dirty, dirty little boys, do you know that?' Mrs Gardiner enunciated each word clearly and slowly. Some of the younger pupils shuffled uneasily, others bit their lips.

The head teacher scanned the faces. 'Last night, when Mrs Garbutt went into the boys' toilets, she was disgusted. *Disgusted!* She came straight away to find me and when I saw the floor and the walls I too was disgusted. The floor was awash—and I do not mean with water!' She stabbed the air with a finger. 'I know full well what you have been up to. You've been seeing who can get highest up the wall.' I suppressed a smirk quickly, and continued to glower. 'Oh, yes,' she continued, 'I know what you've been doing, you dirty little boys.'

At this point, all the boys stared at a small lad with spiky black hair. He was clearly the winner of the contest. Mrs Gardiner's furious gaze settled on him. The boy began to sniffle. 'Don't bother with the crocodile tears, Jimmy Sedgewick. It is not Mrs Garbutt's job to clean puddles up after you. And let me tell you this,' Mrs Gardiner shook a finger at the boys, 'if there is so much as a drop or a drip on the floor today, you will all get down on your hands and knees and clean it up. Is that clear?'

'Yes, Mrs Gardiner,' replied the children in subdued voices.

'Mr Phinn,' continued the head teacher, 'was sent especially from the Education Office about the toilets, and he was appalled when I told him what you have been up to. Just look at his face. See how disgusted he is.'

All eyes focused on me as I sat on my throne. I pulled a particularly gruesome face. There was a pause before the head teacher continued.

'When Mr Phinn goes to the toilet,' said Mrs Gardiner—I looked at her in horror, dreading what was to follow—'he doesn't flip it about like a fireman's hose. Do you, Mr Phinn?'

'N . . . no,' I replied.

'He directs it where it should go. And that is what you boys will do in the future. Is that clear?'

'Yes, Mrs Gardiner,' replied the boys.

'Have you anything to add, Mr Phinn?'

'No, nothing,' I murmured, attempting to take in what I had just heard.

Later in her room, Mrs Gardiner sat behind her desk and remarked, 'I think we made our point, don't you think, Mr Phinn?'

THE FIRST MEETING with the head teacher, Mrs Braddock-Smith, and the governors of the Ugglemattersby Infant School, where I had outlined the suggestions for the amalgamation, had gone amazingly smoothly and everyone present had been strongly in favour of the recommendation. The meeting with the head teacher, Mr Harrison, and governors of the Juniors had been less good humoured, but it appeared that my lucky star was shining brightly, for the predicted 'fly in the ointment', Councillor Sidebottom, was 'down with the flu' and couldn't attend.

The meeting with the parents of the children who attended the two schools had been very well attended, and the general feeling was that the amalgamation was an excellent idea. The two teachers from the Junior School, Mrs Battersby and Mrs Sidebottom, had sat at the back like stone statues: it was clear that they were not in favour of the proposal. Councillor Sidebottom, who had got up from his sick bed, had soon discovered that the parents were vociferously in favour of the proposal. With an eye to the next county elections, he had been remarkably restrained. He had explained that he was in an invidious position and could not speak freely, but he did want to register his opposition. The evening had ended with the parents voting in favour of the change.

Now I was meeting with Mrs Braddock-Smith to discuss the amalgamation in more detail.

'Well, I think,' she said, 'it's the only course of action. There's plenty of room on this site and, let's face it, the Junior School is in decline. It is a sad fact that the Junior School does not provide the sort of education these parents are looking for. In my opinion, it's a very appropriate move. I feel fully confident I can take on the headship of the amalgamated school and—'

'It's not quite as simple as that, Mrs Braddock-Smith,' I told her, irritated by her smugness.

'Oh?'

'The schools will amalgamate and become a county primary school with a new head teacher.'

'A new head teacher!' exclaimed Mrs Braddock-Smith. The colour drained from her face as what I had said sunk in.

'Well, both you and Mr Harrison will be considered for the position and then, if neither of you is appointed, it will go to national advert.'

'You mean I will be in *competition* with Mr Harrison for the post?'

'Yes,' I replied.

She gave a wry smile. 'Well, Mr Phinn, when you compare my track record with that of my colleague down the road, I should think there will be little doubt which one of us is the better suited for the position. You yourself have seen the quality of the education I provide here and, though I say so myself, I feel I run a school second to none in the county.'

'That may very well be the case, Mrs Braddock-Smith,' I told her, 'but I can only advise the appointment will be in the hands of a new governing body,' I said, 'comprising governors from both schools.'

'I see,' said the head teacher. Mrs Braddock-Smith's elation had evaporated like a burst balloon. She rose from her desk in queenly fashion. 'Well,' she said, 'this has come as some surprise. I shall have to see what Archdeacon Richards has to say about all this—and my union. And now, if you will excuse me, Mr Phinn, I have a great deal to do.'

Oh dear, I thought, a minute or so later as I stood at the gate. This situation was likely to be more contentious than I had imagined.

AT THE JUNIOR SCHOOL, Mr Harrison was waiting in the entrance to greet me. He looked a whole lot better than when I had last seen him at the parents' meeting and was actually smiling.

'Good afternoon, Mr Phinn,' he said cheerfully.

'Good afternoon.'

I followed him to his room where he sat at his desk, rubbed his hands together vigorously and asked, 'Cup of tea?'

'No, thank you,' I replied, bemused by his manner. Mr Harrison was grinning like a cat that had got the cream.

I had written to him after my last visit, explaining that I had seen the Chief Inspector with the intention of recommending that a thorough inspection of the school would take place, but the proposed amalgamation of the two schools had changed things.

'As you know,' I said now, 'the plan is to close down this school and move the Juniors in with the Infants up the road.'

He leaned back in his chair. 'I think it's an excellent idea,' he said.

'You do?' I said, taken aback.

'I do,' he said. 'I think a fresh start with a new head teacher will make all the difference.'

As at the meeting with the head teacher of Ugglemattersby Infant School, I explained that, in the first instance, he would be in competition with Mrs Braddock-Smith for the headship of the new school.

'I think Mrs Braddock-Smith deserves the job,' he said.

'You do?'

'I do,' he said. 'She's a very successful head teacher and runs a popular and high-achieving school, as she is always at great pains to point out, and I am certain she will rise admirably to the challenge.' There was undisguised sarcasm in his voice.

'So you won't be applying for the post?' I asked.

'No, I won't,' he told me, a smile still playing across his face. 'You see, I am resigning.' He looked as pleased as Punch.

'Resigning?'

'Yes,' he said. 'The chairman of governors of my last school down in London phoned me a few weeks ago to tell me that the present head teacher is retiring. He asked if I would consider putting in an application for the post. I then received such encouraging letters from my former colleagues urging me to apply. I applied, went for the interview last week and was offered the position.

'Well, congratulations,' I said, and meant it.

'And I do hope that Mrs Braddock-Smith is appointed as the head teacher. She always told me that she welcomed a challenge and I have no doubt that should Mrs Battersby and Mrs Sidebottom be redeployed to the new school, they will provide her with all the challenge she needs.'

8

It was the opening night of *The Dame of Sark* and I was ready to head off home from the Staff Development Centre, shower, change, have some tea and get to the Fettlesham Little Theatre in good time. Despite Raymond's frequent panic attacks the production had fallen into place and it seemed that we might not make total fools of ourselves on the night.

I was tidying up after an English course I had just directed. I was about finished when Mrs Kipling from St Margaret's Church of England Primary School popped her head round the door of the room.

'Hello, Mr Phinn,' she said brightly.

'Good afternoon,' I said.

'I've been here on one of the art courses,' she said. 'It's been truly inspirational. He's such a character isn't he, Mr Clamp, and so very talented.'

'Yes, he is,' I agreed.

'I try to come on all the courses he holds,' she said, beaming. 'Would you like to see my collage. I'm really proud of it.'

'Yes,' I replied, surreptitiously looking at my watch, 'I'd be most interested.'

'It's in the corridor.'

I followed Mrs Kipling and there, propped up on a chair, was a garish jigsaw of material mounted on a large piece of card.

She looked at her handiwork with obvious pride. 'We were asked to express a mood such as happiness, anger, frustration, affection, depression, that sort of thing. I call mine "In the Pink". I shall put it in the entrance hall at school in order to cheer people up.'

'It's very striking,' I commented, thinking to myself that I wouldn't hang such a hideous creation on my toilet wall, let alone in my hall. As I looked closer at the collage, I seemed to recognise some of the material—a bright pink nylon fabric, and had a sudden dreadful thought.

'So where did the material come from for your collage?' I asked casually.

'Mr Clamp brought along black bags containing all sorts of scraps of different textures and in various colours. He told us that he often got old clothes from charity shops. As soon as I saw this pink overall—so wonderfully bright that it sort of shimmers—I commandeered it.'

'It was one of the things that Mr Clamp brought in his black bags?'

'Yes—at least I think so,' replied Mrs Kipling. 'Or was it already out of the black bag when I saw it? Yes! That's it. It was over the back of a chair in the art room.'

Oh dear, I thought. It was Connie's pink overall, I was sure of it. I could imagine the mayhem when she discovered that her trademark uniform had been vandalised.

I helped Mrs Kipling carry her creation out to her car.

'I did wonder,' she said, 'if I should offer to let Mr Clamp display it in the Staff Development Centre but then decided I wanted it back in school.'

'A wise decision,' I murmured.

Back in the Centre, the woman in question, Connie, minus overall, was surveying the art room. 'Just look at this mess,' she complained. 'Everywhere he goes he leaves a trail of debris and destruction, that Mr Clamp. There are bits of cloth all over the place. It's like an explosion at a jumble sale in here.' Connie shook her head. 'I was hoping to get off a bit earlier this afternoon. It's my bingo night.'

'Have you ever won at bingo, Connie?' I asked, changing the subject.

'Not a lot,' she said. 'A few pounds here and there, that's all. I'm always optimistic, mind. I've got my eye on the Christmas accumulator.'

'How long have you been playing bingo for?' I asked.

'Oooh, over twenty years,' she said.

'And you've only won a few pounds? You would have been better putting it into a deposit account,' I told her.

She pursed her lips. 'If I want a financial adviser, Mr Phinn,' she told me, clearly nettled, 'I'll find one in Fettlesham, thank you very much. Bingo might not be the cup of tea for you academical sorts, but I enjoy it.'

I changed the subject again. 'I hear from Mr Pritchard that Willingforth School is taking part in the mathematics display at Dr Gore's conference at Manston Hall next month,' I said. 'Are your grandchildren involved, Connie?'

She smiled. 'Our Lucy is,' she told me. 'She's a real whiz when it comes to sums. Can add up like nobody's business. Miss Pilkington's been having them doing mental arithmetic every morning for the past few weeks.'

'It's an excellent school, Willingforth,' I said. 'Mr Pritchard told me that overall it achieves the best maths results in the county.'

'Oh,' said Connie suddenly, and casting her eyes around, 'speaking of overalls, you haven't seen mine, have you?'

I ARRIVED at Fettlesham Little Theatre during the interval. It appeared, judging by the number thronging the noisy bar area, that the play was going well so far. The worst scenario, which Raymond had predicted in one of his blackest moods, was that the audience would vote with its feet if the play didn't come up to scratch before the interval and we would play the second half to an almost empty auditorium. 'And that frightful Marcia McCrudden, theatre critic of the *Fettlesham Gazette*, will be there,' he had moaned, 'sitting like an evil presence in the front row. I dread to think what she will say about this play.' It seemed, however, that since no one was making for the door when I arrived Raymond's prognosis was unfounded.

I went backstage where I came upon Percy, the stage manager, a round little man with a flushed complexion. He was squatting on a small stool by the fire exit, beneath a large sign that stated in bold red letters: 'NO SMOKING'. He held a smouldering cigarette in one hand and a bottle of brown ale in the other.

'I see the cavalry's arrived,' he said, as he caught sight of me squeezing through the narrow door with my holdall containing cap, Sam Browne belt and boots, my uniform over my arm.

'Good evening, Percy,' I said. 'So, how's the play going?'

'How's it going?' he repeated. He gave a hollow little laugh. 'Raymond, our creative director and revered producer, has buggered off.'

'He's what?' I exclaimed.

'He had one of his paddies at the end of the first half, stormed off and nobody's seen him since. It's always the same on the opening night. He gets into this state, getting himself all wound up and winding everyone else up in the process.'

'It's his artistic temperament,' I said. 'You have to make allowances. So what's upset him?' I asked, hanging the uniform up.

'Well,' said Percy. 'Sharon, you know, the lass playing Cecile, the Dame's maid, she arrives all dolled up to the nines, wrapped up in a great cloak thing. Shortly before the performance started, she takes off the cloak, and all she's got on underneath . . .' Percy paused, and chortled at the memory. 'She were wearing just a strip of a skirt, black fishnet stockings and a blouse that revealed more than a liberty bodice. "You're not going on stage in that get-up," Ray says. "You're supposed to be the Dame's maid, not a common back-street tart." Well, Sharon storms off and when she does walk on stage in the proper costume, what does she do?'

'What *does* she do?' I asked.

'She puts on that daft French accent. She can be a right madam, can that Sharon. Anyway,' Percy continued, 'Ray went ballistic when she comes off stage, just as George Furnival brings in the coffin for the last act.'

'What coffin? There isn't a coffin in the last act.'

'I know that,' said Percy, 'but George told Raymond it would be more dramatic if the young German soldier, Wilhelm Muller, who gets blown up by the mine at the end, were brought on stage in a coffin. He'd got this lovely black affair with brass handles. Course, George never misses a trick and he'd put down the side of the casket: "Furnivals for the Finest in Funerals. Coffins to die for." Well, I won't repeat where Raymond told him to stick his coffin. George didn't take it too kindly. Ray just cracked. "I can't stand any more," he says and buggers off.'

'Well, just make sure that you are there when I go on stage, Percy,' I told him. 'The sound effects are pretty complicated.'

'No worries,' he said. 'It's all in hand.'

I had to admit that I did worry. In terms of sound effects, it was the most demanding part of the play and had only been rehearsed once properly at the dress rehearsal.

THE PRODUCTION WAS SAVED, as ever, by Mrs Cleaver-Canning. In Scene Five, Winco missed out half his lines with the result that we were into the final scene a good five minutes earlier than we should have been. Percy, no doubt still squatting on his stool with his bottle of brown ale, missed the cue for Handel's *Water Music*. Luckily, I was alert to what was happening and I entered on cue with the news that the Germans had handed in their guns and were now clearing the mines in the harbour. This was the point when there was to have been the loud explosion, but nothing was heard. I looked desperately at Mrs Cleaver-Canning.

'What was that?' she exclaimed, ad-libbing and staring into the wings with an excessively dramatic gesture.

'What?' I replied nervously, following her gaze.

'I thought I saw a flash from the harbour.'

'The harbour?'

'Yes, the harbour,' she said, slowly. 'Could it have been a mine exploding?'

'A mine?'

'Please don't keep repeating me, Colonel,' said Mrs Cleaver-Canning. 'Did you not inform me that you had instructed the Germans to dismantle the mines in the harbour? Perchance one has exploded.'

'Ah yes,' I said, 'I believe it could have been a mine.' Some of the audience, aware that things were not going exactly to plan, began to titter. Please let this end, I kept repeating to myself. I was frozen to the spot and quite unable to keep up with Mrs C-C. Then I caught sight of a small woman in black, sitting in the very centre of the front row, holding a notebook. I knew at once it was the feared theatre critic, Marcia McCrudden.

'What's the time?' asked Mrs Cleaver-Canning.

'W-what?' I stuttered. Out of the corner of my eye, I caught sight of the theatre critic scribbling in her notebook which added to my discomfiture.

'I asked if you could tell me the time, Colonel,' she said. 'We're forgetting Mr Churchill,' announced Mrs Cleaver-Canning. She fiddled with the knobs on the wireless. 'You don't mind, do you?'

'No, I'd like to hear it,' I replied, knowing full well that there was no chance of that. I looked into the wings but there was still no sign of Percy. Where the devil was he?

'Flat batteries, I'm afraid,' said Mrs Cleaver-Canning. 'Everything seems to stop working in wartime.'

'Well, I imagine Mr Churchill would have announced that the dear Channel Islands have been liberated, that the war is over and that the cause of freedom has triumphed over the scourge of tyranny.'

Following the Prime Minister's broadcast, the telephone should have rung. The stage was deathly silent, Mrs Cleaver-Canning and I looked at each other for a moment.

She then picked up the receiver. 'I think I'll ring Major Lanz and see what that explosion was.' She dialled a number. 'Hello, hello, is that Major Lanz? A soldier? What? One of ours? The English colonel's here. I'll tell him.' She replaced the receiver. 'A young German soldier's been killed by a mine down at the harbour.'

'Oh,' was all I could manage to say.

At this point Percy finally arrived, offstage right. The wireless came to life with a loud rendering of Handel's *Water Music*, the telephone rang and a loud explosion could be heard. Through the cacophony, Mrs Cleaver-Canning bravely declaimed the final words of the play.

'It goes on, Colonel Graham,' she said. 'It goes on. When will it ever stop?'

IT WAS A BRIGHT but chilly November afternoon as I drove along beneath a pale, cloudless sky on my way back to the office from Willingforth, a small rural village set in the depths of the Dales. The countryside was ready to settle down for the winter. In the corners of fields, where the sun had not reached, I could still see traces of the morning's hoar frost. Here and there, the colour was broken by clumps of ochre-coloured bracken.

Suddenly, as I turned a sharp bend, a small boy, perhaps ten or eleven, ran across the road straight in front of me. I slammed my foot on the brake and screeched to a halt. The boy scrabbled over the dry-stone wall and shot across the fields like a hare.

A moment later three other boys, much bigger, emerged from a small copse at the side of the road, panting. They stopped at the roadside when they caught sight of me, and then moved off down the road, looking back occasionally to see if I was still there.

I started forwards again, driving slowly and keeping my eyes peeled. Half a mile along the road I spotted the boy who had run out in front of me; he was sitting on the verge. I pulled over and wound down the car window.

'Whatever were you playing at, running out in front of me like that?' I asked him angrily and, as I did so, immediately recognised who he was. His wavy red hair was the giveaway.

'I was in an 'urry,' the boy replied, refusing to look at me but staring down mulishly at his feet.

'You might have got yourself killed—Terry Mossup!' I said.

At the sound of his name, the boy looked up, surprised. I had met this young lad a couple of years before when I had gone out to Willingforth Primary School at the request of the head teacher, Miss Pilkington, who wanted my advice on how to deal with a particularly disruptive pupil.

He had come from a deprived background, where there had been some abuse and certainly a great deal of neglect, but was now being fostered by a local doctor and her husband who were trying their best to give the boy some affection and stability. When he had started at the school, Terry had been rude, very naughty and destructive, but Miss Pilkington had persevered. After showing incredible patience and investing a great deal of her own time, she had made real progress with Terry, and the boy's behaviour had improved by leaps and bounds. The head teacher had discovered that the boy had a natural way with animals. He was the only pupil that the school cat would allow to stroke it, and he liked nothing better than feeding the birds at playtime.

'Do you remember me, Terry? Mr Phinn.'

The boy stared up at me, with a suspicious expression.

'Are you a social worker?'

'The school inspector.'

He smiled and nodded. 'Oh, aye, I remember thee,' he said. 'You're the one who asks all them questions.'

'So what school are you at now?' I asked.

'West Challerton 'igh,' he told me.

'And how are you getting on at West Challerton?'

'I'm not,' he said, getting to his feet. 'It's crap.'

'Terry, why were those boys chasing you?' I asked.

He bent down and picked up a stone. 'They gang up on me,' he said. 'Cos I'm little and don't give 'em what they want—money and sweets—but I don't take any crap from 'em.'

'Have you told anyone that these boys are bullying you?'

'I can handle missen,' he said. 'They think they're tough when they're in a gang but on their own they're like all bullies—bloody cowards.' He threw the stone behind him.

'I think perhaps you should tell somebody at school,' I said.

'Naw,' he said dismissively. 'What's the use? They never do owt. You just 'ave to put up wi' it.'

'No, you don't,' I said. 'If you are being bullied, you should tell someone you trust. You must never ignore bullying. Something should be done about it. Have you told your foster parents?'

'Naw, it'd only mek things worse.'

'No, it wouldn't,' I said.

He looked at me, and his face tightened. ''Ow would you know? 'Ave you been fostered, taken away from your mam, always movin' round from one place to another, switchin' schools? Then you get to this new school an' everybody knows you're in care an' kids start to pick on you cos you're different. Then they say things about your mam an' where you come from, an' you get into a scrap and sent to the deputy 'ead an' you can see it in the teacher's eyes—"These kids are all the same—trouble."'

I couldn't reply. What a sad, angry and troubled boy he was, standing on the grassy verge, his eyes filling with tears.

'Terry—' I began.

'See ya,' he said and, with that, the boy set off down the road.

'Terry!' I shouted. 'Will you promise me you will tell someone?'

He turned and called back to me, 'I've told *you*, haven't I?'

IN THE OFFICE I sat at my desk, staring out of the window, wondering just what I could do about Terry Mossup.

'Penny for them,' said Julie, who had just come in.

'I was thinking,' I said. 'About a little boy who leads a life no child should lead.'

'Sounds serious,' said Julie.

'Julie, could you get me the school secretary at West Challerton High on the phone, please? I need to arrange a visit.'

At that moment, David and Sidney arrived in the office—arguing as usual.

'We shall have to agree to disagree,' said David crossly.

'Fine,' said Sidney. Then, after a pause, added, 'But I know I'm right.'

A few minutes later, after I had spoken to West Challerton School, arranging to see the headmaster the next morning, Julie tottered in with a tray of cups of tea for all of us.

'Do you remember, Mr Phinn,' she asked, 'when Mrs Savage told you that her car wouldn't start the other afternoon?'

'Yes,'

'Well, it wasn't that it wouldn't start,' said Julie gleefully. 'She'd been clamped!'

'Mrs Savage clamped!' repeated Sidney. 'Oh goody!'

'Makes a change from Mr Clamp being savaged,' chuckled David.

'According to Marlene on the switchboard,' said Julie, 'she'd parked her car in one of the councillors' bays. She had to show herself at the Admin. Office, and pay a fine to get the clamp taken off. It serves her right. By the way,' she continued, holding up a copy of the *Fettlesham Gazette*, 'you're in the paper.'

'I am?' I asked. I reached for the paper and began looking through it, 'It'll be a review of the play I was in.' I said. 'I'm dreading seeing what it says. The night the critic was there was a humiliating failure.'

'Give it here,' said Sidney, snatching the paper from me. He turned to the page. 'Here it is,' he said, taking a theatrical stance: '"The staging of a wartime classic drama, based on the autobiography of the Dame of Sark, was performed last week by the Fettlesham Literary Players at the Little Theatre. It was warmly received by a most appreciative audience."'

'Does it really say that, Sidney?' I asked. 'That's not bad.'

'Scout's honour.' He read on. '"The undisputed star of the show was Margot Cleaver-Canning who gave an inspired performance as the formidable Dame of Sark. She captured the larger-than-life character superbly, dominating the stage with her imperious presence. She was every inch the powerful matriarchal figure whose courage remained steadfast during the occupation of her island home. Sharon Mawson as Cecile, Mrs Hathaway's French maid, brought sparkling vitality to a very demanding role. She maintained the Breton accent throughout the drama with great authenticity."'

'Sounds a *tour de force* to me,' said David. 'Why didn't you tell us about it?'

'Do I get a mention?' I asked, ignoring him.

'Yes, here you are at the end,' said Sidney. He read in silence.

'Well, go on,' I said. 'What does it say?'

'Perhaps you ought to read it yourself, old boy,' said Sidney.

'No, no,' I said, 'go on Sidney. I don't mind what it says.'

'Very well,' said my colleague. He coughed. '"Gervase Phinn, playing the part of the British Colonel Graham, was ..."' Sidney paused.

'Was what?' I asked.

'"Lacklustre",' said Sidney.

'"Lacklustre"!' I cried.

'That's what it says.' Sidney continued, '"He mumbled through his few lines with little conviction and it was hard to suspend one's disbelief and accept that one so lacking in assertiveness could have been the senior British officer who liberated the island."'

'I was fine at rehearsal,' I said. 'It was the blasted sound effects or, rather, the lack of them that did for me. It put me completely off my stroke.'

'Never mind, Gervase,' said Sidney. 'You have to look on the positive side. You won't be called upon again to give up all those evenings rehearsing. You can now, as the politicians frequently say, spend more time with your family.'

'Yes,' I said, feeling rotten. 'It's just that I didn't think I was that bad.'

THE FOLLOWING MORNING, I went straight from home to West Challerton High School to see the headmaster.

Mr Pennington-Smith was thin and stiff as a broom handle. He had short-cropped iron-grey hair and eyes like blue china marbles behind thick black-framed glasses. He was wearing, as always, a black academic gown.

'And what have we done to deserve a visitation from yet another school inspector?' he asked, with undisguised sarcasm. 'You must enjoy coming to West Challerton,' he continued. 'You seem to spend so much time here.'

It was true that Sidney, David and Geraldine had visited the school frequently in recent months, largely because several areas of weakness had been identified in their reports. Despite his grandiose claims when he had taken over the headship, little had been translated into good practice.

At our first meeting, I had been subjected to a lengthy monologue in which this arrogant man had described his impeccable credentials in the education world and his vast experience. I had bristled when he had launched into a diatribe of the previous headmaster. Under Mr Blunt's leadership, the school had achieved commendable examination results, was relatively successful in sports, had a thriving brass band, staged good-quality drama productions and there was a positive atmosphere. It wasn't the county's flagship school but it certainly was not in the doldrums.

At the school's speech day that I'd attended, it had been clear to me that the emphasis in the school, under Mr Pennington-Smith's leadership, would be on the high achievers. So, when young Andy, standing in my garden, had assessed his headmaster as being 'only bothered abaat bright kids and them what are good at sports,' he reinforced an opinion I had already formed. After a little over a year in the job, things had not altered at all for the better.

'I've come about bullying,' I told Mr Pennington-Smith now.

'Bullying,' he repeated.

'Yes. I have reason to believe that one of your pupils is being bullied.'

'You sound like a policeman, Mr Phinn,' he said. '"Reason to believe"?'

'Yes,' I said. 'I am not certain of the facts but—'

'And you have made a special visit to inform me about one pupil,' he interrupted. 'I would have thought that a telephone call would have sufficed.'

'Perhaps,' I said, 'but I thought I should acquaint you personally with this situation. I am sure that you take bullying as seriously as I do.'

'Well, you had better come to my room,' he said. I followed him down the corridor. He glanced at his shiny watch. 'I can spare you ten minutes.'

He sat at his desk and listened impassively as I related the incident with Terry Mossup.

'But from what you have told me,' he said when I had finished, 'this incident took place off school premises and out of school hours. I can hardly be expected to police society as a whole, Mr Phinn, I deal with things which happen in my school, and have no control over what happens out of it.'

'But would you not agree,' I asked him, 'that the bullying is more than likely to continue on school premises.'

'Of course I'm concerned with the pupils in my school,' he said, 'and I shall take any action I deem fit.'

'May I ask what action you might take?' I asked.

'I shall ask my deputy head teacher, Mr Stipple, to investigate. If, indeed, this is a case of victimisation, I shall deal with these three boys, you can be certain of that. I will not tolerate any form of bullying in West Challerton High School. As you may be aware, I have a very thorough anti-bullying policy. I will get you a copy.' He pressed a buzzer on his desk. A disembodied voice asked, 'Yes, Mr Pennington-Smith?'

'Mrs Rogers, would you bring me a copy of our anti-bullying policy, please?' The headmaster smiled. 'You might wish to take it with you when you leave, Mr Phinn,' he said.

ON MY WAY to the car, I came upon a knot of large boys having a crafty smoke well out of sight of the main building. The cigarettes miraculously disappeared as I approached.

'Morning, boys,' I said cheerfully as I passed.

'Hey up, Mester Phinn,' one of the lads said.

'Hello, Andy,' I said.

'Are tha closin' t'school down, then?' he asked.

'No,' I replied.

'Pity. 'As they 'eard aboat mi Uncle 'arry? 'E's been barred from t'Royal Oak. New landlord got sick on 'im complainin' all t'time so 'e told 'im not to come back an' to tek his pals wi' 'im.'

'All four have been banned?' I asked. 'That's a bit much.'

'Well, to be 'onest, Mester Phinn, it were a bit cheeky-like fer mi Uncle 'arry to get up this pertition an' ask people comin' into t'pub to sign it. Any road, 'e's angry as an 'ungry ferret in a sack.'

'I'll remember to keep out of his way,' I said.

'Well, let us know if there's owt else I can 'elp thee wi'.'

'There is something,' I said, having a sudden inspired thought. 'Could you walk with me to the car?' When we were out of earshot of the other boys, I stopped. 'Andy,' I said, 'there's a boy in the first year here called Terry Mossup. He's a bit of a loner, small for his age with ginger hair.'

'Aye, I reckon I've seen 'im abaat. Allus on 'is own.'

'Well, he's being bullied by three older boys and it occurred to me that—'

He finished my sentence. 'Tha wants me to put a stop to it. No problem, Mester Phinn,' he said. 'I'll fettle it for thee. Nob'dy'll pick on 'im from now on. I 'ates bullies.'

'I don't want you to do anything in particular, Andy,' I said. 'Just keep a watchful eye on Terry.'

The boy winked. 'I follow yer drift, Mester Phinn,' he said knowingly, tapping the side of his nose.

'Thank you,' I said.

ON A MORNING towards the end of November, I arrived at Westgarth Primary School to attend the interview panel for a new deputy head teacher. I knew full well that the chairman of the governors, Mr Parsons, would be there. I had visited this school to speak at a parents' meeting and had found him to be an insufferable individual. He was loud and had a profound sense of his own importance. He had berated me about the decline in educational standards, the lack of discipline in the young and the increase in juvenile crime. I noticed a red sports car parked outside the school, which told me that Dr Gore's representative on the panel, Mrs Savage, had already arrived. This was likely, I thought, to prove a very interesting morning.

I could hear the chairman of the governors' loud and abrasive voice as I approached the head teacher's room. Taking a deep breath I knocked and entered. There were five people present, four of whom were being lectured by Mr Parsons. The speaker stopped when he saw me.

'Good morning,' I said brightly.

'Oh,' said Mr Parsons. 'It's Mr Flynn. We can make a start now you've arrived.' There was the hint of criticism in his voice.

'Phinn,' I said.

'What?'

'It's Mr Phinn,' said Mrs Thornton, the head teacher, moving forward to shake my hand. 'Thank you for coming. You know Mrs Savage, of course,' continued the head teacher, 'but may I introduce two of my governors, Mrs Smethurst and Mrs Curry. And, of course, you've met Mr Parsons.'

'Well,' said the chairman of the governors, 'shall we make a start? I've a business to run and don't want these interviews dragging on.'

'I don't think it will take us long,' the head teacher told him. She turned to me. 'Unfortunately, two of the candidates have pulled out at the last minute so we only have three applicants to consider.

The interviews took place in the school hall. The six of us sat in a row at a long trestle table in front of which was a chair for the interviewee.

First of all, the candidates' application forms were considered and, much to my horror when I heard the name, it became clear that the chairman had a preferred choice who was quite unsuitable. However, one of the candidates seemed eminently suitable and another was a strong possibility.

I had met Miss Pinkney, the first candidate, when I had inspected St Catherine's, a school for those with special needs, some two years earlier and had been very impressed by her teaching. I had arrived in the hall to watch a drama lesson, where I had met this larger-than-life, bubbly middle-aged woman with long hair gathered up in a tortoiseshell comb, dressed in a bright pink and yellow Lycra track suit.

'Come along in, Mr Phinn,' she had boomed. 'Shoes by the door, jacket on a peg. There's a spare leotard if you want to slip into it.' When she had seen the appalled look on my face, she had added, 'Only joking!' She had then informed me that her students, all of whom were disabled but 'very talented', were her 'stars'. It was clear that this teacher had a very positive relationship with the children; she was sensitive, encouraging and good-humoured.

I had met a cheerful and obviously clever young man at St Catherine's whose ambition was to study English at university. Michael, aged sixteen, had been blind since birth but announced when I spoke to him that his blindness was not a 'handicap' nor a 'disability'; it was 'more of an inconvenience' and that if sighted people like myself were a little more considerate and put things back in their proper place, then he wouldn't bang into them.

'So tell me, Michael, what is the best thing about St Catherine's?' I had said to him.

'That's easy,' he had replied without hesitation. 'Miss Pinkney.'

That same Miss Pinkney now entered the hall like a seasoned actress coming on stage. She made a grand entrance, dressed in a multicoloured smock of a dress, with a rope of enormous amber-coloured beads.

'Good morning to you all,' she said. 'May I sit?' Without waiting for an answer, she plonked herself down on the chair and smiled at the panel.

Miss Pinkney answered the questions confidently, and it was clear that she was a highly committed and enthusiastic teacher with the experience, expertise and the force of character to be a first-rate deputy head teacher. When Mr Parsons climbed on his hobbyhorse about declining standards, poor behaviour in the young and lack of discipline, she challenged him.

'My goodness,' she chortled, 'you do sound so dreadfully pessimistic. The picture is not quite as bad as you paint it, you know. On the whole, I have to say that I am very impressed by the youth of today. I love working with them and I have a great deal of faith in them. I know there are the awkward and the demanding youngsters who are hard to cope with, but there are many many children who come from caring, supportive homes and are in the hands of dedicated and talented teachers.'

Out of the corner of my eye, I could see Mrs Thornton beside me nodding. She was obviously impressed.

'What do you think are the keys to educational success?' I asked her.

Miss Pinkney answered without a moment's thought. 'Great expectation and high self-esteem.' She clasped her hands in front of her, displaying a set of large coloured rings. 'I think it's so important to build up a child's feeling of self-worth. I work with dyslexic and autistic youngsters and many have such low self-esteem. I try and convince them that they can achieve great things. I firmly believe that if a teacher expects the moon, perhaps her pupils will go through the roof and dwell among the stars.'

'Ah yes,' said Mr Parsons, 'you work with handicapped children?'

'Disabled,' she said. 'Handicapped is a word we no longer use.'

'Yes, well, I'm not big on political correctness,' mumbled Mr Parsons.

The smile disappeared from Miss Pinkney's face. 'It is not a question of political correctness,' she retorted. 'It is more to do with sensitivity and respect. And, yes, I have worked with these children for a number of years.'

'And don't you think you might find it a bit different working with *normal* children?' asked Mr Parsons.

'Children with a disability are like any other children,' she told him. 'They have the same feelings and fears, likes and dislikes. They enjoy the same things. They can be as delightful, difficult, happy, moody, sad, loving, naughty as any other children. It is just that they have rather more difficulties in life to face than many others.'

When Miss Pinkney had left, Mr Parsons turned to the head teacher. 'Not very appropriate outfit for an interview, was it?' he observed. 'She looked like a gypsy fortune-teller in that coloured tent.' He shook his head. 'And I can't say I liked her manner. Over the top with her answers, I thought. What did you make of her then, Mrs Thornton?' he asked.

'I should prefer to see all the candidates before I express my opinion, Mr Parsons,' she told him.

The second applicant was Mr Hornchurch.

'Take a seat,' said Mr Parsons. I could see from his expression that he was less than impressed with the outfit that this candidate too was wearing: a loud checked jacked, pale grey trousers, pink shirt and a multicoloured tie. 'It occurs to me,' he continued, flicking through the application form, 'that you're a bit on the young side for this position.'

'It is true,' Mr Hornchurch answered, crossing his long legs, 'that I have only been in the profession for a relatively short time, but I feel quite confident about taking on the role of the deputy head teacher.' He went on to give a series of splendid answers, outlining what he had developed at Tarncliffe Primary School, and the results the children in his class had achieved.

'A good school,' he said, 'is cheerful and optimistic, a place where children can learn in a safe and secure environment, where the teachers are enthusiastic and committed, and the leadership is purposeful and dynamic. There should be no bullying or racism, and there should be decent toilets.'

'Toilets?' exclaimed Mr Parsons.

'Yes, of course,' replied Mr Hornchurch. 'You see, if the toilets are clean and attractive, everything else in the school is likely to be the same.'

The third candidate, dressed in a black suit and prim white blouse, looked startled when she saw me. She drew her lips together into a tight little line. It was Mrs Sidebottom from Ugglemattersby Junior School. Mr Parsons was clearly taken with her tidy appearance, for his manner changed. I suppose she looked to him like the good old-fashioned sort of teacher that he wanted.

'Do take a seat, Mrs Sidebottom,' he said amiably. 'I'm sorry you have had to be the last in, but somebody has to be.'

'That's quite all right,' she replied, giving a thin-lipped smile.

'So,' said Mr Parsons, 'can you tell us why you want to leave your present position?'

She smiled wanly. 'As you may know, the Junior School in which I teach at present is due to amalgamate with the Infant School. I really feel that it is time for me to take on greater responsibility. I have to say that I believe in very high standards. In my opinion there needs to be discipline, routine, good order in the classroom, and well-behaved children, attributes which I feel are sadly lacking in society.'

'Indeed,' agreed Mr Parsons. 'I'm constantly saying so myself.'

After the interview panel had each put a question to Mrs Sidebottom, I asked her, 'And how important in a school, do you think, are extra-curricular activities? School concerts, trips out of school, that sort of thing?'

'They have their place, I am sure,' she said, 'but the main function of the teacher is to teach children. In my opinion, such things decorate the margin of the more serious business of a school and should be left largely to the parents.'

'I see,' I said. 'No more questions thank you, Mr Chairman.'

When the time came for the panel to consider the three applicants, Mr Parsons said straight away, 'I have to say that the first two candidates didn't *look* like teachers to me. Neither of them was dressed properly for an interview. Nor was I impressed by their answers—far too airy-fairy. The last candidate looks the part, sounds like a teacher after my own heart and, as far as I'm concerned, she's the one we should appoint.'

'Might we hear what the inspector has to say?' asked Mrs Curry.

I was careful to outline what I considered to be their strengths and weaknesses without indicating which one I favoured. I explained that I had observed all three applicants actually teach so was in a position to comment on their classroom practice.

'Thank you,' said Mr Parsons. 'Now, in my opinion—'

'And might we now hear what the head teacher has to say?' asked Mrs Smethurst. 'After all, it is Mrs Thornton who will be working closely with the successful candidate.'

It was clear to all that Mrs Thornton preferred the first candidate and considered the last totally unsuitable.

'I just don't think,' persisted Mr Parsons, 'that this Miss Pinkney *looks* like a teacher who will fit in here.'

'May I ask, Mr Chairman,' said Mrs Savage, asking a question for the first time, 'if you are judging the candidates *only* on their appearances?'

Bravo, Mrs Savage! I thought to myself.

'Well, that and what I've heard,' he replied, testily.

'I should like to draw your attention to the references,' she continued, 'which indicate that there are strong reservations about the last candidate.'

'Mrs Savage,' said the chairman of governors, 'I don't need to remind you that it is the governors of this school who make the decisions in appointing staff.'

'No, you do not,' replied Mrs Savage, with an edge to her voice. 'It is I who send the "Instruments of Governance" to schools. I shall say this, Mr Chairman, that if the governors decide to ignore Mr Phinn and the head teacher, and they disregard the references, which of course they are at liberty to do, and Mrs Sidebottom turns out to be unsuccessful in this role, then it will be the governors' entire responsibility.'

'There's not much chance of that,' said Mrs Curry. 'My vote goes to Miss Pinkney.'

'And so does mine,' agreed Mrs Smethurst.

'Thank you, colleagues,' said Mrs Savage. 'I take it, then, that I may record that Miss Pinkney is to be offered the position?'

9

'Well, that's another of Dr Gore's little jobs about ready for the off,' I said, snapping the folder shut. It was the last week of November, and I was trying to catch up on paperwork. When two of my colleagues arrived, however, I decided to finish the rest at home. There was little chance of getting anything done when Sidney and David were in the office.

'And what little job is that?' asked David.

'The NACADS Conference,' I told him.

'Well, all I can say, dear boy,' said Sidney, leaning back on his chair 'is that you deserve a medal for working with that disagreeable woman.'

'You have to know how to handle Mrs Savage, Sidney,' I told him. 'You just rub her up the wrong way. Actually, she's not been too bad.'

'The only way I would handle that virago,' said Sidney, 'is to place my hands around that long swan-like white neck and throttle the life out of her. She's unbearable. When I arrived at Manston Hall this morning to drop off my exhibits for your conference, do you know what the woman had done?'

'No,' I said, 'but I have an idea you are going to tell us.'

'She had shrouded those wonderful Italian white marble figures, those beautiful classical figures of Venus and Leda with her swan, with ferns, all over the statues' most beautiful and intimate features.' It looked quite ridiculous. "We can't have delegates coming into a room full of naked women," she told me. "Mrs Savage," I said, "they are statues. They are not delegates at a strippers' convention. The British Museum doesn't cover up the statues of the human form. There is nothing offensive about them. They are works of art."'

'How did you get on with your mathematics display?' I asked David.

'Oh fine,' said David. 'Fortunately the woman in question was busy giving the audiovisual technician a hard time when I took in my materials. I shall put up my display tomorrow afternoon. I've asked Miss Pilkington to bring some of her pupils along on the Sunday to do a demonstration. Wonderfully talented children she's got, all keen and confident.'

'Yes, and I understand Connie's grandchildren are involved,' I said.

'There's another woman I could throttle,' mumbled Sidney. 'She's forever moaning and groaning about the mess I leave.'

'You want to be careful Connie doesn't throttle you first after what you've done,' I told him. I related the incident at the SDC and how Mrs Kipling had used Connie's prized pink overall as part of her collage.

'Oh dear,' said Sidney, laughing. 'You won't tell her, will you? Anyway, then,' he exclaimed, 'Mrs Savage had the brass neck to tell me that she hoped the paintings and sculptures I would be exhibiting would not include anything *risqué*. "Look here," I said,' continued Sidney, '"it is not your function to tell me what I should or what I should not be displaying."'

'Was Lord Manston around?' I asked.

'Who?' Sidney asked.

'Lord Marrick's son and heir. He's in charge of the conference.'

'Tadge?' said David.

'You know him?' I asked.

'Of course, I know him,' said David. 'He's captain at the golf club this year. Decent fellow is Tadge but a bit of a ladies' man.'

'Yes,' I said, 'I detected something of that when Mrs Savage and I were over there for a planning meeting. He couldn't take his eyes off her, nor she off him. They flirted shamelessly!'

'What! Lord what's-his-name and Mrs Savage!' exclaimed Sidney. 'He wants his head examining. She'll eat him up and spit him out.'

'She's a very attractive woman,' said David. 'Anyway, she'll never get her hooks into Tadge. Many have tried, but none have succeeded in landing him. The merry widower is Tadge and likely to stay like that.'

At this point Julie arrived in the office. 'I could hear you right along the corridor, Mr Clamp,' she told him.

'He's been regaling us with the saga of Mrs Savage and the naked statues at Manston Hall,' I told her.

'You'll all be naked and whipped if you don't get over to the Centre. Dr Mullarkey went ages ago,' said Julie.

'Great Scot!' exclaimed Sidney. 'I had forgotten the inspectors' meeting has been brought forward.'

I think we had all forgotten, and the three of us set off post-haste for the Staff Development Centre.

'I HAVE ASKED Mrs Savage to join us this morning,' said Miss de la Mare. 'I thought it would save time if we heard the latest developments from the horse's mouth, so to speak.' Mrs Savage gave a small nod.

'Before I ask Mrs Savage to give us the latest information about the CEO's conference,' said the Chief Inspector, 'I should just like to take this opportunity of thanking you. The past six weeks has been a particularly frenetic and demanding time, and you have all risen to the challenge superbly. You have been more than generous with your time, attending the frequent evening meetings of governors and parents, interviewing head teachers, as well as your regular weekend courses and seminars, quite apart from inspecting schools. You really have worked so very hard, so thank you.'

She was a clever woman was Miss de la Mare. This eulogy was clearly intended for the ears of the CEO's Personal Assistant, who had a somewhat jaundiced view of the school inspectors: they appeared to her to have far too much power, influence and freedom for her liking.

'It's nice to be appreciated,' said David, with just a hint of a smirk.

'And, as a mark of my appreciation,' said Miss de la Mare, 'I should like to invite you all to a small Christmas get-together at the end of the school term on the 18th, here at the Centre. Just a glass of sherry and a few nibbles at the end of the day, about six o'clock, I suggest.'

'Excellent,' said Sidney.

'Now to business,' said the Chief Inspector. She turned to Mrs Savage. 'First of all, Dr Gore's conference. I am exceedingly sorry that I shall not be able to be there myself. Perhaps you might like to update us, Mrs Savage, on how things are progressing.'

'Yes, indeed,' said Mrs Savage, opening the first capacious folder. 'The NACADS Conference, which will take place this weekend at—'

At this point the door burst open and Connie appeared, pulling behind her a large metal trolley on squeaky wheels. She was attired in an electric-blue overall which clashed alarmingly with her copper-coloured hair.

'I'm bringing your elevenses in now, Miss de la Mare,' Connie announced, 'It's in flasks so you can have it at your own convenience.'

Miss de la Mare gave a small, indulgent smile. 'Thank you, Connie.'

Connie manoeuvred the trolley into position at the side of the room and was about to leave when Sidney stretched out a hand to her. 'Your new overall is the *most* wonderful colour, Connie, truly—er, electrifying.'

Connie halted, and looked down at herself. She was obviously quite taken aback by Sidney's praise. 'Well, I don't know, I'm sure,' she said. 'I don't think blue is my colour. But what with my pink overall gone missing, I've had to use this substitution.' She looked up. 'I know I've asked you all before but has *anyone* seen my pink one?'

'I'm afraid I haven't seen it,' said the Chief Inspector.

I shook my head and tried to appear the picture of innocence. David looked pointedly at Sidney who stared heavenwards.

'Well, it's a mystery and no mistake,' said Connie.

'I am sure it will turn up, Connie,' said Miss de la Mare. 'Thank you for the—er, elevenses.'

When Connie had departed, Mrs Savage continued. 'As I was saying, the NACADS Conference at Manston Hall at the weekend appears to be up to speed. Dr Gore was particularly keen that it should have a Yorkshire flavour to it. With that in mind he has secured the concert pianist, Vincent Barrington, himself a Yorkshireman, to entertain the delegates after the Friday evening reception.'

Geraldine, who was so often very quiet at our meetings, suddenly became animated. 'Vincent Barrington!' she exclaimed. 'Oh, that's wonderful! How clever of Dr Gore.'

'Yes, indeed,' purred Mrs Savage. 'This talented young man took third prize in last year's Leeds International Pianoforte Competition.'

'I heard him earlier this year in the Bridgewater Hall, and I would dearly love to come and hear him,' said Geraldine.

'On the Saturday morning,' continued Mrs Savage, 'the Minister of Education and Science, the Right Honourable Sir Bryan Holyoake, QC, MP, will give the keynote lecture. After the buffet lunch, there will be seminars. For the formal dinner on Saturday evening, Dr Gore is delighted to have secured the lawyer, author and raconteur Mr Stephen D. Smith as the after-dinner speaker. He is, of course, another Yorkshireman. Then, on the Sunday morning, the delegates will have the opportunity of viewing the displays, observing the children's demonstrations, joining in the students' workshops and listening, before lunch, to the Young People's Brass Band directed by Mr Gordon of the Music Service.'

Mrs Savage looked up from her file, which she then closed.

'That all sounds excellent,' observed the Chief Inspector. 'Thank you for bringing us up to date, Mrs Savage. Does anyone have any questions for Mrs Savage?' She paused. 'No? Well, then, I think this is a good time to break and have our elevenses, and then we can discuss the school closures.'

WHEN I ARRIVED HOME that evening, I found Christine standing by the kitchen table nursing a sleepy baby, and sitting opposite her was Andy, clutching a large mug of tea.

'Hey up, Mester Phinn,' he said, smiling widely.

'Hello, Andy,' I said as I entered. I kissed Christine and tickled Richard under the chin. 'And how's my little Tricky Dicky been today?' I asked.

'Teething and nappy rash,' replied Christine, 'and he's certainly let me know all about it. He's been tetchy all day. Anyway, since Richard looks as though he might at last go to sleep, I'll take him up.'

I slipped off my jacket, poured myself some tea and then joined Andy at the table. The boy's large pink face looked scrubbed and he was dressed in a clean white shirt, leather jacket and denim jeans.

'You look very smart, Andy,' I told him.

'Young Farmers meetin' toneet, Mester Phinn,' he told me. 'I'm doin' a bit of a talk like, so thowt I'd gerra bit dressed up.'

'Doing a talk,' I said. 'What about?'

'"Preparation for Sheep Breedin"', he said, 'an' I'm reight frit.'

'Go on,' I said, 'there's nothing to be frightened about. From what your Uncle Harry tells me, there's few who know more about sheep than you do.'

At this point, Christine returned. 'And how is your Uncle Harry?' she asked. 'He wasn't too happy last time we saw him.'

'Oh, 'e's been as 'appy as a pig in shit lately. That new landlord at t'Royal Oak is up an' leavin'.'

'I didn't know that,' said Christine. 'My, my!'

'Aye,' said Andy. 'Tha knaas Mester 'ezekiah Longton? 'E were not 'appy abaat all t'change, like rest o' reg'lars. Well, 'e's up an' bought it.'

'Bought the Royal Oak?' I exclaimed.

'Aye, lock, stock an' barrel. There were a big piece abaat it in t'*Fettlesham Gazette*—"Regular buys t'village pub that barred him".'

'What made him think of buying it?' asked Christine.

'Place were goin' dahn't nick. Landlord thowt it'd be filled to burstin' wi' folks out from town, ramblers an' cyclists and such, but it never 'appened. Fact is, 'is trade dropped reight off. Then 'e 'ad this offer to go in wi' a couple o' pals who was openin' a bar in Majorca. That an' t'fact that Mester Longton med him an offer 'e couldn't refuse. Mester Longton 'ad a bit put by, like.'

'So Hezekiah Longton's bought the Royal Oak,' I said. 'Well, well, well.'

'An' from what 'e says, 'e's gunna put things back as they were inside. It'll be a traditional country inn ageean, wi' nowt fancy.'

'And how's young Terry getting on at school?' I asked Andy.

''E's doin' champion,' said the boy. 'Few days after yer were in school, I saw them three bullies follow 'im into t'boys' toilets. I knew what they were up to, so I followed 'em in, and I told 'em face to face—well, more hand to throat, really—that it wasn't very nice to bully little kids. I explained to 'em that if they laid a finger on 'im ageean, I wunt be best pleased. They soon came round to my point o' view an' they 'aven't touched 'im since. Young Terry's been 'elpin me on t'farm, an' I'll tell thee what, Mester Phinn, 'e's reight good wi' beasts. 'E's been a real good 'elp to me.'

'Well, you had better be making tracks to the Young Farmers,' I said. 'I hope your talk goes well.'

'There's a little matter of wages, Mester Phinn. That's reason for comin' to see ya. I've spent all mi brass an' cum to get paid.'

'Of course,' I said, reaching for my wallet. 'You've done a super job for us, Andy, and we are both very grateful.'

'I mean,' said the lad, 'I liked doin' that work for thee, Mester Phinn, but as mi Uncle 'arry is allus remindin' me, nob'dy does owt for nowt in Yorkshire, tha knaas.'

THE MANSTON ESTATE looked magnificent on Friday evening as I drove up the long avenue to the great red-brick house, floodlit from the far side of the gravel sweep in front of the Hall. There was a clear sky above me and frost was already forming on the grass. It was now six o'clock and the delegates were due to arrive in an hour's time for the reception.

A gigantic Christmas tree dominated the impressive entrance hall. It was rather early for a tree but when Tadge had offered one from the estate, we had accepted graciously. However, this was no ordinary Christmas tree—it was white! No flickering fairy lights or coloured baubles for Mrs Savage. The tree was simply but most beautifully decorated with small fuchsia-coloured silk bows. Against the shimmering white of the painted branches, the effect was most dramatic.

My eyes, however, were drawn to Mrs Savage. Wearing a long burgundy-coloured and daringly low-cut dress, which clung to her as if she had been poured into it, and with a pale silk shawl draped around her shoulders, she stood beneath the portrait of the crusty old general, looking for all the world as if she were the chatelaine of Manston Hall.

'Good evening, Mrs Savage,' I said as I approached her. 'You are looking quite splendid, if I may say so.'

'Good evening, Mr Phinn,' she replied. 'And, since this is a special occasion, yes, you may.'

At that moment, Tadge arrived. He gave a low whistle and said, 'My goodness me! How very flippercanorious you are this evening, my dear Brenda.'

I sensed Mrs Savage stiffen. 'Flipperwhaty, Lord Manston?' she enquired.

'Flippercanorious, Mrs Savage. Isn't it a simply splendid word? I discovered it the other day. Elegant, my dear, wonderfully elegant, is what it means. And I think it calls for a toast to the evening.' With that, he turned and walked back across the hall, returning with a bottle of champagne and three glasses, but I politely refused the offer. 'A bit early for me,' I said.

'We are merely making certain that the Moët is at the right temperature,' Tadge said, pouring generous glasses for Mrs Savage and himself.

'In my opinion,' said Mrs Savage, 'there is nothing worse than warm champagne.' She saw me smiling. 'I do want everything to be just right,' she added.

'You're a perfectionist, Brenda,' Tadge commented. 'A true perfectionist.' Mrs Savage accepted the compliment with a slight nod.

'What an amazing Christmas tree!' I said. 'I've never seen one painted white before.'

'Ah, then you've not seen our escutcheon,' Tadge said. 'The white tree has been on our coat of arms since the fifteenth century. Back in the last century, when fir trees became all the fashion, the old Dowager Countess Elvira decided to have the Christmas tree painted white and we've kept up the tradition. Well, if you both will excuse me. I need to make sure the dogs are penned before the guests arrive.' He topped up Mrs Savage's glass, and then strode off, whistling loudly.

At that moment, a young man with curly hair and wearing a long black overcoat walked through the door, and hovered indecisively.

'Round the back, please,' Mrs Savage instructed, pointing over the man's shoulder to the front door.

'I beg your pardon?' he asked, looking thoroughly mystified.

'Would you take the vol-au-vents round the back?' she told him. 'This is not the caterer's entrance.'

'I'm not here with the vol-au-vents,' he replied. 'I'm Vincent Barrington, the pianist.'

'Oh, maestro,' Mrs Savage cooed, changing her tone of voice, gliding towards him and extending a long red-nailed hand. 'I'm so terribly sorry. I foolishly assumed you would be wearing rather different attire.'

'Oh, I don't travel in evening dress,' Vincent Barrington told her amiably, 'since it tends to get creased. It's in the car.'

'Well, it is such a great pleasure to make your acquaintance,' said Mrs Savage. 'I have heard so many wonderful things about you. I'm Brenda Savage, the organiser of the conference.'

'Hello, I'm Gervase Phinn,' I said, offering my hand. 'I am helping Mrs Savage with the conference.'

'Let me show you where you will be giving your recital,' simpered Mrs Savage,' and then I will show you where you can change.'

I stayed in the hall while Mrs Savage took Vincent Barrington to the North Hall and a few minutes later Dr Gore arrived, accompanied by Councillor Peterson.

'Well, Gervase,' said the CEO. 'This looks splendid, quite splendid!'

'And no doubt costing a pretty penny, as well,' grumbled the councillor.

'Not at all,' replied Dr Gore good-humouredly. 'Lord Marrick has kindly allowed us to use Manston Hall without charge, and all other expenses are paid for by NACADS. It would be insensitive, to say the least, for the county to spend money on a conference when we are closing schools to cut costs.'

'Just as well,' mumbled the overweight councillor.

Dr Gore turned back to me. 'Is Lord Marrick about?'

'I'm afraid his plane from Rome has been delayed, Dr Gore. He will be with us in the morning.'

'Oh dear, what a shame. He will miss—'

'And while we're on the subject of closing schools,' interrupted Councillor Peterson, in my opinion, I—'

I quickly made my escape. The very last thing I wanted to hear was George Peterson's undoubtedly biased opinion about school closures.

I found Mrs Savage with Vincent Barrington and Tadge by the grand piano in the North Hall. I thought she was looking rather flushed. No doubt the champagne was having its effect. 'I do so love pianoforte music,' she gushed, 'particularly the works of Brahms and Liszt.' Rather appropriate composers, I thought to myself, considering the state she was getting into.

'Do you have a favourite piece, Mrs Savage?' Vincent Barrington enquired.

'"*Liebestraum*",' she sighed. 'I do so love that melody. It was my dear late husband's favourite.' I saw Mrs Savage's eyes mist over and she began to sniff inelegantly. Perhaps, I thought, there was a sensitive soul after all beneath that icy exterior. But, of course, it could have been the drink.

'Ah, the "Dream of Love",' said the young man. 'I shall play it tonight, especially for you.'

'Really?' simpered Mrs Savage. 'Would you?'

'And what about you, Lord Manston?' he asked.

'I like the works of Schumann,' he said. 'He was my dear late wife's favourite. I would love to hear one of the "Woodland Scenes".'

'Ah yes,' said the concert pianist, 'the great Schumann, who dedicated so much of his work to his beloved Clara. I see I have two romantics here. "You are my heart and my soul," he wrote. "You are the heaven to which I soar."'

'How very beautiful,' sighed Mrs Savage, dabbing her nose with a lace handkerchief. She looked in Tadge's direction and smiled.

This was getting maudlin to say the least, so I left them to it.

THE EVENING, thank heavens, seemed to be a great success. After the reception and buffet, the guests settled down to listen to Vincent Barrington. His playing was superb, and Geraldine, who was next to me, sat totally enraptured. At the end of the recital, the whole audience rose to its feet. Everyone, that is, except Councillor Peterson, who had slept through most of the evening.

'And for an encore,' announced Vincent Barrington, 'I should like to play a piece requested by my elegant hostess. "*Liebestraum*"—the "Dream of Love" by Franz Liszt.' He smiled at Mrs Savage who, true to form, was not going to be relegated to the rear of the hall, and had added a chair to the end of the front row. 'And for Lord Manston, a piece by Schumann: "*Freundliche Landschaft*"—"Friendly Landscape".'

'If you're doing requests,' came a booming voice, 'what about "On Ilkla Mooar Baht 'at"?' It was Councillor Peterson, who had been roused from his slumbers by the applause.

I winced.

'Of course,' said Vincent Barrington. 'It will be my pleasure.'

The guests clapped enthusiastically after the Liszt and Schumann pieces, but they sprang to their feet following a bravura rendering of the good old Yorkshire melody, played in the style of Beethoven, Chopin, Mozart and Rachmaninov. The pianist was indeed a maestro.

THE RT HON SIR BRYAN HOLYOAKE arrived the following morning in a shiny black limousine at precisely nine o'clock. Dr Gore, Lord Marrick, Tadge Manston and I stood a little distance away. The Minister of State for Education and Science was a lean, angular individual with a prominent Roman nose and well-cut silver hair. Sir Bryan was a man of few words. I had been in my job only for a few months when he had visited the Staff Development Centre and, as we had toured the building, he had been embarrassingly uncommunicative. He merely nodded and grunted when spoken to.

'Sir Bryan,' chortled Dr Gore now. 'Such a pleasure to see you again. I trust you have had a pleasant journey?'

'Passable,' he replied.

'Well, let me introduce you to the Earl of Marrick.'

'Morning, Sir Bryan,' growled the peer, who was looking somewhat worn out after his journey back from Italy.

'Good morning, Lord Marrick,' replied the minister.

'Do you know Yorkshire at all?' he was asked.

'A little,' he replied.

'You must spend more time here,' said Lord Marrick. 'God's own county.'

'May I introduce Lord Marrick's son, Sir Bryan—Lord Manston,' said Dr Gore.

'Good morning,' said the minister. He then caught sight of Mrs Savage standing a little behind Tadge, and extended a long white hand. 'And you must be Lady Manston. Good morning.'

'Oh no, Sir Bryan,' simpered Mrs Savage. 'I'm not Lady Manston. I'm a mere minion.' I could think of many words to describe Mrs Savage but 'minion' was not one of them. She was the least obsequious person I knew.

'This is my Personal Assistant,' explained Dr Gore, 'Mrs Brenda Savage, who has organised the conference and next to her is—'

'Ah, yes, Mr Phinn,' said Sir Bryan. 'You took me round the Teachers' Centre where that remarkable janitor—Connie, wasn't it?—kept everything so spick and span.'

'That's right. What a memory you have!' I said. 'She will be very pleased to hear that you remembered her, Sir Bryan.'

The minister became uncharacteristically eager to impart his pet philosophy. 'I make a point of never forgetting a name nor a face, Mr Phinn,' he told me. 'In life, one meets many people, particularly if, as I, one is in the political arena. All people are significant in their own way, and all deserve our attention. Whether one is a chief education officer or a cleaner, a minister of the Crown or a chauffeur, all play their part.'

'Indeed,' said Dr Gore. 'Now, if I may lead the way . . .'

LATER THAT AFTERNOON, when the delegates broke into discussion groups, I rushed home to get my dinner jacket. As I drove through Hawksrill, I smiled as I passed the pub. The brightly painted board with the outline of an oak tree and the lettering THE OAK had been replaced with the original sign featuring the oak tree in full leaf, with the smiling figure of the restored Merry Monarch standing beneath it.

'I see the pub is back as it was,' I said to Christine, as I rootled in a drawer for the studs of my dress shirt. 'That'll please the "gang of four".'

'Yes,' she said. 'I saw Harry earlier when I took Richard out in the buggy for a walk. He was looking almost ecstatic.'

'That makes a change. Oh come on, where are these wretched studs?'

'Are these what you're looking for?' Christine asked, holding up a cupped hand.

'What would I do without you?' I said, pecking her cheek.

THE AFTER-DINNER SPEAKER, a round, jolly man, was a great success and he entertained the delegates for a good forty minutes. Even Mrs Savage managed a smile or two.

On Sunday morning, everything went to plan. My fellow inspectors joined me in the South Hall, and the delegates seemed genuinely interested in the exhibitions we had mounted. After coffee, they returned to the North Hall. Here they listened to a short but impressive performance by the brass band. Finally, Dr Gore gave a rather tedious address, which generated polite applause, and by noon the delegates had all departed.

Mrs Savage and I wandered through the now strangely silent building.

'It went well,' I said.

'Yes, it did,' she said. 'And now we are left to organise all the clearing up.'

'Where's Dr Gore?' I asked.

'I believe he's gone off with Lord Manston for lunch at his golf club.'

I could tell by the tone of her voice that she was distinctly peeved. 'It certainly wouldn't have hurt him to invite us. After all, we did all the work.'

'Ah well, Mrs Savage,' I said with a smile, 'that is the fate of the mere underlings of the powerful. We are the foot soldiers and not the generals, but we too play our small part in the scheme of things.'

10

I was the last inspector to arrive at the SDC for Miss de la Mare's Christmas get-together. Everyone had gathered in the lounge area, which had been decorated with silver streamers and coloured balloons, sprigs of mistletoe and holly. A large Christmas tree, over-decorated with bright baubles and fairy lights, stood in one corner.

I approached Sidney, who was dressed in a black velvet jacket and ostentatious pink bow tie. He was explaining to Geraldine the finer points of modern art. Julie was standing next to them, dressed in an incredibly tight-fitting crimson polo neck, a thin black strip of a skirt and red stilettos. She rolled her eyes and tilted her head in Sidney's direction as I approached, which told me he was in the middle of one of his not-to-be-interrupted monologues.

'It is all a matter of symmetry and balance, my dear Geraldine,' Sidney was telling her, 'and the dexterous juxtaposition of primary colours and—' He caught sight of me and stopped mid-sentence. 'Hail the conquering hero cometh, sound the trumpets, beat the drums.'

'And what is that supposed to mean?' I asked.

'Our esteemed leader, Dr Gore, was singing your praises when he spoke to Miss de la Mare recently—so I have been informed by Julie here.'

'Really?'

'Yes,' said Julie. 'He phoned her up saying how well things had gone and what a good job you did at his conference. Marlene on the switchboard just happened to hear the conversation.'

'I am sure after this last startling success, our malleable colleague will have quite a few more of the CEO's "little jobs" to take on,' said Sidney.

'No fear,' I spluttered.

I left Geraldine and Sidney to continue their discussions and joined Connie. She looked very Christmassy, dressed in a scarlet blouse and a green and red apron. She was watching proceedings with eagle eye.

'Good evening, Connie,' I said. 'You're looking very festive.'

'I don't feel very festive,' she said. 'I'm thinking about all the clearing up that will have to be done when you lot have finished. Them pine needles get everywhere.'

'No overall today?'

'I don't sleep in my overall, you know, Mr Phinn,' she said sharply. 'When the occasion merits it, I do dispensate with it. Incidentally, I have a good idea who walked off with my pink one.'

'Really?' I said with feigned innocence.

'I reckon it was Mr Clamp. He was always making disparaging comments about it, and it's just the sort of thing he would do. Anyways, I won't be requiring any overall after this week, because I'm leaving.'

'You're not!' I exclaimed.

'I am. Finishing at the end of the week.'

'For goodness sake, why didn't you say something?'

'You know I'm not a one for any fuss,' she told me. 'As I put in my letter to Dr Gore, I've done my job to the best of my facility and now I want to enjoy my retirement while I can.'

'But you must have a send-off, Connie,' I said. 'You can't walk out of the door after all these years without a bit of a do.'

'It's been a bit of a do all these forty years, Mr Phinn, having to deal with all the destruction and debris you inspectors leave behind. I don't want no "bit of a do". They had a "bit of a do", as you call it, when my Ted retired from driving buses for forty years. They gave him a clock, ugly shiny gold thing it were, far too fancy for us. I don't know why they always give you a clock at the end. Is it so you can spend the rest of your time looking at it and seeing your life ticking away?'

'I know that you'll be greatly missed, Connie,' I said.

'Well, that's as may be,' she replied, dismissing the compliment with a shrug. 'Any road, when I won on the bingo, I said to Ted—'

'Congratulations! How much did you win?'

Connie shrugged again. 'That's for me to know,' she told me. 'It's given me and Ted a bit of a nest egg, and it will supplicate my pension. So, you see, I won't be needing no overall after this week. Mr Clamp is welcome to it.'

For a moment, I considered telling her the truth, that her prized pink overall would be enshrined forever on the wall at St Margaret's School, but I thought better of it. I somehow didn't feel she would find it amusing.

'I'm sure Sidney didn't take it, you know,' I said.

'Oh, yes he did,' said Connie. 'He went all quiet and guilty-looking when I brought it up at your meeting. I've known him long enough to be wise to his little japes. And if he thinks I'll take that letter he sent me seriously—'

'Letter?'

'He's sent me a joke letter.' She reached for her handbag and found a rather crumpled envelope, which she handed to me. 'He must think my brains are made of porridge to fall for this one.'

I read the letter. I was stunned.

'The Prime Minister has asked me to inform you, in strict confidence, that he has in mind, on the occasion of the forthcoming New Year Honours, to submit your name to The Queen with a recommendation that Her Majesty may be graciously pleased to approve that you be appointed a Member of the Order of the British Empire.'

'Connie, this is no joke,' I told her, running my finger over the embossed crest and address at the top of the letter. 'It's the real thing!'

'Don't be so daft! Who would want to give a medal to a cleaner?' she asked.

'The Queen,' I said, 'that's who. This is an authentic letter from 10 Downing Street. You're getting a medal. This is wonderful,' I said. 'Many many congratulations,' and I planted a little kiss on her cheek.

'Mr Phinn!' Connie squeaked, turning bright pink.

'But it's got to be kept secret until the Honours List is announced in the New Year,' I cautioned her. 'You shouldn't have told me until it's official.'

'Well, I didn't know it was for real,' she said. She looked flustered now. 'You mean I'm getting a medal?'

'You'll now have the letters MBE after your name,' I told her.

'I think I'm going to faint,' she said, resting her hand on the table.

'Don't forget—you mustn't say anything to anybody,' I warned her as I caught sight of Geraldine and Sidney heading in our direction.

'Connie, are we going to get a glass of sherry or not?' asked Sidney. 'We've been here a good half hour and not a sign of any libation.' Connie said nothing. She had a puzzled, faraway look on her face.

'Connie! Are you all right? You look ill,' said Geraldine taking her arm. 'Would you like to sit down?'

'No, I'll be fine, Dr Mullarkey, thank you very much,' she replied vacantly. 'I just feel a bit funny, that's all. I'd better see to the drinks.'

After she'd left the room Sidney said to me, 'I don't know what you were saying to Connie but you appear to have frightened the life out of her.'

'I'll go after her,' I said.

I found Connie in the kitchen, crying. 'Now, now, Connie,' I said, putting my arm around her shoulder. 'Why the tears?'

'I don't know what's the matter with me,' she said, sniffing noisily. 'I've come over all unnecessary, as my mother used to say. To think that anybody would want to give me a medal for cleaning toilets and doing a bit of dusting.'

'You do more than that Connie,' I told her, 'much, much more.'

'Brave people like my father, they get medals,' she said. 'People what make a difference in life. I don't know what he'd make of this, I really don't.'

'He'd be so proud of you,' I said. 'You make a real difference to people's lives, Connie, and if anybody deserves a medal, it's you. Now, come on, dry those eyes and I'll help you with the sherry.'

When we arrived back in the lounge area, we discovered Dr Gore had made an appearance with Mrs Savage. His PA was in conversation with Miss de la Mare and David as I approached them with the tray of sherry.

'So is it a quiet Christmas for you this year, Mrs Savage?' the Chief Inspector was enquiring.

'Good gracious, no, Miss de la Mare,' Mrs Savage replied, giving one of her all-too-familiar patronising smiles. 'Quite the opposite, actually. I'm spending the holiday with a friend in the South of France.'

'Whereabouts?' asked David.

'St Tropez,' Mrs Savage told him. 'And are you familiar with the French Riviera, Mr Pritchard?'

'Not at all, never been,' he replied, helping himself to a glass of sherry. There was mischief in his eyes. 'As a matter of fact, our captain at the golf club has a place in St Tropez. Now that's a coincidence, isn't it?'

'Really,' said Mrs Savage, assuming total disinterest. 'If you will excuse me, Miss de la Mare,' said Mrs Savage, 'I think Dr Gore wants a word.'

Sidney gate-crashed the conversation. 'So what was all that about with Connie?' he asked me.

'She's leaving,' I told him.

'Leaving!' exclaimed Sidney and David together.

'I didn't know about this,' said Miss de la Mare.

'Nobody did,' I said. 'Well, apart from Dr Gore.'

Our discussion was interrupted by Dr Gore who, tapping a spoon on his glass, called for attention.

'Colleagues, friends, before we enjoy the Christmas fare that Connie has prepared for us, I guess it is incumbent upon me to say a few words. This term has been a particularly successful one. Standards in schools have continued to rise, the school closures were effected with the minimum of complaint and only one or two hiccoughs, and my NACADS Conference was a resounding success. Indeed, Sir Bryan told me he was most impressed with the sterling work we undertake in the county.

'But, colleagues, friends, I cannot let this occasion pass without mentioning one particular individual, someone who has been a stalwart in the Education Department—loyal, reliable, and never stinting in the work she has undertaken for many years. She has been a great asset and I would like to acknowledge that this evening.'

Mrs Savage, standing to the right of Dr Gore, gave a slight smile. She reminded me of a film star waiting to receive an Academy Award.

The CEO continued. 'I have discovered that in life there are four kinds of people. There are the wishbones, and they are the dreamers. There are the jawbones, and they are the talkers. There are the knucklebones, and they are the critics. And then there are the backbones, who carry the load and do the work. The person to whom I am referring has been the very backbone of the Department. I speak, of course, of Connie.'

I was watching Mrs Savage, and her face was a picture. She looked like a startled ostrich. In contrast, the colour drained again from Connie's face and she looked deeply uncomfortable.

'Connie wrote to me at the beginning of this month,' continued Dr Gore, saying she wished to leave at the end of this term. She wanted no fuss, no leaving celebration. She wished to retire quietly. Well, for once, Connie, you are not getting your own way.' Dr Gore reached behind him for a large box wrapped in silver paper. 'I should like to present you, on behalf of all in the Education Department, with this gift, in appreciation of your loyal and devoted service over the last forty years.' There was a round of enthusiastic applause. 'And, you know, Connie,' said the CEO, 'if it were up to me, I'd give you a medal.' I knew then who had recommended her for the award.

Connie took the box to the table and loosened the paper from around it. She lifted the lid off the box, and peered inside. 'Oh, goodness me, how . . . lovely!' she said, and drew out a large ugly shiny gold clock.

DURING THE FINAL few weeks of term, teachers and pupils everywhere had been preparing for Christmas. Highly decorated fir trees in large tubs stood in entrance halls, cribs with brightly coloured figures had been dusted down and arranged in classrooms, walls had been decorated with Christmas scenes, and nativity plays had been rehearsed throughout the county. I have always loved the weeks leading up to the year's most celebrated festival, both now and when I was a child myself.

Looking back, I realised I had had a charmed childhood and the very best life could offer—the combination of loving parents and dedicated teachers. Of the many children I have met in the course of teaching and inspecting schools, some have been lucky and have had the very best. Some, with disabilities, had mountains to climb, but they often possessed the determination and strength of character to get to the top. Others would feel the pressure of ambitious parents who wouldn't allow them to have a carefree childhood. And then there were children like Terry—angry, lonely, mixed up, troublesome—who had a hard time of it and, of all children, deserved to have the very best teachers, teachers like Miss Bailey and Mr Hornchurch, who were enthusiastic and good humoured, and who brought compassion, respect and laughter into the lives of the children they taught.

It was a cold, overcast afternoon when I arrived at the final school I would visit that term, Backwatersthwaite Primary. I was looking forward to renewing my acquaintance with the remarkable head teacher, Mr Lapping. Our paths had crossed on various occasions during the intervening years, and he had never failed to impress me.

As I made my way up the narrow path towards the gaunt stone school with its shiny slate roof and high leaded windows, I recalled that first occasion when I had lifted the great iron knocker in the shape of a ram's head and let it fall with a resounding thump. The heavy black door had opened and I had been confronted by a thin, stooping man with frizzy greying hair and the complexion of a corpse. He had had no policy documents, planning materials, lesson plans or curriculum guidelines. When I had asked to see his School Development Plan, he had given a hollow laugh and informed me that he wouldn't recognise such a thing if it were to fly through the window: in his book, education was not about paper and processes, procedures and documentation, it was about *teaching*. Then he had tapped his brow.

'It's all up here, Mr Phinn,' he had said.

Despite the fact that there was nothing written down, I had been highly impressed by everything I had seen and heard. Before I had left, a small nine-year-old with wide eyes and thick bracken-coloured hair had approached to inform me seriously that 'Mester Lapping's a reight good teacher, tha knaws.'

Mr Lapping was now retiring after forty years. I was there that afternoon to wish him the very best in his new life. He was moving south to Canterbury to live nearer to his daughter and grandchildren. I knew he would miss Yorkshire desperately. I had been invited to his farewell party, which was to take place later, but sadly I had had to decline since it clashed with the nativity play at Hawksrill School. I had promised Christine I would be home in time to go to it with her.

Mr Lapping and I were sitting in his office, during the afternoon break. Through the window, I could see that snow had started to fall softly, and the deep valley, where a wide, unhurried river flowed gently beneath the arches of a slender bridge, was speckled in white.

'This is for you, George,' I said, passing him a brightly wrapped present. 'It's to help you remember your days in Yorkshire.'

'How very kind,' he replied. 'May I open it?'

'Of course.'

He stared at the book, then read from the binding: '*Dale Folk: Character Sketches in Prose and Verse* by Dorothy Una Ratcliffe. How wonderful. Thank you so much.'

'The final poem is a particular favourite of mine,' I told him. 'Perhaps I might read it to you and wish you all the very best in your retirement. It's called "The Yorkshire Blessing"—I expect you know it.' I turned to the very last page and read:

> To thi mind—Peace,
> To thi 'eart—Joy,
> To thi soul—Strength
> And Courage
>
> In thine outgoings
> Nowt amiss,
> To thi 'ome comings
> 'Appiness.

'Thank you, Gervase,' he said quietly. 'I shall treasure it.' There were tears in his eyes.

AS I DROVE BACK to Hawksrill in the late afternoon sun, the light dusting of snow making the Dales look ethereal yet peaceful, I thought of my beautiful wife and baby whom I should shortly see. How lucky I was!

The cottage looked welcoming as I parked the car; there were lights behind the closed curtains, and a wisp of smoke curled up from the chimney into the frosty air. As I went through the back door and into the kitchen, the smell of something delicious cooking made me sniff the air appreciatively.

'Hello, darling,' said Christine, who was sitting at the table, with Richard in his carry-cot beside her.

I kissed them both. 'I was determined not to be late today,' I said. 'I really didn't want to miss the Hawksrill play. What time is your mother coming? It's good of her to baby-sit for us.'

'She rang about half an hour ago to say she was just leaving.'

I noticed there was a five-pound note on the table, and went to pick it up. 'Is this mine or yours?' I asked.

'It will be Andy's as soon as he calls round for it,' replied Christine. 'I was expecting him earlier.'

'I don't understand,' I said. 'I paid Andy the other weekend.'

She laughed. 'This is for that bet you had with him—the red-tails are back!'

'What—here?' I asked. I had hoped I'd never see those wretched squirrels again.

'No, not here. Andy called in to say that he had seen a flash of red tails down at Ted Poskitt's farm. Apparently, they've taken up residence in the roof above an old tractor shed.'

'I expect they'll be back here soon enough, then,' I said gloomily. 'The farm's not far away.'

'No,' said Christine, who appeared amazingly calm about the return of the pesky creatures. 'Andy thinks that they will hibernate there, and in the spring they will be so busy thinking about babies that they will probably stay where they are.'

'Oh, good, that's that then,' I said, mightily relieved.

'Don't forget you owe me for the fiver,' she said.

'I won't forget,' I said, crossing the room to put my arms round her. 'Nor will I forget that I am married to the most enchanting girl in the world.'

Christine turned and nuzzled her face into my shoulder. 'And that we have a wonderful son in Richard,' she murmured, 'who would like at least two brothers and perhaps a little sister as well.'

And, in due course, that's just what happened.

GERVASE PHINN

Born: Rotherham, December 27, 1946
Favourite book: *The Selfish Giant* by Oscar Wilde
Website: gervase-phinn.com

RD: You were a teacher for fourteen years before becoming a schools inspector. Was it a relief to get out of the classroom?

GP: No, it wasn't a relief. I always missed the classroom very much. I only moved jobs because I was invited to apply for the post of English adviser for the local authority of Rotherham. Throughout my career, whether I was working as an adviser or an inspector, I always grasped any opportunity to do some teaching—either in primary and infant schools, or at adult night classes. I never thought about doing anything else, really.

RD: What was your education like?

GP: I was in the hands of excellent teachers. I had an A-level English teacher, Miss Wainwright, who was brilliant. She brought Shakespeare to life, was caring, dedicated and believed in me. I was lucky to have a combination of a super family home and an excellent education, too, which inspired me.

RD: And what was your family like when you were growing up?

GP: I come from quite a humble background. My father was a steelworker and I was brought up in a semidetached house in Rotherham. I was one of four children and there wasn't a lot of money, but I was brought up surrounded by love, care and support. My father never raised a hand to us. When my parents were angry they talked it through with us. They never needed to smack us.

RD: Did you always want to write? And how did you get started?

GP: I read English at Leeds University. Like any person studying English, I'd always wanted to write a book, and my great ambition was to be the author of a Penguin paperback. Which has come about! And what I've done over the years is what many writers do: I've written things down about people or places. They're often insignificant little trifles but I've always kept a writer's notebook.

RD: And how did the Dales books—this is the fifth in the collection you've written—come to be published?

GP: The charities Childline and NSPCC were opening a big, new Childline office in Leeds and I was asked to do an after-dinner speech. Esther Rantzen came along and heard me talk, and later invited me onto her show. I was on it three times in all, and my future editor at Penguin, Jenny Dereham, happened to see the programme and rang up to ask if I'd like to show her some examples of my work. It went from there . . .

RD: Was it nerve-racking being on television?

GP: No, because I've always been a bit of an actor. I was in youth theatre as a young man and I've always spoken to large audiences. The biggest was 4,000 teachers in the Newcastle Arena. After that, you can do anything!

Arncliffe Primary School, one of many charming school buildings found in the Yorkshire Dales.

RD: What makes a good teacher?

GP: Good teachers are immensely enthusiastic, and their enthusiasm is infectious. Stanley Matthews, the footballer, once said, 'Wrinkles appear on the face with age, but cynicism and lack of enthusiasm wrinkle the soul.' I think teachers have to be enthusiastic, hard-working, caring, dedicated, sensitive and supportive. They must have the interests of every child, however damaged or repellent, at heart. It's a very demanding job, but I do think it is a most important role in society because you can actually transform a child for good or for ill.

RD: So, where do you think schools are going wrong today?

GP: I honestly don't think the schools are going wrong. The teachers get an extremely bad press. In thirty years I visited hundreds of schools and met thousands of teachers and children and I'm immensely optimistic. I'm afraid those youngsters who are hard-working, come from loving homes and have dedicated teachers, just don't get into the papers.

RD: Is the redoubtable Mrs Savage based on anyone real?

GP: No, she's an invented character, an amalgam of various people I met during my thirty years in education. A very forceful, very overpowering woman, Mrs Savage. But I must say a number of people have said, 'Is that supposed to be me?'!

RD: And is your relationship with Christine in the books autobiographical?

GP: Yes. Christine and I have been married now for thirty years and we have four children. We met and fell in love, and it was all just as I've written it in the books.

RD: What makes you happiest?

GP: Simple things . . . sitting round a dinner table with my wife and family, talking, laughing and exchanging stories.

MICHAEL BYRNES
THE SACRED BONES

For two centuries, deep beneath the raised plateau of Temple Mount in Jerusalem, a burial chamber has remained undisturbed, its cool stone walls ringing with the silence of eternity, its contents hidden from scientists, politicians and leaders of the world's three main religions. Until now . . .

PROLOGUE

Limassol, Cyprus — April 1292

Looking out from the eastern parapet of Kolossi Citadel's square tower, Jacques DeMolay gazed across the open expanse of the Mediterranean, his white mantle and thick auburn beard fluttering against a warm breeze. For a knight nearing fifty, his regal features—long nose, penetrating grey eyes, firm brow, and sculpted cheekbones—were surprisingly youthful. His cropped hair was thick and peppered with grey.

Though he couldn't actually see the shores of the Holy Land, he swore he could smell the perfume of its sweet eucalyptus trees.

It had been almost a year since Acre, the last major Crusader stronghold in the eastern Kingdom of Jerusalem, had fallen to the Egyptian Mamluks. The siege lasted six bloody weeks, until the then Grand Master, Guillaume DeBeaujeu, had thrown down his sword and retreated from the citadel wall. *'Je ne m'enfuis pas . . . Je suis mort.'*—'I'm not running away. I am dead.' Raising up his bloody arm, he had shown them the arrow plunged deep into his side. Then he had fallen, never to rise again.

Now, DeMolay wondered if DeBeaujeu's death had foretold the fate of the very Order itself.

'Monsieur,' a young scribe called. 'He is ready to speak to you.'

DeMolay nodded and followed the boy down the stone steps into the belly of the castle. He was led into a fetid stone chamber where the new Grand Master, a haggard Tibald DeGaudin, lay in a bed.

DeMolay tried to not focus on DeGaudin's bony hands, covered with open sores. His face was ghastly white with yellow eyes bulging from sunken sockets. 'How are you feeling?'

'As well as I look.' He contemplated the blood-red pattée cross that decorated DeMolay's mantle, just above his heart.

'Why am I here?' Regardless of the Grand Master's unfortunate condition, he was first and foremost DeMolay's rival.

'To discuss what will happen when I am gone.' DeGaudin's voice was scratchy. 'There are things you need to know.'

'I know only that you refuse to gather a new army to take back what we have lost,' replied DeMolay defiantly.

'Come now, Jacques. This again? The Pope is dead and with him dies any hope of another crusade. Even you can admit that, without the support of Rome, we have no chance of survival.'

'I will not accept that.'

Pope Nicholas IV, Catholicism's first Franciscan pope and an advocate of the Knights Templar, had tried in vain to garner support for another crusade. He had raised funding to equip twenty ships, even sending emissaries as far as China to foster military alliances. Only days earlier, he had died abruptly in Rome.

'Many in Rome claim that Nicholas's death was no accident.' DeGaudin's tone was conspiratorial. 'He made many enemies, particularly in France.' The Grand Master raised a faltering hand. 'As you know, King Philip has been taking drastic measures to fund his military campaigns. Arresting Jews in order to seize their assets. He's levied a fifty-per-cent tax on French clergy. Pope Nicholas protested these things.'

'Surely you are not saying that Philip had him killed?'

The Grand Master shielded a cough with his sleeve. When he pulled it away, spots of blood dotted the fabric. 'Just know that Philip's ambition is to control Rome. The Church has a much bigger problem to contend with. Jerusalem will have to wait.'

For a long moment, DeMolay was silent. His gaze shifted back to DeGaudin. 'You know what lies beneath Solomon's Temple. How can you ignore such things?'

DeGaudin managed a thin smile. 'Need I remind you that for centuries before we arrived in Jerusalem, others had also fought to protect those secrets? We have only played a small role in this legacy.' He paused. 'I know your intentions. Your will is strong. The men listen to you. And when I am gone, you will no doubt try to have your way.'

'Is that not our duty? Is that not why we swore an oath to God?'

'Perhaps what we have hidden all these years needs to be revealed.'

DeMolay drew close to the Grand Master's haggard face. 'Such revela tions would destroy everything we know.'

'And in its place, something better may emerge.' DeGaudin's voice dropped to a whisper. 'Have faith, my friend. Put down your sword.'

'Never.'

CHAPTER 1

Jerusalem — Present Day

S alvatore Conte never questioned his clients' motives. His many missions had taught him how to remain calm and keep focused. But tonight was different. Tonight he felt uneasy.

The eight men moved through the ancient streets scanning their sur- roundings with infrared night-vision goggles. Entirely clothed in black, each was armed with Heckler & Koch XM8 carbines equipped with 100- round magazines and grenade launchers.

With an abrupt hand signal to hold position, Conte paced ahead.

He knew that his team was just as apprehensive. Though Jerusalem's name meant 'City of Peace', this place defined turmoil. The men had trav- elled separately from a handful of European countries, convening two days earlier at an apartment leased in a quiet part of the Jewish Quarter under one of Conte's numerous aliases, 'Daniel Marrone'.

On arrival Conte had familiarised himself with the web of winding streets surrounding the thirty-five-acre rectangular monument in the centre of the fortified Old City—a massive complex of bulwarks and retaining walls standing thirty-two metres high, which resembled a colossal monolith laid flat upon Mount Moriah's steep ridge. The world's most contested parcel of real estate, the Islamic *Haram-esh-Sharif*, or 'Noble Sanctuary', was more familiar by another name—the Temple Mount.

As the cover of buildings gave way to the towering western wall, Conte motioned two men forward. The wall-mounted floodlights cast long shad- ows into which Conte's men would easily blend. But then so could the Israeli Defense Force soldiers, the IDF.

He peered ahead, his night-vision goggles transforming the shadows to eerie green. The area was clear except for two armed soldiers loitering fifty metres away, smoking.

Glancing over to their intended entry point at Moors' Gate, an elevated gateway on the platform's western wall, Conte quickly surmised there was no way to gain access to the Temple Mount without being detected.

Shifting his fingers along the barrel, he flicked the XM8 to single-shot mode and mounted the rifle on his left shoulder. He aimed for the head, using the glowing butt of the cigarette as a guide. *One shot. One kill.*

His index finger gently squeezed.

There was a muffled retort and he saw the target buckle at the knees.

The scope shifted to the remaining man.

Before the second IDF soldier had begun to comprehend what was happening, Conte had fired again, the round penetrating the man's face.

He watched him collapse and paused. Silence.

Another abrupt hand signal ushered his men onto the walkway approaching Moors' Gate. To his left, he glimpsed the Western Wall Plaza at the embankment's base. Yesterday he had marvelled at the Orthodox Jews—men separated from women by a curtained partition—who gathered here to mourn the ancient temple they believed had once graced this holy place.

A substantial iron gate sealed with a deadbolt denied access. In seconds the lock had been picked and Conte's team funnelled through the tunnelled entrance and fanned out across the broad esplanade beyond.

Past the stout Al-Aqsa Mosque abutting the Temple Mount's southern wall, at the esplanade's centre, a second and much grander mosque stood on an elevated platform, its gilded cupola illuminated against the night sky. The Dome of the Rock—embodiment of Islam's claim over the Holy Land.

Conte led the team to the esplanade's southeast corner where a wide opening accommodated a modern staircase, cascading downwards. He splayed the fingers of his gloved right hand and four men disappeared below the surface. Then he signalled the remaining two men to hunker down in the nearby tree shadows to secure a perimeter.

The air in the passage became moist the further the men descended, then abruptly cold, giving off a mossy aroma. At the base of the steps, they switched on rifle-mounted halogen lights bisecting the darkness to reveal a vaulted space with arched stanchions laid out in neat avenues.

Conte remembered reading that twelfth-century Crusaders had used this subterranean room as a horse stable. Now it was a mosque. Running his light along the room's eastern wall, he was pleased to spot the two brown canvas bags his local contact had promised. 'Gretner,' he addressed his Austrian explosives expert. 'Those are for you.'

The Austrian retrieved them.

Slinging his carbine over his shoulder, Conte took a folded paper from his pocket and switched on a penlight. The map showed the exact location of what they'd been charged to procure. 'Should be just ahead.'

Securing the penlight between his teeth, he used a free hand to unclip an electronic measuring device from his belt. He punched a button on its keypad and a small LCD came to life, activating a thin red laser that cut deep into the darkness. Conte moved diagonally through the chamber, his team close behind. Then he stopped abruptly, verified the measurements on the LCD, and swung the laser till it found the mosque's southern wall. He turned to face the northern wall, the gut of the Temple Mount.

'What we're looking for should be just behind there.' Salvatore Conte rapped a gloved hand on the wall's limestone brickwork.

Setting down the canvas bags, Klaus Gretner held a portable ultrasound device over the wall to gauge density. 'It's about half a metre.'

From the first bag, Conte pulled a sizable handheld coring drill and passed it to Gretner. 'You should have no problem dry-cutting it with that. How many cores you going with?'

'The stone's soft. Six should do it.'

From the second bag, Conte took out a brick of C-4 and began moulding the grey, putty-like explosive into cylinders while the Austrian drilled into the wall's mortar seams. Ten minutes later, six neat cores were packed and plugged with remote detonating caps. Gretner and Conte took cover with the others behind the columns, covering their faces with respirators. Using a handheld transmitter, Gretner triggered a coordinated detonation.

The ear-numbing blast was followed by a rush of debris and dust.

Conte climbed through the gaping opening, followed by the others. They found themselves inside another chamber, its details obscured by the clouds of dust. Even with respirators, the air was difficult to inhale.

Moving forward into the gloom, the men played the halogen lights across a row of ten rectangular forms resting on the floor against the chamber's side wall. Each was about two-thirds of a metre in length, cream-coloured, and slightly tapered from top to bottom.

Conte paused over the box at one end of the row, kneeling to get a better look. Unlike all the others, this was covered in ornate, etched designs. He compared the distinctive carved symbol on the side of the box to the image on a photocopy he pulled from his pocket. A perfect match.

'This is it,' he announced, pocketing the papers. 'Let's keep moving.'

Though they were deep beneath the Temple Mount, Conte knew that the sound of the explosions would have been heard beyond the outer walls.

Gretner stepped forward. 'Looks heavy.' He laid a web of nylon strapping on the floor and he and another man hoisted the box onto the webbing.

'Let's get out of here.' Conte waved the team back through the blast hole and into the mosque.

Emerging onto the esplanade, Conte scanned the area and verified that his two sentries remained posted securely in the shadows. He signalled to them and both men sprinted ahead.

Moments later, when the sentries' silhouettes swept across the opening of Moors' Gate, they were forced back by automatic gunfire emanating from the plaza below.

Motioning for the rest of the team to remain, Conte ran over to the gate, dropping onto his elbows as he neared the opening. Peering out he saw Israeli soldiers and police swarming into the vicinity, blocking the walkways down by the Western Wall Plaza. Someone must have either found the two dead IDF soldiers, or heard the detonation.

The Israelis were hunkered down, waiting for them to make a move. Other entrances provided access to the Temple Mount but Conte was certain the IDF would be sending reinforcements to those gates as well. He knew that the rented van parked in the Kidron Valley was no longer an option. He signalled for the sentries to follow him back to the group and grabbed the encrypted radio transmitter from his belt. 'Come in Alpha One. Over.'

Through the static a choppy voice was just audible.

Conte cut in with the transmitter button. 'We're under fire,' he articulated carefully. 'Pick us up on the southeast corner of the Temple Mount esplanade, beside the Al-Aqsa Mosque. Over.'

A pause. More static.

'Roger. On my way,' a faint voice crackled back. 'Over.'

Conte concealed his relief. Just over the jagged mountain range to the south he detected a dark shadow against the night sky.

The chopper was approaching rapidly.

He clicked his XM8 to fully automatic, activating the grenade launcher.

'We'll need to take those guys down to clear the area,' Conte commanded. On his signal, the mercenaries rushed towards the gate in neat formation, carbines drawn. The chopping sound of rotor blades now had the Israelis' attention, many gazing skywards at the black shadow.

From their position high up on the retaining wall, Conte and his men sprayed the soldiers with a curtain of firepower. Within seconds, eight had fallen. Others were scurrying for cover in the open plaza below, while reinforcements spilled into the area from a network of narrow streets.

The Israeli Air Force Black Hawk suddenly rose over the embankment's southeast corner, its familiar profile temporarily confusing the IDF soldiers. But Conte could also see a group of men manoeuvring to better positions on the embankment's southwest corner.

Sliding his finger to the carbine's second trigger, Conte centred his sights on the cluster of soldiers below and fired. The grenade rocketed off its rifle mount streaming an arc of smoke and orange sparks until it exploded, hurling fragments of stone into the air, forcing the Israelis back in chaos.

The rotor blades were close behind the team now, throwing up a dust storm. The Black Hawk bounced down to rest beside the Al-Aqsa Mosque.

'Go now!' he yelled, waving the team on. 'Get the cargo on board!'

Retreating from the gate, Conte spotted yet more IDF soldiers closing in on the Dome of the Rock platform. It was going to be close, he thought.

The stone box was rapidly stowed in the chopper and then his men clambered aboard. He ducked under the rotor blades, jumping inside.

Under heavy gunfire, the Black Hawk lifted off the platform and tore away from the Temple Mount. Hugging the Ha-Ela Valley floor, it headed southwest across the Negev Desert, well beneath radar range.

Within minutes the lights of the Palestinian settlements along the Gaza Strip came into view, then the dark expanse of the Mediterranean.

Eighty kilometres off Israel's coast, a Hinckley motor yacht was anchored at precise coordinates. The pilot manoeuvred the Black Hawk over the yacht's aft deck, and the box was carefully lowered to the Hinckley's waiting crew. Then one by one the team rappelled down the line. Conte went last.

Setting the autopilot controls to hover, Conte's pilot evacuated the cockpit, stepping over the two dead Israeli pilots who earlier that evening had set out from the Sde Dor air base on a routine surveillance mission along the Egyptian border, blissfully unaware of their heavily armed replacement hidden in the rear.

With cargo and passengers secured, the Hinckley's engines fired up and the craft headed northwest across the Mediterranean. Conte loaded another grenade and found the chopper fifty metres away. A split second afterwards, the latest state-of-the-art in American military technology ripped apart, lighting up the night sky in a flaming ball.

Tel Aviv, Monday: Three Days Later

As the El Al captain announced the flight's final descent into Ben Gurion International, Razak bin Ahmed bin al-Tahini gazed out of his window to watch the Mediterranean yielding to a desert landscape.

Yesterday, he had received a disturbing phone call from the Waqf—the Muslim council that acted as the Temple Mount overseers—summoning him to Jerusalem for assistance in a sensitive matter.

Raised in the Syrian capital of Damascus, Razak was the son of a diplomat. With his father's help he had begun his political career as a liaison between rival Sunni and Shiite factions in Syria. After studying politics in London, he'd returned to the Middle East, where the scope of his duties had broadened to include diplomatic missions to the UN.

For almost a decade, Razak had been intimately involved in Islam's most problematic issues, becoming a reluctant—yet influential—political figure. With its maligned association with radical fanaticism and terrorist acts, the sanctity of Islam in the modern world was increasingly difficult to preserve, and though he aspired to focus on the religious aspects of Islam, he had quickly learned that its political components were inseparable.

And at forty-five, his responsibilities were showing. Premature grey streaks had sprouted from his temples, spreading through thick black hair, and a permanent heaviness showed under his dark, solemn eyes. Of medium height and build, Razak wasn't one to turn heads, though in many circles his knack for diplomacy was sure to leave a lasting impression.

As the Boeing 767 touched down, Razak's thoughts focused on the mysterious altercation in Jerusalem's Old City three days earlier. The worldwide media was circulating reports about a violent exchange that had taken place at the Temple Mount, claiming the lives of thirteen IDF soldiers. Razak knew it was no coincidence that his services were now required here.

He retrieved his suitcase from the baggage claim carousel and made his way to the exit.

Outside the terminal he was greeted by a tall young man with dark features who led him to a white Mercedes 500.

'*Assalaamu alaykum.*'

'*Wa alaykum assalaam,*' Razak replied. 'Is your family well, Akil?'

'Thank you, yes. An honour to have you back, sir.'

Akil took his bag and opened the rear door. Razak dipped into the air-conditioned interior and the young Arab took his place behind the wheel.

'We should be in Jerusalem in under an hour.'

THE OLD CITY, with its prohibitively narrow streets, was off-limits to most vehicular traffic, so the driver reclaimed his reserved spot in a parking lot outside the city walls and Razak made the rest of the journey on foot.

Outside the Jaffa Gate, he was subjected to a thorough body pat down and an exhaustive verification of his credentials by heavily armed IDF guards. Finally, he was funnelled through a metal detector and into a narrow, L-shaped tunnel—a design from centuries earlier meant to slow marauding attackers—that emerged into the busy Christian Quarter. Climbing the sloped cobblestone walkways into the Muslim Quarter, Razak breathed in the complex aromas of the nearby souk—fresh bread, spicy meat, tamarind, charcoal and mint. It took him fifteen minutes to reach the high staircase on Via Dolorosa that climbed up to the Temple Mount's elevated northern gate. There, a second security check was required by the IDF.

As he crossed the Temple Mount's expansive esplanade, towards a squat, two-storey building situated between the sacred Dome of the Rock and Al-Aqsa Mosques, Razak could hear the raucous cries of protestors down near the Western Wall Plaza. Entering the Dome of Learning building, he climbed a flight of stairs and strode down a narrow corridor to a private room where the Waqf officials awaited him.

Inside, nine Arab men were convened around a heavy teak table. Some wore traditional *kaffiyeh* head wraps and business suits; others had opted for turbans and colourful tunics. When Razak entered the room, a hush fell.

At the head of the table, a tall bearded Arab wearing a white headdress stood and raised a hand in greeting.

Razak raised his own. '*Assalaamu alaykum.*'

'*Wa alaykum assalaam,*' the man responded. In his mid-sixties, Farouq bin Alim Abd al-Rahmaan al-Jamir had presence. His lucid grey eyes revealed the burden of many secrets, but showed little of the man within. A scar ran across his left cheek, as a reminder of his days on the battlefield.

Ever since Muslims regained control of the sacred Temple Mount in the thirteenth century, a Waqf 'Keeper' had been appointed as its supreme overseer. That responsibility now lay with Farouq.

As they took their seats Farouq reacquainted Razak with the men round the table, then quickly got to the matter at hand.

'I make no apology for summoning you here at such short notice.' Farouq stared round the table. 'You all know about the incident last Friday.'

A male servant bent to pour Razak a cup of spicy Arabian coffee.

'Enormously troubling,' Farouq continued. 'Sometime in the late evening, a group of men broke into the Marwani Mosque. They used explosives to access a hidden room behind the rear wall.'

The fact that the crime had occurred on a Friday, when Muslims from all over Jerusalem would gather on the Temple Mount for prayer, was particularly troublesome to Razak. He sipped his coffee slowly. 'For what purpose?'

'It seems they have stolen an artefact.' Not for the first time Razak wished the Keeper didn't play his cards so close to his chest.

'Did the explosions damage the mosque?'

'Luckily, no. It seems the damage is restricted to the wall.'

Razak frowned. 'Any idea who could have done this?'

Farouq shook his head. 'Eyewitnesses reported that an Israeli Black Hawk landed outside the Al-Aqsa Mosque and took the thieves away.'

'But that's restricted airspace.' Though he wouldn't admit it, Razak was impressed that anyone could pull off such an operation, especially in Jerusalem. 'How?'

'All we know is that the helicopter was spotted over Gaza minutes after the theft. We're awaiting a full report from the IDF. But let's not forget that thirteen Israelis died in the attack, so to assume Israelis were responsible . . . For now that wouldn't seem to make sense.' He spread his hands and paused. 'The Israelis have agreed to keep this quiet, but ask that we share all information uncovered through our investigations.'

Razak fingered his cup and looked up. 'I'm assuming the police have already begun preliminary investigations?'

'Of course. Problem is, we suspect important facts are being withheld. That's why we've summoned you. Confrontation seems inevitable.'

'If only—' Razak began.

'Time's limited.' One of the silver-haired Waqf elders overrode him. 'It won't be long before the media starts drawing its own conclusions. And we all know what that will lead to.' His grave eyes circled the table to draw support. 'Razak, you know how fragile our role is here in Jerusalem. Our people rely on us to protect this place. There's no knowing how they'll react. Unlike us, they will assume the Israelis are responsible.'

Farouq came in again. 'You can well imagine that Hamas and Hezbollah are anxious to lambaste the Jews for this.' His face darkened. 'They're asking for our support in implicating the Israelis.'

The situation was worse than Razak had imagined. The Waqf was stuck in the middle of a very precarious political situation. 'So what do you wish of me?' he asked, looking round the table.

'Determine who stole the relic,' replied Farouq. 'We need to know who committed this act so justice can be served.'

In the ensuing silence Razak could hear the taunting, muffled sounds of protestors through the window. 'I'll do whatever's necessary,' he said. 'First I'll need to see where this happened.'

Farouq rose to his feet. 'I'll take you there now.'

CHAPTER 2

Vatican City

Charlotte Hennesey was battling with the unforgiving eight-hour time difference, and three espressos earlier that morning hadn't helped to settle her.

As instructed, she was waiting in her guest suite until summoned. Unlike the first-class service that had whisked her from Phoenix to Rome, her accommodation at Vatican City's Domus Sanctae Marthae residence hall was austere: white walls, simple oak furniture, single bed and nightstand.

Seated at the sun-filled window, she gazed out over the tiled roofs of Rome's western sprawl, then looked over at the nightstand's digital clock. It was 3:18 p.m. She was anxious to get to work, but wondered what purpose a geneticist could possibly serve here.

As the head of research and development at BioMapping Solutions, Charlotte typically visited companies looking to apply the latest discoveries in the human genome to their research. Her boss, BMS founder Evan Aldrich, had taken the call almost two weeks ago from a Vatican cleric named Father Patrick Donovan. The priest had requested her services after seeing one of her media interviews concerning the reconstruction of maternal lineage through mapping mitochondrial DNA. Having heard the priest's proposal, Aldrich had agreed to Charlotte's taking on this highly secret project.

At thirty-two, Charlotte was a lithe five foot nine inches, with striking emerald green eyes and a healthily tanned face framed by shoulder-length chestnut hair. With a rare balance of intellect and charm, she'd become her company's media spokesperson in an industry typified by grey scientists. Now her time was split between research and public relations.

Charlotte's thoughts drifted back to Evan Aldrich.

Ten years ago Aldrich had abandoned his secure tenure as a Harvard professor of genetic science to enter the uncertain world of business. Not for money, though when BMS eventually went public he would make a great deal of it. What really drove the man was his belief that the work they did and the choices they made really mattered. It was his passion and genuine charisma that first attracted her to him. The fact that she thought he looked like a movie star didn't hurt either.

Almost a year ago, she and Evan had begun dating, both very cautious about the potential work-related conflicts. But if there could exist a natural fit between two people, Charlotte certainly felt she had found it, and only four months ago things between them had seemed perfect.

Then fate decided to intervene.

A routine blood test taken during her annual medical examination detected abnormally high protein levels in her blood. Further testing followed, including a bone biopsy, then the devastating diagnosis: *multiple myeloma*. Bone cancer.

At first, she was angry. After all, she was practically a vegetarian, rarely drank, and exercised like a fiend. It just didn't make sense, especially because at the time, she felt perfectly fine.

But that wasn't the case now. A week ago, she began taking Melphalan— her first round of low-dose chemotherapy. Now she felt like she was battling a permanent hangover, complete with intermittent waves of nausea.

She didn't have the heart to tell Evan. Not yet, at least. He had already been talking about a more permanent future, even kids. In all fairness to him, she needed to be certain that she would be among the ten per cent who beat this disease before she could commit to anything more serious.

A discreet knock pulled Charlotte from her thoughts.

Reaching the door in four strides, she opened it to see a bespectacled bald man barely her height, dressed in a black suit and shirt. His complexion was smooth and pale. Maybe in his late forties or early fifties, she guessed. Her eyes were immediately drawn to the white priest collar.

'Good afternoon, Dr Hennesey. I'm Father Patrick Donovan.' His English was flavoured with an Irish brogue.

My Vatican admirer, she thought. 'A pleasure to meet you, Father.'

'I appreciate your patience. I apologise for the delay. Shall we go?'

DEEP BENEATH THE TEMPLE MOUNT, Razak and Farouq stood amidst the rubble-strewn floor of the Marwani Mosque. As the Keeper had indicated, the damage to the site had been considerable, yet contained. Pole-mounted spotlights had been erected to illuminate a gaping hole in the rear wall about a metre-and-a-half in diameter.

Approaching the aperture, Razak ran his fingers along its jagged edge, feeling a gummy residue. He peered into the secret chamber beyond.

Farouq appeared beside him holding a piece of masonry. 'See this?' He indicated a smooth arc along one edge of the brick. 'The Israelis found a drill used to make cores that were then packed with explosive.'

Razak examined the brick. 'How could explosives be smuggled into the heart of Jerusalem, past all the checkpoints?'

'Explosives *and* guns. These people were smart.' Farouq peered into the chamber. 'I didn't want to mention it in front of the others, but this seems to suggest that someone on the inside helped them.'

Both men climbed through the hole into the space beyond. Additional pole lights illuminated the inner chamber, clearly carved from Mount Moriah's soft limestone bedrock, with thick stone pillars supporting its rocky ceiling. Against the east wall, Razak detected a line of nine stone boxes, each etched in a language that looked like Hebrew. He moved closer. At one end, a depression in the earth suggested a tenth box had been removed.

Unexpectedly, a voice broke in from the other side of the blast hole. 'Gentlemen. Can I have a moment?'

Razak and Farouq whirled round to find a middle-aged man peering through the aperture. His face was pale and streaked by sunburn, topped off by a nest of unruly brown hair.

'Sorry, do you speak English?' The stranger had a refined English accent.

'We do.' Razak approached the hole.

'Marvellous.' The stranger smiled. 'My Arabic's a little ropey.'

Farouq elbowed Razak aside. 'Who are you?'

'My name is Barton.' He moved to step through the opening. 'Graham Barton, I—'

Farouq threw oversized hands in the air. 'You dare come in here? This is a sacred place!'

Barton stopped in his tracks. 'I'm sorry. I was sent by the Israeli Police Commissioner, to assist you.' He pulled out a letter on police department stationery and offered it to Farouq.

'Need I remind you,' Farouq warned, 'that non-Muslims are banned here?'

'My religious affinities aren't so easily defined.' Barton scowled. There had been a time, long ago, when he regularly attended Anglican services at Holy Trinity Church near his Kensington home in London. But now he considered himself a more secular believer who shunned the establishment.

'I work with the Israeli Antiquities Authority,' Barton persisted. He was already feeling that accepting this job had been a very bad idea. 'Ancient Holy Land antiquities are my speciality and I'm well regarded in my field.' Renowned, in fact, he thought. 'Trained at Oxford University, head curator of antiquities for the Museum of London.'

Farouq was dismissive. 'Credentials do not impress me.'

'Right. But I can save you a lot of time,' Barton added, dodging the Keeper's hostility. 'Besides, the IDF and Israeli police have retained my services. I've been told you're committed to full cooperation.'

Farouq's eyes met Razak's, registering displeasure at the Israelis' tactics.

'I was informed that the incident here possibly involved an ancient relic.' Barton was trying to peer over Razak's shoulder. 'The thieves must have had precise information,' Barton forged on, 'to know the exact whereabouts of a room so well hidden beneath the Temple Mount.'

'A moment, please.' Farouq raised a finger and motioned to the archaeologist to move back through the blast hole.

Sighing, Barton retreated into the mosque.

Razak watched him go. 'Did the Israelis mention this to you?' he asked.

'Not at all,' Farouq replied. 'And I will not permit this. It's an outrage!'

Razak drew a deep breath. He didn't like the idea of allowing this Barton—apparently a delegate from the Jewish authorities—to intervene in such a sensitive investigation. After all, the Israeli police and the IDF had already spent two days inspecting the crime scene without apparent results. However, time wasn't on Razak's side and his knowledge of archaeology and antiquities was limited at best.

'Perhaps he can give us information,' he said. 'Something to start with. It's in everyone's interests to resolve this quickly.'

'Razak, you are a virtuous man. But not everyone's like you. We have to be very careful.'

Razak raised an eyebrow. 'Of course, but do we really have a choice?'

Farouq returned Razak's gaze. Finally, the creases in his brow softened. 'You could be right,' he relented, sighing dramatically. 'Take his letter and check his credentials. Proceed how you see fit. I'm leaving.'

Back out in the mosque, Razak took the letter and instructed the Englishman to wait for him to return, then walked the Keeper to the stairs.

'Keep a close eye on him,' Farouq reminded Razak before disappearing into the sunlight above.

Razak pulled out his cellphone and punched in the number for the Israeli police commissioner who had signed the letter.

Two transfers later a strong, nasal voice came on. 'Major Topol speaking.'

'My name is Razak bin Ahmed bin al-Tahini. I've been commissioned by the Waqf to oversee the investigation at the Temple Mount.'

'Been expecting your call,' Topol said between sips of burnt coffee from a paper cup, clearly unimpressed. 'I take it you've met Mr Barton?'

Razak was thrown by the man's directness. 'Yes, I have.'

'He's good . . . used him before. Very objective.'

Razak refrained from comment. 'I must inform you that his presence in the mosque wasn't well received.'

'Graham Barton has been authorised to act on our behalf,' Topol replied, stifling a yawn. 'I'm sure you'll understand that the nature of this crime requires us to play an equal role in the investigation.'

'But he's an archaeologist, not an investigator,' Razak challenged.

'Sure, but the crime seems to centre on a missing artefact. We felt the investigation could benefit from Barton's knowledge.'

Razak said nothing. It was routine for him to choose silence over confrontation. When negotiating, the opposition often blurted out significant information just to fill the silence.

The policeman lowered his voice and spoke conspiratorially. 'I think we'll both need to put aside our differences so that justice can be served.'

'My colleagues and I share your concern. Can we trust all information will remain confidential until our investigation is complete?'

'You have my word on that. We're looking for a quick, peaceful resolution here. Rumours are spreading like wildfire.'

'I understand.'

'Good luck to you.' The line went dead.

Razak returned to where the Englishman stood near the blast hole, hands folded behind his back, whistling and admiring the Marwani Mosque's impressive interior. Barton turned to him. 'Everything OK?'

He offered his hand. 'Welcome, Mr Barton. My name is Razak.'

CHARLOTTE HENNESEY and Father Donovan strode across the Domus's modern lobby and exited the building into bright sunshine.

'I'm sure you're curious as to why you've been asked to come here,' Father Donovan said.

'The thought had crossed my mind,' she politely replied.

'The Vatican is proficient in theology and faith,' he explained. 'However, you won't be shocked to hear that in the field of natural sciences there are obvious deficiencies in our capabilities.' He offered a self-deprecating smile.

They strolled past Piazza Santa Marta, circling the rear walkways along the apse of the basilica. Charlotte marvelled at its marble exterior.

'Take me for instance,' he offered. '*Prefetto di Biblioteca Apostolica Vaticana* . . . a fancy way of saying head curator of the Vatican Library. My expertise is Church history. I know little about your field, I must confess. But when I saw you on television, I was convinced that you could really help me with a project I've been asked to undertake. Many within these walls have reservations about the intentions of genetic research. I, however, like to keep a more open mind.'

'That's good to know,' she said, smiling. 'What is it that I'll be studying?'

'A relic.' The priest considered enlarging on the idea, but decided against it. 'It's best to see it with your own eyes.'

Heading north they crossed through the lush greenery of the Vatican Gardens, to the straight pathway that ran behind the massive Vatican Museum. Charlotte remembered reading that the Vatican's extensive art collection was housed there, within the former palace of Renaissance-era popes. It was also the place where visitors from around the world came to marvel at the city's most famous exhibit—the Sistine Chapel.

'This place is enchanting,' she said, gazing at the flowers, ornate fountains and fantastic Renaissance architecture. 'Do you actually live here?'

'Oh yes,' Father Donovan said. 'The Vatican is its own world. Everything I need is right within these walls. It's kind of like a college campus.'

'Really?'

He held up both hands. 'Without the night life,' he said with a laugh.

They were just approaching the museum's service entrance. In less than ten minutes they had walked almost the entire width of the country.

RAZAK LED THE ENGLISHMAN over to the blast hole, motioning him into the chamber. Barton's analytical gaze immediately swept the subterranean vault, focusing his attention on the stone boxes.

'So what is this place?' Razak asked.

Barton let out a prolonged breath. 'You're standing in what appears to be an ancient Jewish crypt.'

Razak crossed his arms tightly across his chest. The idea of being amidst death and unreconciled souls underlined his sense of foreboding. And

Jewish, to boot. The place felt instantly smaller. Suffocating.

'And it looks like your thieves removed one of the permanent occupants.' Barton pointed to the rectangular depression in the dirt.

'But aren't those boxes far too small to be coffins?'

'Let me explain.' The archaeologist paused to gather his thoughts. 'During the ancient Jewish burial ritual—the *tahara*—bodies of the deceased were cleaned, then covered with flowers, herbs, spices and oils, and two coins placed over the eyes. Finally the body would be wrapped in a shroud, and placed inside a long niche, or *loculus*.'

'But I still don't see—'

Barton held up a hand. 'Please,' he cut in gently. 'They believed that the body needed to expiate sin, shed it through the process of decaying flesh. So the family would allow the corpse to putrefy for a year, after which they would place the bones in a sacred stone box called an ossuary.'

Razak stared at him. Islamic burial practice—interment within twenty-four hours in a modest tomb facing Mecca—was in stark contrast to elaborate ancient Jewish rituals. 'I see.' He fingered his beard.

'This type of burial was common in this region,' Barton continued, 'but only between roughly 200 BCE to 70 CE. As you can see,' Barton pointed to the row of stone boxes, 'the ossuaries are just large enough to accommodate a dismembered skeleton.'

'Why did they save the bones? Razak thought he knew the answer.

'The ancient Jews believed strongly in their eventual resurrection, ushered in by the coming of the true Messiah.'

'Are ossuaries valuable?'

'Depends. The stone would need to be in pristine condition.' Barton surveyed the nine remaining relics. 'And these look to be in excellent shape. Etchings can be important too. If the engravings are impeccable, it pushes the price up. These ossuaries look fairly standard, however.'

'Then what would one of them be worth?'

Barton pursed his lips. 'Depends. Maybe six thousand pounds. To fetch a high price, it would need to be in perfect condition and purchased by an avid collector or museum. But these days museums tend not to like pieces obtained through the antiquities markets. They need adequate proof that a relic has been excavated from a specific site, validating its authenticity.'

Razak squatted down. This was a lot to absorb. 'So what you're saying is that this stolen ossuary might not be worth much on the open market?'

Barton nodded. 'Absolutely. If its provenance is suspect, the ossuary's value would be severely reduced, which means we can rule out the possibility of a museum or well-known collector as the thief.'

Razak looked up at him. 'Why would someone go to so much trouble— with such violence—to steal just one? Why not steal them all?'

'Good point,' Barton concurred. 'My guess is the thieves knew precisely which ossuary they wanted and were unconcerned about establishing provenance.'

'What does one of those things weigh?'

'About twenty-two kilos, plus the bones . . . around thirty-five in total.'

'And how would one go about shipping it?'

'A standard crate, I'd guess. You'd need to wrap it in a fair amount of packing material. And I've been told that since Friday, all cargo awaiting shipment from Israeli ports is being inspected piece by piece. It would never get through customs.'

'Most likely the IDF secured all roads following the crime,' Razak added. 'That would rule out the ossuary being driven from Israel.'

Quizzically, Barton eyed the Muslim. 'Yes, but aren't the police saying a helicopter was used during the theft?'

Razak nodded. 'That's what eyewitnesses have been saying. And apparently a helicopter was reported over Gaza shortly after the theft.'

'Oh dear, that's not good,' Barton said.

'No it's not,' Razak agreed. 'Not when the helicopter is yet to turn up.'

'There's always a remote possibility that the ossuary is still in Israel.'

Standing, Razak brushed away dust from his trousers, silently cursing the Waqf for involving him in this. 'I think that's unlikely.'

Sensing that the Muslim felt overwhelmed, Barton thought it wise to shift gears. 'I'm no expert on crime scenes,' Barton continued, 'but I believe the ossuary contained more than bones. I would wager those thieves knew exactly what was in it. I'll do my best to see what these inscriptions say.'

'Let's reconvene in the morning,' Razak suggested. 'I'll have Akbar, one of our men from the Waqf, meet you at the top of the steps. He'll escort you down so you can get started. Shall we say around nine o'clock?'

'Right.'

Razak passed him a business card. 'In case you need to contact me.'

Barton glanced at it. Just the name and mobile phone number. 'Thanks. And just for the record, Razak . . . I'm not interested in politics. I'm an archaeologist. Please remember I'm here to help you.'

Razak nodded affably and the two men made their way out of the crypt.

CHAPTER 3

Father Donovan and Charlotte rode a noisy goods lift down one level beneath the Vatican Museum. When the doors opened, the cleric led her out into a wide, fluorescent-lit corridor.

'We're just up ahead,' Father Donovan said, pointing to a wide metal door at the end of the hall.

The priest slid a key card through a reader mounted on the doorframe and a heavy lock disengaged. He opened the door and motioned her inside.

'You can keep this key.' The priest handed it to Charlotte. 'It also opens the rear service door after hours. Please don't lose it.'

She nodded, pocketing it.

Beyond the threshold was a spacious laboratory. The walls were lined with sleek, glass-panelled cabinets housing a broad range of chemical containers and an armada of state-of-the-art scientific gadgetry. Crisp halogen lighting illuminated every stainless-steel surface. An air and purification system regulated the laboratory's humidity and temperature. It was one of the most impressive workspaces she had ever seen.

A man in a crisp white lab coat emerged from a doorway to an adjacent room in the rear of the lab. Seeing him, the priest smiled.

'*Ah, Giovanni, come sta?*'

'*Fantastico, Padre. E lei?*'

'*Bene, grazie.*'

Charlotte watched the man approach to shake the priest's hand. With hazel eyes and thick black and grey hair, he had a pleasant face and a wide smile.

'Dr Giovanni Bersei, I'd like you to meet Dr Charlotte Hennesey, a renowned geneticist from Phoenix, Arizona.'

'A pleasure to meet you, Dr Hennesey,' Bersei replied, in accented English. Like many others who had met Charlotte Hennesey for the first time, he was captivated by her striking green eyes.

'Likewise.' She shook his smooth hand and offered a warm smile.

'Dr Bersei has helped us in the past,' Father Donovan informed her. 'He is an anthropologist whose speciality is ancient Roman culture.' He held out his hands. 'Now I have to go and pick up our delivery from Termini. I'll leave the two of you to get acquainted while I'm gone.'

'Great,' Charlotte said, eyeing Bersei who also seemed pleased with the recommendation.

When Father Donovan had gone Charlotte turned to Bersei wearing a puzzled look. 'Any idea what this is all about?'

'No idea,' he shrugged. 'I've worked for the Vatican in the past, but never had to sign confidentiality agreements. You too, I suppose?'

'Yes. I thought that seemed odd.'

'And I've certainly never been paired up with a geneticist,' he said, puzzled. 'Not that I'm complaining, of course,' he added quickly.

Charlotte laughed. 'So what type of work have you done here in the past?'

'Oh, a few different projects,' Bersei said. 'I suppose my claim to fame are my papers on the ancient catacombs here in Rome. But I'm rarely called into the Vatican itself. It's a bit intimidating, no?'

'Certainly is,' she agreed. 'Lots of guards.'

Bersei stroked his chin. 'Well, Dr Hennesey, let's get you a lab coat. I'm sure Father Donovan will be anxious to start as soon as he returns.'

RETURNING FROM HIS MEETING with the archaeologist, Razak found Farouq in the same room the Waqf council had convened earlier that afternoon. The Keeper wound up his phone call and placed the receiver back in its cradle.

'That was Topol.' Farouq nodded towards the phone. 'Apologising he hadn't contacted us earlier. Offered to pull Barton if we weren't comfortable. I told him I'd speak to you.'

'I think we can trust him,' Razak said. 'And he seems to know what he's talking about.'

'Just be sure to keep a close eye on him,' Farouq reiterated. 'Does he know what was stolen?'

'Yes. An ossuary. He needs time to determine exactly what was in it. He'll conduct a study of the crypt tomorrow. Meanwhile we should request copies of all outgoing shipping manifests at ports and airports for the past three days. According to Barton the consignment would weigh about thirty-five kilos. Have all the roadway checkpoints been secured?'

Farouq grimaced. 'All vehicles are being thoroughly inspected but I doubt they'd risk driving this thing out of Israel.'

'Do you think the helicopter may have flown it out of the country?'

'It hasn't turned up in Israel yet, so the odds are it's already gone. By the way,' Farouq continued without pause, 'the police are looking into a call from a landlady in the Jewish Quarter. A stranger rented a room from her.

He shared it with several men she thought were part of a tour group. They all disappeared late on Friday evening.'

'Think it's anything?'

'Perhaps.' Farouq eyed his notepad. 'The name on the room was Daniel Marrone—the same one used to lease a rental van found abandoned on Haofel Road. It appears to be an alias. The Israelis also ran ballistics tests on the munitions,' he continued. 'The thieves were armed with XM8 assault rifles, manufactured for the United States military.'

'Interesting. But it doesn't seem to make sense.' Razak was frowning.

'What do you mean?'

'Barton says the ossuary is probably only worth a few thousand dollars.'

'Hmm.' He considered it. 'Let's wait and see what he comes up with.'

ON THE WIDE cement walkway along Stazione Termini's loading zone, a young baggage clerk was working a bulky wooden crate onto a hand truck.

'*Tananà*,' a sharp Italian voice cut the air, 'make sure you handle that with care.'

Squinting into the bright summer sunlight, the clerk looked up to see a tall, thickset man dressed in chinos and a white shirt. The stranger didn't look like the type who would respond well to a smart reply. '*Sì, signore.*'

A white Fiat van pulled up at the kerb and Father Patrick Donovan jumped out. 'Everything all right?' he asked.

'Would be if baggage handlers gave a damn about doing their job right.' The young clerk rolled his eyes, careful not to let the Italian see him.

Conte eyed the priest disapprovingly. 'Did you have to wear that get-up? Do you really need to be so damn obvious?' He eyed the van's tags. At least they weren't Vatican City plates.

Father Donovan shrugged and let out a long breath.

'Make yourself useful and open the doors,' Conte instructed him.

Silent, Donovan made his way to the van's rear. Such a brash man, he thought. He hated the idea of working with Conte—a thief, a killer—and deeply regretted that Cardinal Antonio Carlo Santelli, the Vatican secretary of state, had commissioned him for such a momentous task. No one in the Vatican, including Santelli, seemed to know much about Salvatore Conte, except that he was a retired Italian Secret Service operative. According to Santelli, the only sure things about Salvatore Conte were his reliability and his mission-specific twenty-four-digit Cayman Islands bank account number. It was obvious that Santelli had spared no expense—in money or lives—to ensure this project's success. And Donovan reminded himself how much was at stake. If having to contend with the Contes of the world was part of it, then so be it.

'I'll take it from here,' Conte huffed, urging the handler to the side with the wave of a hand. After all that nonsense in Jerusalem, Conte wasn't about to risk having some pimply-faced station porter dropping the damn cargo now.

Wheeling the crate to the rear of the Fiat, Conte motioned for Donovan to help him lift it into the van. With it stowed securely inside, Conte slammed the doors and returned the hand truck to the porter. No tip.

Donovan made his way into the driver's seat and started the engine.

Sighing, Conte paced over to the driver's side and motioned Donovan out of the van. 'When I'm here, you're over there,' the Italian said gruffly, pointing to the passenger seat. 'Get moving.'

THE WHITE FIAT entered Vatican City via the Sant'Anna Gate—one of only two secure vehicle entrances in the fifteen-metre wall that formed a tight three-kilometre perimeter around the 109-acre complex.

Waved through by a Swiss Guard, the Fiat lurched forward down the road that ran behind the Apostolic Palace. Following Donovan's directions, Conte continued through a short tunnel that led out onto a narrow driveway that snaked around the towering edifice of the Vatican Museum complex.

Conte parked the van near the service entrance and unloaded the secret cargo onto a compact dolly. The priest escorted him inside to the goods lift and down one flight.

Entering the lab, Conte parked the dolly to one side. Father Donovan trailed in as the two scientists made their way over.

'Thanks so much for waiting,' Father Donovan said in English. 'Dr Giovanni Bersei, Dr Charlotte Hennesey'—he motioned to them, then over to the mercenary—'this is Salvatore Conte.'

Keeping his distance, Conte straightened, hands on hips. His eyes were immediately glued to Charlotte, roving up and down her body. He grinned. 'If my doctor looked like you, I'd be sick every week.'

Charlotte smiled tightly and diverted her attention to the bulky wooden shipping crate. 'So this is it?' she asked Donovan.

Clearly embarrassed by Conte's crassness, the priest said, 'Yes. Shall we open the crate now?'

Conte grabbed a crowbar off the dolly, and less than thirty seconds later he had stripped the lid away from the crate. Father Donovan placed it gently on the floor.

Glancing briefly at the shipping label, Giovanni Bersei couldn't help but notice the port of origin printed in large bold print: STAZIONE BARI. Bari was an eastern coastal city with a spectacular seaport where wealthy Italians docked their oversized yachts.

'We need to get these two side panels off,' Conte said, claiming one and pointing to the side closer to Bersei.

Bersei stepped forward and lifted the panel easily up and out along grooved tracks, exposing layers of bubble wrap.

Charlotte moved in closer.

'Don't be shy, just tear it away,' Conte instructed the scientists.

As her hands peeled back the last layer of wrapping, Charlotte's fingers ran over a hard flat surface, cold and slick. Seconds later a rectangular surface shrouded in blue-tinted plastic was revealed.

Rubbing his hands together, Donovan looked up at them. 'We'll get it over to the workstation,' he said to Bersei. 'Dr Hennesey, would you please set that rubber matting on top of the table?' He pointed to a thick rubber sheet sitting on a nearby counter.

Conte wheeled the dolly closer to the nearest workstation and Bersei crouched down, cupping his hands round the corners. The mercenary counted down and together they manhandled the solid box up onto the matting.

'If there's nothing else you need,' Conte grumbled, 'I need a drink.'

'That'll be all, Mr Conte,' Donovan replied cordially. 'Thank you.'

Before leaving, Conte turned his back on the scientists and faced the priest. He pointed to his left eye, then at Father Donovan. The message was clear. *Remember, I'll be watching you.* Then he was gone.

Rejoining the scientists, Donovan said, 'Let's get this plastic off.'

'Just a moment,' Bersei said. He disappeared into a rear room, then reappeared holding a lab coat. 'You should wear this.'

'And these.' Charlotte passed the priest a box of latex gloves. 'We don't want to contaminate the specimen.'

Each scientist took a pair, and donned sterile masks and caps.

Charlotte passed Donovan an X-Acto knife from the workstation's tool drawer. 'Would you like to do the honours?'

Drawing a deep breath, the Vatican librarian nodded, took the knife, and began slicing through the plastic shroud. When he finally drew the wrap apart, what he saw made his eyes light up in wonderment.

ONLY WEEKS AGO, Father Patrick Donovan had acquired an astounding manuscript whose ancient parchment pages chronicled the origin of this magnificent relic, complete with detailed sketches and maps to locate its secret resting place. He had tried to imagine what the box would look like, but nothing could have prepared him for this. *Astonishing*.

Giovanni Bersei was circling round the box, squinting. 'This is a burial casket—an ossuary.' His voice was muffled by his mask.

Goosebumps ran up Charlotte's arms.

Bathed in bright halogen light, the ossuary's impressive craftsmanship seemed to come to life. On the front and rear faces, rosettes and hatch patterns had been painstakingly etched. The lid was arched and bevelled along its edges. The sides were flat, one blank, the other bearing a simple relief of a dolphin wrapped round a trident.

Hennesey was momentarily transfixed by the image. 'Father Donovan— what does this symbol mean?'

Still trying to calm himself, Donovan studied it briefly then shook his head. 'Not sure.' It wasn't a complete lie. But—vitally—the symbol identically matched the manuscript's meticulous description of the box.

Bersei ran a gloved finger over the thin gap along the lid's edge. 'There's a seal here.' He pressed it cautiously. 'Most likely wax. It's a good indication that what's inside has been well preserved.'

'I'd like to open this now,' Donovan said. 'Then we'll discuss details of the analysis you will perform.'

Hennesey and Bersei looked at each other, knowing that their seemingly diverse disciplines had indeed found common ground. Opening a sealed burial box implied one thing.

A corpse.

CHARLOTTE AND BERSEI worked the lid's edges with their X-Acto knives, loosening the seal of wax that maintained a tight bond with the ossuary.

When they had finished, Giovanni Bersei set down his knife and looked over at the priest. 'Ready?' he asked.

Donovan nodded and moved to the head of the table.

With fingers hooked underneath the edge of the lid, the two scientists squeezed and applied steady upward pressure, gently moving it from side to side to loosen the remaining wax. There was a small pop as the ancient seal gave way, followed by a hiss of escaping gas. Even through their masks they all detected an acrid smell.

'Probably effluvium,' Bersei observed. 'By-product of decaying bone.'

Donovan swallowed hard, anxiously motioning them to continue. They removed the lid in tandem and placed it on the rubber mat.

BENEATH HIS SURGICAL mask, Father Patrick Donovan was grinning from ear to ear. Inside the ossuary's exposed cavity was a neatly stacked pile of human remains, each bone with a dark, grainy finish resembling carved maple.

Charlotte reached out and touched one, running her finger along a femur. 'These are in extraordinary shape.' She silently wished that her own bones might look so good when her time would come. It seemed like a cruel joke that she had been called halfway round the world for *this*.

Bersei turned sharply to Donovan. 'Whose remains are these?'

'We're not sure.' The librarian avoided eye contact. 'And that's precisely the reason you've both been selected, to help us reconstruct the skeleton's identity.' He touched the ossuary's rim and stared down at the contents again. 'We have reason to believe that this amazing relic may help us to better understand the historical context of the Bible.'

'In what way exactly?' asked Charlotte. She preferred people to say what they meant.

Donovan's eyes were frozen to the bones. 'We won't know until we can accurately date this specimen and reconstruct the physical profile.'

Bersei hesitated, sensing the same thing as Charlotte. The priest seemed to be holding back. 'Much of the success of understanding antiquities relies on knowing specifics relating to its origin. Isn't there anything you know about how this ossuary was procured? Where it came from perhaps?'

Donovan shook his head and straightened. 'We've been provided with little background. You can imagine an acquisition like this has to be approached very cautiously. The price is substantial.'

Charlotte was puzzled. Two prominent scientists lured here at great expense, both having to sign letters of confidentiality. Obviously the Vatican believed the ossuary and its contents were valuable.

'We'll perform a complete study,' Bersei assured him. 'A full pathology report. Physical reconstruction. The works.' He glanced over at Charlotte.

'And I'll be wanting to do a carbon-dating analysis and to draw up a complete genetic profile,' she added.

'Excellent,' said Donovan, clearly pleased. 'Please let me know when you're ready to report your findings. If possible, I'd like to present a prelim-inary report in the next few days.'

The scientists exchanged glances.

'That should be fine,' Bersei said.

Donovan stripped off his gloves, mask and lab coat. 'Please direct any activity through me. I can be reached by dialling extension two-one-one-four on the intercom.' Donovan looked at his watch—6.12. 'Well, it's late. Why don't we call it a day and you can both start fresh tomorrow morning?'

The two scientists agreed.

'Dr Hennesey, have you had a chance to see the basilica since you've arrived?' the priest enquired.

'No.'

'You can't stay in Vatican City without seeing first-hand its heart and soul,' he insisted. 'Would you like to see it now?'

Her eyes lit up. 'If you have time, I'd love that.'

'Giovanni, would like to join us?'

'Sorry, but I must get home to my wife,' he humbly declined. 'She's making osso bucco for dinner.' Bersei leaned closer to Charlotte and whispered loud enough for Donovan to hear. 'You're in good hands. He's the best tour guide in the Vatican.'

THE SUN WAS SINKING over western Rome as they stepped outside. Cypress trees swayed in a gentle breeze. Ambling beside Father Donovan, Charlotte breathed in the garden's fragrant smell.

'Tell me, Dr Hennesey,' Donovan said, 'now that you've seen the relic, are you comfortable with this project?'

'I have to admit that it's not at all what I would have expected. I'm pleasantly surprised, though,' she added. 'Should be very exciting.'

'It will be exciting for us all,' Donovan promised. Nearing the rear of the basilica, he gazed up at it, reverently. 'In the first century, this place where Vatican City now stands was the Vatican Circus, later called Nero's Circus. It was a forum where the emperor Nero held chariot races. Ironic, since he's best known for his persecution of early Christians.'

'He blamed them for the fire that burned down Rome in AD 64. And in AD 67, he crucified St Peter to entertain the crowds.'

Donovan was impressed. 'You're a Christian? Or just a good historian?'

'There was a time when I was good at both.'

'I see.' The priest could sense that religion was a touchy subject, 'You know, back in Ireland we had a saying: "I believe in the sun when it's not shining, I believe in love even when I feel it not, I believe in God even when lie is silent."' He glanced over at Charlotte and saw that she was smiling.

Climbing a set of wide marble steps that accessed the rear of the basilica, Donovan led her to one of the largest bronze doors she'd ever seen. He produced a keycard and slid it through the reader on the doorframe. With hardly any effort, the priest opened the huge door and motioned her inside.

'We're going in through here?'

'Of course. One of the benefits of being a guest of the papacy.'

Entering the basilica's cavernous marble nave, Charlotte felt like she was being transported to another world. She remembered reading that the Notre-Dame cathedral in Paris could easily fit inside this grand basilica. But standing inside it completely distorted her spatial senses.

Her eyes were drawn upwards to Michelangelo's grand coffered cupola. Covered in tiled mosaics, it soared 137 metres above the nave with shafts of sunlight spilling in from its west-facing windows to give it an ethereal glow.

Gradually, her gaze panned down to the famous bronze Baldacchino that stood directly beneath the dome and over the High Altar. Designed by Renaissance genius Giovanni Lorenzo Bernini, its four spiral bronze columns rose twenty-one metres to support a gilded canopy that stretched another six metres upwards.

'Wow,' she gasped.

'Yes, quite magnificent,' Donovan concurred, folding his arms. 'I could easily spend a few hours here giving you a tour, but I find that the basilica is more of a spiritual journey and is best seen alone.' From a wooden kiosk along the wall, he retrieved a guidebook then handed it to Charlotte. 'I must be going now. Enjoy.'

After thanking Father Donovan she slowly began working her way along the side aisle along the basilica's northern wall.

Like most pilgrims who came here, she stopped in front of the thirteenth-century bronze statue that depicted a bearded St Peter seated on a papal throne. He gripped a papal key in his left hand, his right hand raised up as if to deliver a blessing. A few visitors were queuing to touch the statue's outstretched foot. Referring to the guidebook, she read that this ritual was supposed to grant good luck. She wasn't one to believe in superstition, but she convinced herself that given her current circumstances, every little bit could help.

Less than five minutes later, she stepped forward and reached out to place her left hand on the statue's foot. Then she did something she hadn't done in years. She prayed, asking God for strength and guidance.

She had all but abandoned faith eleven years ago, after watching her mother, a devout Catholic, suffering with stomach cancer. God's compassion, Charlotte quickly surmised, was not guaranteed to the pious. Following her mother's death, Charlotte didn't go to church to find answers—she went behind a microscope, convinced that her mum's defect wasn't faith, but simply a genetic imperfection; corrupted coding.

Somehow her father, even after losing his beloved wife so cruelly, had still managed to attend mass every Sunday, still said grace before every meal, was still thankful for every new day. Yet, regardless of her dad's spiritual resolve, she didn't have the heart to tell him about her own illness.

Lacking the structure of religion made her feel spiritually empty—particularly as of late. Did Charlotte Hennesey believe in God? There was no place on earth that could push that question like *this* place. Perhaps she would find the answer here.

Almost forty minutes later, she was circling back beside the Baldacchino again where she came across a haunting sculpture that made her stop dead in her tracks. Tucked into a marble alcove, Bernini's *Monument to Pope Alexander VII* loomed above her on a pedestal. The Pope was immortalised in white marble, kneeling in prayer. Beneath him were various statues depicting Truth, Justice, Prudence and Charity as human figures.

But Charlotte's horrified gaze had instantly blocked those images out and had sharpened on the shrine's central figure—an oversized winged human skeleton forged from bronze, holding out an hourglass in its right hand.

The Angel of Death.

The image seemed to come to life, swooping out to dump more of its wretched cancer into her body. For a moment, she didn't breathe and she could feel tears welling up in her eyes. She almost felt violated, as if it was purposely meant for her.

'Creepy, isn't it,' a voice cut into her thoughts.

Surprised, she gasped. Turning, she saw a figure that seemed equally ominous. Where the hell had *he* come from?

'Bernini was eighty when he designed that one,' Salvatore Conte said, full of himself. 'Guess he was feeling bitter about his golden years.'

Charlotte tried to give him an obligatory smile, but it didn't happen.

'Did you know this place was built by selling indulgences?' Conte glared up at the central dome disapprovingly. 'Back in the fifteen hundreds, Pope Leo the Tenth ran out of money to finish the project, so he basically raised funds by selling Catholics "get-out-of-Hell-free" cards.'

'I take it you don't go to church every Sunday,' she sardonically replied.

Leaning closer, he dropped his voice, 'After all that I've seen, particularly inside these walls,' he said, 'I'm willing to take my chances.'

She tried to understand what he really meant, but there was nothing in his eyes and she certainly wasn't about to ask him to expound.

'Are you visiting or just stalking?'

The remark took him off guard. 'Just seeing the sights,' he replied.

'Well, I've got to get going. Nice seeing you,' she lied. Turning to go, Charlotte felt his hand touch her shoulder. She went rigid and turned back to him with icy eyes. 'What do you want?' She pronounced each word clearly.

Realising his miscalculation, Conte threw his arms up. 'Sorry. I was going to see if you wanted company for dinner. I thought, you're here alone . . . I don't see a wedding ring. Maybe you'd like some conversation. That's all.'

For a long moment, she just stared at him, unable to process the idea that he was actually hitting on her in St Peter's Basilica. 'I've got a boyfriend and I've already made plans, but thank you,' she said, trying her best to be polite.

'Some other time, then,' he replied confidently.

'Good night.' She turned and made her way for the exit.

Tuesday

The rising sun cast a faint glow of deep blue and purple over the Mount of Olives as Razak made his way across the Temple Mount esplanade towards the Dome of the Rock Mosque's golden cupola, its crescent-shaped finial delicately pointing towards Mecca.

No matter how many times he visited this place, it always affected him deeply. Here, history and emotion seemed to drip like dew.

In the seventh century, the Temple Mount had virtually been forgotten, all its previous architecture having been destroyed many times over. But in 687, only a few decades after a Muslim army led by Caliph Omar had conquered Jerusalem, Caliph Abd al-Malik began construction of the Dome of the Rock Mosque as a testament to the site's rebirth and Islam's physical claim over the Holy Land.

Throughout the centuries that followed, Islam had periodically lost its hold over the Temple Mount, most notably to Christian Crusaders during the twelfth and thirteenth centuries. But it was once again under Islamic control and the Waqf had been entrusted to enforce and legitimise that role.

Razak scaled a flight of steps to the mosque's raised platform. Outside the entrance, he removed his shoes, then made his way into the shrine, glancing up at the elaborate inner dome that sat high atop marble columns. Directly beneath the cupola, cordoned by railings, lay a bare stone expanse of Mount Moriah's summit known as 'the Rock'.

The Rock marked the sacred site where, in biblical times, Abraham made to sacrifice his son to God, and where Jacob had dreamt of a ladder to heaven. The Jews proclaimed that a grand temple built by King Solomon once stood here. And the Christians claimed Jesus had preached at that same temple.

But the site was significant to Razak and his people for another reason.

In 621, the Archangel Gabriel had appeared to the great prophet Muhammad in Mecca, presenting him with a winged horse bearing a human face, named El Buraq. Embarking on his *Isra*, or 'night journey', Muhammad was carried by El Buraq to the Temple Mount where he encountered Moses and the great prophets. He was then escorted by Gabriel to the pinnacle of the Rock, where he ascended through the heavens in a glorious light to behold Allah. There, Muhammad was given the five daily prayers by Allah—a core event in his ministry known as the *Miraj*. This rendered the Dome of the Rock the third most important religious site in Islam, behind Mecca—Muhammad's birthplace—and Medina where he established the Islamic movement.

Razak gazed up at the cupola's exquisite tile work. Outside, the muezzin's call echoed from loudspeakers, summoning Muslims to prayer. In front of the mosque's mihrab—the small, arched golden alcove that indicated the direction of Mecca—Razak eased onto his knees and bowed in prayer. After a few minutes, he stood and circled back to the mosque entrance, where he put on his shoes and made his way outside.

He still had a couple more hours until his meeting with Barton, so he strolled down into the Muslim Quarter and had coffee and breakfast at a small café on Via Dolorosa.

At 9 a.m., he crossed the Temple Mount esplanade and descended into the Marwani Mosque. Climbing through the blast hole into the crypt, Akbar—the guard watching over Barton—signalled that everything was fine. Razak nodded and waved him out into the mosque.

Graham Barton was crouched in a corner transcribing an inscription on one of the ossuaries.

'Good morning, Mr Barton,' Razak said in English.

The archaeologist sprang to his feet.

'Looks like you've been busy.' Razak eyed the small stacks of rubbings

Barton had laid out on the floor. 'What have you found out so far?'

'It's an extraordinary discovery. This crypt belonged to a Jewish man named Yosef.' Barton pointed to a box at one end. 'And each of these ossuaries is inscribed in Hebrew with the names of his family members.'

Unimpressed, Razak sought meaningful information. 'Yosef *who*?'

Barton shrugged. 'Ancient Jews weren't terribly specific when it came to names. They rarely used family names, at least for burial purposes.'

Razak eyed the inscriptions carved into the sides of the nine boxes.

'Each one identifies whose remains are inside. Those are his four daughters,' Barton indicated the cluster at the beginning of the line-up. 'Three sons,' he motioned to the next three, then to one beside Yosef's, 'his loving wife, Sarah.' He drew a deep breath. 'But there's an etching on the back wall that provides more detail.' Grabbing a flashlight, he motioned for Razak to follow him into the shadowy recess. 'See that?' Barton illuminated an ornate stone tablet. 'It lists the inventory of ossuaries contained in this chamber.'

The Muslim stepped closer. 'So the missing ossuary should be listed here.' Counting nine lines of text, Razak's eyes were drawn to a deep gouge in the rock beneath the last line. 'I'm only seeing nine entries.'

'Correct. And those nine are the names that match the remaining ossuaries. But this entry here,' Barton trained the light on the disfigured rock, 'probably identified the tenth ossuary.' He tapped it with his finger.

Razak strolled round the chamber holding out his hands. 'Of all places, why would the crypt be located here?'

He had a good point, Barton thought. 'Normally we'd expect crypts to be outside the city walls. But it's certainly possible this site was chosen for security reasons. In the first century, the Roman garrison was situated adjacent to the northern wall of the Temple Mount. The centurions would police the crowds, ready to quell any disturbances.'

'And what do Roman centurions have to do with this crypt?'

'Everything. Remember, in ancient times there were no safes or lockboxes. The only way to protect treasures or valuables was with an army.'

'Then perhaps the tenth ossuary didn't contain human remains. Could it have protected some kind of treasure? I'm not seeing why anyone would go through such great trouble to steal bones.'

'It's impossible to draw any conclusions,' Barton replied. 'But inside these remaining nine boxes we may find some more clues.' He handed Razak a pair of rubber gloves. 'Which is why you'll need these.'

A horrified look came over the Muslim.

CHAPTER 4

The two scientists convened in the lab at 8 a.m., both heading directly to the rear break room where Giovanni Bersei instructed Charlotte Hennesey on how to use what he considered to be the lab's most vital piece of equipment—the Gaggia automatic coffee machine.

'Tell me. How was your visit to the basilica last night?'

Rolling her eyes, she gave him a quick summary that ended with her retelling of the unpleasant encounter with Salvatore Conte. She told him that it had disturbed her so much she'd decided to turn in early to catch up on her sleep. 'And how did your wife's osso bucco turn out?'

He made a sour face. 'Not so good. Carmela is many things, but a good cook is not one of them.'

She hit him lightly on the shoulder. 'I hope you haven't told her that.'

'Are you crazy? I value my life.'

They both laughed and moved into the main room, donning lab coats, masks and latex gloves. The ossuary, with its mysterious skeleton, was just as they had left it yesterday.

Positioned on opposite sides of the workstation, the scientists began removing the bones one at a time, carefully placing them onto the rubber matting. Slowly the reassembled skeletal frame came together: the longer bones of the legs and arms, the pelvis and ribs, the segments of spinal vertebrae, the skull, and finally the delicate bones of the hands and feet.

Bersei performed a quick visual inspection. 'Looks like all two hundred and six bones are here.' He grabbed a Canon EOS digital camera and snapped some shots of the completed skeleton.

Charlotte peered down. 'OK. Let's figure out cause of death.'

From the workstation drawer, she pulled out two pairs of Orascoptic goggles. Giving one pair to Bersei and putting the other on, she flipped the telescoping lenses over her eyes.

They began with the skull, both bending closer to study it with detail.

'Looks perfect,' Bersei said peering through his goggles.

Charlotte sized up the dimensions and contours. 'Square chin, pronounced supraorbital ridges. It looks like we're dealing with a male.'

'You may be right.' Bersei tilted the skull back and rotated it, examining the inner cavity. 'The sutures are still visible, but have all fused.'

Verifying his observation, Charlotte knew the concept. The younger the specimen, the more pronounced the joining lines would appear; the older the specimen, the lines would become indiscernible. 'That means we're looking at age twenty to thirty, minimum?'

'I'd agree with that.' Bersei turned the skull over a few times, scanning its surfaces. 'I'm not seeing any indications of head trauma.'

Both scientists turned their attention to the mandible.

'These teeth are in magnificent shape,' Charlotte said. 'This guy had a full set. I don't even see an indication of periodontal disease.'

They moved to the cervical region, analysing intently, searching for abnormalities in the neck.

'I'm not seeing any spurs,' Charlotte remarked. 'No ridging or ossification here.'

'No fusion either,' Bersei added. 'Actually, the discs don't appear to have degenerated at all.' He motioned towards the rib cage. 'Let's keep moving.'

Charlotte's eyebrows shot up. 'Wait. That's interesting.'

Following her finger to the centre of the chest area, Bersei focused on the flat bones of the sternum and spotted it immediately. 'That's a huge tear.'

'Sure is. Do you think that might have happened when the rib cage was detached to fit into the ossuary?'

'Perhaps.' His tone was cautious. Bersei shifted his focus to the adjacent shoulder. 'Look here.'

She followed his lead. 'You've got a good eye. The humerus and clavicle were separated from the scapula?'

'Agreed. But it doesn't look like it happened post-mortem. The tears are fibrous. See here. Where the tissue separated suggests the breakage happened before the tissue dried.'

'What do you think . . . a dislocation?'

'A very violent dislocation.' Bersei's tone was troubled. 'But it certainly didn't kill him. You take those ribs.' He indicated the ones closest to her. 'And I'll take these.'

Time seemed suspended as they worked on the ribs, meticulously analysing each surface.

'You seeing what I'm seeing?' Charlotte asked, after a while.

'The deep grooves?' Bersei's head was down. 'Absolutely.'

Some of the ribs were unscathed, but most looked like they'd been raked with thick nails to produce long, scalloped gouges.

'What could've done this?' Her voice had sunk to a whisper.

'I think I may know. Do you see traces of metal deposit?'

'Yes. Is this something that happened post-mortem?'

'I'd have to say no,' Bersei told her. 'You'll notice those marks only appear on the anterior fascia.' He peered over the flip-down telescoping lenses. 'If the bones look this bad, the muscle and skin that covered them must have looked far worse . . . Probably shredded.' Holding her gaze, he drew a breath then said, 'Looks to me like this man was flayed.'

'You mean whipped?'

Bersei nodded slowly. 'That's right. Those markings are from a barbed whip.' He bent lower and began working on the upper segments of lumbar vertebrae, while Charlotte started scrutinising the lower ones.

'Everything looks good here,' she said.

'Agreed.' Bersei glanced at the compact structure of the pelvic bones that provided definitive clues relating to gender. 'Definitely male.' He ran his fingers along the contours of bone where the genitalia would be. 'The sciatic notch is narrow, the preauricular area's got no indentations and flattens. No babies coming out through there.'

So far Giovanni Bersei was pleased. Determining gender from skeletal remains was never easy as the most obvious gender-specific traits occurred in the soft tissues, not the bones.

'So—arms or legs?' he enquired.

'Arms first.'

They shifted along the skeleton, starting with the humerus and working down to the paired set of each arm's lower half—the ulna and radius.

Something caught Charlotte's eye and she moved even closer to sharpen the lens's resolution. There was significant damage to the inner surfaces of the bones above the wrist. 'Looks like these bones went through a grinder.'

'It's on this side too. The damage is contained to just above the wrist,' Bersei confirmed. 'Do you see any oxidation?'

'Yeah, could be metallic residue. Hang on.' She repositioned the lens. 'Fibres have been lodged in the bone. Your side?'

'Yes. Get a sample of that. Looks like wood.'

Charlotte went into the tool drawer, removed a pair of tweezers and a small plastic vial, and proceeded to pluck away the fibres from the bone.

Meanwhile, Bersei was already moving down near the skeleton's feet. He bent over to get a better look at something there, then waved her closer. 'Come take a look.'

Nestled in the upper notches of each foot were deep, gritty patches scooped into the bones. Two bones in the left foot had been fractured.

'Look at the damage between the second and third metatarsals,' Bersei noted. 'It's similar to the arms.'

'Same rust-coloured streaking,' Hennesey added. 'Definitely came from some kind of impaled metal.'

'Judging from the fractures in the second metatarsal on the left foot, it was a nail. Do you see where the point hit the bone and split it?'

Hennesey saw a diamond-shaped indentation stamped in the fissure's midpoint and detected more wood splinters. 'Unbelievable. Looks like the nail missed the first time.' Thinking that one human could inflict this kind of damage on another nauseated her.

'Most likely because the feet were nailed on top of one another,' Dr Bersei stated flatly. He noticed another oddity in the area of the knees and positioned himself for a better view. 'Look at this.'

Charlotte focused on the knee joint. The damage was immediately apparent.'Oh, God. Look at those tears in the cartilage. His knees were broken?'

'Yes, of course.' Bersei straightened and flipped his lenses up. His face was ashen. 'It's quite clear what happened here. This man was crucified.'

'SURELY YOU DON'T expect me to desecrate the remains of the dead?' Utterly insulted, Razak folded his arms across his chest and frowned at Barton. 'Have you no conscience?'

'It's important, Razak. The only clues we have are in this room. Every possibility must be explored.'

For a few seconds, the crypt was deathly silent.

'All right,' Razak finally yielded. 'But this you will do alone.'

Relieved, Barton knelt in front of the first ossuary and clasped the sides of the flat stone lid. He glanced over at Razak. The Muslim had turned his back to him and seemed to be chanting prayers. Drawing a deep breath, Barton jostled the lid loose, pulling it away, and began his analysis of the contents.

Two hours after he had opened the first ossuary, Barton was just replacing the skeletal remains that he had taken out of the seventh ossuary. Though forensic anthropology wasn't his speciality, he understood the fundamentals. Certainly, the names on each ossuary eliminated much of the speculation concerning gender, but as he worked his way along the line of ossuaries the clues present on the skull sutures, joints, and pelvic bones led him to certain conclusions regarding the age of these skeletons. The four females—the daughters, he guessed—deceased very young, ranging in age between late teens and early twenties. The three younger males—by the same logic, the sons—also seemed to fall into the same range. As far as Barton could tell, their remains showed no outright anomalies. No telling signs of trauma. It seemed uncanny that all could have died so young. Even in the first century, where life expectancy might have been as low as thirty-five, this seemed statistically improbable. In fact, it appeared as if they'd all died at the same time. Strange.

Barton stood up to stretch. 'Still doing OK over there?' He glanced across the chamber where the Muslim was seated, facing the wall.

'Yes. How much longer will you need?'

'Just two more to go. Say half an hour?'

The Muslim nodded.

The archaeologist rolled his neck then squatted down in front of the eighth ossuary containing Yosef's spouse, Sarah. Having established a good system by now, he deftly pulled away the lid, flipped it, and rested it on the stone floor so it could be used as a pallet for the extracted bones.

Graham Barton was starting to lose hope that anything extraordinary was contained in these boxes. Could the thieves really have known this and purposely left these behind like Razak had suggested? Certainly the contents within the tenth ossuary couldn't have been as pedestrian as these.

Palming the skull, Barton rotated it. The fusion along the sutures suggested that Sarah had probably been in her late thirties. He set it down on the lid. Then, one by one, he plucked the remaining bones out and stacked them neatly beside the skull. All accounted for and all normal.

Reverently returning Sarah's bones to her ossuary and replacing the lid, Barton squatted in front of the ninth ossuary with little enthusiasm. 'Come on Yosef, talk to me.' Reaching out, he gripped the lid. This time, he was surprised when the top didn't budge. He tried again. Nothing.

'Hmm. That's odd.'

'What is it?' Razak called out.

'This last ossuary's been sealed.' Barton ran the flashlight over its seam. It looked like some kind of fatty wax. He removed a Swiss Army knife from his pocket, and with a blade he loosened the seal enough to free the lid.

'Right then,' he muttered, wiping sweat from his brow. Clasping the lid lengthwise, he coaxed it away, flipped it, and set it on the floor. An unpleasant odour rose up from the box's exposed cavity, making him gasp.

Grabbing the flashlight, he shone it downwards and began unpacking the bones. When he came to the skull, he flipped it round and lit it up. Judging from the substantial wear on the remaining teeth, Yosef had been in his late sixties or early seventies at the time of death. As he took the last of the bones out from the ossuary, Barton was surprised to see a small rectangular metal plate on the bottom of the box. He worked the Swiss Army blade under the plate, prising it away, uncovering a small niche carved into the ossuary's base. And in it was a metal cylinder no longer than fifteen centimetres. Barton smiled. 'That's my boy.' He grabbed it and held it up.

'Did you find something?' Razak's voice echoed across the crypt.

'A clue.' Barton bounced to his feet and walked over to a pole light. 'Come and have a look.'

Razak got up and went and stood beside Barton. The cylinder—most likely bronze—had small caps on both ends. 'Are you going to open it?'

'Of course.' Without hesitation, he pulled one cap free and looked inside. He spotted something rolled up. 'Aha. I think we have a scroll.'

Barton tapped the cylinder a few times until the scroll fell into his palm. 'Vellum. And excellently preserved.' Very gingerly, he unfurled it. It was filled with ancient Greek text. He glanced up at Razak.

'Bingo.'

HAVING SPENT the past two hours completing a comprehensive journal chronicling the forensic examination—digital photos, written descriptions, case notes—the two scientists sipped their espressos in the lab's cramped break room. Both were steeped in thought.

'You're certain that what we're seeing here is the result of crucifixion, not some other form of torture?' Charlotte said eventually.

'Certain. And I'll tell you why.' Bersei drained his coffee. 'First off, you have to understand *why* the Romans crucified criminals. It was intended to send a message to all citizens that Rome was in control. It was considered a dishonourable way to die and was reserved for criminals of low social status and enemies of the state.'

Charlotte looked at him curiously. 'How do you know all this?'

'A few years ago I published a study on crucifixion, funded by the Pontifical Commission. I tested established theories regarding how it kills the victim. Crucifixion was practiced for centuries and it's hugely relevant to understanding the early Roman government.

'Before they were crucified, criminals were scourged, usually with a cane or whip. In the case of our man, it seems the scourging was performed with a *flagrum*—a vicious, multi-thong whip with metal barbs.'

'That explains why the ribs were so badly scarred.'

'*Sì*. And that was just the beginning. Crucifixion itself was far, far worse. The criminal was impaled on a cruciform by spikes, eighteen centimetres or so long, driven through the wrists and feet. A rope was bound round the arms to provide additional support when the body was hung upright. We know that the familiar images of crucifixion depict victims being nailed to the cross through the hands . . .'

Charlotte knew where this was going. 'But the small bones and weak flesh in the hands couldn't support the weight of a body, right?'

'Exactly. So to support the weight, iron spikes would be driven into the wrist along with a large wooden washer to prevent slippage. Right here.' Bersei pointed to a spot just above the crease of his wrist. 'It would've crushed the median nerve, sending shock waves of excruciating pain up the arm. The hands would have been instantly paralysed.'

Hideous images of nails pounding into flesh came into her mind's eye. 'That explains the shoulder dislocation.'

'It also explains the gouge patterns we see in the wrists—evidence of extreme pressure against the bones. Grinding. Like the weight of the body was suspended on nails.'

Hennesey dropped her cup into the sink. 'I can't drink any more.'

Bersei put his hand on her arm. 'Are you OK?'

She rubbed her eyes. 'Keep going. I'm fine.'

'The feet would have been laid over one another, then nailed into the post,' the Italian continued. 'It wouldn't have been easy as the victim would have been flailing about.'

Charlotte felt as if she was going to faint. She took a deep breath.

Folding his hands, Bersei paused to marshal his thoughts. 'The fact is, no one thing kills the victim. Overall trauma eventually does that. Scourging, impalement, exposure to the elements . . . they all contribute. Depending on the victim's health before execution, death could take days.'

'And we already know that this man was extremely healthy.'

Bersei nodded. 'The damage we saw to the ribs suggests that the scourging alone should have killed him. He must have suffered horribly. Which brings me to my last point.'

Charlotte's stomach contracted. She knew he was about to lay it on her even thicker.

'If the criminal wasn't moving through the process quickly enough,' Bersei continued, 'they'd break the knees with a large metal club. Without the support of the legs, the full weight of the body would pull across the rib cage. With the lungs constricted, the victim would struggle desperately to breathe. Meanwhile what little blood remained would begin to settle lower into the legs and torso.'

Fighting to remain objective, Charlotte pondered the consequences of the punishment's final stage. 'Then basically the criminal would have expired from asphyxiation and heart failure, right?'

'Right. Dehydration and trauma could also speed up the process.' He paused. 'The victim would be kept on the cross for days, until death came.'

'Then what?'

Lips pulled tight, Bersei offered his explanation. 'The corpses would be tossed to the ground, then vultures, dogs, and other beasts would feed on them. The Romans were very systematic about refusing a criminal a proper burial. Any remnants were burnt, thereby denying victims any possibility of eventual afterlife, reincarnation, or resurrection.'

'The ultimate punishment.' Charlotte cast her eyes to the floor.

A moment of silence fell over the break room.

'Who do you think this guy was?' she finally asked.

Bersei shrugged. 'Could be any one of thousands crucified by the Romans. Prior to this, the only crucified remains ever found was a heel bone with a nail driven through it. The fact that what we're looking at represents the first intact crucified *body* recovered makes it extraordinarily valuable.'

Charlotte inclined her head. 'That explains why the Vatican's gone to so much trouble to bring us here. But how on earth could they have known the man had been crucified? How did they know they'd need your expertise?'

Bersei considered this. 'It's no surprise they called me here. Having worked in the catacombs for years, I've come across many skeletons. But let's hold off on the theories until we study the ossuary further. After all, the physical remains tell only part of the story.'

DOWN THE CORRIDOR from the lab, in a cramped space normally used for storage, a network of cables cascaded down to the computer hard drive, feeding live video and audio transmissions from the laboratory and its adjoining break room. Wearing headphones, Salvatore Conte was diligently recording all of the scientists' activity, as directed by Cardinal Santelli. Wireless links were also monitoring all phone calls in and out of Charlotte

Hennesey's dorm rooms and Giovanni Bersei's personal residence.

On a separate computer monitor, Conte brought up the home page for the Cayman Islands bank where he had opened a new account under one of his pseudonyms. Entering his user name and password, he made sure that Cardinal Santelli had made good on his end of the bargain.

Earlier that morning, he'd had a candid discussion with the cardinal concerning a bonus payment for expedited delivery of the relics as well as additional hazard pay for himself and his colleagues. Surprisingly, the cardinal hadn't protested, readily agreeing to the additional expense. The money was wire transferred through one of the Vatican's outside banking affiliates, bearing no audit trail back within these walls.

As a teen, Salvatore Conte had been a high achiever at Nunziatella Military School in Naples and upon graduation went off to fulfil the State's mandatory military conscription. It wasn't long before his unique abilities—both physical and intellectual—earned him a position in the SISDE, the Italian Secret Service, where he had excelled at any job thrown at him.

His decision to leave the SISDE almost five years ago had been a good one. Having established plenty of contacts during his time with them, there was never a shortage of clients. Among them was the Vatican—a tiny country that considered itself virtually impregnable with its high walls, its nifty security system—and its mercenary army. Conte had taken the liberty of paying a visit to its top guy to remind him that no system was impenetrable.

He could still recall the look on the old bastard's face when Santelli—the man he knew was the brains of the operation—came strolling into his office that morning, only to see Conte sitting at his impeccably organised desk playing solitaire on his computer, which he had hacked into with a portable password unscrambler.

Appalled, the cardinal had yelled, 'Who the hell are you?'

'Your security consultant,' Conte quickly replied in kind, standing and rounding the desk to offer a personalised business card with his alias and an encrypted mobile telephone number. 'I was in the area and wanted to introduce myself and go over some deficiencies in your security system.'

It had taken a minute or two for Santelli to calm down, to try to rationalise how anyone could have circumvented the Vatican's tight security layers. All the while, he had been contemplating the intercom on his desk. Conte explained the myriad services he could provide, running through a laundry list of services that the cardinal pretended to be offended by. But Conte had seen the SISDE file on this guy—particularly the one related to the infamous

Banco Ambrosiano scandal—and he knew the cardinal was no stranger to nefarious deeds.

Smiling, Conte was wide-eyed as he read his account balance: 6.5 million euros. After deducting overhead expenses and the cut owed to his team members, he was left with a cool net of 4 million euros.

Not bad for a few days' work.

CHAPTER 5

Chinon, France — March 3, 1314

In a dim, cramped cell beneath the Fort du Coudray, Jacques DeMolay sat against the dungeon wall watching three rats fight over the scrap of bread he had thrown to them. The smell of excrement hung in the air.

Now seventy years old, DeMolay's heavily scarred body—once robust— had turned haggard. For six years the Grand Master had been festering in this godforsaken pit, having fallen victim to the political ploys of France's King Philip IV and his cohort, Pope Clement V.

So many Templars had died in the name of Christ in the Holy Land. DeMolay felt like shouting out the lies that those sanctimonious bastards had propagated to undermine that sacrifice. But no one would ever believe the amazing things he had learned and the equally amazing relics still hidden beneath the site of Solomon's Temple in Jerusalem that attested to those truths. DeMolay took solace in knowing that some day the truth would be discovered . . . and woe to all who tried to deny it, he thought.

Not a day had gone by when he didn't think back to his conversation with Tibald DeGaudin. Perhaps he should have heeded the coward's advice.

Beyond the iron bars he heard sounds emanating from down the passage, metal keys jingling, approaching footsteps. Seconds later, a cloaked figure materialised outside the cell. The heavy smell of cologne left no doubt that Pope Clement had finally made an appearance, flanked by two guards.

A nasal, French voice cut the air. 'You look like hell, Jacques. Even worse than usual.'

DeMolay glared up at the corpulent pontiff who shielded his nose with an embroidered handkerchief. Gold, jewel-encrusted rings, including the papal fisherman's ring, covered his soft, manicured fingers and his dangling gold pectoral cross winked in the light of a nearby torch. DeMolay spoke, painfully forcing his cracked lips to move. 'You look . . . pretty.'

'Now, now, Grand Master. Let us not make this personal.'

'It has never been anything *but* personal,' DeMolay reminded him.

Clement lowered the handkerchief and smiled. 'What did you want to talk to me about? Are you finally ready to confess?'

DeMolay's icy gaze drilled into the Pope—a man two decades his junior. 'You know I will not disavow my brothers and my own honour.'

Four years earlier, DeMolay had been presented with no less than 127 accusations against the Order, outlandish charges that included devil worship and sexual perversion. And just two years ago, on March 22, 1312, Clement had issued a papal bull entitled '*Vox in excelso*', formally disbanding the Order.

'You have already taken our money and our land.' DeMolay's tone showed his disgust for this man. 'You've tortured hundreds of my men to extract false confessions, burned alive another fifty-four—all honourable men who dedicated their lives to preserve the Church's holy throne.'

Clement was impervious to his barbs. 'You know that if you do not end this stubbornness, you will be executed by the Inquisitors . . . You and your men are as archaic as what you stand for, honour or no honour. It's more than twenty years since you lost control over the Holy Land.'

'We both know that Rome was unwilling to support our efforts,' DeMolay said. 'We needed more men and they weren't sent. We were outnumbered ten to one. It was money then and it's money now.'

The Pope waved his hand dismissively. 'I would hate to think I have travelled this far merely to dredge up old misgivings. Why am I here?'

'To make a deal.'

Clement laughed. 'You are in no position to bargain.'

'I want you to reinstate the Order. Not for my sake, but for your own.'

'Come now, Jacques, you cannot be serious.'

DeMolay forged on, determination flickering in his gaze. 'After Acre fell, there was no time to return to Jerusalem. We had to leave many treasures behind. Valuable treasures that could easily fall into Muslim hands. And if they do, the entire future of your great Church could be in jeopardy.'

The Pope looked at him quizzically. He sized up the prisoner—a man he had never considered a liar. 'I am listening.'

DeMolay couldn't believe what he was about to do. But having waited for six long years, he had come to the dismal conclusion that the surviving Templars would not endure another year if something drastic did not happen. With remorse, he had resigned himself to divulging the Order's most coveted secret. 'There is an ancient book that has remained under the protection of the Order for over two centuries. It is called the *Ephemeris Conlusio*.'

'The *Journal of Secrets*? The Pope's tone was impatient. 'What secrets?'

For the next fifteen minutes, the Templar Grand Master recounted a remarkable story of a discovery so profound that if it were true, history itself hung in the balance. The Pope listened intently.

When the Grand Master had finished, he sat perfectly still, waiting for the pontiff to respond.

After almost a minute of brooding, Clement finally spoke, his tone less confident now, almost afraid. 'And you left this book in Jerusalem?'

'We had no choice. The city had already been seized.'

'That is quite a story,' Clement admitted. 'Why now do you tell it to me?'

'So you can reverse the injustice that has befallen the Order. We need to raise a new army to reclaim what has been lost. If not, I think you realise the consequences.' DeMolay could see by Clement's expression that he did.

'Even if I were to exonerate the Templars,' he thought out loud, 'I would have to convince Philip to do the same.' Doubtful, he shook his head. 'After all that has happened, I do not think that he will concede.'

'You must try,' DeMolay urged. He knew that he had succeeded in finding Clement's one vulnerability. 'Give me your word that you will try.'

Clement had expected today to be the day when he would finally break DeMolay and thus put an end to this whole charade. Suddenly, he realised he needed the old man more than ever. 'As you wish. You have my word.'

'Before you leave here, I want it in writing. I need reassurance.'

'I cannot do such a thing.'

'Without my support, you will never recover the book . . . and what it is meant to find,' DeMolay insisted. 'I am your only hope.'

The pontiff considered the idea for a long moment. 'So be it.' He instructed one of the guards to fetch his scribe. 'And if Philip does not agree?'

'Then it is of no matter what fate holds for me or my men . . . for you, King Philip, and all of Christendom will be doomed.'

Vatican City
In the Apostolic Palace, Father Donovan sat at a heavy oak desk in an expansive library that could only be entered by passing through a complex series of key-encrypted entryways and a contingent of Swiss Guards.

The *Archivum Secretum Apostolicum Vaticanum*—the Vatican Secret Archive.

Over the years the Vatican had enhanced the security system here, recognising that there were no treasures in Vatican City more valuable than its secrets. From rejected scriptural works blending philosophy, pagan mythology, and the Christ story, to the writings of Renaissance heretics like Galileo, the Vatican Archive was a depository for centuries of works banned by past pontiffs, as well as Vatican City's legal documents. Father Donovan still marvelled at how he had become the trusted custodian.

Straight out of the seminary, Donovan had joined Dublin's Christchurch Cathedral as a resident priest. But his passion for history and books had soon earned him recognition as a biblical historian and, two years ago, he had begun a highly successful biblical history programme at University College, Dublin. His lectures and papers on early Christian Scriptures had eventually caught the attention of Ireland's pre-eminent cardinal, Daniel Michael Shaunessey. Donovan accompanied Shaunessey on a visit to Vatican City, where he introduced him to the cardinal who oversaw the Vatican Library. Four months later, a compelling offer was extended to Donovan for a position inside Vatican City, managing its archives.

That had been twelve years ago. And never could he have imagined that one day he would be intimately involved in the single largest scandal in Church history—and all because of a book.

Poring over the yellowed, parchment pages of the archive's latest acquisition, Donovan was scanning the leather-bound *Ephemeris Conlusio*—the Journal of Secrets. In recognition of the blood spilled acquiring the relic now being studied in the Vatican Museum, he needed reassurance that the ossuary had met all the criteria described in the text. Studying a meticulous drawing of the ossuary, Donovan exhaled with relief when his eyes came across a precise match with the symbol carved onto the box's side.

It was almost impossible for the librarian to imagine how he had come to this juncture—the result of a shocking series of events set into motion by a single phone call he had received one rainy afternoon just two weeks earlier.

Donovan had been deeply absorbed in an eighteenth-century study on the nature of heresy when the phone rang.

'Is this Father Patrick Donovan, the curator of the Vatican's Secret Archive?' said the voice.

Donovan couldn't quite place the accent. 'Who is this?'

'Who I am is of no concern to you. I possess something that you want.'

'I don't have time for opaqueness,' Donovan responded. 'Be specific.'

'I have the *Ephemeris Conlusio*.'

'That book is a legend,' Donovan's voice cracked. 'Pure myth.' He stood up and began pacing nervously as he awaited a response.

'Your legend is now being held in my hand.'

Donovan's heart began to race. 'If you really do possess the *Ephemeris Conlusio* then tell me, who is the author?'

The caller told him and Donovan was amazed.

'Catholicism's prime enemy, am I not correct?'

Outside the window, the sky darkened and the rain intensified.

On the spot, Donovan decided that only if the caller could reveal the book's most profound contents would he consider the claim credible. 'Legend has it the *Ephemeris Conlusio* contains a map. Do you know what it's meant to locate?'

Donovan's lower lip quivered as the caller provided a precise description of the legendary relics.

'Do you want to sell the book?' Donovan's mouth was dry.

'It's not that simple.'

Now Donovan feared the worst, painfully aware that this stranger could potentially wound the Church very deeply, perhaps even fatally. 'Are you trying to blackmail the Vatican?'

The man cackled. 'It's not about money,' he hissed. 'Once you've seen what I have to offer, you will know what I'm after. And what you have to do . . . and will want to do. *That* will be my payment.'

'The Vatican would need to determine authenticity before any terms could be discussed. I'd need you to fax me a page from the book.'

'Give me your number.' The caller was hesitant. 'I will stay on this line.'

Donovan twice repeated his office's private fax number.

A long minute passed before the fax machine rang. The printed message was spat out seconds later. Donovan held it close to the light. The remarkably authentic Greek text left him momentarily breathless. Shaking, he returned the phone to his ear. 'Where did you find this?'

'That is not important. You are probably the only man at the Vatican who understands the profound implications of this book. I have chosen you to be my voice to the Holy See.'

There was a long pause.

'Do you want the book or not?'

Another pause.

'Of course,' he finally said.

Donovan had made arrangements to meet the anonymous caller's messenger two days later in the Caffè Greco on Via Condotti. Two armed plain-clothes Swiss Guards sat at a nearby table, but there had been no drama requiring their intervention. The messenger appeared at the agreed time and discreetly passed a leather satchel over to Donovan.

Opening it in the sanctuary of his office, Donovan had found a handwritten note and a newspaper clipping inside. The note had read: *Use the map to find the relics. Act quickly to find them before the Jews do. Should you require assistance, call me.* A phone number was listed below the message. Salvatore Conte had told him later that it had been a one-time-use cell-phone and that each of his subsequent communications with the insider was routed to a new phone number—all untraceable. Using these secure channels, the insider had coordinated with Conte to procure explosives and certain tools needed to extract the ossuary.

The Jews? Confused, the priest had read the clipping from the *Jerusalem Post* and realised exactly what had prompted this meeting. Digging deeper inside the satchel, his hands had come upon the smooth leather covers of the *Ephemeris Conlusio*.

THOUGH THE MAIN offices of the Israeli Antiquities Authority, the IAA, are located in Tel Aviv, a temporary office had been set up just three weeks earlier, inside the Wohl Archaeological Museum.

As Barton hurried towards the front door of the building he groaned inwardly when he saw the gold BMW saloon with police markings parked outside. He should have known his inspection of the crime scene would have the police and IDF breathing down his neck.

Descending into the Wohl's subterranean gallery, he moved past the restored mosaics and ritual baths of a lavish, excavated Herodian-era villa.

The IAA had recently launched a huge digitising campaign to catalogue its enormous collection—from vellums to pottery, pagan statuary to ossuaries, and, having pioneered similar programmes in the UK, Barton had been the ideal candidate to head up the initiative. Waiting in his temporary office at the rear of the gallery were the two men who only yesterday had asked for his help in the investigation—the Jerusalem District police commissioner Major General Jakob Topol and the IDF's head of domestic intelligence, Major General Ari Teleksen. Each had claimed a metal folding chair on the guest-side of his makeshift desk.

'Gentlemen.' Barton put down his briefcase and sat opposite them.

Teleksen was in his late fifties, thickset, with the face of a pitbull. He sat with his arms folded, making no effort to conceal the two missing fingers of his left hand. As Israel's most celebrated veteran counterterrorism agent, he retained a coldness befitting someone who'd seen far too much. 'We'd like to hear the results of your preliminary analysis.' His voice echoed off the bare walls.

Barton stroked his chin as he gathered his thoughts. 'The explosion breached the rear wall of the Marwani Mosque. Definitely professional.'

'We know that,' Teleksen impatiently replied. 'But for what purpose?'

'To access a hidden burial crypt.'

'Crypt?' Topol was staring at him. Clearly the junior of the two, his uniform more befitted a commercial jet pilot—a powder-blue collared shirt with rank-marking epaulettes on each shoulder, and navy-blue trousers. Middle-aged with a thick frame, his face was angular with deep-set eyes. 'What was stolen?'

'I'm speculating, but it seems to have been a burial box. An ossuary. It probably contained a disassembled human skeleton.'

'What I'm interested in here is motives,' Teleksen replied. 'You mean to tell me that we've lost thirteen IDF men for a box of bones?'

Barton nodded. 'The theft seems to have been coordinated by someone who knew exactly what the box contained.'

'What good would a box of bones be to anyone?' Teleksen made no effort to temper his scorn. He dipped into his jacket's breast pocket and pulled out a packet of cigarettes. Tapping one out, he skipped the formality of asking Barton if smoking here was OK and lit it up with a silver Zippo.

'Difficult to say,' Barton replied. 'We'd have to speculate on what could have been inside.'

There was a very long silence. The two lawmen exchanged looks.

'Any theories?' Teleksen took a deep drag of the cigarette and exhaled, the smoke curling in tendrils from his nostrils.

'Not yet.'

Topol was more level-headed. 'Was there anything else of value that could've been in the crypt?'

'No.' Barton was emphatic. 'It wasn't customary to leave valuables in crypts. This isn't ancient Egypt, Major General.'

'Did you find any evidence that could lead us to the perpetrators? Anything that might suggest Palestinian involvement?' Teleksen pursued.

'As of yet, nothing obvious.'

'Isn't there any way of tracking down this ossuary?' Teleksen was losing patience.

'Perhaps.' Barton regarded both men levelly. 'I'll be monitoring the antiquities markets closely. That's the most likely place it'll turn up.' He reached into his briefcase for a sheet of paper and pushed it towards Topol. 'Here's a basic drawing of what the ossuary probably looks like. I suggest you circulate this among your men, particularly at checkpoints.'

Topol stowed it away.

'I think you might be missing a very important part of all this,' Barton added quietly. 'A crypt beneath the Temple Mount would reinforce the Zionist notion that a Jewish temple once stood above it. Perhaps you should share that information with the prime minister.' Barton was playing off the idea that every Israeli Jew clung to the hope that one day solid evidence supporting Jewish exclusivity to the Temple Mount would be discovered.

Teleksen shifted uneasily.

'So don't be too surprised if this investigation leads to a much larger discovery,' Barton added.

'Anything else?' Topol queried.

For a split second, he thought about divulging his discovery of the scroll now back inside its cylinder in his trouser pocket. 'Not at this point.'

'I hardly need to remind you what's at stake here,' Teleksen said firmly. 'We're teetering on the verge of a very unpleasant confrontation with Hamas and the Palestinian Authority. Plenty of people on their side are ready to use any excuse to accuse us of a terrorist act against Islam.'

Barton looked at them. 'I'll do all I can to find the ossuary.'

Teleksen took a final drag that burned the cigarette down to its filter. 'If you find this box, notify us immediately.' He tossed the butt onto the floor and stubbed it out with his right foot. Both men stood and made their way out into the gallery.

Barton quickly closed the door and excitedly pulled out the cylinder from his pocket. Uncapping it, he tapped the scroll out onto his desk. From a nearby shelf, he retrieved a pair of latex gloves and slipped them on. After delicately opening the vellum, he slid it face-up into a plastic Ziploc bag, then gently ironed it flat with his hand. The neatly written text confirmed that he would need a translator, because Greek was not his strong point.

And as far as he was concerned, there was only one man in Jerusalem whom he considered an expert.

LEAVING THE WOHL Archaeological Museum, Barton quickly made his way through the Christian Quarter to the Church of the Holy Sepulchre.

Christian pilgrims flocked to Jerusalem to retrace Christ's footsteps along the fourteen 'stations' from flagellation to crucifixion known as the 'Stations of the Cross'. The journey would begin at a Franciscan monastery on the Via Dolorosa, just beneath the Temple Mount's northern wall—the site where many Christians maintained that Christ had taken up the cross after being scourged and crowned with thorns. Stations ten to fourteen—where Christ was stripped, nailed to the cross, died, and was taken from the cross—were commemorated in this church.

There weren't many tourists here today. Barton made his way through the main entrance, and circled a small mausoleum embellished with elaborate gold ornamentation that was sited beneath the church's massive rotunda. Inside this structure was the most sacred site in the church—a marble slab that covered the rock where Christ had been laid out for burial.

'Graham?' a warm voice called out. 'Is that you?'

Barton turned to face a corpulent old priest with a long white beard, dressed in the ceremonial garb of the Greek Orthodox Church: a flowing black soutane and a substantial black pipe hat.

'Father Demetrios.' The archaeologist smiled.

The priest clasped Barton with both his pudgy hands and pulled him slightly closer. 'What brings you back to Jerusalem?'

It had been almost a year and a half since Barton first met the priest to arrange for an exhibition of some of the Sepulchre's Crusader-era relics and crucifixes in the Museum of London. Father Demetrios had graciously loaned the items to the museum in exchange for a generous donation.

'I was hoping you'd be able to help me translate an old document.'

'Of course,' the priest replied cheerily. 'Come, walk with me.'

Strolling beside Father Demetrios, he eyed the numerous clerics milling about the space. The Greek clergy was compelled by a long-standing Ottoman decree to share this space with the church's other resident sects—Roman Catholics, Ethiopians, Syrians, Armenians and Copts—and throughout the Sepulchre, each had erected their own elaborate chapels.

'Rumour has it that the Israelis have called you in to assist in the investigation at the Temple Mount,' the priest whispered. 'Is there any truth to that?'

'I'd rather not say.'

'I don't blame you. But if it is true, please tread lightly, Graham.'

The priest led him into the Greek Orthodox chapel known as 'the Centre of the World', named for a stone basin in its centre that marked the spot ancient mapmakers had designated as the divide between east and west. In front of the altar, the priest made the sign of the cross, then turned to Barton. 'Show me what you have, Graham.'

Barton pulled the plastic-sealed vellum from his breast pocket and handed it over.

The priest held the document against the ambient glow of an ornate candelabrum and began to study the text intently. Seconds later a blanched expression came over him and his lower lip sagged. 'Oh my.'

'What is it?'

The priest looked concerned. Scared. 'Where did you find this?' he asked.

Barton considered telling him. 'I can't say. I'm sorry.'

'I see.' By the look in his eye, it was obvious that the priest already knew the answer. 'Let us go downstairs.' Father Demetrios motioned for Barton to follow. He led him down a staircase that wound beneath the nave.

Barton was pondering how the ancient words could have so spooked the old priest. Deeper they went, until stone walls gave way to cool, hewn earth.

Standing in what looked like a cave, the priest finally stopped. 'You know this place?'

'Of course,' Barton said, scanning the low-hanging rocky ceiling that bore telltale marks of mining activity. 'The old quarry.' His eyes wandered briefly to the wall behind the priest where hundreds of Knights Templar equilateral crosses had been carved into the rock—twelfth-century graffiti.

'The tomb,' the priest corrected him, pointing to the long burial niches carved into the far wall. 'Though I know your reservations in wanting to accept this idea.'

Where Helena was also lucky enough to unearth Christ's cross, he wanted to say, but curbed his response. The fact that Emperor Constantine's elderly mother had selected this site—formerly a Roman temple where pagans once worshipped Venus—left little doubt that its authenticity was questionable. But he wasn't about to offend with blasphemy.

'Why have you brought me here? Is it something about this scroll?'

'Everything about it.' His voice was solemn. 'I don't know where you found this, Graham. But if it wasn't from here—and I know it's not—I caution you. Be very, very careful. If you promise me you'll remember what I've said, I will write down your translation.'

'You have my word.'

'Good.' The priest let out a deep breath. 'Let me have your pen and paper.'

CHAPTER 6

Each time Father Patrick Donovan walked down the Apostolic Palace's grand corridor he felt intimidated. This was the apex of Christendom's hierarchy. Adjoining the far end of the Vatican Museum, it housed the offices of the Pope and the secretary of state.

Tall porticos ran along one side of the corridor, overlooking the Piazza San Pietro—Bernini's massive, elliptical courtyard, completed in 1667. Four sweeping arcs of colonnades embraced the space, pinpointing at its centre Caligula's obelisk that had been brought to Rome from the Nile Delta in AD 37.

The looming double door at the end of the corridor was flanked by two Swiss Guards in full costume billowing gold- and Medici blue-striped tunics and pantaloons, red berets and white gloves. Each carried an eight-foot-long pole called a 'halberd'—a sixteenth-century weapon that combined speared tip, axe blade and grappling hook. Donovan noticed that both soldiers also carried holstered Berettas.

He stopped two metres in front of the doorway.

'*Buona sera, Padre. Si chiama?*' The guard was demanding his name.

'Father Patrick Donovan,' he responded in Italian. 'I have been summoned by His Eminence, Cardinal Santelli.'

The guard disappeared into the room beyond. In a few moments he re-emerged. 'He is ready to see you.'

The librarian was ushered into an expansive antechamber furnished in marble and wood. Santelli's personal assistant, the young Father James Martin, manned a lone desk, his face blank and withdrawn.

'You may go right in,' Father Martin said, motioning to a huge oak door.

Opening the door to the sumptuous room, Donovan saw a purple skull-cap and the familiar mound of thick silver hair poking over the back of a tall leather chair.

The Vatican secretary of state was facing a window that neatly framed St Peter's Basilica, a phone held to his right ear, frail hands gesticulating. When he swivelled round, Donovan was met by the bloodshot eyes, bushy eyebrows and heavy jowls of Cardinal Antonio Carlo Santelli. The cardinal motioned him towards an armchair in front of the mahogany desk.

As the Vatican's highest-ranking cardinal, Santelli was charged with overseeing the political and diplomatic issues of the Holy See, accountable only to the Pope himself.

While the cardinal wrapped up his conversation, Donovan took in this inner sanctum of the pontifical machine. Santelli's immense desk was bare, save for a short stack of reports arranged at a perfect perpendicular. In the corner, a marble-topped credenza supported a replica of Michelangelo's *Pietà*. Three Raphaels hung—almost casually—on the walls.

His gaze circled back to Santelli.

'Advise him the final decision will be made by the Holy Father,' the cardinal was saying in Italian. Santelli was always direct. 'Call me when it's done.' He replaced the phone and looked up. 'Prompt as always, Patrick.'

Donovan smiled.

'After the appalling mess left behind in Jerusalem, I trust you're bringing me good news. Tell me all our efforts have been worthy of such sacrifice.'

Donovan forced himself to look Santelli in the eye. 'There's enough evidence to lead me to believe the ossuary's genuine. More tests need to be done, but so far the evidence is compelling.'

The cardinal grimaced. 'But is there a body?'

Donovan nodded. 'Just as the manuscript suggested.'

'And when will these scientists be ready to make a presentation?'

'I requested that they prepare something for Friday.'

'Good.' The cardinal saw that Donovan was preoccupied. 'Cheer up, Father Donovan. You've just helped give this great institution new life.'

CHARLOTTE HENNESEY WAS still grappling with the notion that the ossuary's skeletal remains suggested that the thirty-something male subject exhibited multiple signs of trauma resulting from crucifixion.

She and Bersei were now preparing to establish further evidence reinforcing the subject's identity, and estimating date of death. Carbon dating would need to be performed on the bone, and the ossuary itself would need to be examined closely for any telling clues. Charlotte pointed to the fused symbol of the dolphin and trident on the side of the ossuary. 'Think we'll be able to determine what that means?'

'I'm fairly certain it's a pagan symbol,' Bersei continued. 'It's funny, I know I've seen it somewhere before. First, let's figure out if this patina's legitimate.'

'While you finish analysing the ossuary, I'll work on preparing a bone sample for carbon dating.' She motioned across the room to the skeleton

'Sounds good. By the way,' Bersei reached for his notepad and jotted something down. 'Here's the name and number of my contact at an AMS lab here in Rome.' He tore off a sheet. 'Say we're doing work for the Vatican and need immediate results. That should get his attention.'

Hennesey read it. 'Antonio Ciardini?'

'Pronounced Char-dini. Old friend of mine, plus he owes me a favour.'

While Charlotte phoned the Affiliated Medical Services lab, Bersei began his analysis of the ossuary. Dimming the lights above the workstation, he swept each surface with an ultraviolet light wand. Looking through the Orascoptic's goggles' crisp lenses, the first thing he noticed was that the patina had been scuffed in many areas, particularly along the sides. Glowing under the black light, the abrasive marks were long and wide. Straps, he guessed, though no trace fibres had been left behind. Probably new nylon webbing. He concluded that the marks were fresh.

It wasn't that shocking. He'd often seen relics that had been handled improperly during excavation and shipment, but this type of disregard for the past always offended him. He had read that the James ossuary had been cracked during shipment. By comparison, the damage here was forgivable.

After mounting the digital camera on a tabletop tripod, powering it up and deactivating its flash, he snapped some shots. Then he turned off the black light and set the workstation lighting higher.

Next, painstakingly inspecting every edge and surface, Bersei hunted for any evidence that the patina had been manually transplanted. Had the box been inscribed after it was found, the geological residue would exhibit obvious inconsistencies. However, the lengthy examination showed no suspicious scrapes or gouges. The patina appeared to be bonded evenly across all the ossuary's limestone surfaces.

He used a small blade to scrape samples from selected areas, placing the material on glass slides and clearly marking each one. After collecting fifteen samples, he moved to another workstation equipped with an electron microscope and loaded the first specimen.

Super-magnified and projected onto an adjacent computer monitor, the dried minerals and deposits that formed the patina looked like greyish-beige cauliflower. He saved a detailed profile of the sample in a database, removed the first slide and continued along the tray to the last sample image. He then entered a command to cross-check for inconsistencies. If any part of the patina had been artificially 'manufactured' the program would spot it, but as far as he could tell, the results substantiated that the ossuary's etchings pre-dated the formation of the patina. It was more than reasonable to conclude that the dolphin and trident symbol on the ossuary did indeed date from the same time as the bones. If he could figure out what it meant, it might help identify the crucified man.

WATCHING GIOVANNI BERSEI at work on the other side of the lab, Charlotte picked up the cordless phone and dialled the number he had given her.

'*Salve.*'

For a moment, she didn't know what to say. She'd expected a switchboard or assistant, perhaps even voicemail, and wondered if she'd accidentally dialled someone's residence.

'Signore Antonio Ciardini?'

'*Sì.*'

'This is Dr Charlotte Hennesey speaking. Giovanni Bersei suggested I contact you. I'm sorry—I didn't know I'd be calling your home.'

'You've dialled my mobile. Quite all right.' His English was impressive. 'What can I do for my good friend Giovanni?'

Everyone seemed to like Dr Bersei. 'He and I are working on a unique project here in the Vatican. We've been asked to examine an ancient bone sample and we'd like to date the specimen.'

His voice went up a notch. 'Bone specimens in the Vatican? That's an odd pairing. Though there are those tombs beneath St Peter's Basilica . . .'

'Yes, well . . .' She couldn't elaborate. 'I hate to trouble you, but Dr Bersei was wondering if you might be able to speed up the results?'

'For Giovanni, sure. The bone—is it in good condition? Clean?'

'It's extremely well preserved.'

'Good. Then I suggest you send a sample of at least a gram.'

'Got that. And there's a wood splinter that we'd like to date as well.'

'Preferably ten milligrams for wood.'

'Ten is no problem. Dr Bersei was wondering if you could call us as soon as the results are available?'

'So that's why he had you call, Dr Hennesey.' Ciardini let loose with a big belly laugh. 'I'll do my best to get them done within a couple of hours.'

'Thank you. The samples will be with you soon as possible. *Ciao.*'

Returning the receiver to its wall-mounted cradle, she went back to the workstation. Studying the skeleton, she finally settled on a splintered fragment from the left foot's fractured metatarsal. With a pair of tweezers,

Charlotte carefully broke away a piece and sealed it in a plastic vial. From the drawer, she retrieved the wood splinter she had taken during the initial pathological analysis, and placed the two specimens in a padded envelope.

To thoroughly re-create the skeleton's physical profile, Charlotte would also need to sample the skeleton's deoxyribonucleic acid, or DNA. Contained within the core of all human cells, the ribbon-like nucleotide acids held the coding that determined every human physical attribute. She'd read that scientists had been able to study DNA in Egyptian mummies almost 5,000 years old, so she was confident that the skeleton's DNA would not have degraded beyond the point of being able to study it. This kind of genetic examination required sophisticated equipment and Charlotte knew the fastest and most reliable facility for such testing was at BioMapping Solutions, under Evan Aldrich's watchful eye.

Glancing at her watch, she picked up the phone and dialled Phoenix. A quarter to five. Even with the eight-hour difference, she knew Evan was an inveterate early bird.

'Aldrich.' That was the way he always answered: to the point. Another thing she loved about him.

'Hey there. It's the Rome field office calling in.'

Hearing her voice, he immediately sounded cheerful. 'How are operations at Christianity Central?'

'Good. How are things back home?' She touched one of her earrings, remembering he had given them to her for her last birthday.

'Same old. So what's shaking at the Vatican?'

'It's amazing. I've been analysing ancient skeletal remains. Standard forensic stuff so far, but fascinating. I wish you could see this.'

'Hope it's worth our time.' He paused. 'I'm assuming you didn't call just to chat.'

After her abrupt—make that icy—departure last Sunday, she knew he was referring to relationship issues. Evan had slept at her house the previous evening. A night of passion that led to an early-morning discussion about 'taking things to the next level'. Still not having told him about her cancer, she'd been quick to dodge the issue and she hadn't left on the best of terms. Fixing things between them was important, but now was not the time.

'The specimen's bones are in incredibly good shape and I was hoping to impress the locals with some DNA-mapping magic,' she explained. 'Think BMS might be interested?' There was a pause that she knew was most likely disappointment.

After a long moment, he said, 'Sounds like it would be good PR.'

'Is the new gene scanner ready?'

'We're already in the beta testing stage. Get me your sample—something small like a tarsal would be best—and I'll run it through. It'll be a good test.'

'Thanks, Evan. I'll see if they'll let me send it for overnight delivery.'

'Say hi to the Pope for me. And Charlotte . . .'

Here it comes, she thought. 'Yeah?'

'It isn't just my best scientist I miss around here.'

She smiled. 'I miss you, too. Bye.'

Charlotte returned to the workstation, trying to fight off the surge of regret welling inside her. She should have told him why she couldn't be with him the way he wanted. Why making any long-term emotional commitment would be irresponsible. Drawing a calming breath, she resigned herself to the fact that when she returned to Phoenix, she would tell him everything. Then they would figure out how to move forward.

Bagging the metatarsal, she stuffed the sample into a DHL box. As she wrote BMS's address on the shipping label, she tried to suppress a sudden bout of homesickness. Dr Bersei joined her at the workstation. 'Far as I can tell, the patina wasn't tampered with. It's the real thing. You?'

'I had a nice conversation with Signore Ciardini,' she said, managing a smile. 'Very charming man. He'll have the results for us tomorrow.'

'What's that package you're working on?'

'Another sample I hope will provide a genetic profile for our man.' She held it up. 'I'm sending it to Phoenix for DNA analysis.'

Bersei glanced at his watch—just past five. 'We got a lot done today. I've got to get home for dinner. Carmela's making chicken saltimbocca and my oldest daughter is stopping by. Tomorrow maybe we can take a look inside the box, and I'll see if I can't decipher that dolphin symbol.'

'You have a good evening, Giovanni. Thanks for everything.'

'You're welcome. See you in the morning.'

As the door closed behind him, just for a moment, Charlotte Hennesey envied him.

Wednesday

Razak sat on the verandah of his apartment in the Muslim Quarter overlooking the Temple Mount and its Western Wall Plaza. Throngs of protestors had been gathering since sunrise and now he could see news crews from around the world queuing to get past the police cordons.

Tuned to *Al-Jazeera*, the volume on Razak's TV was set low, providing a quiet buzz in the background. The mood in Jerusalem was tense. Armoured vehicles were now posted at all Israeli checkpoints, as well as the main gates to Old Jerusalem. The IDF had doubled its border patrols.

People were demanding answers, needing someone to blame. Israel was gearing up its defence, ready for yet another confrontation.

Razak tried to focus on formulating a plan for diffusing the tension, at least temporarily. Damage control.

The mobile phone interrupted his thoughts.

'Sorry to bother you. It's Graham Barton. I've got the transcription back on that scroll we found.'

'What does it say?'

'Something astounding,' Barton promised. 'But not something we should discuss over the telephone. Can you meet me to go over this?'

'Of course.' It was hard for Razak to deny the upbeat archaeologist's infectious enthusiasm. 'When?'

'How about noon at *Abu Shukri* on El-Wad Road?'

Razak glanced at his watch. 'I will see you at noon.' Maybe, thought Razak, this is the break I've been waiting for.

CHARLOTTE HENNESEY turned to see the clock's digital readout blinking 7:00 in thick lines of annoying red light. The sun was glaring through the thin curtains that covered the windows and she dropped her head back onto the pillow. Though the small bed was quite comfortable, she had not slept well.

Hanging on the wall directly above her head was a crucifix. Her eyes locked onto it. Against her will, images of hammers pounding huge nails through skin and muscle again crept into her thoughts.

Dragging herself out of bed, she stumbled to her travel bag and wrestled the cap off a bottle of Melphalan. She took out one of the tiny white pills and swilled it down with some water. Next came a fistful of supplements to counteract the havoc it would wreak on her immune system.

After brushing her teeth, she showered and dressed, and soon she was making her way out of the door.

Giovanni was already well into his work, hunched over a metal cabinet and fiddling with some computer cables, when Charlotte entered the lab. He looked up, smiled and then waved her over. 'You're going to like this. It's a laser scanner used for 3-D imaging.'

The rectangular unit stood about three feet high, with an empty inner chamber and glass door. The controls were mounted on the side.

Charlotte eyed it critically. 'Looks like a mini bar,' she said.

He laughed. 'Never thought of that. Why don't you get some coffee and I'll show you how to work it,' he said, connecting a USB cable from the back of the unit into his laptop's data port.

Five minutes later Charlotte was suited up and ready to go.

'With this we scan every bone and reassemble the skeleton in the computer's imaging software,' Bersei explained. 'Then the CAD program analyses them and re-creates the image of what our mystery man looked like when he was flesh and blood. I'll do the first one; you can do the rest.'

Bersei reached out for the skull, cradling its toothy mandible with one hand, globular mass in the other, and mounted it in the scanning chamber. Working the mouse, it took him a few seconds to adjust the program settings, but less than a minute later, a perfect digitised replica of the skull popped up on the laptop screen.

'There you go. A 3-D copy. Now the image can be manipulated however we want.' He ran his finger over the laptop's touchpad so the onscreen skull rotated and flipped on command. 'Why don't you try one?' He opened the scanner door and removed the skull.

Charlotte picked up a segment of spine and closed it in the scanner. Clicking the 'SCAN' button, she watched the luminescent lasers as they played over the bones. After a minute, the imaging was complete.

Bersei was watching over her shoulder. '*Perfetto*. Let me know when you're finished,' he said. 'Then I'll show you how to piece it all together.'

While she worked on scanning another spinal segment, Bersei looked into the ossuary to examine the thick coat of dust that covered the base of its interior. He would need to empty the material out and pass it through the spectrometer. He assumed that he would find some desiccated flesh and loose stone dust—perhaps trace amounts of the flowers and spices traditionally used in ancient Jewish burial rituals.

What he didn't expect was the small, circular object he found in his scoop. Removing it with gloved fingers, and lightly dusting its surface with a delicate brush, Bersei saw it was stamped metal.

A coin.

Taking a stiffer brush from the tool tray, he beckoned Charlotte over.

'Take a look at this.' Bersei held the coin out for her.

Her eyes narrowed as she peered at it. 'A coin? Good stuff, Giovanni.'

'Yes. It'll make dating the relic far easier.'

He passed her the small coin and swivelled back to the computer terminal, keying in the search criteria: 'roman coins LIZ'.

Charlotte studied it intently. On its face was a symbol that looked like a backwards question mark, circled by a ring of text. The flip side revealed three capital letters—LIZ.

'Here we go,' Bersei murmured. The first hits had come back instantly. He clicked the most relevant link, which brought up an online coin seller named 'Forum Ancient Coins'.

'What did you find?'

Scrolling down a list of ancient coins for sale, he found an exact image of the coin Charlotte held between her fingers and enlarged it. 'Interesting. Says here it was issued by Pontius Pilate,' Bersei pointed out.

Charlotte was taken aback as she bent over to get a better look. 'The Pontius Pilate . . . as in the guy in the Bible?'

'You know, he *was* a real historical figure,' Bersei confirmed. He silently read some onscreen text that accompanied the image. 'Says Pilate issued three coins during his decade-long tenure, which began in AD 26,' he summarised. 'All were minted in Caesarea in the years AD 29, 30, and 31.'

'So these Roman numerals L-I-Z tell us the specific date?'

'Technically, those are *Greek* numerals. Back then, Hellenic culture was still very influential on daily life in Judea. And, yes, they do indicate the actual date of issue,' Bersei explained. 'You see those ancient Greek words encircling the coin? They say "of Tiberius Emperor".'

'How do you know that?'

'I happen to read ancient Greek fluently. It was a common language in the early Roman Empire.'

'Impressive.'

He grinned. 'Anyway, Tiberius's reign began in the year AD 14. Now the L is just an abbreviation for the word "year". The I is equal to ten, the Z is seven—add them together and you get seventeen. Therefore, this coin was minted during the seventeenth year of Tiberius's reign.'

'And what about this other symbol—this reverse question-mark thing?'

'Yes. It says here the *littus* symbolises a staff that was held by an augur.'

'An augur?'

'A kind of priest. Likened to an oracle and commissioned by Rome.'

Looking back to the monitor, Charlotte noticed the remarkably low bid price for Pilate's relic. 'Twenty-two dollars? How could a coin almost two thousand years old be worth only that much?'

'Supply and demand, I guess,' Bersei explained. 'Back in the day, this would have been the equivalent of your American penny.'

Her brow furrowed. 'Why do you think it was in the ossuary?'

'Easy. Placing coins on the eyes of the dead was part of Jewish burial practice. Kept the eyelids closed to protect the soul until the flesh decayed.'

'Hmm.'

Reaching into the ossuary, he fished around for a few seconds then plucked something from the dust and held it up. A second coin. 'Two eyes. Two coins.' Bersei examined both sides. 'A perfect match.'

'So the bones must have been buried in the same year, right?'

'Not necessarily. But most likely, yes.'

She gazed at the skeleton. 'Pontius Pilate and a crucified body. You don't think—'

Bersei held a hand up, knowing what she was about to suggest. 'Let's not go there,' he urged. 'Like I said, the Romans executed thousands by crucifixion. And, I'm a good Catholic boy,' he added with a smile.

CHAPTER 7

At precisely twelve o'clock, Razak strolled over to the table where Graham Barton was seated in front of the tiny open-air café, drinking black coffee and reading the *Jerusalem Post*. Seeing Razak, Barton folded the paper and stood to greet him.

Razak smiled. 'Good morning, Graham.'

Barton offered a hand and Razak accepted.

'Please sit.' The archaeologist motioned to the chair opposite.

'This was a fine choice.'

'I thought you'd like it.' Barton had purposely selected this popular small café in the Muslim Quarter since, as of late, he'd been hearing rumblings that Jewish shopkeepers weren't taking kindly to Muslim guests.

Pulling in his chair, Razak was immediately approached by a young male Palestinian waiter, painfully thin, just sprouting a sparse beard.

'Will you eat, Graham?'

'Yes, if you have time. What do you recommend?'

Razak turned to the waiter and rattled off a few dishes—the restaurant's famous hummous with black beans and roasted pine nuts, pitta bread 'hot please,' he specified, falafel, two shwarma kabobs, and a pot of mint tea.

Once the waiter had retreated to the rear kitchen, he said. 'Tell me, what have you found out?'

Barton's face lit up. 'Something quite extraordinary.' He reached into his shirt pocket and pulled out a folded sheet of paper. 'See here?' He opened the paper and laid it out for Razak. 'On top is a photocopy of the original text, below it, the English cipher.'

Briefly, Razak admired the beautiful handwriting of the ancient script. Then his eyes skipped down the page to the translation: *'Having fulfilled God's will, I, Joseph of Arimathea and my beloved family wait here for the glorious day when our fallen Messiah shall return to reclaim God's testimony from beneath Abraham's altar.'*

Razak's expression showed his confusion. 'Who is this Joseph?'

The waiter returned with a steaming pot of tea and Barton waited for him to leave before answering. 'Joseph is the man whose skeleton is in the ninth ossuary. You see, the Hebrew name "Yosef" translates in English to "Joseph". Have you ever heard of Joseph of Arimathea?'

Razak shook his head.

'I'm not surprised. He's an obscure first-century biblical figure who appears only briefly in the New Testament.'

Sipping his tea, Razak suddenly looked uneasy. 'And what does the book say about him?'

The Englishman spread his hands on the table. 'The Gospels of Mark and Luke state that Joseph was a prominent member of the Sanhedrin—the council of seventy-one Jewish sages who acted as the supreme court of ancient Judea. The Gospels also suggest that Joseph was a close confidant of a very famous, charismatic Jew named Joshua.'

The name didn't register. 'Am I supposed to know this Joshua?'

'Oh, you know him,' Barton replied confidently. 'Some Hebrew translations refer to him as *"Yeshua"*. But his Arabic name is *"Isa"*.'

Razak's eyes went wide. 'Jesus?'

'Following Jesus' death, Joseph was said to have gone to Gaul—modern-day France—where he preached Jesus' teachings. Supposedly, somewhere around 63 CE, he even spent time in Glastonbury in England, where he acquired land and built England's first monastery.'

Sipping more tea, Razak raised his eyebrows. 'Go on.'

'Fast forward to the Middle Ages and Joseph becomes a cult hero. A legend surfaces claiming that Joseph possessed Jesus' crown of thorns and the chalice he drank from at the Last Supper.' Barton paused. 'Some believed that Joseph collected the blood of Jesus' crucified body in that cup. Better known as "the Holy Grail", the cup was believed to possess healing powers and granted its owner immortality.'

'Surely you're not suggesting that the thieves thought the missing ossuary contained the Holy Grail?'

'No. I'd certainly not push that idea,' Barton continued tentatively. 'But I decided to do a bit more research on Joseph of Arimathea using the most convenient and relevant handbook available.' He held up a book.

Razak's eyes bored into its title: *Holy Bible: New International Version.* 'More legend,' he said cynically.

Knowing that the New Testament would be a touchy matter, Barton expected this reaction. Muslims revered Jesus as one in a long series of human prophets that included Abraham, Moses, and Allah's final servant, Muhammad. Under no circumstances would Islam accept any prophet as an equal to God himself. It was this pillar of Islamic faith that rendered the Christian concept of the Trinity absolute blasphemy. To Muslims, the New Testament is a gross misinterpretation of Jesus' life.

Ignoring the jibe, Barton forged on, 'There are detailed accounts of the prophet Jesus in the Gospels of Matthew, Mark, Luke and John. Each specifically mentions Joseph of Arimathea.' Barton flipped open the Bible to a section marked by a Post-It note. 'All four accounts essentially say the same thing, so I'll just read this first excerpt from Matthew:

'As evening approached, there came a rich man from Arimathea, named Joseph, who had himself become a disciple of Jesus. Going to Pilate, he asked for Jesus' body, and Pilate ordered that it be given to him. Joseph took the body, wrapped it in a clean linen cloth, and placed it in his own new tomb that he had cut out of the rock. He rolled a big stone in front of the entrance to the tomb and went away.'

Barton raised his eyes from the pages. 'I'll read that one sentence again. "Joseph took the body, wrapped it in a clean linen cloth, and placed it in his own new tomb that he had cut out of the rock."'

Razak's mouth gaped open. 'Surely you don't think—'

The waiter appeared suddenly and Razak stopped mid-sentence, waiting for the young man to set down the plates and leave before continuing.

Razak took a deep breath. 'I see where you're going with this, Graham. It is a very dangerous theory indeed.' He took some bread and hummous.

'We have to at least entertain the idea that the thieves may have truly believed that the missing ossuary contained the remains of Jesus,' Barton continued softly. 'And this scroll we found in the ninth ossuary clearly references the Messiah.'

As he explained this to Razak, Barton was beginning to feel the full weight of Father Demetrios's subtle warning. The words on this scroll could potentially undermine traditional commemoration of Christ's mysterious benefactor, because the *loculi* deep beneath the Church of the Holy Sepulchre were believed to have belonged to Joseph.

Razak stared at the archaeologist. 'You should eat your bread while it's still hot.'

'Look. I'm not saying I believe all this.' Barton tore off some bread and spooned some hummous onto his plate. 'I'm simply suggesting a motive that would make that missing ossuary the ultimate relic.'

Razak finished chewing, swallowed and said, 'I'm sure you'll understand that I can't possibly accept the idea that this missing ossuary contained Jesus' body. Remember, Mr Barton, that unlike the misguided men who wrote that book,' he pointed at the Bible, 'the Qur'an speaks the literal words of Allah using the great prophet Muhammad—peace be upon him— as his messenger. As Muslims we've been told the truth. Jesus didn't die a mortal death but was reclaimed by Allah and ascended to heaven.' He dipped some more bread into the hummous. 'Besides, don't Christians claim Jesus rose from the dead and ascended into heaven?'

'Absolutely,' Barton said. 'But the Gospels were drafted decades after Jesus' ministry, following a long period of oral tradition. I don't need to tell you how that can affect the integrity of what we read today. I might also point out that ancient interpretations of resurrection had much more to do with a spiritual transformation than a physical one.'

Razak shook his head. 'How could anyone believe those stories?'

'Well,' Barton carefully countered, 'you need to keep in mind that the target audience for the Gospels were pagan converts. Those people believed in divine gods who died tragically and were resurrected gloriously. Early Christian leaders, particularly Paul of Tarsus—a Hellenistic, philosophical Jew—knew Jesus needed to fit these criteria. We can't discount the idea that he embellished the story. And of twenty-seven books in the New Testament, he alone is thought to have written fourteen of them.' Razak turned his attention back to the transcription. 'And what about the rest of this . . . what does it all mean?' He read the second part of the transcription: '"To reclaim God's testimony from beneath Abraham's altar."'

Barton was hoping to avoid this part of the discussion. 'Ah.' He paused. 'Abraham's altar is most likely referring to Mount Moriah.'

'Where the prophet Ibrahim was told to sacrifice Ismaeel, son of Hagar,' the Muslim stated flatly.

Barton let the interpretation slide. Though the Torah clearly stated that Abraham was to sacrifice *Isaac*, the son of his wife Sarah, Muslims traced their lineage back to Ismaeel—the son born to Sarah's handmaiden, Hagar. It was yet another example of the two religions trying to claim as its own the Old Testament's most revered patriarch—the man credited with complete submission to the one true God.

'And this reference to "God's testimony",' Razak added. 'Sounds as if it is a physical thing that is "beneath Abraham's altar". I don't understand.'

A shiver ran down Barton's arm. 'I'm still trying to determine what that means,' he lied. 'I'll need to do a bit more research.'

Razak nodded. 'I trust you'll let me know what you discover. Where do we go from here?'

Barton thought about it. Oddly, his thoughts kept drifting to the chamber beneath the Temple Mount, and how it lacked some of the features typical in first-century crypts. 'Actually, I think we'll need to go back to the crypt.'

'Let's hold off on that until tomorrow,' Razak suggested. 'I received a very interesting call from a good friend who heard I was involved in this investigation. He says he has some information that might help us out.'

'What kind of information?'

'I'm not sure, actually,' Razak said. 'He wouldn't say over the phone. I was going to go and see him this afternoon. Maybe you should come along.'

'I'd like that. What time?'

Razak looked down at his watch. 'Can you meet me in the car park outside the Jaffa Gate around two?'

'I'll be there.'

OPPOSITE THE CAFÉ on El Wad, a forgettable young man was seated on a bench reading a newspaper and sipping coffee, enjoying the mild afternoon. Occasionally he inconspicuously glanced over to the archaeologist and Muslim delegate. The small headphones plugged into his ears, seemingly connected to an iPod, were transmitting the amazing conversation that was taking place to the IDF's Jerusalem outpost.

BRINGING UP the skeletal scans in full-screen view, Giovanni Bersei scrolled down the grid of miniature images. 'That's great, Charlotte. All we have to do now is ask the computer to assemble the skeleton.'

He clicked on a series of menu options and seconds later the screen flashed back a 3-D image of the skeleton. The program had scrutinised each bone's smallest detail to re-create the condition of joints and cartilage attachments, providing an accurate picture of the fully reassembled skeletal frame. It had even maintained the minute, awful detail resulting from cruci-fixion—the gouges on the ribs and damage to the wrists, feet and knees.

'Extraordinary.' Bersei eyed the onscreen image—an assembled version of what lay on the workstation behind them. 'That's probably just the way our man looked prior to being placed in the ossuary.'

'What about the flesh?'

He held his hands out as if trying to slow a speeding car. 'One step at a time.' He worked the mouse again. 'Now we'll ask the computer to assign muscle mass to the skeletal frame. The software will measure every bone to estimate its density and re-create its ligament attachment points.'

The screen refreshed.

This time the program had clothed a fibrous weave of lean musculature over the skeletal form. The man had been perfectly proportioned.

Charlotte leaned in closer. 'Looks very fit,' she said matter-of-factly.

'No McDonald's back then,' Giovanni said as he manipulated the mouse. 'Let's add some skin here.' He clicked a command.

Almost instantly the screen refreshed again. The 3-D image looked like a Bernini marble sculpture with its smooth 'flesh' The image omitted all hair, including eyebrows. The eyes were smooth, colourless orbs.

'This is where your DNA analysis will help fill in the blanks,' Bersei con-tinued. 'The program accepts genetic information—it re-creates everything from eye and skin colour to hair density, hairline, body hair, and so on.'

'Go in on the face.'

Bersei held the mouse button to drag a white lined frame round the image and clicked to zoom.

A ghostly form filled the screen, its features well defined, yet soft, with a long sloping nose, full lips and a strong chin. There was a pronounced jaw line with a firm brow and wide eyes.

Bersei seemed satisfied. 'For now this is the program's best re-creation. He was a handsome devil.'

The intercom suddenly came to life. Father Donovan apologised for the interruption, but was patching through a call from a Signore Ciardini.

'Probably our carbon-dating results,' Bersei said. 'Why don't you take that call and I'll continue my work on the ossuary.'

Bersei returned to his workstation, while Charlotte made her way to the phone. As he finished removing the powdery dust layer from the bottom of the ossuary, a thin outline of a rectangular form gradually emerged.

Taking a small blade, he carefully levered up what looked like a metal plate to reveal a hollowed-out compartment. Inside were the shadowy forms of three long, tapered objects. Reaching into the ossuary, Bersei withdrew one of them. It was surprisingly heavy, easily eighteen centimetres long with a knobby, blunted end that tapered into a shaft of wrought edges.

A nail.

Placing it on a steel tray, he stared at it, disbelief flooding back.

He pulled the two remaining nails from the ossuary, and aligned all three on the tray. 'Oh my,' he gasped, sinking back into his chair.

Across the lab Charlotte had just hung up the phone.

'You've got to see what I've just found,' he called over to her.

Charlotte approached the workstation. By Bersei's blanched look she knew that the ossuary had offered up yet another of its secrets.

He pointed mutely to the three metal objects. 'I think it's safe to say that these are the nails used to crucify this man . . . whoever he was.'

'Where did you find them?'

'Take a look.' He pointed with his chin.

She positioned herself above the ossuary, scanning its exposed cavity. Her eyes caught the faint outline of a second recess carved even deeper into the compartment. 'Wait,' she called sharply, swinging the retractable lighting arm over the ossuary. 'Looks like you missed something.'

Nestled in a carved niche at the very bottom of the ossuary was something that resembled a metal test tube.

Above the white fabric of their masks, the scientists exchanged looks.

'I've just about had all I can take right now,' Giovanni motioned to the cylinder. 'You do the honours.'

Charlotte reached down and her fingers closed round smooth metal. With infinite care, she withdrew it from the ossuary.

Turning her hand over, she rolled the tarnished tubular casing along her latex covered palm—a stark contrast of old and new. Both ends were sealed by round metal caps. There were no distinguishing marks or inscriptions.

'A container of some kind?' Her eyes were on him, searching for an explanation, but Bersei could not speak. Charlotte rotated it. The metal looked similar to the coins. Was it bronze? 'OK. Here goes.' She held the cylinder over a tray, took hold of the cap sealing one end, and twisted. A muffled cracking sound indicated the wax seal had broken.

The cap came free.

Fellow conspirators, the two scientists gazed at one another. Tilting the cylinder closer to the light, she glimpsed something rolled up inside.

'What do you see?' Bersei's voice was hoarse with tension.

'It looks like a scroll.'

'Handle it extremely carefully. It's probably very brittle.'

Gently tapping the unopened end of the cylinder, Charlotte gently coaxed the scroll from the tube. It slid onto the tray.

Bersei reached out and gingerly rolled it back and forth with his index finger. He exhaled heavily. 'Looks like it's in excellent condition.'

'Is that parchment?'

Bersei studied it. 'Most likely calfskin.'

'We can't just unfurl it, can we?'

'It looks remarkably well preserved, but there will be strict procedures. We can't risk any damage.' His expression hardened. 'Don't you think there's just too much evidence here?'

'Perhaps. But I've got some really interesting news for you.'

'The carbon-dating results?'

She nodded. 'That bone sample was so good that it's ninety-eight point seven per cent certain the bones date from between AD 5 and 71.'

Uncertainty was growing in Bersei's eyes again. That narrow time range was almost incredible. With his left hand, he massaged a cramp that was setting into the base of his neck. Stress. 'This is compelling news.'

'And the wood splinter—which, by the way, is from a type of walnut tree indigenous to a region in Israel—there's an eighty-nine point six per cent degree of certainty that it dates from between AD 18 and 34.'

Bersei's eyes jumped over to the skeleton as if it had suddenly come to life. 'When do you think you'll have the results of the genetic analysis?'

'We might have them tomorrow.'

He stared down at the scroll. 'Good. Let's go ahead and document all this,' he suggested.

Charlotte got the digital camera, turned it on and started snapping shots of the ossuary's interior while Bersei carefully returned the scroll to its metal housing and sealed the cap.

AN HOUR SOUTHWEST of Jerusalem, the lush farmlands of Israel's transformed desert began to fade back into arid landscape as Razak drove down Highway 4 towards the Gaza border.

'Have you ever been on that side of the fence?' Barton motioned with his eyes through the distant tall posts and steel wiring of the separation fence that ran along the Gaza Strip's fifty-one-kilometre border, cutting away the tiny sliver of land from Israel's southern coast.

'Only once,' Razak replied in a dreary tone. He did not elaborate.

Seeing as Barton would be only one of a handful of Europeans in the tiny place inhabited by almost 1.3 million Palestinians, he would have preferred a more reassuring response from Razak—especially since Westerners were prime targets for abduction by Islamic militants.

Up ahead, the road was snarled for almost three kilometres with idling vehicles awaiting clearance through the Erez Crossing.

'Who exactly is this contact we're meeting?' Barton asked.

'An old school friend of mine. A man who shares many of my concerns for the future of the Middle East,' Razak explained. 'If you don't mind, I'd like to request that you let me do all the talking.'

'Agreed.'

It took almost two hours before they reached the expansive metal canopy that shielded the IDF border-patrol guards from the sun. Tanks and armoured vehicles were positioned on both sides of the gate.

Razak turned to Barton. 'Do you still have that letter the Israeli police gave you?'

'Certainly.'

'Good. I have a feeling we may need it.'

Finally the guards, armed and wearing full combat gear, waved Razak forward. A scrawny young Israeli stepped towards the car. 'Open your rear compartment and let me see your papers,' he stated in rough Arabic.

Razak pushed the boot-release button and handed over their passports.

Two soldiers paced along either side of the car, running mirrors under the chassis, then made their way to the rear to inspect the boot.

The guard crouched slightly to get a look at Barton. 'Not from here, I see.' Grimacing, he shifted his gaze back to Razak and said, 'You must be crazy going in there, especially now. What's your business?'

Presenting Barton's letter, Razak explained that the Israeli police had commissioned them to aid in the Temple Mount investigation. The guard seemed satisfied.

'Go, but be careful,' he warned. 'Past this gate, you're on your own.'

Razak nodded then pulled ahead, letting out a prolonged sigh of relief.

Fifteen minutes later, Gaza City's unimpressive skyline came into view. The concentration of buildings tightened as Razak drove through the crowded downtown streets where the bombed-out façades were lasting reminders of Israel's frequent missile attacks.

For a long while, both men remained quiet, each taking in the bleakness of it all. 'This is awful,' Barton finally said.

'Over a million people packed into a tiny parcel of land.' Razak's tone was grim. 'Horrible sanitary conditions, political instability . . .'

'The perfect recipe for discontent.'

Parking alongside the kerb, Razak paid a Palestinian boy with a round face forty Israeli shekels to watch the car. The streets were mobbed. The hot, lifeless air smelt of sewage.

'We're meeting him over there,' Razak said, motioning with his eyes to a tiny outdoor café. 'Let's go.'

THE CONTACT—a Palestinian with a sturdy frame and a bearded, smooth face—was already seated at a table, sipping mint tea from a clear glass. He called over to Razak.

Smiling, Razak greeted the man with a blessing and a handshake, then introduced the man to Barton by his first name—Taheem.

Barton smiled and extended a hand in greeting. Taheem's grin faded noticeably as he looked round before reciprocating the gesture. 'Please, sit.'

'Will it be all right if we speak in English?' Razak asked.

Taheem hesitated momentarily. 'Of course.'

'So, tell me, my friend. How are things here?'

Shaking his head, Taheem rolled his eyes. 'You'd think the Israeli pullout would have helped matters. Far from it. Funding from the UN and the West has dried up. And now, with this incident in Jerusalem . . .' His eyes shifted to somewhere off in the distance.

'I know it must be difficult.'

'I'm just happy that I have no family here,' Taheem added. 'And you? How are things?'

Razak smiled. 'Everything's fine.'

'Glad to hear that.' He called for the waiter to bring two more teas.

'As you might imagine,' Razak said in a hushed tone, 'I'm anxious to know what you've heard about the theft.'

Taheem paused while the waiter set down the two glasses for Razak and Barton, then said, 'You know about the helicopter?'

'Yes,' Razak said. 'The Israelis are still trying to find it.'

He looked surprised. 'Then you *don't* know. They've already found it.'

'What?'

Sipping his tea, Barton listened in silent astonishment, trying to ignore the neat line of bullet holes that ran along the café's cinderblock façade.

'I heard that a Palestinian fisherman caught some things in his nets three days ago. Pieces from a helicopter—seat cushions, flotation vests . . . and the head of a pilot wearing an Israeli flight helmet.'

Razak was shocked. 'But how can it be that no one knows this?'

Taheem scanned the area before answering. 'Rumour has it that the Shin Bet killed the fisherman before he spoke to anyone. But not before he had told his brother—a dear friend of mine.'

'But why was the helicopter in pieces?'

'The night of the theft, many heard it flying low over the rooftops and out to sea. Minutes later, some saw an explosion over the horizon.'

Suddenly feeling helpless, Razak knew that Taheem's story confirmed his lingering fear that both the ossuary and the helicopter were long gone. He exchanged an uneasy glance with Barton.

'There's more,' Taheem said. He leaned in closer. 'I was also told that someone inside Jerusalem coordinated the whole thing.'

'But—'

Before the words escaped Razak's mouth, Taheem's face suddenly exploded outwards, spewing blood and flesh onto the wall. Instinctively, Razak catapulted forward onto the ground, pulling Barton down beside him as Taheem's lifeless torso teetered forward onto the tabletop.

A few nearby pedestrians screamed and scurried away.

'Jesus!' Barton yelled, shaking in fear. 'What on earth was that!'

The silent shot had been so precise, Razak knew instantly. 'Sniper.'

A second round hammered into the thick wooden tabletop.

'We've got to get out of here right now.' Scrambling to remove the car key from his pocket, Razak continued, 'We'll split up and meet at the car. Run fast and low through the crowd. Go!'

Both men sprang out from the café, racing in opposite directions.

Barton did his best to avoid running into the pedestrians, feeling remorseful as he strategically kept them in the sniper's line of fire. Out of the corner of his eye, he could see Razak cutting swiftly through the crowds in the street.

The car's lights blinked as Razak remotely disengaged the door locks. Barton scrambled to open the door. Diving inside the car and pulling the door shut, he glanced over to see the young Palestinian boy holding the driver's door open as if he were a valet. A split second later, Razak weaved deftly through the traffic and spilled into the car. He thrust the key into the ignition as the boy closed the door behind him. Razak waved the clueless kid away just as the sniper managed a clean shot through the boy's temple.

Now pandemonium broke out—people running off in all directions.

Throwing the gearstick into drive, Razak slammed his foot on the accelerator. For the next few minutes, he focused on angling his way through the narrow streets, backtracking through the city towards the main highway.

Without warning, the rear of the car lurched to the right amid the deafening crunch of metal and glass as Razak and Barton were jerked sideways.

Somehow, Razak managed to regain control of the car. His head swivelled to glimpse a Fiat saloon with a mangled front end that had spun out and was manoeuvring to continue its pursuit. When he saw the man in the passenger seat leaning out the window, aiming at them with an AK-47, he yelled over at Barton, 'Get down!'

The archaeologist sank below the seat just as a string of bullets took out the car's windscreen, glass fragments showering down on him.

Razak sped through two more intersections before swinging a wide turn onto the highway, heading north. Adrenaline buzzing through him, Razak pressed the accelerator all the way to the floor. Miraculously, the car's rear end had endured the collision, though the steering wheel was pulling hard to the left. He glanced down at Barton. 'You OK?'

'Are they still behind us?'

Razak eyed the rearview mirror as more shots pinged off the rear of the car. 'Yes. But I don't think they'll be able to keep up.'

The Fiat—now belching grey smoke from its twisted grill—was quickly losing ground. Sighing with relief, Razak tried to settle his breathing.

A half-kilometre from the border crossing, the pursuers came to an abrupt stop. 'You can come up now,' he told Barton.

Barton settled back into his seat, shaking glass fragments out of his hair, as Razak wound the car through the barricades. Alarmed by the condition of the car, the guards drew their rifles as it came to a stop by the guard shelter.

Then the same young guard who had allowed them entry into Gaza stepped forward and crouched down beside Razak's blown-out window.

'That was fast,' he said smugly. 'Hope you enjoyed your stay.'

Just after five o'clock, Father Donovan entered the lab.

'Working late again, I see,' he said, eyeing the skeleton.

'We want to make sure that the Vatican gets the best value for its money,' Bersei replied. 'Would you like a quick overview of our findings?'

The priest perked up visibly. 'Yes, indeed.'

For the next fifteen minutes, the scientists gave Donovan a basic summary of the forensic study and carbon-dating results, and showed him the additional relics hidden in the ossuary's secret compartment.

Judging from the priest's reaction to the preliminary findings—ranging from genuine surprise, to tempered concern over the nature of the skeleton's signs of crucifixion—Charlotte sensed that maybe he had no advance knowledge of the ossuary's contents.

'Father Donovan,' Bersei concluded, 'this is one of the most remarkable archaeological discoveries I've ever laid eyes upon. The Vatican has a priceless relic here.'

Watching the priest closely, Charlotte saw that Donovan's expression showed that he was pleased, but even more so, relieved.

'I don't want to rush things,' the priest said, his eyes wandering once more over to the skeleton. 'But do you think you might be able to formally present your findings on Friday?'

Bersei looked over to Charlotte to see if she concurred with the idea. She nodded and Bersei turned back to Donovan. 'It will take some preparation, but we can do it,' he said.

'Very good,' Donovan said.

'If there's nothing else, Father,' Bersei said, 'I'll have to be on my way. Don't want to keep my wife waiting.'

Bersei disappeared into the break room to hang up his lab coat.

'He's quite the family man,' Charlotte whispered to Donovan.

'Oh, yes,' Donovan agreed. 'Dr Bersei is very kind . . . a gentle soul.' The priest paused for a moment and added, 'Tell me, Dr Hennesey, have you ever visited Rome before?'

'No, and I haven't even had time to venture across the river yet.'

'May I suggest a tour for you?'

'I'd love that.' She genuinely appreciated the priest's kindness.

'If you don't have plans this evening, I'd highly recommend the Night Walking Tour,' he offered. 'It begins at Piazza Navona, just across the Ponte Sant'Angelo Bridge, at six thirty. Takes about three hours. You'll get a great overview of all the major sights in the old city.'

'Sounds perfect.'

'I'll call to reserve you a place.'

An hour later Charlotte entered the expansive Piazza Navona, with its immense Italian baroque fountain at its centre—*Fontana dei Quattro Fiumi*. A group of people were already assembling around a lanky Italian man with a badge, presumably the tour guide. Charlotte waited patiently on the fringe, admiring the fountain's huge obelisk and four Bernini sculptures representing the great rivers—the Ganges, the Danube, the Nile, and the Rio de la Plata—as muscular male giants.

Moments later the tall guide came over to her, looking down at a list of confirmed attendees. 'You must be Dr Charlotte Hennesey,' he said cheerily in near-perfect English, ticking a handwritten note at the bottom of his roster. 'My name is Marco. Father Donovan called ahead for you.'

'That's right,' she replied. 'Thank you for taking me on such short notice.'

Marco led the group first on an amazing journey through the city's famous circular temple, the Pantheon, completed in AD 125 by Emperor Hadrian. There, Charlotte marvelled at its expansive inner dome that seemed to defy the rules of physics, as the sun melted through the wide oculus that hovered at its centre.

Then it was off to the junction of three roads—*tre vie*—to admire Nicola Salvi's enormous baroque Trevi Fountain with its seahorse-riding tritons guiding Neptune's shell chariot. A few blocks away came the eye-catching white marble monument that Romans compared to a colossal wedding cake plonked down in the centre of Old Rome. Inaugurated in 1925, Il Vittoriano honoured Victor Emmanuel II, the first king of a unified Italy.

By the time the tour had made its way up Capitoline Hill and through the crumbling arches and columns of the Imperial Forums, the sun was fading over the horizon and Charlotte Hennesey was completely lost in the shadows of an ancient empire.

Thursday

At 9 a.m., Barton negotiated his way past Akbar and through the blast hole into the crypt. Razak was already there, wearing neatly pressed chinos and a white shirt. 'Have you told Farouq what we discovered yesterday?'

Razak shook his head and held a finger to his lips, pointing towards Akbar. He drew Barton by the arm towards the rear of the chamber. 'I don't think he's ready for that just yet,' he whispered. Last night, he had barely slept, trying to figure out who'd sent the sniper. He could only guess that the

Shin Bet, Israel's most secret and lethal intelligence branch was looking to tie up some loose ends. Now, he feared, there was a good chance that he and Barton might share Taheem's fate. 'Remember, you mustn't tell anyone what we heard or what happened yesterday. We don't know what the consequences could be.'

Barton nodded.

Razak let go of his arm. 'So what brings us back here?'

The archaeologist collected his thoughts. 'As I mentioned yesterday, I've been giving the concept of a crypt considerable thought. There are certain facts that simply don't add up.' Barton's eyes roved the walls. 'I have been thinking about Joseph of Arimathea—his status, power and money. I'm troubled that this crypt lacks many of the features I'd have expected to see in the tomb of a wealthy family. There are no ornate carvings, no pilasters, frescoes or mosaics. Nothing.'

Razak inclined his head, trying to remain patient. To a Muslim it wasn't striking. 'Perhaps this Joseph was a man of humility?'

'Maybe. But remember how I explained to you that in those days the body was allowed to decompose for twelve months before being placed in the ossuary? You'd expect to see at least one small niche called a *loculus*—a small tunnel about two metres deep—where the body would have been laid out.'

Razak eyed the walls. 'I don't see one.'

'Precisely,' Barton agreed, motioning to the ossuaries. 'And I have a feeling that this family all died at once.'

Razak's brow furrowed. 'How can you tell?'

'These remaining skeletons seem like they came out of a family photo.' He turned towards the nine ossuaries. 'An old father, a slightly younger mother, and none of the children making it past their late twenties. One would expect at least some of the children to reach their later years.'

'That is odd.'

'Furthermore,' Barton's eyes canvassed the space, 'do you see any sign of an entrance?'

Razak scanned the bedrock on all but one side. 'Looks like the only way in was the opening covered by the stone wall.' He pointed to the blast hole.

Barton nodded. 'Exactly. And look at this.' Moving towards the blast hole, he motioned Razak to follow. 'See?' Barton spread his hands, indicating the depth of the wall. 'This wall's about half a metre thick. But look here. See how these stones'—he tapped the side facing them—'are the same as those used to construct the Marwani Mosque. Coincidence? Perhaps not.'

Razak was getting it. He studied the space that the stone wall had filled. 'What do you think this means?'

'It strongly suggests that our thieves weren't the first intruders here. It seems clear to me that this room wasn't designed to be a crypt.'

The Muslim stared at him blankly.

'This room is a *vault* specifically built for concealment and security,' Barton explained. 'Somehow it was built in conjunction with Solomon's Stables. And I think I know who was responsible.'

Razak mulled over the history of this place, in particular the notion that the area now converted to the Marwani Mosque was once a horse stable, built by . . . his face slackened. 'The Knights Templar?'

Barton smiled and shook his head knowingly. 'Correct! It's a long shot, but most archaeologists credit them with constructing Solomon's Stables.'

The Poor Knights of Christ and the Temple of Solomon had been founded in 1118 CE, after the first Christian Crusade. The Knights Templar were an order of militant, monastic mercenaries commissioned by the papacy to protect the reclaimed kingdom of Jerusalem from neighbouring Muslim tribes, ensuring safe passage for pilgrims. They had remained in control of the Temple Mount until slaughtered by a Muslim force led by Saladin in the twelfth century.

'These ossuaries were transferred here from another site where the proper rituals would have taken place initially. If we go with the theory that this is a vault,' Barton continued, 'it would suggest the Templar Knights might have constructed it to protect the ossuaries.'

'Or treasure,' Razak responded swiftly. 'Let's not forget that possibility.'

'True, the Templars amassed a fortune, mostly plundered. Eventually, they became bankers. Prior to embarking on their journey to the Holy Land, European pilgrims would deposit money with a local Templar lodge where they'd be given an encrypted depository note. Upon their arrival, they'd exchange the note for local currency.'

'Then how can you be so sure this vault didn't contain their loot?'

'We'll never know for sure,' Barton admitted. 'But it seems highly unlikely they'd seal away assets so permanently.' He ambled over to the ossuaries again, scrutinising them, searching for an explanation. 'If the ossuaries were transferred here to be locked away, then where were they originally found?' he muttered quietly, thinking aloud.

'This Joseph of Arimathea.' Razak spread his hands. 'I'm assuming he was from somewhere called Arimathea—correct?'

Barton nodded. 'That's what the Scriptures imply.'

'Then perhaps the original crypt was there, in Joseph's own land?'

'Perhaps,' Barton replied unenthusiastically. 'The problem is that no one knows what place Arimathea really referred to. Some think it was a Judean hill town. But that's all conjecture.'

'Assuming you're on the right track, how do you suppose the thieves found this place?' Visualising Taheem's horrid, blown-out face, Razak felt an urgent need to link this to something the authorities would find useful— something that could help to bring closure to their investigation.

Barton let out a long breath and ran his fingers through his hair. 'The only thing I can think of is that the thief got hold of an ancient text that identifies this burial spot.'

'But who could possess something like that?'

'I'm not sure. Sometimes these ancient scrolls or books have been lying around in plain sight, untranslated, in museum rooms—for decades. Maybe some fanatical Christian museum employee,' he said half-heartedly.

Razak looked sceptical.

'And you've seen nothing in the antiquities markets yet for the ossuary?'

Barton shook his head. 'I checked again this morning. Nothing.'

CHAPTER 8

Shortly after 9 a.m., Father Patrick Donovan buzzed the lab intercom, announcing a call for Charlotte from the United States.

She made her way to the phone, sliding the mask off her face. 'Charlotte Hennesey speaking.'

'It's me, Evan.'

Hearing his voice come through the small speaker, her stomach fluttered. 'Hi, Evan. What time is it there?'

'Very early, or very late, depending on how you want to look at it. Anyway, I just finished running a scan on your sample.'

Something in his voice didn't sound right. She waited for him to continue.

'I began with a simple spectral karyotype to get a preliminary idea of the DNA's quality. You know . . . basic plot of chromosome pairs. That's when I noticed something very odd.'

'What is it? Is something wrong?'

'Yes, Charlotte. The result was forty-eight XY.'

In a spectral karyotype, DNA strands called chromosomes are marked with fluorescent die and colour-sorted into pairs to detect genetic aberrations. Since every human inherits twenty-two chromosomes from each parent, an X sex chromosome from the mother, and an additional sex chromosome from the father, a typical result would be forty-six XX for females and forty-six XY for males.

Forty-*eight* XY? Hennesey twisted an earring between thumb and forefinger, trying to let that one sink in. The good news was that the gender was definitely male. But Aldrich was suggesting that an extra pair of non-sex chromosomes, or 'autosomes', had appeared.

'We have a mutation here.'

'What kind?' She kept her voice low so as not to draw Bersei's attention.

'Not sure yet. Got to adjust the gene scanner to handle the additional strands. But I've emailed basic coding for the genetic profile to you.'

'Great. That'll give me a good head start.'

'How much longer do you think you'll be in Rome?'

'I don't know. Maybe a few more days. I might want to take a couple more just to explore the city. It's wonderful here.'

'Has the Vatican briefed you fully about the work?'

'Yes, but we're being told everything here is in strictest confidence. I had to sign a letter of confidentiality.'

'That's OK—I just don't want BMS involved in anything shady.'

What had he discovered that made him so nervous? she wondered. 'Did you happen to run the genetic profile to determine ethnicity?'

There was a brief silence. 'Actually, I did. That's the other weird thing. I found nothing. No matches.'

'But that's impossible. Did you include Middle Eastern profiles?'

'Yeah.'

'How about Jewish profiles?'

'Already checked it. Nothing there.'

'Could it have something to do with the anomaly you found?'

'I'd say so. I'll let you know what I find. Anything else?'

She hesitated, huddling closer to the wall. 'I miss you,' she finally whispered. 'And I'm really sorry that I didn't leave on a better note. I just . . . I'd like to talk to you when I get back. There's some stuff you need to know.'

At first, he didn't respond. 'I'd like that.'

'I'll see you soon. Don't forget me.'

'Impossible,' he said.

Bersei appeared beside her as she returned the phone to the cradle. 'Everything all right?'

'Seems so,' she said, flashing a smile. 'I got the DNA profile from the lab. We have the missing information we need.'

Bersei watched over her shoulder as Charlotte brought up the web browser and accessed her email account. Within seconds, she'd retrieved Aldrich's data file, and opened the spreadsheet for Bersei to inspect.

He scrolled through the data.

'How does it look?'

'Incredibly specific. Looks like I can plug the data right into the program,' he said as he formatted the file for import, then clicked to update the profile.

After a few agonising seconds, the enhanced reconstruction flashed back onto the monitor.

IT WASN'T WHAT either scientist expected. Both stared in amazement at the screen. The new data had transformed the statue-like image of the skeletal scans into a complete 3-D human apparition.

Astonished at the final result, Bersei's hand was covering his mouth. 'What would you say is his ethnic origin?'

Charlotte shrugged. It looked like maybe Aldrich had been correct after all. 'I'm not sure he has one.' Her words sounded totally implausible.

Blending dark and light, the assigned skin pigmentation added an eerily lifelike quality, defining muscles and highlighting features.

Giovanni zoomed in on the face.

Though unmistakably masculine, the image exuded a subtle androgyny. With their hypnotic aquamarine irises, the eyes were wide, tapering slightly upwards in the corners beneath slender eyebrows. The long nose broadened slightly above full, mocha-coloured lips. Blackish-brown wisps formed a thick hairline that pinched in hard corners at the temples. The facial hair was similarly coloured and thick, mostly evident along the angular jaw line.

'Quite a handsome specimen,' Bersei said in a very clinical tone.

'I'd say he's perfect,' Charlotte replied. 'I don't mean in a male model sort of way . . . but he's unlike anyone I've ever seen.' And nothing about the image suggested a genetic defect, unless perfection was considered a flaw. Now she wondered what Aldrich's prototype scanner had detected. Could it have malfunctioned?

Tilting his head sideways, Bersei said, 'If you took all the typical ethnic characteristics of humanity and put them in a blender, this would probably be the end result. Its absolutely fascinating.'

'Now what?'

Bersei looked haunted, as if the image was almost torturing him. 'I'm really not sure. We've performed a full forensic examination'—he began counting off with his fingers—'carbon dating, a complete genetic profile. The only major item left is the symbol on the ossuary.'

'Well, if you want to look into that,' Charlotte suggested, 'I can begin preparing our preliminary presentation for Father Donovan.'

'That sounds like a plan. Who knows, maybe that symbol has something to tell us about this guy.'

Bersei returned to his workstation and turned on the digital camera. Humming softly to himself, he proceeded to snap several close-ups of the ossuary's single relief, uploading the images onto the computer terminal.

Marvelling at the quality of the engraver's work, he ran his finger over the raised symbol carved onto the ossuary's side. From the outset, this image had perplexed him. The ossuary was clearly of Jewish origin, yet the dolphin and the trident were primarily pagan symbols.

Back at the computer, he brought up the web browser. He began with simple search criteria: *trident*. Almost instantly, a flood of hits came back at him. He began clicking through the most relevant ones.

The trident itself had many meanings. Hindus called it the *trishul*, or 'the sacred three', symbolising creation, preservation and destruction. In the Middle East, it was associated with lightning. Its alter ego, the pitchfork, later found its way into Christian art to symbolise the devil.

The dolphin was equally mysterious. In ancient times, these intelligent mammals were revered for their devotion to saving the lives of shipwrecked sailors. Romans also used dolphins to signify the journey souls would take far to the ends of the sea to their final resting place on the Blessed Isles.

The dolphin and trident seemed to first appear together in Greek mythology, both symbolising the power of Neptune, the sea god. His trident was a gift from the one-eyed titans, the Cyclopes. When the god was angered, he'd pound the ocean floor with it to stir the waters, causing storms.

Bersei was certain there had to be more that he was missing.

Another hit came back, linking to ancient coins minted by Pompey, a Roman general in the first century BC. On the front of the coin was an image of the general's head flanked on both sides by a dolphin and a trident.

Bersei recalled that, early in his career, he had invaded Jerusalem.

He leaned forward.

After his siege of Jerusalem in 64 BC, Pompey had ordered the crucifixion of thousands of Jewish zealots—all in a single day.

Crucifixion. Jerusalem.

Could this be the connection? But Bersei still wasn't satisfied. He vaguely recalled seeing this exact depiction somewhere else.

The hunt continued. Using various search phrases, like 'dolphin round trident', he finally found a clear hit. Clicking the link, he was astounded when the exact image on the ossuary filled the screen.

'Now we're getting somewhere,' he muttered. Scrolling down, he read the text that accompanied the image.

The words hit him like a stone. He read it again, dumbfounded. 'Charlotte,' he called out. 'You have to see this.'

Two seconds later, she was at his side. 'What is it?'

Bersei pointed at the computer screen. 'The meaning behind the relief on the ossuary.' His voice was quiet as he slumped back in his chair.

Charlotte read the text aloud: 'Adopted by early Christians, the dolphin intertwined around the trident is a portrayal of . . .'

The low drone of the ventilation system became suddenly pronounced.

'. . . Christ's crucifixion.' Her voice trembled as she uttered the words, which seemed to hang in the air like vapour.

It took Charlotte a moment until the full impact hit her. 'Oh my God.' A vice tightened in her stomach and she had to look away.

'I should have known.' Bersei's strained voice sounded tormented, weak. 'The dolphin shuttles spirits to the afterlife. The trident, the sacred three, representing the Trinity.'

'No way. This isn't right.' She looked down at him.

'I *know* the ossuary's patina is genuine,' Bersei protested, 'including the residue covering this relief. The mineral content could only have come from one place—Israel. And the evidence we saw on the bones indicates scourging and crucifixion. We even have the nails and pieces of wood.' He threw his hands up in surrender. 'Just how much more obvious could all this be?'

Her mind went momentarily blank. 'If this is really the body of . . . Jesus Christ'—it almost hurt for her to say it—'how profound this is.' Charlotte pictured the crucifix hanging over her bed. 'But it *can't* be. Everyone knows the crucifixion story. The Bible describes it in minute detail and it doesn't agree with this.' She strode briskly to the workstation.

'What are you doing?' Bersei was out of his chair.

'Here. See for yourself.' She jabbed a shaking finger at the brow of the skeleton's skull. 'Do you see any evidence of thorns?'

Scrutinising the skull intently, Giovanni failed to detect even minute scratches. 'But surely thorns could not inflict damage on the bone itself?'

Moving round the side of the workstation, Charlotte was now down by the legs. 'What about this? Broken knees?' She pointed at them. 'I don't remember these being mentioned in the Bible. Wasn't it a spear in Jesus' side that finished him off?' She turned to the anthropologist and studied his face intently. 'Giovanni, you don't *really* think these are the remains of Jesus Christ, do you?'

He ran his fingers through his hair and sighed. 'There's always the possibility that this symbol was only meant to honour Christ,' he offered. 'This man,' he pointed to the skeleton, 'could merely have been some early Christian, a martyr perhaps.' He shrugged. 'But you saw the genetic profile. It's not like any man we've ever seen. I'd have to say that I'm pretty certain about this.'

'But it's only a symbol,' she protested. 'How can you be sure?'

Bersei was taken aback by the American's passionate denial. He wished he could feel as strongly. 'Come with me.' He motioned for her to follow.

'Where are we going?' She called after the Italian, pacing behind him into the corridor.

'I'll explain in a minute. You'll see.'

Phoenix, Arizona

Evan Aldrich threaded his way past the workstations heaped with scientific gadgetry, making for the glass-panelled enclosure to the rear of BMS's main laboratory.

Once inside, he closed the door, reached into his lab coat and removed a sealed glass vial, which he set down next to a high-powered microscope. He pulled on a pair of latex gloves.

There was a brief knock and the door opened.

'Morning, Evan. What's happening?'

Glancing over, he found Lydia Campbell, his managing technician for genetic research, poking her head round the doorframe. Aldrich's hand reflexively moved to cover the vial. 'Got some samples I need to have another look at.'

'Well, you know where I am if you need anything. Coffee?'

He shook his head with a smile and the door closed behind her.

An hour later, he slipped the vial—now filled with a clear serum—back into his pocket. Feeling an overwhelming urgency to tell Charlotte what he'd found, he reached for the phone . . . but pulled back. This was far too astounding for an open phone line or an unencrypted email.

Aldrich headed directly for his office and plonked himself down in front of his computer. Logging onto his Continental Airlines frequent-flier account page, he booked a first-class ticket on the next flight to Rome.

THE KEEPER OF THE TEMPLE MOUNT had just hung up his phone in utter disbelief, his hands shaking.

The caller had been a voice from the past—a dark past that still haunted Farouq. The last time he'd heard that unmistakable baritone was just past 6 p.m. on November 11, 1995. That was the day the Shin Bet had abducted him on a side street in Gaza, pulling him into the back of a van. They had bound his limbs and slipped a black hood over his head.

As the van sped off, the interrogation began, carried out by the man who now held the second highest position in the IDF power structure. Back then the ambitious Israeli was hunting down the Engineer—a Palestinian named Yahya Ayyash who was recruiting suicide bombers to launch attacks on Israeli civilians. One of their prime suspects was Farouq, who had alleged ties to the Engineer's primary supporter—Hamas.

By the time he'd been tossed from the van in a desolate location not far from the Israeli border, Farouq had suffered three broken ribs, four fractured fingers, cigarette burns to the chest, and seven missing teeth.

But he smiled, blood oozing through his broken mouth, knowing that he had not uttered one word about the whereabouts of the Engineer. No Israeli would ever break him.

He also took great pleasure in knowing that the blood on his face was not only his own. Even hooded and bound he had managed to bite Teleksen's hand, clamping his teeth into the despicable Israeli flesh until nerves severed and bones cracked. The Israeli had whimpered like a dog.

Shortly after, the Engineer was assassinated by a rigged explosive cellphone, and Ari Teleksen was promoted to *Aluf*—major general. Farouq had seen him a few times since then—news reports mostly—always identifiable by the hand the Keeper had disfigured that night long ago in Gaza.

Now Teleksen had the audacity to call with what initially seemed to be a request for a favour. But after a lengthy explanation, it had become clear that the request would benefit Farouq's cause equally well.

'Akbar?' Farouq called out to the corridor.

A moment later, the hulking bodyguard appeared in the doorway.

Farouq's eyes briefly sized him up. 'You're a strong boy. I need you to do something for me.'

THE TWO SCIENTISTS rode the elevator up one level and the doors opened into the main gallery that stood above the lab—the Vatican Museum's Pio Christian Gallery.

As they exited the elevator, Bersei quietly explained, 'You see, Charlotte, for three centuries after Jesus' death, early Christians did not portray his image. However, archaeological evidence indicates they used other familiar images to depict Jesus.'

Bersei waved a hand at massive marble reliefs mounted on the gallery walls. 'Those are relics from the early fourth century, a time when Emperor Diocletian began his campaign of persecution—burning churches and killing Christians who wouldn't denounce their faith. It's also a time when early Christians secretly convened in the catacombs outside Rome to pray among the dead martyrs and saints laid to rest there.'

They had stopped in front of a three-foot-high marble statue. 'Here we are.' Bersei turned to her. 'Do you know what this image portrays?'

Looking at it, she saw a young man with long curled hair, dressed in a tunic. A lamb was slung over his shoulders and he was holding its legs with both hands. Hanging at his side was a pouch containing a lyre.

'Looks like a shepherd.'

'Not bad. It's actually called "The Good Shepherd". It was found in the catacombs. This is how early Christians depicted Jesus.'

Charlotte gave the statue another once-over. 'You're kidding me.' The shepherd was boyish, its design Greco-Roman—not biblical.

'Keep in mind that this representation wasn't intended to resemble Jesus. It was an attempt to embody the ideal he represented—the protector, the shepherd.'

'Just like the dolphin and the trident represent salvation and divinity.' Now she knew why he had brought her up here.

'Exactly.'

'Why though? Why didn't they worship icons or the crucifix?'

'First off, it would've sent a clear message to the Romans that they were indeed Christians. Not wise in an era of systematic persecution. And second, early Christians didn't embrace the notion of iconography. In fact Peter forbade such things. Images of the crucifix didn't exist until Constantine came along.'

'That guy again.'

'Sure. He's the forefather of the modern faith. Constantine changed all the rules when he came to power in the fourth century. That's also when Christ was transformed into a true cult hero—a divine being. Crucifixes sprouted up, grand cathedrals built and the Bible formally compiled.'

'It's amazing, I wasn't really taught anything about Constantine—and I went to a Catholic high school!'

Bersei took a deep breath. 'In AD 312, the Roman Empire was split between two factions of emperors—Constantine in the west and his ally Licinius in the east, versus Maximinus and Maxentius. Constantine had decided that the sun god, Sol Invictus, had pre-ordained him to be the sole ruler of the empire, so with an army made up of an obscure group known as Christians, he battled his way through northern Italy to within ten miles of Rome. The armies clashed in a bloody battle and miraculously Constantine emerged victorious.

'Owing a debt to his soldiers, perhaps even inspired by the power and persuasion of their passionate faith, Constantine embraced their religion at the national level. However, to appease the pagan masses who had yet to assimilate into the new religion, Constantine craftily blended many pagan concepts into early Christianity.'

'Such as?'

Bersei laced his fingers together, eyes scanning the gallery. 'The solar halo for instance. Constantine had coins minted in 315 depicting Sol Invictus, the sun god, on them—a *solar-haloed* Sol Invictus in a flowing robe that looks remarkably similar to later Jesus iconography.'

'Interesting.'

'Constantine also cleverly coincided the celebration of Christ's birth with the December 25th pagan winter solstice celebration of Sol Invictus's birthday. Of course, I think you won't be surprised when you hear that the Christian day of worship, once celebrated on Saturday, the Jewish Sabbath, was also moved to a more special day of the week.'

'*Sun*day.'

He nodded. 'Known in Constantine's time as *dies Solis*.' His expression clouded. 'Then something even more profound emerges during Constantine's reign. The emphasis on Jesus' physical rather than spiritual resurrection.'

'What do you mean?'

'The early Greek Gospels used wording that suggested Christ's body wasn't necessarily reanimated, but transformed.'

'But in the Bible, Jesus walked out of the tomb and appeared to the disciples after his death, didn't he?' All those years of Catechism and Catholic school had drilled this stuff into her head.

'Sure. Jesus disappeared from the tomb,' he readily agreed. Then a knowing grin swept across Bersei's face. 'Though none of the Gospels say *how*. In some accounts Jesus had the ability to walk through walls and materialise from out of nowhere. Those aren't attributes associated with a reanimated physical body.'

'Then why does the Church emphasise his physical death and physical resurrection?'

He smiled. 'My guess goes something like this. Egypt, particularly Alexandria, was a very influential cultural centre in the Roman Empire. There, cults worshipped Osiris, the god of the underworld, who was horribly murdered by a rival god named Seth—cut to pieces in fact. Osiris' wife collected his body parts and returned them to the temple and performed rituals so that three days later, the god resurrected.'

'Sounds a lot like Easter,' she concurred. 'Are you suggesting the Gospels were altered?'

An older couple were dawdling close by, intrigued by the two people in white lab coats. Bersei drew closer to Charlotte. 'Largely untouched, but perhaps reinterpreted in key areas,' he said 'You have to understand that if what we're looking at downstairs is the physical body of Christ, it doesn't contradict the original Gospels. But it certainly creates a big problem for a Church that's taken some liberties in its scriptural interpretations.'

'I'd say,' she readily agreed. 'What do you think Christians would think if our findings were made public?'

'They'd think what they want to think. Just like you and me The evidence is remarkable, but inconsistent. So the faithful would remain faithful, like they have through other controversies. Don't get me wrong, it would certainly be an enormous dilemma for Christianity. And a public relations nightmare once the press got hold of it.'

'Any possibility this could be a fake?'

Bersei exhaled slowly. 'It would have to be one hell of a hoax, but you never know.'

CHAPTER 9

By the time Graham Barton returned to his rented flat in Jabotinsky Street in modern Jerusalem, it was already eight thirty in the evening. After all that had happened today, he was looking forward to a full glass of cabernet sauvignon and a long night's rest.

If the rising discontent stemming from the Temple Mount theft was not soon remedied he knew that the violence would unravel this city. Barton felt obligated to come up with real answers that might help the situation. But after the harrowing experience he and Razak had endured in Gaza, he was wondering if the Israelis knew more than they were letting on. He was also concerned that the gunmen might still be anxious to find him and Razak. Who were they working for? he wondered.

As he inserted his key into the front-door lock, he barely registered three figures coming up the stairwell. He leaned back to get a better view. That's when Topol and two burly, uniformed officers rounded the corner.

Topol gave him a cursory nod. 'Good evening, Mr Barton.'

A sense of foreboding swept over the Englishman. He eyed the policemen's holstered handguns. 'Good evening to you, Commander.'

'I'm glad you're here.' Topol's dark eyes were hard, unblinking. 'It will make our visit more meaningful.'

Heart drumming in his chest, Barton replied, 'Why would that be?'

'Please, let's talk inside.' The major general motioned to the door.

Hesitantly, Barton made his way into the apartment and switched on the lights. The policemen crowded in behind him.

Topol got right to the point. 'I've been asked to search your residence.'

Barton was stupefied. 'What? Why would you want to do that?'

'I'd rather not get into that just yet. I have secured proper authorisation.' He flashed an official-looking document and handed it to Barton. 'You can read this while we proceed.' Topol nodded to the two officers and straight away they disappeared into the next room.

'Can I please have everything from your pockets?'

'What is this? Am I am being arrested?'

'For now, we're just talking,' Topol explained. 'If you'd feel more comfortable at the station we can go there.'

Barton nodded compliantly.

'Your pockets, please,' Topol insisted, pointing to the table.

One way or another, the major would have his way, Barton realised. Trying not to look alarmed, he began emptying the contents of his pockets onto the table: a wallet, UK passport, keys to the Wohl, bus tickets.

'I have received a very disturbing phone call from the Waqf. It seems some things have gone missing,' Topol said.

The sounds coming from the rear of the apartment were less than subtle—drawers being opened, furniture being moved around.

Barton dipped into his breast pocket and withdrew the bronze cylinder, certain it would ignite the policeman's curiosity. Lastly came the Ziploc containing the vellum and its accompanying folded transcription. Setting it down on the table, he tried to gauge Topol's expression.

Eyebrows raised, the major eyed the vellum's strange text. 'Since the inception of this investigation, I've had suspicions that an insider could have helped organise this theft. The head of the Waqf has similar concerns.'

Barton's shoulders sank. 'I'm not sure what you're implying.'

'The theft required extremely sophisticated movements of weapons and explosives,' the policeman sneered. 'Not to mention skilled manpower. Only someone with high-level clearance could have handled such transactions. Someone well-versed in the Temple Mount's history. Someone who knew what treasure lay in the vault. The Waqf suggests that person is you.'

Barton felt suffocated. 'You must be joking.'

'An Israeli helicopter and two pilots are still missing . . .'

Barton saw the major's eyes shift down when he said this. Could he have known about the meeting in Gaza? Did he know about the fisherman and the recovered debris from the Black Hawk?

'Sources indicate these pilots may have been involved in the theft . . .' Topol elaborated. 'Perhaps someone on the inside gave them incentives.'

'You know there's no way I'm involved in this.'

The major was stone-faced, recalling yesterday's late-night discussion with Teleksen. They had agreed a quick solution to this affair was essential. 'I've been told you've made quite a name for yourself procuring rare antiquities for European clients.'

'Museums,' the archaeologist clarified.

'Given the nature of your work with the IAA, you've also been given high-level clearance in the Old City. You've been moving equipment in and out at will . . . many times without inspection.'

'How could I have got explosives into the city?' Graham Barton's tone was stronger now. 'There are detectors all over the place.'

'Apparently quite easily. Our chemists analysed the residue of the plastic explosive. Seems it was missing the chemical marker that would allow it to be detected—dimethyl dinitrobutane. You see, Mr Barton . . . those explosives were military grade. Perhaps provided to you by our missing pilots.'

One of the officers stormed into the room and momentarily broke the tension. He was hauling something in a large plastic sheath.

Barton eyed the package. What the hell was in the bag?

Topol removed the plastic and read out the model name on the motor housing—Flex BHI 822 VR. Topol ran his finger over the long hollow drum attached to its chuck. 'A coring drill. This part of your toolbox?'

Shortly following the theft, Topol's forensic crime team had found the drill abandoned on the floor. No prints. That morning, Topol had ensured all documentation concerning it had been struck from records.

The archaeologist's complexion turned grey. 'I've never seen that thing before in my life,' he said weakly. Could this really be happening?

'And what do you have here?' Topol leaned over and snatched the vellum off the table. 'Seems to be an ancient document.' He unfolded the sheet of paper containing the photocopy and accompanying transcription. 'I'm no biblical scholar, Mr Barton, but this looks to me like something that implies a burial chamber hidden beneath Mount Moriah. And if I'm not mistaken, wasn't Joseph of Arimathea somehow connected to Jesus Christ and legends about the Holy Grail—a priceless relic for those who believe?'

There was a sarcastic tone to Topol's voice that only reaffirmed his suspicion that, somehow, he already knew about the scroll. Perspiration started to bead on Barton's forehead. The walls were closing in.

'You were given access to the crime scene and in return you tampered with key evidence—scratching inscriptions from the wall, removing the remaining ossuaries.'

'What?' Barton was aghast. 'Are you completely out of your mind?'

'You heard me. The Waqf insists that the remaining nine ossuaries have mysteriously vanished. It seems that the thief is still among us.'

That the ossuaries had suddenly vanished was truly disturbing, but something about the major's first accusation struck even harder. 'Scratching inscriptions from the wall? What does that mean?'

From his jacket, Topol produced a picture and handed it to Barton. 'That picture was taken by my forensic team a day before you arrived.'

Stunned, Barton saw that the image was of the stone tablet affixed to the crypt wall. Nine names were listed . . . and one perfectly clear relief depicting a dolphin intertwined round a trident. He had seen this symbol before, and knew its origin well. Its implications shook him to the core.

Friday

Opening the front door of his townhouse overlooking Villa Borghese's manicured park, a robed and barefoot Giovanni Bersei retrieved the morning's delivery of *Il Messaggero* from the front step. The sun was barely glowing a deep blue above the neighbouring rooftops, and the lamp posts lining the empty street were still casting a warm glow. This was his favourite time of the day.

Turning to go back inside, he paused to glance over at the iron railing that hung loosely from its mount on his home's stucco façade. Carmela had been after him for three weeks to fix it. Today would be the day the job would get done, he vowed. Closing the door, he went directly to the kitchen.

The coffee pot, dutifully set on a timer, was already full. He poured himself some coffee and sat for a long moment enjoying the silence. Cupping the heavy porcelain mug in his hands, he slowly sipped the hot liquid, savouring the deep, rich flavour.

Last night, he hadn't slept well at all, his mind endlessly churning over the ossuary, the skeleton and the symbol that accompanied the relics. The mere possibility that he had touched the physical remains of Jesus Christ had left him feeling ashamed and vulnerable. Bersei was a practising Catholic. He went to church each Sunday and prayed often. And this morning, he was going to be asked by the Vatican to explain his findings. How could anyone explain what he had witnessed over the past days?

Scratching the grey stubble on his chin, he put on his reading glasses and began scanning the newspaper's front page. A headline on the bottom of the front page read: MUSLIMS AND JEWS ENRAGED OVER RUMOURED THEFT AT TEMPLE MOUNT. He ignored it, flipping directly to the funnies. Then, almost as an afterthought, he turned back to the front page.

Though articles sensationalising the political problems in the Holy Land were regular media fodder, these past few days he'd noticed that they had dominated the headlines even more than usual. The piece's accompanying photo showed Israeli soldiers and police trying to hold back violent protestors just outside the famous Wailing Wall.

He read the report.

Following Friday's violence at Jerusalem's Temple Mount, Islamic officials are pressuring the Israeli government to release details concerning the mysterious explosion that inflicted serious damage to the site. Resident Jews are demanding answers as to why thirteen Israeli Defense Force soldiers were killed during a firefight that erupted shortly after the explosion. Many have criticised Israeli officials for ignoring rumours that the incident involved religious artefacts stolen from the site.

'Religious artefacts?' he muttered aloud.

'What, love?' Carmela emerged from the doorway. She bent to kiss him on the head before making her way to the cupboard for a mug, her fuzzy pink slippers scuffing along the tiled floor.

'Probably nothing. Just reading about all this turmoil in Israel.'

'They'll never get along,' she said, pouring coffee into her favourite mug. 'They all just want to kill one another.'

He directed his attention back to the newspaper. The article went on to say that efforts towards a more formal and lasting peace accord between Israelis and Palestinians had once again been tabled.

'Will you be home early tonight?'

'Should be,' he said, preoccupied.

Carmela pushed down on the newspaper to get his attention. 'Then maybe you can find some time to fix that railing.'

Grinning, Bersei said, 'I'll see what I can do.'

'I'm going up to take a shower.' Sipping her coffee, she shuffled away.

Bersei turned the page to where the article continued . . . and felt like he had been punched in the gut. Staring up at him was a photofit rendition of a man who looked all too familiar. The caption read: *The suspect is said to be a Caucasian male, approximately 180 centimetres tall and 88 kilos. Authorities state he is travelling under the assumed identity of Daniel Marrone and are looking for any information concerning his whereabouts.*

He collapsed back into his chair.

The only possible explanation could be that the Vatican was somehow involved in this. But that was *impossible* . . . Or was it?

Bersei tried to reconcile the timing of the events over the past few days. This theft in Jerusalem had occurred last Friday. A week ago. Both he and Charlotte had arrived in Vatican City shortly afterwards. She'd flown into Rome on Sunday afternoon. He'd arrived on Monday morning, just before Father Donovan and Salvatore Conte returned with the mysterious crate.

Of course. Recalling the woven impressions left on the ossuary's patina, he no longer suspected a careless extraction, but a *rushed* one. A theft?

He remembered Father Donovan's expression when he opened the crate—anxiety . . . and something else playing in his eyes. The crate's Eurostar shipping label was still imprinted into his brain. Bari, the vibrant tourist spot on Italy's east coast faced the Adriatic with direct sea routes to the Mediterranean . . . and Israel. A boat cruising at twenty knots—just over thirty-seven kilometres an hour—would take perhaps two days. Allowing for two and a half days at sea and another half-day traversing Italy, the shipment fitted comfortably into the time frame.

He went back to the news article. Thirteen Israeli soldiers killed. The thieves had been sophisticated and no meaningful clues had been found.

Was the Vatican *really* capable of pulling off an operation like that? It didn't make sense. Certainly Father Donovan—*a cleric for Christ's sake!*—wasn't capable of such a thing.

But Salvatore Conte . . . He eyed the photofit and felt nothing but fear.

Bersei considered a second theory. Maybe the Vatican had bought the ossuary from whoever stole it and had been unwittingly caught up in the incident? One thing was certain: somehow the relics sitting in the Vatican basement had a very questionable provenance.

He wrestled with how to deal with all this. Should he consult with Charlotte? Or should he go to the authorities?

Setting the paper down, Giovanni went over to the phone and asked the operator to connect him to the local substation for the *Carabinieri*—Italy's military police force. A young male voice picked up the call and when Giovanni requested to speak to the duty detective the young man informed him that Detective Perardi wasn't expected in until nine thirty.

'Can I have his voicemail , please?' Giovanni requested in Italian.

He left a brief message, requesting a meeting later in the morning to discuss a possible Roman link to the theft in Jerusalem, then hurried upstairs to put on his clothes. He would need to act quickly.

PARKING HIS VESPA in the staff car park for the Vatican Museum, Giovanni quickly made his way through the rear service entrance to the lab, using his keycard to unlock the door. Looking over his shoulder to check that the basement corridor was still clear, he ducked inside and went directly to the workstation.

The spikes and coins sat on the tray. Beside them lay the last of the ossuary's mysteries—the scroll cylinder. There was something about it that stirred him. If his foreboding about all of this was correct, there'd be no future opportunity to read it.

He picked up the cylinder and removed the unsealed cap. Then with a pounding heart he teased out the scroll. Glancing quickly round the room, he swore he felt invisible eyes boring into him.

Delicately smoothing out the calfskin, Bersei could immediately see that it had been magnificently preserved. There were countless possibilities of what this document might contain.

His fingers were shaking uncontrollably as he held it up.

Studying the neat text intently, he saw that it was Koine Greek, the unofficial *lingua franca* of the Roman Empire until the fourth century. Below the text was a detailed drawing that looked remarkably familiar.

As he read the ancient message—clear and brief—his tension began to subside and for a moment, he sat there in silence. Refocusing his attention on the accompanying drawing his brow tightened. Again he felt as though he'd seen this imagery before. But where? Think. *Think*.

That's when it hit him. Bersei's face blanched. *Of course*!

He had definitely seen this image before, and the place it was meant to depict was only a few kilometres away on the outskirts of Rome, deep beneath the city. Instantly he knew that he would need to go there in order to substantiate his claim against the Vatican. But he needed information that could be used by the *Carabinieri* to investigate the case.

Scrambling over to the photocopier that sat in the corner of the room, he flattened the scroll onto the glass, closed the lid and made a copy. Returning the scroll to the cylinder, he placed it beside the other relics. Then he folded the copy and stuck it in his pocket.

Nerves ablaze, Bersei linked his laptop to the main computer terminal and began copying files onto its hard drive—the skeleton's complete profile, pictures of the ossuary and its accompanying relics, carbon-dating results—everything. When the last file had finished copying, he folded the laptop and packed it into its carrying bag.

'Hey, Giovanni,' a familiar voice called over to him.

He spun around. Charlotte. He hadn't even heard her come in.

Walking past him, she noticed that he looked awful. 'Everything OK?'

He didn't know what say. 'You're here early.'

'I didn't sleep well. Are you going somewhere?'

'I have an appointment I need to go to.'

'Oh.' She looked at her watch. 'You'll be back for the meeting, right?'

He slung the bag over his shoulder, avoiding her eyes. 'I'm not sure, actually. Something important has come up.'

'Something's wrong, Giovanni. Tell me what it is.'

'Not here,' he said. 'Walk out with me and I'll explain.'

Bersei opened the main door and poked his head out into the corridor. Everything was clear. He motioned her to follow.

Quietly, they slipped outside, easing the door closed behind them.

IN THE MAKESHIFT surveillance room, Salvatore Conte snatched the phone from its console.

Santelli answered on the second ring and Conte could tell by his groggy voice that he'd woken the old man. 'We have a real problem down here.'

The cardinal knew what was coming. 'Have they found out?'

'Just Bersei. And right now he's on his way out the door with copies of everything on his way to the *Carabinieri*.'

'Very unfortunate.' A sigh. 'You know what you must do.'

BERSEI DIDN'T SAY a word until he and Charlotte were safely outside the museum's confines. He headed straight for his parked Vespa.

'I think the Vatican is involved in something bad,' he said to her in a hushed tone. 'Something to do with the ossuary.'

'What are you talking about?'

'Too much to explain right now.' Stowing the laptop bag in the scooter's rear compartment, he mounted the bike and put a key in the ignition. 'You need to trust me on this. You'll be safe here, don't worry.'

'Giovanni, please.' She grabbed his arm tightly. 'You're not going anywhere,' she said, 'until you tell me what you're talking about.'

Bersei looked at her, his gaze filled with concern. 'I think that ossuary was stolen. It may be linked to a theft in Jerusalem that left many people dead. There's someone I need to speak to about what we've found.'

For a moment, she said nothing. 'Are you sure?'

'No, I'm not. That's why I'm trying to leave you out of this. If I'm wrong, this could turn out badly for me. I don't want you dragged down too.'

'Is there anything I can do to help?'

'Just pretend we didn't have this conversation. Hopefully I'm wrong about everything.' He looked down at her hand. 'Please, let me go.'

Charlotte loosened her grip. 'Be careful.' She watched as Bersei rode off round the corner of the building.

As THE ELEVATOR DOORS slid apart, Charlotte hesitated before stepping out into the basement corridor. Surely the Vatican couldn't be involved in a theft, she tried to convince herself. But what if Giovanni was right?

Halfway down the corridor, she noticed that one of the solid metal doors was slightly ajar. It hadn't been earlier—she was sure of that. Curious, she stepped up to the door and knocked. 'Hello? Anyone there?'

No answer. She reached out and pushed the door open.

Stepping into the tiny room lined with empty shelves, she stood in front of a very peculiar workstation—a bank of monitors, a computer, a set of headphones. Her eyes followed a bundle of wires that led out from the computer, crept up the wall and disappeared into an opening in the ceiling. The system was in sleep mode.

Sitting in a chair positioned in front of the equipment, she tried to imagine what purpose this all served. Finally, she couldn't help but reach down to press a key on the keyboard. The monitors flickered and hummed as the the software activated what appeared to be the last program that had been in use. It took Charlotte a moment to piece together the familiar collage of camera images that spread out before her. On one of the onscreen viewing panels, there was a chambermaid cleaning a small room. Charlotte's stomach sank when she saw her own luggage beside the bed. On a second panel she saw a familiar set of toiletries lining the vanity shelf.

'Conte,' she seethed. 'That pervert.'

She studied a number of other hidden cameras transmitting from the lab and the break room—live feeds, judging by the time and date counters on the bottom of each panel. He'd been watching and listening the whole time.

In that moment she knew that Giovanni had been right.

CHAPTER 10

In the Secret Archive, Father Donovan placed the *Ephemeris Conlusio* codex next to the plastic-sealed document bearing reference number *D 217*—'The Chinon Parchment'—and closed the door. There was a small hiss as a vacuum pump pulled all the air out from the compartment.

Secrets. Donovan was no stranger to them. Perhaps that was why he felt so connected to books and solitude.

Many who were drawn to the Catholic priesthood would attribute their decision to some kind of vocational calling. Donovan had turned to the Church for a more sobering cause—survival.

As a young boy, he'd grown up in Belfast during the tumultuous sixties and seventies, when the violence between the Catholics and Protestants was at its peak. In 1969 he'd watched his house, and dozens of others around it, burnt to the ground by rioting loyalists. He could also vividly recall the IRA's retaliatory bombings. At fifteen, he had been lured into a street gang that ran errands for the IRA.

On his seventeenth birthday, Donovan's life was changed for ever. He was drinking at a local pub with his two best friends, Sean and Michael. They had got into a shouting match with a group of drunken Protestants. It hadn't taken long for fists to start flying.

Though no stranger to street fighting, Donovan's wiry frame and swift hands had been no match for the two men that teamed up on him. While one of the Protestants had pinned him to the ground, the second landed body blows, seemingly intent on beating him to death.

Suppressed rage had flooded into him as he envisioned the glowing embers of his home. Donovan had reacted on instinct, fighting his way back onto his feet, flipping open a jackknife and plunging it deep into the stomach of the attacker who had held him down. The man had fallen, horrified as he tried to hold back the gush of blood flooding out of his abdomen. The remaining Protestants had stood frozen in disbelief as the Catholics fled.

Donovan remembered the dread he had felt next day when the papers and TV reported that a local Protestant man had been stabbed to death. He realised that he needed to leave Belfast before he became its next victim.

The seminary had provided him with a safe haven and the hope of God's forgiveness. He'd always been a good student and the solitude of priesthood reignited his passion for reading. He found peace in history and Scripture. Seeing his remarkable dedication to learning, the Diocese of Dublin had sponsored his university training. Perhaps, Donovan thought, it was his obsession with books that had helped to save him.

Now, it was a book that seemed to threaten everything he held sacred. The very institution that had protected him was under attack.

He stared through the glass panel at the *Ephemeris Conlusio*—the lost Scripture that had set in motion the momentous events in Jerusalem. Only two weeks ago he had presented this incredible discovery to the Vatican secretary of state. He remembered the meeting with Santelli as clear as day.

'IT'S NOT OFTEN I receive such urgent requests for an appointment from the Vatican Library.' Cardinal Santelli's hands lay folded on his desk.

Seated opposite, Father Donovan clutched his leather satchel. 'Apologies for the short notice, Eminence. But I hope you'll agree that the reason I've come here warrants your immediate attention . . .'

'What is it?' Santelli looked bored.

Donovan was unsure exactly where to begin. 'You recall a few years back when the Chinon Parchment was discovered in the Secret Archive?'

'Clement's secret dismissal of charges against the Knights Templar?'

'Correct. I came to you with further documents detailing the clandestine meeting between Clement V and Jacques DeMolay, the Templar Grand Master.' Donovan swallowed hard. 'The Pope's account specifically mentioned a book called the *Ephemeris Conlusio*, supposedly containing information about the Templars' hidden relics.'

'A crude attempt to restore the Templar Order,' Santelli interjected.

'But DeMolay's negotiations had to be quite compelling for Clement to have exonerated the Templars after ordering their disbandment.'

'A fabrication. No book was ever produced by Jacques DeMolay.'

'Agreed.' Donovan dug into his satchel and retrieved the book. 'Because it wasn't in his possession.'

Santelli shifted his chair. 'What is that you have there?'

'This is the *Ephemeris Conlusio*.'

Santelli was bewildered. This was one legend he had always hoped to be pure fantasy. 'You're not suggesting . . .'

'Yes,' he confidently replied. 'Let me explain.'

Donovan recounted the history of Jacques DeMolay's imprisonment, his secret discussion with Clement, his subsequent trial and execution. 'Pope Clement V died one month after DeMolay from what many accounts say was severe dysentery—a hideous death. Seven months later, King Philip IV died mysteriously during a hunt. Many speculated that the Knights Templar had exacted their revenge.'

Santelli looked spooked. 'Poisoned?'

'Perhaps.' Donovan shrugged. 'Meanwhile the Holy Land had been fully reclaimed by the Muslims, the Chinon Parchment gathered dust in the Secret Archive, and the *Ephemeris Conlusio*—this book—faded into history. Until I received a phone call this week.' Donovan summarised his phone conversation with the mystery caller, then described the transaction with the caller's messenger in Caffè Greco.

'Have you read it?' Santelli asked when Donovan finished.

Donovan nodded. 'It says many disturbing things. Apparently this book isn't a Templar document *per se*. It's a journal written by Joseph of Arimathea, chronicling many events specific to Christ's ministry. Eyewitness accounts of miracles, like his healing the lame and lepers. His teachings, his travels with the disciples, the events leading to Jesus' apprehension and crucifixion. Most of Joseph's account is in agreement with the Gospels . . . with some minor discrepancies. According to Joseph of Arimathea, he himself secretly negotiated with Pontius Pilate to remove Christ from the cross, in exchange for a hefty sum.'

'A bribe?'

'Yes.' Donovan took a deep breath. 'In the New Testament, Jesus' body was supposedly laid out for burial in Joseph's family crypt.'

'Before you continue, this Templar relic . . . the book. Is it authentic?'

'I had the parchment, leather, and ink dated. The origin is unquestionably first century. But this book isn't the relic Jacques DeMolay implied. It's merely a means of finding the real treasure he alluded to.'

Santelli stared at him.

'Joseph describes Jesus' burial rituals in vivid detail. How the body was cleaned, wrapped in linen and then bound. Coins were placed over the eyes.' Donovan's voice sank an octave. 'He claims that the body was laid out in Joseph's tomb . . . for twelve months.'

'*A year*?' Santelli was aghast.

'According to Joseph there never was a physical resurrection. You see . . .' Donovan locked eyes with the cardinal. 'Christ died a mortal death.'

It wasn't the first time Santelli had heard this theory. 'But we've been through all this before—assertions about early Christians seeing resurrection as being spiritual not physical.' He gestured at the book dismissively. 'This *Ephemeris Conlusio* is a clear contradiction to Scripture.'

'I'm afraid there's more.'

Santelli watched silently as Donovan reached into his satchel and removed a furled, yellow scroll. Carefully, he laid it out on the desk.

The Cardinal leaned in. 'What is this?'

'A one-dimensional technical illustration—a kind of map, actually—of the Temple Mount in Jerusalem.' He indicated the elongated rectangle. Then he pointed to the image drawn on top of it. 'This is the Jewish Temple that was built by Herod the Great, later destroyed by the Romans. As you know, the Dome of the Rock Mosque is there now.'

Santelli looked up sharply. 'The Temple Mount?'

'Yes,' Donovan confirmed. 'This is Joseph of Arimathea's representation of how it appeared in AD 30 during the time of Christ.'

Donovan explained that Joseph's writings described the temple in great detail—its rectangular courtyards and sacred Tabernacle; its storage houses for oil and wood; the water basins used to consecrate sacrificial offerings and the wooden pyres to burn sacred animals during Passover.

'But it's this spot here'—Donovan pointed to the small square that Joseph had drawn inside the gut of the platform—'that's most important. It's meant to show the location of Jesus' crypt. Joseph includes specific measurements as to its proximity from the Temple Mount's outer walls.'

For a few seconds Santelli remained perfectly still.

'I have researched the site in great detail,' Donovan continued. 'I'm absolutely certain that the secret crypt is still there. I believe that the Knights Templar discovered the crypt and secured it.'

'How can you be so sure?'

Donovan carefully turned the ancient pages of the *Ephemeris Conlusio*, stopping on a group of crude sketches. 'Those items are the relics that Joseph of Arimathea buried in the crypt. The bones, coins, and nails. Plus the ossuary, of course.'

Santelli crossed himself.

'If these relics had ever been discovered, we probably wouldn't even be sitting here having this conversation.' Donovan retrieved yet another document from his satchel. 'Then there's this recent article from the *Jerusalem Post*, which our mysterious benefactor included with the book.'

Santelli snatched it away and read the *Post*'s headline: JEWISH AND MUSLIM ARCHAEOLOGISTS CLEARED TO EXCAVATE BENEATH TEMPLE MOUNT.

Donovan gave Santelli time to absorb the rest of the article, then spoke up. 'Since Israeli peace accords don't permit digging on the site, the Templar Knights are the Temple Mount's last known excavators. But in 1996 the Muslim trust that oversees the site was permitted to clear rubble from a vast chamber beneath the platform once used by the Templars as a stable, and blocked off since their occupation. The messenger who delivered this book was an Arab. I am fairly certain that the *Ephemeris Conlusio* must have been discovered by the Muslims during their excavations.'

'But why have they waited until now to present it?'

'At first, I too was suspicious,' Donovan confessed. 'Though now I've got a good idea as to why.' From the satchel he retrieved a modern drawing—his own. 'When the area had been cleared, the Muslims converted that space into what is now the Marwani Mosque. Here's an aerial plan of the the Temple Mount as it stands today. Using Joseph's measurements, I've calculated the precise location of the crypt. I've marked in red the Marwani Mosque, situated about eleven metres below the esplanade.'

Santelli grasped what Donovan was implying. 'My God, it's right next to the secret chamber.'

'Directly abutting the mosque's rear wall. Muslim and Jewish archaeologists already suspect that chambers exist beneath the Temple Mount and they'll be performing surface scans to detect them.'

Santelli's face was drained. 'Then they will find this place.'

'It would be impossible to miss,' Donovan grimly confirmed. 'If the relics described in the *Ephemeris Conlusio* are real, there's a good chance that the physical remains of Christ may be unearthed in a few weeks. That is why I have come here today. To ask you . . . what can we do?'

'I think that's all too clear, Patrick,' Santelli's voice was brisk. 'We must retrieve those relics from beneath the Temple Mount. Over one billion Christians depend on the Gospels of Jesus Christ. To disrupt their faith is to disrupt social order. This isn't just a matter of theology.'

'But the political situation in Israel is far too complicated to obtain them through diplomacy,' Donovan reminded the cardinal.

'Who said anything about diplomacy?' Santelli reached over to the intercom on his desk. 'Father Martin? In my phone list, you'll find a "Salvatore Conte". Please summon him to my office immediately.'

CHAPTER 11

Veering off the congested Via Nomentana through the Villa Torlonia park entrance, Giovanni Bersei slowed along a narrow bike path, the Vespa's engine purring softly.

Here, beneath the sprawling English gardens, where a flurry of joggers and cyclists went about their exercise regimens, a labyrinth of Jewish crypts formed just over nine kilometres of what had recently proved to be Rome's oldest catacombs. And somewhere in this subterranean realm, he was certain, lay part of an ancient secret tied to Jesus Christ.

Glancing up at the weathered neoclassical edifice that made this place famous—the palatial villa where Benito Mussolini had once resided—Bersei angled the Vespa towards a set of low buildings at the rear. Here were the stables where excavations in 1918 had accidentally uncovered the first burial chambers. He killed the Vespa's engine and dismounted behind some shrubs. He rocked the scooter onto its kickstand, then, opening the rear cargo box, he removed his laptop bag and a sturdy flashlight, then stowed his helmet inside.

It was only ten minutes to nine. Most likely, the place would still be locked up. Bersei tried the door. It opened. Inside the crude foyer an elderly docent sat behind a desk, reading a novel. A smile broke across his face.

'*Ah, Signore Bersei.*' He placed his book down. '*Come sta?*'

'*Bene grazie, Mario. E lei?*'

'Better and better every day,' the old man boasted in thick Italian.

'Glad you're an early bird. I thought I'd be standing outside for a while.'

'They have me here at eight nowadays, just in case anyone feels motivated to get some work done. They're trying to speed up the restoration.'

Intensive conservation efforts had been underway for more than a decade. Noxious gases still present in the deep recesses of the subterranean labyrinth of crypts had only prolonged the delay.

Bersei pointed to the book. 'I see you're keeping busy.'

The old man shrugged. 'Catching up on my reading. What brings you back here?'

It had been a while since Bersei's last visit. Two years, in fact. This was only one of over sixty Roman burial sites he had surveyed for the Pontifical Commission over the years. 'The latest carbon-dating results have me second-guessing some of my original assumptions. Just want to have a second look at some of the *hypogea*. Do you need my card?' Bersei pulled out his wallet, flipping it open to a laminated identification card granting him full access to most of the city's historic sites.

Mario waved it away. 'I'll log you in,' he said, passing him a piece of paper. 'Here's an updated map for you.'

Bersei eyed the revised plan of tunnels and galleries. The passageways had evolved haphazardly over centuries of expansion like a pattern of cracks in a crazed piece of pottery. 'I won't be long. Would you mind if I left this with you for a little while?' He held up the laptop bag.

'No problem. I'll keep it behind the desk.'

He made his way across the foyer and flicked on his flashlight, angling it low to illuminate the stone steps that plunged into pure blackness.

At the base of the steps, Bersei paused to adjust his breathing to the frigid, damp air. It was remarkable that so many frescoes had been preserved down here, in an unforgiving environment that had completely ravaged the corpses that once occupied its thousands of niches. Barely any bones had been uncovered during the excavations, most having been stolen by charlatans who had turned a profit by passing them off as the relics of saints.

He pointed the light down the narrow passageway that dissolved into total darkness only a few metres ahead. The *necropolis*, he thought. 'City of the dead.' He shielded his nose from the mouldy smell and, swallowing hard, Bersei pushed forward.

'CAN I HELP YOU?' the docent set down his book for the second time and studied the rugged-looking man standing in front of his desk. 'I'm afraid the exhibit isn't open to the public,' he continued, smiling wryly. 'So unless you have proper identification, I'll have to ask you to leave.'

Power wielded by the powerless. Conte disregarded the old man's request, ogling the visitor's sign-in sheet. Only one name was listed there; the only name that mattered. This was going to be easy. He slid his left hand into his coat pocket and calmly withdrew a small syringe. Clasping the docent by the back of his neck, Conte thrust the needle deep into neck muscle, injecting Tubarine—a drug used during heart surgery to paralyse the cardiac tissue. Never knowing when he might need it, Conte always kept a lethal dose in his possession. Whoever found the old man would assume he'd had a heart attack.

As he crumpled to the floor, Conte stepped smartly away and rummaged through the desk drawers until he found a flashlight. He noticed Bersei's laptop bag and made a mental note to take it with him on his way out. Then he reached down to the corpse and yanked away a set of keys.

From beneath his coat, he drew his Glock 9mm. Flashlight on, he stepped down into the darkness and pulled the door shut behind him, engaging its meaty lock.

FOR FIFTEEN MINUTES, Giovanni Bersei worked his way deeper into the Villa Torlonia catacomb, stopping intermittently to refer to the map. Without the diagram, this zigzag of tunnels would have been impossible to navigate. So many of the passages—most of which terminated in dead ends—looked the same, and being underground he had little sense of direction.

Judging from the scale of the map, he figured he'd walked just under half a kilometre from the entrance. His destination was very close now.

Ahead, the left wall gave way to a sweeping archway—an entrance to a chamber called a *cubiculum*. Bersei referenced the map again to confirm that he had found the right cell then moved into the space beyond.

In the centre of the ornately tiled floor, he craned back his head and aimed the flashlight upwards. If he remembered correctly, what he'd most wanted to see would be here.

HIS FLASHLIGHT momentarily switched off, Salvatore Conte listened intently for the distant sounds echoing through the stone maze. Totally unaware of his pursuer, the anthropologist was making no effort to conceal the scraping sounds of his footsteps against the tunnel floor.

Conte was close now. Very close.

He poked his head around the corner of the wall. About forty metres down the narrow passage, a faint glow spilled out from an arched opening. He placed his flashlight on the ground, then reaching behind his back, he tucked the Glock into his belt.

GIOVANNI BERSEI'S gaze was transfixed on the amazing fresco that covered the lofty vault.

In the centre was a menorah, the seven-branched candelabrum of the Jewish Temple, contained within concentric circles like a sunburst, centred upon a large cross—a cruciform—wrapped by grapevine tendrils. Between the equal arms of the cross were four half circles arranged to match the points of a compass. Each contained the symbol carved onto the ossuary's side—a dolphin wrapped round a trident, the early Christian symbol for Jesus Christ, the Saviour.

Trembling, Bersei tucked the flashlight in his armpit and reached into his breast pocket for the photocopy of the scroll.

'My God,' Bersei muttered. A virtual reproduction of the ceiling fresco was drawn beneath the Greek text written almost two millennia earlier by Joseph of Arimathea. If this commingling of Jewish and Christian motifs wasn't overwhelming enough, the fact that Joseph was somehow linked to this place was mind-boggling.

Bersei turned his attention to an opening in the *cubiculum*'s rear wall. If the place followed standard crypt design, a funerary preparation room would adjoin the burial room.

He could barely control his excitement as he moved into the adjoining chamber. The walls of this space were cleanly carved into *loculi*, shelves where bodies were laid out to decompose.

Amazing.

Bersei counted the niches. *Ten.*

Nine of the shelves were fairly plain, save for some ornamental stone mouldings. But on the rear wall, one *loculus* stood out because of the intricate rosettes and hatch patterns that framed it. Undoubtedly, it was the handiwork of the same stone craftsman who had decorated the ossuary.

Bersei paced forward, mouth agape. He pointed the light into the carved grotto, just large enough to store a prostrate body. Empty, of course. Now the light caught a symbol carved into the top edge of the frame. A dolphin wrapped round a trident.

Could Joseph of Arimathea really have transported Christ's body to Rome? And if so, why? Bersei tried to wrap his head round the idea. Protection, perhaps? But wasn't there an empty tomb in a church in Jerusalem? Maybe this explained why the Gospels said it had been found empty.

'Dr Bersei?' Abruptly, a sharp voice invaded the silence.

Startled, Bersei pivoted, swinging the light behind him. Half expecting to see a ghastly apparition, he was even more terrified when the cylinder of light played on Salvatore Conte's hard features. Heart thundering against his ribs, Bersei lowered the beam. 'How did you get down here?' He feared he already knew the answer.

Conte ignored the question. 'What are you looking for, Doctor?'

Bersei didn't answer.

Conte strode up to him and snatched the photocopy from his hand.

'It's merely research. Nothing more.' Bersei retreated a step, his back pressing against the crypt wall.

'You must think I'm an idiot. I know you've taken files from the lab. Do you intend to give them to Detective Perardi too?'

Bersei went mute. How could Conte have known about Perardi? That call was made from his home. A sinking feeling came over him. Could the Vatican have been so ruthless as to tap his telephone?

'Stealing's one thing. Stealing from the Vatican . . . Now that's just un-Christian.' Conte turned and stepped away to the centre of the chamber purposely displaying the Glock stuffed in his belt for dramatic effect. 'Come here and give me more light.' He moved into the centre of the cubiculum.

Reluctantly, Giovanni Bersei shuffled into the antechamber and shone his light high up into its vault. The beam oscillated in his shaking hand.

Conte absorbed the fresco's complex imagery for a few seconds, then compared it to the image on the paper. 'So this is what you've found,' he said, impressed. 'Who would have thought that box had origins here?'

Bersei frowned.

'I take it you think Joseph of Arimathea brought Jesus' body here first,' Conte continued, 'before shipping the bones back to that sandbox in the Holy Land. I don't even think the Vatican librarian or the Pope's cronies could have thought this far ahead.'

Bersei was stupefied by Conte's casual disregard for what this all really meant. More so, he was horrified that Conte had just confirmed his suspicions of the Vatican's knowledge of the theft. Salvatore Conte had made it all possible. The master thief. The Israeli death count scrolled through his mind's eye. Thirteen dead. What was one more life for a man like this?

Calmly, Conte folded the paper and slipped it into his trouser pocket. Then he was coolly reaching behind his back for the Glock.

Correctly anticipating what was coming, Bersei reacted on survival impulse, slamming his flashlight against the stone wall behind him. There was a harsh clatter of metal and the cubiculum plunged into utter darkness.

An instant later, Conte squeezed off a shot, the muzzle flash strobing the darkness, just long enough to see that the scientist had already scrambled away on his knees. He fired again—another flash, followed by a ricochet that almost clipped Conte's ear. Though his intention was merely to scare the scientist, not actually shoot him, he'd have to aim better.

He stopped to listen. To Conte's surprise, fast-moving steps confirmed that the anthropologist had gone deeper into the maze.

Retrieving his own flashlight, Conte began his pursuit, sprinting along the tunnel, the amber glow of light swinging with each pump of his arms.

GIOVANNI BERSEI had a good head start, but the uncertainty of the catacomb's layout, filled with long tunnels that ran hundreds of metres to dead ends, had him panic-stricken. He needed to keep his wits about him, above all to remember the map.

Running through the uneven stone corridors, each footfall echoed loudly behind him, an aural trail for Conte. As he progressed deeper into the pure black, the air was putrid with the acrid smells.

His right shoulder bounced off the wall and he spun slightly, almost tripping over himself, disorientated. Slowing momentarily to regain his balance, he began to move again, only to career into a wall face-first.

Panting wildly, he thrust his arms to the right, groping, searching for an opening, praying that this wasn't a dead end. Finally his hands found a void. The passageway hadn't terminated; it simply angled hard to the left.

Bersei rounded the corner and sprinted through the darkness, running purely on faith that he wouldn't crash again. Seconds later, his feet tangled on something low to the floor and he slammed hard onto the stone paving. He'd landed on what felt like paint cans, his head colliding loudly against some kind of metal case.

A blinding light shot into his eyes as intense pain racked his skull. He swore furiously, thinking the flash was a by-product of the head blow. But opening his eyes, he stared directly into an illuminated work light and saw that he had run directly into a section of the tunnel where restoration was still underway. Tools, brushes and cans were strewn throughout the passage. A thick cord had lassoed his ankles and downed the pole light onto its switch. He yanked the mess away, snapping back to his feet.

The footsteps behind him were faster now, closing in.

The toolbox that he'd collided with lay open, a ball-pein hammer sitting in its top tray. He grabbed it and ran.

CONTE ROUNDED the corner where a mysterious light spilled out into the tunnel. He was beginning to feel a bit light-headed from the acrid air now filling his lungs. Slowing to navigate the mess of tools blocking the passage, he planted a firm kick on the work light and it fizzled out.

Up ahead, the passage forked in three directions. He raced to the intersection, paused, striving to control his breathing, and listened. Nothing. Finally he had to make a choice.

INSIDE STATION ZION'S cramped detaining cell, Graham Barton stared hopelessly at the solid metal door. He'd been framed as the mastermind behind the Temple Mount theft. Deep down he knew that the powers were aligned against him for a reason—perhaps an expedient political one.

The door opened and he looked up at a familiar figure.

Razak.

Clearly upset, the Muslim crossed to the remaining chair as the door closed behind him and was locked from the outside.

'Quite a predicament you're in, Graham,' his tone was disappointed. The police had presented such strong evidence against the archaeologist that he couldn't help but feel he'd been played for a fool.

'It's a set-up,' Barton insisted. 'I had nothing to do with this crime. You of all people should know that.'

'I like you. You seem to be a good man, but they said that things only the thieves could have possessed were discovered in your apartment.'

'Someone planted that drill,' Barton protested. 'And you know as well as me that the scroll was in that ossuary.'

Razak spread his hands. 'I had my back turned,' he reminded him.

'Right. I see.' Disappointment clouded the archaeologist's face. 'You're part of this, too.'

'What about the other ossuaries?'

Barton was exasperated. 'How could a man my size move nine ossuaries weighing thirty-three kilos each right from under the eyes of the Waqf and police?' he said. 'And I was never there without you present.'

Razak was silent, eyes cast down.

'And even if I'd been able to take them, where would I have hidden them? In my flat? They've already searched there. Next you're going to assume that I defaced the tablet in the crypt because I saw it before you did.'

The Muslim's eyes shot up. 'What do you mean by that?'

'The tenth entry on the tablet. Remember it was scratched away?'

Now Razak knew what he was referring to. 'Yes.'

'Well, tonight Major Topol conveniently showed me a photograph taken *before* I was brought in. It showed the symbol that was originally there.'

Razak didn't like that. 'And what was it?'

'A dolphin wrapped round a trident, an early Christian symbol for Jesus.'

Razak shook his head. 'I don't know what to believe.'

'You must help me, Razak. You're the only one who knows the truth.'

'Truth's a rare commodity in this part of the world.' Razak glanced away. 'Even if the truth existed, I don't know if I'd recognise it.' He began to feel a keen responsibility for the Englishman. Barton's intuition about the theft had been virtually flawless, yet here he was awaiting charges. And Razak had seen these tactics used many times in the past by the Israeli authorities.

'Is there any hope for me?'

Raza spread his hands. 'There's always hope.'

'You're not going to pursue this investigation, are you?'

'You have to understand our position.' Razak was beginning to wonder if he understood it himself. 'Already news of your arrest has started to ease tensions. Discussions are resuming. People have someone to blame—and a man who's not a Jew or a Muslim.'

'Very convenient.' The archaeologist knew nothing more would be done.

'The real problem we're facing is political.' Razak rose to his feet and knocked on the cell door. Before leaving, he paused and said, 'I will do my best to help. But I cannot attest to things that I'm unsure of. I know you can respect that.' With a sinking feeling, he made his way outside.

HUDDLED INSIDE a *loculus* high on the passage wall, Giovanni Bersei was sucking in shallow breaths, desperate to steady himself, hoping that Conte would choose the wrong tunnel and wander aimlessly into the catacomb. He tightened his grip round the ball-pein hammer's handle.

Minutes passed. Silence returned.

A little more time and he would consider climbing back out into the tunnel. But the idea was short-lived, because a faint glow of light suddenly played along the craggy wall opposite the niche.

Conte was coming.

Having searched two tunnels unsuccessfully, Conte had backtracked to the area where Bersei had stumbled over the tools. Pacing down the third passage, he felt the slightest breeze. The air here was less putrid. Maybe there was a ventilation shaft nearby.

Moving slowly through the tunnel, Conte detected a dim light far ahead. Daylight? Panic suddenly overcame him. Perhaps it was a ventilation shaft, but it looked wide enough to provide an escape route. He broke into a sprint.

About ten metres ahead, a dark form suddenly arced out from high on the wall, too fast for even the mercenary to react. It cracked him hard in the right temple and felled him flat on his back, his head slamming against the ground with a hollow thud. The flashlight skittered across the tunnel floor. The Glock, however, remained fast in his grasp.

Dazed, Conte barely discerned a figure crawling out from the wall like a reanimated corpse. Hitting the floor, Bersei scrambled for the light.

Suddenly, through blurry double vision, Conte saw something cartwheeling through the air. It struck him hard in the chest. Raising the Glock, he blindly squeezed off a shot.

BERSEI FOCUSED on the luminous cone of sunlight at the end of the passage. Maybe, just maybe, he'd get out of this appalling place alive.

But only a couple of metres from the cone, Bersei slid to a stop, just before a gaping opening in the floor where the sunlight flowed down a wide, ragged shaft, four, perhaps five storeys deep.

The lower galleries. Three more levels below, her reminded himself. The restorers must have opened the ventilation shaft to help release lingering subterranean gases.

Christ, help me. His eyes drifted up to the light source. A heavy iron grate sealed the opening high above. Despair closed in on him like a vice.

Suddenly from behind, he heard a slight noise. Turning, he just had time to see Conte's body launched in midair like a projectile. The assassin's feet caught Bersei in the chest, throwing him back violently across the mouth of the shaft, slamming his body against the wall beyond.

For a split second, Bersei was suspended on the wall, his feet caught on the small ridge that formed a rim round the opening. But the force of the impact made him teeter forward uncontrollably. The jagged rocks pinwheeled round him as he plummeted head-first down the shaft.

Conte stared down at Giovanni Bersei's body, which was bent into an unnatural shape at the bottom of the shaft, blood oozing from his skull. The hunter smiled. A clean kill that would appear to be an unfortunate accident. Backtracking through the tunnels, he made his way into the foyer. He returned the keys to the dead docent, grabbed the laptop bag and left, closing the door behind him. All things considered, it had been a good job.

CHAPTER 12

At ten to ten, Father Patrick Donovan entered the lab looking like he hadn't slept in days. 'Good morning, Dr Hennesey.'

Seated by the ossuary, Charlotte forced her eyes up from the relic. Donovan looked round the lab. 'Is Dr Bersei here?'

'He hasn't come in yet,' she said. Bending the truth was not something she was good at.

'That's strange. I hope everything is OK.'

'I know what you mean. Doesn't seem like him to be late.'

'Especially for something so important,' Donovan added. 'Think you can handle the presentation without him?'

'Sure,' she replied, her insides roiling. How could she possibly go through with this alone? What if Bersei was right?

Donovan checked his watch. 'Let's get going. I don't want to be late.'

AT THE GUARDED ENTRY to Cardinal Santelli's office, Donovan and Charlotte were quickly cleared and escorted by a Swiss Guard into the antechamber where Father Martin got up from his desk to greet them.

'Good to see you again, James.' Donovan shook the young priest's hand. As he introduced Charlotte, the intercom on Martin's desk suddenly came to life. 'James.' A rough voice tore through the tiny speaker. 'I asked you for that report ten minutes ago. What the hell are you waiting for?'

The young priest smiled tightly. 'Excuse me for a moment.' He pressed the intercom's button. 'Father Donovan and Dr Hennesey have arrived.'

'Well, what are you waiting for? Send them in!'

Rolling his eyes, Father Martin led them into Santelli's office. The cardinal acknowledged the visitors with a nod.

'He's all yours,' Martin whispered to Donovan as he retreated.

Seeing Santelli's intimidating figure seated behind the desk, Charlotte realised that she'd been so preoccupied with Bersei's claims and Conte's creepy spy room that she'd failed to discuss etiquette with Donovan. Now the cardinal stood up, tall and rigid, his face pleasant yet firm.

'Good morning, Father Donovan.' The cardinal extended his right hand.

'Eminence.' Donovan stepped forward and bowed slightly to kiss Santelli's sacred ring. 'Eminence Antonio Carlo Santelli, may I introduce you to Dr Charlotte Hennesey.'

Santelli was grinning widely. 'I've heard much about you, Dr Hennesey.'

A feeling of panic came over Charlotte as he closed in for a greeting. Perhaps sensing it, he offered her a standard handshake. Relieved, she shook his enormous paw. 'An honour to meet you, Eminence.'

'Thank you, my dear. You are very kind. Come, let us sit.' Cupping his hand on her shoulder, he motioned across the office to a circular mahogany conference table. When they had all settled into their leather armchairs, Donovan apologised on behalf of Dr Bersei who could not attend the meeting due to a personal crisis.

The cardinal looked alarmed. 'Nothing serious, I hope?'

The librarian was hoping the same thing. 'I'm sure he's fine.'

'That means you have the floor, Dr Hennesey.'

Charlotte handed Santelli a neatly bound report and gave Donovan a second copy. Flipping open her laptop, she walked the two men through a PowerPoint slideshow of crisp, colour photos of the skeletal aberrations: the gouges, fractured knees, damaged wrists and feet. 'On the basis of what you see here, both Dr Bersei and myself concluded that this male specimen interred in the ossuary—who was otherwise in perfect health—died in his early thirties as a result of . . . execution.'

Santelli managed to look surprised. 'Execution?'

She glanced to Donovan who seemed equally puzzled, but nodded for her to continue. 'He was crucified.'

The words hung in the air for a long moment.

Santelli leaned forward and held the geneticist's gaze. 'I see.'

'Furthermore, we also found these objects inside the ossuary.' Determined to steady her hands, Charlotte removed the three separate plastic bags from her carrying case. Laying the first one down, she tried not to let the spikes hit too hard against the burnished tabletop. Next came the sealed bag with the two coins. The third contained the metal cylinder.

Santelli and Donovan examined each object closely.

'We submitted a bone sample and some wood splinters for radiocarbon dating.' She passed across two copies of the dating certificates Ciardini had sent over. 'As you can see, both samples date to the early first century.'

She brought up the 3-D skeletal imaging and swivelled the laptop towards them. 'Scanning the skeleton, we calibrated the specimen's muscle mass, then incorporated the basic genetic profile found in the specimen's DNA. In this way we reconstructed the man's appearance at the time of death. And here he is.'

She tapped the mouse button and the screen refreshed—pigmented skin, eyes alive with colour, the hair dark and full.

Both men were astounded.

'That's absolutely . . . extraordinary,' Santelli muttered.

As they studied the image, she eyed both of them in turn. Could these two clerics possibly be involved in a theft that had left people dead? 'Lastly, Dr Bersei was able to decipher the meaning behind this symbol carved onto the side of the ossuary.' She held up a photo clearly showing the dolphin wrapped round a trident, and explained the significance of each symbol separately. 'The fusing of these two pagan symbols was how first-century Christians represented . . . Jesus Christ.'

Santelli and Donovan exchanged uneasy glances.

Mission accomplished, Charlotte thought.

Silence fell over the room.

SANTELLI WAS THE FIRST to speak. 'Are you telling us, Dr Hennesey, that you believe these are the mortal remains of Jesus Christ?'

Swallowing hard, Charlotte felt a bolt of energy shoot through her system—fight or flight.

'At face value,' she began, 'the evidence is compelling. But there are discrepancies in the pathology report and contradictions to accounts in the Bible. For example, we found no evidence that a spear was thrust into the rib cage as the Bible states. And this man's knees were broken.' She went on to detail how the Romans speeded up death with a metal club.

Father Donovan's attention wandered momentarily as he thought about this anticipated inconsistency. He knew Charlotte was referring to the Gospel of John, which stated that a Roman soldier pierced Jesus' side with a spear to help expedite his agonising death:

When they came to Jesus, they did not break His legs since they saw that He was already dead . . . For these things happened so that the Scripture would be fulfilled: Not one of His bones will be broken.

Interestingly, none of the Synoptic Gospels—Matthew, Mark or Luke made mention of this event. Donovan could only surmise that the Gospel of John included this embellished account to convince Jews that Jesus had been the true Messiah foretold by Old Testament prophets—'so that the Scripture would be fulfilled'.

'But most importantly,' Charlotte went on, pointing to the monitor, 'his genetic make-up isn't what you'd expect of someone born in ancient Judea. I carefully reviewed the DNA's gene sequencing and it doesn't match any documented Middle Eastern profiles for Jews or Arabs.'

Now both Santelli and Donovan looked perplexed.

Santelli tilted his head to one side. 'So, Dr Hennesey, are you telling us that you *don't* believe that these are actually Jesus' remains?'

Their eyes met in a silent stand-off.

For an instant, she thought back to her conversation with Bersei—how he'd said that people might have been killed for these relics. The cardinal's shifty gaze was starting to convince her that Giovanni's suspicions might just have been right. 'From what I've seen here, claiming these to be the actual remains of Jesus Christ would be a long shot. There is a very real possibility that this is some kind of first-century forgery.'

'That's a relief,' said Donovan.

Taken aback, Charlotte looked at him sharply. 'Why's that?'

Opening the satchel he had brought with him, he produced the *Ephemeris Conlusio*. 'Let me explain.'

CAREFULLY RESTING the ancient manuscript on the mahogany table, Father Donovan turned to her. 'You know, of course, that the Vatican has been extremely concerned about the ossuary's provenance.'

Charlotte eyed the book curiously.

'And there was a very good reason why,' he explained. 'But first, I need to give you some background. Many Jews living in ancient Judea maintained that Jesus—the self-proclaimed son of God—hadn't fulfilled the messianic criteria outlined in the Old Testament. And they were right.'

That's an odd admission, she thought.

'The Messiah foretold by the prophets was supposed to be a warrior empowered by God to free the Promised Land from tyranny and oppression.' Donovan was speaking quickly, his face animated. 'The Messiah was supposed to rebuild the Holy Temple. The Messiah was supposed to conquer Rome. Yet in reading the Scriptures, you find Jesus advocating peace. Here was a man telling the Jews to pay their taxes and accept their lot in life. In return he promised them eternity with God.'

Charlotte realised that Donovan needed to tell this story.

'Jesus knew Rome couldn't be defeated. He was trying to prevent a massive Jewish rebellion that would have ended in a massacre by the Romans. But many chose not to listen.' Donovan's voice was solemn. 'Less than thirty years after Christ's death, the Jews finally revolted. The Roman response was swift and brutal. They besieged Jerusalem and after they'd taken the city, they slaughtered every man, woman and child. Jerusalem and the second temple were razed to the ground. Just as Jesus had predicted.' He paused, and Charlotte watched his hands migrate to the *Ephemeris Conlusio*, where they rested flatly on its cover, as if protecting it.

'That book has something to do with all this?' she asked.

Donovan answered her with a question. 'You're familiar with Christ's resurrection story, the empty tomb?'

'Of course.' Having gone to an all-girls Catholic high school, she knew plenty about Scripture. 'Jesus was crucified and buried. Three days later he rose from the dead and reappeared to his disciples.'

'Absolutely.' Donovan was pleased. 'Which brings us to this.' He gently patted the book's cover. 'This is a journal written by Joseph of Arimathea.'

Charlotte was amazed. '*The* Joseph of Arimathea?'

'Yes. The man who buried Christ.' Father Donovan opened the volume revealed pages in ancient Greek. He looked up. 'For centuries the Vatican has feared rebuttal of Christ's role as the Messiah. This book provides many reasons why.' Stealing a quick glance at Santelli, Donovan braced himself not to let his voice waver. So far, it seemed that the cardinal was satisfied with his performance. 'Though portrayed as Christ's advocate in the New Testament, in fact Joseph of Arimathea was secretly working to undermine Jesus' ministry. You see, Jesus posed a substantial risk to the Jewish elite. He had harshly criticised Jewish authority, particularly those priests who had turned God's house into a travesty.'

Charlotte recalled Matthew's portrayal of Jesus entering the Jewish temple, ransacking merchants' and moneychangers' tables.

'Jesus had found fault with the Jewish ruling class,' Donovan went on, 'so it was no surprise that it was the Jewish priests who sent their own guards to apprehend him. After Jesus was executed, Joseph of Arimathea was chosen by the Sanhedrin to approach Pontius Pilate to negotiate the release of the body. Convinced by Joseph that it would prevent Jesus' followers from removing the body from the cross, Pilate granted his request.'

Charlotte knew body language. Though Donovan was telling his story confidently, his eyes were shifting.

'But why would Jesus' followers even want to steal his body?' she asked.

'In order to declare a resurrection and portray Jesus as divine.'

'So Joseph of Arimathea procured the body to protect it?'

'That's right.' Donovan forced himself to look at her.

'And the resurrection?' She swallowed hard. 'Did it really happen?'

'Of course,' Donovan replied. 'The body was secretly placed in Joseph's tomb—a location unbeknownst to Jesus' followers. But three days later it had disappeared.'

'Was it stolen?'

Donovan felt Santelli's judicious gaze digging into him. 'Four separate New Testament accounts tell us that three days later Jesus rose up from the tomb. Then he reappeared to his followers and ascended to heaven.'

Charlotte didn't know what to think. 'But what about the ossuary, the crucified corpse . . . and this symbol of Christ? Does this book say what it all really means?'

Composed now, Donovan leafed through the *Ephemeris Conlusio* almost to the end, carefully setting it back in front of her. Charlotte studied the pages, taking in detailed drawings of the ossuary and its contents.

'After Joseph's secret deal with Pilate,' Donovan explained levelly, 'the disciples caused quite a stir in Jerusalem when they discovered that Jesus' body had gone. The body's disappearance allowed them to claim that a resurrection had occurred. Naturally, Pilate came down hard on Joseph of Arimathea, insisting that he fix the problem.' Donovan pointed to the ossuary. 'And that's when Joseph concocted this idea.'

'So if these bones aren't Jesus' . . .'

Smiling, Donovan spun his hands, encouraging her to think it through.

'. . . that means Joseph of Arimathea must have *replaced* the body?'

She thought she heard Santelli sigh in relief.

'According to Joseph's account, he acquired *another* crucified corpse—one of two bodies that still remained on a cross on top of Golgotha . . . a criminal killed the same day as Jesus. The body was subjected to standard Jewish burial rituals and allowed to decay for a year. A brilliant fabrication intended to prove Christ never left the tomb. An attempt to discredit early Christianity in order to preserve the Jewish aristocracy.'

She let that sink in. Father Donovan's argument did agree with the inconsistencies she'd cited earlier, particularly the odd genetic profile and the clubbed knees. The skeleton could have belonged to some criminal from a backwater Roman province. But the fact still remained that the priest's interpretation was all that she had to go by. She looked at the priest sharply. 'It's obvious Joseph's plan failed. So why is it that no one previously discovered all this?'

Donovan shrugged. 'I believe Joseph died or was killed during those first twelve months, before the body was finally prepared. We'll never really know. Let's just be thankful that his scheme was never carried out. Because unlike today, where skilled scientists can detect foul play, in ancient times, a physical body could have been extremely problematic.'

'And the ossuary was found only recently?' She braced herself.

'The *Ephemeris Conlusio* was obtained by the Vatican in the early fourteenth century. But it wasn't taken seriously until a lone archaeologist unearthed a tomb just north of Jerusalem a few weeks ago. He knew that if he approached us discreetly we'd pay him very handsomely for it.'

Momentarily perplexed, Charlotte let the explanation roll over in her mind a couple times. Possibly Bersei had jumped to the wrong conclusion. But what had he discovered that made him so sure of his claims? 'A first-century relic of a crucified man bearing the symbol of Christ,' she murmured. 'A priceless artefact . . . for all the wrong reasons.'

'Exactly. This was a seemingly authentic discovery that, without proper explanation, may have caused needless hardship for the Christian faith. Now, thanks to your hard work, I'm certain we've closed this case.'

Charlotte's eyes wandered back to the opened manuscript where Joseph's drawings inventoried the ossuary and all its contents. Then she noticed something. The scroll cylinder wasn't included there. Her brow furrowed.

'Is something wrong?' Donovan asked.

Taking the plastic-sheathed cylinder in her hand, she said, 'Why isn't this shown there?' She motioned to the drawings.

Donovan suddenly looked nervous. 'Not sure,' he said, shaking his head. He tentatively glanced over at Santelli.

'Why don't you open it?' Santelli suggested boldly.

Taken aback, Charlotte said. 'We were waiting to . . .'

'Nothing to worry about, Dr Hennesey,' Santelli cut in. 'Father Donovan is an expert in handling ancient documents.'

'OK.' She handed the bagged cylinder to the white-faced librarian.

'Go ahead, Patrick,' Santelli urged. 'Open it.'

Amazed that the cardinal could be so brazen, Donovan proceeded to open the bag. Withdrawing the cylinder, he removed the loose end cap and tipped the scroll out onto the table. 'Here we go.' With the utmost care, he unfurled the scroll on top of the plastic and held it flat with both hands. Seeing what was there, he felt instantly relieved.

All eyes took in what had been inked onto the ancient vellum. The focal point was a Jewish menorah superimposed over a cross. The symbol that was on the ossuary's side was repeated at the end of each arm of the cross.

'What does this all mean?' Santelli asked Donovan.

'I'm not sure,' he admitted. He tried to conceal the fact that he noticed the edge of the scroll that faced towards him looked freshly cut. He rested his thumbs flat over the edge to conceal the marks.

'Whatever it means, it's beautiful,' Charlotte interjected.

'Yes, it is,' Donovan agreed, smiling.

'Well, then, Dr Hennesey,' Santelli spoke up. 'You've done a brilliant job. We cannot thank you enough. Just please be diligent in adhering to our request not to discuss this with anyone.'

'You have my word,' she promised.

'Excellent. If you don't mind, I'll have Father Martin escort you out. I have a few items to discuss with Father Donovan.'

LEAVING THE APOSTOLIC PALACE, Charlotte headed directly to the lab to see if Bersei had returned.

She slid her keycard through the reader next to the lab door and made her way into the darkened room. Groping for the control panel she flicked on the light switches.

When the lights came on, she couldn't believe what she was seeing. The entire lab was empty—the ossuary, the bones, the relics, the computers . . . all gone. Fearing the worst, she turned the lights off again and doubled-back to the door. That's when she heard footsteps in the corridor. They stopped and she could see a shadow moving into the light penetrating in from beneath the door.

Lunging back into the darkened lab, Charlotte crouched low to the floor. The hair on the back of her neck prickled as the door creaked open. She held her breath and steadied the laptop bag with both hands, remaining perfectly still. A very long moment went by. Then, pulling the door closed behind him, the intruder moved slowly into the room, snaked between the workstations and back towards the break room.

The second Charlotte sensed that the intruder had gone into the break room, she sprang up and lunged for the door. As her hand turned the handle, she glimpsed Conte returning into the lab, his face twisted into a snarl. Without looking back she sprinted down the corridor, heading directly for the fire exit. She shoved the door back hard on its hinges, and practically flew up the staircase, still clutching the laptop tightly to her side.

At the top of the landing, she wheeled towards the entrance to the museum, quietly easing the door closed behind her.

MOVING QUICKLY through the Pio Christian gallery, Charlotte slipped out the building's main entrance, joining the crowds loitering in the courtyard. Conte was nowhere in sight.

Determined to get out of Vatican City she hurried towards the short tunnel that passed beneath the city's old ramparts, and emerged into the small village that clustered in the shadow of the Apostolic Palace's rear edifice. Turning onto Borgo Pio, her eyes reached for the Sant'Anna Gate and the Swiss Guards who manned it. Had Conte called ahead to alert them? Would they try to detain her in this public place?

Then, only twenty metres from the gate, she saw him. Hands on his hips and breathing heavily, Conte had positioned himself between her and the gate, daring her to take another step. Knowing that there was no going back now, she broke into a sprint, eyes focused on the gate.

Conte reacted instantly, shooting out onto the roadway. He lunged in front of Charlotte, stopping her in her tracks. 'You're not going anywhere with that,' he growled, eyeing the laptop bag. For some reason, the geneti cist didn't look scared. Then she did something he hadn't expected.

She screamed.

For a moment, Conte was paralysed.

'Help!' Charlotte screamed again, louder this time.

The guards at the gate started running towards her, Berettas drawn.

When she saw Conte's attention momentarily shift to the approaching guards, she took the opportunity to do something she'd been thinking about since the moment she met this creep. Bending slightly at the knees, she swept a powerful left foot at his crotch, landing a perfect shot.

Conte buckled. Retching, he had to put his hands to the ground to not fall flat on his face. 'You bitch!'

The two guards arrived and planted themselves on opposite sides, guns levelled at his head. 'Stay still!' one of them commanded.

'What's going on here?' the second one asked Charlotte in English.

'This man was threatening me, trying to take my bag.'

The first guard was asking Conte for identification.

'I'm not . . .'—he spit out vomit and bile—'carrying it on me.' He was sure Santelli wouldn't approve of name-dropping in this situation. For now, he'd have to play the game.

The second guard had also asked Charlotte for identification, which she readily provided. The ornate papal crest on her guest badge showed she was a guest of the secretariat. 'You're free to go, Dr Hennesey.'

He turned to Conte. 'And you'll need to come with us, *signore*.'

Conte had no option but to comply.

Breathing a sigh of relief, Charlotte made her way to the gate. Once safely outside Vatican City, she waved down a taxi and told the driver to take her to Fiumicino Airport. *Rapidamente!*

As soon as the taxi driver hit the autostrada Charlotte pulled out her cell-phone and called Evan Aldrich. So what if it was still the middle of the night in Phoenix? He picked up almost instantly.

'Evan?'

'Hey, Charlie. I was just thinking about you. Everything OK?'

'No. Not at all.' Lowering her voice, she gave him a brief rundown of what had transpired. 'I'm heading to the airport now.'

'I was going to surprise you, but . . . I was actually on my way there to see you. In fact, my flight just arrived at Fiumicino. I'm at the baggage carousel right now. I'll tell you where to meet me.'

CHAPTER 13

An hour northeast of Rome, Salvatore Conte's rented black Alfa Romeo saloon climbed the SS5 autostrada along the Apennine mountain range into Monte Scuncole. A light drizzle sprayed the windscreen. Trying to settle his thoughts, Patrick Donovan stared out of the misty passenger window at the patchwork of vineyards in the valley below.

Following Charlotte Hennesey's hasty departure earlier that morning, and Conte's embarrassing bail-out from the Swiss Guard detention centre, a profoundly anxious Cardinal Santelli had given him specific instructions: 'See to it that this chapter of the Church's history disappears without trace. Destroy the ossuary and everything it contains . . . the manuscript too.'

Conte turned into a narrow, unpaved road. Thick grass scraped the car's undercarriage. He braked, then killed the engine.

Emerging from the car, both men circled to the back. Conte grabbed a couple of shovels from the boot and pushed one into Donovan's hands. 'We'll need to dig deep.'

Conte thrust his shovel into the soil. The smell of fresh earth filled the damp air. The light rain had resumed.

'Whose bones do you really believe are in that ossuary?' the mercenary asked. Salvatore Conte wasn't questioning his own faith. That was something he'd abandoned long ago.

Donovan replied, 'For all we know, these really are the bones of Jesus Christ. Our primary duty is to protect the Church.'

'Well, if that's Jesus in that box'—the mercenary pointed to the car's boot—'I'd say you're protecting an enormous lie.'

Donovan hadn't expected a man like Conte to understand the broader implications of all this. Two millennia of human history would be fundamentally affected by the ossuary and its contents. What spiritual belief remained in this chaotic, materialistic world needed to be preserved. 'I'm surprised. You don't strike me as someone who'd give a shit about that.'

Surprised by the priest's language, Conte shot him a look. Suddenly the task before him seemed easier. 'I don't actually. Besides, if there was a God,' he said, 'men like you and me wouldn't exist.'

Donovan was disgusted by the idea that he and Conte shared any commonalities, but knew that perhaps he was right. *I am part of this.*

'What really happened to Dr Bersei?' Donovan's tone was forceful. Somehow he knew his own fate was linked to Conte's answer.

'He got what he deserved and I spared you the dirty work.' Conte's hard face was twisted. 'That's all you need to know.'

'Why was he in the catacombs?' Donovan felt a swell of anger.

'He figured out that the picture on that scroll they found matched a fresco in the catacombs. Seems Bersei thought that Jesus was originally dried out in a crypt there.'

Donovan's eyes went wide. Could it be? Had he found the actual tomb?

'Let me give you some advice,' Conte added. 'Don't get too attached to the girl, either. Santelli told me all that nonsense you fed her about the book. Nice story. But she already has too much information. Did the cardinal tell you she skipped off with her laptop . . . loaded up with all the data?'

'No, he didn't.' No wonder Santelli was a bundle of nerves about all this—the whole thing was on the verge of unravelling.

'It's not good. I've got to fix that too and her blood will be on your hands.'

Donovan's jaw tensed as he thrust his shovel into the earth, the latent anger pushed deep down in his soul fighting its way to the surface.

It took them almost three hours to carve out the five-foot-deep pit. It could easily accommodate the ossuary *and* a body, Donovan thought.

At last Conte threw his shovel to the ground. 'Looks good.' Both men were lathered in soil and sweat. 'Let's get the ossuary.'

They walked back to the saloon. Conte leaned into the boot and lifted the ossuary's lid. Resting on top of the bones was the *Ephemeris Conlusio* and two thick grey blocks that resembled moulded clay.

Donovan pointed to the C-4. 'Is that—'

'Oh, I think a man with your background should know. Or didn't the IRA use this stuff to blow up Protestant shopfronts in Belfast?'

How on earth could he have known that?

'Best to blow it apart underground, wouldn't you agree?'

Donovan wondered if Conte would hit him on the head with a shovel, then push him into the hole and detonate the explosives.

The two men heaved the ossuary out of the boot, lugging it over to the edge of the pit.

'Drop on three.' Conte counted down.

Father Donovan felt a sudden dread as he watched the ossuary hit the earth with a dull thud. The lid slammed back onto the base, producing a crack along its etchings.

Conte turned round for his spade. One solid blow to Donovan's skull should do it. The C-4 would do the rest. From the corner of his eye, he noticed Donovan crouching down as if to tie his shoe.

The priest rose to his feet, aiming a silver handgun directly at his chest. A standard-issue Beretta, most likely lifted from the Swiss Guard barracks.

'Drop the shovel,' Donovan demanded.

Shaking his head chastisingly, Conte squatted to rest the shovel on the spongy grass, then quickly went for the Glock strapped round his right ankle, beneath his trouser leg.

The first shot struck Conte in the right hand. The slug ripped cleanly through flesh and bone, grazing the mercenary's ankle as it exited. Blood bubbled out from the hole and his damaged hand curled into a tight claw.

'Stand up,' Donovan demanded, daring to level the gun at Conte's head.

At first, it looked as if the mercenary would comply. But what happened next was far too fast for him. Conte sprang forward, burying a shoulder in Donovan's chest, forcing him back and then down.

Remarkably, the priest managed to maintain his grip on the Beretta. Conte reached for it with his left hand, but miscalculated, cupping the muzzle. A second shot cracked through the air and Conte screamed out in frustration. Now his good hand had been mangled too.

Badly wounded, Conte still managed to force Donovan's gun-hand down to the ground. Cocking his elbow back, he landed a shot just below the priest's wrist, forcing the Beretta away. Thrashing viciously, Donovan tried to escape from under the assassin, but to no avail. Conte let go of the priest's arm to prepare another elbow-shot, giving him a fraction of a second to strike. He jabbed hard with his fist on the side of Conte's head.

Momentarily dazed, Conte teetered to one side, allowing Donovan to stagger to his feet. Seeing there was no chance of getting the Beretta, the priest ran away in the direction of the autostrada.

After a few seconds, the pain subsided, but Conte was still seeing a haze of stars. He tried grabbing the fumbled Beretta, but neither crippled hand would obey. Abandoning the weapon, Conte sprang to his feet in pursuit.

Donovan knew it was only a matter of time until Conte caught up. *Please, Lord, help me get through this*. He heard Conte's hoarse panting a couple of paces behind him. Calling on all his reserve energy, Donovan pushed his body to the limit.

Five metres . . . Two metres . . . As Donovan's feet hit the autostrada's tarmac he barely registered a fast-approaching car on the periphery of his field of vision. A blaring horn, headlights. By some miracle, the car veered behind him . . . just as Conte's feet touched the roadway.

Donovan turned to see Conte's legs bend and snap in the wrong direction against the car's front end, his body hurled up onto the bonnet, striking the windscreen, tumbling over the roof and onto the roadway.

Trying to compensate for the sudden manoeuvre, the Mercedes's anti-lock brakes and traction control system simultaneously went into action. But on the rain-slicked tarmac the car careered into a large fir tree in a horrible cacophony of twisting metal and breaking glass. The driver—a young female with long blonde hair, who apparently hadn't been wearing a seat belt—was ejected through the windscreen and hung limp across the bonnet of the car, neck broken, blood everywhere.

There was nothing Donovan could do for her.

Conte was down, but, remarkably, still moving.

Donovan staggered over to the assassin. There was no way he was going to gamble that Salvatore Conte was going to have even the slightest chance of making it out alive. He clawed for the handgun still strapped to Conte's right ankle, tearing it free. As he jabbed it against Conte's right temple, he murmured, 'God forgive me,' and squeezed the trigger.

FATHER PATRICK DONOVAN dragged Conte's body into a thicket of bushes by the side of the road. Stripping the mercenary of his wallet, he came across a syringe and a vial of clear liquid, and pocketed them too.

He ran back along the track to the pit, easing himself down into it. He gently pulled the two bricks of C-4 from the ossuary, leaving them in the hole. With little room to manoeuvre, he managed to coax the ossuary up to the rim of the pit. Struggling to catch his breath, he climbed out.

Moving the Alfa closer, Donovan made a final effort to hoist the ossuary into the boot and stowed the shovels behind the box. Slamming the lid, he ducked into the driver's seat, a dirty, bloody mess. His muscles were aching and fatigue swept over him. But, overall, he was pleased. God had protected him . . . and he knew why. This injustice needed to be undone.

SEATED AT HIS kitchen table, sipping a late-afternoon tea, Razak was interrupted by his cellphone . He picked it up. '*As-Salaam*?'

'I saw you on television.'

The voice was vaguely familiar. 'Who is this?'

'A friend.'

Razak set down his glass.

'I know who stole the ossuary,' the voice stated flatly.

Razak straightened in his chair. 'I don't know what you're talking about.'

'Yes, you do. You delivered a package to me a few weeks ago in Rome. You gave me your card and said to call if there were any problems.'

Razak recalled the bald priest, sitting in the Caffè Greco with wiry fingers wrapped tightly round a pint of lager. Razak remembered that the leather satchel he had given the priest contained a confidential dossier. 'I'm listening,' he replied tentatively.

'The book contained very detailed information about an ossuary buried deep beneath the Temple Mount in a hidden chamber. There were nine other ossuaries there, too. Am I not correct?'

'OK.' Razak's voice was encouraging. Not quite an admission.

'And I have the tenth ossuary.'

Razak paused, stupefied. 'You killed thirteen men? Desecrated a holy site?'

'No,' the caller cut in, insistent. 'But I know who did.'

'And how do I know you're telling the truth?'

'Because I'm going to give the ossuary back to you . . . So you can put an end to this, as you see fit.'

At first, Razak didn't know what to say. 'And why would you do that?'

'I see what is happening there, in Jerusalem,' the man continued. 'Too many innocent people have already suffered.'

Razak couldn't help but ask: 'What was inside the ossuary that made it so valuable?'

There was a long pause. 'Something very profound.'

'Will the contents be returned with the box?'

'Unfortunately, I cannot allow that.'

Razak dared another question. 'Was it really *his* remains inside the box?'

The caller hesitated, clearly knowing whom Razak was referring to. 'There's no way to know for sure. For your own safety, please don't ask any more about this. Just let me know where you'd like it delivered.'

Razak pictured Barton sitting in an Israeli prison cell. Then he considered how Farouq—the force behind the delivery of the book that had set everything in motion—had played him for a fool. Razak decided to give the caller a shipping address. 'When should I expect it?'

'I'll have it to you as soon as possible.'

'And the book?' Razak enquired.

'I'll be sure to include that as well.'

'And for the record,' the caller added, 'the English archaeologist being held by Israeli police had nothing to do with all this.'

'I suspected that,' Razak replied. 'And the real thieves?'

Another pause. 'Justice has its own way of finding the guilty.'

Saturday

After dawn prayer, Razak headed straight for the Qur'anic teaching school on the Temple Mount. He hadn't slept at all last night, after the shocking phone call he'd received from the priest he had met in Rome three weeks ago. The Israeli police were right. Only an insider could have abetted the thieves. Now it was clear Graham Barton wasn't the insider.

The Keeper's office was empty.

Razak stood motionless for a moment, struggling with what to do. Reluctantly, he circled behind the desk and searched its drawers.

Inside, he discovered an array of items that included a litre of Wild Turkey bourbon that, since the Qur'an strictly forbade drinking alcohol, Razak fervently hoped Farouq had confiscated from someone. There was an ornate casket but it was locked. Finally, he found what he was looking for: a key ring. Snatching it up, he made his way out of the building.

Traversing the esplanade, Razak was unaware of the Keeper trailing discreetly behind him.

Negotiating his way through the Al-Aqsa Mosque's prayer hall, Razak stopped at a locked door on the rear corridor. One by one, he tried the keys. Finally, a silver key slid easily into the lock, which clicked and gave way. Razak depressed the door handle. Beyond the threshold the windowless room was dark. Moving inside, Razak fumbled for the light switch and the overhead strip lights crackled to life.

Razak's face slackened in bewilderment.

Along the rear wall of the storage room, nine ossuaries were neatly arranged. 'Allah save us,' Razak muttered in Arabic.

From the corner of his eye he detected a figure in the doorway and spun round.

Farouq.

'You've done well, Razak.' Farouq crossed his arms. 'You mustn't be troubled by this. They will shortly disappear.'

'What have you done?'

'A noble deed to help our people,' the Keeper stated flatly. 'Don't concern yourself with the small sacrifices that need to be made.'

'Small sacrifices? You framed an innocent man.'

'Barton? Innocent? None of *them* are innocent, Razak.'

'You sent me to Rome to deliver a package to the Vatican—a book that led them to perpetrate this unthinkable crime.'

'Razak.' Farouq shook his head in disappointment. 'You haven't grasped the seriousness of our situation here. Here in Jerusalem what we protect isn't just a patch of land or a sacred shrine. Islam is everything.'

'But this isn't a war.'

'It's been a war since the very beginning. Ever since the Christians and Jews decided to reclaim this forgotten land made sacred by the great prophet Muhammad, Allah grant him peace.'

'What was it that I delivered to Rome for you?'

Farouq contemplated the question. 'If I tell you, will you feel at peace with what has happened?'

'Perhaps.'

Farouq turned towards the door. 'Come with me.'

INSIDE FAROUQ'S OFFICE, Razak awaited the Keeper's explanation for enabling Christians to violate the Temple Mount—a deed so vile and deceitful that no motive seemed good enough.

The old man held out his hand. 'My keys, please.'

Razak dropped the key ring in the old man's palm.

Reaching beneath his desk, Farouq withdrew the small, rectangular casket and cradled it on his lap.

'When we began excavating the Marwani Mosque in 1996,' he began, 'tons of rubble were thoroughly sifted through and examined. The last thing we needed was some relic misconstrued as belonging to the Jewish temple.'

'You mean Solomon's Temple?'

He nodded. 'Archaeological evidence substantiating that claim has yet to surface and, as such, strengthens our position here.' Farouq's gruff voice rose slightly. 'But as you are aware, the Jews managed to persuade the Israeli government to study the whole platform's structural integrity, citing a bulge in the outer wall.' Farouq moved in his seat. 'The Israeli Antiquities Authority convinced many people—including some of our own—that this work was essential. Their studies were to have begun just days from now.'

Razak knew where this was going. 'So you knew that the hidden crypt would be discovered? How did you know it even existed?'

He patted the casket. 'This was unearthed a few years ago.'

Razak's eyes combed the stamped bronze exterior of the casket. The design appeared Islamic, but the symbols—mainly ornate cruciforms—were undoubtedly Christian. 'What does that seal mean?'

'Two medieval knights in full armour, sharing a single lance and one galloping horse, symbolises those who swore to rid this land of Muslim influence. The Christian knights of Solomon's Temple. The Knights Templar. It was found beneath the floor of the Marwani Mosque when an earth-moving machine broke a stone slab.'

'And what was inside?'

Farouq tapped the lid. 'A manuscript called the *Ephemeris Conlusio*. You delivered it to Rome three weeks ago. We needed the Catholics' help.'

Razak folded his arms. 'I'm assuming that this book indicated the vault's precise location?'

'There was a drawing accompanied by precise measurements.' Farouq went on to describe Joseph of Arimathea's account of Jesus' capture, crucifixion and burial, the revelation of the ossuary and its relics substantiating Jesus' crucifixion and mortal death.

'If this was true, it would violate the Qur'an's teachings.'

'Absolutely. You know our position when it comes to Jesus. Allah raised him up to heaven before his enemies could do him any harm—no arrest, no crucifixion . . . and certainly no burial. Now do you understand the necessity of eliminating this threat?'

'So you let the Catholics do your dirty work. And it gave you total deniability.' Once again, religion and politics had become inseparable.

'Since the threat was even more damaging to them, I knew the Catholics would act quickly to extract this relic,' Farouq continued smoothly. 'It would enable them to preserve their institution. In return we would strengthen our own position here by eliminating a threat that contradicts the Prophet's teachings. And before you pass judgment, let me show you one more thing.' He opened his desk drawer and produced a sheet of paper, which he laid out for Razak. 'Take a good look at this.'

Razak studied a crude sketch of rectangles accompanied by some text that appeared to be Greek. 'What's this?'

'Joseph's map of the Temple Mount—the same map the thieves had used to determine the ossuary's exact location. Notice that structure on top?'

Nodding, Razak felt choked.

'That's the Jewish temple Joseph so vividly describes in these pages.'

'Then it did exist after all.' Razak felt the breath sucked out of him.

Farouq smiled. 'Perhaps. Once we've permanently disposed of the remaining nine ossuaries, all archaeological evidence will be removed.'

Razak was at a loss. If it was true that the Western Wall had definitely once supported a temple, it legitimised Jewish claims to the platform.

'There is something you didn't deliver to Rome. Something you need to know.' Farouq unhinged the casket's lid. 'I found one other document in this Templar box. Another journal, not written by Joseph of Arimathea.'

'Whose journal is it?'

From the box, the Keeper pulled out a frail-looking scroll. 'That of the Templar Knight who discovered the ossuaries in the first place.'

CHAPTER 14

In their suite at the Fiumicino Hilton, Evan and Charlotte sipped coffee as they relaxed in armchairs facing the sun-filled window, overlooking the airport's busy runways. Not exactly classical Italian romance but Charlotte had insisted that she wouldn't feel safe going back into Rome.

She pulled her bathrobe snug and eyed Evan affectionately. Finally, she had achieved a good night's sleep. All it had taken were a couple of glasses of wine and a sleeping pill. The unexpected and utterly gratifying bout of lovemaking hadn't hurt, either. Having told Evan all about the incredible events that had taken place over the past few days, she'd shown him the astounding presentation stored on her laptop.

'I've missed you, Evan,' she said. 'I'm sorry about how I've been acting.'

'I've not exactly been on best behaviour either.' He smiled. 'Hey, I've been dying to show you something, Charlie. You have no idea.'

Getting up, he slalomed round the room-service cart and went directly to his bag. Unzipping its side pouch, she watched him take out a small box, a key ring, and what looked like a vial.

She shot him a look. 'What's going on?'

'First off, this is for you,' he said. 'It's the real reason I came here.' Smiling, he held out the small box in the palm of his hand.

Seeing it, her heart skipped a beat. It looked like a jewellery box . . .

'Go ahead. Open it.'

She glanced at him. Not exactly the most romantic approach.

'It's that bone sample you sent me.'

'Oh,' she said, feeling simultaneously relieved and disappointed. Pulling the lid away, she stared down at the metatarsal sitting on white gauze.

'You remember that anomaly we discussed?' Aldrich uncapped the tiny flash drive that dangled off his key ring and inserted it into her laptop. 'I thought the scanner was malfunctioning when I saw this,' he explained, activating a file. A video clip began loading and she leaned closer.

'Here we go. The first thing you'll see is the karyotype. I'll pause it when it comes up.' As playback began Aldrich froze the image.

Charlotte scrutinised the image. As soon as her eyes lit on the twenty-third chromosome set, she spotted something odd. One expected each chromosome to exhibit visible bands along its length. Pair twenty-three didn't have any banding. 'What's with twenty-three?'

'Exactly.' Aldrich brought up another screen showing a super-magnified cell nucleus. The chromosomes and nucleotide material were present in their natural, unordered state. 'I marked the twenty-third chromosome pair.' Aldrich pointed to two bright yellow circles on the screen.

'Got it.'

'Watch closely, Charlie. Here comes the extraction.'

'What?'

'I'll explain in a sec.' On the screen a hollow glass needle penetrated the nuclear membrane and some chromosome pairs—though not the twenty-third pair were extracted. The needle retracted from the nucleus and the membrane shrank back over the puncture.

'Now watch this.'

That's when she saw something remarkable unfold. The unbanded twin chromosomes—still inside the cell's nucleus—instantly began to divide, churning out new chromosome pairs to replace the extracted material. The spontaneous regeneration stopped once the nucleus had reached its odd equilibrium—forty-eight chromosomes.

'What did I just see?' She tore her eyes from the screen. '*Evan?*'

He looked up at her intently. 'A huge biological discovery. That's what you just saw. I'll play it again.'

And there it was, just as Evan had said—the most remarkable biological process she had ever witnessed—spontaneous genetic regeneration.

Charlotte covered her mouth. 'It's scientifically impossible for any human chromosome to replicate exact copies of other sets. There's DNA from the mother, the father . . . a complex genetic code.'

'Violates everything we know as scientists,' he stated flatly. 'Want to hear more?'

'You mean this gets better?'

'Much.' Aldrich collected himself. 'I performed a thorough analysis using the new gene scanner and mapped out the DNA's coding, comparing it with published genome maps. And I found that the sample you'd sent me registered less than *ten per cent* of the total expected genetic material found in the standard human genome.'

Charlotte shook her head in disbelief. 'I don't understand.'

'Me neither,' Aldrich replied. 'So I did a lot more testing. Using our new system to compare the genome to all known anomalies, I came up with . . . ready for this? *No matches.* Nothing! Not a single one!'

For a moment her rational mind shut down. No explanation came.

A flawless genome implied the absence of an evolutionary process. An organism in its purest, most unadulterated form.

Perfection, she thought. But how could a *human* possibly exhibit that kind of profile?

Evan Aldrich waved a hand at the screen. 'This DNA could take stem-cell research to a new level. I mean, this is *perfect* DNA in a viral form!' He spoke slowly. 'It got me thinking about the consequences of making this public. At first I thought how many lives could be saved, the effect on disease. Then I envisioned biotech companies scrambling to customise cures for the rich. And even if the poor got a look in, the result would be devastating. Widespread longevity would lead to unprecedented population growth that would place enormous strain on all the world's resources.'

She felt overwhelmed. 'I see what you mean, but—'

'Let me finish,' he urged. 'There's a point to all this.' He reached over and held the vial up in front of her. 'This.'

CARDINAL ANTONIO CARLO SANTELLI stared dejectedly out of his office window at the expanse of Piazza San Pietro and the giant obelisk at its centre that glowed pure white in the morning sunlight.

Late yesterday morning, after personally seeing to Conte's release from the Swiss Guard detention cell, he'd given the mercenary the go-ahead to eliminate the last complications that could implicate the Vatican in the Jerusalem debacle: the ossuary and its contents, of course; Patrick

Donovan, Charlotte Hennesey and her lover, Evan Aldrich.

Yet more blood on his hands.

Last night, he had expected an update from Conte to confirm that both the relics had been eliminated. No call had come. Now he was starting to worry that the mercenary had double-crossed him.

Worse, only minutes ago, he'd heard a news report concerning the death of a docent at the Torlonia catacombs. A routine police inquiry prompted by the death led investigators to search the catacombs to locate the person listed on a visitors' sign-in sheet found in the docent's office. Giovanni Bersei's broken body had been found at the base of a shaft.

Any minute now, Santelli expected a call from the investigators.

Another scandal.

In each hand, Santelli held the two halves of the scroll the scientists had found in Christ's ossuary. In his left hand was the sketched ceiling fresco in Joseph's crypt deep within the Torlonia catacombs. In his right hand was the Greek text that preceded the drawing, which he had asked Conte to separate from the picture, fearing it might contain some overt message. His glance shifted to Father Donovan's transcription of the text:

May faith guide us in our solemn vow to protect the sanctity of God.
Here lay his son, awaiting his final resurrection so that the souls of
all men may be judged. Let these bones not dissuade the faithful.
The spirit is the eternal truth.
May God have mercy on us all.
His loyal servant, Joseph of Arimathea

The intercom came to life, pulling the cardinal from his thoughts.

'Eminence, I'm sorry to bother you, but . . . Father Donovan is here to see you.' Father Martin sounded flustered. 'I told him you weren't available, but he's refusing to leave.'

Alarmed, the cardinal collapsed into his chair, hands gripping the armrests. *Donovan?* Impossible. Santelli opened the top drawer of his desk, confirming that the Beretta was still there. 'Send him in.'

Seconds later, the office door opened.

As Patrick Donovan made his way into the room, Santelli saw that he had deep bruises under each eye. He eyed the bulky leather bag that the priest gripped in his left hand.

Donovan sat in the leather chair opposite the cardinal and placed the bag on his lap. 'I came to show you something.' He patted the bag.

Had Santelli not been sitting in one of the most secure rooms in Vatican City, protected by metal and explosives detectors, he might have thought that inside the bag was some kind of weapon or bomb. But nothing like that could have made it this far.

'But first, I must ask you why you tried to have me killed?'

'That's a very serious accusation, Patrick.'

'It certainly is.'

'Are you wearing a wire? A recording device? Is that what this is about?'

Donovan shook his head. 'You know that it would have been detected before I made it through the door.'

The priest was right. This inner sanctum was designed to be foolproof. Santelli motioned to the satchel. 'So what have you brought me?'

'Something you must see with your own eyes.' Donovan stood and placed the satchel on Santelli's impossibly neat desk, glaring at the cardinal.

Irritated, Santelli levered himself out of his chair. 'Fine, Patrick. If looking in your bag will make you go away . . . so be it.' He opened the zip.

Santelli's face went a ghastly white as he stared at the human skull and bones, the ultimate relic. When he looked up, his eyes had lost their fiery glow. 'You sanctimonious bastard. You'll go to hell for this.'

'I wanted you to make your peace with Him before I perform a proper burial,' said Donovan. He'd felt terrible carrying the sacred bones around in a bag. But yesterday afternoon, he had stopped at DHL to arrange for the ossuary to be airfreighted immediately to Jerusalem. The manuscript had been sent separately to Razak. The spikes and coins were stowed in the rental car's glove compartment alongside the Beretta.

What happened next was a blur.

Yanking his hands out from his pockets, Donovan clasped the old man's wrist with his right hand, simultaneously revealing the small plastic syringe with his left. Thrusting it deep into the cardinal's upper arm, he pressed down on the plunger.

With a look of utter disbelief, the cardinal collapsed into his chair, and grabbed the site of the injection. Before he could yell for Father Martin, the Tubarine clamped down on his heart. Santelli buckled over in agony, his hands clawing for the pain, trying to tear it from his chest.

Donovan watched the body give a last convulsive shake. 'God's will,' he said quietly. He wasn't sure what the syringe had contained, but was fairly certain it had been Conte's method for killing the docent at the catacombs.

Murder violated everything he held sacred, but unless Santelli was taken down, Charlotte Hennesey would surely die, and an innocent archaeologist would shoulder the blame for a crime he hadn't committed.

Carefully gathering up the satchel, Donovan exited into the antechamber, advising Father Martin that the cardinal wished not to be disturbed.

RAZAK WAITED for Farouq to put on his reading glasses, all the while staring at the ancient scroll intently.

Clearing his throat, the Keeper began to read out loud.

'*December 12, Anno Dominae 1133.*

'*In Jerusalem, there has existed for centuries Christians who believe that Christ died a mortal death and that only his spirit rose from the tomb to appear to his disciples. They call themselves the "Order of Qumran".*

'*Through careful study, I began to understand that their beliefs were rooted in true faith and reverence. Their God was our God. Their Christ was our Christ. Interpretation was all that seemed to divide us.*

'*On the 11th day of October, 1133, Jerusalem was attacked by Muslim warriors. Our Christian brothers of Qumran fell and their leader, Zachariah, was wounded and dying when I found him. In his possession was an old book. Knowing that none of his brothers had survived the attack, he gave it to me. He whispered that the book contained an ancient secret long protected by his people—the location of the chamber where Christ's body had been interred.*

'*I employed trusted scribes to translate the book's writings, a journal written in Greek by a scholarly man named Joseph of Arimathea. A map drawn by Joseph marked the location of Christ's body, in a tomb buried beneath the site of Solomon's Temple.*

'*I ordered my men to find Joseph's tomb. After weeks of digging and breaching three ancient walls, we reached solid earth and a massive circular stone concealing a hidden chamber. Inside I found nine stone boxes inscribed with the names of Joseph and his family. To my amazement, a tenth box bore the sacred symbol of Jesus Christ, and in it were human bones and relics.*

'*To uphold my oath to protect God and His Son Jesus Christ, I have secured these wondrous relics beneath Solomon's Temple. For if the old man taught truth, these bones may one day be brought back to life so that the souls of all men might be saved. I have named Joseph of Arimathea's book* Ephemeris Conlusio. *In it are the secrets of our salvation.*

'May God forgive me for my deeds.

'His faithful servant, Hugues de Payen'

Farouq carefully rolled up the yellowed parchment and returned it to the casket. He removed his glasses and sat back, waiting for Razak's response.

Finally Razak spoke up. 'Tell me if I've got this right. In the twelfth century, the Knights Templar befriended a group of radical Christians who gave them the *Ephemeris Conlusio*, which led them to Jesus' body, buried in a secret room beneath this very platform. The Templars secured the crypt and secreted that casket together with the *Ephemeris Conlusio* beneath the floor. You found the casket during excavations here in 1997.'

'That is all correct.'

Razak tried to absorb it. Why would the Templars have hidden such extraordinary relics? It was possible that this knowledge had been retained as insurance—perhaps even blackmail—against the Church. It certainly helped explain the Templars' rise to power. But the piety in Hugues de Payen's letter had suggested something else. Perhaps the Templars had retained noble intentions? 'How did you convince the Vatican to take action?'

'Easily. I spoke to Father Patrick Donovan, the Vatican Library's head curator. I knew he would have been aware of the *Ephemeris Conlusio*'s existence and its implications. A few days later you delivered it to him in Rome. I correctly assumed that he would escalate things fast.'

'You took a very big risk doing all of this.'

'I acted as I saw fit, Razak, my friend. Averting discovery of Jesus' body preserves the teachings of both Islam and Christianity. Very regrettably, lives have been sacrificed in the process . . . but if we'd done nothing, there would have been a much higher death toll—both physical and spiritual—of both Muslims and Christians. Only the Jews would have gained at our expense.'

'How do you feel having learned of the contradictions to our teachings?'

Farouq stared at the ceiling. 'None of this should mean that we question our faith, Razak. It may mean we need to dig deeper for meaning. Even if those stolen bones truly were Jesus' remains, I will not waver in my faith. Not over some old bones.'

Razak recalled Barton saying something about pre-biblical texts viewing resurrection as a spiritual transformation—not a physical one. Perhaps the meaning of 'resurrection' had evolved into a more literal definition over the centuries. 'And Solomon's Temple?' he said, finally.

The Keeper pursed his lips. 'No one truly owns this place except Allah. For now, the Jews have regained control of Israel. But our very presence here, on this site, reminds them that this could be reversed. Ultimately, it is up to Allah.' Farouq circled round the desk and placed a hand on Razak's shoulder. 'Let us go to the mosque to pray.'

ALDRICH MOVED CLOSER to Charlotte. 'Charlie, what if I told you we could wipe away any disease with one injection— a serum so powerful that it can recode damaged DNA?'

Her mouth opened, but no words came. She stared from the vial, to Evan, and back again. Could it be?

'When I was at your house last week, I saw the medication in your refrigerator— the Melphalan . . . with your name on it.'

Her eyes welled up with tears. 'I've been meaning to tell you, but—' She collapsed in his arms.

'It's OK,' he said softly. 'Myeloma is one tough cancer. I know this must be tearing you up. And I know it's probably why you've been distant lately.'

Sobbing, she nodded. 'I . . . I haven't told anyone.'

'I can take the tough stuff, Charlie,' he said earnestly. 'You need to be able to trust me.'

Nodding, she reached over for the tissue box on the nightstand. 'I've got to tell my dad, too.' She dabbed the tears away.

'You're not going to have to tell him.'

'What are you talking about?'

He cradled the precious vial. 'I'd like you to be the first in my clinical trial.'

She wiped her eyes. 'Come on, Evan, it can't be that easy.'

'That's what I thought, too. But I think you'll agree that when it comes to genetics, I know what I'm talking about. I'm absolutely certain about this.'

She studied the vial again, this time more seriously. 'So . . . if I agree to this, you mean I just shoot this stuff into my body?'

'Yes. I've customised this serum to target your bones and blood cells.'

He looked at the vial, then back at her.

Time seemed suspended as she contemplated the dismal alternative of staying with the chemotherapy. No doubt, even if she were to control this incurable thing raging in her bones, those treatments would eliminate any hope of having children. Best-case scenario, she might live another ten or fifteen years. She'd never even make it to fifty.

'Well?'

She smiled, knowing that she could trust him. She recalled the Angel of Death in St Peter's, flipping the hourglass. 'OK.'

'Great.' He was grinning ear to ear. 'But just answer me one question. Who on earth *was* this guy?'

ST PETER'S BASILICA had closed promptly at 7 p.m. and the vast, dimmed interior was empty, except for one figure carrying a black bag.

Father Donovan moved to the front of the towering Baldacchino where a marble balustrade circled round a sunken grotto directly below the papal altar. Pausing to bless himself, he opened the side gate and crept down the semicircular staircase to an elaborate marble shrine. This was the most holy ground in Vatican City—the *Sepulcrum Sancti Petri Apostoli*. St Peter's tomb.

Donovan recalled Joseph's final passage in the *Ephemeris Conlusio*:

> *On this night, I am to be the guest of the emperor Nero in his palace, and so too, my wife and children. With much sadness, I have agreed, though I know his evil intent. Those of us who celebrate the teachings of Jesus have refused to pay tribute to him. For this, many he has burned alive. But for my loyal service to Rome, Nero has made known to me that my death and the deaths of my beloved family will be humane. The food we eat tonight will be poisoned.*
>
> *Rome is vast and there is no place he will not find us. The only protection we have comes from God.*
>
> *It has been agreed that our bodies will be given to my brother, Simon Peter, to be buried in my crypt beside Jesus. Once all have been freed from flesh, Peter will journey back to Jerusalem. Beneath the great temple will Jesus be interred, for this I promised to Him before His execution . . .*

Once Peter had fulfilled his duties, he had returned to Rome to continue preaching Jesus' teachings. Shortly thereafter, he was imprisoned by Nero and sentenced to death by being crucified upside down.

Keep moving, Donovan silently urged himself.

Directly beneath the Baldacchino's base, between red marble columns, was a small glass-enclosed niche containing a golden mosaic depicting a haloed Christ. In front of the mosaic was a golden casket—an ossuary. Inside were kept the bones of St Peter himself, extracted from a tomb that was discovered beneath the Baldacchino during excavations in 1950.

From his pocket, Donovan produced the gold key he had removed from a safe in the Vatican's Secret Archive. He set down the bag, then smoothly inserted the key into a lock on the niche's frame. The hinges let out a low moan as he eased the door open. Knowing that he had little time, Donovan reached out and grabbed the box's cover, pulling it up and away.

As expected, the ossuary was empty.

Following carbon dating, the saint's bones had been returned to the humble Constantine-era crypt where it was originally found. Few knew that this box was only meant to commemorate the first pope.

'God have mercy on me,' he whispered reverently.

Reciting the Lord's Prayer, he transferred the bones from the leather bag into the ossuary and replaced the lid.

As he closed the glass door and turned the lock, he heard noises emanating from above, within the basilica. A door opening. Urgent footsteps.

'*Padre Donovan*,' a deep voice called out in Italian. 'Are you in here?'

Peering through the balustrade, he could see three figures—two Swiss Guards and a priest.

Trapped!

He wondered how they had found him so quickly. Then he remembered he'd used his keycard to enter the basilica. Each key-swipe logged his location into the Swiss Guard's security system.

Trying his best to remain calm, he climbed up the steps and opened the gate. 'Yes, I'm over here,' he called out.

The two guards made their way quickly over to him, with the cleric trailing cautiously behind.

'Just finishing my prayers,' Donovan offered, confidently.

'Father Donovan.' The shorter guard's voice was curt. 'We need you to come with us.'

The librarian eyed the guard's gleaming Beretta and thought about yesterday, when he and Santelli had dropped by the barracks to retrieve Conte. The Swiss Guard's gunsmith had half a dozen weapons set out for maintenance. Amidst all the excitement, no one had even noticed Donovan slip the gun and a few clips of ammunition into his pocket.

Managing a smile, Donovan said, 'Is there a problem?'

'Yes,' the cleric responded, stepping into view. It was Father Martin. Had he brought the guards to arrest him?

'There's a major problem,' Martin stated severely. 'Shortly after you left Cardinal Santelli's office this evening, His Eminence was found dead.'

Donovan gasped, trying his best to look surprised. 'That's awful.'

'It seems that he suffered a heart attack,' Father Martin explained.

Studying Martin's face, Donovan swore he detected a lie.

'Very unfortunate,' Father Martin said quietly. Earlier that evening, he had listened in on Donovan's discussion with Santelli, using the cardinal's phone as an intercom. He was almost certain that Father Donovan had exacted revenge on the scheming old man, though he could only wonder how. Didn't the metal detectors register all weapons? But had he been in Donovan's position, he would have done the same. *Not only is the Church better off without that bastard Santelli*, Father Martin thought, *but so am I.* 'We need your help in collecting his legal papers from the archive.'

Donovan raised his head, eyes gleaming. 'Certainly. We can go there now.'

Martin offered a reassuring smile. 'Bless you, Father.'

Sunday

Graham Barton had never been so glad to see the dusty streets of Jerusalem. He drew a deep, invigorating breath, savouring the familiar smell of cypress and eucalyptus. It was a lovely morning. He grinned when he saw Razak standing at the bottom of the steps of the police station.

'I've heard that in Jerusalem being framed happens often.' Razak embraced Barton. 'But justice has a way of finding the guilty.'

'It certainly does. Speaking of which,' Barton said, confused, 'how did you manage this? What convinced the Israelis it wasn't me?'

'You'll find out soon enough,' Razak replied. 'I brought a gift for you.' He held out a thick envelope that looked like it contained a large book.

'What's this?'

'A copy of one of the exhibits presented as evidence in your defence,' Razak answered cryptically. 'There's a lot of history inside that envelope. You should read it. It says many interesting things.'

FAROUQ SAT on his verandah, overlooking the red-tiled roofs and weathered facades of the Old City's Muslim Quarter.

He felt good. Israel was once again teetering on the verge of violent confrontation, the struggle for Palestinian liberation was alive and well, and the faith of all—the vital fire required to keep the conflict burning—was strong. Smiling, he sipped his mint tea.

Suddenly, the doorbell rang.

No visitors were expected that morning. Scowling, the old man made his way back inside just as the bell rang again. 'I'm coming!' he yelled.

Opening the front door, he was surprised to find a yellow DHL delivery van parked out front, the Palestinian driver standing on the stoop.

'You have a large package,' said the uniformed man. 'Where would you like me to put it?'

The Keeper's face showed his puzzlement. He wasn't expecting anything. 'In the garage. I'll open the door.'

Inside, Farouq pushed the garage door button and the door slowly rolled back. The driver was waiting on the other side with the delivery. He lowered the crate onto the cement floor of the garage, rolled the handtruck back to the van and drove away.

Farouq eyed the shipping label. The package had come from Rome. The sender's name was a Daniel Marrone.

Suddenly the Keeper felt light-headed.

It took Farouq ten minutes to gather the courage to open the crate. Stripping away the bubble wrap, his fingers detected the cold touch of stone. A sinking feeling came over him. First the book. Now this? Pulling away the last of the wrapping, he stared vacantly at the beautiful etchings on the ossuary's fractured lid.

Without warning, figures suddenly materialised in the garage opening.

'Stay right there,' a voice commanded in Arabic.

Farouq stood bolt upright to see four men, each with a gun targeting his chest. They wore plain clothes and bulletproof vests, and he knew immediately who had sent them. Shin Bet agents. Ghosts from his past.

Ari Teleksen appeared round the corner, his saggy jowls raised on both sides by a sardonic smile. A cigarette dangled between his stern lips. He exhaled a plume of smoke, knowing it would offend the Muslim. 'Farouq al-Jamir,' Teleksen's haunting baritone filled the garage. 'Thought I'd bring you the owner's manual for your delivery. You seem to have left it in your office.' Gripped between the three fingers of his disfigured hand, he held up a plastic-covered ream of papers. 'If you'd like to see the original, maybe I can talk to my friends at the Israeli Antiquities Authority.'

Farouq recognised the photocopy of the *Ephemeris Conlusio*. 'Just like old times, eh?' Teleksen was grinning. 'Ready to go for a ride?' For the first time in a long while, Farouq felt afraid. Very afraid.

MICHAEL BYRNES

Born: New Jersey, March 3, 1950
Home: Florida
Hobbies: playing the guitar and basketball

RD: It must take huge discipline to run your own company and write books. To what do you attribute your ability to get things done?
MB: I just start writing without worrying about criticism or having a perfectly clear path. My passion for the subject matter provides structure and drive. I literally obsess about the story until it's finished. That's probably not so healthy, but it certainly keeps me on track.

RD: In 1997, after working at a large American insurance company for four years and moving up through the sales ranks, you co-founded your own brokerage business with a partner. Do you prefer being your own boss?
MB: Being self-employed provides lots of flexibility, so it's difficult to imagine working in a corporate environment again. However, my clients keep me humble and remind me that if I want to succeed, I'll always have a 'boss'.

RD: And what part of your work do you enjoy the most?
MB: I certainly don't enjoy all the paperwork that plagues insurance! But I've always been intrigued and challenged by the art of consultative selling. There are a lot of personality types out there and I've had to find a way to communicate effectively with all of them!

RD: What triggered your career as a writer?
MB: According to my mom, even as a kid I had a knack for writing. Art too. And I've been playing guitar for over twenty years. So the need to write or express myself artistically has always been there.

RD: What was the hardest part of putting together this, your first novel?
MB: Amassing the huge body of research necessary to bring the story to life. I had to gain proficiency in so many different disciplines: religion, history, geography, genetics, archaeology, forensic anthropology . . .

RD: Have you visited Rome and Jerusalem?
MB: Yes, I've been to both. 'Magical' is the word that best describes these cities. In fact, I was just in Jerusalem this March taking lots of pictures and videos for the sequel to *The Sacred Bones*, which I'm now finishing.

RD: Was it the Dome of the Rock that partly inspired the plot for _The Sacred Bones_?

MB: The Dome of the Rock and the Temple Mount embody the story. So I made both sites 'characters' in the book. Also, having grown up a Catholic, I was always fascinated by the historical Jesus and the use of the crucifix as the central icon for the faith.

RD: What was your reaction when you recently read in the press that a tomb had actually been found in Jerusalem back in 1980?

MB: The uncanny similarities—ten ossuaries, DNA, ties to the Jesus story—astounded me. I immediately sent a copy of my book to Hollywood director James Cameron, who's since produced a documentary about the site.

RD: How do you like to relax when not working or writing?

I really enjoy spending time with my wife and two young daughters. We play together, cook together and have lots of parties. I find great satisfaction and joy in watching my kids grow.

RD: Do you have any unfulfilled ambitions, especially non-literary ones?

RD: Right now, I can't handle many more ambitions! But I thrive on tackling new challenges, professionally and personally. So I'm thrilled when I think about where the road of life may take me.

JERUSALEM'S HIDDEN TREASURES

In 2007, after publication of _The Sacred Bones_, Michael Byrnes learned of a remarkable coincidence: a burial chamber, similar to the one he had imagined for his novel, had been found in the Jerusalem suburb of Talpiot in 1980. Furthermore, director Simcha Jacobovici was making a television documentary about the controversial archaeological findings for the Discovery Channel. In Byrnes's novel, the ossuary containing the sacred bones is stolen from a chamber deep beneath the Western Wall Plaza of the Temple Mount in Jerusalem, pictured below. The gilded cupola of the Dome of the Rock Mosque dominates the skyline behind the towering wall.

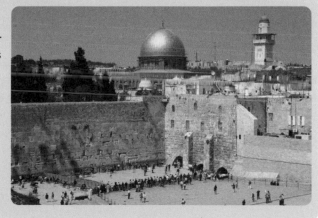

the Island

VICTORIA HISLOP

Alexis looked down at the little Cretan village shimmering in the afternoon sun, the white houses and the harbour fringed by a blindingly blue sea. Could this timeless, idyllic place, lost in a haze among the olive groves, be the key to her mother's secret past? Might it even provide the solution to her own future?

Plaka, 1953

A cold wind whipped through the narrow streets of Plaka and the chill of the autumnal air encircled the woman, paralysing her body and mind with a numbness that almost blocked her senses but could do nothing to alleviate her grief. As she stumbled the last few metres to the jetty she leaned heavily on her father, as if every step brought a stab of pain. But her pain was not physical. Her body was as strong as that of any young woman who had spent her life breathing the pure Cretan air, and her skin was as youthful and her eyes as intensely brown as those of any girl on this island.

The little boat, unstable with its cargo of oddly shaped bundles lashed together with string, bobbed and lurched on the sea. The elderly man lowered himself in slowly and, with one hand trying to hold the craft steady, then reached out to help his daughter. Once she was safely on board he wrapped her protectively in a blanket to shield her from the elements. The only visible indication then that she was not simply another piece of cargo were the long strands of dark hair that flew and danced freely in the wind. He carefully released his vessel from its mooring—there was nothing more to be said or done—and their journey began.

This was not the start of a short trip to deliver supplies. It was the beginning of a one-way journey to start a new life. Life in a leper colony. Life on Spinalonga.

PART 1

CHAPTER ONE
Plaka, 2001

Unfurled from its mooring, the rope flew through the air and sprayed the woman's bare arms with droplets of seawater. They soon dried, and, as the sun beat down on her from a cloudless sky, she noticed that her skin sparkled with intricate patterns of salty crystals, like a tattoo in diamonds. Alexis was the only passenger in the small, battered boat, and, as it chugged towards the lonely, unpeopled island ahead of them, she shuddered as she thought of all the men and women who had travelled there before her.

Spinalonga. She played with the word, rolling it around her tongue like an olive stone. As the boat approached the great Venetian fortification that fronted the sea, she felt both the pull of its past and an overpowering sense of what it still meant in the present. This, she speculated, might be a place where history was still warm, not stone cold, where the inhabitants were real, not mythical. How different, then, from the ancient palaces and sites she had spent the past few weeks, months—even years—visiting.

Alexis could have spent another day clambering over the ruins of Knossos, conjuring up in her mind from those chunky fragments how life had been lived there over 4,000 years before. Of late, however, she had begun to feel that this was a past so remote as to be almost beyond the reach of her imagination, and certainly beyond her caring. Though she had a degree in archaeology and a job in a museum, she felt her interest in the subject waning by the day. Her father was an academic with a passion for his subject. To him there was no ancient civilisation too far in the past to arouse his interest, but for Alexis, now twenty-five, the bullock she had passed on the road earlier that day had considerably more reality and relevance to her life than the Minotaur at the centre of the legendary Cretan labyrinth ever could.

The direction her career was taking was not, currently, the burning issue in her life. More pressing was her dilemma over Ed. All the while they soaked up the late summer rays on their Greek island holiday, a line was slowly being drawn under the era of a once promising love affair. Theirs was a relationship that had blossomed in the rarefied microcosm of a university, but, three years on, it was like a sickly cutting that had failed to survive being transplanted from greenhouse to border.

Ed was handsome, and it was his good looks that sometimes annoyed Alexis as much as anything. Certainly they added to his air of arrogance and enviable self-belief. They had got together in an 'opposites attract' sort of way, Alexis with her pale skin and dark hair and eyes and Ed with his blond, blue-eyed, almost Aryan looks. Sometimes, however, she felt her own wilder nature being bleached out by Ed's need for discipline and order; even the small measure of spontaneity she craved seemed anathema to him.

Everything had always gone Ed's way. He was one of life's golden boys: effortlessly top of the class and unchallenged victor ludorum year after year. The perfect head boy. A job in a top law firm. It would hurt to see his bubble burst. He had been brought up to believe that the world was his oyster, but Alexis had begun to see that she could not be enclosed within it. In spite of Ed's expectations that she would be moving in to his smart apartment in Kensington in the autumn, she had begun questioning the point of living with him if their intention wasn't to marry. And was he the man she would want as father of her children? Such uncertainties had circled in her mind for weeks, even months now, and sooner or later she would have to be bold enough to do something about them.

How can I be twenty-five and so *hopelessly* uncertain of the future? she asked herself. By the time her mother, Sofia, had been Alexis's age, she had been married for several years and had two children. How could she have been so settled and mature when Alexis still felt such a child? If she knew more about how her mother had approached life, perhaps it would help her to make her own decisions.

Sofia had always been extremely guarded about her background, though, and this sense that she was hiding something from her children cast a shadow of mistrust. Sofia Fielding appeared not just to have buried her roots but to have trodden down hard on the earth above them.

Alexis had only one clue to her mother's past: a faded wedding photograph that had stood on Sofia's bedside table for as long as Alexis could remember, the ornate silver frame worn thin with polishing. In early childhood, when Alexis used her parents' big lumpy bed as a trampoline, the image of the smiling but rather stiffly posed couple in the picture had floated up and down in front of her. Sometimes she had asked her mother questions about the beautiful lady in lace and the chiselled, platinum-haired man. Sofia had only given the briefest of answers: that they were her Aunt

Maria and Uncle Nikolaos, that they had lived in Crete and that they were now both dead. This information had satisfied Alexis then—but now she needed to know more. It had been the only framed photograph in the house, apart from those of herself and her younger brother Nick. This couple had clearly been significant in her mother's childhood and yet Sofia always refused to talk about them. As Alexis grew into adolescence she had learned to respect her mother's desire for privacy—it was as keen as her own teenage instinct to avoid communication—but she had grown beyond all that now. She needed to know more.

On the night before she was to leave for her holiday, she had gone to her parents' home, a Victorian terraced house in a quiet Battersea street. It had always been a family tradition to eat out at the local Greek taverna before either Alexis or Nick left for a new university term or a trip abroad, but this time Alexis had another motive for the visit. She wanted her mother's advice on what to do about Ed and, just as importantly, she planned to ask her a few questions about her past.

Arriving a good hour early, Alexis let herself into the house, dropped her heavy rucksack onto the tiled floor and tossed her key into the tarnished brass tray on the hall shelf.

'Hi, Mum!' she called into the silent space of the hallway. Guessing that her mother would be upstairs, she took the steps two at a time, and as she entered her parents' room she marvelled as usual at its extreme orderliness. A modest collection of beads was strung across the corner of the mirror and three bottles of perfume stood neatly lined up on Sofia's dressing table. Otherwise the room was entirely devoid of clutter. There were no clues to her mother's personality or past.

If the sparse minimalism of the master bedroom made it Sofia's space, the dark, messy study, where books were piled in towering columns on the floor, was Marcus's. Her father enjoyed working in this ruined temple of books; it reminded him of being in the midst of an archaeological dig, where every stone had been carefully labelled even if they all looked to the untrained eye like so many bits of abandoned rubble. It was always warm in the study, and as a child Alexis had often sneaked in to read a book, curled up on the soft leather chair that was the cosiest and most embracing seat in the house.

'Hello,' said Sofia, greeting her daughter's reflection in the mirror. She was simultaneously combing her short, blonde-streaked hair and rummaging in a small jewellery box. 'I'm nearly ready,' she added, fastening some coral earrings that matched her blouse.

Though Alexis would never have known it, a knot tightened in Sofia's stomach as she prepared for this family ritual. The moment reminded her of all those nights before her daughter's university terms began when she feigned jollity but felt anguished that Alexis would soon be gone. Sofia's ability to hide her emotions seemed to strengthen in proportion to the feelings she was suppressing.

'Hello, Mum,' Alexis said quietly. 'When's Dad back?'

'Quite soon, I hope. He knows you've got to be up early tomorrow so he promised not to be late.'

Alexis picked up the familiar silver frame and took a deep breath, summoning up courage to force her way into the no-go region of her mother's past, as though she was ducking under the striped tape that cordoned off the scene of a crime.

'Could I . . .' asked Alexis, 'could I go and see where you grew up?' Apart from her Christian name the only outward sign Alexis had of her maternal origins were her dark brown eyes, which she used now to full effect, locking her mother in her gaze. 'We're going to Crete at the end of our trip and it would be such a waste to miss the chance.'

Sofia was a woman who found it hard to show her feelings, to embrace. Reticence was her natural state, and so her immediate response was to search for an excuse. Something stopped her, however. Marcus had often said that Alexis would always be their child, but not forever *a* child. Now, seeing in front of her this independent young woman, whose questioning eyes were engaging with her own in such an adult way, this was finally confirmed. Instead of clamming up, Sofia responded with unexpected warmth.

'Yes . . .' she said hesitantly. 'I suppose you could.' Then, more certainly: 'Yes, it would be a good opportunity. I'll write a note for you to take to Fortini Davaras. She's lived in the village where I was born for her whole life and married the owner of the local taverna—so you might even get a good meal.'

Alexis shone with excitement. 'Thanks, Mum . . . Where exactly is the village?' she added. 'In relation to Hania?'

'It's about two hours east of Iraklion,' Sofia said. 'So from Hania it might take you four or five hours. After dinner I'll write the letter and show you exactly where Plaka is on a map.'

The careless bang of the front door announced Marcus's return from the university library. A bespectacled bear of a man with thick silvery hair, who probably weighed as much as his wife and daughter combined, he greeted Alexis with a huge smile as she ran down from her mother's room and flew into his arms in just the way she had done since she was three years old.

'Dad!' said Alexis simply, and even that was superfluous.

'My beautiful girl,' he said, enveloping her in the sort of warm and comfortable embrace that only fathers of such generous proportions can offer.

They left for the restaurant soon after, a five-minute walk from the house. Nestling in the row of glossy wine bars, overpriced patisseries and trendy fusion restaurants, Taverna Loukakis was the constant. It had opened not long after the Fieldings had bought their house and in the meantime had seen a hundred other shops and eating places come and go. For more than twenty years almost every landmark of the Fieldings' lives had been celebrated there. The owner, Gregorio, greeted the trio as the old friends they were, and so ritualistic were their visits that he knew even before they sat down what they would order.

It was a light-hearted evening. The three of them had not been together for several months and Alexis had much to catch up on, not least all the tales of Nick's love life. In Manchester doing postgraduate work, Alexis's brother was in no hurry to grow up and his family were constantly amazed at the complexity of his relationships.

As the evening progressed, Alexis felt a growing excitement that at last she might have the opportunity to delve further into her family history. In spite of the tensions she knew would have to be faced on her holiday, at least the visit to her mother's birthplace was something she could look forward to.

They finished their meal, politely drank the complimentary raki to the halfway mark, then left for home. Alexis would sleep in her old room tonight, and she was looking forward to those few hours in her childhood bed before she would have to get up to take the underground to Heathrow in the morning. She felt strangely contented in spite of the fact that she had singularly failed to ask her mother's advice about Ed. It seemed much more important at this very moment that she was going, with her mother's full cooperation, to visit Sofia's birthplace. All her pressing anxieties over the more distant future were, for a time, put aside.

When they returned from the restaurant, Alexis made her mother some coffee, while Sofia sat at the kitchen table composing the letter to Fortini. She rejected three drafts before finally sealing an envelope and passing it to her daughter. The whole process was conducted in silence, absorbing Sofia completely. Alexis had sensed that if she spoke the spell might be broken and her mother might have a change of heart after all.

FOR TWO AND A HALF weeks now, Sofia's letter had sat in the safe inner pocket of Alexis's bag, as precious as her passport. It had travelled with her from Athens and onwards on the fume-filled, sometimes storm-tossed ferries to Paros, Santorini and now Crete. They had arrived on the island a few days earlier and found a room to rent on the seafront in Hania—an easy task at this stage of the season when most holidaymakers had already departed.

These were the last days of their holiday, and having reluctantly visited Knossos and the archaeological museum at Iraklion, Ed was keen to spend a few days on the beach. Alexis, however, had other plans.

'I'm going to visit an old friend of my mother's tomorrow,' she announced as they sat in a harbourside taverna waiting to give their order. 'She lives the other side of Iraklion, so I'll be gone most of the day.'

It was the first time she had mentioned her pilgrimage to Ed and she braced herself for his reaction.

'Terrific!' he snapped resentfully. 'Presumably you're taking the car?'

'Yes, if that's OK. It would take me days if I had to go on buses.'

'Well, I suppose I don't really have a choice, do I? And I certainly don't want to come with you.'

Ed's angry eyes flashed at her like sapphires as his suntanned face disappeared behind his menu. He would sulk for the rest of the evening but Alexis could take that given that she had rather sprung this on him. What was harder to cope with was his total lack of interest in her plan, not even asking the name of the person she was going to visit.

Shortly after the sun had risen over the hills the following morning, she crept out of bed and left their hotel.

Something unexpected had come to her attention when she looked Plaka up in her guidebook. There was an island opposite the village just off the coast, and although the entry for it was minimal, missable even, it had captured her imagination:

SPINALONGA: Dominated by a massive Venetian fortress, this island was seized by the Turks in the eighteenth century. The majority of Turks left Crete when it was declared autonomous in 1898 but the inhabitants of Spinalonga refused to give up their lucrative smuggling trade until 1903, when the island was turned into a leper colony. In 1941, Crete was invaded by the Germans, but the presence of lepers meant Spinalonga was left alone. Abandoned in 1957.

It appeared that the raison d'être of Plaka itself had been to act as a supply centre for the leper colony, and it intrigued Alexis that her mother had made no mention of this at all. As she sat at the wheel of the hired Cinquecento, she hoped she might have time to visit Spinalonga.

The journey took her eastwards past Iraklion, and along the smooth, straight coastal road that passed through the insanely overdeveloped modern strips of Hersonisos and Mallia.

Passing mile upon mile of olive groves and, in places where the ground became flatter, huge plantations of reddening tomatoes and ripening grapes, she eventually turned off the main road and began the final stage of her journey towards Plaka. From here, the road narrowed and she was forced to drive in a more leisurely way to avoid small piles of rocks and, from time to time, a goat ambling in front of her as the road began to climb into the mountains. After one particularly sharp hairpin bend she drew in to the side, her tyres crackling on the gravelly surface. Way below her, in the blindingly blue waters of the Gulf of Mirabello, she could see the great arc of an almost circular natural harbour, and, just where the arms of it seemed to join in embrace, there was a piece of land that looked like a small, rounded hillock. From a distance, it appeared to be connected to the mainland, but from her map Alexis knew this was the island of Spinalonga and that to reach it there was a strip of water to be crossed. The remains of the Venetian fortress were clearly visible at one end and, behind it, fainter but still distinct, a series of lines mapped out; these were its streets. So there it was: the empty island abandoned less than fifty years ago after thousands of years of continuous habitation.

She drove the last few miles of her journey down to Plaka slowly, the windows wound down to let in the warm breeze and the fragrant smell of thyme. It was two o'clock in the afternoon when she finally rattled to a halt in the silent village square. It was a ghostly time to arrive in a Greek village. Dogs played dead in the shade and a few cats prowled for scraps. There were no other signs of life, simply some vague indications that people had been there not long before—an abandoned moped leaning against a tree, a backgammon set lying open on a bench. The village probably looked exactly as it had done in the 1970s when her mother had left.

Alexis had decided that she would try to visit the island of Spinalonga before she tracked down Fortini Davaras, because once she had found the elderly woman it might then seem rude to go off on a boat trip. It was clear to Alexis that she would be pushed to get back to Hania that night, but just for now she would enjoy her afternoon and would deal with the logistics of ringing Ed and finding somewhere to stay later on.

Deciding to take the guidebook at its word (*Try the bar in the small fishing village of Plaka where, for a few thousand drachma, there is usually a fisherman willing to take you across*), she made her way purposefully across the square and pushed aside the sticky rainbow of plastic strips that hung in the doorway of the village bar. Staring into the gloom, Alexis could just about make out the shape of a woman seated behind the bar.

'*Nero, parakalo*,' she said, hesitantly.

The woman reached into the fridge for some chilled mineral water which she poured carefully into a tall, straight-edged glass, adding a thick wedge of rough-skinned lemon. 'English?' she asked, as she passed it to Alexis.

Alexis nodded. It was a half-truth after all. It took her just one word to communicate her next wish. 'Spinalonga?' she said.

The woman turned on her heel and vanished through a little doorway behind the bar. Alexis could hear the muffled yells of 'Gerasimo! Gerasimo!' and, soon after, the sound of footsteps on a wooden staircase. An elderly man, bleary-eyed from his disturbed siesta, appeared. The woman gabbled away at him, and the only word that meant anything to Alexis was 'drachma', which was repeated several times. It was quite clear that, in no uncertain terms, he was being told that there was good money to be earned here.

The woman turned back to Alexis and, grabbing her order pad from the bar, scribbled down some figures and a diagram. Alexis deduced from this that her return trip to Spinalonga, with a two-hour stop on the island, would cost 20,000 drachma, around £35. She nodded and smiled at the boatman, who nodded gravely back at her. It was then that it dawned on Alexis that there was more to the ferryman's silence than she had realised. He could not have spoken even if he had wished. Gerasimo was dumb.

It was a short walk to the quayside where the fisherman's battered old boat was moored. They walked in silence past the sleeping dogs and the shuttered buildings, and Alexis castigated herself for not getting her mother to teach her some useful vocabulary—presumably Sofia could still speak Greek fluently even if her daughter had never heard her utter a word. The only sounds were the soft padding of their own rubber-soled feet and the relentless chorus of the cicadas. Even the sea was flat and soundless. Alexis muttered a polite '*efharisto*'—'thank you'—as Gerasimo helped her on board, at which he made a small grunting sound and touched the brim of his battered straw hat in reply.

So here she was being ferried on this 500-metre journey by a man who occasionally smiled, but no more. He was as leather-faced as any Cretan fisherman who had spent decades on storm-tossed seas, battling the elements by night and mending his nets in the baking sunshine by day. His features betrayed nothing. They were simply the quiet features of resigned old age and a reflection of all that he had lived through in the previous century.

Now approaching Spinalonga, Alexis gathered up her camera and the plastic two-litre bottle of water that the woman in the café had pressed upon her, indicating that she must drink plenty. As the boat bumped against the jetty, the old man offered her a hand and she stepped onto the deserted quay. She noticed then that the engine was still running. The old man was not, it appeared, intending to stay. They managed to communicate to each other that he would return in two hours, and she watched as he slowly turned the boat and set off back in the direction of Plaka.

Alexis was now stranded on Spinalonga and felt a wave of fear sweep over her. Supposing Gerasimo forgot her? Her dependency suddenly felt like a millstone and she resolved to pull herself together. She would embrace this period of solitude—her few hours of isolation were a mere pinprick of time compared with the life sentence of loneliness that past inhabitants of Spinalonga must have faced.

The massive stone walls of the Venetian fortification loomed above her. How was she to get past this apparently impregnable obstacle? It was then that she noticed, in the rounded section of the wall, a tiny, dark opening in the pale expanse of stonework. She stepped into a long tunnel that curved away to block the view of what lay at its far end. The dark, claustrophobic passageway went on for some metres, but when Alexis re-emerged into the dazzling early afternoon light she stopped, transfixed.

She was at the lower end of a long street lined on both sides with small two-storey houses. At one time this might have looked like any village in Crete, but these buildings had been reduced to a state of semi-dereliction. Window frames hung at strange angles on broken hinges and shutters twitched and creaked in the slight sea breeze. She walked hesitantly down the dusty street, taking in everything she saw: a church on her right with a solid carved door, a building that, judging by its large ground-floor window frames, had evidently been a shop, and a slightly grander detached building with a wooden balcony, arched doorway and the remains of a walled garden. A profound, eerie silence hung over it all.

In the downstairs rooms of the houses clumps of bright wild flowers grew in abundance, and on the upper storeys wallflowers peeped out from between cracks in the plaster. Many of the house numbers were still visible, focusing Alexis's imagination on the fact that behind each of these front doors real lives had been lived. She continued to stroll, spellbound. It was like sleepwalking, there was something entirely unreal about it all.

She passed what must have been a café, a larger hall and a building with rows of concrete basins, which she deduced must have been a laundry. Next to them were the remains of an ugly three-storey block with functional cast-iron balcony railings. The scale of the building was in strange contrast with the little houses, and it was odd to think that when this building was put up, around seventy years ago, it would have been thought the height of modernity. Now its huge windows gaped open to the sea breeze and electric wires hung down from the ceilings like clumps of coagulated spaghetti. It was almost the saddest building of all.

Beyond the town she came to an overgrown path that led away to a spot beyond all signs of civilisation. It was a natural promontory with a sheer drop into the sea hundreds of feet below. Here she allowed herself to imagine the misery of the lepers and to wonder whether in desperation they might ever have come to this place to contemplate ending it all. She stared out towards the curved horizon, so absorbed by her surroundings, so entirely immersed in the dense atmosphere of the place, that all thoughts of her own situation were suspended.

Retracing her steps into the silent town, Alexis rested for a while on a stone doorstep, gulping back some of the bottled water she had carried with her. Nothing stirred except for the occasional lizard scuttling through the dry leaves that now carpeted the floors of these decaying homes. Through a gap in the derelict house in front of her she caught a glimpse across the sea to Plaka. She could only begin to imagine how much its proximity must have tantalised the lepers.

What stories could the walls of this town tell? They would have seen great suffering. It went without saying that being a leper, stuck out here on this rock, must have been as bad a card as life could deal. Alexis was, however, well practised in making deductions from archaeological fragments, and she could tell from what remained of this place that life here had held a more complex range of emotions for the inhabitants than simply misery and despair. If their existence had been entirely abject, why would there have been a café? Why was there a building that could only have been a town hall? That this tiny island had been a community, not just a place to come to die, was clear from the remains of the infrastructure.

Time had passed quickly. When Alexis glanced at her watch she saw that it was already five o'clock. She leapt up, her heart pounding. Though she had enjoyed the silence and the peace, she did not relish the idea of being left here. She hurried back through the long dark tunnel and out onto the quay on the other side. The old fisherman was sitting in his boat waiting for her, and immediately she appeared, he twisted the key to start the motor. Clearly he had no intention of staying around longer than necessary.

The journey back to Plaka was over within minutes. With a sense of relief she spotted the comfortingly familiar hire car parked just opposite the bar. By now the village had come to life. Outside doorways women sat talking, and under the trees in the open space by the bar a group of men were huddled over a game of cards, a pall of smoke from their strong cigarettes hanging in the air. Back at the bar, they were greeted by the woman, who Alexis reckoned was the old man's wife. Having counted out a handful of scruffy notes, Alexis rummaged inside her backpack for the crumpled envelope containing Sofia's letter. She showed the address to the woman, who registered immediate recognition. Taking Alexis by the arm, she led her out into the street and pointed to a taverna about fifty metres down the road. Like an oasis, its painted blue chairs and checked indigo and white tablecloths seemed to summon Alexis. It was much too early for the local people to eat, but the moment she was greeted by the restaurant's owner, Stephanos, she knew she would be happy to sit there by herself and watch the sun go down.

'Is Fortini Davaras here today?' Alexis asked the moustachioed owner tentatively in English, as he led her to a table on the seafront. 'My mother knew her when she was growing up here. I have a letter for her.'

Stephanos, who knew a great deal more English than the woman at the bar, replied warmly that his wife was indeed there and would come out to see her as soon as she had finished preparing today's dishes. He suggested meanwhile that he bring her a selection of local specialities. With a glass of chilled retsina in her hand and some coarse bread on the table in front of her to sate her immediate hunger, Alexis felt a wave of contentment pass over her.

Stephanos returned with a series of small white plates stacked up his arm, each one charged with a tiny portion of something tasty and freshly prepared from his kitchen—prawns, stuffed zucchini flowers, tzatziki and miniature cheese pies. Alexis wondered if she had ever felt such hunger or been presented with such delicious-looking food.

As he approached her table, Stephanos had noticed her gazing out towards the island. He was intrigued by this lone Englishwoman who had, as Ariana, Gerasimo's wife, explained, spent the afternoon on Spinalonga.

'What did you think of the island?' he asked.

'It surprised me,' she replied. 'I expected it to be melancholy—and it was—but there was much more to it than that. It was obvious that the people who lived there did more than just sit around feeling sorry for themselves. At least that's how it seemed to me. Am I right?'

'May I sit down?' asked Stephanos, not waiting for an answer before scraping a chair across the floor and perching on it. 'My wife had a friend who used to live there,' he said. 'She is one of the few people round here who still has any connections with the island. Everyone else went as far away as possible once the cure had been found. Apart from old Gerasimo.'

'Gerasimo . . . was a leper?' asked Alexis slightly aghast. That would explain his haste to get away from the island once he had dropped her off.

By now, other customers were arriving and Stephanos got up from the wicker-seated chair to show them to their tables and present them with menus. The sun had fallen below the horizon and the sky had turned a deep pink. Swallows dived and swooped, catching insects on the rapidly cooling air. Alexis had eaten everything that Stephanos had put in front of her but she was still hungry.

Just as she was wondering whether to go into the kitchen to choose what to have next, as was perfectly acceptable for customers in Crete, the waitress arrived and set down an oval platter. 'This is today's catch,' she said. 'It is *barbouni*. Red mullet in English, I think. I hope I have cooked it as you like it—just grilled with fresh herbs.'

Alexis was astonished. Not just by the perfectly presented dish. Not even by the woman's soft, almost accentless English. What took her by surprise was her beauty. She had always wondered what kind of face could possibly have launched a thousand ships. It must have been one like this.

'Thank you,' she said finally. 'That looks wonderful.'

The vision seemed about to turn away, but then she paused. 'My husband said you were asking for me. I am Fortini Davaras.'

Alexis looked up in surprise. This woman was slim, scarcely lined, and her hair, piled high on her head, was still the colour of ripe chestnuts. She was not the old woman Alexis had been expecting to meet.

Alexis got uncertainly to her feet. 'I have a letter for you,' she said, recovering. 'From my mother, Sofia Fielding.'

Fortini Davaras's face lit up. 'You're Sofia's daughter! My goodness, how wonderful!' she said. 'How is she? How is she?'

Fortini accepted with huge enthusiasm the letter that Alexis held out to her, hugging it to her chest as though Sofia herself were there in person. 'I am so happy. I haven't heard from her since her aunt died a few years ago. I was worried when some of my last letters went unanswered.'

All of this was news to Alexis. How odd that she had never once seen a letter bearing a Greek postmark in the house. It seemed that her mother had gone to great lengths to conceal this correspondence.

By now Fortini was holding Alexis by the shoulders and scrutinising her face with her almond-shaped eyes. 'Let me see—yes, yes, you do look a bit like her. You look even more like poor Anna.'

Anna? On all those occasions when she had tried to extract information from her mother about the sepia-toned aunt and uncle who had brought her up, Alexis had never heard this name. 'Your mother's mother,' Fortini added quickly, immediately spotting the quizzical look on the girl's face.

'Come on, sit down, sit down. You must eat the *barbouni*,' said Fortini.

By now Alexis had almost lost her appetite, all but knocked backwards by the scale of her mother's secretiveness, but she felt it polite to cooperate and the two women sat down.

In spite of the fact that she wanted to ask all the questions—she was bursting with them—Alexis found herself answering Fortini's questions very openly. This woman was old enough to be her grandmother and yet it wasn't long before Alexis was confiding in her.

'My mother has always been secretive about her early life,' she said. 'All I know is that she was born near here and that she left when she was eighteen and never came back.'

'She really hasn't told you any more than that?' Fortini asked.

'No, nothing at all. That's partly why I'm here. I want to know more. I want to know what made her turn her back on the past like that.'

'But why now?' enquired Fortini.

'Oh, lots of reasons,' said Alexis, looking down at her plate. 'But mostly it's to do with my boyfriend. I've realised lately how lucky my mother was to find my father—I'd always assumed their relationship was typical.'

'I'm glad they're happy. It was a bit of a whirlwind at the time.'

'I've come to feel that if I find out more about my mother, it might help me. She was fortunate to meet someone she could care so much about, but how did she *know* he would be the right person for ever? I've been with Ed for five years and I'm not sure whether we should be together or not.'

This statement was uncharacteristic of the normally pragmatic Alexis and she was aware that she had strayed off the agenda. Besides, how could she expect this Greek woman, kindly as she was, to be interested in her?

Stephanos approached at this moment to clear the dishes, and within minutes he was back with cups of coffee and two generous balloons of molasses-coloured brandy. Other customers had come and gone during the evening and, once again, the table Alexis occupied was the only one in use.

Warmed by the hot coffee and even more so by the fiery Metaxa, Alexis asked Fortini how long she had known her mother.

'From the day she was born,' the older woman replied. But she stopped there, feeling a great weight of responsibility. Who was she to tell this girl things about her family's past that her own mother had clearly wanted to conceal from her? It was only at that moment that Fortini remembered the letter. She pulled it out of her apron and slit it open.

Dear Fortini,

Please forgive me for being out of touch for so long. I know I don't need to explain the reasons to you, but believe me when I tell you that I think of you often. This is my daughter, Alexis. Will you treat her as kindly as you always treated me—I hardly need to ask it, do I?

Alexis is very curious about her history—it's understandable, but I have found it almost impossible to tell her anything. Isn't it odd how the passage of time can make it harder than ever to bring things out into the open? Will you answer her questions? I think you will be able to give her a truer account than I ever could. Paint a picture of it all for her, Fortini. Will you show her where I was born—I know she will be interested in that—and take her to Agios Nikolaos?

This comes with much love to you and Stephanos.

Thank you, Fortini.

Yours ever, Sofia

When she had finished reading the letter, Fortini looked across at Alexis, who was studying her with curiosity.

'Your mother has asked me to tell you all about your family,' said Fortini, 'but it's not really a bedtime story. We close the taverna on Sunday and Monday. Why don't you stay with us for a couple of days? I would be delighted if you would.' Fortini's eyes glittered in the darkness. They looked watery—with tears or excitement, Alexis couldn't tell.

She knew that this might be the one chance she was offered in her lifetime to grab at the fragments of her own history before they were dissipated in the breeze. She understood that there was only one response to the invitation, even though she realised that to stay was an act of almost callous disregard for Ed. Just a brief text message would be all it would take. 'Thank you,' she said quietly. 'I'd love to stay.'

IT WAS NEARLY TEN when luminous sunshine came streaming through the gap between the thick hessian curtains and threw a beam across Alexis's pillow. As it woke her she instinctively slid further under the sheets. In the past fortnight she had slept in several unfamiliar rooms and each time she surfaced there was a moment of confusion as she adjusted to her surroundings.

When she got up and drew back the curtains she was greeted by the dazzling vista of a sparkling sea and the island of Spinalonga, which, in the shimmering heat, seemed farther away, more remote than it had yesterday.

She had had no intention of staying in Plaka overnight, and for that reason she had set off from Hania with nothing more than a map and her camera. Fortini, however, had come to her rescue, lending her everything she needed—one of Stephanos's shirts to sleep in, and a clean if rather threadbare towel. This morning, at the end of her bed, she found a floral shirt—not at all her style, and the pinks and blues looked incongruous with her khaki shorts, but after the heat and dust of the previous day she was glad for the change of clothing.

Alexis splashed her face with cold water at the basin in the corner and then wandered down the dark back stairway and found herself in the restaurant kitchen, drawn there by the powerful aroma of strong, freshly brewed coffee. Fortini sat at a huge, gnarled table in the middle of the room.

'*Kalimera*, Alexis!' she said warmly, rising to greet her.

She was wearing a blouse similar to the one she had lent Alexis, though Fortini's was in shades of ochre that matched the full skirt that billowed out from her slender waist and nearly reached her ankles. The first impression of her beauty, which had struck Alexis so forcibly the night before, had not been wrong.

'Did you sleep well?' asked Fortini.

Alexis stifled a yawn, nodded and then smiled at Fortini, who was now busily loading a tray with a coffeepot, some generously proportioned cups and saucers, and a loaf that she had just removed from the oven.

Alexis followed Fortini out through a set of the ubiquitous plastic strips and onto the terrace, where all last night's tables had been stripped of their paper cloths and now looked strangely bare with their red Formica tops.

The two women chose a table overlooking the sea. The September sunshine had a clear brilliance and a kindly warmth, and the women sat down opposite one another beneath the shade of an awning. After pouring the dense black liquid into cups Fortini put her hand on Alexis's.

'I'm so pleased you have come,' she said. 'You can't imagine how pleased. I was very hurt when your mother stopped writing—I understood perfectly, but it broke such an important link with the past.'

'I had no idea she used to write to you,' said Alexis, feeling as though she should apologise on her mother's behalf.

'The very beginning of her life was difficult,' continued Fortini, 'but we all tried, we really did, to make her happy and to do our best for her.'

Looking at Alexis's slightly puzzled expression, Fortini realised that she had to slow her pace. She gave herself a moment to think about how to start.

Alexis began to feel slightly edgy. The impregnable safe of her mother's past, which had been locked her entire life, was now to be opened. She stared out across the sea at the pale outline of Spinalonga and remembered her solitary afternoon there, already with nostalgia. Pandora regretted opening her box. Would it be the same for her?

Fortini spotted the direction of her gaze.

'Your great-grandmother lived on that island,' she said. 'She was a leper.' She didn't expect her words to sound quite so blunt, quite so heartless, and she saw straight away that they had made Alexis wince.

'A *leper*?' Alexis asked in a voice that was almost choked with shock. Though she knew her reaction was irrational, she was horrified to hear that her own flesh and blood had been leprous.

For Fortini, who had grown up in the shadow of the colony, leprosy had always been a fact of life. She had seen more lepers arrive in Plaka to cross over the water to Spinalonga than she could count. But she understood Alexis's reaction. It was the natural response for someone whose knowledge of leprosy came from the image of a bell-swinging sufferer crying, 'Unclean! Unclean!'

'Let me explain more,' she offered. 'Leprosy isn't a rampantly fast-spreading disease like the plague. It sometimes takes ages to develop—those images you have seen of people who are so terribly maimed are of those who have suffered for years, maybe decades. There are two strains of leprosy, one much slower to develop than the other. Both are curable now. Your great-grandmother was unfortunate. She had the faster-developing of the two types and neither time nor history was on her side.'

Alexis was ashamed of her initial reaction, but the revelation that a member of her family had been a leper had been a bolt out of the blue.

'Your great-grandmother may have been the one with the disease, but your great-grandfather, Georgios, bore deep scars too. He used to make deliveries to the island with his fishing boat, and it meant that he watched on an almost daily basis as she was gradually destroyed by the disease. You do know how it happens, don't you? Leprosy can affect nerve endings, and the result of this is that you can't feel it if you burn or cut yourself. That's why people with leprosy are so vulnerable to inflicting permanent damage on themselves with consequences that can be disastrous.'

Fortini paused, and smiled. 'I don't want your image of your mother's family to be dominated by disease. It wasn't like that,' she added. 'Look. I've got some photographs of them here.'

On the big wooden tray propped against the coffeepot there was a tatty manila envelope. Fortini opened it and the contents spilled out onto the table. Some of the photographs were no bigger than train tickets, others were postcard size; many had faded almost to invisibility.

The first photo Alexis focused on was one she recognised. It was the picture that her mother had next to her bed. She picked it up.

'That's your great-aunt Maria and great-uncle Nikolaos,' said Fortini, with a detectable hint of pride. 'And this one,' she said, pulling out a battered picture from the bottom of the pile, 'was the last picture taken of your great-grandparents and their two girls all together.'

She passed it to Alexis. The man was about the same height as the woman, but broad-shouldered. He had dark, wavy hair, a clipped moustache, a strong nose, and eyes that smiled even though the expression he maintained for this studio photograph was serious and posed. The woman next to him was slim, long-necked and strikingly beautiful; her hair was wound into plaits coiled up on top of her head, and her smile was broad and spontaneous. Seated in front of them were two girls in cotton dresses. One had strong, thick hair worn loose about her shoulders and her eyes were slanted almost like a cat's. She had mischief in her eyes and plump lips that did not smile. The other had neatly plaited hair, more delicate features and a nose that wrinkled as she smiled demurely at the camera.

'That's Maria,' said Fortini, pointing at the child who smiled. 'And that's Anna, your grandmother,' she said, indicating the other. 'And those are their parents, Eleni and Georgios.'

She spread the pictures out on the table, and occasionally the breeze lifted them gently from its surface and seemed to bring them to life.

There was also a picture of Anna arm in arm with a man in full traditional Cretan dress. It was a wedding picture.

'So that must be my grandfather,' said Alexis. 'Anna looks really beautiful there,' she added admiringly. 'Really happy.'

'Mmm . . . the radiance of young love,' said Fortini. There was a hint of sarcasm in her voice that took Alexis by surprise, and she was about to quiz her further when another picture surfaced which seized her interest.

'That looks like my mother!' she exclaimed. The little girl in the photograph had a distinctive aquiline nose and a sweet but rather shy smile.

Like any collection of family photographs, it was a random selection that told only fragments of a story. The real tale would be revealed by the pictures that were missing or never even taken at all.

'It all began here in Plaka,' said Fortini. 'Just behind us, over there. That's where the Petrakis family lived.'

She pointed to a small house on the corner. It was a tatty, whitewashed building, as shabby as every other home in the ramshackle village, but charming nevertheless. Its plastered walls were flaking and the shutters, repainted time and time again, were a shade of bright aqua that had peeled and cracked in the heat. A balcony, perched above the doorway, sagged under the weight of several huge urns from which flame-red geraniums cascaded downwards, as though making their escape through the carved wooden railings. It was typical of almost every home on every Greek island and could have been built at any time in the past few hundred years.

'That's where your grandmother and her sister grew up. Maria was my best friend; she was just over a year younger than Anna. Their father, Georgios, was a fisherman, like most of the local men, and Eleni, his wife, was a teacher at the local elementary school in Elounda, the town you must have come through to reach us here. She loved children—not just her own daughters, but all the children who were in her classes. I think Anna found that difficult. She hated sharing anything, especially her mother's affection. But Eleni was generous in every way and had enough time for all her children, whether they were her own flesh and blood or simply her pupils. When I was little I probably spent more time at the Petrakis place than I did at my own, but the tables turned later on and Anna and Maria more or less lived with us.

'Our playground at that time, and for our whole childhood, was the beach. We never tired of it. We would swim each day from late May to early October. During the winter months, when the tides were higher, there was usually something washed up on the beach for us to inspect: jellyfish, eels, octopus and the odd turtle. Whatever the season, we would go back to Anna and Maria's as it was getting dark and the fragrant smell of warm pastry often greeted us when we arrived—Eleni would make us fresh cheese pies and I'd usually be nibbling on one as I trudged home at bedtime.'

'It does sound an idyllic way to grow up,' interrupted Alexis, beguiled by Fortini's descriptions of this perfect childhood. What she really wanted to find out, though, was how it all came to an end. 'How did Eleni catch leprosy?' she asked abruptly. 'Were lepers allowed off the island?'

'No, of course they weren't. That was why the island was feared so much. Back at the beginning of the last century, the government had declared that all lepers in Crete should be confined on Spinalonga. People did everything they could to conceal symptoms, because the consequences of being diagnosed were so horrific. It was hardly surprising that Eleni was vulnerable to leprosy. She never gave a second thought to the risk of catching infections from her pupils—she couldn't teach them without having them sitting close, and if a child fell in the dusty schoolyard she would be the first to scoop the little one up. And it turned out that one of her pupils did have leprosy.' Fortini paused.

'Do you think the parents knew their child was infected?'

'Almost certainly,' replied Fortini. 'They knew they would never see the child again if anyone found out. There was only one responsible action Eleni could take once she knew she was infected—and she took it. She gave instructions that every child in the school should be checked so that the sufferer could be identified, and, sure enough, there was a nine-year-old boy, called Dimitri, whose wretched parents had to endure the horror of having their son taken away from them.'

'That must have been very difficult for Eleni to do—particularly if she had that kind of relationship with her pupils,' said Alexis thoughtfully.

'Yes, it was awful. Awful for everyone concerned,' replied Fortini.

Alexis's lips had dried and she hardly trusted herself to speak in case no sound came. To help the moment pass, she moved her empty cup towards Fortini, who filled it once more and pushed it back across the table.

As she stirred sugar into the dark, swirling liquid, Alexis said, 'Why has my mother never told me any of this?' she asked.

'She had her reasons, I'm sure,' said Fortini, knowing that there was so much more left to tell. 'Perhaps when you get back to England she'll explain why she was so secretive.'

OVER THE NEXT few days Fortini told Alexis everything she knew of her family's history. The two women strolled along the coastal paths, sat for hours over the dinner table and made journeys to local towns and villages in Alexis's hired car, with Fortini laying the pieces of the Petrakis jigsaw before them. These were days during which Alexis felt herself grow older and wiser, and Fortini, in retelling so much of her past, felt herself young again. The half-century that separated the two women disappeared to vanishing point, and as they strolled arm in arm, they might even have been mistaken for sisters.

PART 2

CHAPTER TWO
1939

Early May brings Crete its most perfect and heaven-sent days. On one such day, when the trees were heavy with blossom and the very last of the mountain snows had melted into crystal streams, Eleni left for Spinalonga. In cruel contrast to this blackest of events, the sky was a brilliant, cloudless blue. A crowd had gathered to watch, to weep, to wave a final goodbye, to their beloved 'Kyria Petrakis'.

Eleni Petrakis was loved in Plaka and the surrounding villages. She had a magnetism that attracted children and adults alike to her and was admired and respected by them all. The reason was simple. For Eleni, teaching was a vocation, and her enthusiasm touched the children like a torch. 'If they love it they will learn it' was her mantra.

But it was not just a favourite teacher who would be making her way over the water to Spinalonga that day. The children were saying goodbye to a friend as well: nine-year-old Dimitri, whose parents had gone to great lengths for a year or more to conceal the signs of his leprosy. Each month there had been some new attempt to hide his blemishes—his knee-length shorts were replaced by long trousers, open sandals by heavy boots, and in the summer he was banned from swimming in the sea lest the patches on his back should be noticed. 'Say you're afraid of the waves!' pleaded his mother, always knowing that sooner or later he would be found out.

Anyone unacquainted with the extraordinary circumstances of this summer morning might well have assumed that the crowd had gathered for a funeral. They were nearly a hundred in number, mostly women and children, and there was a sad stillness about them. They stood in the village square silent, waiting, breathing in unison. In an adjacent side street, Eleni Petrakis opened her front door and was confronted by the sight of this great mass of people. Her instinct was to retreat inside, but this was not an option. Georgios was waiting for her by the jetty, his boat already loaded up with her possessions. Anna and Maria remained behind the closed door, spared the sight of their mother's reducing figure. The last few minutes with them had been the most agonising of Eleni's life. She felt the strongest desire to hold them, to crush them in her embrace, to feel their hot tears on her skin, to still their shaking bodies. But she could do none of these things. Not without risk. Their faces were contorted with grief and their eyes swollen with crying. There was nothing left to say. Their mother was leaving. She would not be coming back that evening. There would be no return.

This was the hardest moment of Eleni's life and now the least private. She was watched by rows of sad eyes. She knew they were there to wish her farewell but never before had she yearned so much to be alone. Every face in the crowd was familiar to her, each was one she loved. 'Goodbye,' she said softly. 'Goodbye.' She kept her distance from them. Her old instincts to embrace had died a sudden death ten days ago, that fateful morning when she had noticed the strange patches on the back of her leg. They were unmistakable. Now, the words from Leviticus resounded inside her head:

As the leprosy appeareth in the skin of the flesh, he is a leprous man, he is unclean: the priest shall pronounce him utterly unclean . . . And the leper in whom the plague is, his clothes shall be rent and his head bare and he shall put a covering upon his upper lip and shall cry 'Unclean, Unclean.'

This Old Testament passage had been heard in churches for hundreds of years, and the image of a leper as a man, woman or even child to be cast out of society was deeply ingrained.

As Eleni approached the jetty, the crowd remained silent. One child cried, but was hushed by its mother. One false emotional move and these grieving people would lose their composure. The control, the formality would be gone and the dignity of this farewell would be no more. Though the few hundred metres had seemed an impossible distance, Eleni's walk to the jetty was nearly over, and she turned round to look at the throng for the last time. Her house was out of sight now, but she knew the shutters would remain closed and that her daughters would be weeping in the darkness.

Suddenly there were cries to be heard. They were the loud, heartbreaking sobs of a grown woman, and her display of grief was as unchecked as Eleni's was controlled. For a moment Eleni halted. These sounds seemed to be the precise outward expression of everything she felt inside, but she knew she was not their author. The crowd stirred, taking their eyes off Eleni and looking back towards the far corner of the square where a mule had been tethered to a tree and, close by, a man and a woman stood. Though he had all but disappeared within the woman's embrace, there was also a boy. The woman's arms were wrapped round his body as though she would never let go. 'My boy!' she cried despairingly. 'My boy, my darling boy!' Her husband was at their side. 'Katerina,' he coaxed. 'Dimitri must go. The boat is waiting.' Gently he prised the mother's arms away from the child. She spoke her son's name one final time, softly, 'Dimitri . . .' but the boy did not look up. His gaze was fixed on the dusty ground. 'Come, Dimitri,' his father said firmly. And the boy followed his father to the water's edge.

The final goodbye between father and son was a brief, almost manly one. Eleni, aware of this awkwardness, greeted Dimitri, her focus now solely on the boy whose life, from this moment on, would be her greatest responsibility. 'Come,' she said, encouragingly. 'Let's go and see our new home.' And she took the child's hand and helped him onto the boat as though they were going on an adventure and the boxes packed around them contained supplies for a picnic.

The crowd watched the departure, maintaining its silence. There was no protocol for this moment. Should they wave? Should they shout goodbye? Skin paled, stomachs contracted, hearts felt heavy. While some had ambivalent feelings about the boy, blaming him for Eleni's situation and for the unease they now had about their own children's health, at this moment they felt only pity for the two unfortunates who were leaving their families behind for ever. Georgios stood watching, his arms wrapped tightly across his chest, his head bowed. He thought that if he stood like this, his body tense, rigid, he could subdue his raging emotions and prevent them from spilling out as huge involuntary cries of anguish. Inside, though, he was stricken with grief. I must do this, he told himself, as though it is just another ordinary boat journey. To the thousand crossings he had already made would be added this one and a thousand more. Georgios pushed the boat away from the jetty and soon his oars were engaged in the usual battle with the current. For a short while the crowd watched, but as the figures became less distinct they began to disperse.

The last to turn away and leave the square were a woman of about Eleni's own age and a girl. The woman was Savina Angelopoulos, who had grown up with Eleni, and the girl was her daughter Fortini, who was the best friend of Eleni's youngest daughter, Maria. When the little boat had all but disappeared, the two of them turned and walked swiftly across the square to the house from which Eleni had emerged some time earlier. The faded green shutters were closed, but the front door was unlocked and mother and daughter stepped inside. Soon Savina would hold the girls and provide the embrace that their own mother, in her wisdom, had been unable to give.

AS THE BOAT neared the island, Eleni held Dimitri's hand ever more tightly. She was glad that this poor boy would have someone to care for him and at that moment did not give a second thought to the irony of the position. She would nurture him as though he were her own son.

Georgios guided the boat expertly towards the jetty and soon he was helping his wife and Dimitri onto dry land. Almost subconsciously, he found himself avoiding contact with the boy's bare skin as he helped him out of the boat. He then concentrated fiercely on tying the boat fast so that he could unload the boxes safely onto the quay, distracting himself from the thought of leaving the island without his wife.

Now that they were on Spinalonga, it seemed to both Eleni and Dimitri that they had crossed a wide ocean and that their old lives were already a million miles away.

Before Eleni had thought to look round once more, Georgios had gone. They had agreed the night before that there would be no goodbyes between them, and they had both been true to their resolve. Georgios was already a hundred metres away, his hat pulled down low so that the boat's dark strips of wood were all that lay in his field of vision.

A CLUSTER OF PEOPLE were standing outside the fortress wall, waiting for them. Eleni held out her hand to the man who came forward to greet them. It was a gesture that demonstrated an acceptance that this was her new home. She found herself reaching out to take a hand that was as bent as a shepherd's crook, a hand so badly deformed now by leprosy that the elderly man could not grasp Eleni's outstretched hand. But his smile said enough, and Eleni responded with a polite 'Kalimera'. Dimitri stood back, silent.

He would remain in this state of shock for several more days.

It was a custom on Spinalonga for new members of the colony to be received with some degree of formality by the island leader, Petros Kontomaris. He had been voted in, along with a group of elders, by the 300 or so inhabitants in the annual election. It was Kontomaris's duty to welcome all newcomers, and only he and a handful of other appointed individuals were permitted to come and go through the gateway.

Eleni and Dimitri followed Petros Kontomaris through the tunnel, their hands locked together. The scene that greeted them was a surprise. In the narrow street ahead of them was a throng of people. It looked just like market day in Plaka. People went to and fro with baskets full of produce, a priest emerged from a church doorway and two elderly women made their way slowly up the street, riding sidesaddle on their weary-looking donkeys. Some turned to stare at the new arrivals and several nodded their heads in a gesture of greeting. Eleni looked around her, anxious not to be rude but unable to contain her curiosity. What had always been rumoured was true. Most of the lepers looked as she did: ostensibly unblemished.

The small group continued to walk up the street, followed by an elderly man who led two donkeys bearing their possessions. Petros Kontomaris chatted to Eleni. 'We have a house for you,' he explained. 'It became vacant last week.'

In Spinalonga, vacancies were created only by death. People continued to arrive regardless of whether there was space, and this meant that the island was overcrowded. The previous year, just when existing buildings were reaching the limit of their capacity, an ugly but functional block had been completed and a housing crisis averted. Once again, every islander had some privacy. The man who made the final decision on where new-comers should live was Kontomaris. He regarded Eleni and Dimitri as a special case; they were to be treated as mother and son, and for that reason he had decided that they should not be housed in the new block, but should take over the newly vacant house in the high street.

'Kyria Petrakis,' he said. 'This is to be your home.'

At the end of the central street, where the shops ended, and standing back from the road, stood a single house. It struck Eleni that it bore more than a little resemblance to her own home. Then she told herself she must stop thinking in this way—this old stone house in front of her *was* her home. Kontomaris unlocked the door and held it open for her. The interior was dark, even on this bright day, and her heart sank. For the hundredth time that day, the limits of her bravery were tested. This was undoubtedly the best there was and it was imperative that she pretend to be pleased.

'I'll leave you to settle in,' Kontomaris said. 'My wife will be over to see you later and she will show you round the colony.'

'Your wife?' exclaimed Eleni with more surprise in her voice than she had quite intended. But he was used to such a reaction.

'Yes, my wife. We met and married here. It's not unusual, you know.'

'No, no, I'm sure it isn't,' said Eleni, abashed, realising that she had much to learn. Kontomaris gave the slightest of bows and left. Eleni and Dimitri were now alone, and they both stood looking about them in the day-time darkness. Apart from a threadbare rug, all that furnished the room was a wooden chest, a small table and two spindly wooden chairs. Tears pricked Eleni's eyes. Her life was reduced to this. Once again, though, there was an imperative for false cheer.

'Come on, Dimitri, shall we go and look upstairs?'

They crossed the unlit room and climbed the stairs. At the top were two doors. Eleni opened the left-hand one and went in, throwing open the shutters. The light poured in. The windows looked over the street and from here the sparkle of the sea could be seen in the distance. Eleni left Dimitri standing there and went into the other bedroom, which was smaller and somehow greyer. She returned to the first, where Dimitri still stood.

'This one will be your room,' she announced.

'My room?' he asked incredulously. 'Just for me?' He had always shared a room with his two brothers and two sisters. For the first time his small face showed some expression.

As they descended the stairs a cockroach scuttled across the room and disappeared behind the wooden chest in the corner. Eleni would hunt it out later, but for now she would light the three oil lamps which would help to brighten this gloomy dwelling. Opening her box of possessions she found paper and pencil and began to make a list. Georgios would be back in a few days and Eleni knew that he would fulfil her requirements to the very last letter.

Dimitri sat and watched Eleni as she drew up her inventory of essentials. He was slightly in awe of this woman who only yesterday had been his teacher and now was to be his mother, his *meetera*. But he would never call her by any name other than 'Kyria Petrakis'. He wondered what his real mother was doing now. She would probably be stirring the big cooking pot, preparing the evening meal. His throat tightened until it hurt so much the tears flowed down his face. Then Kyria Petrakis was by his side, holding him close and whispering: 'Everything will be all right, Dimitri . . . Everything will be all right.' If only he believed her.

That afternoon they unpacked their boxes. Surrounding themselves with a few familiar objects should have lifted their mood, but each time a new possession emerged it came with all the associations of their past lives.

One of Eleni's treasures was a small clock, a gift from her parents on her wedding day. She placed it in the centre of the mantelpiece and a gentle tick-tocking now filled the long silences. It struck on the hour, and at precisely three o'clock, before the chimes had quite died away, there was a gentle knock on the door.

Eleni opened the door wide to admit her visitor, a small, round-faced woman with flecks of silver in her hair. '*Kalispera*,' said Eleni. 'Kyrios Kontomaris told me to expect your visit. Please come in.'

'This must be Dimitri,' said the woman immediately, walking over to the boy, who remained seated, his head resting in his hands. 'Come,' she said, holding out her hand to him. 'I am going to show you round. My name is Elpida Kontomaris, but please call me Elpida.'

There was a note of forced jollity in her voice and the kind of enthusiasm you would summon up if you were taking a terrified child to have a tooth pulled. They emerged into the late-afternoon light and turned right.

'The most important thing is the water supply,' she began. 'This'—she pointed to a huge cistern at the foot of the hill—'is where we collect our water. It's a sociable place and we all spend plenty of time here chatting and catching up with each other's news.'

In truth, the fact that they had to trudge several hundred metres downhill to fetch water and then all the way back with it angered her beyond words. But, as usual, Elpida put on a brave front for her introduction to the island and presented only the positive aspects of it all. She showed Eleni Petrakis the few shops as though they were the finest in Iraklion, pointed out where the bi-weekly market was held and where they did their laundry. She also took her to the pharmacy, which for many was the most important building of all. She told her the times when the baker's oven was lit and where the *kafenion* was situated, tucked away down a little side street. The priest would call on her later, but meanwhile she indicated where he lived and took them to the church. She enthused to the boy about the puppet shows, which were put on for the children once a week in the town hall, and finally she pointed out the schoolhouse, which stood empty today, but on three mornings each week contained the island's small population of children.

She attempted to prise a smile out of the boy by describing the fun and games they had together, but his face remained impassive.

What she refrained from speaking of today, especially in front of the boy, was the restlessness that was brewing on Spinalonga.

As the wife of the island leader she was in a difficult position. Petros Kontomaris had been elected by the people of Spinalonga, but his most important task was to act as mediator between the government and a vociferous and sometimes radical minority in the leper colony who felt that they were being badly treated and who agitated constantly for improvements to the island's facilities. Elpida had seen huge changes since she had arrived, and most of these had been achieved through her husband's endeavours. Kontomaris had negotiated a monthly allowance of twenty-five drachma for every inhabitant, a grant to build the new block of flats, a decent pharmacy and clinic and regular visits from a doctor from the mainland. He had also constructed a plan that allocated land to each person who wished to cultivate their own fruit and vegetables to sell at the weekly market. In short, he had done everything he humanly could, but the population of Spinalonga always wanted more and Elpida was not sure that her husband had the energy to fulfil their expectations. He was in his late fifties, like her, but his health was failing. Leprosy was beginning to win the battle for his body.

The rumbles of dissatisfaction grew by the day, the water situation being the main focus of unrest, particularly in the summer. The Venetian water system, constructed hundreds of years earlier, collected rainwater in tunnelled watersheds and stored it in underground tanks to prevent evaporation. It was ingeniously simple, but the tunnels were now beginning to crumble. Additionally, fresh water was brought over from the mainland every week, but there was never enough to keep more than 200 people well washed and watered. In the winter it was electricity they needed as the generator, which had been installed a couple of years earlier, had packed up after only three weeks and had never worked again. Requests for new parts were ignored and the machinery stood abandoned, covered now with a tangle of weeds.

Water and electricity were not luxuries but necessities, and the inhabitants of Spinalonga seethed with anger that the government's commitment to making their lives better was at best perfunctory.

All they could do was try to make their voices heard, and that was where Petros's powers of argument and diplomacy became their most valuable weapon. Elpida had to maintain some distance between herself and the rest of the community but her ear was continually bent, mostly by the women, who regarded her as a conduit to her husband. She was tired of it all and secretly pressured Petros not to stand in the next election.

As she led Eleni and Dimitri around the little streets of the island, Elpida kept all this to herself. She saw Dimitri clutch the edge of Eleni's billowing skirt as they walked, as if for comfort, and sighed to herself. What sort of future did the boy have in this place?

Eleni found the gentle tug at her skirt reassuring. It reminded her that she was not alone and had someone to care for. Only yesterday she had had a husband and daughters, and the day before a hundred eager faces at school had looked up into hers. All of them had needed her and she had thrived on that. This new reality was hard to grasp. Suddenly she could feel huge tears well up in her eyes. For the first time she lost control. Her throat contracted as if to deny her another breath and she took one desperate gasp to drag air into her lungs. Elpida, until now so matter-of-fact, so businesslike, turned to face her and grasped her by the arms. Dimitri looked up at both women as the tears coursed freely down his teacher's cheeks.

'Don't be afraid to cry,' said Elpida gently. 'The boy will see plenty of tears here. Believe me, they're shed freely on Spinalonga.'

Eleni buried her head in Elpida's shoulder and Dimitri looked away, embarrassed. By good fortune they had come to a halt outside Elpida's house, and she led Eleni firmly inside. As the official residence of the island leader, the house was one of the buildings dating from the island's period of occupation by the Venetians, with a wooden balcony, which could almost be described as grand, and a porticoed front door.

The dwelling provided an extraordinary contrast with almost every other home on the island and was secretly coveted by everyone on Spinalonga. Floor-to-ceiling windows allowed light to flood in on three sides, and an ornate crystal lamp hung down into the middle of the room on a long, dusty chain, the small, irregular shapes of coloured crystal projecting a kaleidoscopic pattern onto the pastel walls.

The furniture was worn but comfortable, and Elpida gestured to Eleni to take a seat. Dimitri wandered about the room, examining the framed photos and staring into a glass-fronted cabinet that housed precious pieces of Kontomaris memorabilia: an etched silver jug, a row of lace bobbins, some pieces of precious china and, most intriguingly of all, row upon row of tiny soldiers. He stood gazing into the cabinet for some minutes, not looking beyond the glass at these objects but mesmerised by the reflection of Kyria Kontomaris with her arms wrapped round Kyria Petrakis, comforting her as she wept. He watched for some moments and then refocused on the soldiers so neatly arranged in their regiments.

When he turned round to face the women, Kyria Petrakis had regained her composure and reached out both hands towards him. 'Dimitri,' she said, 'I am sorry.'

Her crying had shocked and embarrassed him, but now the thought suddenly occurred to him that she might be missing her children as much as he was missing his mother. He took Kyria Petrakis's hands and squeezed them hard. 'Don't be sorry,' he said.

Elpida disappeared into her kitchen to make coffee for Eleni and lemonade for Dimitri. When she returned she found her visitors sitting, talking quietly. The boy's eyes lit up when he saw his drink and he had soon drained it to the bottom. As for Eleni, whether it was the sweetness of the coffee or the kindness, she could not tell, but she felt herself enveloped in Elpida's warm concern. It had always been her role to dispense such sympathy and she found it harder to receive than to give.

The afternoon light was beginning to fade. For a few minutes they sat absorbed in their own thoughts, the silence broken only by the careful clink of their cups. When they had all finished their drinks, Elpida spoke.

'Shall we continue our walk?' she asked, rising out of her seat. 'There's someone waiting to meet you.'

Eleni and Dimitri followed her from the house. Dimitri was reluctant to leave. He had liked this house where the light shone in rainbow patterns and the chairs were softer than anything he had ever slept on, and hoped he might go back one day to take a closer look at the soldiers in the cabinet.

Farther up the street a functional building, several hundred years newer than the leader's residence, was their next stop.

Eleni and Dimitri's arrival had coincided with one of the three days on which the doctor came from the mainland to visit the hospital. The doctor who had put himself forward for what many of his colleagues thought was a dangerous and foolhardy assignment was Christos Lapakis. He was a jovial fellow in his early thirties, well liked by the staff in the dermatovenereology department at the hospital in Agios Nikolaos, and loved by his patients on Spinalonga. His great girth was a reflection of his belief that the here and now was all you had so you might as well enjoy it.

Dr Lapakis spent his time on Spinalonga treating wounds and advising his patients on all the extra precautions they could take and how exercise could help them. His emphasis on cleanliness, sanitation and physiotherapy had improved the health and lifted the morale of many on the island. When he had first arrived, he had discovered something akin to apathy among the inhabitants. Their sense of abandonment was catastrophic and the psychological damage inflicted by being on the island was actually greater than the physical harm caused by the disease.

Christos Lapakis treated both their minds and their bodies. He told them that there always had to be hope and that they should never give up. He was authoritative but often blunt: 'You will die if you don't wash your wounds,' he would say. He was pragmatic and told them the truth dispassionately, but also with enough feeling to show that he cared. Lapakis was a great supporter of Kontomaris and gave him all the backing he could in lobbying for the freshwater supply that could transform the island and the prognosis of many who lived there.

'Here's the hospital,' said Elpida. 'Dr Lapakis is expecting you.'

They found themselves in a space as cool and white as a sepulchre and sat on the bench that ran down one side of the room. They were not seated for long. The doctor soon came out to greet them, and in turn, the woman and the boy were examined. The pale-faced Dimitri had a few large dry patches on his back and legs, indicating that at this stage he had the less damaging, tuberculoid strain of the disease. The smaller, shinier lesions on Eleni Petrakis's legs and feet worried Dr Lapakis much more. Without any doubt she had the more virulent, lepromatous form.

The boy's prognosis is not too bad, Lapakis mused. But that poor woman, she's not long for this island. His face, however, did not betray the merest hint of what he had discovered.

CHAPTER THREE

When Eleni left for Spinalonga, Anna was twelve and Maria ten. Georgios was faced with managing the job of homemaking single-handedly and, more importantly, the task of bringing up the girls without their mother. Of the two, Anna had always been the more difficult. She had been obstreperous to the point of uncontrollability even before she could walk, and from the day her younger sister was born it seemed she was furious with life.

Maria had an altogether gentler nature, and she fell naturally into the role of peacekeeper even if she often had to fight an instinct to react against Anna's aggression. Unlike Anna, Maria did not find domestic work belittling, and enjoyed helping her father clean and cook, a tendency for which Georgios silently thanked God.

To the world at large, Georgios seemed a man of few words. Those who knew him better saw his uncommunicative behaviour as a reflection of a quiet stoicism, a quality that stood him in good stead now that his circumstances had changed so drastically.

Life for Georgios had rarely been anything but tough. He was a fisherman like his father and grandfather before him, and like them he had become hardened to long stretches spent at sea, battling against the wild waves. A Cretan fisherman never questioned his lot. For him it was fate, not choice.

For several years before Eleni had been exiled there, Georgios had supplemented his income by making deliveries to Spinalonga. Nowadays he had a boat with a motor and would go there once a week with crates of essential items, dropping them off on the jetty for collection by the lepers.

For the first few days after Eleni left, Georgios dared not leave his daughters for a moment. Their distress seemed to intensify the longer their mother was away. Although kind neighbours came with food, Georgios still had the responsibility of getting the girls to eat. One evening, when he faced the task of cooking a meal himself, his woeful inadequacy at the stove almost brought a smile to Maria's lips. Anna, though, could only mock her father's efforts.

'I'm not eating this!' she cried, throwing her fork down into her plate of mutton stew. 'A starving *animal* wouldn't eat it!' With that she burst into tears for the tenth time that day and flounced from the room. It was the third night that she had eaten nothing but bread.

'Starvation will soon crack her stubbornness,' her father said lightly to Maria, who silently chewed a piece of the overcooked meat.

The day eventually came when they had to return to school, and as soon as Anna and Maria had something other than their mother to focus on, their grief began to abate. This was also the day when Georgios could point the prow of his boat once more towards Spinalonga. With a curious mix of dread and excitement he made his way across the narrow strip of water. Eleni would not know he was coming, and a message would have to be sent to alert her to his arrival. But news travelled fast on Spinalonga, and, before he had even tied his boat to the mooring post, Eleni had appeared round the corner of the huge wall.

What could they say? How could they react? They did not touch though they desperately wanted to. Instead they just spoke each other's names. They were words they had uttered a thousand times before, but today their syllables sounded like noises with no meaning. At that moment Georgios wished he had not come. He had mourned his wife this last week, and yet here she was, just as she always had been, as vivid and lovely as ever, which only added to the unbearable ache of their impending separation.

Eleni's time on the island had been full of activity and had passed quickly, but when she heard that Georgios's boat had been spotted on its way from Plaka, her emotions were thrown into turmoil. Now that he was standing there before her, his deep green eyes gazing into hers, there was only one focus for her thoughts: how much she loved this broad-shouldered man and how much it hurt her to the core of her being to be separated from him.

They asked almost formally about each other's health, and Eleni enquired after the girls. How could he respond, except with an answer that only just brushed the surface of the truth? Once they had got used to it all he would be able to tell her honestly how they were. The only truth today was in Eleni's answer to Georgios's question.

'What's it like in there?' He nodded in the direction of the stone wall.

'Dimitri and I have a house all to ourselves,' she told him, 'and it's not unlike our home in Plaka. We have our own courtyard and by next spring we should have a herb garden, if you can bring me some seeds. There are roses already in bloom on our doorstep. It's not bad really.'

Georgios was relieved to hear such words. Eleni now produced a folded sheet of paper from her pocket, and an envelope, and gave them to him.

'This is a list of things we need for the house, and a letter for the girls.'

Georgios noted the use of 'we' and a pang of envy hit him. Once, 'we' had included Anna, Maria and himself, he reflected, now 'we' meant the child who had taken Eleni away from them. Georgios was finding it hard to believe that God had not deserted them all. One moment he had been the head of a household; the next he was just a man with two daughters.

It was time for Georgios to go. The girls would be back from school soon. 'I shall be across again soon,' he promised. 'And I'll bring everything you've asked for.'

'Let's agree on something,' said Eleni. 'Shall we *not* say goodbye? There's no real sense in the word.'

'You're right,' responded Georgios. 'We'll have no goodbyes.'

They smiled and turned away from each other, Eleni towards the shadowy entrance and Georgios to his boat. Neither looked back.

Georgios visited the island more regularly and his meetings with Eleni were his oxygen. He lived for those moments when she would appear through the archway in the wall and they would sit together on the stone mooring posts or in the shade of the pines that grew, as if for the purpose, out of the dry earth. Georgios would tell her how the girls were, what they had been doing, and would confide in her about Anna's behaviour.

'Sometimes it's as though she has the devil in her,' said Georgios one day as they sat talking. 'She doesn't seem to get any easier with time.'

'Well, it's just as well that Maria isn't the same,' replied Eleni.

'That's probably why Anna is so disobedient half the time, because Maria doesn't seem to have a wicked bone in her body,' reflected Georgios. 'And I thought tantrums were meant to be something children grew out of.'

'I'm sorry to leave you with such a burden, Georgios, I really am,' sighed Eleni, knowing that she would give anything to be facing the battle of wills involved in bringing Anna up instead of being stuck on this island.

GEORGIOS WAS NOT even forty when Eleni left, but over the next few months he was to age beyond recognition. His hair turned from olive black to the silvery grey of the eucalyptus, and people seemed always to refer to him as 'Poor Georgios'. It became his name.

Fortini's mother Savina Angelopoulos did as much as she was able, while managing her own home too. On still, moonless nights, knowing that there could be a rich catch, Georgios would want to go out fishing, and it became a regular event for Maria and Fortini to sleep, top to tail, in the latter's narrow bed, with Anna on the floor next to them, two thick blankets for her mattress. Maria and Anna also found they were eating more meals at the Angelopoulos home than their own. On those nights there would be eight at the table: Fortini and her two brothers, Antonis and Angelos, her parents, and Georgios, Anna and Maria. Some days, Savina would try to teach Anna and Maria how to keep their house tidy, how to beat a carpet and how to make up a bed, but quite often she would end up doing it all for them. Anna had no interest in anything domestic. Why should she learn to patch a sheet, gut a fish or bake a loaf? She was determined that she would never need such skills and from an early age had a powerful urge to escape from what she regarded as pointless domestic drudgery. While Maria simply accepted her lot, knowing that complaining achieved nothing and just made things worse, her sister had no such wisdom. 'Why do *I* have to go and get the bread every morning?' she complained one day.

'You don't,' her father replied patiently. 'Maria gets it every other day.'

'Well, why can't she get it *every* day? I'm the oldest and I don't see why I have to get bread for her.'

'If everyone questioned why they should do things for each other, the world would stop turning. Now, go and get the bread. Right this minute!'

Georgios's fist came down on the table. He was weary of Anna turning every domestic task she was asked to perform into an argument.

On Spinalonga, meanwhile, the first really disagreeable encounter Eleni experienced on the island was with Kristina Kroustalakis, the woman who ran the school.

'I don't expect her to like me,' she commented to Georgios, 'but she's acting like an animal that's been driven into a tight corner.'

'Why does she do that?' asked Georgios one day, already knowing the answer.

'She's a useless teacher, who doesn't care a drachma for the children— and she knows that's what I think of her,' answered Eleni.

Georgios sighed. Eleni had never been reticent about her views.

Almost as soon as they had arrived, Eleni had seen that the school had little to offer Dimitri. After his first day, he returned silent and sullen, and when she enquired what he had done in class his reply was 'Nothing'.

'What do you mean "nothing"? You must have done something.'

'The teacher was writing all the letters and numbers on the board and I was sent to the back of the class for saying that I already knew them. Then the oldest children were allowed to do some really easy sums and when I shouted out one of the answers I was sent out of the room.'

After this, Eleni started to teach Dimitri herself, and then other children began to come to her for lessons. Soon those who had barely been able to distinguish their letters and numbers could read and do their sums, and within a few months her house was filled with children on five mornings a week.

The tension between Kristina Kroustalakis and Eleni began to build up. It was evident to almost everyone that Eleni should take over the school and that the valuable teacher's stipend should be hers. Kristina Kroustalakis refused to consider even the possibility of sharing her role, but Eleni was invited to put her case before the elders. She brought with her examples of the work the children had been doing both before and after she arrived.

'But this simply shows natural progress,' protested one elder, known to be a friend of Kyria Kroustalakis. To most of them there, however, the evidence was plain, and the elders voted in favour of removing the established teacher from her position and installing Eleni instead.

The school provided Dimitri with almost everything he needed: a structure to his day, stimulation for his mind, and companionship, in the form of a new friend, Nikos. In some ways this life was an improvement on how things used to be. The small, dark-eyed boy now endured less hardship and fewer worries than had burdened him as the oldest of five children in a peasant family. Each afternoon, however, when he left the school building to return home, he would become aware of the undercurrents of adult disquiet. He would hear snatches of conversation in the café or whispered discussions between people as they talked in the street.

There was the endlessly recycled discussion over whether they would be getting a new generator and the perennial debate over the water supply, as well as whispers about an increased 'pension' for every member of the colony. The smallest events, as well as the larger ones, such as illness and death, were anticipated and endlessly mulled over. One day, though, something took place for which there had been no build-up and little forewarning, but which was to have a huge impact on the life of the island.

One evening a few months after Dimitri and Eleni had arrived they were eating supper when they were disturbed by an insistent banging on the door. It was Elpida, out of breath and flushed with excitement.

'Eleni, please come,' she panted. 'There are boatloads of them—*boatloads*—and they need our help. Come!'

Eleni knew Elpida well enough by now to realise that if she said help was called for, no questions needed to be asked. Dimitri's curiosity was aroused. He dropped his cutlery and followed the women.

'They're from Athens,' Elpida gasped as they hastened down the twilit street. 'Georgios has already brought over two boatloads and he's about to arrive with the third. They're mostly men, but I noticed a few women as well.'

By now they had reached the tunnel that led to the quay. Eleni turned to Dimitri and told him to go back to the house and finish his supper. Then the two women hurried on and were soon out of sight.

Even from the end of the tunnel, Dimitri could hear the muffled echo of male voices, and he was more curious than ever about what was causing the commotion. Looking furtively behind him, he darted into the dark passageway, making sure he kept close to the sides. As he turned the corner he could see quite clearly what the fuss was all about.

New inhabitants usually arrived one by one and slipped as discreetly into the community as they could. On the quayside tonight, however, there was no such calm. As they tumbled off Georgios's small boat, many of the new arrivals lost their balance before landing heavily on the stony ground. They shouted, writhed and howled, and from his shadowy position, Dimitri could see the the newcomers were all wearing strange jackets that trapped their arms behind their backs.

The boy watched as Eleni and Elpida bent down and undid the straps that kept these people tied up like packages and, one by one, released them from their hessian prisons. Lying in heaps on the ground these creatures seemed less than human. The boy was both fascinated and fearful as the newcomers slowly unfurled themselves and stood upright, regaining a little dignity. Even from where he stood, he could feel the anger and aggression that emanated from them. Gathering around one particular man, who appeared to be attempting to calm them, several talked at once, their voices raised.

Dimitri counted. There were eighteen of them here, and Georgios was turning his boat round for his return trip to Plaka where he would collect one more boatload.

A FEW DAYS before, Georgios had taken a letter from Athens across to Petros Kontomaris warning him of the lepers' imminent arrival. The island leader decided to keep his own counsel. The prospect of nearly two dozen new patients arriving simultaneously on Spinalonga would send the islanders into a state of panic. All Kontomaris had been told was that these lepers had created trouble at the hospital in Athens—and as a consequence had been shipped like cattle to Plaka. From there, Georgios was to bring them on the final stretch of their journey to Spinalonga.

Georgios returned with the last five passengers. When they reached Spinalonga, the previous arrivals were wandering about. It was the first time in thirty-six hours that they had stood upright. The four women among them remained in a quiet huddle. Petros Kontomaris was walking from one person to another asking for names, ages, occupations and number of years since diagnosis. Every additional minute that he could detain them here with this bureaucracy gave him more time for some kind of inspiration about where, in heaven's name, these people were going to be housed. By the time he had finished, one thing was very clear. The new arrivals on his list were mostly trained professionals: lawyer, teacher, doctor, master stonemason, editor, engineer . . . This was an entirely different category of folk from those who made up the bulk of the population on Spinalonga, and

Kontomaris felt slightly fearful of this band of Athenian citizens who had arrived in the guise of beggars.

It was time now to take them into their new world. Kontomaris led the group through the tunnel and into the square, where they came to a halt. The island leader turned to face them.

'Apart from the women, who will be housed in a room in the block at the top of the hill, you will be accommodated temporarily in the town hall. Your arrival swells our number by ten per cent and we now expect the government to provide money for new housing, as they have long promised.'

A crowd of islanders had gathered round the newcomers and now there was a murmur of unrest as they heard the announcement. The town hall was where the social life of Spinalonga, such as it was, took place, and to commandeer it was to strip the islanders of a key resource. But where else was there? Nowhere. It had to be the town hall.

The first few days were tense. Everyone waited to see what impact these twenty-three new arrivals would have, but for forty-eight hours most of them were hardly seen, many lying impassively on their improvised bedding. Dr Lapakis visited them and noted that they were all suffering not just from leprosy but also from the rigours of a journey without adequate food or water and without shade from the relentless sun. It would take each one of them several weeks to recover from the months, perhaps years, of mistreatment they had endured even before their journey from Athens.

Lapakis had heard how there was no discernible difference between conditions in the leprosy hospital and those in the city jail. All the patients had been treated barbarically, and this group who had arrived in Crete had been the driving force behind a rebellion. Mostly professional, educated people, they had led a hunger strike, smuggled out letters to friends and politicians, and stirred up dissent. Rather than agreeing to any change, however, the governor of the hospital had decided to evict them; or, as he preferred to term it, 'transfer them to more suitable accommodation' on Spinalonga.

The women were visited each day by Elpida. They were soon recovered enough to have their tour of the island and even to begin planning how they would make use of the small plot of ground that had been cleared for them to grow vegetables. They recognised very quickly that this life was an improvement on the old. From their window on the second floor they could see the sun rise, and during their first days on the island they were entranced by the sight of the slow-breaking dawn.

Just as Eleni had done, they turned the space they were given into a home. Embroidered cotton cloths hung across the windows at night and woven rugs spread across their beds transformed the room.

For the men, it was a different story. They languished on their beds for several days. Kontomaris organised for food to be brought to the hall, but at first the islanders' offerings were scarcely touched. On the fourth day, however, Nikos Papadimitriou emerged, blinking, into the sunlight. Forty-five years old and a lawyer, Papadimitriou had once been at the centre of Athenian life. Now he was the leader and spokesman for a group of lepers, playing this role with just as much energy as he had put into his legal career.

Though sharp-tongued, Papadimitriou had great charm and could always gather supporters. His great ally and friend was Mihalis Kouris, an engineer who had, like Papadimitriou, been in the Athenian hospital for nearly five years. That day, as Kontomaris took them around Spinalonga, the two men asked a constant stream of questions. 'So where is the water source?' 'How long have you been waiting for the generator?' 'How often does the doctor visit?' 'What are the current building plans?'

Kontomaris answered their questions as well as he could, but could tell by their every grunt and sigh that they were rarely satisfied with the answers. He had worked tirelessly for six years to improve things, and it was a thankless task. As he strolled out beyond the town towards the cemetery, he wondered why he had bothered at all. Papadimitriou's insistent questioning made him want to sit down and weep. He decided that he would tell the Athenians the bald facts.

Stopping in his tracks he turned to face the two men and said, 'I'll tell you everything you want to know. But, if I do that, the burden becomes yours too. Do you understand?'

They nodded in assent, and Kontomaris began to give them the details of all the island's shortcomings, all the issues currently under negotiation. Then the three of them went back to the leader's house and, with Papadimitriou and Kouris's fresh perspective on the island's facilities, drew up a new plan. This included works in progress, projects to be started and finished within the coming year, and an outline of what would be undertaken in the forthcoming five-year period. Within weeks, their proposals were ready to be submitted to the government. Papadimitriou's law firm in Athens, a family practice of some influence, became involved. 'Everyone on this island is a citizen of Greece,' he insisted. 'They have rights.' To the amazement of everyone—apart from Papadimitriou himself—within a month the government had agreed to provide the money they had asked for.

The other Athenians, once they had risen from their torpor, threw themselves into new building projects. No longer were they abandoned invalids but members of a community where everyone had to pull their weight. It was now late September, and though temperatures were more moderate, the issue of water was still pressing. Something had to be done to the crumbling water tunnels and Mihalis Kouris was the man to do it.

Once repairs were complete, everyone looked to the heavens for rain, and one night in early November their prayers were answered. In a spectacular display of sound and light, the skies opened. Pebble-sized hailstones bounced down, sending goats scampering for safety on the hillsides, as flashes of lightning bathed the landscape in an apocalyptic luminescence. Next morning the islanders woke to find their watersheds brimful of cool, clear water. Having resolved the most pressing issue of all, the Athenians then turned their attention to creating homes for themselves. With the sort of industry and efficiency rarely seen on Crete, the derelict houses in the area between the main street and sea were restored and raised up out of the rubble. Well before the first snowfall crowned Mount Dhikti they were ready to be occupied and the town hall was once again available for everyone.

Then, as winter approached, the campaign for the generator began to bear fruit as a letter arrived from Athens promising all the parts that were required. As Eleni wrote in a letter to Anna and Maria: *The generator is going to make so much difference to our lives. There was one here once before so some of the electric fittings are already in place and two of the men from Athens are expert in how to make it all work (thank goodness). Every house is promised at least one light and a small heater.*

Anna read the letter in the dying light of a winter's afternoon. A low fire burned in the grate but she could see her breath on the cold air. Why did her mother have to write so often? Did she really think that they all wanted to hear of her warm, contented and now well-lit life with that boy? Her father made them reply to every letter he brought from the island and Anna struggled over every word. She was not happy and she was not going to pretend.

Maria read her mother's letter and showed it to her father.

'It's good news, isn't it?' Georgios commented. 'And it's all thanks to those Athenians.'

Before the sharpness of the December winds arrived, the island had warmth and electric light.

Georgios and Eleni decided that for a few days before and after Christmas Georgios would not cross the choppy waters to visit Eleni. Not just because the vicious wind would bite into his hands and face until they were raw, but because his daughters needed him. After early-morning Mass on Christmas Day Georgios and his daughters feasted with the Angelopoulos family on pork and delicious *kourambiethes*, sweet nutty biscuits baked by Savina.

Things were not so different on Spinalonga. The children sang in the square, helped bake the seasonal loaves known as *christopsomo*, Christ's bread. For Dimitri it was the first time he had enjoyed such plentiful food.

On January 1, St Basil's Day, Georgios visited Eleni once again, bringing her presents from the children and from Savina. The ending of the old year and the beginning of the new was a watershed, a milestone that took the Petrakis family into a different era. Although Anna and Maria still missed their mother, they now knew that they could survive without her.

CHAPTER FOUR
1940

After its best winter in years came Spinalonga's most glorious spring. It was not just the carpets of wild flowers that spread across the northern slopes and peeped out of every crack in the rocks that made it so, but also the sense of new life that had been breathed into the community.

Spinalonga's main street, only a few months earlier a series of dilapidated buildings, was now a smart row of shops with shutters and doors freshly painted in deep blues and greens. The *kafenion* was flourishing and a new taverna opened specialising in *kakavia*, freshly made fish soup.

As Kontomaris's strength began to fail, the leader relied more and more on Papadimitriou, and the popularity of the Athenian grew among the islanders. The men and women respected him for what he had achieved in such a short time, and soon he enjoyed a sort of hero worship.

Although the Athenian had ambitions, he was not a ruthless man, and he would not stand for election unless Kontomaris was ready to retire.

'Papadimitriou, I'm more than ready to give up this position,' the older man said one night in early March over a game of backgammon. 'I've told you that a thousand times. The job needs fresh blood—and look at what you have done for the island already! My supporters will back you, there's no question of it. Believe me, I'm just too weary now.'

Papadimitriou was unsurprised at this last comment. During the six months since his arrival he had seen Kontomaris's condition deteriorate.

'I'll take it on if you really are ready to let go,' he said quietly, 'but there's one other thing I want you to know. If I do win the election, I shall not want to live in your house.'

'But it isn't my house,' retorted Kontomaris. 'It's the leader's house. It goes with the position and always has done.'

Papadimitriou drew on his cigarette and decided to let the matter rest. The issue might be hypothetical in any case since the election was not entirely a *fait accompli*. It would be contested by two others, one of whom had been on the island for some six or seven years.

When the annual elections were held in late March, however, Papadimitriou won by a clear majority. The population had voted with their hearts, but also with wisdom. It was a pivotal moment in the civilising of the island.

'Fellow inhabitants of Spinalonga,' he said. 'My wishes for this island are your wishes too.' He was speaking to the crowd gathered in the small square outside the town hall on the night following the election. 'We have already made Spinalonga a more civilised place, and in some ways it is now an even better place to live than the towns and villages that serve us.' He waved his hand in the direction of Plaka. 'We have electricity when Plaka does not. We have diligent medical staff and the most dedicated of teachers. On the mainland, many people are living at subsistence level, starving when we are not. Last week, some of them rowed out to us from Elounda. Rumours of our new prosperity had reached them and they came to ask *us* for food. Is that not a turnaround?'

A murmur of assent rippled through the throng. Someone shouted out from the crowd: 'Three cheers for Papadimitriou!' When the cheers died down, he added one final note to his message.

'There is one thing that binds us together. The disease of leprosy. While we have life, let us make it as good as we can—this must be our common purpose.' He raised his hand in the air, pointing his finger upwards into the sky, a sign of celebration and victory. 'To Spinalonga!' he shouted.

The crowd mirrored the gesture, and with a cry that was heard across the water in Plaka they cried out in unison: 'To Spinalonga!'

THE NEXT AFTERNOON, Elpida Kontomaris began to pack her possessions. Within a day or two she and Petros would need to move out of the house and into Papadimitriou's current accommodation. She had expected this moment for a long time but it did not lessen the feeling of dread.

A gentle tap on the door interrupted her thoughts. When Elpida opened it, a large, darkly dressed male figure filled the frame. It was Papadimitriou.

'*Kalispera*, Kyria Kontomaris. May I come in?' he asked.

'Yes . . . please do,' she answered, moving away from the door.

'I have only one thing to say,' he told her as they stood facing each other, surrounded by the half-filled crates of books, china and photographs. 'There is no need for you to move out of here. I have no intention of taking this house away from you. Petros has given so much of his life to being leader of this island that I have decided to endow him with it.'

'But it's where the leader has always lived,' Elpida protested. 'It's yours now, and besides, Petros wouldn't hear of it.'

'I have no interest in what has happened in the past,' replied Papadimitriou. 'I'm in charge now. What I want you to do is unpack all your things from these boxes and put them back exactly where they were. I'll come back later to make sure you've done that.'

Elpida's eyes glistened with tears. 'It's so kind of you,' she said, extending both her hands towards him. Before Papadimitriou went on his way, she asked him to eat with them that evening. She cooked as no one else on Spinalonga, and only a fool would ever turn down such an invitation.

When Kontomaris arrived home later that day, his duties as leader finally completed, there was a lightness in his step. As he entered his house, the fragrant smells of baking wafted over him and an apron-clad Elpida came towards him, her arms outstretched in welcome.

'It's all over,' he murmured as they embraced. 'At long last it's over.'

As he glanced up, he noticed that the room looked just as it always had. There was no sign of the half-filled crates that had been standing about the room when he had left that morning.

'Why haven't you packed?' There was more than a note of irritation in his voice. He was weary and the fact that nothing seemed even vaguely ready to be transported to their new home upset him greatly.

'I packed and then I unpacked,' Elpida replied mysteriously. 'We're staying here.'

Precisely on cue, there was a knock at the door. It was Papadimitriou.

'Kyria Kontomaris invited me to eat with you,' he said simply.

Once they were all seated and a generous glass of ouzo had been poured for each of them, Kontomaris regained his composure. 'I think there's been some kind of conspiracy,' he said. 'I should be angry, but I know you both well enough to realise I've no choice in this matter.'

His smile belied the formality of his words. He was secretly delighted at Papadimitriou's generosity, not least because he knew how much it meant to his wife. The three of them toasted each other in ratification of the deal that had been struck, and the issue of the leader's house was never mentioned between them again.

WORK CONTINUED apace with the renovation of the island. Papadimitriou's efforts had not merely been an electioneering ploy. Repairing and rebuilding went on until everyone had a decent place to live, their own oven—usually in the courtyard in front of their home—and, even more importantly for their sense of pride, a private outdoor latrine.

The social aspect of their lives was also enhanced, however, when Panos Sklavounis, an Athenian who had once been an actor, took Papadimitriou to one side with a suggestion.

'Boredom is growing like a fungus here,' he said. 'What people need is entertainment. Lots of them can't look forward to next year, but they might as well have something to look forward to next week.'

'I see your point and I agree entirely,' responded Papadimitriou. 'But what do you propose?'

'Entertainment. Large-scale entertainment,' replied Sklavounis grandly.

'Which means what?' asked Papadimitriou.

'Movies,' said Sklavounis.

Six months earlier, such a proposal would have seemed as laughable as telling the lepers they could swim across to Elounda to visit the cinema. Now, however, it was not beyond the realms of possibility.

'Well, we have a generator,' said Papadimitriou, 'which is a good start. What else do we need?'

Sklavounis was quick to reply. He had already worked out how many people could fit into the town hall and where he could get a projector, a screen and the film reels. He had also, very importantly, done the figures. Given that many of the lepers were now earning some kind of income, an entry fee could be charged to the new cinema and the cost of the entire enterprise might eventually cover itself.

Within a few weeks of his initial request, posters appeared around the town for a showing of *The Apaches of Athens*.

That Saturday evening, nearly 200 people queued outside the town hall to see the film, and the same enthusiasm greeted the film the following Saturday.

A few weeks later, however, Georgios was to bring a newsreel from Athens that brought the audience sharply up to date with the sinister events that were taking place in the outside world. Though copies of Crete's weekly newspaper made their way to the island, and radios occasionally crackled with the latest news bulletin, no one had had any idea of the scale of the growing havoc being wreaked across Europe by Nazi Germany. At this stage these outrages seemed remote and the inhabitants of Spinalonga had other more immediate things to concern them. Easter was approaching and Papadimitriou made sure this year the commemoration of Christ's resurrection was to be no less extravagant in expression than anything held on Crete or in mainland Greece itself.

Lent had been strictly observed. Most people had gone without meat and fish for forty days, and, in the final week, wine and olive oil had been consigned to the darkest recesses. By Thursday of Passion Week, the wooden cross in the little church of St Panteleimon was laden with lemon blossom and a long line formed down the street to mourn Christ and kiss his feet. This was a melancholy moment, and all the more so when the worshippers looked on the icon of St Panteleimon, who was, as the more cynical of the lepers described him, the supposed patron saint of healing.

However cynical the islanders might be about the healing powers of the saint, they all joined in Christ's great funeral procession the next day. A coffin was decorated with flowers and solemnly carried through the streets.

Saturday was meant to be a quiet day of mourning. Everyone was busy, however. Eleni organised the children into a working party to paint eggs and then decorate them with tiny leaf stencils. Meanwhile other women baked the traditional cakes. Once all the chores were done, people again visited the church to decorate it with sprigs of rosemary, laurel leaves and myrtle branches, and by early evening a bittersweet smell emanated from the building and the air was heavy with anticipation and incense.

At midnight, the candles that had burned inside the crowded church were extinguished. In silence the priest lit a single candle.

'Come and receive the light,' he commanded. Papa Kazakos spoke the sacred words with reverence, but also with directness, and one by one the islanders closest to him reached out with tapers, and from these the light was shared around until the church became a flickering forest of flames.

'*Christos anesti!*' Papa Kazakos proclaimed. Christ is risen.

'*Christos anesti! Christos anesti!*' the crowd shouted back in unison.

Then it was time to carry the lighted candles carefully home.

'Come, Dimitri,' Eleni encouraged the boy. 'Let's see if we can get this home without it going out.'

If they could reach their house with the candle still lit, it would bring good luck for a whole year, and on this still night it was perfectly feasible. Within minutes every home had a candle glowing in its window.

The final stage of the ritual was the lighting of the bonfire, the symbolic burning of the traitor Judas Iscariot. All day people had brought their spare kindling, and now the priest lit the pyre and there was more rejoicing as it crackled and then finally went up with a roar while rockets soared into the sky all around. The celebrations had begun. In every far-flung village, town and city, from Plaka to Athens, there would be great merrymaking, and this year it would be as noisy on Spinalonga as anywhere across the land.

WHAT WAS LEFT of April became a period of intense activity. Several more lepers had arrived from Athens in March, and this meant more restoration work was needed. Repairs to the Venetian water tanks were completed, front doors and shutters had another coat of paint and the loose tiles on the church roof were fastened into place.

As Spinalonga rose from its own ashes, Eleni began to decline. For months she had pretended to herself that there had been no development of the disease, but then she began to notice daily changes. The lumps on her feet had multiplied, and now she walked without feeling in them.

'Isn't there anything the doctor can do to help?' Georgios asked quietly.

'No,' she said. 'I think we have to face that.'

'How is Dimitri?' he asked, trying to change the subject.

'He's fine. He's being very helpful now that I'm finding it harder to walk. In the last few months he's grown a lot and can carry the groceries for me.'

By the end of May, life had settled into its usual summer pattern of long siestas and sultry nights. Flies buzzed around and a haze of heat settled over the island from midday till dusk. Scarcely anything moved during these hours of simmering heat, but there was plenty happening on Spinalonga. Occasionally there was even a marriage. Such major events, and the burgeoning social life on the island, soon created the need for a newspaper. Yiannis Solomonidis, formerly a journalist in Athens, took charge and, once he had got hold of a press, printed fifty copies of a weekly newssheet, the *Spinalonga Star*. These were passed around and devoured with interest.

One day in November there was a significant event that went unreported by the newspaper. Not a word recorded the visit of a mysterious dark-haired man whose smart appearance would have made him blend into a crowd in Iraklion. In Plaka, however, he was noticed by several people because it was rare for someone to be seen in the village wearing a suit.

DR LAPAKIS HAD informed Georgios that he was expecting a visitor who would need to be brought across to Spinalonga and returned to Plaka a few hours later. His name was Nikolaos Kyritsis. In his early thirties, with thick black hair and prominent cheekbones, he was slight by comparison with most Cretans and a well-cut suit accentuated his slender build.

Kyritsis looked incongruous on the Plaka quayside. He had no baggage and no tearful family, as did most of the people Georgios took across. The only other people who went to Spinalonga were Dr Lapakis and the occasional government representative making a quick visit to assess financial requests. This man was the first real visitor Georgios had ever taken there, and he overcame his usual reticence with strangers and spoke to him.

'What's your business on the island?'

'I'm a doctor,' the man replied.

'But there's already a doctor there. I took him this morning.'

'Yes, I know. It's Dr Lapakis I'm going to visit. He is a friend and colleague of mine from many years back.'

'You aren't a leper, are you?' asked Georgios.

'No,' answered the stranger, his face almost creasing into a smile. 'And one day none of the people on the island will be either.'

This was a bold statement and Georgios's heart quickened at the thought. Eleni's condition had been getting visibly worse in the past few months. Today, for the first time since Georgios had taken her to Spinalonga, eighteen months earlier, his heart lifted. Just a little.

PAPADIMITRIOU had been waiting on the quayside to greet the doctor and now, as the two men walked up the main street, he grilled Kyritsis about the latest research.

Kyritsis had not expected this cross-examination, but then he had not anticipated meeting someone like Papadimitriou.

'It's early days,' he said cautiously. 'I'm part of a widespread research programme being funded by the Pasteur Foundation, but it's not just the cure we're hunting for. I want to make sure that we are doing all we can in the areas of treatment and prevention—I don't want the cure, if and when it's found, to be too late for everyone here.'

Papadimitriou, a consummate actor, concealed his disappointment by laughing it off: 'That's too bad. I'd promised my family I'd be back in Athens by Christmas, so I was relying on you for a magic potion.'

Kyritsis was a realist. He knew it could be some years before these people received successful treatment and he would not raise their hopes. Leprosy was not going to vanish overnight.

As the men walked together to the hospital, Kyritsis took in the sights and sounds around him with some incredulity. It looked like any normal village, albeit less run-down than many in that part of Crete. Except for the occasional inhabitant he spotted with an enlarged ear lobe or perhaps a crippled foot, the people living there could have been ordinary folk going about their business. At this time of year there were few faces in full view. Men wore their caps pulled down and their collars turned up and women had their woollen shawls furled tightly round their heads and shoulders, protecting themselves from the elements.

Lapakis was at the front entrance to greet Kyritsis, and, after embracing his visitor in a spontaneous display of genuine affection, he took him on a swift guided tour of the outpatients' clinic, the treatment rooms and finally the ward, where the shutters were closed and only a few faint streaks of light filtered through.

'All these patients are in a reactive state,' said Lapakis quietly, leaning against the door frame. This was the phase of leprosy where the symptoms of the disease intensified, sometimes for days or even weeks. During their time in this state patients were in terrible pain, with a raging fever and agonising sores. Lepra reaction could leave them sicker than before, but sometimes it indicated that the body was struggling to eliminate the disease.

As the two men stood looking into the overcrowded room, most of the patients were quiet. One moaned intermittently and another, whom Kyritsis thought was a woman but could not be sure, groaned. Lapakis and Kyritsis withdrew from the doorway. It seemed intrusive to stand there.

'Come to my office,' said Lapakis. 'We'll talk there.'

He led Kyritsis down a dark corridor to the very last door on the left. Unlike the ward, this was a room with a view. Huge windows looked out towards Plaka and the mountains that rose up behind it.

'So what brought you back to Crete, my friend? I was so glad to get your letter, but you didn't really say why you were coming here.'

The two men began to speak with the easy intimacy of those who had spent their student years together. They had both been at medical school in

Athens, and, although six years had passed since they had last met, they were able to pick up their friendship as if they had never been apart.

'It's quite simple, really,' said Kyritsis. 'I'd grown tired of Athens, and, when I saw a post advertised at the hospital in Iraklion in the Department of Dermatovenereology, I applied. I knew I'd be able to continue my research into leprosy, and Spinalonga is altogether a perfect place for a case study. Would you be happy for me to make occasional visits—and, more importantly, do you think the patients would tolerate it?'

'I certainly have no objection, and I am sure they wouldn't either.'

'At some point, there might even be some new treatments to try out—though I'm not promising anything dramatic.'

Lapakis sat at his desk. He had listened intently and his heart had lifted with every word that Kyritsis had spoken. For six long years he had been the only doctor prepared to visit Spinalonga, and during that time he had treated a relentless stream of the sick and the dying.

He did have some help now, in the form of Athina Manakis. She had been a doctor in Athens before discovering that she had leprosy. Athina Manakis's twenty-five years' experience and her willingness to work every hour except those when she slept made her invaluable. If Lapakis had believed in God, he would have thanked Him heartily.

Now, out of the blue—or, more accurately, out of the grey of this November day—Nikolaos Kyritsis had arrived, asking if he could make regular visits. Lapakis could have wept with relief. His had been a lonely and thankless job and now his isolation had come to an end.

'Please,' he said. 'Come as often as you wish. I can't tell you how delighted I would be. Tell me what you'd be doing exactly.'

'Well,' said Kyritsis, 'there are people in the field of leprosy research who are sure that we are getting closer to a cure. I'm still attached to the Pasteur Institute in Athens and our director-general is very keen to push things forward. In my opinion we're still a long way off, but every case study helps build a picture of how we can prevent the disease spreading.'

'So what's your plan exactly?'

'What I need are a few dozen cases that I can monitor very minutely over the next few months, even years, if it works out that way.'

'I've got records of everyone who has been here since I came in 1934,' said Lapakis. 'I make detailed notes on their state when they arrive and record every change as it happens. They're in age order—it seemed as logical a way as any. Why don't you go through them and pull out the ones you'd like to see, and when you next visit I can make appointments for the individuals to come and meet you.'

He tugged open the heavy top drawer of the filing cabinet nearest to him and with a sweep of his arm he gave Kyritsis an open invitation to browse.

'I'll leave you to it,' he said. 'I'd better get back to the ward.'

An hour and a half later, when Lapakis returned to his office, there was a stack of files on the floor; the name on the top one was 'Eleni Petrakis'.

'You met her husband this morning,' said Lapakis. 'He's the boatman.'

They made a note of all the chosen patients, then Kyritsis glanced at the clock on the wall. It was time to go. Before he entered the disinfectant room to spray himself the two men shook hands firmly. Lapakis then led him back down the hill to the tunnel entrance and Kyritsis continued alone to the quayside, where Georgios was waiting.

Few words were exchanged on the return journey to the mainland, but, when they reached Plaka, Kyritsis asked Georgios whether he could be there on the same day the following week to take him across to Spinalonga. For some reason he could not quite fathom, Georgios felt glad to know that the new doctor, as he thought of him, would be back.

THROUGH THE BITTER cold of December, January and February and the howling gales of March, Nikolaos Kyritsis continued to visit every Wednesday. Neither he nor Georgios was a man for small talk, but they did strike up short conversations as they crossed to the island.

'Kyrie Petrakis, how are you today?' Kyritsis would ask.

'I'm well, God willing,' Georgios would reply with caution.

'And how is your wife?' the doctor would ask, a question that made Georgios feel like a man with an ordinary married life. Neither of them dwelt on the irony that the person asking knew the answer better than anyone.

By April, the winds had lost their bite and there was a subtle change in the air. The earth was warming up. Purple spring anemones and pale pink orchids had broken through. Everyone welcomed the change of season, but there were also less positive changes in the air.

War had raged in Europe for some time, but that very month Greece itself was overrun. The colony's newspaper, the *Spinalonga Star*, carried regular bulletins on the situation, and the newsreels that came with the weekly film stirred the population into a state of anxiety. What they feared most then happened: the Germans turned their sights on Crete.

CHAPTER FIVE

'Maria, Maria!' screamed Anna from the street below her sister's window. 'They're here! The Germans are here!' There was panic in her voice, and as Maria galloped two steps at a time down the stairs, she fully expected to hear the sound of steel-tipped boots marching down the street.

'Where?' Maria demanded breathlessly, colliding with her sister in the street. 'Where are they? I can't see them.'

'They're not right here, you idiot,' retorted Anna. 'Not yet, anyway, but they are here on Crete and they could be coming this way.'

Anyone who knew Anna well would have spotted a hint of excitement in her voice. Her view was that anything that broke the monotony of an existence governed by the pattern of the seasons was to be welcomed.

Anna had run all the way from Fortini's house, where a group of them had been gathered around a crackling radio to hear the news that German paratroopers had landed in the west of Crete. Now the girls both raced to the village square. It was late afternoon but the bar was overflowing with men and, unusually, women, all clamouring to listen to the radio.

The broadcast information was stark and limited. 'At around six o'clock this morning a number of paratroopers landed on Cretan soil near the airfield of Maleme, near Hania. They are all believed to be dead.'

As usual, thought Maria, Anna had overreacted.

There was tension in the air, however. Athens had fallen four weeks earlier and the German flag now fluttered over the Acropolis. But to Maria, who had never been there, Athens seemed a long way off, and her sense of security was reinforced by what the adults were saying.

'They haven't got a chance!' scoffed Vangelis Lidaki, the bar owner. 'The mainland's one thing, but not Crete. Look at our landscape! They couldn't *begin* to get across our mountains with their tanks!'

'We didn't manage to keep the Turks out,' retorted Pavlos Angelopoulos.

'Or the Venetians,' piped up a voice in the crowd.

'Well, if this lot come anywhere near here, they'll get more than they bargained for,' growled another, punching a fist into his open palm.

This was not an empty threat, and all those in the room knew it. Even if

Crete had been invaded in the past, the inhabitants had always put up the fiercest resistance. The history of their island was a long catalogue of fighting, reprisals and nationalism, and among males over the age of fourteen there were few untrained in the use of a lethal weapon.

Savina Angelopoulos, who stood in the doorway with Fortini and the two Petrakis girls, did not share the confidence of the menfolk, despite the presence of tens of thousands of Allied troops on Crete. The men wanted to believe that the killing of a few hundred Germans who had landed by parachute was the end of the story. Savina felt instinctively that it was not.

Within a week, the true picture was clearer. Each day everyone congregated at the bar, as more pieces of the story would drift over from the west like thistle seeds carried on the air. It seemed that although many of the men who had dropped from the sky had died, a worrying number of them had survived and the airfield had been used to land thousands more. The tide was turning in the Germans' favour, and within a week of the first landings Germany claimed Crete as its own.

That night, everyone gathered in the bar once again.

'Why weren't we ready?' demanded Antonis Angelopoulos, banging his glass down on the metal table. 'It was obvious they'd come by air.' Beneath dark lashes, his hooded green eyes flashed with anger.

'No, it wasn't,' said his brother Angelos, with a dismissive wave of his pudgy hand. 'That's the last thing anyone expected.'

Not for the first time Pavlos wondered why his sons could never agree on anything. He delivered his own verdict. 'I'm with Angelos,' he said. 'No one imagined an air attack. It's a suicidal way to invade this place—dropping out of the sky to be shot as you land!'

Pavlos was right. For many of them it had been little more than suicide, but the Germans thought nothing of sacrificing a few thousand men in order to achieve their aim, and before the Allies had organised themselves to react, the key airfield of Maleme was in their hands.

For the first few days, Plaka went about its business as usual, its inhabitants in a state of shock that it had been allowed to happen at all. News filtered through that the picture was bleaker than anyone had imagined. The 40,000 combined Greek and Allied troops on Crete had been routed and thousands of Allies had to be evacuated with huge loss of life. The desire to take up arms against the Germans began to spread like a religious fervour. The villagers were not afraid of bloodshed. Many of them looked forward to picking up a weapon.

It became reality for the people of Plaka when a small battalion of German soldiers arrived in the village early one morning.

'Open up!' shouted the soldiers, banging on a door with their rifle.

Despite not having a word of common language, the family understood the command, and those that followed. They were to vacate their home by midday or face the consequences.

Day to day, there was little substantial news of what was going on elsewhere on Crete, but there was plenty of rumour, including talk that small groups of Allies were moving east towards Sitia. One night, as dusk fell, four heavily disguised British soldiers came down from the hills. They were welcomed warmly. It was not just the hunger for news that drew people to them; it was also the innate desire of the villagers to be hospitable and to treat every stranger as though he might have been sent from God. The men, who had been sleeping in an abandoned shepherd's hut, ate and drank everything that was offered, but only after a Greek-speaking member of the group had given a first-hand account of the events on the northwest coast.

'The last thing we expected was for the Germans to come by air—and certainly not in those numbers,' he said. 'The Germans have never before encountered the kind of resistance they are meeting in Crete. It has taken them completely by surprise. But it's only fair to warn you that they have dealt brutally with several villages over in the west. They've razed them to the ground—even the churches and the schools—'

He was unable to continue. Uproar broke out in the room.

'Shall we resist them?' roared Pavlos Angelopoulos over the hubbub.

'Yes,' shouted the forty or so men in reply.

'To the death!' roared Angelopoulos.

'To the death!' echoed the crowd.

Even though the Germans rarely ventured out after dark, men took turns to keep watch at the door of the bar. They talked long into the small hours of the morning, until the air was thick with smoke and silvery forests of empty raki bottles sat on the tables. The soldiers rose to go just before dawn. From now on they were in hiding. Tens of thousands of Allied troops had been evacuated to Alexandria a few days earlier and those left had to avoid capture by the Germans if they were to perform their vital intelligence operations. This group was on its way to Sitia, where the Italians had already landed and taken control.

In the Englishmen's view, the farewells and embraces were long and affectionate for such a short acquaintance, but the Cretans thought nothing of putting on such an emotional display. While the men had been drinking, some of the wives had come to the bar with parcels of provisions that would last them a fortnight. They were fulsome in their gratitude. '*Efharisto*, *efharisto*,' repeated one of them over and over again.

'It's nothing,' the villagers said. 'You are helping us. It is we who should be saying thank you.'

While they were all still in the bar, Antonis Angelopoulos, the older of Fortini's brothers, had slipped into the house to gather a few possessions: a sharp knife, a woollen blanket, a spare shirt and a small pistol that his father had given him at the age of eighteen. At the last minute he grabbed his wooden flute. He did not know when he would be home again and he could not leave it behind.

Just as he was fastening the buckle of his leather bag, Savina appeared in the doorway, woken by the the scrape of the pistol on the rough wall as it was lifted from its hook. Antonis had not wanted to be seen by his mother. She might try to stop him.

'What are you doing?' she asked.

'I'm going to help them. I'm going to guide those soldiers—they won't last a day in the mountains without someone who knows the terrain.' Antonis launched into a passionate defence of his actions, expecting fierce opposition. To his surprise, however, his mother nodded in agreement.

'You're right,' she said, adding in a rather matter-of-fact fashion: 'It's our duty to support them however we can.'

Savina held her son for a fleeting moment and then he was gone.

'Keep safe,' his mother murmured to his shadow, though he was already out of earshot. 'Promise me you'll keep safe.'

GEORGIOS RELATED all of this to Eleni when he visited the following day.

'Poor Savina!' she exclaimed hoarsely. 'She'll be worried sick.'

'Someone has to do it—and that young man was ready for an adventure,' replied Georgios flippantly, trying to make light of Antonis's departure.

'But how long will he be away?'

'Nobody knows. That's like asking how long this war is going to last.'

'Have the Germans been causing any trouble?'

'You would hardly know they were there,' answered Georgios. 'They patrol up and down in the day but at night they're nowhere to be seen.'

The last thing Georgios wanted to do was make Eleni aware of the sense of menace that now pervaded the atmosphere. He changed the subject.

'But how are you feeling, Eleni?'

His wife's health was beginning to fail. The lesions on her face had spread and her voice had become gravelly.

'My throat is a bit sore,' she admitted, 'but I'm sure it's just a cold. Tell me about the girls.'

Georgios knew not to dwell on the subject of her health, so he said, 'Anna seems a bit happier at the moment. She's working hard at school but she's not much better round the house. In fact she's probably lazier than ever. And Maria seems so quiet at the moment. I think she's even more anxious about the occupation than Anna.'

At moments like these Eleni felt overwhelmed with guilt that her daughters were growing up without her. She said, 'I feel more isolated than ever. I can't even share the danger you're in.' She fought against the possibility of breaking down in front of her husband. It would not help.

'We're not in danger, Eleni.'

His words were a lie, of course. The Cretan resistance had become more organised and several more men from the village had left to play their role in the unfolding events of the war. This added to the sense of anticipation that sooner or later life might change dramatically. Villages just like theirs, where men had become *andarte*, members of the Resistance, were being marked out by the Germans and targeted for the most brutal reprisals.

One day early in 1942 a group of children, including Anna and Maria, were taking the long walk home from school along the water's edge.

'Look!' shouted Maria. 'Look—it's snowing!'

Maria was the first to realise the truth. It was not snow that was falling from the sky. It was paper, dropped by a small aircraft which had buzzed overhead moments earlier. Anna grabbed one as it floated down towards her.

'Look at this,' she said. 'It's from the Germans.' They clustered around to read the leaflet, which warned them against giving shelter. IF YOU ARE FOUND GUILTY, it concluded, RETRIBUTION WILL BE HARSH AND SWIFT FOR YOUR ENTIRE VILLAGE.

'We must take some of these back to our parents,' suggested one, gathering a handful before they blew away. 'We need to warn them.' They trudged home, their hearts pounding with fear.

Other villages had been similarly targeted with this warning, but the effect was not the one the Germans had hoped for.

'You're crazy,' said Anna, as her father read the leaflet and shrugged his shoulders. 'How can you dismiss it like that? These *andarte* are putting all our lives at risk. Just for the sake of their own little adventures!'

Georgios struggled to control his temper. 'Do you really think they are doing it for themselves? Freezing to death in caves and living off grass like *animals*! How dare you?'

Anna shrank. She loved to provoke these scenes but had rarely seen her father vent such fury.

'You haven't seen them when they stagger into the bar at dead of night,' he continued, 'almost dying of hunger, their bones almost piercing their cheeks! They're doing it for you, Anna, and me and Maria.'

'And for our mother,' said Maria quietly from the corner.

Everything Georgios said was true. Levels of starvation were, by now, reaching such heights that it was not unheard of for local people to accept what was known as the 'Deutsche drachma' for a tip-off about the where-abouts of Resistance fighters. Hunger could corrupt even honest people, and the danger of betrayal meant that Antonis and all like him made only rare and brief visits to their families, knowing that their presence might endanger those they loved the most.

Throughout the war, the only place that really remained immune from the Germans was Spinalonga. As a result of the occupation, Nikolaos Kyritsis's visits had ceased, since unnecessary travel to and from Iraklion was regarded with suspicion by the occupying troops. Loath as he was to do it, Kyritsis abandoned his research for the time being; the needs of the wounded and dying in the field hospitals around Iraklion could not be ignored. He was so exhausted he rarely thought of the lepers who had briefly been the focus of his efforts, but the absence of Dr Kyritsis was the worst side effect of the war on the inhabitants of Spinalonga. While he had made his weekly visits they had nurtured hopes for the future. Now, once again, the present was their only certainty.

Georgios's routine of coming and going from the island was not inter-rupted. The Germans feared Spinalonga, with its hundreds of lepers living just across the water, and they had allowed deliveries to continue. The last thing they wanted was for any of them to leave the island to search out their own supplies on the mainland.

On Spinalonga, candles were lit daily for those suffering on the main-land. The islanders were well aware that the Cretans were living in fear of German cruelty, and prayed for a swift end to the occupation.

Dr Lapakis, who believed in the power of medicine rather than divine intervention, began to grow disillusioned. He knew that research and testing had been more or less abandoned. He had sent letters to Kyritsis in Iraklion, but since they had gone unanswered for many months, he came to the conclusion that his colleague must be dealing with more pressing issues. Lapakis increased the number of visits he made to Spinalonga from three to six days a week. Some of the lepers needed constant attention, and Athina Manakis could not cope alone. One such patient was Eleni.

Georgios would never forget the day he came to the island and saw, instead of the slender silhouette of his wife, the squatter figure of Elpida, her friend. His heartbeat had quickened. What had happened to Eleni? It was the first time she had not been there to greet him. Elpida spoke first.

'Don't worry, Georgios,' she said, trying to inject reassurance into her voice. 'Eleni is fine.'

'Where is she then?' There was a note of panic in his tone.

'She has to spend a few days in the hospital. Dr Lapakis is keeping her under observation for a while until her throat improves.'

'And *will* it improve?' he asked.

'I hope so,' said Elpida. 'The doctors are doing everything they can.'

Her statement was noncommittal. Elpida knew no more about the chances of Eleni's survival than Georgios himself.

The fisherman left the packages he was delivering and returned to Plaka. For the next four months Eleni lay in the hospital, too ill to struggle through the tunnel to meet Georgios. Every evening when he brought Lapakis back to Plaka, the doctor would tell him, 'Her body is still fighting the disease,' or 'I think her temperature has gone down slightly today.'

But Lapakis soon realised that he was building false hopes, and that the more these were reinforced the harder it would be when the final days came, as he knew they would. The lesions on Eleni's legs, back, neck and face had now multiplied, and she lay racked with pain.

It was during this phase that Elpida took Dimitri to see Eleni. He was now living at the Kontomaris house, an arrangement they had all hoped would be temporary but which was now looking as if it might be permanent.

'Hello, Dimitri,' Eleni said weakly. Then, turning her head towards Elpida, she managed just two more words: 'Thank you.'

Her voice was very quiet but Elpida knew what her words had acknowledged: that the boy was now in her capable hands. This at least might give her some peace of mind.

Eleni had been moved into a small room so that in the dead of night, when the agony worsened and her groans were continuous, she wouldn't disturb the other patients. Athina Manakis tended to her in those dark hours, spooning watery soup between her lips and sponging down her fiery brow. One night, however, Eleni ceased to be able to swallow.

It was when Lapakis found her gasping for breath the next morning that he realised his patient had entered a new and perhaps final stage.

'Kyria Petrakis, I need to look at your throat,' he said gently, glancing up at Dr Manakis, who was standing on the other side of the bed. With the new sores round her lips, he knew that even getting her to open her mouth wide enough to look inside would be uncomfortable. The examination only confirmed his fears. She didn't have long.

He sat down beside Eleni and took her hand. It was the point he had reached with so many patients, when he knew that there was nothing more he could do for them, except keep them company for the last hours. As he sat listening to her increasingly laboured breathing, he gazed through the huge window, with its view across the water to Plaka, and thought of Georgios, who would be setting off towards Spinalonga later that day. It may have been for two, maybe even three hours that he sat like this before the end finally came. Eleni's last breath was a futile struggle for another that failed to come.

Georgios was puzzled that Dr Lapakis was already waiting on the quay-side when he arrived. It was unusual for his passenger to be there first, but there was also something in his manner that made Georgios nervous.

'Can we stay here a moment?' Lapakis asked him, conscious that he must break the news here and now and give Georgios time to compose him-self before they were back in Plaka and he had to confront his daughters. He held out his hand to Georgios to help him off the boat, and Georgios knew even before the doctor spoke that his hopes were about to be destroyed.

They sat down on the low stone wall that had been built round the pine trees and both men looked out across the sea.

'She's dead,' Georgios said quietly. It was not just the lines of distress left on Lapakis's face by a gruelling day that had given the news away. A man can simply feel it in the air when his wife is no longer there.

'I am so, so sorry,' said the doctor. 'There was nothing we could do in the end. She died peacefully.' It was an untruth that he had told before and would willingly tell again.

Dr Lapakis had his arm round Georgios's shoulders, and the older man, head in hands, now shed such heavy and copious tears that they splashed his dirty shoes and darkened the dust around his feet. They sat like this for more than an hour, and it was nearly seven o'clock, the sky almost dark, when the tears no longer coursed down his face and the first intense tidal wave of grief had passed.

'The girls will be wondering where I am,' he said. 'We must get back.'

As they bumped up and down across the water towards the lights of Plaka, Georgios confessed to Lapakis that he had kept the seriousness of Eleni's condition from his daughters.

'You were right to do that,' Lapakis said comfortingly. 'Only a month ago I still believed she could win the fight. It's never wrong to have hope.'

It was much later than usual when Georgios arrived home, and the moment he walked in the door the girls knew something was wrong.

'It's our mother, isn't it?' demanded Anna. 'Something has happened!'

Georgios's face crumpled and he gripped the back of a chair.

Maria stepped forward and put her arms round him. 'Sit down, Father,' she said. 'Tell us what's happened . . . please.'

Georgios sat at the table trying to compose himself. A few minutes elapsed before he could speak.

'Your mother . . . is dead.' He almost choked on the words.

'Dead!' shrieked Anna. 'But we didn't know she was going to *die*!'

Anna had never accepted that her mother's illness could have only one real, inevitable conclusion. Georgios's decision to keep the news of her deterioration from them meant that news of her death now came as a huge shock to them both.

Anna's first reaction was one of anger that their father had not given them any warning and that this cataclysmic event had come out of the blue. The finality of Eleni's death was hard to grasp. They had always cherished the hope that she would return, and, as talk of a cure had increased, their hopes had risen. But now this.

Anna's sobs were audible as far as the village square. Maria's tears did not come so easily. She looked at her father and saw a man physically diminished by grief. His life had been turned upside down when Eleni was exiled, but now it was changed beyond repair.

For forty days an oil lamp burned in the front room as a mark of respect and the doors and windows of their home remained closed. Eleni had been buried on Spinalonga, but she was remembered in Plaka by the lighting of a single candle in the church of Agia Marina, where the sea was so close it lapped against the church steps.

After a few months, Maria, and even Anna, moved beyond the stages of mourning. For a time, their own personal tragedy had eclipsed wider world events, but when they emerged from their cocoon of grief, all continued to go on around them just as it had before.

In April, the daring kidnap of General Kreipe, commander of the Sebastopol Division in Crete, added to the state of tension across the island. With the help of members of the Resistance, Kreipe had been ambushed by Allied troops disguised as Germans and shipped off to Egypt; he was the Allies' most valuable prisoner of war. There were fears that the reprisals for this audacious abduction might be more barbaric than ever.

'How much longer can we stand this?' Vangelis Lidaki's wife asked after listening to his description of the awful burnt-out villages the bar owner had seen on his way back from Neapoli. 'If we stopped helping the *andarte*, we could sleep easy in our beds.'

The debate continued in the bar long into the night. To surrender and cooperate went against everything that was instinctive to most Cretans. They should resist, they should fight. Besides, they liked fighting. From a minor argument to a decade-old blood feud between families, the men thrived on conflict. Many of the women, by contrast, prayed hard for peace and thought their prayers had been answered as they detected sinking morale among their occupiers.

One night Antonis visited briefly to reassure his parents he was still alive. He brought with him a newssheet produced by the British, which gave the impression that the enemy's position was weakening, spread rumours of a British landing and exaggerated the success of Resistance activities. '*Kapitulation*' was the theme, and the Germans would wake to the sight of huge letter Ks daubed liberally on their sentry boxes, barrack walls and vehicles.

Such attempts to undermine the Germans may have been small in themselves, but they helped to change the bigger picture. The tide was turning throughout Europe, and cracks had appeared in the Nazis' firm hold on the Continent. In Crete, morale was now so low that German troops were starting to withdraw; some, even, to desert.

It was Maria who noticed that the small garrison in Plaka had cleared out. At six o'clock sharp there was always a show of force, a supposedly intimidating march through the main street and back again with the occasional interrogation of someone en route.

'Something's strange,' she said to Fortini. 'Something's different.'

It did not take long to work it out. It was now ten past six and the familiar sound of steel-capped boots had not been heard.

'You're right,' replied Fortini. 'It's quiet.'

Within an hour word had swept around the village that the German garrison had gone. That evening the square was filled with people celebrating the release of their own small corner of the island.

Only days later, on October 11, 1944, Iraklion was liberated. Remarkably, given all the bloodshed of the previous few years, the German troops were escorted out of the city gate without any loss of life; the violence was saved for anyone who was perceived to have collaborated. German troops did, however, continue to occupy parts of western Crete until the following summer.

Vangelis Lidaki had the radio blaring in the bar as he washed glasses from the night before, and was mildly irritated when the music was suddenly interrupted for a news announcement. His ears pricked up, however, when he caught the solemnity of the tone.

'Today, May the 8th, 1945, the Germans have officially surrendered. Within a few days all enemy troops will have withdrawn from the Hania area and Crete will once again be free.'

The music resumed and Lidaki wondered if the announcement had just been a trick of his own mind. He stuck his head out of the door of the bar and saw Georgios hastening towards him.

'Have you heard?' he asked.

'I have!' replied Lidaki.

It was true then. The tyranny was over. Though the people of Crete had always believed that they would drive the enemy from their island, when the moment came their joy was unrestrained.

PART 3

Chapter Six
1945

W ithin a fortnight of the end of occupation it was the feast of Agios Konstandinos, and this saint's day was the excuse to hold a celebration to end all celebrations. A cloud had lifted and madness descended in its place. Fatted goats and well-fed sheep rotated on spits the length and breadth of Crete and fireworks crackled in the sky.

The girls of Plaka donned their finery. They had been to church, but their minds were on things other than the sacred nature of the event. Anna had become a well-practised flirt. She was never happier than when she was in the company of boys and could toss her mane of hair and flash her engaging smile, knowing that her audience would not look away.

'Tonight's going to be special,' announced Anna. 'I can feel it in the air.'

'Why's that, then?' asked Fortini.

'Most of the boys are back, that's why,' she answered.

There were several dozen young men in the village, mere boys when they had left to fight with the *andarte*. Some of them had now joined the Communists in their struggle against right-wing forces. Fortini's brother Antonis was one of those who had returned to Plaka. During the four years he had been away in the Resistance, Antonis had grown wiry and strong. Now he had not only a moustache but a beard, too, and his time in the mountains, enduring extremes of heat and cold, had given him a sense of indestructibility.

It was the romantic figure of Antonis that Anna had set her heart on that night. He was lean and slim-hipped, and when the dancing began Anna was determined to make him notice her. If he failed to, he would be the only man in the village who had. Everyone was aware of Anna, not only because she was half a head taller than most of the other girls, but because her hair was longer, wavier and glossier than all the rest. The whites of her huge oval eyes were bright and her pearly teeth gleamed as she laughed and chattered with her friends, supremely conscious of her beauty.

The smell of roasting lamb wafted in the air and brought with it the anticipation of pleasure. Tables and chairs had been set out on three sides of the square and on the fourth a long trestle table took the weight of a dozen dishes piled high with cheese pies and spicy sausages, sweet pastries and pyramids of oranges and ripe apricots. There was a strict order of events. Eating and drinking would come later. Before that there would be dancing.

At first the boys and men all stood talking together and the girls stood apart, giggling excitedly. The separation was not to last. The band struck up and the swirling and stamping of feet began. Men and women rose from their seats and girls and boys broke away from their huddles. Soon the dusty space was filled. Anna knew as the inner female circle rotated that sooner or later she find herself opposite Antonis and that for a few moments they would dance together before moving on. How can I make him see me as someone more than his little sister's friend? she asked herself.

She did not have to try. Antonis stood in front of her. The slow *pentozali* dance gave her a few moments to study the pair of fathomless eyes that looked out through the black tassled fringe of his *sariki*, the traditional headdress that showed he had graduated into manhood.

Anna flashed her broad smile at this boy who had become a man, but he did not return it. The ebony eyes had instead fixed on hers and held them until she was almost relieved when it was time for him to move on to his next partner. The dance ended and she returned to her friends, who now spectated as some of the men, Antonis among them, leapt and reeled before them in a dizzying display.

As Antonis rotated and the music of lute, lyre and drum built to a climax, Anna was certain that this handsome warrior was dancing for her alone. The audience clapped and cheered as the men finished their acrobatics.

Anna was bold. She broke away from her friends and approached Antonis, who was pouring himself a glass of wine. He had barely noticed her before tonight. Before the occupation Anna had seemed just a little girl; now a shapely, voluptuous woman had taken her place.

'Hello, Antonis,' she said. 'You must have been practising your dancing while you were away,' she said, 'to be able to do those steps.'

'We saw nothing but goats in the mountains,' Antonis replied, laughing. 'But they're nimble, so maybe we learnt a thing or two from them.'

'Can we dance again soon?' she asked, over the noisy strains of the lyre.

'Yes,' he said, his face now breaking into a smile.

'Good. I'll be waiting. Over there,' she said, and returned to her friends.

Antonis had the feeling that Anna had offered herself to him for more than a *pentozali*. When a suitable dance began, he went up to her, took her by the hand and led her into the circle. Holding her round the waist, he now inhaled the indescribably sensual smell of her sweat, an essence of more intoxicating sweetness than anything he had ever breathed in before. When the dance finished, he felt her hot breath in his ear.

'Meet me behind the church,' she whispered.

Anna knew that a stroll to the church, even during such wild celebrations, was normal on a saint's day. She made her way swiftly to the alleyway behind the church and within moments Antonis was there too, fumbling to find her in the darkness. Her parted lips immediately sought his.

Antonis could feel real desire in her kiss. There was no mistaking it. Every part of his being craved for this lascivious kiss to continue. His mind was working swiftly. Here he was back for good and expected to marry and settle down in the community, and here in his arms was a woman eager for love who had been waiting, quite literally, on his doorstep, just as she had been since childhood. She had to be his. It was meant to be.

They separated from their embrace. 'We must get back to the square,' said Anna, knowing that her father would notice her absence if she was away for much longer. 'But let's go separately.'

She slipped out of the shadows and into the church, where she spent a few minutes lighting a candle before an image of the Virgin and Child, her lips, still wet from Antonis's, moving silently in prayer.

As she returned to the square there was a slight commotion in the street. A large saloon car had drawn up, one of few on the island. Anna paused to watch the passengers as they climbed out. The driver, a distinguished man in his sixties, was immediately recognisable as Alexandros Vandoulakis, the head of the wealthy landowning family from Elounda. He was a popular man, and his wife Eleftheria was well liked too. They employed a dozen or so men in the village, including Antonis since his return. They were generous with the men's wages, though some said, sarcastically, that they could afford to be. Theirs was a fortune of rare magnitude. It was not just the thousands of hectares of olive groves that were the source of their wealth. They owned a similar amount of land on the fertile Lasithi plateau, where they grew huge crops of potatoes, cereals and apples, providing them with an all-year-round income. The cool climate of the plateau, 800 metres up, rarely failed and the green fields were verdant with moisture provided by the melting snows of the mountains that encircled it. Alexandros and Eleftheria Vandoulakis often spent the months of high summer in Neapoli, twenty or so kilometres away, where they had a grand town house, leaving the estate in Elounda to be managed by their son Andreas.

It was, however, no surprise that such a well-to-do family should turn out to celebrate with fishermen, shepherds and men who worked the land. Both rich and poor had equal cause to celebrate their liberation, and the wealthy landowning families could not throw a better party, however great their fortune.

From the back seat of the car emerged the two Vandoulakis daughters and finally their older brother, Andreas. They were immediately welcomed by some of the villagers and given a good table with the best view of the dancing. Andreas, however, did not sit for long.

'Come on,' he said to his sisters. 'Let's join in with the dancing.'

He grabbed them both and pulled them into the circle, where they blended in with the crowd of dancers, dressed as they were in the same costumes as the villagers. Anna watched. It struck her that if her friends were going to have the opportunity to dance with Andreas Vandoulakis, then so was she. She joined the next *pentozali* and, just as she had done with Antonis not an hour earlier, fixed Andreas in her gaze.

The dance soon came to an end. The lamb was now roasted and being cut into thick chunks, platters of which were passed around for the villagers to feast on. Andreas was back with his family but his mind was elsewhere.

At the age of twenty-five, he was being pressurised by his parents to find a wife. Alexandros and Eleftheria were frustrated by his rejection of every single one of the daughters of their friends and acquaintances, even though all of them would have been more than generously dowried.

'Who's that girl, the one with the amazing hair?' he asked his sisters, gesturing towards Anna.

'How should we know?' they chorused. 'She's just one of the local girls.'

'She's beautiful,' he said. 'That's what I'd like my wife to look like.'

As he got up, Eleftheria gave Alexandros a knowing look. Her view was that, given the lack of impact any dowry would have on Andreas's life, what did it really matter whom he married? She just wanted her son to be happy, and if that meant flying in the face of convention, then so be it. Eleftheria herself had come from a considerably humbler background than Alexandros, but it had not significantly affected their lives.

Andreas had walked right up to the crowd of girls, who were sitting in a circle eating the tender meat with their fingers. There was nothing particularly remarkable about Andreas, who had inherited his father's strong features and his mother's sallow complexion, but his family background lent him a bearing that set him apart from the other young men.

'Anyone care to dance?' he asked casually, looking directly at Anna. His was the attitude of a man confident of his superior social situation and there was only one response. To get up and take his hand.

The candles on the tables had guttered and burned out, but by now the moon had risen and was casting its bright glow. Both raki and wine had flowed and the musicians, emboldened by the atmosphere, played faster and faster until the dancers once again appeared to fly through the air. Andreas held Anna close. It was the time of night when the tradition of swapping partners during the dance could be ignored, and he decided he was not going to exchange her for anyone.

Alexandros and Eleftheria Vandoulakis watched their son courting this woman, but they were not the only ones to do so. Antonis sat at a table with his friends, drinking himself into a stupor as he realised that the man he worked for was in the process of seducing the girl he desired. What hope did he have of keeping Anna for himself when he was in competition with the most eligible man this side of Agios Nikolaos?

The Vandoulakis family eventually rose to leave. Andreas's mother knew that her son would not want to come home with them, but in the interests of respectability and the reputation of this village beauty he had taken such a liking to, they all knew that it was important that he should.

'I have to go now,' Andreas said to Anna, 'but I want to see you again. I'll have a note delivered to you tomorrow, telling you when we can meet.'

He spoke like a man used to issuing orders and expecting them to be carried out. Anna had no objection to that, for once realising that acquiescence was the right response. It could, after all, be her route out of Plaka.

THE NEXT MORNING one of the Vandoulakis labourers delivered an envelope to Anna's house. She sat down at the table and, with trembling hands, broke the seal. She wanted to savour the moment. What was she going to find? An articulate outpouring of passion? Words that exploded on the page like fireworks? Like any eighteen-year-old girl anticipating such poetry, she was bound to be disappointed by the letter on the table in front of her:

Dear Anna,
I wish to meet you again. Please come to lunch with your father on
Sunday next. My mother and father look forward to meeting you both.
Yours,
Andreas Vandoulakis

Though the content excited her, the formality of the letter chilled her. Anna thought that because Andreas had enjoyed a superior education he might be masterful with words, but there was about as much emotion in this hastily scribbled note as in a book of Ancient Greek grammar.

The lunch duly took place, and many thereafter. Anna was always chaperoned by her father in accordance with the strict etiquette observed by people both rich and poor for such situations. On the first half-dozen occasions, father and daughter were collected at midday by a servant in Alexandros Vandoulakis's car and taken to the grand, porticoed town house in Neapoli where the family spent the summer months. They returned home again at three thirty precisely. The pattern was always the same. On arrival they would be shown into an airy reception room where Eleftheria Vandoulakis would offer them a small plate of sweet preserve and a tiny glass of liqueur. Then they all processed into the gloomy dining room, where oil paintings of fierce moustachioed ancestors glared down from panelled walls.

Eleftheria did all she could to make her guests feel relaxed; many years earlier she had been through the same ordeal when she was vetted by the previous generation of the Vandoulakis family, and she remembered the unbearable stiffness of it all as though it was yesterday. In spite of the woman's kind efforts, however, conversation was stilted and both Georgios and Anna were painfully conscious that they were on trial.

By the time of the seventh meeting, the Vandoulakis family had decamped to the sprawling house on the large estate in Elounda, which was where they spent the months between September and April. Anna was now growing impatient. She and Andreas had not been alone together since the dance they had had in May, and, as she moaned one evening to Fortini and Savina, 'That was hardly being on our own, with the whole village watching us! Why does it all take so long?'

'Because if it's the right thing for both of you and for both families there is no need to hurry,' answered Savina, wisely.

It took until spring of the following year for Alexandros Vandoulakis to satisfy himself that, in spite of the differences in their wealth and social situation, it would not be a mistake if his son made Anna his bride. She was, after all, exceedingly handsome, bright enough and clearly devoted to Andreas. One day, after yet another lunch, the two fathers returned to the reception room alone. Alexandros Vandoulakis was blunt.

'We are all aware of the inequality of this potential union but my wife has persuaded me that Andreas will be happier with your daughter than with any other woman he has ever met, so as long as Anna performs her duties as wife and mother we can find no real objections.'

'I can't offer you much of a dowry,' said Georgios, stating the obvious.

'We are perfectly aware of that,' replied Alexandros. 'Her dowry would be her promise to be a good wife and to do all she can in helping to manage the estate. I'll be retiring in a few years and Andreas will have a great deal on his shoulders.'

'I am sure she'll do her best,' Georgios said simply. He felt out of his depth, intimidated by the scale of this family's power and wealth. But what mattered was whether Anna could become accustomed to such grandeur. There was no evidence that she felt anything but perfectly at ease in the Vandoulakis home. She could sip delicately from a glass, eat daintily and say the right things as though she had been born to do it. He, of course, knew that she was simply acting a role.

'What is as important as anything is that Anna's education has been a good one. Your wife taught her well, Kyrie Petrakis.'

At the mention of Eleni, Georgios maintained his silence. The Vandoulakis family knew that Anna's mother had died a few years earlier, but more than that he did not intend them to find out.

When they returned home that afternoon, Maria was waiting for them.

'Well?' she said. 'Has he asked you?'

'Not yet,' replied Anna. 'But I know it's going to happen, I just know it.'

Maria knew that what her sister wanted more than anything in the world was to become Anna Vandoulakis, and she wanted it for her too. It would take her out of Plaka and into the other world she had always fantasised about, where she would not have to cook, clean, darn or spin.

'He will, I'm sure,' Maria said. 'He obviously loves you. *Everyone* says so.'

'Who's everyone?' Anna asked sharply.

'I don't know really, but Fortini says everyone on the estate thinks so.'

'And what does Fortini know?'

Maria knew that she had said too much. Fortini had confided in Maria about her brother's infatuation with Anna and how it aggravated him to hear the other estate workers talk of nothing but the impending engagement. Poor Antonis. She knew he was not yet used to being at the beck and call of Andrea Vandoulakis, his young master. The roamings of the last few years, though tough, had had a joyful freedom about them and he was finding it hard to get used to the daily routine of being a labourer on the Vandoulakis estate. If that were not enough, Maria had seen him watching Andreas dancing with Anna at the feast of Agios Konstandinos and she knew he realised that the odds were stacked against him.

Anna bullied Maria until she told her.

'It's Antonis. He's obsessed with you, you must know that. He tells Fortini all the estate gossip and everyone's saying that Andreas is about to ask you to marry him.'

For a moment Anna basked in the knowledge that she was the centre of attention and speculation and wanted to know more.

'What else are they saying? Go on, Maria, tell me!'

'They're saying he's marrying beneath him.'

It was not what Anna expected and certainly not what she wanted to hear. She responded with vehemence.

'What do I care about what they think? Why *shouldn't* I marry Andreas Vandoulakis? I certainly wouldn't have married someone like Antonis Angelopoulos. He doesn't own more than the shirt he stands up in!'

'That's no way to talk about our best friend's brother—and, anyway, the reason he has nothing is that he was away fighting for his country while other people stayed at home and lined their own pockets.'

Maria's parting shot was one barbed comment too many, and Anna fled wailing from the house.

IN SPITE OF the opinions of the estate workers and the residual misgivings of Alexandros Vandoulakis, the engagement took place in April. When the moment finally came and Andreas asked Anna for her hand after dinner one night, she felt little emotion. She had played the scene through in her mind so often that when it actually took place she felt numb.

'Anna,' said Andreas. 'I have something to ask you. Will you marry me?'

There was nothing romantic about the proposal, but Anna had finally reached her goal, cocking a snook at those who might have thought she was not up to marriage into a landed family. These were her first thoughts as she accepted Andreas's hand and kissed him fully and passionately on the lips.

A lavish party was thrown to celebrate the engagement, and as was customary, gifts were then lavished on Anna by her future in-laws. Beautiful clothes, silk underwear and expensive trinkets were purchased for her so that, although her own father could provide very little, she would not be lacking for anything by the time she finally became a Vandoulakis.

The following year, no expense was spared for the wedding, which was to be held in March. Before the service in Elounda, the guests arrived at the Vandoulakis home. They were a curious mix. Wealthy people from Elounda, Agios Nikolaos and Neapoli mixed with the estate workers and dozens of folk from Plaka. When they caught sight of Anna, the people from her old village gasped. Enough gold coins to fill a bank vault jangled across her chest and heavily jewelled earrings hung from her ears. In the rich red of her traditional bridal gown she could have stepped from the pages of the *Tales of the Arabian Nights*.

Georgios looked at her with pride and some bemusement, marvelling that this was his own daughter. He wished at this moment that Eleni was here to see their first-born looking so beautiful.

Maria had helped Anna to get ready that morning. Her sister's hands had trembled so violently that she had had to do up every button for her.

'Tell me it's really happening,' Anna had said. 'I can't believe I'm actually going to be Kyria Vandoulakis!'

'It's all real,' Maria had reassured her, wondering as she spoke what the reality of going to live in a grand house would be like. She hoped it would mean more than fine jewellery and smart clothes. Even for Anna such things might have their limitations.

The mix of guests made this an unusual event, but even more unconventional was that the prenuptial feast was held in the groom's house rather than the bride's. The smart ladies of Neapoli tittered at the very thought, just as they had done when they heard that the Vandoulakis boy was marrying a poor fisherman's daughter. But for Cretans both rich and poor the rituals of the marriage ceremony were the same. Two *stephana*, the marriage crowns made from dried flowers and grasses and linked by a ribbon, were placed on the heads of the couple by the priest, and then exchanged three times to cement their union. For much of the time, the words of the sacred ritual were lost in the chatter of the congregation, but when the bride and groom finally joined hands with the priest, a hush spread around the church. Now they performed a sedate dance round the altar, the Isaiah Dance, and the guests knew that soon they would be outside in the sunshine.

Following the carriage of the bride and groom, everyone trooped back to the Vandoulakis home, where trestle tables were laid out for another feast. People ate, drank and danced until dawn, when a volley of gunshots marked the end of the celebrations.

AFTER THE WEDDING, Anna more or less vanished from life in Plaka. At first, she visited once a week to see her father, but, as time went on, she began to send a car down to collect him instead.

She spent each day in the company of Eleftheria and her friends, enjoying a level of leisure that bordered on idleness. She longed to make changes to the two family homes, relieving them of their dark drapes and sombre furnishings. She nagged Andreas until he took his mother aside to ask for permission, and Eleftheria in turn consulted the real head of the household.

'I don't want the big house altered too much,' said Alexandros Vandoulakis to his wife, referring to the house in Elounda. 'But Anna can give the house in Neapoli a lick of paint if she'd like to.'

The new bride threw herself into the task and was soon carried away on a wave of enthusiasm for fabrics and wallpapers, making endless trips to an importer of fine French and Italian goods who had a smart shop in Agios

Nikolaos. It kept her busy and absorbed, and Andreas benefited, finding her in a lively and buoyant mood at the end of each day.

Another of her duties was to manage the *panegyria*, or saint's day, celebrations that the Vandoulakis family threw for their workers. At these feasts she would sometimes feel the eyes of Antonis Angelopoulos on her and she would look up to meet his steely glare.

Anna's marriage brought a change not only to her own status; her departure also meant a change in Maria's. Much of her younger sister's energy had gone into pleasing and pacifying Anna. Now that she was no longer there Maria could put renewed energy into running the Petrakis home.

There was no question in Maria's mind that she should be doing anything other than looking after her father, even if she had once entertained fantasies of standing, chalk in hand, at the front of a class, as her mother had done. All such aspirations had long since faded.

Maria and Fortini shared the joys and the limitations of Plaka life, and, in all the time they performed their duties, it did not occur to them that they had any real cause for complaint. There was water to fetch from the village pump, wood to be collected for their ovens, sweeping, spinning, cooking and the beating of rugs. Maria would regularly collect honey from her hives on the thyme-covered hillside overlooking Plaka; and Fortini's grandmother showed them how to dye wool with extracts of iris, hibiscus and chrysanthemum petals, and how to weave coloured grasses into elaborate baskets and mats. Other women passed on to them their knowledge of the magical benefits of locally grown herbs, and they would walk into the mountains to find wild sage, cistus and camomile for their healing powers. Maria would always have the right potion to minister to her father, if he was sick, and soon her reputation for mixing remedies spread around the village.

However onerous Maria's domestic tasks might have seemed to anyone living in a city, there was always time for chatter and intrigue. Fortini's house was a focal point for this, and the serious business of gossip was conducted in the innocent context of sewing and embroidery. This not only kept the girls' hands busy but also gave them the opportunity to prepare for the future. Every pillowcase, cushion, tablecloth and runner in the house of a married woman had been woven or embroidered by herself, her mother or her mother's mother. Anna had been an exception.

At certain times of year, the girls turned their hands to the seasonal tasks. They would join the fray at grape harvest and be the first into the troughs to tread the juicy fruit. Then they would be among the crowd who would beat the olive trees to make the fruit cascade down into baskets in autumn. Such days were full of laughter and flirtation, and the completion of these communal tasks would be marked with dancing and merrymaking.

One by one, members of this coterie of young women found husbands, or, as was more generally the case, husbands were found for them. When Fortini announced her own engagement, Maria saw her world coming to an end. She displayed only pleasure and delight, however, quietly castigating herself for her feelings of envy as she anticipated the rest of her life spent with the widowed crones, crocheting lace as the sun went down.

Fortini, like Maria, was now twenty-two years old. Her father had supplied the taverna on the seafront for many years, and the owner, Stavros Davaras, was a good friend. His son, Stephanos, would one day take over the business and Pavlos Angelopoulos regarded Stephanos as a good match for his daughter. The pair had known each other since childhood and were confident that they could develop feelings for each other. The great consolation for Maria was that Fortini would be living no farther away from her now than she had been before.

Determined not to betray her dismay at finding herself the last of a diminishing group, Maria threw herself more enthusiastically than ever into her filial duties. Her devotion to Georgios was admired in the village, but at the same time her lack of a husband reduced her status; to be left on the shelf was a daily public humiliation. She would not consider a man from another village, for it was unthinkable that Georgios should uproot himself and therefore unimaginable that Maria would ever move either. There was, she reflected, as much chance of marriage as there was of seeing her beloved mother walk through the door.

CHAPTER SEVEN
1951

Anna was now four years married and thriving on her new status. She loved Andreas dutifully, and willingly responded to his passion for her. To everyone around her, Anna seemed a faultless wife. She was aware, however, that the family was awaiting the announcement of a pregnancy. The lack of a baby did not bother her at all. She was enjoying this carefree time far too much to want to lose it to motherhood.

Anna was now gradually transforming the house in Elounda to her own taste in spite of her father-in-law's penchant for the sombre style favoured by his generation. One day in late autumn, on her return from a shopping trip to Agios Nikolaos, she rushed into the kitchen and planted a kiss on the back of the head of the familiar figure seated at the table.

'Hello, darling,' she said. 'How was the press today?'

It had been the first day of olive pressing, a significant date in the calendar, when the press was used for the first time in many months, and it was always touch and go whether the machinery would perform. The golden liquid that poured from press to *pithoi* was the basis of the family's wealth and, as Anna saw it, each jar was another metre of fabric, another tailored dress to be fitted to her curves.

As she walked across the room, chattering about the minutiae of her day, her coat hugged her breasts and hips like an embrace before falling away almost to the ground in extravagant swirls of fabric, the emerald-green silk lining rustling against her legs. Today, to keep the biting November winds at bay, a fur collar rose up to her neck to warm her ears. She was putting water on to prepare some coffee when the man at the table rose from his chair. Anna turned and let out a scream of surprise.

'Who are *you*?' she asked in a strangulated voice. 'I . . . I thought you were my husband.'

'So I gathered.' The man smiled, clearly amused by her confusion.

As the two stood face to face, Anna saw that the man she had greeted so affectionately, though clearly *not* her husband, was in every way very like him. The breadth of his shoulders, his hair and, now that he was standing, even his height seemed to match Andreas's exactly. When he spoke, Anna's mouth went dry. What trick was this?

'I'm Manoli Vandoulakis,' he said, holding out his hand. 'You must be Anna.'

Anna knew of the existence of a cousin and had heard Manoli's name mentioned a few times in conversation, but little more than that.

'Manoli.' She repeated the name. It was pleasing. 'The similarity between you and Andreas is uncanny.'

'I haven't seen Andreas for ten years, but we were very alike. People were always mistaking us for twins.'

Anna could see that, but she could also see other things that actually made this version of her husband very different from the original. Though Manoli had the same broad shoulders as Andreas, he was actually thinner.

He had laughter in his eyes and deep lines round them. Life was there to be enjoyed, you could see it in his smile.

At that moment, Andreas and his father returned and there were exclamations of delight and amazement when they saw Manoli standing there. Soon the three men were sitting around a bottle of raki and Anna excused herself to make arrangements for dinner. When Eleftheria arrived an hour or so later, both she and Manoli wept tears of joy as they embraced.

Manoli Vandoulakis was a free-spirited youth who had spent the past ten years, largely on mainland Greece, squandering a sizeable inheritance. His mother had died in childbirth and his father had passed away five years later at the age of thirty, of a heart attack. Manoli had grown up hearing dark murmurings of how his father had died of a broken heart, and whether or not this was true, it made him resolve to live as though each day might be his last. It was a philosophy that made perfect sense to him, and even his uncle Alexandros, who since the death of Yiannis Vandoulakis had been his guardian, could not stop him.

Ten years earlier, he had left home. Apart from the occasional letter to his aunt and uncle to reassure them that he was still alive, he had had little contact with his family. Alexandros was aware that if his older brother Yiannis had not died so young, it would be Manoli who would now be in line to inherit the Vandoulakis estate, rather than his own son. But such thoughts were hypothetical. Instead of the promise of land, when he had reached the age of eighteen Manoli had come into a small cash fortune. It was this money that he had squandered in Rome, Belgrade and Athens.

'The high life had a high price,' he confided to Andreas soon after his return. 'The best women were like good wine, expensive but worth every drachma.' Now, however, all he had left were the coins in his pocket and a promise from his uncle that he would employ him on the estate.

His return proved timely. Alexandros Vandoulakis was due to retire the following year and Andreas needed a helping hand in managing the estate. They all felt it would be better for Manoli to take on the role of manager than for them to employ an outsider, even if Alexandros had some doubts about whether his nephew would really buckle down to it.

In December Alexandros provided Manoli with a house of his own. His uncle expected him to get married in the future and for this purpose insisted that he should live in his own home. The house had belonged to the estate manager in the days when Alexandros had paid an outsider to perform the role. It was set at the end of a short driveway a kilometre from the main house, and with its four bedrooms and large drawing room was considered a substantial home for a bachelor. Manoli, however, continued to be a regular visitor at the main house. He wanted to be fed and pampered, just like Alexandros and Andreas, and here were two women to do just that for him.

To his uncle's surprise, Manoli worked quite hard, though he did not have the same commitment as Andreas. His son would always take his lunch to the fields to save time, but his nephew preferred to get out of the harsh sun and had taken to coming in to eat his lunch in the Vandoulakis kitchen. Anna had no objection. Manoli made her laugh, and her appreciation of his teasing humour and the way her eyes sparkled when she held his gaze were enough to keep him from the olive groves well into the afternoon.

Sometimes Eleftheria was there rather than in Neapoli and feared that her nephew was not pulling his weight on the estate. 'Men shouldn't hang around the house in the day,' she once remarked to Anna. 'It's a woman's territory. Theirs is outside.'

Anna chose to ignore her mother-in-law's disapproving comment. In her view, the closeness of the kinship between them sanctioned their friendship. It was the custom that a woman enjoyed much greater freedom once married, so at first no one questioned Anna's liberty to spend an hour a day, sometimes even more, with her 'cousin'. But soon tongues started to wag.

One lunchtime that spring, Manoli had lingered even longer than usual. Anna sensed his recklessness and for once shuddered at the danger she was putting herself in. He had picked some meadow flowers that day and had presented her with a bouquet. It was a romantic gesture and she was charmed, especially when he pulled one from the bunch and carefully placed it in the front of her blouse. His touch was subtle and she was not certain whether the contact of his fingers on her breast was accidental. A moment later, when she felt his gentle touch on her neck, the doubt was gone. I ought to stop this, she thought. Otherwise I could lose everything. She addressed Manoli with her usual haughtiness. It was their game: while he was extravagantly flirtatious, she treated him as her inferior.

'Look, young man,' she said. 'As you know, I'm spoken for. You can take your flowers elsewhere.'

'Can I indeed?' Manoli answered. 'And exactly where shall I take them?'

'Well, my sister isn't yet spoken for. You could take them to her.' As if the true Anna was somewhere very distant, she heard a voice saying: 'I shall invite her to lunch next Sunday. You'll like her.'

The following Sunday was the feast of Agios Georgios, so it was a perfect excuse for inviting Maria and her father to visit. These days it was a duty rather than a particular pleasure to see them both; she felt she had nothing in common with her tedious little sister and little to say to her father. Georgios, on the other hand was delighted to receive the invitation.

'Maria, look! Anna has invited us to lunch on Sunday.'

'That's kind of her ladyship,' said Maria with uncharacteristic sarcasm, though she was secretly pleased that they had been invited. She yearned to strengthen the bond with her sister, as their mother would have wanted, but nevertheless she felt some trepidation as the day approached.

Anna cringed as she heard the spluttering sound of her father's newly acquired truck in the driveway and with little enthusiasm made her way slowly down the big staircase to greet them. Manoli, who had already arrived, had got to the front door well before her and thrown it open.

Maria was not at all what he had expected. She had the biggest brown eyes he had ever seen and they looked at him with wide-eyed surprise.

'I'm Manoli,' he said, striding towards her with outstretched hand, adding: 'Andreas's cousin.'

So negligent was Anna in her correspondence that Maria and Georgios had known nothing of the arrival of the long-lost relative.

Manoli was always in his element with a pretty girl, but never more so than with one like this, who added innocence to such sweet beauty.

Throughout lunch Manoli dominated Anna's younger sister with his play-ful talk, and although she was unused to such flippancy, she parried his witty remarks intelligently. Her unaffected personality made her different from most of the women he'd met; she was without artifice and had a naivety that he found unexpectedly alluring.

Anna watched as Manoli drew Maria into his magnetic field, telling her stories and making her laugh. Before the meal was over, she realised what she had done. She had given Manoli away, handed him like a gift-wrapped parcel to her sister. And now she wanted him back.

THE ACCEPTED PATTERNS of behaviour between men and women in Plaka were very different from those found in the cities where Manoli had lived. He had been perfectly aware of this when he had visited Anna on all those occasions, and had known that he was playing with fire. In Anna he had seen a bored, isolated woman who had separated herself from the village where she had grown up, but who now floated in a friendless social vacuum. A woman with eyes that so hungrily sought his, and lips that spread themselves into such a generous smile, it would have been rude to ignore her.

Maria was quite different. Not only did she lack her sister's ambition to marry outside the village, she seemed without desire to marry at all. Manoli would not have admitted it to himself, but it was largely her lack of interest that attracted him. He had all the time in the world, though, and was confident that sooner or later she would be won over. Manoli had much on his side. Perhaps the most important factor was that Fortini had protected Maria from the gossip about Manoli and Anna. The source of the endless flow of stories was Fortini's brother Antonis. It was more than five years since that kiss, which had meant nothing to Anna and far too much to Antonis, but the sense of having been cast aside still rankled. He despised Anna and had watched with malicious satisfaction the comings and goings of her husband's cousin, which he reported to Fortini whenever he called in for supper at the taverna

'He was there for two hours one lunchtime last week,' he gloated.

'I don't want to hear your stories,' Fortini said brusquely to Antonis as she poured him a raki. 'And, above all, I don't want Maria to hear them.'

'Why not? Her sister is a tart. Don't you think she knows that already?'

'Of course she doesn't know that. And nor do you. So what if her husband's cousin comes to visit her? He's family, why shouldn't he?'

'Just the occasional visit would be one thing, but not virtually every day. Even family don't visit each other that often.'

'Well, whatever you think, Maria mustn't know—and nor must Georgios. He has suffered quite enough. You're to keep your mouth shut. I mean it.'

Fortini glared at him. She was as protective of Georgios and Maria Petrakis as she would have been of her own flesh and blood. Besides, she held out hope that Manoli might one day notice Maria. Since the lunch on the feast of Agios Georgios, Maria had chatted incessantly about him.

Manoli had been seen a few times in the village. With his connection to Georgios he had found a warm welcome among the men of Plaka and soon became a regular fixture at the bar, often playing backgammon and discussing island politics beneath a thick pall of cigarette smoke. Even in this small village, events on mainland Greece aroused passion and fury.

'The Communists are to blame!' exclaimed Lidaki, banging his fist on the top of the bar.

'How can you say that?' answered another voice. 'If it wasn't for the monarchy, the mainland wouldn't be in half the mess it is.' And so they went on, sometimes into the small hours.

Manoli had a broader world view than others in the bar—many had never been further than Iraklion—and he brought a new perspective to the argument. Though he was careful not to brag of the casual conquests that had been a recurring theme of his travels, he entertained them all with stories of Italians, Yugoslavians and their brothers on mainland Greece.

Even Antonis, who had ceased to skulk in the corner whenever his boss's rakish cousin appeared, now greeted him warmly. Music was their common bond. During his travelling years, Manoli's lyre had been both a companion and his security, and the only possession of any value that he had not gambled away. Likewise, Antonis's wooden flute, his *thiaboli*, had been his constant companion during his years in the Resistance. Its mellow sounds had filled a hundred different caves and shepherds' huts, the notes soothing the hearts and souls of his companions. As different as Manoli and Antonis were, music was a neutral space where wealth and hierarchy played no part. When the two men played in the bar, their haunting melodies cast a spell over their audience.

Though everyone was aware of the great wealth that Manoli's parents had enjoyed, and of the fortune that he himself had frittered away, most of the villagers now accepted him as someone just like themselves, who needed to work hard for a living. For Manoli, the simplicity of this more settled life had its own rewards. The bonds between childhood friends, the loyalty to family and a way of life that had not changed for centuries, all had great appeal. If he could secure a woman like Maria as his wife, it would complete his sense of belonging.

He knew he could not mention his intentions to Anna, and he was not visiting her so much now. She had been predictably brittle with him when he last visited.

'Well, thanks for coming to see me,' she said tartly.

'I don't think I should come at lunchtime any more,' said Manoli. 'People are muttering about me not pulling my weight.'

'Suit yourself,' Anna snapped. 'You've obviously finished your little game with me and I assume you're now playing it with someone else.'

With that she marched out of the room.

Manoli would miss the sparkle in Anna's eyes, but it was a price he was prepared to pay.

Since there was no one at home preparing him meals, Manoli often ate in one of the tavernas in Elounda or in Plaka and each Friday he went to Fortini's taverna, which she and Stephanos had now taken over from Stephanos's father. One visit in July, he sat there looking out to sea towards Spinalonga, wondering idly what it must be like over on the leper's island, when his eye was caught by a little boat, with two people in it, chugging its way from the island in the dusk.

'Stephanos!' he called, as the boat came into the harbour. 'Is that Maria with Georgios? You don't usually see a woman out fishing, do you?'

'They haven't been fishing,' replied Stephanos. 'They've been making one of their deliveries to the leper colony.'

'Oh,' said Manoli, chewing thoughtfully. 'I suppose someone has to.'

'Georgios has been doing it for years. He mostly does it for—'

Fortini, who had been hovering in the background, saw where this conversation might lead and dived forward with a plate of sliced aubergines. 'Here you are, Manoli! These are freshly cooked. I hope you like them. Would you excuse us a moment?'

She grabbed her husband's arm and led him back to the kitchen.

'You must be careful!' she exclaimed. 'We *all* have to forget that Anna and Maria's mother was ever on Spinalonga. *We* know it's nothing to be ashamed of, but Alexandros Vandoulakis might not see it that way.'

Stephanos was shamefaced.

'I know, I know. It slips my mind sometimes, that's all,' he muttered. 'Manoli comes in here so often, I forget that he's connected with Anna.'

'It's not just Anna I'm thinking of. Maria has feelings for Manoli. They met at Anna's house and she hasn't stopped talking about him since.'

'Really? Well, he looks a bit of a rogue to me,' replied Stephanos sceptically, yet he understood what his wife was getting at and realised that he and Fortini had a role to play in bringing these two together.

The following Friday, as soon as Manoli appeared, Fortini slipped out of a side door and ran to the Petrakis house. Georgios had gone to the bar to play backgammon and Maria now sat reading.

'Maria, he's there,' Fortini said breathlessly. 'Manoli is at the taverna. Why don't you come down and see him.'

'I can't,' said Maria. 'What would my father think?'

'For heaven's sake,' replied Fortini, grabbing her friend by the arm. 'You're twenty-three, Maria. Be bold. Your father needn't even know.'

Maria resisted, but only feebly. 'What do I say to him?' she asked anxiously.

'Don't worry,' Fortini reassured her. 'Men like Manoli never allow that to be your concern, at least not for long. He'll have plenty to say.'

Fortini was right. When they arrived at the taverna, Manoli was in charge of the situation immediately. He did not question why Maria was there, but invited her to join him at his table, asking her what she had been doing since they had last met, and how her father was. Then, more boldly than a man normally did in these situations, he said, 'There's a new cinema opened in Agios Nikolaos. Would you come there with me?'

Maria blushed deeply. 'That would be very nice,' she said. 'But it's not really the done thing around here . . . going to the cinema with someone you hardly know.'

'I tell you what, I shall ask Fortini and Stephanos to come as well. They can act as chaperones. Let's go on Monday, the day the taverna shuts.'

So before she knew it, a date was agreed. In a mere three days from now they would all go to Agios Nikolaos.

Manoli's manners were impeccable and their outings became a weekly event. Each Monday, the four of them would set off to spend an evening watching the latest movie, followed by supper.

Laughter characterised their times together, and they were often bent double with amusement at Manoli's jokes and antics. Maria began to allow herself the luxury of a daydream and to imagine that she could spend the rest of her days looking at this handsome, lined face, aged by life and laughter. Sometimes when he looked straight into her eyes she felt the invisible hairs on her neck stand on end. It was a new experience to be so flattered and teased. Maria had never enjoyed such carefree happiness and began to think this euphoria was love.

Although she knew that Georgios was delighted to see his daughter being wooed by this charming man, weighing on Maria's conscience was what would become of her father if she should marry. With most marriage arrangements, the girl left her own family and moved in with her new husband's parents. Clearly that would not happen with Manoli since he had no parents, but equally impossible was the idea that he might move into their small Plaka home. The problem went round and round in her mind, and not once did it seem absurd that Manoli had not yet even kissed her.

Manoli was on his best behaviour and had long since decided that the only way he would win Maria was by conducting himself faultlessly. His desire for her was intense but the waiting had a delicious novelty. In the early months of this courtship, when he gazed at her pale oval face framed by its halo of dark plaited hair, she would look down bashfully, afraid to meet his eye. As time went on, however, he watched her grow bolder and stare back. Though he had deflowered dozens of girls in his past, even he could not disgrace the lovely Maria and, more importantly, a voice inside urged him to hold back. It was time to settle down.

From a distance, Anna smouldered with envy and resentment when she learned from her father that Manoli was wooing Maria. Was this just to provoke her? If only she could show Manoli that she really did not care. There was no such opportunity, however, and the fury built up inside her.

Andreas, dismayed by her strange mood, repeatedly asked her what was wrong and was told not to bother her. He gave up. He had sensed for a while that the halcyon days of early marriage were over and he now busied himself more and more on the estate. Eleftheria noticed the change too, and she assumed that Anna's irritability had something to do with the fact that she had so far failed to conceive a child.

One February evening, six months after the weekly nights out had begun, Manoli went to find Georgios in the bar. The old man was sitting alone, reading the local newspaper.

'Georgios, may I sit down?' Manoli asked politely.

'Yes,' Georgios replied, returning to his paper. 'I don't own the place, do I?'

'There's something I want to ask you. I'll get to the point. I would like to marry your daughter. Will you agree to it?'

Georgios folded the newspaper carefully and placed it on the table. To Manoli it seemed an age before he spoke.

'Agree to it? Of course I will! You've been courting the most beautiful girl in the village for over half a year—it's about time!'

Georgios's blustering response concealed his absolute joy at the request. Not just one, but now two of his daughters were to become part of the most powerful family in the province. Both their futures were now secure. It was the best a father could possibly hope for. Behind Manoli's head he could see the twinkling lights of Spinalonga. If only Eleni could share this moment.

He put out his hand to seize Manoli's, momentarily lost for words.

'Thank you. I will look after her, but between us we will look after you too,' said Manoli, fully aware of the lonely situation Maria's marriage could put her father in.

'Hey! We need your best *tsikoudia*!' he called out to Lidaki. 'We have something to celebrate here. It's a miracle. I'm no longer an orphan!'

'What are you talking about?' said Vangelis Lidaki, sauntering over with a bottle and two glasses, well used now to Manoli's verbal stunts.

'Georgios has agreed to be my father-in-law. I am to marry Maria!'

There were a few others in the bar that evening, and even before Maria knew anything about it, the menfolk of Plaka were toasting their future.

Later that night, when Georgios returned home, Maria was getting ready for bed. As her father came in through the door, she noticed an unfamiliar expression on his face. It was suffused with excitement and delight.

'Maria,' he said, reaching out to grab her by both arms, 'Manoli has asked for your hand in marriage.'

For a moment she bowed her head, pleasure and pain somehow mixed in equal measure. 'What answer did you give him?' she asked in a whisper.

'The one you would have wanted me to. Yes, of course!'

In all her life Maria had not felt this unfamiliar mingling of emotions. Her heart felt like a cauldron of ingredients that declined to blend. Her chest tightened with anxiety. What was this? She was fairly certain she loved Manoli. With his charm and wit, it was not hard to do so. But a host of worries began to gnaw at her. What would happen to her father?

'It's wonderful, Father. Wonderful. But I can't leave you here alone.'

'Don't worry about me. I can stay here—I wouldn't want to move out of Plaka. There's still too much for me to do here.'

'What do you mean?' she asked, although she knew what he meant.

'Spinalonga. Dr Lapakis relies on me, and so do all the islanders.'

There were as many comings and goings to and from the leper colony as ever, with new arrivals and supplies to be delivered, as well as building materials for the refurbishment that was being carried out. Georgios was an essential part of the whole operation.

'You do understand, don't you, Maria?' Georgios said.

'Of course I do, Father.' Maria knew that this was his vocation and his way of maintaining a connection with Eleni. 'I don't mind, as long as you come to see us as often as you can—and anyway we'll be in Plaka to see you most days.'

Georgios knew Maria would be true to her word, unlike Anna.

THE ENGAGEMENT between Manoli and Maria was cemented one month later with a party to which the whole of Plaka was invited. Both of them felt as if they had been blessed by good fortune. Maria was surprised and thankful to find herself marrying for love. For his part, Manoli loved the idea of marriage. He now relished the prospect of being looked after and even of having children.

The night of the engagement party the village square teemed with merrymakers. Stephanos carried around huge trays of food and Maria and

Manoli mingled with the crowd. To everyone's amazement and concern, however, Anna did not come to the party. She sent her excuses with Andreas, who arrived at the celebrations with his parents.

When the party was in full swing Manoli took his cousin to one side.

'Andreas,' he asked, almost shouting to be heard above the din of the band and the singing, 'would you agree to be our wedding sponsor?'

The wedding sponsor, the *koumbaros*, was a key figure in the marriage ceremony and, God willing, the sponsor would become the godparent of the first child.

'Nothing would delight me more, cousin! I'd be honoured,' Andreas said, and in truth he would have been wounded if Manoli had not asked him.

Maria received the first of many gifts for her trousseau that evening, and the merrymaking continued into the small hours, after which the village became the quietest place on Crete. Even the dogs would be too tired to bark until the sun was well over the horizon.

When Andreas arrived home everyone was asleep. Alexandros and Eleftheria had returned before him and the house was eerily silent and dark. He crept into the bedroom and heard Anna stir.

'Hello, Anna,' he whispered quietly, in case she was still asleep.

The truth was that Anna had not had a wink of sleep that night. She had tossed and turned, crazed with anger as she pictured her sister's beaming smile and Manoli's dark eyes fixed on her as they lapped up the compliments from all the well-wishers at the party.

When Andreas switched on the bedside light she rolled over.

'Well,' she said. 'Was it fun?'

'It was a great celebration,' he answered, not looking at his wife as he undressed and so failing to take in the look on her tear-stained face. 'And Manoli has asked me to be *koumbaros*!'

The issuing of such an invitation had been inevitable but to Anna it seemed as if her nose was being rubbed in her sister's happiness. In the shadows, her eyes pricked as she rolled over to bury her face in the pillow.

'Good night, Anna. Sleep tight.' Andreas climbed into bed. Within seconds the bed vibrated with his snores.

SPRING ARRIVED with an explosion of buds and blossom, and by summertime plans for the wedding were well under way. The date was set for October, and the marriage would be toasted with the first wines from the season's crops.

Maria and Manoli continued their weekly outings, still in the company of Fortini and Stephanos. A girl's virginity was an unspoken prerequisite of the marriage contract and the powers of temptation were well recognised.

One May evening, when the four of them were sitting over a drink in Agios Nikolaos, Maria noticed that Fortini looked slightly flushed.

'What is it, Fortini? You look like the cat that's got the cream!'

'That's exactly how I feel . . . We're having a baby!' she blurted out.

'You're pregnant! That's such wonderful news,' said Maria, grasping her friend's hands. 'When's it due?'

'I think in about six months—it's very early days.'

'That's only a month after our wedding—I'll have to come back to Plaka to see you every other day,' Maria said, bubbling with enthusiasm.

In August, bemused by her sister's complete lack of interest in her forth-coming nuptials, Maria decided that she and Manoli should call on her. It was a bold move. No invitation had been issued and Maria wanted to get to the bottom of why her sister was behaving in this way.

When they drew up outside the Vandoulakis home, Maria was the first to get out of the car. She was impatient for this encounter. Her fiancé knocked on the door three times. Eventually it was opened by Eleftheria, who was surprised to see Manoli and Maria. It was rare that anyone should call unannounced, but everyone knew that Manoli was not the type to bother about etiquette and she embraced him warmly.

'Come in, come in,' she fussed. 'It's so nice to see you. I'll get us some-thing to eat and some drinks . . .'

'We've really come to see Anna,' said Manoli, interrupting. 'How is she? She's been rather out of touch—for months.'

'Has she? Oh, I see. I didn't realise. I'll go up and let her know you're here.' Eleftheria bustled out of the room.

From her bedroom window, Anna had seen the car draw up. What should she do? She had managed to avoid such a confrontation for as long as she possibly could, believing that if only she could keep away from Manoli her feelings for him might gradually fade. Yet the intensity of her passion for this vivacious version of her husband was as strong as it had been that day he had tucked a flower between her breasts. She longed to see that sparkling smile, but she knew that any such meeting would now be with Maria, and that would mean a reminder that Manoli could never be hers.

Eleftheria tapped gently on her door. 'Anna, your sister and her fiancé are here!' she called, without entering. 'Will you come and see them?'

Without ever having been taken into her confidence, Eleftheria had harboured her suspicions about Anna's feelings for Manoli. She had been the only person who had known quite how often he had called on her, and the only person who had known full well that Anna was not ill on the day of her sister's engagement party. It was all beginning to make sense. She knocked on the door again. 'Anna? Are you coming?'

Anna delivered a sharp retort. '*Yes,* I *am* coming. I'll be down when I'm ready.'

A few moments later, her vermilion lipstick freshly applied, Anna took a deep breath, threw open her bedroom door and went downstairs. She swept across the room and pecked her sister politely on the cheek. Then she turned to Manoli, holding out a pale, limp hand to shake his.

'Hello,' she said, smiling. 'This is such a surprise. Such a nice surprise.' And in so many ways it *was* nice to see this man, this obsession of hers, in the flesh, looking even more rugged, more desirable than she had remembered. She found she was still holding his hand. She pulled away.

'I felt it had been such a long time since I saw you,' said Maria. 'Time is moving on and you know we are getting married in October, don't you?'

'Yes, yes, that's marvellous news. Truly marvellous.'

Eleftheria bustled in now with a tray of glasses and a row of little plates piled with olives, cubes of feta cheese, almonds and warm spinach pies. She continued to bustle about as she took a decanter from the sideboard and poured everyone a drink.

They all took a seat. Anna perched on the edge of hers; Manoli sat back, totally at ease. Though conversation was stilted, Anna kept some sort of dialogue going. She knew it was her role.

'Tell me about Father. How is he?'

It was hard to tell whether Anna really cared, but it had certainly never occurred to Maria that she did not.

'He's fine. He's very pleased about our wedding, but he is adamant about staying where he is in Plaka,' she said.

She had always made plenty of excuses for her sister's apparent lack of concern—her distance from Plaka, her new duties as a wife; now that similar changes were soon to affect her, it would be a great help if Anna would begin to play more of a role with their father. She was about to broach the subject when there were voices in the hallway.

Alexandros and Andreas had returned from an inspection of their land up on the Lasithi plateau, and though the cousins saw each other regularly to discuss the affairs of the estate, they embraced now like long-lost friends. More drinks were poured and the two men of the house sat down.

Maria detected a tension but could not put her finger on the cause. Anna seemed perfectly happy making conversation, but she could not help noticing that most of her comments were directed at Manoli rather than her.

Manoli had forgotten the strength of his attraction to Anna. There was something so gloriously coquettish about her. Even though he was engaged, the old rogue in Manoli still lurked close to the surface.

Eleftheria could see a difference in Anna. Tonight she was animated, her cheeks flushed, as she listened to Manoli with an almost fawning appreciation. As usual, Manoli dominated the conversation. Anna tried not to be infuriated when he kept referring to Maria as his 'beautiful fiancée', but the way he was looking at her now, speaking to her as though there was no one else in the room, made it plain that he had not forgotten their flirtation.

It was almost dark by the time Maria and Manoli rose to go.

'There is just one thing, Anna,' Maria said, determined not to leave without achieving her mission. 'Would you come and visit Father soon? I know you are busy, but I think he would really appreciate it.'

'Yes, yes, I will,' said Anna with unusual deference to her younger sister. 'I've been neglectful. I'll come down to Plaka in a few weeks' time. What about the first Wednesday in September? Would that be convenient?'

It was a casual, throwaway question, but somehow full of malice. Anna knew perfectly well that a Wednesday in September was the same for Maria as any Wednesday. Also, Maria had expected Anna to suggest something sooner. She was impeccable in her reply, however.

'That would be lovely,' she said. 'I know Father will look forward to it.'

MARIA WAS NOW counting the days until her marriage: only four weeks to go. She wished they would pass more quickly, but the fact that she would be leaving her father still weighed heavily on her mind and she resolved to do everything she possibly could to ease the transition. The most practical step she could take would be to tidy up the house for when Georgios would be there alone. She had put this task off during the hot summer months, but it was much cooler now and today was the perfect day to do such a job.

As Maria worked, she listened to the radio, humming along to the music that crackled over the airwaves. One of her favourite Mikis Theodorakis songs was on the radio. She turned the volume up high, then kicked off her shoes to climb onto a chair so that she could reach into the back of a tall cupboard. As she stepped up, she noticed a strange mark on her foot. Her heart missed a beat. In some lights it might scarcely have been visible. It was like a shadow but in reverse, a patch of dry skin that was slightly paler than the rest. It almost looked as though she had burned her foot in the sun and the skin had peeled off to leave the lighter pigment underneath. Perhaps it was nothing at all to worry about, but she felt sick with anxiety.

That night was the most troubled Maria had ever endured. She lay awake almost until dawn, tossing and turning. When she finally fell into a brief and fitful sleep, she dreamt of her mother and of huge stormy seas that wrecked Spinalonga as though it were a great ship. It was a relief when day broke. She would go and confide in Fortini. Her friend was always up by six o'clock, preparing food for the day ahead. It seemed especially tough, given that she was now seven months' pregnant.

'Maria! What are you doing here so early?' Fortini exclaimed. She could see that there was something on her friend's mind. 'Let's have some coffee.' She stopped working and they sat down together in the kitchen. 'Are you getting nervous about the wedding or something?' she asked.

Maria looked up at Fortini, the shadows under her eyes as dark as her untouched coffee and her eyes welled with tears.

'Maria, what is it?' Fortini reached out and covered her friend's hand.

'It's this,' said Maria. She stood up and put her foot on the chair, pointing to the faded patch of dry skin. 'Can you see it?'

Fortini leaned over. She now understood why her friend had looked so anxious. Everyone in Plaka was familiar with the first visible symptoms of leprosy, and this looked very like one of them.

'What do I do?' Maria said quietly, tears now pouring down her cheeks.

Fortini was calm. 'For a start, you mustn't let anyone round here know about this. It could be nothing. You need to get a proper diagnosis. Your father brings that doctor home from the island nearly every day, doesn't he? Why don't you ask him to have a look?'

'Dr Lapakis is a good friend of Father's, but he's almost too close and someone might get to hear of it. There was another doctor. He used to come over before the war. I think he worked in Iraklion. Father would know.'

'Why don't you try to see him then? You've plenty of excuses for going to Iraklion with your wedding round the corner.'

'But it means telling my father,' Maria sobbed. She tried to wipe the tears from her face, but still they flowed. There was no avoiding this. Even if it could be kept secret from everyone else, Georgios would *have* to know.

Maria returned home. It was only eight o'clock but Georgios was already out, and she knew she would have to wait until the evening to speak to him. She would distract herself by continuing with the cleaning she had begun the day before, and she threw herself into it with renewed vigour and energy, polishing furniture until it gleamed and picking the dust with her fingernail from the darkest corners of every cupboard and drawer.

Just before Georgios was due to arrive home there was a knock at the door, which was then opened from the outside. It was Anna. 'Hello, Maria. what are you doing?' asked Anna, entering the room. 'Don't you ever stop working?'

'Hello, Anna. I'm getting the house ready for when Father is on his own,' answered Maria quietly, and as she spoke she remembered that it was the day that Anna had promised to visit. In her anxiety it had slipped her mind.

Anna did not reply. She stood looking at her sister, transfixed. Maria shifted uncomfortably and climbed down from a stool. Her sister's eyes followed her but they were trained on her bare feet. She had noticed the sinister mark and it was too late for Maria to conceal it.

'What's that patch on your foot?' she demanded, bending down to have a closer look at her foot.

'I don't know,' said Maria defensively. 'Probably nothing, but I am going to have it checked.'

'Have you told Father about it? And has Manoli seen it?' Anna asked.

'Neither of them knows about it yet,' answered Maria.

'Well, if you're not going to tell them, then I'm going to. It looks like leprosy to me,' Anna said.

'Look,' said Maria, 'I shall tell Father tonight. But no one else is to know. It may be nothing.'

'Well, as soon as you know the truth, you're to come and let me know.'

Anna's tone was distinctly bullying, and the thought even crossed Maria's mind that she was relishing the thought of her sister being leprous.

'If I haven't heard from you within a fortnight or so, I'll be back.'

With that she was gone, and a faint whiff of French perfume was the only evidence that she had ever been there.

That night, Maria told Georgios that Anna had called in, but had been unable to wait for his return. Then she showed him her foot.

'It's Dr Kyritsis we ought to go and see,' he said. 'He works at the big hospital in Iraklion. I'll write to him straight away for an appointment.'

He said little more than that, but his stomach churned with fear.

CHAPTER EIGHT

After breakfast on Monday, September 17, Georgios and Maria set off on the three-hour trip to Iraklion. It was a long and often windswept journey along the coast, and as they approached the city, the noise of trucks and construction work deafened them. Georgios had not visited the city since the war, and apart from the hefty city walls, which had stubbornly withstood German bombardment, most of it had changed beyond recognition. Eventually they spotted the hospital and Georgios pulled up outside.

Ten minutes later a nurse was escorting them into Dr Kyritsis's office.

If the war had transformed the face of Iraklion, it had left an even greater mark on Dr Kyritsis. Though his slim figure was unchanged, the thick black hair had turned silver-grey and the previously unlined face now bore clear signs of age and overwork. He looked every one of his forty-two years.

'Kyrie Petrakis,' he said, taking Georgios's hand.

'This is my daughter Maria,' said Georgios.

'Despineda Petrakis. It's many years since I saw you but I do remember you as a child,' said Dr Kyritsis, shaking her hand. 'Please, do sit down and tell me why you have come.'

Maria began, nervously at first, to describe her symptoms.

'Two weeks ago, I noticed a pale mark on my left foot. It's slightly dry and a little numb. With my mother's history I couldn't ignore it.'

'And is it just this one area? Or are there others?'

Maria looked across at her father. Since the discovery of the first mark, she had found several others. 'No,' she replied. 'There are some others.'

'I will need to examine them, and if I think it necessary we will have to take some skin smears.'

Dr Kyritsis got up and Maria followed him into his surgery, leaving Georgios to contemplate the anatomical drawings that lined the walls. First of all Kyritsis examined the lesions on her foot and back. He then tested them for sensitivity, first using a feather and then a pin. There was no doubt in his mind that there was some impairment to nerve endings, but whether it was leprosy he was not one hundred per cent certain.

'I am sorry, Despineda Petrakis, I will have to take some smears. I am afraid it will leave your skin a little sore afterwards.'

Maria sat in silence as Kyritsis and a nurse gathered the required instruments. The scalpel was razor sharp. Kyritsis took a smear from her back, and the nurse then applied some antiseptic ointment and cotton wool.

Once the bleeding had stopped, Maria was helped from the couch by the nurse and they returned to Dr Kyritsis's office, where Georgios was waiting.

'Well,' said the doctor. 'I will have the results within a few days. Come and see me again in a week and I will give you my diagnosis.'

It was the longest week of Maria's life. She sent a message to Manoli that she was unwell and would not be able to see him for a few days. Although she tried to occupy herself with practical tasks, nothing was enough to distract her from what might happen the following Monday.

The Friday before they were due to return to Iraklion, Anna called on her. She was eager to know: had Maria been to have tests? What were the results? Why did she not know? There was no implied sympathy or concern in her questions, and Maria was disturbed by the vindictive note of enthusiasm she had detected in Anna's reaction to the situation. Maria answered her sister in monosyllables and eventually Anna went on her way.

Monday arrived, eventually, and Maria and Georgios repeated the journey to Iraklion. This time the doctor's demeanour seemed different. Maria's file was on his desk and he opened it and shut it again, as though there was something he needed to check. There was not, of course. Dr Kyritsis knew exactly what he had to say. He came straight to the point.

'Despineda Petrakis, I am afraid that there are bacteria in your lesions to indicate that leprosy is present in your body. I am sorry it's bad news.'

He hated these moments. He was not sure for whom the news was more devastating, the daughter or the father. The girl was the spitting image of her late mother, and he was keenly aware of this cruel repetition of history.

The pair sat in silence, their worst fears realised, and Kyritsis tried to give them some reassurance while the terrible news sank in.

'This is very hard news for you and I am terribly sorry to deliver it. You must be reassured, however, that great advances have been made in the study of leprosy in the past few years and I very much hope you will benefit from it, Despineda Petrakis.'

Maria could hear the doctor speaking but he sounded as though he was a very long distance away. It was only when she heard her name that she looked up.

'It could be eight or ten years before your condition develops,' he was saying. 'Your leprosy type is, at present, neural, and if you remain in otherwise good health it should not progress to the lepromatous type.'

What is he saying? thought Maria. That I am effectively condemned to death but that it will take me a long time to die?

'So,' her voice was almost a whisper, 'what happens next?'

For the first time since she had entered the room, Maria looked directly at Kyritsis. She could see from his steady gaze that he was unafraid of the truth, and that he would tell her whatever needed to be told. For her father's sake, if not her own, she must be brave. She must not cry.

'I shall write a letter to Dr Lapakis to explain the situation, and within the next week or so you will have to join the colony on Spinalonga. I would advise you to say as little as possible to anyone, except those who are closest to you. People still have very out-of-date ideas about leprosy and think you can catch it just by being in the same room as a victim.'

At this point Georgios spoke up.

'We know,' he said. 'You can't live opposite Spinalonga for long without knowing what most people think of lepers.' He stood up. 'I think we should go now, Maria. The doctor has told us what we need to know.'

'Yes, thank you.' Maria was now completely composed. She knew where she would be spending the rest of her life. Not with Manoli near Elounda, but alone on Spinalonga.

Kyritsis opened the door for them. 'Just one final thing,' he said. 'I have been in correspondence with Dr Lapakis and I shall be resuming my visits to Spinalonga. I will, therefore, be involved with your treatment.'

They both listened to his words of comfort. It was kind of him to be so solicitous, but it did not help.

Maria and Georgios emerged from the hospital into the bright sunlight. All around them people went about their business, oblivious to the grief of the two individuals who stood there. How Maria envied them the trivial tasks of their routine that in a few days would be lost to her. In the space of an hour, her life and her father's had changed totally.

WHEN THEY ARRIVED back in Plaka, Anna's car was parked outside their house. She was the last person in the world Maria wanted to see. However Anna still had a key and had let herself into the house. It was almost dark by now and she was sitting in the twilight waiting for their return. There was no mistaking that their news was bad. Their downcast faces said it all, but Anna, insensitive as ever, shattered their silence.

'Well?' she said. 'What was the result?'

'The result was positive. I have leprosy,' her sister replied.

The words were stark. Even Anna now let the silence linger. All three of them standing in this room knew exactly what this meant.

'I will go and see Manoli now,' said Georgios decisively. 'And then Alexandros and Eleftheria Vandoulakis tomorrow. They all need to know as soon as possible.'

With that he left. His daughters sat on together for a while, though they had little to say to each other.

Georgios knew Manoli would be at the bar in the village. He strode in and spoke bluntly. 'I need to talk to you, Manoli,' he said. 'Alone.'

They withdrew to a corner table, out of earshot of everyone else.

'I have bad news, I'm afraid. Maria will not be able to marry you.'

'What's happened? Why not? Tell me!' There was sheer disbelief in Manoli's voice. He knew Maria had not been well for a few days, but had assumed it was something minor. 'You have to tell me what's wrong!'

'She has leprosy.'

'Leprosy!'

'Yes, leprosy. The day after tomorrow I will be taking her to Spinalonga.'

'How did she get it?' Manoli asked, immediately worried for himself.

What should Georgios tell him? It could take many years before the symptoms of leprosy made themselves evident, and it was possible that Maria had been infected by her mother all those years ago. He thought of Anna and the implications this might have for her.

'I don't know. But it's highly unlikely that anyone will have caught it from her,' he answered.

'I don't know what to say. It's such terrible news.'

Manoli moved his chair away from Georgios. It was an unconscious gesture, but one full of meaning. Georgios looked at him and was surprised by what he saw. Manoli was shocked, but by no means destroyed.

Manoli felt very sad for Maria. Leprosy, as far as he knew, was the most terrible fate for any human being. But it was not the end of his world. Though he had loved her, he had also loved a dozen other women in his life, and he was realistic. His affections would sooner or later find another object; Maria had not been his one and only true love.

Georgios took his leave. He had to be up early to call on Alexandros and Eleftheria. When he arrived at the Vandoulakis house the following morning the four of them were already waiting for him.

Knowing that it was only a matter of time before the truth of her family history came out, Anna had confessed to Andreas that her mother had died on Spinalonga. She calculated that her honesty might appear to be a virtue in this situation. She was to be disappointed. Even though Alexandros Vandoulakis was an intelligent man, his views on leprosy were no different from those of an ignorant peasant: that the disease was hereditary and that its presence in a family was a curse.

'Why did you keep Eleni's leprosy secret?' he demanded of Georgios. 'You have brought shame upon our family!'

Eleftheria tried to restrain him, but he was determined to continue.

'For the sake of our dignity, we will keep Anna within our family, though we shall never forgive the way you have deceived us. Only one thing could have made this situation more serious and that is if our nephew Manoli had already married your daughter Maria. From now on Anna will visit you in Plaka, but you are no longer welcome here, Georgios.'

There was not one word of concern for Maria, not a moment's thought for her plight. On the drive back to Plaka, Georgios sobbed as he lamented the final fragmentation of his family.

WHEN GEORGIOS ARRIVED home, he found that Fortini was already there helping Maria. They both looked up from their conversation as he walked in, and knew from his pale and battered demeanour that the encounter with the Vandoulakis family had been difficult.

He left the two women to get on with their preparations for Maria's departure, though there was little to do. It was only a few weeks ago that she had been preparing her trousseau, so boxes already stood in the corner of the room. As she lifted the presents of nightwear and lingerie out, Maria's tears dripped onto the finely stitched silk.

'Why don't you take them?' said Fortini. 'Why shouldn't you have fine things on Spinalonga?'

'You're right, I suppose; they might make life more bearable.' She repacked them and shut the box. 'So what else do you think I should take?' she asked bravely.

'Well, your father will be delivering several times a week, so we can always send you anything you need. But why not take some of your herbs? There's bound to be someone there who would benefit from them.' They spent the rest of the day going over what Maria might need on the island. It was an effective distraction from the impending catastrophe of her departure. Fortini kept up a gentle flow of conversation that lasted until it was dark. When the moment came for her to depart, she said, 'I'm not going to say goodbye. Not just because it hurts, but because it isn't goodbye. I'll be coming with your father to do the occasional delivery.'

'It would be wonderful to think that you might come and see me,' said Maria, feeling a sudden surge of courage. She knew that many people on the island had not seen a relative for years. She at least would have a regular chance to see her father, and now her best friend too.

'So that's that. No goodbyes,' said Fortini with bravado. 'Just a "see you next week then".' She did not embrace her friend for even she worried about such proximity, especially with her unborn child.

'But what about the baby?'

'The baby isn't due until November, and, anyway, Stephanos can take care of it when I come across to see you.' No one, not even Fortini, could quite put to one side the fear that leprosy could be spread by even the most superficial human contact.

Once Fortini had gone, Maria was alone for the first time in several days. She spent the next few hours rereading her mother's letters, trying to picture what it was like on Spinalonga. Her reverie was disturbed by a sharp knock on the door.

It was Manoli.

'Maria,' he said breathlessly. 'I just wanted to say goodbye. I'm terribly sorry it's all had to end like this.'

He did not hold out his hands or embrace her. Not that she would have expected either. What she would have hoped for was at least a greater sense of sorrow, but his eyes would not meet hers. His demeanour confirmed to Maria what she had half suspected, that Manoli's great passion would soon find another recipient. Her throat tightened. 'Goodbye.' Within moments he had gone and once again the door was closed. Maria felt as hollow as the silence that once again filled the house.

Georgios had yet to return. He had spent the last day of his daughter's freedom engaged in mending his nets, cleaning his boat.

Maria had made supper for them as usual, and at about seven in the evening they sat down opposite each other, though neither of them had any appetite. They spoke of trivial things, such as what Maria had packed in her boxes, as well as more important ones like when she would next see her father on the island and how often Savina would expect him for supper at the Angelopoulos house each week. At nine in the evening, both exhausted, they retired to bed.

By six thirty the following morning, Georgios had loaded Maria's boxes onto his boat and now returned to the house to collect her. Still vivid in his mind, as though it had happened only yesterday, was Eleni's departure. That May day the sun had shone on the crowd of friends and schoolchildren as his wife had left them. This morning there was deadly silence in the village. Maria would simply disappear.

A cold wind whipped through the narrow streets of Plaka and the chill of the autumnal air encircled Maria, paralysing her body and mind with a numbness that almost blocked her senses but could do nothing to alleviate her grief. As she stumbled the last few metres to the jetty she leaned heavily on her father, as if every step brought a stab of pain. But her pain was not physical. Her body was as strong as that of any young woman who had spent her life breathing the pure Cretan air, and her skin was as youthful and her eyes as intensely brown as those of any girl on this island.

The little boat, unstable with its cargo of oddly shaped bundles lashed together with string, bobbed and lurched on the sea. Georgios lowered himself in slowly, then reached out to help his daughter. Once she was safely on board he wrapped her protectively in a blanket to shield her from the elements. The only visible indication then that she was not simply another piece of cargo were the long strands of dark hair that flew and danced freely in the wind. He carefully released his vessel from its mooring— there was nothing more to be said or done—and their journey began. This was not the start of a short trip to deliver supplies. It was the beginning of Maria's one-way journey to start a new life. Life on Spinalonga.

Chapter Nine

For a few minutes they stood alone on the quay. Georgios was not going to leave her until someone came to meet them.

'Maria, be brave,' said Georgios quietly. 'I'll be back soon. Come and see me if you can.'

He held both her hands in his. To hell with it if he got leprosy. Perhaps that would be the kindest solution because he could then come and live with Maria. Though if that happened they would be hard pushed to find anyone else to make the deliveries to Spinalonga.

'Of course I'll come if it's allowed,' she answered.

'I'm sure it will be. Look,' said Georgios, pointing to the figure emerging through the long tunnel that passed through the old fortress wall. 'Here comes Nikos Papadimitriou, the island leader. I sent him a note yesterday to say I'd be bringing you today.'

'Welcome to Spinalonga,' Papadimitriou said, addressing Maria. How he could have such levity in his tone baffled her, but it distracted her for a moment. 'Your boxes will be carried to your home shortly. Shall we go?'

He indicated that she should follow him up the few steps into the tunnel.

'Before we go,' Maria said hastily, 'can I ask permission to come and see my father when he brings Dr Lapakis and does his deliveries?'

'Why, certainly!' boomed Papadimitriou. 'I assumed that would be the arrangement. I know you won't try to escape.'

Georgios wanted to put the moment of parting behind him. He knew that one or other of them had to turn away first, and today he waited for his daughter to make that move. He had always regretted his hasty departure when Eleni arrived on the island fourteen years ago. So great had been his grief that he had set off in his boat before they had even said goodbye.

Maria followed Papadimitriou into the tunnel. He walked slowly, leaning heavily on his stick, and eventually they saw the light at the other end. Maria's emergence from the darkness of the tunnel into her new world was as much of a surprise for her as for any new arrival. In spite of her mother's letters, which had been full of description and colour, nothing had prepared her for what she now saw. A long road with a row of shops, still shuttered, houses with window boxes and urns full of late-flowering geraniums, and one or two grander homes with carved wooden balconies. The fragrance of freshly baked bread and pastries filled the street.

'Despineda Petrakis, before I show you to your new home, come and meet my wife,' said Papadimitriou. 'She has made breakfast for you.'

They turned left into a small side street, which in turn led into a courtyard with houses opening off it. Papadimitriou opened the door of one of these and ducked inside.

The interior of the house was bright and ordered. There was a kitchen off the main room and stairs that led up to another floor.

'Let me introduce my wife. Katerina, this is Maria.'

The two women shook hands. In spite of everything that Eleni had told her to the contrary in her many letters, Maria had still expected the place to be inhabited by the lame and the deformed, and she was surprised at the woman's elegance and beauty. Katerina was younger than her grey-haired husband and Maria surmised that she must be in her late forties.

The table was set with embroidered linen and fine china. When they were all seated, Katerina filled the cups with hot black coffee.

'There is a small house next door that is vacant,' said Papadimitriou. 'We thought you might like that, unless you prefer to share a flat.'

'I think I would rather be on my own,' said Maria. 'If it's all right.'

There was a plate of fresh pastries on the table and Maria devoured one hungrily. She had eaten very little for several days.

'Do you remember my mother, Eleni Petrakis?' she asked.

'Of course we do! She was a wonderful lady and a brilliant teacher too,' replied Katerina. 'Everyone thought so.'

Papadimitriou stood up. It was now after eight o'clock and it was time for the island leader to be in his office. 'I shall no doubt see you again very soon, Despineda Petrakis. I shall leave you in Katerina's capable hands. She will take you on a tour of the island this morning.'

'Thank you for making me feel so welcome,' responded Maria.

'Shall we finish our coffee and start the tour,' Katerina said brightly when Papadimitriou had left. 'I don't know how much you know about Spinalonga, but it's not a bad place to live. The only problems come from being cooped up with the same people for your whole life. Coming from Athens I found that hard to get used to at first.'

'I've spent my life in Plaka,' said Maria, 'so I'm accustomed to that.'

Maria tightened her shawl about her shoulders as they left the house. When they turned into the main street, the shops were open. People came and went about their business, either on foot, or with mules or with donkey and cart. Everyone looked busy and purposeful. There was the *pantopoleion*, the general store that sold everything for the house, displaying its wares in profusion at the front of the building; a grocer whose windows were piled high with cans of olive oil; the knife-maker; the raki store; and the baker, whose rows of freshly baked loaves drew in every passer-by. Most important of all, for the men of the island at least, was the bar, which was run by the youthful and popular Gerasimo Mandakis. Already a few customers sat drinking coffee.

Just before they came to the church, there was a single-storey building. Katerina told Maria that this was the school. They peered in through the window and saw a young man standing at the front of a class of children.

'So who is the teacher these days?' asked Maria.

'For a while one of my fellow Athenians took over, but then he died. Your mother had trained another teacher, though. He was very young when he took over but the children adore him.'

'What's his name?'

'Dimitri Limonias.'

'Dimitri Limonias! He was the boy who came over here at the same time as my mother. We were told that it was he who had infected her.'

As occasionally happened with leprosy, Dimitri's symptoms had hardly developed since he had first been diagnosed, and now here he was, in charge of the school. Maria felt a momentary pang of resentment.

'There seems to be a large number of children,' she commented. 'Where do they all come from? Are their parents here too?'

'On the whole they're children who contracted leprosy on the mainland and were sent here. People try not to have children at all when they come to Spinalonga, but if a baby is born healthy it's taken away and adopted on the mainland. We've had one or two such tragic cases recently.'

'That's desperately sad. Who looks after the children who are sent here?'

'Most of them are fostered. Nikos and I had one such child. They're all well cared for.'

The two women continued on up the main street. Above them on the hill towered the hospital. 'I'll take you up there later on,' said Katerina, following Maria's gaze. 'Dr Lapakis likes to see all new arrivals.'

They walked round to the north side of the island, where human habitation ran out and eagles soared in the sky above. Here Spinalonga took the full blast of the wind from the northeast and the sea crashed on the rocks far below them, sending its spray high into the air. It began to drizzle now and the path was becoming slippery.

'Come on,' Katerina said. 'Let's go back. Your boxes will have been brought up by now. I'll show you your new home and help you unpack.'

As they descended the path, Maria noticed dozens of separate, carefully cultivated areas of land where, against the odds created by the elements, people were growing vegetable crops.

They passed a chapel that looked out across the huge expanse of sea, then reached the walled cemetery.

'Your mother was buried here,' Katerina said to Maria. 'It's where everyone ends up on Spinalonga.'

Katerina had not meant her words to sound so blunt, but in any case Maria did not react. She was keeping her emotions in check.

Just before they came full circle they passed a house with a large balcony and a portico; it was the grandest house Maria had yet seen on the island.

'Officially that's the home of the island leader,' Katerina told her, 'but when Nikos took over he didn't want to push the previous leader and his wife out of their home, so they stayed where they were. Elpida Kontomaris still lives there.'

Maria recognised the name immediately. Elpida had been her mother's best friend. The harsh fact was that her mother seemed to have been out-lived by nearly all around her.

'My mother used to write about Elpida Kontomaris,' Maria said. 'She was her best friend.'

By now they had returned to the cluster of houses they'd left earlier. Katerina led Maria towards a rust-coloured front door and took a key from her pocket, which she gave to Maria. It seemed dark inside, but with the flick of a switch the main room was cheered up just a little. There was a dampness about it, as though it had been uninhabited for some time, and the room was sparsely furnished: one dark table, two chairs and a sofa against the wall. A shepherd's hut in the mountains would have been more hospitable.

'I'll stay and help you unpack,' said Katerina bossily.

Maria was determined to hide her feelings about this hovel and could only do so if she was left here on her own. 'That's very kind of you,' she said firmly, 'but I don't want to impose any more on your time.'

'Very well,' said Katerina. 'But I'll pop back later this afternoon to see if there is anything I can do. You know where I am if you need me.'

Maria was glad to be alone with her thoughts, but it was then that despondency overtook her. All those hours of self-control and false good cheer for her father, for the Papadimitrious and for herself had been a strain, and the awfulness of what had happened now engulfed her. She locked the front door and went upstairs to the bedroom. A hard bed and a straw mattress were all the room contained, except for a small wooden icon of the Virgin nailed to the wall. Maria lay down, her knees pulled in towards her chest, and sobbed. How long she remained so she was not sure, since she eventually fell into fitful, nightmarish sleep.

Somewhere in the profound darkness of her deep underwater dream, she heard the distant sound of drums and felt herself being pulled to the surface. Now she could hear that the steady percussive beat was not a drum at all but the sound of someone knocking on her front door. She descended the narrow staircase and as she unlocked and opened the door, she saw two women standing there in the twilight.

'Maria! Are you all right?' cried Katerina. 'We have been knocking on the door for an hour. I thought you might have . . . done yourself harm.'

There was a strong basis for her anxiety. In the past there had been a few newcomers who had tried to kill themselves, some of them successfully.

'Yes, I'm fine. Really. I must have fallen asleep . . . Come in.'

Maria opened the door wide and stepped aside to let the two women in.

'I must introduce you,' Katerina said. 'This is Elpida Kontomaris.'

The older woman took hold of Maria's hands.

'I can see so much of your mother in you,' she said. 'I loved your mother, she was one of the best friends I ever had.'

'Kyria Kontomaris, I know your name so well. In her letters, my mother told me of your friendship.'

Elpida surveyed the bare, cold room. Maria's boxes stood unopened and it was obvious that this bewildered young woman had not even attempted to unpack. It was still a dead man's house.

'Look, why don't you come and stay with me tonight?' she asked kindly. 'I have a spare room, so it will be no trouble.'

Maria had no hesitation in accepting. She remembered passing Elpida's house earlier that day. Yes, that was where she would like to be tonight.

FOR THE NEXT few nights Maria slept in Elpida Kontomaris's house and during the day returned to her own little house and worked hard to transform it into a home, whitewashing her walls and recoating the old front door with a bright, fresh green. She unpacked her books, her photographs and a selection of small pictures, which she hung on the wall, then ironed her embroidered cotton cloths, spreading them on the table and on some comfortable chairs that Elpida had decided she no longer needed. She put up a shelf and arranged the jars of dried herbs she had brought with her, and scrubbed the kitchen until it gleamed.

Having overslept and missed it on that first afternoon of despair, Maria went later that week for her appointment with Dr Lapakis. He noted her symptoms and drew the location of her lesions on a diagrammatic outline of the body, comparing his observations with the information that Dr Kyritsis had sent him and noting that there was now one more lesion on her back. This alarmed him. Maria was in good general health at present, but if anything happened to change this, Kyritsis's hope that she had a good chance of survival might come to nothing.

Three days later Maria went to meet her father. As she watched his boat approaching she could see that he had another passenger besides Lapakis today. This was unusual. For a fleeting moment she wondered if it was Manoli, breaking all the rules to come to visit her. She had thought much about what life with Manoli would have been like and had begun to question how he would have reacted in difficult times. As soon as she could distinguish the figure in the boat, however, she saw that it was Dr Kyritsis.

As they bumped gently into the quay, Georgios threw the rope to Maria, who tied it expertly to a post.

'Maria . . . I am so pleased to see you,' he said, concealing his anxiety for his daughter.

'How are you, Maria?' enquired Kyritsis, stepping nimbly from the boat.

'I feel one hundred per cent well, Dr Kyritsis,' she replied.

He paused to look at her. This young woman seemed so out of place here, so perfect and so incongruous.

Leaving Maria to talk to her father, the two doctors disappeared through the tunnel. It was more than a dozen years since Nikolaos Kyritsis had last visited, and the transformation of the island astonished him. When they reached the hospital, he was even more amazed. The original building was just as it had been, but a huge extension had been added.

'It's astonishing!' he exclaimed. 'It's all here. Just as you planned.'

'Only after plenty of blood, sweat and tears, I can assure you,' Dr Lapakis replied. He showed Kyritsis proudly around the hospital. The rooms in the new wing were lofty, with windows that reached from floor to ceiling. In the winter, the sturdy shutters and thick walls shielded patients from the howling gales, and in the summer the windows were thrown open to receive the soothing sea breezes. Everywhere was spotlessly clean and Kyritsis noticed that each room had its own shower and washing cubicle.

'Finally I've got a hospital where patients can be treated as they should be,' said Lapakis as they walked to his office. 'And, moreover, a place where they can have some self-respect.'

'It's very impressive, Christos,' said Kyritsis. 'It looks exceptionally clean and comfortable.'

'Yes, but good conditions aren't all they want. More than anything they want to get better and leave this place.' Lapakis spoke wearily.

The islanders knew that drug treatments were being worked on, but little seemed to have come their way, and as yet a cure was no more than a dream.

'Look, we've got to be optimistic,' said Kyritsis. 'There are some drug treatments under trial at the moment. They don't work overnight, but do you think some of the patients here would be prepared to try them?'

'I'm sure they would, Nikolaos. What do they have to lose?'

'Actually, quite a lot at this stage . . .' replied Kyritsis thoughtfully. 'It's all sulphur-based, as you probably know, and unless the patient is in good health the side effects can be disastrous. At the Leprosy Congress I've just been to there were even reports of suicide being attributed to this new treatment.'

'Well, we'll have to think very carefully about which, if any, of our patients act as guinea pigs.'

Kyritsis walked back to the quayside. It was now midday and as the doctor emerged from the tunnel and the choppy October sea came into view, he saw Georgios's boat bobbing up and down a hundred metres or so off the shore as arranged. A woman stood on the quayside. She was looking out to sea but heard his step and turned. As she did so, her long hair blew around her face and two large oval eyes gazed at him with hope.

Many years earlier, before the war, Kyritsis had visited Florence and seen Botticelli's captivating image of the *Birth of Venus*. With the grey-green sea behind her and her long hair caught by the wind, Maria strongly evoked the painting, and for a moment Kyritsis was stopped in his tracks. He thought her more beautiful then than anyone he had ever seen.

'Dr Kyritsis,' she said, rousing him from his reverie with the sound of his own name. 'Dr Kyritsis, my father is here.'

'Yes, yes, thank you,' he blustered, aware that he must have been staring.

Maria held the boat fast as the doctor climbed in, and then she released it and tossed him the rope. As Kyritsis caught it he looked up at her. The face of Venus herself could not have been more perfect.

To MARIA'S SURPRISE, her first few weeks on the island passed quickly. One evening Elpida invited her to meet Dimitri Limonias. Both approached the meeting with some trepidation.

'Your mother was extremely kind to me,' Dimitri began, once drinks were poured and both were seated. 'She treated me like her own son.'

'She loved you like her own son,' said Maria. 'That's why.'

'I know that everyone believed that I was responsible for giving her the disease,' said Dimitri hesitantly. 'But I've talked to Dr Lapakis about this at length and he thinks it is highly improbable that the bacteria were passed from me to your mother.'

'None of that matters now,' said Maria. 'I'm not here to blame you. I just thought it would be good to meet. You're almost like a brother after all.'

'That's a very generous thing to say,' he said. 'I don't feel as though I have much of a family any more. My parents have both died and my brothers and sisters were never exactly in the habit of writing letters.'

Several hours passed as the two talked about the island, the school and Eleni. Dimitri had been lucky. During his time on Spinalonga he had enjoyed the loving care of Eleni and then Elpida. One was an experienced mother and the other had treated him as the precious child she had always yearned for. Maria was glad to have met this quasi half-brother, and the pair would regularly meet for coffee or supper, which she would cook while Dimitri enthused about his work. Spending time with someone who was driven by his working life made Maria realise that being a leper was not going to dominate her every waking hour. A fortnightly appointment at the hospital, a house to keep neat and tidy, a small allotment to tend to—along with the meetings with her father, these were the cornerstones of her existence.

But soon she realised she needed something more to occupy her, and she picked a battered notebook off her shelf. It contained all her handwritten instructions on the use of herbs. *For healing and cure*, she had written on the title page in her schoolgirl script. In the context of leprosy, those words looked so naive, so far-fetched. There were, however, plenty of routine ailments that people suffered from on Spinalonga, and if she could relieve them of those, then it would be a worthwhile contribution.

Maria was bubbling over with news of her plans when Fortini came to visit her one day. She told her friend how she planned to scour the uninhabited, rocky part of the island for herbs as soon as spring came.

'Even on those limestone cliffs with the salt spray there's apparently plenty of sage, cistus, oregano, rosemary and thyme. I'll need to get approval from Dr Lapakis, but once I've done that I'll advertise my remedies in the *Spinalonga Star*,' she told Fortini, who, on this chilly day, was warmed to see her dear friend so full of fire and enthusiasm.

'But tell me what's going on in Plaka,' Maria asked, never one to keep the conversation one-sided.

'Not much really. Mother says that Antonis is as grumpy as ever and it's high time he found himself a wife, but Angelos has met a girl in Elounda that he seems keen on. Perhaps one of my brothers might soon be married.'

'And what about Manoli?' asked Maria quietly. 'Has he been around?'

'Antonis hasn't seen him much . . . Are you sad about him, Maria?'

'It probably sounds awful, but I don't miss him as much as I thought I would. Do you think that's strange?'

'No, I think it's probably a good thing.' Since Fortini had been on the receiving end of Antonis's gossip about Maria's fiancé all those months ago, she had never entirely trusted Manoli anyway.

Maria looked down at her friend's swollen belly. 'Is the baby kicking?'

'Yes,' replied Fortini. 'All the time now.'

'Perhaps you shouldn't be coming across now,' said Maria. 'If you're not careful you'll be giving birth in my father's boat.'

'As soon as I've had the baby I'll be straight back,' Fortini reassured her. She was nearing the end of her pregnancy and beginning to worry about the rough waters she had to cross to see her friend. 'And I'll write. I promise.'

By now Georgios had established a firm routine for seeing his daughter on Spinalonga. Though he came and went more often, they decided to limit themselves to three encounters a week, on Mondays, Wednesdays and Fridays. These days were the high points of her week.

In December, Georgios brought the exciting news that Fortini had given birth to a son, called Mattheos.

By the following week, Maria had embroidered a tiny pillowcase with the baby's name and date of birth and filled it with dried lavender. *Put it in his cradle*, she wrote in a note to Fortini. *It'll help him to sleep.*

By April, Fortini was ready to come and see Maria again. Even with her new responsibilities as a mother, she still knew the minutiae of everything that happened in Plaka.

'Have you seen my sister lately?' Maria asked her friend.

'No. Not for a long time,' Fortini said thoughtfully.

Georgios had told Maria that Anna came to see him quite regularly, but now she wondered if that were really true. If Anna had turned up in her shiny car, Fortini would have known about it. The Vandoulakis family had been extremely angry when they learned of Maria's leprosy and it did not surprise her that Anna had not written to her. Neither would it really surprise her if her father had lied about her sister's visits.

'Antonis sees her from time to time at work,' Fortini said at last.

'Does he say how she looks?'

'Fine, I think.' Fortini knew what Maria was really asking. Was her sister pregnant? After all those years of marriage, it was high time that Anna had a child. If not, there must be a problem.

'Look, I probably shouldn't tell you this, but Antonis has seen Manoli coming and going from Anna's house when Andreas is out.'

'That's allowed, isn't it? He is family.'

'Yes, but even members of your family don't visit *every* day.'

Maria found herself being defensive. 'Well it sounds to me as though Antonis is spying.'

'He isn't spying, Maria. I think your sister and Manoli have grown rather close. Manoli visits during the day when Andreas is out.'

'Well, why doesn't Andreas do something about it?'

'Because he has absolutely no idea what's going on,' said Fortini. 'But I'm sure the whole thing will just fade out.'

The two women sat in silence for a moment. Suddenly Maria remembered her sister's edgy behaviour all those months ago when she and Manoli had visited. It was perfectly feasible that something was going on between them. Her sister was more than capable of such infidelity.

As ever, Maria's thoughts were with her father. She felt keenly, even in anticipation, his ever-deepening shame. Her eyes pricked with tears of anger and frustration. She knew Manoli would never be hers but it was hard to bear the idea of him being with her sister.

The two sat in silence until Maria introduced a new subject. 'I've started using my herbs again,' she said, 'with some success. People are beginning to come to me now with their ailments.'

They continued to chat, though Fortini's revelation about Anna weighed heavily on their minds.

The relationship between Anna and Manoli did not, as Fortini predicted, fade out. On the contrary, the spark between them was rekindled and a fire soon smouldered. Manoli had been faithful to Maria while they were engaged. She was perfect, a virgin, his Agia Maria, and undoubtedly she would have made him a happy man. But now the period of mourning the loss of his fiancée had passed he was drawn back to Anna, like a moth to a flame.

CHAPTER TEN

Within a few weeks of Kyritsis's first visit the two doctors had short-listed the cases that they would monitor for suitability for drug treatment. Maria's name was among them. She was young, healthy, and in all ways an ideal candidate, yet for reasons that Kyritsis could not explain, he did not want to include her in the first group that they would begin to inject several months from now. It was the first action he had taken in perhaps his entire career that was not governed by reason. Not enough was known about the side effects of some of the drugs and he did not want Maria to be in the front line of an experiment.

As the months passed, Maria, for her part, began to look forward to the days when Kyritsis came across, and always made sure she was at the quayside to meet her father and the silver-haired doctor. One summer day Kyritsis stopped to talk. He had heard from Dr Lapakis of Maria's skills with herbal cures. A firm believer in modern medicine, he had long been sceptical about the power of the sweet, gentle flowers that grew on the mountainsides, but when several of the patients he saw on Spinalonga talked of the relief they had experienced through some of Maria's tinctures, he was prepared to relax his cynicism.

'I know conviction when I see it,' he said. 'I've also seen some real evidence that these things can work. I can hardly remain a sceptic, can I?'

'No, you can't. I'm glad you admit it,' said Maria, with a note of triumph. It gave her huge satisfaction to realise that she had persuaded this man to change his views. Even greater was her satisfaction when she looked at him and saw his face break into a smile. It transformed him.

Kyritsis had not been given to smiling in the past. Other people's misery was the cornerstone of his life and rarely gave him cause for levity or pleasure. He lived alone in Iraklion, working long days in the hospital, and the few waking hours he had outside it were spent reading. Now, at last, there was something else in his life: the beauty of a woman's face. To his colleagues and the lepers who were now regular patients he was just the same as he always had been: a dedicated, single-minded—some would say humourless—scientist. For Maria he had become a different person. Whether he would be her salvation in the long term she did not know, but every time he crossed the water her pulse quickened and she became a woman again, not just a patient waiting on this rock to die.

Though the temperatures began to drop during those first days of autumn, Maria felt an increasing warmth in Nikolaos Kyritsis. When he arrived on the island each Wednesday he would stop to talk to her. First of all it would be just for five minutes, but as time went on it was for longer on each occasion. Eventually, he asked Georgios to bring him over at eight thirty rather than nine so they could talk before his first hospital appointment. Georgios observed that the days when Maria had come to see him were over. She still met the boat, but not to see her father.

Usually a man of few words, Kyritsis talked to Maria about his work back in Iraklion and explained the research with which he was involved. He told her about his travels to international conferences and about the various cures that were being tried out. Occasionally he had to remind himself that this woman was a patient and might eventually be a recipient of the drug therapy that was being trialled on Spinalonga. How strange, he found himself thinking, to have found such friendship on this small island. Not only his old friend, Christos Lapakis, but this young woman too.

By late October the winter winds were gaining strength and would soon penetrate the thickest overcoats and the heaviest of woollen wraps. It seemed to Maria that it was uncivilised to stand outside in the perishing cold talking to Dr Kyritsis, but the thought of giving up their conversations was unbearable. They seemed never to run out of things to say, even though she felt she had so little of interest to tell him.

'I want to know what it's really like to live here,' he said to her one day as the wind gusted around them.

'But you see the island every week. You must be as familiar with how it looks as I am,' she said, rather puzzled by his statement.

'I see it as an outsider passing through. That's very different,' he replied.

'Would you like to come to my house and have some coffee?' As the words came out she hardly recognised her own voice.

'Coffee?' Kyritsis had heard her clearly enough, but repeated the word for want of something to say in response. 'Yes, I think I would,' he said.

They walked together through the tunnel. Both had passed through the Venetian walls a hundred times, but this was a different kind of journey. Kyritsis had not walked a street in the company of a woman for years, and Maria felt self-conscious in a way she thought she had left behind with childhood. Someone might see them and jump to the wrong conclusion. 'It's the doctor!' she wanted to shout, as she led him to her house, desperate as she was to spare herself from gossip.

While Maria busied herself making some coffee, Kyritsis looked about the room. It was much more comfortable and colourful than his own small apartment in Iraklion. He noticed the embroidered cloths, the picture of the young Kyria Petrakis with Maria and another girl on the wall. He saw a neat row of books, a jug containing leafy sprigs from an olive tree and bunches of lavender and herbs hanging to dry from the ceiling. He saw order and domesticity and was warmed by them both.

Now that they were on Maria's terrain, he felt he could get her to talk about herself. There was one burning question he wanted to ask. He knew so much about the disease, its symptoms, its epidemiology, its pathology, but of course he did not know what it really *felt* like to have leprosy.

'How does it feel . . .' he ventured, 'to be a leper?'

The question seemed so personal, but Maria did not hesitate to answer.

'In some ways I feel no different now than I did a year ago,' she said, 'but for someone like me who's not affected by the disease day to day, it's a bit like being in prison. Except there are no locks on the door, no bars.'

As she said this, her mind went back to that cold autumn morning when she had left Plaka to come to Spinalonga. Life on a leper colony had certainly not been what she had wished for, but she wondered what it would have been like had she married Manoli. She realised now that circumstances might have spared her. This was a man who had betrayed his own family, and with whom she had not once had a conversation that touched anything deeper or broader than the olive harvest, or whether to attend the saint's day celebrations in Elounda. His *joie de vivre* had attracted her at first, but she realised that perhaps there was no more to him than that. Life with Manoli might have been just another kind of life sentence.

'There are lots of good things, though,' she added. 'Wonderful people like Elpida Kontomaris and the Papadimitrious and Dimitri. They have such spirit and they never, ever complain.'

When she had finished speaking, Maria poured coffee into a cup and passed it to Kyritsis. She noticed, too late, that his hand trembled violently, and when he took the coffee, the cup clattered to the ground. There was an awkward silence before Maria rushed to the sink to get a cloth. She sensed his profound embarrassment and was keen to relieve him of it.

'I'm terribly sorry,' he said. 'It was so clumsy of me.'

'Don't worry, it's fine,' she said, mopping up, collecting the pieces of china in a dustpan as she did so. 'As long as you didn't burn yourself.'

It was, in fact, a special cup, one of a set that had belonged to her mother, but Maria realised that she did not mind at all. It was almost a relief that Kyritsis was not so perfect as he outwardly appeared.

'Perhaps I shouldn't have come,' Kyritsis mumbled.

'Of course you should have come. I invited you and I would have been miserable if you hadn't.'

Maria's spontaneous outburst surprised her. Now they were even. Both had lost their composure.

'Please stay and have some more coffee.'

Maria's eyes looked into the doctor's so imploringly that he could do nothing but accept. She took another cup from the rack, and this time, once the coffee was poured into it, she left it on the table for him to pick up.

They both sipped without speaking. Sometimes there is awkwardness in silence, but not this time. Eventually Maria broke the spell.

'I hear a few people have started some drug treatment. Is it going to work?' It was a question she had been longing to ask.

'It's quite early days, Maria,' he answered. 'But we have to hold out a little hope. We are aware of some contraindications to the treatment, which is why we have to be cautious at this stage. The key thing, though, is that any improvement generally takes place over the very long term.'

'It's no magic potion then,' said Maria, trying not to sound disappointed.

'No, I'm afraid it's not,' said Kyritsis. 'It'll be a while before we really know if anyone will ever be fully cured. No one will be leaving quite yet.'

'So that means you might be able to come for coffee another time?'

'I very much hope so. You make such good coffee.'

Dr Kyritsis knew his answer sounded gauche and that it implied he was only interested in coming because of the quality of her coffee. 'Well, I had better be going now,' he said, trying to cover his embarrassment. 'Thank you.' With that rather stiff farewell, he left.

As she cleared the cups, Maria heard herself humming. The sensation could only be described as a lightness of heart, an unfamiliar feeling in a grey place. As soon as she had tidied up, she bundled some of her herb jars into a basket and set off to see Elpida, who had been suffering griping stomachache.

The elderly woman was in bed, pale but propped up on her pillows.

'Elpida, how are you feeling today?'

'I am actually feeling much better,' she said. 'Thanks to you.'

'It's thanks to nature, not to me,' Maria corrected her. 'I'm going to make another infusion for you. Have a cupful now, one in about three hours, and then I will come back this evening to give you a third.'

As soon as she had made sure that Elpida was comfortable, Maria made her way to 'the block', as the large apartment building at the end of the main street was unaffectionately known.

Today Maria went there because four of the apartments were home to lepers who could no longer fend for themselves. These were the cases whose ulcerated feet had led to amputation, whose claw-like hands rendered them incapable of even the simplest domestic tasks and whose faces were hideously scarred, deformed beyond recognition. Every one of the dozen or so extreme cases who lived here matched the biblical image of the leper, and were as far along the hellish road to disfigurement as anyone could be while still being perceptibly human. These people lived on the very brink of despair, but the efforts of Maria and a few other women like her never allowed them to go over it.

What these people cherished more than anything was their privacy. For one young woman, whose nose had been destroyed by leprosy and whose eyes were held permanently open through facial paralysis, the stares of her fellow colonists were insupportable. Another, slightly older woman had lost one of her hands. She was paying the highest price for the severe burns she had inflicted on herself while cooking for her family before coming to the island. Her remaining hand was fixed in a claw.

Maria shopped and cooked for these end-stage cases. She hardly noticed their deformities any more, as she served them lunch and, in some cases, helped to feed them. As she lifted spoons of rice to their lips, she hoped that Eleni had never suffered as these people did.

Most people on the mainland imagined that all lepers were as ravaged by the disease as these extreme cases. The very thought of their proximity repulsed them, fearing that the bacillus that had infected the islanders could be airborne into their own homes. Even in Plaka there were people with such misconceptions. In the past few years, a secondary reason for resenting the colony had brewed. Greatly exaggerated stories of the wealth of the Athenians who were living on Spinalonga had whipped people up into a state of increasing rancour, particularly in the poorer hillside communities. One minute they feared the idea that they too might end up on Spinalonga; the next they seethed with envy at the idea that the colonists might be living more comfortable lives than they were themselves.

One day in February a rumour was sparked by the idle comment of one man, and, like a forest fire from a carelessly dropped match, it spread with frightening speed through every village from Elounda in the south to Vilhadia on the northern coast. It was said that the mayor in Sellia had taken his ten-year-old son to hospital in Iraklion to have tests for suspected leprosy. Perhaps the disease was spreading from the island to the mainland. A ringleader in each village and the long-incubated feelings of fear and loathing were all it took for anger to boil over, and within a day people began to descend angrily on Plaka, intent on the island's destruction. If Spinalonga was sacked, they reasoned, no further lepers could be sent there and the Greek government would be forced to relocate the colony.

The mob planned to take every fishing boat they could lay their hands on and, under cover of darkness, torch the island. By five o'clock that Wednesday afternoon there was a gathering of 200 men on the Plaka quayside. Georgios had to force his way through them to find his boat. As he prepared to go over to collect Dr Kyritsis, he caught snatches of conversation.

'Who's got the petrol?'

'Make sure there's plenty!'

One of the ringleaders spotted the old man getting into his boat and shouted aggressively, 'Where do you think you're going?'

'I'm going across to collect one of the doctors,' he answered.

'What good can doctors do for lepers?' the ringleader sneered.

As the group laughed and jeered, Georgios pushed his boat away from the quay. His whole body quaked with fear and his hand trembled violently on the tiller. Never had the journey seemed longer.

Kyritsis was waiting, as usual, on the quayside. It had been an arduous day and he was eager to get home. In the half-light, he could hardly see Georgios's face under his hat, but the old man's voice was unusually audible.

'Dr Kyritsis,' he almost choked, 'there's a crowd over there. I think they're planning to attack Spinalonga!'

'What do you mean?'

'Hundreds of them have arrived. They're getting some boats together and they've got cans of petrol. They could be on their way any time now.'

Kyritsis was dumbstruck both by the stupidity of these people and by fear for the islanders. It would only waste valuable minutes if he went back inside the great walls to warn the lepers. He had to get to the mainland to talk these lunatics out of their plan.

'We need to get back—*fast*,' he urged Georgios.

Georgios swung the boat round. This time the wind and tide were behind him and the caïque covered the distance in no time at all. By now the people on the quayside had lit their torches, and as the small boat reached the shore the crowd parted to make way for a tall, broad-shouldered man who was clearly their spokesman.

'So who are *you*?' he mocked, as Kyritsis disembarked. 'Coming and going from the leper colony as freely as you like?'

The noisy, excitable crowd fell silent to listen to the exchange.

'My name is Dr Kyritsis. I am treating a number of patients on the island with new drug therapy. There are signs that this could lead to a cure.'

'Oh!' The man laughed sarcastically. 'Listen, everybody! Do you hear that? The lepers are going to get better.'

'There is a very strong chance of it.'

'Well, supposing we don't believe that?'

'It doesn't matter if *you* don't believe it.' Kyritsis was dramatic in his emphasis. He focused on the ringleader. He could see that this bully would be nothing without his mob.

'So why is that then?' the man said, surveying the crowd who stood expectantly on the quayside. Maybe he had misjudged this slight man who seemed to command more attention than he had anticipated.

'If you lay so much as a finger on a single one of those lepers out there,' said Kyritsis, 'you will find yourself in a prison cell darker and deeper than your worst nightmares. If even *one* of those lepers dies, you will be tried and convicted for murder. I will see to it personally.'

There was a stir among the crowd and then it fell silent again. The leader sensed he had lost them. Kyritsis's voice penetrated the silence.

'Now, what do you plan to do? Go home quietly or do your worst?'

People turned to each other and small huddles formed. One by one, torches were extinguished and the crowd returned quietly to their vehicles. All their resolve to destroy Spinalonga had evaporated.

As the leader made his way alone back to the main street, he cast a backward glance at the doctor.

'We'll be looking out for that cure,' he shouted. 'And if it doesn't come, we'll be back. You mark my words.'

IT DID NOT take long for word to get around Spinalonga that Dr Kyritsis had single-handedly quelled an uprising against the island. He returned the following Wednesday as hero of the hour. Maria was on the quayside to meet him, a familiar figure in her green coat, and today a broad smile stretched across her face.

'Thank you, Dr Kyritsis,' she said, before he had even stepped off the boat. 'My father told me how you stood up to those men and everyone here is so grateful for what you did.'

By now Kyritsis was on dry land. He knew that what had given him the courage to stand up to the mob had been the possibility that the woman he loved had been in danger. He could not deny it. It was Maria he had been desperate to save. Now, every part of him wanted to take her in his arms and declare his love—he had thought of little else all week—but such spontaneous behaviour went against a lifetime of reticence.

'Anyone would have done the same. It was nothing,' he said quietly. 'I did it for you.'

Such unguarded words. He knew he should be more careful.

'And for everyone on this island,' he added hastily.

Maria said nothing and Kyritsis had no idea whether she had even heard him. As usual they walked together through the tunnel, but, as they reached the exit, the usual view of the main street was obscured. The reason for this soon became clear. Nearly every inhabitant of the island who was fit enough had gathered to greet the doctor and to express their gratitude. As Kyritsis emerged, applause broke out and stopped him in his tracks.

Papadimitriou stepped forward. 'Dr Kyritsis. On behalf of every inhabitant of this island, I would like to thank you for what you did last week. We understand that you saved us from invasion and in all likelihood from injury or death. Everyone here will be eternally grateful to you for that.'

Expectant eyes gazed at him. They wanted to hear his voice.

'You people have as much right to life as anyone on the mainland. As long as I have anything to do with it, no one will destroy this place.'

Once again applause broke out, and then the islanders drifted away. Kyritsis had been overwhelmed by the ovation and was relieved when he was no longer the centre of so much attention. Papadimitriou was now at his side and walking along with him.

'Let me accompany you to the hospital,' he said, unaware that this deprived the doctor of precious moments with Maria. Standing among the milling crowd, Maria knew that Kyritsis could not come to her house. She watched his figure receding and returned to her home.

'Good morning, Nikolaos!' cried Lapakis teasingly, as he entered the hospital. 'The finest doctor in Crete, and now the Saint of Spinalonga!'

'Oh, come on, Christos,' replied Kyritsis, slightly abashed. 'You know you would have done the same.'

'I'm not sure, you know. By all accounts they were pretty rough.'

'Well, all that was last week,' said Kyritsis, brushing the episode to one side. 'Let's get on with today's issues. How are our test patients doing?'

'Let's go into my office and I'll put you in the picture.'

On Lapakis's desk was a tower of files. One by one he gave his friend a brief description of the current state of each of the fifteen patients receiving the drug treatment. Most were reacting positively, though not all.

'Two of them are in a severely reactive state,' said Lapakis. 'One of them has had a temperature of around a hundred and four degrees since you last came, and the other kept the whole island awake last night with her screams. She keeps asking how she can have no sensation in her arms and legs and yet feel such terrible pain. I haven't got an answer for her.'

'I'll take a look at her, but I think the best thing now would be to withdraw the treatment. There's a good chance that there might be some spontaneous healing and the sulphone could do some damage if that's the case.'

When they had gone through the notes, it was time for the two doctors to do the ward rounds. It was a grim business. One of the patients wept in agony as Lapakis applied a solution of trichloroacetic acid to dry the lesions. Another listened quietly as Kyritsis suggested that the best way of dealing with the dead bones in his fingers would be amputation. For another there was a visible surge of optimism as Lapakis described the tendon transplant he planned to do on his foot to enable him to walk again. At each bedside, the doctors agreed with the patient what the next stage would be.

The first of the outpatients then began to arrive, and it wasn't until midafternoon that it was time to see the patients who were receiving the new treatment. One thing was clear: several months into the trial, the new doses of drug therapy were producing encouraging results and the side effects that Dr Kyritsis had been wary of had not materialised in most cases.

'We've taken all our guinea pigs up from twenty-five to three hundred milligrams of dapsone twice a week now,' said Dr Lapakis. 'That's the most I can give them, isn't it?'

'I certainly wouldn't recommend anything higher, and if that's giving us these results I think we should regard it as the upper limit, especially given that we will continue treatment for several years after the patient's leprosy has ceased to be active.'

'What about starting the treatment with the next group?'

Lapakis was both excited and impatient. He had a gut feeling that after all these years of talk, a turning point had been reached.

'Yes, there's no point in waiting. I think we should select the next fifteen as soon as possible,' said Kyritsis. With every bone in his body, he wanted to make sure that Maria was among the list of names, but he knew it would be unprofessional to exert his influence.

THE FOLLOWING MONDAY, Fortini arrived on the island as usual, and she was clearly bursting with news.

'Anna's pregnant!'

'At last,' Maria said, unsure whether this news was good or bad. 'Does my father know?'

'He can't do, otherwise he would have said something to you, surely?'

'I suppose he would,' Maria said thoughtfully. 'How did you find out?'

'Through Antonis, of course. By all accounts the estate has been buzzing with speculation for weeks! But they've announced it officially now. She's three and a half months gone.'

In her first few months of pregnancy, Anna had been racked by sickness, and once the vomiting subsided there was a new problem. She began to bleed. The only way she might save this baby now was to have complete bed rest. It seemed, however, that the child was determined to cling on, and in the fourteenth week everything stabilised. To Andreas's great relief, Anna then rose from her bed. She now wore more voluminous clothes, under which her belly slowly swelled.

The forthcoming child was cause for celebration on the estate. Andreas threw open his cellar, and early one evening under the trees outside the house all his workers came to drink the best of the previous year's wine. Manoli was there too, and his was the loudest voice among them as they toasted the baby's safe arrival.

Maria listened in disbelief as Fortini described these recent events.

'I can't believe she hasn't made a point of going to see Father,' she said. 'She never thinks of anyone but herself, does she? Do I tell him or wait until she gets round to it?'

'Well, if I were you, I would tell him yourself. Otherwise he's bound to hear it from someone else.'

They sat in silence. The expectation of a child was normally a cause for great excitement. Not this time, though.

'Presumably it's Andreas's?'

Maria had said the unsayable.

'I don't know. My hunch is that even Anna doesn't know, but Antonis says that gossip is still rife and there's plenty of speculation.

'I'll tell Father about Anna when he comes to collect Dr Lapakis,' said Maria at last. 'I'll tell him as though it's the best news ever and say Anna has been too sick to come to see him. It's half true anyway.'

That afternoon, after Georgios had off-loaded all the boxes he was delivering, he went and sat with the two women on the bench by the wall. 'Father, there's some news. Some really good news,' Maria began, doing her best to sound enthusiastic. Georgios paused. The only good news he ever hoped for was that Maria might one day say she could come home.

'Anna is having a baby,' she said simply.

'Anna?' he said vaguely, as though he had almost forgotten who she was. The truth was that he had not seen his elder daughter for over a year. Initially this had been a great sadness, but with the passage of time he began to forget about his daughter.

'That's good,' he said at last, struggling to find a response. 'When?'

'It's due in August,' replied Maria. 'Why don't you write to her?'

'Yes, perhaps I should. It would be a good excuse to get in touch.' He would ask Maria's help in composing a letter later that week, but there was no hurry.

Two days later it was time for Kyritsis's visit. When he came to Spinalonga he had to rise at 5 a.m., and after his long journey from Iraklion the last few miles were full of anticipation for the taste of coffee on his lips. He could see Maria waiting for him, and today he inwardly rehearsed the words he wanted to say to her. In his head he saw a version of himself that was articulate but full of passion, calm but fired with emotion, but as he got off the boat, he knew that he should not be so hasty. Though she looked at him with the eyes of a friend, she spoke to him with the voice of a patient. As her doctor he realised that his dreams of confessing his love were but that. Dreams. It was out of the question to cross the barrier created by his position.

They walked through the tunnel as usual and as always the cups were on the table and Maria had brewed some coffee.

'We've had some very encouraging results from the drug testing,' he said, resolving to keep his emotions in check. 'Some of the patients are really showing an improvement.'

'I know,' she said. 'Dimitri Limonias is one of them, and I was talking to him yesterday. He says he can already feel a change.'

'Much of that could be psychological,' said Kyritsis. 'Being put on any kind of treatment tends to give patients a huge boost. Dr Lapakis is compiling a list of people from whom we will select the next group. Ultimately, we hope almost everyone on Spinalonga will be given the new drugs.'

He wanted to say that he hoped she would be on that list. He wanted to say that all his years of research and testing would be worthwhile if she was saved. He wanted to say that he loved her. None of those words came.

Much as he would have liked to linger in Maria's pretty home, he knew that they would be waiting for him up at the hospital. Wednesdays were like a shaft of sunlight in the darkness of a strenuous, overworked week for

Dr Lapakis and Dr Manakis. The extra workload that had been created for these two doctors in administering the drug therapy, and dealing with the side effects, was taking them over the edge of endurance. Soon Kyritsis would have to consider increasing the frequency of his visits.

Two WEEKS LATER, Dr Lapakis had short-listed his next group of candidates for treatment. Maria was one of them. One Wednesday in mid-March, when the tight buds on the almond trees were bursting into blossom, Kyritsis went to find Maria in her house. It was six o'clock and she was surprised to hear a knock on the door at that time. She was even more amazed to see the doctor standing there, when she knew he was usually hurrying to meet her father at the quay.

'Dr Kyritsis. Come in . . . What can I get for you?'

The evening light glowed burnt amber through the gauze curtains. It was as though the village outside was going up in flames, and for all Kyritsis cared at this moment, this could have been the case.

To Maria's surprise, he took both her hands. 'You're going to start treatment next week,' he said, looking directly into her eyes. Then, with absolute certainty, he added, 'One day you're going to leave this island.'

There were so many words he had rehearsed, but when the moment came he declared his love with a soundless gesture. For Maria, the cool fingers that grasped hers and lightly pressed them were more intimate, more articulate, than any arrangement of words about love.

Maria looked up. Their eyes and hands were now locked together and she felt an overwhelming sense of peace and wholeness. Neither of them knew how long they stood like this, though it was enough time for one era of their lives to end and another to begin.

'I will see you next week,' Kyritsis said finally. 'By then I hope Dr Lapakis will have given you a date for starting treatment. Goodbye, Maria.'

As he left her house, Maria watched Kyritsis's slight frame until it disappeared round the corner and out of sight. She felt she had known him for ever. It was in fact more than half her life ago that she had first set eyes on him, when he first came to visit Spinalonga in the days before the German occupation. Though he had made little impression then, she now found it hard to remember what it had felt like *not* to love him.

When Fortini arrived the following Monday, it was patently obvious to her that something had happened to her oldest friend. Maria was radiant.

'You look as though you have been cured,' Fortini joked, putting her bag down on the quayside. 'Come on, tell me. What's happened?'

'Dr Kyritsis—' Maria began.

'As if I couldn't have guessed,' teased Fortini, who had noticed how often Maria had spoken of the doctor in the past few months. 'Go on . . .'

'I don't know what to tell you, really. He held my hands, and said that I would be starting treatment soon and that I might one day leave this island . . . and he said it as though he cared.'

This might have seemed feeble evidence of love to Fortini, who had never even met Kyritsis properly, but who was she to judge? In front of her, though, she had the sight of her greatest friend suffused with happiness. That much was very real.

Maria's course of treatment began that month. Her symptoms had been slow to develop since she arrived on the island, but she felt an extraordinary relief, nevertheless, that finally something was being done to combat the disease. Though it had not yet devastated her body, it had already done plenty of damage to her life.

THE SPRINGTIME WIND, the Sokoros, blew from the south, finding its way between the mountains to the Gulf of Mirabello, where it whipped the sea into a white frenzy. Meanwhile on land the trees, full of leaves in bud, began to whisper. Now that it was nearly May, the sun came out strongly and reliably each day and drenched the landscape in blue, gold, green, yellow and purple.

Over half the population of Spinalonga were now being given dapsone. They knew it did not mean an overnight cure, but at least it gave them hope. Not everyone thrived, however. In July, having started her course only two weeks earlier, Elpida Kontomaris went into lepra reaction. Whether or not it was a consequence of the treatment the doctors could not be sure, but they stopped giving her the injections straight away and did what they could to relieve the agony she was in. Her temperature raged out of control, her body was covered in ulcerated sores, and every nerve felt tender.

Maria went to visit her in the hospital and, against all the rules, Dr Lapakis allowed her into the small ward where Elpida lay. Through her half-closed eyes, she recognised Maria.

'Maria,' she whispered hoarsely, 'they can't do anything for me. I've been ill for so long. I just want to go now. I want to be with Petros . . . Please tell them to let me go,' she pleaded.

Sitting on an old wooden chair by her bed, Maria took the woman's limp, sweating hand. Was this, she wondered, the same violent death that her own mother had suffered? She had not been there to say farewell to her mother, but she would stay with Elpida until the end.

At some point during that hot night, Athina Manakis came to relieve her. 'Go and get some rest,' she said. 'I'll stay with Elpida for a while.'

By now, Elpida's breathing was shallow. For the first time, it seemed that she was out of pain. Maria knew she might not have long now.

'I'll stay,' she said firmly. 'I must.'

Maria's instincts were right. A short while later, in the quietest hour of the night, Elpida gave a final sigh and was gone. Maria wept until her body was drained of tears and energy. Her grief was not just for the elderly woman who had given her so much friendship since she had arrived on the island, but for her own mother.

The funeral was an event that brought everyone on the island pouring down to the little church of St Panteleimon. The priest conducted the service in the doorway so that those who stood outside could share it with those who were crammed into the cool interior. When the chanting and prayers were over, the flower-covered coffin was carried at the head of a long procession up the hill to the cemetery.

It was the last week of July, and the saint's day for St Panteleimon was on the 27th of the month. It seemed both a good and a bad time for such a celebration. On the one hand, with one of the most beloved members of the community so recently buried, the patron saint of healing seemed not to have been doing his job. On the other, many people on Spinalonga who had been receiving the drug treatment were showing signs of recovery, and for those, at least, it seemed as though a miracle might take place.

Special breads and pastries were baked the night before the festival, and on the day itself people filed through the church to light their candles and say a prayer. In the evening there was dancing and the singing of *mantinades*, and the people of Plaka could hear the occasional strains of lyre and bouzouki as they drifted across the water in the breeze.

As if to balance death with birth, news came at the end of August that Anna's daughter had been born. The arrival of a child in the Vandoulakis family after nearly a decade of waiting was a reason for great thanksgiving and celebration in both the family and the community beyond it. No one welcomed the disruption of the natural order that occurred when the people who owned the land and provided jobs failed to produce children. Now that Anna Vandoulakis had given birth to one child, none doubted that she would produce another and that the next time it would be a boy. That would ensure that the old patterns would continue for the next generation.

The baptism was to take place in the church in Elounda, and Georgios had been invited. The birth had softened Alexandros Vandoulakis's attitude towards Georgios, and he now felt that it was an appropriate moment for reconciliation. As Georgios sat on a hard wooden seat at the back of the church waiting, along with dozens of others, for his daughter and her husband to arrive with the baby, he watched Manoli, who sat next to Alexandros and Eleftheria at the front of the church, talking animatedly to the people in the row behind him. He was as handsome as ever, his dark hair slightly longer than Georgios remembered it and his teeth gleaming white against his tanned skin. He must miss Maria, he mused, to have still not found another girl to be his wife. Then the congregation rose. The priest had entered and was processing down the aisle, followed by Andreas and Anna. She carried a tiny bundle of white lace.

Georgios was immediately struck by the appearance of his daughter. He expected to see the radiance of motherhood, but instead it was an almost gaunt figure who wafted past him, with Andreas, rather stiff and upright and as aware as ever of his place in the world, at her side.

The buzz of lively chatter stopped and a hush descended on the congregation. Though the sleeping baby was blissfully unaware of anything but the warmth of her mother's arms round her, it was a significant moment. Until baptised, Sofia, as she was to be named, was exposed to the 'evil eye', but after that her spiritual safety would be guaranteed.

As the rest of the gathering once again took their seats, Manoli stepped forward. Aside from the priest and the baby, he was the key figure at the baptism: the *nonos*, the godfather. In the final stage of the ritual, after the waters had washed away the baby's non-existent sins, Manoli was handed the baby. A pure white ribbon was hung round his shoulders by the priest, then knotted to create a symbolic circle embracing both man and child: the spiritual bond between them was forged. Manoli looked down at the baby's sweet face and smiled. Sofia was awake now, and her dark, innocent eyes gazed unfocused into his. On his face she would have seen a look of pure adoration, and no one doubted for a second that he would forever love and cherish his godchild, his precious *filiotsa*.

After the baptism, Georgios hung back as the crowd made their way out of the church and into the sunshine outside. As Anna turned to leave she spotted him and waved enthusiastically across the sea of people. 'Father,' she said brightly, when she reached him 'I'm so pleased you could come.'

'If you really are so pleased I came, why haven't you been to see me? I've not been anywhere,' he said, adding pointedly, 'except Spinalonga.'

'I'm sorry, Father, but I wasn't well at the beginning or end of the pregnancy, and these summer months have been so hot and uncomfortable.'

There was no point in being critical of Anna. She had always managed to twist criticism round and make the accuser feel guilty.

'Can I meet my granddaughter?'

Manoli had lingered at the front of the church while a group gathered round him to admire his goddaughter. Now he made his way up the aisle towards the man who had so nearly become his father-in-law. They greeted each other and Georgios studied what he could see of his little granddaughter, buried in many layers of lace.

'She's beautiful, isn't she?' said Manoli, smiling proprietorially.

'From what I can see of her she is,' replied Georgios.

'Just like her mother!' continued Manoli, glancing up at Anna with laughter in his eyes.

He had not really given Maria a second thought for months, but felt he ought to enquire after her. 'How is Maria?' he asked, his voice full of concern. It was the question Anna should have asked, and she now stood quietly to hear the answer, wondering after all whether Manoli still carried a flame for her sister.

'She is quite well and her symptoms haven't really got worse since she's been there,' he said. 'She spends most of her time helping the lepers who can't look after themselves.'

What he did not mention was that most of the islanders were now undergoing treatment. There was no point in making too much of it, because even he did not know what it really meant. He did not believe there could be a cure for leprosy and he would not let himself indulge in such a dream.

As he finished speaking, Andreas came over.

'Kalispera Georgios. How are you?' he asked rather formally. The appropriate niceties were exchanged and then the moment came for them all to leave the church. Alexandros and Eleftheria Vandoulakis hovered in the background. Privately Eleftheria felt a great deal of pity for Georgios Petrakis. She did not, however, have the guts to say so. This would have been to defy her husband, who felt as keenly as ever the shame and stigma of having such a close connection with the leper colony.

The wall of shimmering heat that met Georgios when he emerged from the church made him feel light-headed. He blinked in the glare and was about to try to slip away unnoticed when Anna appeared at his side.

'Father, you must come and have a drink with us. I insist on it,' she said. 'It'll bring the baby bad luck if you don't.'

Georgios believed as much in the influence of fate and the importance of trying to ward off evil spirits as he did in God and all his saints, and he could not therefore refuse his daughter's invitation.

The party was already in full swing when he parked his truck under a lemon tree at the side of the long driveway that led to the Vandoulakis home. On the terrace outside the house, a group of musicians was playing, and though the dancing had not yet begun, there was a keen sense of anticipation. A long trestle table was laid out with rows of glasses, and people helped themselves from barrels of wine and took platefuls of *meze*, small cubes of feta cheese, plump olives and freshly made *dolmades*. Georgios stood for a while before helping himself to some food.

When the dancing began the old man looked on, glass in hand, as Manoli whirled his partner round and round until it made onlookers dizzy to watch. His lithe figure and energetic steps made him the centre of attention, as did his smile and the way in which he shouted instructions and encouragement. He saw in front of him a man with the rare ability to live for the moment, and his sheer abandon showed he did not give a damn what people thought.

Georgios found his daughter standing by his side. He could feel the heat from her body, even before he saw she was there, but until the music stopped there was no purpose in speaking. Georgios could sense her agitation at not being among the dancers, and when the music stopped and new people filtered into the circle and others bowed out, she quickly slipped in to take her place. Next to Manoli.

A different tune struck up. This one was more sedate, more stately, and the dancers held their heads high and rocked backwards and forwards and to left and right. Georgios watched for a few moments. As he caught sight of Anna through the forest of arms and spinning bodies he could see that she had relaxed. She was smiling and making comments to her partner.

While his daughter was immersed in the dance, Georgios took the opportunity to leave. Long after his small truck had bumped its way down the track, he could still hear the strains of music in the air. Back in Plaka, he stopped at the bar. It was where he would find a quiet place to sit and think about the day, and wonder at the strong current that flowed between his daughter and Andreas's cousin.

LIFE ON SPINALONGA continued as before. Dr Lapakis came and went each day and Dr Kyritsis increased his visits from once to three times each week. One particular autumn evening, as he made his journey from Spinalonga to Plaka, something struck him forcibly. Dusk had already fallen; the sun had dropped behind the mountains, plunging the coastline into darkness. When he looked round, however, he saw that Spinalonga was still bathed in the golden glow of the last of the sun's rays. It seemed to Kyritsis the right way round.

It was Plaka that had many of the qualities you would expect of an island—insular, sealed against the outside world—whereas Spinalonga hummed with life and energy. Its newspaper, the *Spinalonga Star*, carried digests of world news along with comment and opinion. There were also reviews of films that were due to be shown in forthcoming months, and extracts from new books. Perhaps because they dreamed of leaving, they continually looked outwards, beyond the place where they lived.

The *kafenion* and the taverna overflowed with customers in the evening and now even had competition in the form of a second small taverna. The allotments round the back of the island were yielding good crops, and there was plenty to buy and sell in the twice-weekly market. The island had never been in such good shape.

Occasionally Maria allowed herself a moment of frustrated outburst.

'It's almost more agonising now that I know there's a chance we might be cured,' she told Fortini, gripping her hands together. 'Can we dream or should we just be happy with the present?'

'It's never a bad thing to be content with the present,' said Fortini, as they sat on the bench by the quay.

Maria knew her friend was right. One thing that did prey on her mind, however, was the consequence for her of being cured.

'What would happen then?' she asked. 'If I was no longer on Spinalonga, I would never see Dr Kyritsis again.'

'Of course you would,' Fortini said, who was crocheting the edge of a baby's coat as they talked. She was pregnant again. 'If you weren't living here he'd no longer be your doctor and things might be different.'

'I know you're right, but it fills me with dread,' said Maria.

'Has he still not said anything to you?'

'No, nothing,' Maria confirmed.

'But he comes to see you every week. Doesn't that say enough?'

'Not quite,' Maria said bluntly. 'Though I do understand why he can't say anything. It wouldn't be the right thing to do.'

MARIA BETRAYED none of her anxiety when she saw Kyritsis. Instead she threw herself more vigorously than ever into her work, helping those she looked after in 'the block'.

Unbeknown to her, the doctors were testing and retesting the patients who had been the first to receive the treatment, just over a year before, and five of them appeared to be entirely free of the bacillus. One of these was Dimitri Limonias.

At the tail end of one long and arduous day, Kyritsis and Lapakis sat down to review the results. Something had become very obvious.

'You know, I think we'll soon have a good case for letting these patients go, don't you?' said Kyritsis with a rare smile.

'I do,' replied Lapakis. 'But we'll need government approval first and they may be reluctant to give it so soon.'

'I'll request their release on condition that they continue to have treatment for a few months afterwards and checkups for a year after that.'

'Agreed. Once we've got government authority, we'll tell the patients.'

Weeks passed before a letter came. It stated that the patients would have to test negative for a year before they could be let off the island. Kyritsis was disappointed by this delay, but even so it meant that a dozen islanders could soon be gone.

The first few healthy patients greeted the announcement with tears of joy, but when Dr Kyritsis told Dimitri Limonias the good news, the young teacher felt as though the numbness that used to afflict his hands had returned and taken his tongue. Spinalonga was his home now and the colonists were his family. His face was very disfigured on one side, which in the outside world would single him out for attention. And who would teach in the school?

'I would rather remain here while I have a function,' he said to Kyritsis, 'than go out into the unknown.'

He was not alone in his reluctance to leave. Others also feared that the visible legacy of the disease would always mark them out, and they needed reassurance that they might be able to reintegrate.

In spite of the misgivings of Dimitri and a few others, it was a momentous development in the island's history, and the pattern of recovery continued during the following year.

'By the end of this year we'll be out of a job,' said the sardonic Lapakis.

'I never thought that unemployment would be my aim in life,' replied Athina Manakis, 'but it is now.'

By late spring, save for a few dozen cases who had reacted badly to the treatment or who had not responded at all, it was clear that the summer could bring a widespread departure from the island.

In Lapakis's office, the island leader and the three doctors gathered to discuss how the success of the cure should be marked.

'I want the world to know that people are leaving because they're cured,' said Papadimitriou. 'I think we should all leave together, rather than sneaking away, and I want a celebration, a feast of thanksgiving, on the mainland.'

'We have those who aren't cured to think about too,' said Manakis. 'There's nothing for them to celebrate.'

'The patients who are facing longer-term treatment,' said Kyritsis diplomatically, 'will also be leaving the island, we hope.'

'How's that?' asked Papadimitriou.

'I am awaiting authority for them to be transferred to a hospital in Athens,' he answered. 'They will receive better care there, and in any case the government won't fund Spinalonga once there are too few people here.'

'In that case,' said Lapakis, 'may I suggest that we allow the sick to leave the island before the cured? I think it would be easier for them that way.'

They were all in agreement. Papadimitriou would have his public display of this new freedom, and those who were yet to be cured would be tactfully transferred to the Hospital of Santa Barbara in Athens. All that remained now was to set a date. It was agreed that August 25, the feast of Agios Titos, would be the historic day. The only one among them who harboured any misgivings about the fact that Spinalonga's days as a leper colony were now numbered was Kyritsis. He might never see Maria again.

CHAPTER ELEVEN
1957

The day for departure came. This time it was not only Georgios who went to the island, but half a dozen other village fishermen who finally believed they had nothing to fear and would help ferry people away from Spinalonga.

A farewell service had been held in the tiny church of St Panteleimon the previous day, but people had filed through the church to light candles and mumble their prayers for many days before. They came to give thanks, and they prayed to God that He would give them the courage to face whatever the world across that narrow strip of water brought them. Even those who had not a mark, not a blemish, to indicate that they had been leprous, were full of trepidation that they would never be able to live a normal life.

The elderly and those still sick were helped on board first. Donkeys plodded back and forth through the tunnel pulling carts piled high with boxes. A mountain of goods built up on the quayside, turning a long-held dream of departure into reality.

Kyritsis was on the quay at Plaka, ensuring that those who were being taken to Athens to continue treatment were carefully dealt with.

Among the last few left on the island were Lapakis and Maria. As Maria took a last look up the main street, memories rolled one after the other into her mind, overlapping and colliding. The extraordinary friendships she had formed, the merrymaking on feast days, the satisfaction in helping people who needed her. It was as if no time at all had elapsed since she had stood on this spot for the first time four years ago.

Lapakis was making his way down the street towards Maria and read all this in her face. For him, as well, life was to bring new uncertainties. He would spend a few months in Athens with the lepers who still needed treatment, but after that his own life was unmapped.

'Come on,' he said, when at last he stood beside Maria. 'We should go. Your father will be waiting for us.'

They both turned now and walked through the tunnel. Georgios sat on the wall in the shade of a mimosa tree, watching for his daughter to emerge. The last boat had departed ten minutes earlier and the quayside was now deserted. Perhaps there had been a hitch, Georgios thought in a panic. Perhaps the doctor had not signed her papers.

At that moment, Maria emerged from the black semicircle of the tunnel and ran towards him, her arms outstretched, all second thoughts and doubts about leaving the island forgotten as she embraced her father. Wordlessly he basked in the sensation of her silky hair against his rough skin.

'Shall we go?' Maria asked eventually.

Her possessions were already on board. Lapakis, who had emerged from the tunnel soon after Maria, got on first and helped her onto the boat. Their life on Spinalonga was over.

Georgios untethered his old caïque and pushed it away from the quayside. Then, nimbly for a man his age, he jumped aboard and swung the boat round so that it was soon speeding away from the island.

The little harbour in Plaka was crowded. The noisiest contingent were friends of the Athenians, here to celebrate this epoch-making day. Tomorrow they would all make their way back to Iraklion, but for now they would teach Plaka a thing or two about the art of making merry.

Fortini and Stephanos were there to greet Maria, along with Mattheos, their little brown-eyed boy, who danced about with excitement in the heady atmosphere, and their new baby Petros.

'Welcome home, Maria,' said Stephanos. He had stood back as his wife embraced her friend, waiting his turn. 'We are so glad you are back.'

He began to load Maria's boxes onto his pick-up truck. It was only a short distance to the Petrakis house, but too far to carry everything by hand. Leaving Georgios to tie up the boat, the two women set off across the square. By the time they arrived at Georgios's house, Stephanos had already unloaded the boxes inside the door. Maria felt a pricking sensation on the back of her neck. Nothing had changed since the day she left, but the walls themselves seemed to have absorbed the profound misery that had been endured within them. Everything appeared to be the same, but nothing was as it had been.

When Georgios walked in a few moments later, he found Stephanos, Fortini, Petros and Mattheos, who was clutching a small posy of flowers, and Maria all crowded into the little house. At last it seemed that some fragments of his life were fitting back together. His beautiful daughter was standing in front of him, and, in his eyes, she was lovelier than ever.

'Well,' said Fortini. 'I shouldn't stay too long—there's food still to be prepared. We'll see you both back in the square.'

Half an hour later, changed into a different dress and with her hair brushed until it gleamed, Maria was ready to face the inhabitants of Plaka. She knew many would be scrutinising her for signs of the disease. They would be disappointed. She did not bear the slightest trace.

Maria and her father walked together towards the square.

'I won't believe it until I see it,' said Georgios, 'but your sister has said she might come tonight. I got a note from her yesterday.'

Like any parent he yearned for this reunion, but Maria did not relish the prospect of meeting Anna tonight. Celebration, not reconciliation, was the purpose of today.

IN HER ELOUNDA HOME, Anna was preparing herself for the party in Plaka, carefully pinning her hair and meticulously applying lipstick to her full lips. Sitting on her grandmother's lap, Sofia watched intently.

'Aren't you ready yet?' Andreas asked Anna coldly, ignoring both his mother and his daughter.

'Almost,' she replied, spraying herself with a cloud of French perfume.

'Can we go then?' he snapped.

Anna seemed oblivious to her husband's icy tones. Eleftheria was not, and she wondered whether Andreas had, at last, woken up to the familiarity that now existed between his wife and Manoli.

'Night-night, sweetheart.' Anna turned to her little daughter, whose chubby arms reached out towards her. 'Be good.' And with that she planted a perfect imprint of her lips on Sofia's forehead and left the room.

Andreas was already waiting in the car. He knew why his wife was taking such meticulous care with her appearance. He had finally faced the fact that his wife was being unfaithful to him when he had found an earring under his pillow. Anna was always meticulous about removing her jewellery before she went to bed. He had said nothing when he saw the glint of gold against the white linen as he climbed between the sheets, but his heart had turned to ice.

Two days after that he came home in the early afternoon, parking his car some distance away and walking the last fifty metres to his house. He was not surprised to see Manoli's truck parked outside. Quietly he opened the front door and stepped inside. Suddenly the silence was shattered by a woman's wail. Andreas was sickened by the sound of his wife's ecstasy. His instinct was to leap up the stairs two at a time, and tear them both limb from limb, but something stopped him. He needed time to think.

As Maria approached the square an immense crowd was already gathered there. She spotted Dimitri standing at the centre of a small group along with Gerasimo Mandakis, who had run the colony's *kafenion*.

The last few hours had been so momentous that she had given little thought to Dr Kyritsis. There had been no goodbye, so she was sure they would meet again. Now, as she entered the crowd, Maria felt her heart lurch. There he was, sitting at one of the long tables with Dr Lapakis. The doctors were deep in conversation, but Lapakis looked up and noticed her.

'Maria!' he exclaimed, getting to his feet. 'What a great day for you. What is it like being home after all this time?'

Fortunately it was not a question she was expected to answer, for she would not have known where to begin. At this moment, Papadimitriou approached the two men who were responsible for giving the islanders a new life. There would be a thousand toasts later, but the island leader wanted to be the first to say thank you.

As Lapakis talked to the Papadimitrious, Kyritsis drew Maria to one side. 'Can I have a moment of your time somewhere else?' he asked.

'We could walk to the church,' she answered. 'I want to light a candle.'

As they walked the length of the empty street a sense of impatience overwhelmed Kyritsis. Enough of this woman's life had been taken away by the disease and every second seemed one too many to lose. By the entrance to the church door, he turned to face her.

'I have something to say. It's very simple indeed,' he said, holding her by her shoulders. 'I would like you to marry me.'

It was a statement, not a question. And it was as if no reply was required. For some time now, there had been no real doubt in Maria's mind that Kyritsis loved her, but she had forced herself to banish daydreams.

As though she needed persuasion that he meant what he had said, he filled her silence. 'There has never been anyone who has affected me as you have. If you don't wish to marry me, I shall go away and you need never think of me again. But either way, I need to know now.'

So it *was* a question. 'Yes,' was the husky response she gave.

'You will?' Kyritsis seemed astounded. His face broke into a smile and Maria's mirrored it, dazzlingly. Uncertainly at first, and then with increasing passion, he kissed her.

'We must return to the celebrations,' said Kyritsis eventually. 'People might wonder where we are.'

By the time they got back to the square, a huge circle had formed and a slow *pentozali* dance was in progress. As Kyritsis and Maria took their places, even Georgios joined in. The man who had so often sat in the shadows at any event had come forward and now whole-heartedly joined the merrymaking.

ANNA AND ANDREAS were nearly in Plaka now. Neither had spoken throughout the journey. It had occurred to Andreas that Manoli might resume his engagement to Maria, and as they approached the village he broke the silence, taking pleasure in provoking his wife with the suggestion.

'Manoli? Marry Maria? Over my dead body!' she screamed with a passion he had never seen in her before.

'Why shouldn't he? They were engaged before,' he taunted.

'Shut up. Just shut up!' She lashed out at him as he parked the car.

The violence of Anna's response had shocked even Andreas.

'My God!' he roared, defending himself from the hard blows that rained down on him. 'You love him, don't you? Go on, admit it, Anna! I'm not a complete fool, you know. I came home early one day last week and he was there with you. How long . . . ?'

Anna was now crying and laughing at the same time, hysterical. 'Years,' she spluttered. 'Years and years . . .'

It seemed to Andreas that Anna's scarlet lips smiled as though even now she was lost in some kind of ecstasy. Her denial would have given him a place to retreat, the possibility that he was wrong, but her admission was the greatest mockery of all. He had to wipe that grin from her face.

In one deft movement he reached inside his jacket pocket and drew out his pistol. Anna was not even looking. She was delirious with laughter.

'I've never . . .' she gasped, now completely crazed with the excitement of telling him the truth, 'I've never loved anyone as much as Manoli.' Her words lashed out like a whip, cracking the air around Andreas.

IN THE MAIN SQUARE, Kyritsis watched as the first of the fireworks was let off. Rockets would be sent into the air every hour until midnight, each one exploding with a violent bang and a shower of sparks that were reflected like gems in the still sea.

As the first volley of fireworks came to an end there was a moment's quiet before the band struck up again. Before they could do so, however, there were two more loud and unexpected bangs. Kyritsis turned his face upwards, expecting to see a shower of glittering sparks descending from the sky, but there was none.

A commotion had broken out around a car parked near the square. It had been seen drawing up only a few minutes earlier, and now a woman lay sprawled in the passenger seat. Kyritsis started to run towards it. For a moment, disbelief that such an act of violence could intrude on this merrymaking almost paralysed the crowd, but they cleared a path to let him through.

Kyritsis felt the woman's pulse. There was still a sign of life.

'We need to move her,' he said to Dr Lapakis, who was now at his side. Rugs and pillows had miraculously appeared from a nearby house and the two men carefully lifted the woman down onto the ground.

Maria had worked her way to the front of the crowd. As they laid the woman down on the blanket, she realised who it was that they held in their bloodstained embrace. Many in the crowd now recognised her too and there was a collective gasp of horror.

There was no mistaking her. Raven-haired, full-bosomed and clad in a dress that no one else at this gathering could have afforded in a month of feast days, it was, without any doubt at all, Anna Vandoulakis.

'It's my sister,' she whispered through her sobs to Kyritsis. 'My sister.'

Someone in the crowd was heard to shout: 'Find Georgios!' and seconds later Georgios was kneeling by Maria's side, weeping silently at the sight of his elder daughter, whose life was ebbing away before them all.

'Why? Why?' repeated Georgios through his tears, when it was all over.

Maria knew the answer but she was not going to tell him. He would learn the truth soon enough.

ANNA'S FUNERAL was not to take place in Plaka's main church, but in the chapel on the outskirts of the village. This small building overlooked the sea and had an uninterrupted view of Spinalonga, where the remains of Anna's mother lay in the ground.

Less than forty-eight hours after the death, a small, darkly clad group gathered in the damp chapel. The Vandoulakis family was not represented. They had remained within the four walls of the Elounda house since Andreas had been found in the church at Plaka, still with a gun in his hand, and had been taken away under police escort. All except Manoli, who had disappeared without trace.

Maria, Georgios, Kyritsis, Fortini, Savina and Pavlos stood with their heads bowed as the priest prayed over the coffin. Wafts of incense billowed from the censer as lengthy intercessions were said for the forgiveness of sins before the comforting words of the Lord's Prayer. When it was time for the interment, tears and perspiration mingled to flow down their cheeks as the coffin was lowered into the ground.

Maria went home with her father. He wanted sleep, he said. Fortini and her parents returned to the taverna to find Stephanos, who had been minding Mattheos and Petros. It was the quiet midafternoon hour. Not a soul stirred.

Kyritsis would wait for Maria in the square. She needed to get away from Plaka for a few hours and they planned to drive to Elounda, to find a small *kafenion* she remembered by the water's edge. It would be the first journey she had made in four years and the first opportunity Maria and Kyritsis had had to be alone since the night of the feast.

For perhaps one hour her life had held such promise, such a future, but now the great step forward had been counteracted by several back.

When he looked back on this moment some weeks later, Kyritsis blamed himself for rushing in. His overexcitement at the prospect of their future together bubbled over into talk of his apartment in Iraklion and how he hoped it would be adequate for them.

'It isn't very spacious, but there is a study and a separate guest room,' he said. 'It's very convenient for the hospital.'

He took her hands across the table. She looked troubled. Of course she did. They had just buried her sister, and here he was wanting to talk about the practicalities of their life together.

'I can't marry you,' she said suddenly. 'I have to look after my father.'

Kyritsis was shocked. Within minutes, though, he saw it made perfect sense. How could this woman, whom he had been drawn to as much by her integrity and selflessness as by her beauty, be expected to leave her bereaved and distressed father? One part of him wanted to protest, but instead he spoke with such understanding and forgiveness that it almost broke her heart.

'You're right to stay,' he said. 'And that's why I love you, Maria. Because you know what's right and you do it. But I shall never love anyone else.'

Maria eased her hands away from Kyritsis's grasp and sat with her head bowed, her tears flowing freely now. She could not stop them. The restrained grief at the graveside had only temporarily held back the overwhelming sorrow that now burst its dam. The fact that Kyritsis was so reasonable made her weep all the more.

Kyritsis sat looking at the top of Maria's bowed head. When the shaking had subsided, he touched her gently on the shoulder.

'Maria,' he whispered. 'Shall we go?'

They walked away from their table, hand in hand. As they drove back to Plaka, in silence, the sapphire-blue water still sparkled, but the sky had begun to change. At last this terrible day was beginning to fade.

When they reached the village, the doctor spoke.

'Will you write to me and tell me how you are? Tell me how life is for you in the free world?' he asked with forced enthusiasm.

Maria nodded.

It was pointless prolonging the moment. Kyritsis parked outside Maria's house and got out to open the passenger door. Face to face they stood, and then for a few seconds they held each other. They did not so much embrace as cling to each other, like children in a storm. Then, with great strength of will, they simultaneously released each other. Maria immediately turned away and went into her house. Kyritsis climbed back into his car and drove away. He would not stop until he got back to Iraklion.

ANNA'S DEATH left a trail of other disrupted and destroyed lives. Not just her sister's, but her father's and her husband's, and her daughter's too. Sofia was not yet two years old, and it was not long before she noticed the absence of her parents. Her grandparents told her that they had both gone away for a while. She cried at first, and then began the process of forgetting. As for Alexandros and Eleftheria Vandoulakis, in one evening they had lost their son, their hopes for the future and the reputation of the family. Everything that had ever worried Alexandros about Andreas marrying beneath his class had been fulfilled to the letter. And when Manoli's absence was brought to their attention they worked out for themselves what had led to the horrifying events of the feast of Agios Titos.

Andreas's trial in Agios Nikolaos lasted three days. Eleftheria and Alexandros sat impassively in the gallery, gaunt with anxiety and shame. The circumstances of the murder were hung out and aired for the whole of Crete to salivate over, and the daily newspaper ran every last sensational detail.

CHAPTER TWELVE
1958

For several months there was no communication between the Vandoulakis and Petrakis families. There was Sofia to consider, however, and for her sake this ice age had to pass. Even Alexandros, given time to reflect, began to see that it was not only his own family who had suffered, and that the damage sustained had been heavy on both sides. It was the responsibility of all of them to knit some kind of a life together for the little girl's sake.

Alexandros wrote to Georgios, saying it was time to put aside the past, and asking him and Maria to join them for lunch the following Sunday.

Some kind of rapprochement was forged between the families after that, with unspoken acknowledgment that there was fault on both sides for the catastrophe that had damaged them all. Sofia, from the very beginning, was well cushioned. She lived with her grandparents but every week she would go down to Plaka and spend a day with her other grandfather and Maria, who would take her out on boat trips, catch fish and crabs and sea urchins, and go for walks along the cliff path. At six o'clock, when they delivered Sofia back to her grandparents' house near Elounda, they would all be tired out. Sofia had the adoring attention of three grandparents. In some ways, she was lucky.

FOR MANY MONTHS Kyritsis continued his work at the hospital in Iraklion, where people came in waves to be treated by the doctor who was known to have brought the cure for leprosy to Crete. There should have been nothing more rewarding than seeing his patients walk away from him free of the disease. All he felt, however, was a terrible emptiness. He lived the same disciplined and dedicated existence he had always lived: into the hospital on the dot of seven thirty in the morning and out again at nearly eight at night, but each day became more of an effort than the last as he dragged himself from his bed and back to the hospital.

It was during this time that he received a letter from Dr Lapakis, who, since Spinalonga had closed, was now married and working as head of dermatovenereology at the general hospital in Agios Nikolaos.

> *My dear Nikolaos,*
>
> *I wonder how you are. I fully intended to get in touch with you earlier, but life has been busy back here in Agios Nikolaos and the hospital has greatly expanded since I was here full time.*
>
> *I am writing to let you know that I am planning to give up my job here because my wife wants to live closer to her parents in Rethimnon. It occurred to me that you might be interested in taking over my department. The hospital is expanding rapidly. Meanwhile, I thought I should let you know of my plans.*
>
> *Yours,*
> *Christos*

Although nothing had ever been said, his old friend Lapakis knew that his colleague had formed a bond with Maria Petrakis, and he had been dismayed to learn that Kyritsis had returned to Iraklion alone. He surmised that Maria had felt obliged to stay with her father.

Kyritsis read and reread the letter before putting it into the top pocket of his white coat. Although a job in Agios Nikolaos would close all kinds of doors in his career, there was one door in his life that would open: the opportunity to live closer to Maria. That night he wrote a letter of application for the post. As Lapakis had known, Kyritsis was overqualified for the job and the hospital was delighted, if mystified, that someone of his calibre should have applied. He was summoned for interview and offered the post.

Less than a month later, one Sunday afternoon in May, Kyritsis set off to Plaka, which was only twenty-five minutes' drive away from his new home near the hospital. When Maria opened her front door to find Kyritsis standing there, she paled with surprise.

'Nikolaos!' she gasped.

She moved aside and Kyritsis stepped over the threshold. She looked at his back as he passed her, the same neat, straight back that she had watched so many times when he had left her home to walk up the main street of Spinalonga to the hospital. Suddenly it seemed only a moment since she had been on the island, daydreaming of a future.

Maria trembled as she laid out cups and saucers, and soon she and Kyritsis were sipping their coffee just as they used to on Spinalonga.

'I've moved,' Kyritsis said. 'To Agios Nikolaos.'

'Agios Nikolaos?' Maria almost choked on the words. Astonishment and delight mingled in equal measure.

Kyritsis leaned forward. For the third time in her life Maria heard the words: 'Marry me.'

She knew that Georgios was able to look after himself now. They had come to terms with Anna's death and little Sofia had brought pleasure and distraction into their lives. The distance to Agios Nikolaos meant that Maria could visit her father several times a week and still see Sofia as well. Before she took her next breath she had given him her answer.

Georgios returned soon after. He had not been as happy since the day he learned that Maria was cured. By the next day, news had travelled all around Plaka that Maria Petrakis was to marry the man who had cured her, and preparations for the wedding began immediately.

On the morning of the wedding, they woke up to a clear May day. Every last inhabitant of the village emerged to follow the bridal procession the short distance from Maria's home to the church. As the pair stood at the altar, the priest crowned them with woven halos of flowers and grasses. There was absolute silence in the church and the crowd standing in the sunshine outside were hushed as they strained to hear the words of the ceremony.

When finally, the deed was done, sugared almonds were distributed to everyone in the congregation and all of those who stood outside. They were a symbol of the abundance and joy that everyone hoped Maria and Kyritsis would now enjoy. There was not a soul who wished them anything else.

Georgios had sat in the front pew of the church with Eleftheria and Alexandros Vandoulakis. It was a public symbol of their reconciliation, and between them sat little Sofia, charmed and excited by the pageantry and colour of the wedding. For Georgios there was a strong sense of a new beginning. It was the first time in years that he had felt at peace.

When Maria emerged from the church with her silver-haired groom, the crowd cheered and then trailed after them in the sunshine to the taverna, where the merrymaking would begin. The feast that Stephanos laid on for all the guests that night was munificent. Wine flowed and corks popped from bottles of *tsikoudia* long into the night. Under the stars, the musicians plucked and bowed until the dancers' feet were numb.

The couple spent the first two nights of their marriage in a grand hotel overlooking the harbour in Agios Nikolaos, but they were both eager to begin the next stage of their lives. It would be the first time Maria had lived in a town, and she relished the prospect. Their marital home was on a steep hill close to the hospital, and, with its wrought-iron balcony and floor-to-ceiling windows, was grand and spacious. For the first time in her life Maria had a fridge and a telephone.

For a few months, life could not have been more perfect. Maria loved her new home, and soon it was decorated to her taste and hung with the samplers she had embroidered, as well as photos of her family. One morning in early September, however, Georgios telephoned her; she knew immediately that something was amiss.

'It's Eleftheria,' he said. 'She passed away this morning.'

In the past few months Georgios had grown close to the Vandoulakis couple, and Maria could detect the sorrow in his voice. Eleftheria's funeral was held a few days later, and it was only at the end of the ceremony, when Maria saw her little niece hand in hand with her two grandfathers, that the reality of the situation dawned on her. Sofia needed a mother. The little girl was only just three years old—what was to happen to her? Suppose Alexandros died too? Georgios would never manage to look after her on his own. As for her father, the judge had passed a harsh sentence that ensured he would not be out of prison until Sofia was at least sixteen.

Two days later, having telephoned ahead to let him know they would like to come, Maria and Nikolaos Kyritsis found themselves in Alexandros Vandoulakis's drawing room.

'Sofia has already gone to bed,' he began, pouring them both a drink. 'Otherwise she would be here to say hello to you.'

'It's about Sofia that we've come,' began Maria.

'I thought it might be,' said Vandoulakis. 'The matter scarcely warrants discussion.'

Maria paled. Perhaps they had made a terrible faux pas in coming.

'Eleftheria and I had a discussion a few months ago on this very subject,' Vandoulakis began. 'We talked about what would happen to Sofia if one of us died—though of course we were assuming it would be me who would go first. What we agreed was that if one of us were left on our own, the very best thing for our granddaughter would be if she went to live with you,' he said, addressing them both. 'Would you consider it? I know you are very fond of her, Maria, and you are the closest of all her blood relations.'

For a few moments Maria struggled to speak, but Kyritsis managed to say everything that was necessary.

The next day, when Kyritsis had finished work at the hospital, he and Maria returned to the Vandoulakis home and between them began to prepare Sofia for the next stage of her life. By the end of the following week she had moved to the house in Agios Nikolaos.

At first Maria was nervous. Within a year of leaving Spinalonga she had become a wife and now, almost overnight, the mother of a three-year-old. She need not have feared, however. Sofia led the way and adapted happily to being with a couple who were so much more energetic than her grandparents. She loved the company of other children, which she soon found in abundance in their very own street.

As soon as Sofia went to school, Maria began to train for a job in the hospital dispensary. It seemed a perfect complement to her work with natural herbs, which she also continued to practise. Once a week Maria drove Sofia to her paternal grandfather's house, where she would spend the night in the bedroom that was kept for her there. The next day, when Maria collected her, they would usually continue to Plaka, where they saw Georgios. Almost every visit they would see Fortini too and Sofia would play on the beach below the taverna with Mattheos and Petros.

Life continued in this happy and settled way, and eventually the knowledge that Maria and Nikolaos were not her real parents slipped out of memory's reach. The house where they lived in Agios Nikolaos was all she would ever be able to recollect of early childhood.

When Sofia was nine, Alexandros Vandoulakis passed away peacefully in his sleep. He left a generous lump sum of money in trust for Sofia. Three years later, Georgios became bedridden after a chest infection and moved to the house in Agios Nikolaos to be cared for by Maria. One autumn day, two years later, he died. The funeral was held in Plaka and the church was filled with well over a hundred villagers, who remembered the taciturn fisherman with great affection.

ONE CHILLY MORNING, early the next year, a typed envelope bearing an Iraklion postmark arrived. It was addressed to 'The Guardians of Sofia Vandoulakis'. Maria's stomach lurched when she saw the name. It was not one that Sofia had ever known she possessed and Maria snatched the letter up from the doormat and immediately stashed it at the back of a drawer until Nikolaos arrived home from the hospital. Sofia had gone to bed an hour earlier. With some formality, Nikolaos slit the envelope open with his silver opener and drew out a stiff sheet of paper.

> To Whom It May Concern
> We regret to inform you that Andreas Vandoulakis passed away on
> January 7th. The cause of death was pneumonia. Burial will take
> place on January 14th. Please confirm receipt of this letter.
> Yours faithfully,
> Governor, Prison of Iraklion

For a few moments, neither of them spoke. It was so hard to believe that the life of such a privileged individual had finally ended in a damp prison cell. Without speaking, Nikolaos returned the letter to its envelope and crossed the room to lock it in his bureau. There was no chance that Sofia would ever find it there.

Two days later, Maria was the only mourner as Andreas's coffin was lowered into a pauper's grave. Neither of his sisters attended. As far as they were concerned their brother had been as good as dead for a very long time.

By now it was the late 1960s and the first wave of tourists began to arrive in Agios Nikolaos, which became a magnet for northern Europeans beguiled by the sunshine, the warm sea and the cheap wine. Sofia was fourteen and becoming wilful, hanging around in the town with boys from France and Germany who were only too pleased to keep the company of a beautiful Greek girl with glorious waist-length hair.

'She's inherited her mother's looks,' despaired Maria late one night when

Sofia had failed to return home. 'But it now looks as though she might have her character too.'

Though she was rebellious in some ways, Sofia worked hard at school, and when she reached the age of eighteen it was time to consider university. Maria assumed that Sofia would go to Iraklion for her studies, but she wanted to go to Athens. Never having left Crete herself, Maria was filled with trepidation at Sofia's ambition.

'The university in Iraklion is as good as any on the mainland,' she said, appealing to Sofia.

'I'm sure it is,' Sofia replied, showing a determination that nothing could bend. 'But I want to go farther afield to Athens or Thessalonika. There's so much happening out there.'

She was displaying a desire to travel that was natural for a girl at her stage of life. Nowadays everyone of her age seemed keen to go off and see more of the world, but Maria couldn't help but think that Manoli would have talked like that, about Crete being a small island on a very large planet. There was something strangely familiar about this wanderlust.

By the time June came, Sofia had made her decision. She was going to Athens and her parents would not stand in her way. The night before she sailed away Maria and Nikolaos decided it was their duty to tell her they were not her true parents.

PART 4

CHAPTER THIRTEEN

As Fortini reached this point in the story, she was suddenly overwhelmed by the responsibility of describing the emotions of someone who was more than capable of telling her own tale. Although she knew as well as anyone else alive how Sofia must have felt, who could tell the story better than she who had taken the blows of truth first-hand? It was Sofia who, on that August night, had tried and repeatedly failed to catch her breath when her parents revealed they were not really her parents at all; she who had had to face the fact that her real mother was no longer alive, and that there was no certainty about the identity of her natural father.

Fortini realised there was only one thing to do, and all it would take was a phone call to Sofia in London. She slipped away, leaving Alexis to contemplate the now familiar view of Spinalonga.

As soon as she picked up the telephone, Sofia knew who it was who was calling. 'Fortini! Is that you?' she said.

'It is me. How are you, Sofia?'

'Very well, thank you. Has my daughter Alexis been to visit you?'

'She most certainly has and she's still here now. We've had a very rewarding time together and I've done almost everything you asked.'

There was a moment's hesitation at the other end of the line.

'Sofia, how long would it take for you to get here? I've told Alexis all I can, but there are some things that I don't feel right about telling her. Could you get here before she leaves?'

Still silence at the other end.

'Sofia? Are you still there?'

'Yes, I'm still here . . .'

It was such a spontaneous invitation. There were a thousand reasons why Sofia could not drop everything and fly out to Greece, but there were enough very good reasons why she should.

'Look, I'll see if I can get a flight. It would be lovely to come to Plaka after all this time.'

Sofia had no problem getting an afternoon flight to Athens. She packed a bag and left a message on Marcus's answering machine to explain where she was going. Take-off was on time, and by eight o'clock she was speeding in a taxi towards Piraeus, where she caught the night boat to Iraklion.

The following morning, less than twenty-four hours since the telephone conversation between the two women, Fortini saw a car drawing up in the side road near the taverna. A well-rounded blonde woman stepped out. Fortini realised immediately who it was. She hurried out to meet her.

'Sofia, you're here!' she exclaimed. 'I wasn't sure you'd come!'

'Of course I've come. I've wanted to come back for years but there just never seemed the right moment.' Sofia paused and looked around her. 'It all looks just the same.'

'Nothing much has changed,' Fortini said. 'You know what it's like. The local shop paints its shutters a different colour and there's an outcry!'

Fortini had not told Alexis about her mother's impending arrival, and when the younger woman appeared on the terrace, bleary-eyed with sleep, she was astounded to see Sofia.

'Mum?' was all she could say.

'Yes, it is me,' replied Sofia. 'Fortini invited me and it seemed a good opportunity to come over.'

'It's such a surprise!' her daughter replied.

The three women sat round a table drinking coffee.

'How has your trip been?' asked Sofia.

'Oh, so-so,' said Alexis with a shrug. 'Until I got here. And then it became much more interesting. I've had a fantastic time in Plaka.'

'Is Ed here with you?' Sofia asked.

'No. I left him in Hania,' Alexis said, looking down at her coffee. Suddenly she felt a pang of guilt that she had abandoned him for so long. 'But I plan to go back tomorrow,' she added.

'Well,' said Fortini, 'we haven't got much time then.'

All three of them knew that there was an agenda. Why else would Sofia have come? Alexis's head was still spinning from everything that Fortini had told her over the past few days, but she knew there was a final chapter. This was what her mother was here to provide.

WHEN SOFIA returned from an evening saying goodbye to her friends, she found her father pacing up and down the room. Her mother sat on the edge of a chair, her hands clasped tightly together.

'I'm sorry I'm so late,' Sofia said. 'But you didn't have to wait up.'

'Sofia, we wanted to talk to you,' said her father gently. 'There are one or two things we feel you should know before you go to Athens tomorrow.'

Now her mother took over. After all, most of it was her story.

'It's hard to know where to begin,' she said. 'But there are a few things we want to tell you about our family . . .'

That night they told her everything, just as Fortini had related it to Alexis. Not the slightest suspicion or unguarded word had given Sofia any forewarning, and she was totally ill-equipped to deal with such revelations. She had never questioned that she was the product of these two people who sat in front of her. Why should she? But she was no more a blood relation of the man she had always called Father than of any man she might meet in the street. She had loved her parents unquestioningly, but now that they were not her parents, were her feelings for them different? In the space of an hour, her entire life history had changed. It had dissolved behind her and when she looked back, there was a void. A blank. A nothingness.

She received the news silently and felt sick. Not for a moment did she think of how Maria and Kyritsis might be feeling. No. This was *her* story, *her* life that they had falsified, and she was angry.

'Why didn't you tell me all this before?' she screamed.

'We wanted to protect you,' said Kyritsis firmly. 'There seemed no need to tell you before.'

'We have loved you as your own parents would have loved you,' interjected Maria pleadingly.

She was desperate enough to be losing her only child to university, but even more distressed that the girl who stood in front of her and looked at her as though she were a stranger would no longer regard her as her mother.

At this moment, however, Sofia just saw the couple before her as people who had lied to her, conspired against her, even. She was eighteen, irrational, and resolved now in her desire to invent a future for herself where she would be in command of the facts. Her anger gave way to a *froideur* that chilled the hearts of the people who loved her most in the world. 'I'll see you in the morning,' she said. 'The boat leaves at nine.'

With that, she turned on her heel.

The following morning Sofia was up at dawn doing her final packing, and at eight o'clock she and Kyritsis loaded her luggage into the car. Neither of them spoke. All three of them drove down to the port, and when the moment came, Sofia's farewells were perfunctory.

She kissed each of them on both cheeks.

'Goodbye,' she said, with finality. 'I'll write.'

Maria and Kyritsis watched the ferry pull away from its moorings, but of Sofia there was no sign. Only when the boat was a speck on the horizon did they turn away. The emptiness was unbearable.

For Sofia, the journey to Athens became a flight from her past, from the stigma of leprosy and the uncertainty of her parentage. A few months into her first term, she was ready to write.

Dear Mother and Father (or should I call you Uncle and Aunt?),

I am sorry things were so difficult when I left. I was terribly shocked. I can't even begin to put it into words and I still feel sick when I think about it all. Anyway, I am just writing to let you know that I am settling in well here and I am enjoying my lectures.

I will write again. I promise.

Love,

Sofia

The letter said everything and nothing. They continued to receive notes that were descriptive and often enthusiastic but gave away little of how Sofia was feeling. At the end of the first year, they were bitterly disappointed, if not entirely surprised, when she did not return for the holidays.

She had decided to spend the summer trying to trace Manoli. She followed a few leads around Athens and then other parts of Greece, but after a while the trail, such as it was, went cold. Even if she found this man, she realised, she would not know for sure if he were her father. Would she, in any case, prefer her father to have been a murderer who had killed her mother, or an adulterer who had abandoned her? It was not much of a choice.

At the beginning of her second year, she met someone who turned out to be a much more significant figure in her life than her father, whoever he might have been. He was an Englishman by the name of Marcus Fielding and he was on sabbatical at the university for a year. He was big and bearish and looked permanently crumpled in a way that only an Englishman could.

He met Sofia in his first month at the university and thought her the most beautiful woman he had ever seen. Though she seemed quite worldly, she was not unapproachable, and he was astonished when she accepted an invitation from him. Within weeks they were inseparable, and when it was time for Marcus to return to England she made the decision that she would forgo the rest of her course in order to go with him.

'I have no ties,' she said one night. 'I'm an orphan.'

When he protested, she assured him it was true.

'No, really, I am,' she said. 'I have an uncle and aunt who brought me up but they're in Crete. They won't mind me going to London.'

She said no more about her upbringing and Marcus did not pursue it, but what he did insist on was that they should marry. Sofia needed no persuasion. She was completely and passionately in love with this man and knew beyond a shadow of a doubt that he would never let her down.

One chilly February day, they married in a South London registry office. The informal invitation had stood on the high shelf above Maria and Nikolaos's fireplace for a few weeks. It would be the first time they had seen Sofia since the day she had sailed out of their lives, and they approached the wedding with a mixture of excitement and trepidation.

They liked Marcus instantly. Sofia could not have found herself a kinder, more dependable man, and to see her so content and secure was as much as they could have wished for, even if it was tainted by the fact that there was little likelihood now that she would ever return to settle in Crete. Maria and

Nikolaos remained at each other's side throughout the wedding, husband acting as translator for his wife, who spoke no English.

In 1990, at the age of eighty, Dr Kyritsis died. Several short obituaries appeared in British newspapers, praising him for his contribution to leprosy research, and Sofia carefully cut them out and filed them away. In spite of an age gap of nearly twenty years, Maria survived him by only a few years. Sofia flew out to Crete for her aunt's funeral and was overwhelmed by guilt and loss. She realised that her eighteen-year-old self had shown nothing but self-centred ingratitude in the way she had left Crete all those years before, but it was too late now to make amends. Far, far too late.

Marcus had known better than to ask too many questions and went along with Sofia's desire to avoid any reference to her past, but as the children grew up she began to fear that they might one day discover what sort of people their ancestors had been, and her stomach churned. Looking at Alexis now, Sofia wished she had been more open.

'I am so sorry,' she said to Alexis, 'that I've never told you this before.'

'But why are you so ashamed of it all?' Alexis asked, leaning forward. 'It's your life story, sort of, but at the same time you played no part in it.'

'These people were my flesh and blood. Lepers, adulterers, murderers—'

'For goodness' sake, Mum, some of these people were heroic. Take your uncle and aunt—their love survived everything, and your uncle's work saved hundreds, if not thousands, of people. And your grandfather! What an example he'd be to people nowadays, never complaining, never disowning anyone, suffering it all in silence.'

'But what about my mother?'

'Well, I'm glad she wasn't *my* mother, but I wouldn't blame her entirely. It was just the way she was made.'

'You're very forgiving, Alexis. She was certainly flawed, but shouldn't she have fought harder against her natural instincts?'

'We all should, I suppose, but not everyone has the strength. And Manoli exploited her weakness—just as people like that always do.'

There was a pause. Sofia fiddled anxiously with her earring as though there was something she wanted to say but she couldn't quite spit it out.

'But you know who behaved worse than anyone?' she eventually blurted out. 'It was me. I turned my back on those two kind, wonderful people. They'd given me everything and I rejected them! I just turned my back on them. And now it's too late to say sorry.'

Tears welled up in Sofia's eyes. Alexis had never seen her mother cry.

'You mustn't be too hard on yourself,' she whispered, putting an arm round her mother. 'It's understandable that you were so angry and upset.'

'But I still feel so guilty about it, and I have done for so many years.'

'Well, I don't think you need to. It's the past, Mum,' said Alexis, pulling her closer. 'From everything I've heard about Maria, I think she probably forgave you. And they came to your wedding, didn't they? I'm sure Maria wasn't bitter—I don't think she had it in her.'

'I hope you're right,' said Sofia, struggling to suppress her tears. She looked away towards the island and slowly regained her composure.

Fortini had listened quietly to this exchange between mother and daughter. She could see that Alexis was making Sofia look at the past from a new perspective, and decided to leave them alone together for a while.

The taverna was closed that night, but Mattheos, who was soon to take over his parents' business, now arrived. He had grown into a mountain of a man, and Sofia and he embraced enthusiastically.

'It's good to see you, Sofia,' he said warmly. 'It's been so long.'

Mattheos began to lay a long table. One more guest was still to arrive. Fortini had telephoned her brother Antonis earlier that day, and at nine o'clock he arrived from Sitia. He was now very grey and quite stooped, but he still had those dark, romantic eyes that had drawn Anna to him all those years ago. After a few drinks he lost his shyness about speaking English.

'Your mother was the most beautiful woman I ever saw,' he said to Sofia, adding as an afterthought, 'apart from my own wife, of course.'

He sat quietly for a moment before he spoke again. 'Her beauty was a gift as well as a curse, and a woman like her will always drive some men to extreme behaviour. It wasn't all her fault, you know.'

Alexis watched her mother's face and could see that she understood.

'*Efharisto*,' Sofia said quietly. Thank you.

It was well past midnight, and the candles had long since guttered to extinction before everyone round the table got up to leave. Only a few hours later both Alexis and Sofia needed to be on the road. Fond promises were made to return the following year for a longer stay.

Alexis drove her mother to Iraklion, where Sofia was to catch the night ferry to Athens. There was not a moment of silence on the journey as their conversation flowed. Once she had dropped off her mother, who would happily spend the day in the city's museums before catching the ferry to Piraeus that night, Alexis carried on towards Hania.

Nearly three hours later she arrived back at the hotel. Ed was sitting in a bar overlooking the beach, alone and gazing out to sea. Alexis moved towards him quietly and took a seat at his table. The scrape of her chair alerted him to Alexis's presence and he looked round, startled by the noise.

'Where the *hell* have you been?' he shouted.

Apart from the message she had left for him four days earlier to say that she would be staying in Plaka for a couple of nights, she had not contacted him. Her mobile phone had been switched off.

'Look,' she said, knowing she had been wrong to be so out of touch, 'I'm really sorry. It all got very involved and somehow I lost track of time. Then my mum came over and—'

'What do you mean, your mum came over? So you were having some kind of family reunion and forgot to tell me about it! Thanks a lot!'

'Listen . . .' Alexis began. 'It was really important.'

'For God's sake, Alexis!' he groaned with sarcasm. '*What* is more important? Buggering off to see your mother, who you can visit any day of the week when you're at home, or having this holiday with me?'

Ed did not expect an answer to this. He had already sauntered across to the bar to get himself another drink, his back turned to Alexis. She could see the anger and resentment in the line of his shoulders, and while they were still turned she slipped quickly and silently away. It took her a matter of minutes to stuff all her clothes into a bag and scribble him a note.

Sorry it's ended like this. You never did listen.

It was the end. She could admit it to herself now. There was no love left.

ALEXIS WAS SOON back on the road to Iraklion. She would have to put her foot down if she was to reach it by seven o'clock, in time to return the hire car and catch the ferry, which left at eight.

As she drove along the smooth road, which hugged the coastline and gave her a continuous and spectacular view of the sparkling azure sea, a feeling of euphoria swept over her. There was nothing quite like the sense of abandon she got at the wheel of a car.

With only moments to spare, she dealt with the irritations of dispensing with the hired car, purchased her ticket for the ferry and climbed the ramp which took her onto the ship.

Somewhere on this boat, she knew she would find her mother. She walked through the two lounges, occupied by big family groups returning to mainland Greece after their holidays, but when she could not find her mother on this level she went up on deck.

In the fading light she saw Sofia at the far end, towards the prow. She was sitting alone, her small travel bag at her feet, looking across at the twinkling lights of Iraklion and the vaulted arches of the great arsenal built by the Venetians in the sixteenth-century fortress.

It was Sofia's turn to be surprised by the sight of her daughter.

'Alexis! What are you doing here?' she exclaimed. 'I thought you were going back to Hania. Where's Ed?'

'Still in Hania. I left him there.'

There was little need to explain, but Alexis wanted to talk.

'It's all over. I realised how pointless it was, how halfhearted,' she began. 'When I sat listening to Fortini describe your family and what they went through, what really struck me was how powerfully they loved each other. It was through sickness and health, thick and thin, until death parted them . . . I knew I didn't feel like that about Ed—and I certainly wouldn't feel like that about him in twenty, or even ten years' time.'

In the decades since Sofia had turned her back on the people and the place that had nurtured her into adulthood, she had never perceived it all so clearly. At last she saw not humiliation but heroism, not perfidy but passion, not leprosy but love.

Everything was in the open now, the wounds were exposed to the air and there was no shame in any of it. She no longer had anything to hide, and for the first time her tears flowed unchecked.

As the cumbersome ferry moved slowly out of the harbour and blasted its horn into the night air, Alexis and Sofia stood against the rails, catching the breeze on their faces. Arms entwined, they looked back across the pitch-black water until, gradually, the lights of Crete faded into the distance.

VICTORIA HISLOP

Born: June 8, 1959, Bromley, Kent
Relaxation: playing tennis and walking
Website: www.victoriahislop.com

RD: You are already a successful travel writer, so what inspired you to write *The Island*, your first novel?

VH: Ian and I were on a family holiday in Crete with the children, who must have been about nine and eleven and quite happy not to do any sightseeing, but spend all day on a beach, but Ian always wants something to do. We had already dragged the kids in and out of lots of churches and round all the ancient Minoan sites. I then delved into the guidebook and read about the island of Spinalonga, which was a leper colony between 1903 and 1957. To get to the island meant we had to take a little boat trip, which was a real bonus, because if the children didn't like what was at the end of it at least they had a trip there and back to enjoy! So off we went, late one afternoon. And it's actually very much as I describe it when Alexis gets off the boat and she promptly finds herself in this derelict village. For some reason I was instantly and completely spellbound by it.

RD: Are you able to explain why you were so affected by the village?

VH: I am quite responsive to atmosphere. Since writing the book, I've met people who have a great deal more knowledge of Spinalonga than I do, and who've read books written in Greek by people who lived there, and they all say to me, 'It's exactly what it was like. But how did you know?' And I didn't know. I just *felt* it. And I think one reason why people have responded to the book is that I didn't go there and think 'what a miserable place, how awful it must have been', I sensed that the people there had had a really varied life: there was a church, for instance, a bakery, a laundry and some quite pretty houses. People with leprosy had been lifted out of their lives and forced into this community, knowing that, unless there was a cure, they wouldn't be able to leave the island again. They would die there . . . So that's how it came to me—going to the island, finding the hairs on my arms literally standing up, and waking up next morning haunted by what I'd felt. I am not saying that the island was haunted, but I think that people always leave behind something of themselves—how could they not?

RD: But your story is fictional?

VH: Oh, yes. The island was, in reality, governed slightly differently. I made up the infrastructure, although there were lots of things I didn't make up. I ransacked four or five local guidebooks for facts. There was a school, for example, and they had a newspaper—they actually had a satirical newspaper, but when I read about that I thought, 'I'm not going to include that because people will think I made it up!' Since Ian is well known as the Editor of *Private Eye*, I reckoned it could have seemed laughable.

RD: You were named Newcomer of the Year at the 2007 Galaxy British Book Awards. Why do you think *The Island* is such a winner?

VH: I think it's an incredibly simple book and it's quite emotional. I'm sure people love to have an excuse to cry. I do feel there's something about weeping which gives tremendous relief, and I cried a lot when I was writing it. A friend of mine died of breast cancer just as I wrote the part about Eleni's death on Spinalonga. I felt so sad, because my friend was so young. I suppose I just put those feelings on the page.

The book is kind of me really. It's not detached.

RD: Did you enjoy essay writing at school?

VH: I did win an essay prize at my primary school and I remember being very pleased when I was given a book token. But I stopped all creative writing when I was fourteen. I don't think schools encourage it enough. By the A-level stage you aren't doing any, it's all comprehension.

RD: Has this experience encouraged you to write more novels?

VH: I've nearly finished my second book and I'm finding it just as exciting, if not so unique, as my first. As a journalist, it was very restricting sticking to nonfiction, because I've realised that when you're writing fiction, there are no rules! It's like the difference between walking and flying—I can create these characters, these people, out of nowhere. You wake up in the morning and you're thinking about them. It's a bit like meeting someone for the first time. They've already got fair hair and blue eyes, or whatever, when they arrive. Then as time goes on I find out more about them and they evolve. You have to move round the characters and observe them.

RD: Do you have dreams and hopes for the future?

VH: That my children (Emily, sixteen and William, thirteen) will have fulfilling and happy lives. I think they are growing up in a much more challenging and competitive world than I did and I already hugely admire their grip on the issues they face. The Sixties and Seventies were gentle by comparison with the decades they have known.

Illustrations and Photos:
Page 4–5: Jeffery Deaver © Jerry Bauer; Gervase Phinn courtesy of the Penguin Group;
Michael Byrnes © Elizabeth Castillo; Victoria Hislop © nickcunard.co.uk.
The Sleeping Doll: 6–8: image: Photonica; illustration: Narrinder Singh @ velvet tamarind;
page 164 © Jerry Bauer.
Heart of the Dales: 166–8: illustration: Warwick Johnson-Cadwell @ EastWing; page 280:
courtesy of the Penguin Group; page 281: Yorkshire school © Simon Miles Photography.
The Sacred Bones: 282–4: image: Getty Images; illustration: Curtis Cozier; page 422:
© Elizabeth Castillo; page 423: Temple Mount © The Travel Library/Rex Features.
The Island: 424–6 : illustration: Greek landscape © Charles Dragazis www.dragazis.com;
boat © Photonica/Toby Marshall; page 574 © nickcunard.co.uk; page 575: Spinalonga
© Walter Bibikow/JAI/Corbis.
Dustjacket spine: Getty Images; **back dustjacket:** Victoria Hislop © *Publishing News*.

Printed and bound by GGP Media GmbH, Pössneck, Germany

020-249 DJ0000-1